A Long Pull

Allan Harris & Jason Gray

CASTLE ROCK · 2007

ISBN 978-0-578-01003-8

I'm at a good place right now, so I'd like to tell you my story, starting nine months ago. I'm telling it like a NASA countdown, T minus twenty, T minus nineteen, because after all the missteps, faulty parts and deteriorating conditions, I'm finally ready to lift off. I won't blame you if it seems more like a time bomb counting down to detonation.

T - 20

People tell me things. Why, I don't know, because everyone knows I give as good as I get. I don't believe in secrets, other than as conversation pieces.

What I hear from you, about your job or wife or golf game, could very well be passed along to the next guy, embellished as necessary. I'm a story-teller, but I can't just make this stuff up. I have to get my stories somewhere.

So here goes.

This young guy in a business suit had been coming into my coffeeshop for the past couple days. Nice guy, easy smile, introverted in a way that invites conversation. Blushed whenever Charlotte asked him something more personal than *What can I get for you?* He would give her a polite and short answer and then promptly ask a return question, to deflect attention back to her.

Charlotte knew she made this gentleman—all gentlemen—nervous, and not so secretly she enjoyed it. I'd like to think she kept the banter flying and their nerves firing as a sales technique, to build our customer base. But it was for the tips. Nervous sexual tension equals tips. So the banter flew and the tip jar grew.

Even though I'm right there pulling shots and frothing milk, you would never know I'm listening to these conversations, because all the while I'm humming or singing or letting the customer know that her tall white chocolate mocha is ready. But I know the best way to keep 'em coming back—besides hiring cute underdressed employees—is to personalize a dig, a gentle flattering dig. And this sort of tailored teasing can only be achieved by listening.

So when this well-dressed young man came in for the third day in a row, I was prepared. Charlotte said, "Hi there, what can I get for you?"

Speaking for this gentleman, I said, "Your phone number?" He blushed like a fire engine. Charlotte told me to shut up with a suffering sigh. And the next thing you know, with Charlotte off washing dishes and me lounging on the counter with a little time on my hands, he's telling me about a girl.

Kevin was his name, from San Francisco, and he was supposedly in town to audit the local Wells Fargo branch. His real mission, though, was to make time with this girl, Andrea. How this came to be, how he received this golden opportunity, well, I will never cease to be amazed how well life can work out.

Kevin met Andrea at Colorado State University. Kevin was the caring, stable shoulder that Andrea always cried on whenever she and her college sweetheart—not Kevin—had a fight, which was often, often enough that Kevin fell in love. A month before graduation three years ago, Andrea accepted a marriage proposal from her cyclical boyfriend during one of their reconciliations. Her fiancé had it goin' on, earning a degree in mechanical engineering and going to work for one of Denver's top construction firms, with the knowledge that he would eventually open a Denver branch for his father's successful North Dakota construction company. And so the crestfallen accountant Kevin took an internal auditor job with Wells Fargo in San Fran, resigned to never again set eyes or hands upon his old flame.

"Wow, a mechanical engineer," I said to Kevin. "Sounds like she made the right choice." I can be a smart ass. Not sarcastic, because I actually like people. But a smart ass. Which is a decent segue to tell you about this woman named Francesca who walked into my shop the next day.

"Hey there," I greeted her. "What can I get for you?"

"You have a sandwich board on your sidewalk," said Francesca, a pointy-chinned lady with puffy hair, a dingy scoop of ice cream on a pale sugar cone.

"We don't serve sandwiches, sorry."

"No," she said, instantly exasperated, "your sandwich board."

"I don't know what you want," I said.

"On your sidewalk," Francesca snapped. "You have a sandwich board advertising your store."

My only real customer perked up his ears behind the screen of his laptop. Terrence is a wannabe author who writes his novels for two hours darn near every day of the five years I've owned the shop. He's the best unpublished writer I know.

I like having an audience during times like this, especially one with an ear for snappy dialogue. "A sign board. Yes I do."

"It's called a sandwich board," Francesca corrected. "And it's against town regulations. We have an ordinance against it."

"Well not really."

"Yes. Really."

Among the downtown merchants, Francesca is affectionately known as the sign nazi, which gives you a feel for the not-so-affectionate labels. Signage infractions are her specialty, but she also excels at badgering the police to enforce wintertime parking violations, and keeping the state health department current on potential health code offenses.

Francesca wouldn't approach the counter. She dug through her satchel. "Here's the relevant section of the ordinance." She put the photocopy on the nearest table.

"I'm familiar with it. It's Sally, right?"

Francesca glared. "It's Francesca."

"Frannie, this is a waste of your time. And of course mine. The town has never enforced that statute."

"We have no choice. We've had a complaint."

"Really? Someone complained? Gimme a break. Who?"

After a long internal debate, Francesca decided to make this into a fun guessing game. "A fellow retailer."

Wouldn't have been fun in any case, but I already knew the answer. "Would this retailer sell bad coffee, by any chance?"

"What's going on?" Charlotte carried an armload of cups from storage.

"I'm being busted for an illegal sign board."

"Oh that's crap." Charlotte dumped her load and returned to the storage room without a glance at the scowling nazi.

Francesca looked over my shoulder toward the kitchen, hoping to score a couple more obvious violations. "Compliance is serious, Mr. Lawson."

"Frannie, a week from now we'll be ten below zero and under two feet of snow." It was late October and beautiful outside, Indian summer they called it. But winter was coming, and always with a vengeance. That knowledge—and because the golf courses were closed—made it hard to enjoy the nice weather. "People will be dying on the sidewalks if they can't find the place with the hot coffee. It's not just serious, Frannie. It's life and death."

"You have one week to comply, Mr. Lawson."

"Or what?" I asked.

"Or what, what?" she said.

Before getting into a bad Abbott & Costello routine, I answered, "What's the fine? What's the penalty if I don't comply?"

She put her weight on one leg and a hand on her hip. "The maximum penalty is thirty days in jail."

"What's the minimum?"

"I surely don't know, Mr. Lawson."

"I'll take the minimum." This got a chuckle from Terrence, pretending not to be listening.

Craig sauntered through the shop hauling two five-gallon pails of beans from our roaster across the alley. Craig was co-assistant manager with Charlotte, a brooding, hardworking guy who had his business degree but hated office buildings. He had a full black mustache—rare these days—and a wide flat torso. Craig Sterling is the closest thing to a misogynist I've ever met. At the same time, he's a crusader against the objectification of women—I suppose that getting turned on by women's body parts gets in the way of hating them.

Craig eyeballed Francesca as he duckwalked to the freezer. He dropped the pails with a bang and opened the freezer door, using it as a screen in order to roll his eyes at me. Maybe it was his general contempt for women, and maybe he was a pretty good judge of character.

And yes, we keep our beans in the freezer, and yes, I recommend you do the same at home, and yes of course, I am aware that many coffeeshop owners believe this is bad for the beans. And no I will not debate this issue without getting angry.

"Mr. Lawson," said Francesca, "you have a week to comply or respond."

"I'll take your 'respond' option. And I don't even need a week. No."

"What's that?"

"My response. No."

Terrence chortled, and quickly put his cup to his lips. Maybe that little exchange would make it in his novel.

Francesca puffed out her itty-bitty chest. "You have one week. Good day."

"You're not going to tell me who it was?"

Francesca raised her eyebrows and lowered her eyes, which isn't the most difficult maneuver in the world, but does take practice. "You may come down to the city administration building if you wish to see a copy of the complaint." With a last glance at the filled-to-bursting garbage can, Francesca walked out, stopping on the sidewalk to make record in her notebook.

I cleaned, whistled, seethed. Terrence sauntered to the table where a copy of the ordinance lay. "You want to see this?"

"I already know what it says. Our economic development committee voted to recommend to city council that they do away with it. Outlawing sign boards doesn't make sense, because the town won't let us alter the building signage above the first floor."

Charlotte returned with another armful of supplies, and stopped to listen. A package of napkins tumbled to the floor. Craig stared with a tiny smirk and a little nod, waiting. I hoped he wouldn't cuff her for her clumsiness.

"Historical preservation," I was saying. "All these downtown buildings are on the historic register."

"We have historic buildings?" Charlotte was dubious.

"It's all relative. So since the downtown businesses might actually need to announce our presence to the occasional out-of-towner who's running out of gas and accidentally takes the business loop instead of the exit with all the gas stations and fast food shops and great big neon blinking signs, the city council agreed that the sandwich board ordinance is a non-issue. They couldn't bring themselves to get rid of it, but they won't vote to enforce it."

"Somebody doesn't like our sign?" Charlotte pouted.

"Charlotte designed it," I told Terrence.

"It's a beautiful sign," he said.

"Thank you." Charlotte continued to pout as she unpacked the supplies. "Hey," she exclaimed, suddenly all excited, slapping Craig on the leg to prove it. "Did you hear Edna Applejack might be getting out?"

"Is that a new cereal?" I asked.

"Her appeal was successful?" said Terrence, squeaky with excitement.

"My friend Tonya's dad is a judge, so this might be confidential," said Charlotte. During my year in college, this was the breathless tone women used when they discussed the latest developments in their favorite soaps. "It sounds like the conviction will be reduced from second degree to third degree, or something like that. But the judge isn't going to rule until spring."

"Second degree what?" I asked. "Burns?"

"Murder," said Charlotte. Still kneeling, she put her hands on her hips. "You honestly haven't heard the story of Edna Applejack?"

"What kind of coffeeshop owner are you?" Terrence piled on.

At the time I got a little defensive, my pride wounded. In retrospect they were right. How did I not see Edna coming?

"Edna is a North Dakota legend," said Terrence.

"How long ago did they put her away?"

"I don't know, what was it?" Terrence pondered.

"Ten and a half years ago," said Charlotte.

"Old news," I told them.

"Not if she gets out," said Terrence.

"Whatever," I said, heading for my office. "I gotta run."

"Are you going over to Town Hall to see who complained about your sign?" Terrence asked.

"I already know," I called back.

"It's that stupid...Mexican fellow," said Charlotte.

"Did you mean 'spic'?" Craig asked.

"No I didn't. I would be afraid to use that term, in case you're one." Charlotte giggled and crawled away, out of Craig's reach.

"Maybe I am," he said.

"Are you bragging or apologizing?" she asked.

Craig shook his head, knowing better than to take it any further.

"Is it the guy who owns the campus coffeeshop?" Terrence asked.

I leaned out of my office. "Would you say Hernandes's shop is by the campus? I wouldn't. He's a good mile from the bridge. The way the streets run along the river, his place is no closer to campus than we are."

"Sounds like you pulled out a yardstick and measured it," Terrence joked.

"I'm going by my odometer."

I was hot to open another shop on the Jamestown College campus, but the private school was aware that its well-to-do students were a retailing gold mine. And so the College owned and operated every convenience store, hamburger grill and vending machine on campus. And regularly reminded the city council to keep the surrounding square mile zoned strictly residential, or else. Nobody wanted to contemplate the 'or else'. This is a college town, Jamestown College-town. The billboard off Interstate 94 proclaims us the "Home of the Big Buffalo", but the gargantuan bison statue on the hill is a figurehead. The College operates all the levers of power. My downtown location is about as close as any business can get to the campus.

I was hot to open a second shop, period. Here, there, anywhere. A second, and a third. A whole chain of coffeeshops. Unfortunately, this was impossible.

"Brian, what the hell are you doing here?" Terrence asked me, somewhat out of the blue. Maybe that wasn't the exact day he asked me this particular question, but ask it he did, like one of the sorry bastards from Billy Joel's *Piano Man*, sitting at the bar and putting bread in my jar. And I think it's relevant to this story. "I've been around, here and there and all over the place," Terrence said, "and let me tell you, you're bigger than this place. You could be running a chain of shops on the coast where they appreciate good coffee and a good personality."

"Tell me about it."

I'll tell you about it, later. On the day in question I was pissed off all over again that this Hernandes character was advertising his place as a campus coffeeshop, when he was nowhere near the college. And a bigger issue was burning me, that day and every day, 'til the day I die: why is it that no one would think of becoming a golf pro without a few skills, yet the only prerequisite to opening a coffeeshop is a failed career and a caffeine addiction? I can't count how many times customers have come in and admired my establishment, with dollar signs in their eyes.

"I love coffee," they say. "I should do a coffee shop."

I try to smile. My head almost explodes. Then I envision this potential competitor swimming and finally drowning in debt. "Yeah, you'd be good at it," I say, as sincere as I can muster.

Hernandes was the perfect example. He was doing everything wrong, and sooner or later he was going to have to call it quits. But in the meantime he was taking business away from me. The timing couldn't have been worse.

But back to Kevin the auditor, the San Francisco cheat, a bit player in this tale, but responsible for so much that follows. He was almost gleeful over his good fortune. Of Wells Fargo's five thousand branches, he managed to get himself staffed on an audit in the little North Dakota town where his old flame lived. At a time when her marriage was falling apart. Is life amazing or what?

Granted Kevin didn't know me well enough to worry about my loose storyteller's lips. But auditors are known for their critical thinking skills, the ability to connect the dots and recognize a problem, right? So how do you figure him regaling me with poorly told tales of how he mooned over this Andrea girl in college, always there to comfort her but never really getting any; and how he called her the week before this audit started and learned that, just like old times, she was having serious trouble with her man; and how, just like the old blue-ball days, they had gone out drinking, and even spent a couple hours in his hotel room, where nothing had really happened; and how Andrea and her husband, whose name is Rick, Kevin tells me, moved here a few months ago from Denver to help out with his family's construction business while his brother underwent chemo treatment—I mean, being a coffeeshop owner in a town this size, wouldn't you figure that I might know this Rick guy? Because I do.

T - 19

I told Charlotte and Craig I was running to Sam's Club for supplies, and then walked to Town Hall two blocks away. That's where I parked. There were a limited number of spaces behind my shop, and I liked them available for the morning commuters. The Chamber of Commerce forgot to confiscate my parking permit after I rotated off the board, so I helped myself to the Town Hall employee lot. Given that I did Taekwondo once a week, and played on a city-league basketball team for a few weeks in the winter, I didn't need the exercise—the two-block walk morning and afternoon was probably fitness overkill. But I never complained.

This time I went inside. The help desk in the hall was vacant, so I headed for the offices beyond. No doubt by design, the translucent glass was tinted such a dingy gray that the administration office looked closed. I barged in and waited for the lady behind the desk to look up. I waited for two full seconds, maybe a little less. "Hi Molly," I read her nameplate. "Brian Lawson from James River Valley Coffee. I had a complaint against my sign board. I'd like to get a copy of the complaint." Molly couldn't find a good stopping point in her paper clipping project. "You're busy, so just point me to the copier. Although if it's double-sided—"

"Francesca has the complaint," Molly said without looking up. With her blob of unnaturally dark hair and pinched face, Molly could have been Frannie's younger sister. "She's not back yet from making her rounds."

"Francesca…is that her real name? Because it sounds made-up. I don't think it fits her. Do you?"

"That's her name."

"What do you call her for short?"

"She doesn't like it shortened."

"No, I don't suppose." Frannie it was then.

I saw Mark Andersen the town manager in his corner office, pretending to talk on the phone and praying I wouldn't come back there. I knew that he had received many, many complaints about Frannie. How many complaints do you have to get about an employee before you let her go? Ten? Fifty? A hundred? Charlotte was an amazing employee, but I would still have to let her go on her 50th complaint. Tops.

The last time I called, I had to pause in mid-complaint for all the sighing from Mark. When he quieted down, I resumed my complaint. "I'm not accusing Frannie of puncturing my inflatable meadowlark, but she did draw a chalk circle around it. I had customers wondering if someone died on my sidewalk."

"Duly noted. I'm glad you called. Thank you for your concern and input."

Was that a recorded message? What does Frannie have over the city? Photos? Sex tapes? Racketeering? Enron? A person this ill-equipped to deal with the public should be mowing ditches and emptying wastebaskets at midnight. Must be nice to work for a city that has no balls.

So instead of beating my head against Mark Andersen, Town Wall, I drove straight to the source.

South from my shop on Main Street, Jamestown's main drag, I turned left at the Hardees, drove three blocks past a string of warehouses fronted by tall security fences, turned left again into a fifty-year-old collection of single-story ramblers housing very little disposable income, and then made a final right onto a street the width of a four-lane highway. Here sat Uncommon Grounds.

"Uncommon Grounds". The name screamed coffee, but no imagination. There are over two hundred Uncommon Grounds in the country, none of them affiliated. Uncommon Grounds, Common Grounds, Muddy Waters, House That Brews, The Beanery, Java Hut...I could go on. I would be embarrassed to use any of these names. Sure, James River Valley Coffee isn't the most creative name in the world. But as far as I know, I didn't rip anyone off.

The building formerly housed a printing shop. Now it was a retail strip, Beads!, Calvert's Tax & Accounting, Replay Sports, and a couple businesses still To Be Determined. Hernandes thought he scored a real coup landing an endcap in a redeveloped commercial strip overlooking the James River, with the campus only a hundred yards away on the opposite bank. But it was a mile down to the nearest bridge, so the students stayed on campus and drank terrible coffee made from bulk foodservice beans brewed by ladies in hairnets.

Which was also a fair description of Hernandes's coffee.

As for all the shoppers working up powerful thirsts combing strip malls for outrageous deals, somebody should have told Hernandes that while coffee is certainly consumed twenty-four hours a day by rich college kids, for the rest of us it's mostly in the morning on the way to work. If you aren't a convenient stop on the way to the office, you're wasting your time.

The heavy door went unwillingly, the plate glass shuddering and chattering. Every head, all six of them, swiveled to check me out, then returned to reading, conversing, or for one elderly gent in a backwards ballcap, staring at the east wall and picturing the river sparkling in the mid-afternoon sun as if through a window.

The room was long and narrow, fifty feet to the counter at the back. The only light was from shaded lamps perched on rickety end tables, and a fluorescent strip above the kitchen. Fluorescent lights, a staple of a classy coffeeshop. The walls were painted in swirling coffee gradients, a band of French roast at the bottom, cream and sugar across the middle, café au lait at the top. It did make me think of coffee—first time I've ever feared drowning in it.

"Hey Charlie," I greeted one of my customers, nose buried in a book.

"Oh, hey, Brian. I was just trying to get a little peace and quiet," he struggled to explain. "Your store is always so busy..."

I patted him on the shoulder like a disappointed parent. I took his book and checked the cover. "Harry Potter. I've heard it's good." I slammed it shut. "Oops. I think I lost your place."

"Hey, no problem," said Charlie, eager to suffer any penance I dished out. "So what brings you all the way over here..."

I continued the trek to the counter, snaking through dirty beat-up couches and easy chairs, the end tables, and small mangers filled with highbrow magazines. I unholstered my buzzing cellphone from my hip. "Go."

"Honey," said my fiancée Isabel, "these aren't walkie-talkies. They're phones. You're supposed to say hello."

"Hi. Jerry and I are playing golf at three, but I haven't picked up the pheasants from Joshua yet. Can you run get them? I have the marinade ready to go, but the birds need some prep. They need to be quartered, and then tossed in a Ziploc baggie with the marinade. Can you do it?"

"Sure, sweetie. What time are Joshua and Denise coming over?"

"And Jerry and Amber. Seven. I shouldn't be much later than that."

"The three of us can stay busy until you get there." Isabel was impossible to rattle. I like having people over. Sometimes it's planned, sometimes it isn't. I could give Isabel no heads-up, no warning whatsoever, just show up at her condo with friends in tow, and regardless whether she was fast asleep or in her pj's eating ice cream and watching her favorite television show, she would be delighted. She would get to her feet—I wanted to say "spring" to her feet, but that's not the way Isabel moved—and help me commence to entertaining. Isabel liked people. All people. Her best quality, and her biggest downfall.

"Who's in the shop today?" Isabel asked.

"I saw Charlie." The man behind the counter tried not to stare as he listened to my side of the conversation.

"No one else?" Isabel asked.

"I didn't recognize anyone else, no."

"Where are you?"

"The new shop. You know, the one cleverly hidden in the industrial park down by the river. I'm paying them a social call."

"Mm. Nice. You know, I didn't think that sounded like your music in the background. What is that?"

"Sitar, if I'm not mistaken."

"I kind of like that music."

"I'll call you back, okay?" I hung up and greeted the counter man, slim and slightly effeminate, or European, dressed in earth tones. His glossy black hair lay tight to his head, accentuating bulging eyeballs. For someone who had supposedly spent thirty years in the cutthroat Manhattan investment banking scene, his brown skin was unnaturally smooth. Jamestown was founded by men who priced pelts like that by the pallet. "Brian Lawson," I introduced myself. "Welcome to the neighborhood."

"Bill Hernandes." He felt obligated to reach across the counter. "Hernandes with an 's'. It's Portuguese."

I shook his hand. Thought about pulling him off his feet and across the clutter of cute clipstand menus, folk band flyers, coffee-themed knickknacks, and jars, for tips, pens, biscotti, and suggestions, to slap him awake from the nightmare he was putting me through.

You might look at the competition Hernandes was bringing to town and say, hey, it's capitalism, good for America, good for Jamestown. I say guys like Hernandes are the suicide bombers of the retail world—they have no chance to survive, no apparent love for their own financial lives, and they're eager to take everyone else down with them. The only difference being there's no need for a whack-job imam to implant the delusions of financial grandeur—these guys are spiritually self-guided, hanging out at coffeeshops until they're convinced all they have to do is open their own shop, and that mansion and all those virgins will be theirs in a few short years.

Hernandes eyed me warily. "Are you here for, or what do you…can I get you something?"

"Americano would be great. So how's business all the way out here? Slow like now?"

"No, no. This is the first time today the line isn't out the door." He was a terrible liar. Unless he was talking about his line of angry creditors, I hoped. "People are loving us. Feel free to look around."

"Thanks. Love what you've done with the place." I strolled amongst his few customers as I talked, bumping the occasional elbow. "And here everybody was certain the city council was wasting the town's money. You know, paying to clean up all the toxic printing chemicals that had soaked through the floor and contaminated the soil."

"No, it was worth it," said Hernandes, coming around the counter. "Not much to clean." He tried to usher me back to the register.

"I kept hearing the words Superfund, Three Mile Island, Chernobyl…" I looked around apprehensively. "Wish I had a Geiger counter…. I heard they did a terrible job."

"No. Top-notch. Drink…?" Hernandes sounded like he was being strangled.

"Americano," I reminded him, completing my tour and returning to the counter. "Have you met Brian Smith? He's the—"

"City council president." Hernandes finished. "Great guy. And Carolyn and Ted, and—"

"Doug, John, Jennifer, Dawn. That's all seven, I believe."

"They bent over backward to make me feel welcome." Hernandes fumbled with the tamper, losing half the coffee out of the portafilter. "Cammie, could you come out here and make an Americano?" He spoke slowly; I could tell he was working hard to eliminate his accent. "I want to talk to Brian here."

A plump girl wearing a pink stretch shirt with a lacy sewed-on camisole appeared from the back. "Americano?"

"Thanks Cammie," I said. "Cammie. Is that a nickname?"

She mumbled something unintelligible as she studied the barista instruction manual with a frown.

I pointed at Cammie. "That's one thing I've always prided myself on."

"Hmm?" Hernandes was watching her closely.

"The ability to fix drinks and work the crowd at the same time. I think it's essential to an upbeat, high-energy store."

Hernandes's eyes kept darting to Cammie, who was twisting knobs and punching buttons like I had never seen. "Uh-huh, true," he intoned.

I waited until I had his full attention. "Do you have time to sit down?"

Hernandes thought this over, wide eyes on me, if not really studying me. Maybe it was those eyeballs, too big for their sockets, giving him the wary chinchilla look. Maybe it was the way he kept grooming his smooth shiny hair. "Okay. Yes. Cammie…" He blinked, like he was fighting off a mild aneurysm. "Make two of those, please?" He pointed me to the nearest table, shoved too close against a bookcase filled with old and from what I could see, worthless books. Hernandes waited until I was seated before perching his butt in the chair. He folded his hands on the table. "So—"

"So I received a complaint today."

"Oh, yes?"

"My sign board is an issue."

"Well, yes, I understand sandwich boards are a code violation. It's a potential safety issue. It's important to allow free access on the sidewalks—"

"It's just advertising, Bill. You have a nice storefront. If anyone ever finds their way back here, they'll spot you. But the downtown businesses need sign boards, because of signage restrictions on our buildings."

"It would be nice if we were all treated equally, wouldn't it?"

Don't try to match wits, Billy. "Of course that's not possible," I said, and thanked Cammie as she brought our drinks. I looked for eye contact from her, received none.

"Of course that's not possible," Hernandes echoed. "Fairness isn't always possible. But it's important that businesses have a level playing field."

"Those sound like contradictory concepts. Right?" I chuckled, and Hernandes chuckled with me, with no idea why. "You either compete and accept the consequences, or you spend all your time looking for handouts and favors, am I right?" My chuckles faded to a sigh. "So did you file that complaint?"

Hernandes stopped mid-chuckle. "No I did not file that complaint."

"Good." Liar. "Because we have to stick together. This isn't a competition. If we increase the public's coffee knowledge, we all win." One bad lie deserved another.

"Couldn't agree more." Hernandes forced a smile. "How's business?"

"Great." I beamed as I rose, and stuck out my hand. I was furious. "I gotta run. Stop by sometime." *And get a good cup of coffee.* "You can check out my sign board, see what's on special."

"You're uh, you're not going to pull your sandwich board?"

"Not a chance." I bared my coffee-stained teeth (a must in the industry). "Take care now." I flicked Charlie's book as I passed. "Charlie. Stay focused."

I was all the way to the door when Hernandes said, "Please, uh…please don't disturb my customers."

My cell buzzed as I climbed in the van. "Hey Mike."

Mike McEwen owns Jamestown's biggest construction company. Commercial, residential, they build it all. Mike runs it with his wife and his son—whose name is Rick, by the way. "Brian, how are you? Making any money down there today?"

"A buck or two. I hear you're sending a little my way tomorrow. We're planning on having the coffee ready to go by noon."

"That's why I'm calling. Not about the coffee. The meeting. I want to make sure you're going to attend."

"Hadn't planned on it."

"So change your plans." Mike spoke like a Mafia don with a Scandinavian accent. "We'll be discussing the retail center we're putting up by the new hospital. I want you to have first dibs on the anchor pad."

"The Bluffs, huh?" I stalled. Even with the new hospital nearby, I honestly didn't think it was a prime location. But maybe that was sour grapes, because I couldn't afford it anyway. "Isabel mentioned it."

Isabel McEwen. My fiancée. Mike's daughter. Rick's sister. Andrea's sister-in-law. Which *almost* obligated me to challenge Kevin the Wells Fargo auditor to a duel to defend the family honor.

"Probably because she hears me talking about the Bluffs all the time," said Mike. Iz works in Mike's office while she waits on the school district to reinstate her teaching license. She's been waiting for six years. Given the nature of her infraction, it was my opinion she shouldn't hold her breath.

I continued to stall. "I thought you handled construction and left the developing to someone else." I came upon a car idling at the last intersection before Main Street. The man behind the wheel looked lost and confused.

"I do have some influence, you know," said Mike.

I had the ultimate respect for Mike. He started McEwen Construction while in college and built it into a very profitable business. He had recently lost his youngest son Brent to an infection, after the poor guy made a miraculous turnaround from his cancer and seemed to be on the mend. Mike grieved mightily in private but never said a word in public—although I knew from Iz they were suing the hospital—and never took a day off. He was faithful to his customers, and generous to his friends. He and his wife Valerie loved me like a son. Which was five years in the making and still a little premature.

"Hold on a second, Mike." I pulled alongside the lost motorist and leaned out the window. "You looking for the coffeeshop?"

"I am!" He was pleasantly surprised to find a savior.

"Follow me." I waited for him to make a U-turn. "Sorry Mike. Helping out a lost customer. So you were saying…"

"I'm saying I have more than a little pull deciding who gets in the Bluffs. And you need to be in there. It's the centerpiece of one of the biggest developments Jamestown has ever seen."

"How about when they painted the big buffalo's balls blue?"

"That was some development," Mike agreed. "So I'll see you tomorrow?"

I have no problem saying pretty much anything to pretty much anyone. But telling Mike 'no thanks' was difficult. "I appreciate the offer. But I'm not sure I'm going to be interested."

"Just come and listen to the details—you'll get too excited to stop."

"I hate it when that happens."

"Yeah, well, it doesn't happen to me anymore. Not without those purple pills. Which reminds me…Margie," he called to his secretary, "get me a glass of water, would you?"

"I hope it's not too late," I said.

"Me too," said Mike. "So get ready to expand, Mr. Coffee."

"Unfortunately, Mike, my finances aren't that flexible, at the moment."

Mike gave an impatient grunt. "I'm not short on cash. Your investment would be intellectual. And some sweat equity to get the place up and running."

"Mike, come on…"

"I've seen the hours you put in, my friend. You're worth the risk."

Mike just didn't understand what it took to make money in this business. Hell, I didn't. He didn't know I had already been down the road he was trying to take me, a few years back in California. I knew where that road led. Lupus.

I learned coffee from Dougie Fosseton, owner of the Davis Drip in my hometown. This was back in the day when coffee and I were both young, when coffeeshops struggled to find customers in the waning days before household income rose above that critical threshold, where lattés could be re-classified from extravagance to staple. Sure, Folgers crystals and Mr. Coffee machines were thousands of years old. But coffee as we know it today was barely out of its adolescence.

Dougie Fosseton was a legend. On the rare occasion he was in the house, customers came out of the woodwork, lined up out the door, to get a Fosseton latté. He would entertain the crowds with tales from his childhood on the plan-tations of Sumatra and his kidnapping by pirates of the Celebes Sea.

Not so surprisingly, Dougie could be a raving lunatic. Whenever his em-ployees hacked him off, which was often, he would chew ass like I have never ever seen. But Dougie took a liking to me.

"Java man," that's what Dougie called me, "you remind me of me." This horrified me, Dougie was badly browned and wrinkly. "Java man, I'm going to open up the vault for you."

Dougie showed me what he called his "patented" roasting technique, which, thank goodness, wasn't—it's a great method and I've been using it for free ever since. If I wasn't in school or playing sports, I was with Dougie, learning how to find the best green beans and getting to know his favorite growers and brokers. It wasn't long before he took me off the bar, so he could teach me the business. I was a sponge and he was a river of knowledge. It takes a big sponge, an oversized sponge, to soak up that much knowledge. I owe him so much. God damn him for all eternity for refusing to show me his "patented" latté preparation technique—but whatever, I was clearly his pro-tégé, and I should be eternally grateful for that.

One day during my sophomore year at Cal-Davis, a supplier screwed up our order, and we ended up dangerously low on beans. Dougie sent me to Sac-ramento to beg for a hundred pounds from his competitors. I returned with the hundred pounds, and an extra thousand, with orders to roast them for his com-petitors. Dougie got excited. I became his wholesale bean salesman, hitting the road every weekend. Whether it's retail customers or fellow retailers, selling coffee comes natural to me. Working two days a week, I was the Central Cali-fornia Whole-Salesman of the Year (Small Business Division). I still remem-ber the Salisbury steak they served at the banquet. Scrumptious.

My future was clear and bright. I couldn't wait to graduate from college. In fact I didn't wait. I wasn't surprised or bothered by Dad's explosion and Mom's tears when I announced that a degree wasn't necessary. I hugged them and promised that I would make them proud. I was in love. While the memory makes me a little sick to my stomach now, I can still feel the giddy exhilaration over the plan to open my own chain of coffeeshops.

The day after my twenty-first birthday, I ended my apprenticeship at the Drip and started my own coffeeshop, Central Valley Coffee, a few blocks away. I bought the building from a dry cleaner, and if anybody knows easy access, if anyone knows parking, it's the drycleaner. Customers got in, they got out. And in between they were greeted warmly, usually by the right name. They caught some singing, not so good that they felt like they were being entertained, like they had to listen, like a compliment was necessary. Serious conversations could take place in my shop, under the cover of my voice, the music—looking back, a little heavy on the REM and the Squeeze—and the hiss and squeal of the frothing wand.

People loved my shop. The service was prompt and courteous, the atmosphere unbeatable. And of course the coffee was topnotch. I was kicking Dougie Fosseton's ass. CVC was on everyone's lips.

"So when are you going to open another shop?"

I heard that one all the time.

"Do you have a shop on the north end of town?"

Variations of that one, on a regular basis.

"I'm from San Fran. When are you going to open a shop there?"

That was one of my favorites. "Someday," I would say, believing it.

Business was great—although I was puzzled at how little money that meant. Quite the mystery, and Sherlock Holmes I am not. I couldn't wait to get bigger. Then I heard the owner of Timbuktu Coffee in Sacramento was looking to sell. I jumped on it. My banker—from Wells Fargo, coincidentally—jumped on me, ready to ride that dark-coffee horse all the way to the finish line. I was a heavy favorite, you could say.

Profits started out small, and never grew from there. For every new customer who swore allegiance to me, one would leave. Dougie Fosseton cleaned up the Davis Drip's act, taught his employees to smile, and started billing himself as a campus coffeehouse. Fucking liar, he was nowhere near the campus.

"Hi Brian," a customer would greet me. "Where were you yesterday?"

I got really tired of hearing that question. "At the other shop," I would say. "I alternate days."

Pretty soon, so did my customers. And when they couldn't remember whether today was Brian day, they just didn't come.

I looked like a success. People see big fat margins in every $1.75 cup of coffee and every $3.50 latté. At the same time everyone recognizes that America is the land of cutthroat competition, and if competition is good at anything, it's squeezing margins down to the pennies. No one seems to see the mutual exclusivity in these two concepts.

Two years after he had sold me his shop, the former owner of Timbuktu

Coffee decided to get back in the business. "Coming Soon!" signs were popping up all across Sacramento, "Timbuktoo Coffee!"

I called him. "Joe, I'm not using Timbuktu—with a 'u'. You can have it back."

"No way," said Joe. "Timbuktoo—with two o's—is even better."

I'll tell you what was better. His new location. Location, location, location. Joe was opening his new shop in the spot he should have been in from the start. I knew it was a great corner, but the price had been too steep for me. Joe scored a big coup. He had to outbid a drycleaner for that site.

To top it off, Starbucks was coming. I had heard enough about them to know that I had to increase my volume and my margins, pronto. I welcomed the challenge. I really did. My business model was unique, and customers raved about my coffee. I just needed more of them, and to become a fixture in their lives. To cut costs I let three employees go.

For two years I was a maniac, working multiple shifts by day and doing all the roasting by night. My free time consisted of dealing with personality clashes among my few remaining employees, and shuttling back and forth between Davis and Sacramento, making the twenty-minute trip five times a day to cover gaps in the work schedule. Not paying salaries is a pretty good way to pad the margins.

But my volume wouldn't budge. New customers would come in—and old ones would leave. I felt like I won their hearts and their business when I was present, then lost them when I wasn't. Same for my employees. They laughed when I was with them, and grumbled when I was at the other shop.

I was slipping. I forgot customers' names, drinks and stories, and both shops suffered for it. Customers and employees alike resented me for not being there every second of the day. My business was a dike that had two leaks, and all I could do was run back and forth, taking turns plugging them. At least that's the dream I kept having.

I was in too deep, and too wigged out to realize it. I was desperate for volume, for name recognition, for cachet.

So when the opportunity to sign on to a neighborhood retail development project in Berkeley dropped in my lap, I took it. The People's Republic of Berkeley, hotbed of anti-capitalism; where disposable income flows like water, grows on trees, and makes millionaires out of second-rate entrepreneurs; where smart bankers line up to finance construction, inventory, payroll, the new car and the company van—where I was going to vault over that hump.

And then I got tired. I ran out of gas.

I couldn't get out of bed. Of course I did, but it was hard for those around me to tell. I dreaded the hour drive to my other shops. All that quiet time to contemplate my misery and worry about the newest problem with the landlord or a customer or an employee that I was going to hear about as soon as I stepped in the door.

So I rehired two of my ex-employees and cut my Sacramento time in half. Which was exactly what happened to my revenue. Without me there, my regulars stopped coming. Without regulars laughing and filling seats and creating a vibrant atmosphere, the walk-up customer started walking on by. Luckily the Berkeley financing came in handy to pay off the mounting deficits from the Sacramento shop. Call me Ponzi. I had to lay off one of the very same employees I had already hired, laid off, and hired again. He walked outside and keyed my car and spit on my windshield, and I understood completely.

The Berkeley strip was nearly finished, and I was halfway through the detailing of my space when I pulled the plug—I didn't actually call it quits, I had my accountant call the developer and tell them I had lupus.

AND NOW here was Mike McEwen, pushing me toward another flare-up. I'm honest with people about my problems. For every dilemma they share with me, I probably divulge two of my own. But my inability to be successful in the coffee industry wasn't a problem. It was the defining crisis of my life. I couldn't discuss it with my friends, I couldn't discuss it with my father, and I couldn't discuss it with Mike. I wouldn't discuss it. I just wanted to solve it.

And then there was the North Dakota issue, which can be summed up by noting that Sinatra didn't sing, "North Dakota, if I can make it there, I'll make it anywhere". The dark secret I kept from my Jamestown friends, employees and customers, was that I was increasingly embarrassed to be there. This was my own little psychosis to be sure, but like any other mental illness it was all too real, and it was a diagnosis I sure as hell couldn't confide to Mike, the most rabid North Dakota booster I knew.

So I was going to have to disappoint him, with no explanation. The least I could do was a good deed for his family. An idea had been percolating for the past twenty-four hours, since my last visit from Kevin the Wells Fargo auditor, but didn't fully bubble into my consciousness until that moment. "Mike, I can't make your meeting tomorrow, but why don't you have Rick come down and pick up the coffee. Around eleven."

"He can fill you in on the Bluffs. The Bluffs," Mike savored. "Nice, huh?"

"It's a good name."

"You bet your butt. I'll have Rick come see you tomorrow. It's a no-brainer, Brian. A sure thing. You'll slay 'em there."

"Don't tell Rick. Just tell him to go get the coffee. 'Fetch the coffee, boy.'"

"'And bring me a muffin!'" Mike laughed. "It's a plan, Mr. Coffee."

T - 18

When people tell me things, interesting, troubling, shocking things, I don't react. While listening politely to your story, I'm stripping out the names and building an anecdote around the high points. I'll pretend the most scandalous gossip is yesterday's news, even if it keeps me awake at night.

I've listened to a bit of bragging about inappropriate actions, some already in the books and some still in the planning stage. More often I'm made privy to an ongoing miscommunication, a misunderstanding in process between a Jack and a Jane—more often a Jane and a Jeanie—that's bound to lead to hurt feelings. Because I know so many people from my five years here, I'll often get to hear both sides. And because I've been a sounding board for a lot of my customers' dilemmas during my fifteen years in the business, like Dr. Laura I'm usually aware of the correct course. With a few words I could put things right; I could bring Jane and Jeanie together to clear up the confusion and mend that broken fence. Theoretically.

In practice, I would lose customers. As soon as I become a participant, everything changes. What was heartfelt sharing becomes cruel gossip. Rifts and lifelong enemies are made over what could have been a minor dust-up. It becomes uncomfortable for them to come into my shop. I lose customers.

And truly, my customers don't confide in me to hear a solution. It's Coffeeshop Owners Are From Mars, Coffeeshop Customers Are From Venus. It's their loss, but my customers aren't here to tap into my problem-solving skills. They aren't looking for my unique insights. They simply want to talk, to tell their side. To get a chuckle or a groan. To be a storyteller, too.

They want to impress me. They know I've got a ton of stories; they'd like to see how one of theirs stacks up. Maybe a few weeks later they'll even hear me retelling it to another customer—with the names changed and the scenario tweaked, because as much as people like gossip, they're better able to relish the human comedy without actual personalities getting in the way. It's like seeing their Real Life Adventure story published in *Reader's Digest*. It makes their day.

So why this time? Why didn't I just sit back and watch, and listen, and craft a titillating anecdote from Kevin the auditor's ill-advised chatter? Was my decision to get involved, at the risk of losing customers—at a time when I desperately needed each and every one—a favor to Mike and the McEwen family? Is it possible I'm that altruistic? Or was there more to it?

I don't know. I screwed up, okay? Sure, I could psychoanalyze my motives in retrospect…actually no, I can't. I didn't waste a second on the *whether* at the time, so why should I dwell on it now? I'm a little impulsive. Okay, a lot. I trust my instincts—it's an efficient process, allowing me to skip past the *whether* I should do something and get right to the *what* and the *how*.

As this story moves along, it's going to be really tempting to ask *why*—why did Brian just say that? Why in the world would he do that? Don't fall into that trap. Just accept that I did, and let me focus on what I do best, telling you the *what* and the *how*.

Kevin the Wells Fargo auditor was sitting at what had become his spot over the course of a few days. My shop sits on the corner of Main Street and Second Avenue in the heart of downtown. There are three tables on the floor and another smaller table on the dais in the front display window, where the former Herberger's department store put their fall, winter and spring collections, which varied only by the thickness of the scarves. A couch and two easy chairs sit against the interior wall…

I hate to interrupt, but now's the perfect time to point out another critical comparison to Hernandes. My couches are comfortable, not old. My colors are rich and subdued, not dark. My place is clean. This is a college town, but it's still North Dakota. Farmers. When they walk in, they're thinking value, not ambiance. They're not convinced that a store devoted solely to coffee is such a great idea, and the sight of a bunch of lounging, lecturing, tea-sipping hippies only confirms their suspicions. Hernandes was trying to recreate Soho, Haight-Ashbury and the Paris Left Bank, all rolled into one. Or maybe he just liked a dingy, dirty looking shop. If only I had the luxury to have sat back and waited for that sonofabitch to fail.

I have thirty feet of stainless steel tabletop bolted to the wall, the last couple yards running alongside the counter, with enough room to squeeze in a bar chair. Kevin the auditor loved that seat.

"So how do you find the time to come down here for a couple hours every day?" I asked him during a long lull between customers, seconds after Steve from the Jamestown *Sun* left without selling me an ad, flyer or coupon, a few moments before Rick McEwen walked in.

"For one thing, we schedule too much time for these audits," said Kevin. "Two weeks is ridiculous. I could be done by Tuesday; but I'm budgeted for fieldwork all the way to Friday. I could wrap it up early and show a big positive variance. But auditors live by an unwritten rule: never bust the budget for the next guy."

"You sound like honorable fellows."

"Most of us." Kevin had endearing qualities. He smiled a lot, with nice teeth. Good skin. A little skinnier than I liked to see a man. I was a touch heavy those days. I considered myself a really, really good-looking Jack Black, and an athlete who had grown a gut from working all the time. That's where I was coming from.

"Then there's my technique," Kevin continued. "I slam the bank employees in the morning, first thing, before they can book enough meetings to avoid me. I prepare my list of documents and analyses the night before—"

"Unless you're otherwise occupied."

"True." Slight grin. "I slap this To Do list on them, always with double the documents I actually need pulled. Then I come here for a couple hours. You'd be amazed—I can find a great place like this in just about every town I visit."

"I'm flattered you think this is a great place."

"It's true."

"A little less happy to hear I'm a dime a dozen."

"Actually this is the best coffeeshop I've ever been in."

"Go on with your story."

Kevin debated the need for more groveling, deciding it was safe to continue. "When I show up again after lunch, the bank staff is usually only halfway done with my list. I tell them, 'That's good enough, I'll make do'. They are so thankful. They think I'm a wonderful guy. It's a pretty good system."

"I know quite a few of the people who work at that Wells Fargo branch. I should have probably told you."

Kevin's soft hazel eyes widened. "You won't say anything, will you?"

"Naaww." That's when Rick McEwen entered. "Hey, here's somebody I want you to meet."

Rick is tall, with a tall head. When you add it up, I'd say six-three. His hair is thin and flat to his head. Like baby hair. He has piercing eyes and a thin nose. All that being said, understand that he's a pretty good looking man. I don't think it's just my opinion. For a straight man, I consider myself a fair and objective judge of male beauty.

"Rick," I greeted him. "Here for the coffee?"

"So I hear," said Rick.

"'Hey boy,'" I impersonated Mike, "'you don't seem to be too busy. Like usual. Why don't you run fetch us some coffee.'"

"For never having been to our office," said Rick, "you have a pretty good idea of what goes on there."

"I'm sorry to hear that," I sympathized. "Hey, there's somebody you should meet. Rick, Kevin." They shook hands, and I started filling in the blanks for them. "Kevin's from San Fran, but he went to CSU in Fort Collins. Didn't you graduate from CSU?"

"I did." Rick nodded at Kevin. "You do look familiar. San Francisco, huh? What brings you to North Dakota, for crying out loud?"

"Kevin's an auditor for Wells Fargo," I answered for him because I think his mouth was dry.

"Really." Rick took a step closer, which I knew wasn't unusual for him. Kevin probably didn't. Rick is running a lifelong experiment on people's reaction to an invasion of their personal space. "What was your major?" he demanded. As a related study of the human response to social discomfort, Rick's habit is to make questions sound like threats.

"Accounting," said Kevin, softly, almost as an apology, sitting as far back as the corner would allow.

It's worth noting that for all his size and aggressive habits, Rick is the least threatening guy I know. You can't rile him. You know the old saying, silent waters run deep, and often conceal a twenty-foot man-eating shark? That isn't Rick at all. The man just wants to work. He loves construction—loves it from the moment he wakes up until the second he falls asleep, early, maybe eight-thirty, after a big dinner and a couple glasses of wine. Rick found his life's calling, and is at total inner peace with who he is and where he's heading. He wasn't going to hurt Kevin. He's the only guy I know who could actually take Jesus's advice and turn the other cheek, and not feel like a complete wuss.

"What year did you graduate?" Rick demanded. At this point, because of his natural Inquisitional conversational style, I couldn't tell whether Rick was aware that he might have cornered a fox fresh from his henhouse.

"Oh-two," said Kevin, squirming in his chair with a burnt amber flush on his cheeks, exhibiting all the signs of a fox caught with feathers on his lips. But then again that could have been solely due to having a strange man practically sitting in his lap.

I decided to end the uncertainty. "Rick, didn't your wife graduate in accounting?"

"Business management. She did take a few accounting classes. Maybe you know her," Rick said to Kevin. "Andrea Goldine."

The skin below Kevin's eyebrows went white. "Yeah. Yeah I do—well, did, I did, back then." Was he guessing I had manipulated this meeting to set him up? No, Kevin was thinking one thing and one thing only, *oh God, forgive me my sins and deliver me from the beating I am about to receive.* Me, I was feeling pretty good about myself. I was a helper.

Rick was seeing Kevin through slits.

"Hey." Andrea McEwen had entered the shop without my noticing, to stand behind her husband Rick. "So this is where you go when you leave the house." Andrea had a sassy mouth with Rick. They had moved to town a year ago (when Brent McEwen's oncologist pronounced his cancer incurable and given him a few months to live—they arrived just in time to watch Rick's younger brother make a miraculous recovery, and then suffer a quick, shocking death). I had chatted with Andrea at a few McEwen family functions. Except for the occasional sarcastic comment directed at her husband, she didn't seem able or willing to mesh with the McEwens' tight rhythms.

Rick raised his arm to look down at her through the notch of his armpit. "Speak of the devil." He dropped his arm around Andrea's shoulders—a good foot below his—and pulled her forward, further damming up the chute between counter and tabletop, Kevin's only escape route, if you don't count melting into a puddle of goo and seeping between the floorboards. "And no," said Rick, "I don't come here. I go a lot of places. Here isn't one of them."

"Rick is the errand boy this morning," I said, watching the interplay between Kevin and Andrea. This was a little more than I had bargained for.

"My old man thinks he's funny," said Rick. "I'm going to teach him a lesson, though. Set me up with two dozen muffins."

"I can't help you there," I said. "Unless you want those." I tapped the top of the display case, where a couple tipped muffins and a few loose cookies lay in the crumbs of the previous days' pastries. And there was a croissant, which for the life of me I couldn't remember buying. "I don't recommend it."

Rick shook his head to dislodge the disturbing vision. "I'll pass. How about if you whip up a few lattés and cappuccinos to go? Something pricey."

"Five of each?" I nodded to my employee Sam at the espresso machine, all six-foot-seven and two hundred sixty pounds of him. When he screwed up, we blamed it on his height, and when he did something great, we wrote it off to his unfair height advantage.

"I'm on it," said Sam. No contest, he made the best lattés on staff. But so could we all, if we were as tall as him.

"I've never seen you two together outside of family functions," I said to Rick and Andrea. "And in my shop no less."

"And I doubt you'll see it again anytime soon," said Andrea, average looking, petite, long in the hair, compact in the torso. She was prettier than usual that day, perhaps thanks to spending a few additional minutes on the makeup. Maybe just the extra cleavage and leg she was showing. "Rick is a workaholic. Unless you're wearing a hardhat and steel-toed boots, Rick won't spend much time with you."

"Put on chaps and spurs, then maybe we can talk," said Rick. "Hey." He waggled his hand at Kevin, who looked startled to find himself still visible. "This is—"

"I know Kevin," Andrea short-circuited the introduction. She gave Kevin a wry smile, while he stared at the floor and perspired. Nice poker face, Kevin. Andrea crossed her arms in disapproval. "I should have known you two would find each other." She looked up at Rick. "Can't I have a friend all to myself?"

Rick spread his arms as far as the tight quarters would allow and shrugged. "We were getting along so well, but if that's the way you're going to be…he's yours." I couldn't get a read on his mental state.

"Yeah, right," said Andrea, whose clipped syntax meshed well with her husband's. "I know how men are. Now you two are buddies, and I'm out of the picture. Fine." Very cool, very calculated. Andrea was determined to hold on to both her men. Dangerous game, I thought to myself.

My goal had been to fire a warning shot across Kevin's bow, before he dropped anchor in the McEwen harbor, before I found my self seconding Rick on the foggy moors at dawn, dueling pistols from fifteen paces. I wasn't looking for an in-store exchange of accusations and, God help me, admissions. So far it was all very jokey, but it was banter I couldn't enjoy. Trouble was brewing, and I prayed for thirty customers to stampede through my door. Then again, I always prayed for that.

Terrence and his laptop walked in. Good enough. "Terrence!"

"I got him, Brian," said Sam. I could have tried to elbow that big boy out of the way, but I would have lost. "Hoodilee-hoo, Terrence."

"Hoodilee-hoo, big guy." Terrence ignored me, too polite to interrupt the conversation I appeared to be enjoying in the corner.

"So let me get this straight," Rick grilled Kevin again. "You're just in town for a few days? Where are you staying? The Holiday Inn?"

"At the Buffalo Motel, actually." Kevin looked miserable. "It's a little seedy, but I like to get some of the local flavor when I travel."

"Our firm built the addition on the Buffalo Motel last year," said Rick.

"I'm pretty sure I'm in the old part," said Kevin. A warm puff of panic wafted across the counter.

"I've heard that when Wells Fargo hires auditors," I spoke to Andrea, "tact isn't a quality they look for. Just a rumor I heard."

"Then Rick should have been an auditor," said Andrea. She looked up at him, her arms still crossed, maintaining her sassy pout. If she felt any guilt, she was hiding it very well. "Tact is definitely not his strong suit."

"If I wasn't tactful," Rick retorted, "I'd be accusing you two of getting busy at the Buffalo Motel."

"Like you would care," said Andrea.

"Just as long as it doesn't interfere with our regular schedule." Rick gave me a wink. "So are those expensive coffee creations ready?"

"Almost done," Sam called out.

"Let me grab the brewed coffee," I volunteered.

"I'll pull around back to load it up," said Rick.

"God," said Andrea. "How much coffee do you people drink?"

"You should be able to carry it out the front door," I told Rick, while I gave myself silent props. Kevin had been scared shitless; it looked like everyone was going to walk away in one piece; and Rick wasn't going to bring up the new retail center. That was my favorite part. Although I was pretty pleased to have saved a marriage. I had no doubt Kevin, who may have wet himself, would be wrapping up his audit a few days ahead of schedule, next year's budget be damned.

Sam helped Rick out the door with the drinks and pump pots, leaving Andrea behind with Kevin, while I went about my business, refilling the portafilters, wiping down the bar, flushing hot water through the espresso machine, whistling while I worked.

"That was interesting," said Andrea to Kevin. "I suppose I should have told him you were in town."

"Does he know who I am?" Kevin hissed. "No way. Does he?"

"Only what I told him back then," said Andrea, calm and slightly bored. "That you and I hung out sometimes. That you were always a good friend whenever he was being a dick to me. Don't worry about it—I could have told him you were my hot passionate lover and it wouldn't have mattered. Rick doesn't have a jealous bone in his body."

"That wouldn't have been my read," said Kevin.

Yes, I was eavesdropping.

"He seemed ready to beat the hell out of me," said Kevin.

"He couldn't if he wanted to," said Andrea. "He never works out."

Andrea moved in tight to Kevin, fingers touching his arm. Kevin couldn't take his eyes off the door, waiting for Rick to walk back in, bearing arms. "Just from observation," I joined the conversation, "I'd have to say that if it came down to a battle to the death between Rick and Kevin—say there's only one spot left on the rescue boat before the ship sinks—I'm taking Rick. No offense; but honestly, he'd rip your head off."

"I don't know," said Andrea. "Kevin has some decent muscles under there." She tugged at the sleeve of his polo shirt. "If I remember right."

Like I said, dangerous game. "Were you two an item at CSU?"

"Not really," said Kevin.

"I wouldn't say that." Andrea shook her hair back and fingered it into place for the waiting barrette clenched between her teeth. In this position she highlighted a flexible spine and a sleek throat. Like I said, Andrea wasn't skinny, but she knew how to smokescreen her lack of a waist. That morning she had chosen apparel that revealed a generous stretch of tanned leg and more than a hint of cleavage, all currently on full display.

Kevin was suddenly antsy in a different way. Exuberance barely contained. The possibility that at any second Death could come a-bursting through my front door was a fuzzy memory. He was dying to touch those legs, and plumb that cleavage. He had exchanged fear for lust, right then and there. This guy was in too deep.

When the show was over, I asked Andrea, "What can I get you?"

"Do I have to buy something to stay here?" Andrea teased.

"I'm afraid so."

"Then you're going to have to kick me out."

"I know you're not afraid of me." I'm tall enough, but not imposing. Even though I played sports in school, I never packed on a lot of upper-body muscle. I was content to go with my God-given abilities, a strategy that freed up a generous amount of high school party time while the other guys were in the weight room, and still allowed me to letter four years in basketball. As a teenager my underdeveloped torso created the illusion that my head was too big for my body, when in fact it was exactly the right size. I'm not going to call it the perfect fix, but now that I've added a few pounds around the middle, everything looks more proportionate.

"Are you afraid of me?" I thought I should check, just in case.

"No," Andrea confirmed.

"I don't blame you. But did you get a look at Sam?"

On cue my whopper of an employee returned through the front door, filling it with his thick shoulders and round buzz-cut head. Sam was my personal bodyguard. Not that I had any confidence he would defend me in a barroom brawl. Maybe pick me up and carry me out of harm's way.

"It's not obvious, but that guy has some anger issues, Sam," I called to him, "just calm down. Control your temper—Sam, *Sam*. Come on now, just because this lady is causing trouble is no reason to start swinging."

Sam had played this game way too often, for his tastes. But he did his best to threaten, puffing up his chest and sucking in his gut as he lumbered into the chute, bumping Andrea's shoulder with his belly and glaring down at her. Andrea craned her neck to glare right back, and Sam broke into his goofy grin. He struggled to regain form. "Am I going to have to get tough with you?"

"Please don't push him," I cautioned. "I don't want this to get ugly."

Andrea continued staring up at Sam. "How tall are you?"

"How big am I? Are you saying I'm fat?"

"Don't deck her, Sam," I soothed. "Last week my liability insurance lapsed." This was no joke; certain bills you can stretch, and some you can't.

"Really," said Andrea, "how tall are you? Seven feet?"

"Six-eight," Kevin guessed, happy-go-lucky audit playboy once more.

"Six-two," I scoffed.

"I was six-two in seventh grade," said Sam.

"No way," I argued. "No one's that tall. No one."

"Go beat him up," Andrea urged with a giggle, turning Sam around and giving him a push. "Go beat him up."

I stared at Sam as he came around the counter and ambled toward me. "You are going to have to work on your focus. What did I tell you to do? Didn't I say to kick her out? You want a paycheck or a pink slip, big guy?"

Sam shrugged and grinned.

"Get out of here," I yelled, modest anger in my voice. "Go roast some beans, why don't you?!" Most people had caught my act enough to laugh. Every so often I shocked a customer. Probably drove them to Hernandes's shop, if they could find it.

Andrea was chuckling. "You are too much."

"He is," said Kevin. "I've truly never been in a shop like this, and I've been all over the past couple years. You can feel the clock ticking in every other coffeeshop, the employees waiting for you to leave. Here, it's more like I'm being entertained in Brian's living room."

"You still have to leave at some point." I wasn't in the mood for flattery from this guy. And I was listening to Craig my manager giving Sam gentle direction:

"Did you get the order ready for the Lutheran Bible study group?"

"No."

"Don't you think you should?"

"Definitely."

"When?"

"Soon."

"No, now. Go!"

Craig had no people skills, and the kids I hired were too self-confident to notice. Perfect work environment.

"You're seriously not drinking anything?" I harped on Andrea. "Seriously?"

"Brian, I've been here a year and never come into your shop. Obviously I'm not a coffee drinker."

"You're not going to order a single solitary thing?" I pushed.

"Not a thing." She spread her arms wide, a tough-guy pose. "If you want me out, looks like you'll need to do it yourself."

"If you're going to be that way, I guess you can stay. I don't want to see you sipping on Kevin's mocha, though."

Kevin pulled his drink closer.

"Don't worry," said Andrea. "I don't like coffee. Plus," she said with a nasty little grin, "I heard that new coffeeshop close to the campus has the best joe in town."

That almost hurt my feelings. I froze with my back to them, then threw down the coffee-stained towel I had just picked up. "That cuts it." I pointed at the door. "Out."

T - 17

The next time I saw Andrea was early January, during a blizzard, outside Martin's Restaurant & Bakery. I was picking my way along the sidewalk carrying a to-go bag when she staggered through the bank of plowed snow separating street and sidewalk and fell in next to me. I mean fell. I saw it coming the whole way and caught her arm, holding her upright until she got her feet under her. At no time were my chicken and dumplings in danger of sloshing out of the Styrofoam container. I looked around, waiting for the applause. Never an audience when you need one.

"Thanks," said Andrea. She checked to ensure her papers remained secured by the rubber band. "Good thing I don't weigh much, or your back would be out."

If she didn't weigh much, then my feat wasn't all that spectacular. And in fact Andrea's weight was not insubstantial. That gal weighed more than she looked. But I held my tongue. Chivalry was a bitter pill to swallow.

Andrea bent over and brushed snow off her fur-lined pointy-toed boots. A car drove by and launched a glop of dirty salted slush over the plow-bank, landing an inch from Andrea's suede boot. She straightened up and sighed. "Nice winter we're having, don't you think?"

"Winter in Jamestown is hell on earth. Only a lot colder. So, lady…"

Andrea scowled. "It's Andrea."

"Right, right." I pointed at myself. "Brian."

"Oh yeah," Andrea ladled on the sarcasm, "now I remember. I guess neither of us is spending a lot of time at the McEwen house lately."

"I've been busy."

"Mm, sure."

I inched down the sidewalk toward my shop, eager to be on my way. Without knowing what had transpired the past three months, you might assume it was because I was hungry for those dumplings, or because I was wearing shorts. "By the way," I said, "thanks for not coming into my shop anymore. I don't like trouble with non-coffee drinkers."

"Really." Andrea perked up at the challenge, inching along with me. "What if I came in for a pastry? Would you serve me?"

"A, we don't call them pastries. Around here they're baked goods. B, I don't sell pastries. Not edible ones, anyway. And C, even if I did sell them, not a chance. No coffee, no service. I'm sorry, but that's my policy."

"If that's the way it's going to be…"

"'Fraid so. Don't let me interrupt your business." I nodded to her papers.

She clutched the packet to her chest, and checked out my bare legs. "Nice shorts. What is it today, five below zero?"

"I don't wear pants much. Or ever." Not true, I took Christmas or Easter off, one or the other.

"Aren't you the tough guy."

"Just the only one to realize that if you warm the top, the legs will follow. Your top is the key. I'll stop just short of saying your legs are irrelevant."

"You," said Andrea, "are ridiculous. I suppose your legs are too nice to hide."

"If I'm attractive to the opposite sex, if there's anything remotely appealing about me, it's my legs." I was a hoopster with a soccer player's legs. "And my hair, I suppose." I don't ask for glamour hair, just hair I can take for granted, hair that's going to show up for work each and every day and do its job, which is of course to allow me to nonchalantly run my fingers through it and come away looking no worse than before. "And my eyes…well, enough about me."

"No, go on."

"That's probably enough self-affirmation for one day." Gotta say it to myself you know. It's like a never-ending six-step program.

"Like you need it," said Andrea. "You walk on water, at least as far as Rick's family is concerned."

"Not for long," I muttered.

Andrea wore a devilish look. "I heard you and Isabel are having problems."

"Is that what you heard?"

A snowplow rumbled down the middle of Main Street, leaving an imposing two-foot berm behind the few cars parked in front of my shop. I had asked the city not to do that—was that Frannie the sign nazi driving the plow? A couple came out of my shop and stood in front of their blocked car, shaking their heads. Former customers, I like to call them. I wanted to tell them "it's not my fault, call the city; talk to Frannie". But of course it didn't work that way. If it happened in front of my shop, it was my fault.

"But I also heard you're still engaged," Andrea pressed for clarity.

None really existed. Iz and I had been engaged for eighteen months following three years of steady dating. Nearly from Day One I've known about the sordid episode from her past, the reason Iz is no longer a teacher. But our protracted courtship was always more a function of my shaky financial condition than my hang-up with Iz's indiscretion. Not sure whether it had been subconsciously festering inside me, or whether it was simply a case of finally coming to my senses (or losing them), but 'round about last September my hang-up became a full-blown *issue*.

After spending Christmas with my folks, I had returned to town intent on breaking up. Isabel protested long and tearfully. I have to admit her family entered into the calculation. They were just so vulnerable. Mike especially. He still got weepy at any reference to Brent, or hospitals, or children. The last year had been an emotional time for everyone, but Mike's sensitivity was off the charts. I loved the McEwens, and they were gaga for me. I couldn't kick that family when they were down. So I let Isabel downgrade my breakup demand to a trial separation.

"Technically, we are still engaged," I told Andrea.

"How does that work?"

"It was a poorly executed breakup. No balls, I guess."

Andrea smirked. "She wouldn't let you end it, you mean. Maybe two balls are enough in any relationship."

She was hammering me, deservedly. I started to respect her, at least her tongue.

In truth the temperature was twenty degrees warmer than Andrea's estimate; still, we were standing in a blizzard. The snow was piling up on our feet, the wind periodically whipping a frigid reminder up my shorts. Glad I wasn't a boxer man. Andrea's winter coat was all fashion, no function. We were both shivering, but Andrea was in no hurry to get inside. "If you don't mind my asking," she probed for more Tales Of The Eunuch, "why did you break up?"

"I'd rather not get into it." I started walking. "How about Isabel? Have you seen her lately? How's she doing?" It sounded like a throwaway line at that point, but I was concerned about her.

"Not great." Andrea didn't seem overly sympathetic toward her ex-sister-in-law. In fact, I'd say that Isabel's misery was a day-brightener for Andrea. "I think she's confused about what you're thinking. She was pretty sure you were going to get married."

"Engagements will do that to a person. So…" I wanted to bring this conversation to a close. "…out shopping?"

Andrea chuckled humorlessly. "Legal business. Is that lunch?"

"Sophie, one of the owners at Martin's, she gives me the occasional lunch in exchange for free coffee."

"Sounds like a good arrangement."

"For her. Have you tasted our coffee?" I paused for effect. "No, I guess you wouldn't know how good it is. Well then, have you eaten at Martin's?"

"I don't go out to eat," Andrea stated.

"Let's just say that Sophie definitely comes in for an extra-large three-shot caramel latté ten times more often than I ever grab a dry little half-sandwich and cup of watery soup from her. But hey, whatever. I don't keep track, and that way it doesn't get to me."

"I'll bet you cry like a baby when she walks into your shop."

That was a good one. And true. Sophie was a schoolyard bully following me into the bathroom every day and stealing my lunch money. "I hold back my tears, because Sophie is pretty cute. Easy on the eyes, I think that's the term."

Andrea grimaced and lost interest in the conversation.

"My lunch is getting cold," I announced. "And your papers are wet."

Andrea looked forlornly into the distance. Snowflakes collected on her eyelids. She was so damn tiny. Tiny little feet taking tiny, careful steps. A slippery patch of sidewalk, a gust of wind, and the next thing you know she's under Frannie's blade, to be found in June when the snow berm melted, frozen stiff like an ancient underdressed pygmy cavewoman. If she was parked more than a block away, I honestly didn't think she would make it in this weather.

We were now in front of my shop. "C'mon in. I'll give you a plastic bag for your papers. Hey, check that out. That's some sandwich board, huh?"

Andrea looked at the white hump. A soggy cardboard corner poked through the drift. "It's covered with snow. You can't read it."

"I don't care. I know what it says."

Like snow gods riding personal blizzards we swept into my empty shop.

"You're getting snow on my clean floor," Sam complained from behind the counter.

"This is just a sample of the drift sitting on our sidewalk," I explained.

"You think that's a good excuse?"

"I guess what I'm trying to say is, shovel."

"You don't have to yell," said Sam, slamming his towel on the countertop and storming out onto the floor. I have no clue what Sam's genuine anger is like, but his fake stuff is a little whiney.

"I'm sorry." I pretended to feel bad for his pretend hurt feelings over my very real order. "You know how emotional I get."

"Some customers like to play in the snow." Sam grew closer and closer, taller and taller. When I hired him he was a six-foot-two senior at Jamestown High, a few pounds shy of being a fat kid. As a Jamestown College junior he had grown another five inches and still managed to maintain the exact same figure, scaled up. Big kid.

If all of my employees came to blows—say I made sure Craig wasn't packing his Saturday Night Special and I confiscated smiling Sara's switchblade, and made Dana promise not to use her black magic. Say that I then took them to a deserted island and told them I was going to sail away for an hour (I've given this a lot of thought—possibly too much), and that when I returned, the last person standing would get time-and-a-half for the next three weekends. Assuming no alliances sprang up, Charlotte would be our winner. She has a scary-sexy mean streak. My employees know not to test her. And if she thinks she's protecting me, then look out. Even though she's ten years younger than me, she has a mother hen mentality, keeping me safe from unwanted callers, customers and collectors. No woman was good enough for me, as far as Charlotte was concerned. Even Isabel—pleasant, generous and, unless you knew her dark secret, which I don't believe Charlotte did, impossible to fault. Charlotte knew I was avoiding Iz, and approved.

Yes, Charlotte would win the prize. The giant, the misogynist, the grinning time bomb, the Goth, the Eagle Scout, they'd all be moaning in the sand at Charlotte's feet. Of course I couldn't afford to pay up, but it's the healthy competition that's important.

Sam towered over us. "Why do I always have to go out and shovel?"

"Because the only other job I have is to redo the menu board above the counter. And your handwriting sucks, frankly."

"Good point." Sam's expression turned grim as he eyeballed Andrea. "Hey. Maybe you could make her do it."

"Sure, I'll rewrite the menu," said Andrea.

"Deal," I said.

"Aagh." Sam hung his head.

I headed for my office. "I need to get this lady a plastic bag for her papers." Grab-assing with Andrea didn't feel right, if someone were to walk into the shop. Even if no one did. "Shovel Bodiners sidewalk next door, too," I called over my shoulder. "His son's gone today, and I don't want the old man to have a stroke on my sidewalk."

When I emerged with a Herberger's bag, Sam was talking to Andrea, shifting from foot to foot, wearing a big goofy grin, the skin below his buzz cut a flushed, happy pink. "That sounds like a great job," he was saying. "Andrea's interviewing to be a research assistant at the hospital," I was informed.

"Oh, hey. Good for you. Who with?"

"It's just an interview," said Andrea. "I don't even know if I want the job, but it would be a good fit. My business degree specialized in lab science, and I worked in a genetics lab at CSU. But this would be a lot different. I didn't understand most of what they explained to me. I'm sure they're wondering why they should hire me."

"Because you're short enough to reach the supplies in the lower cupboards," I suggested. "So who did you say you interviewed with?"

"I would probably be a shared resource for more than one scientist."

Besides their money, all I ask of my customers is to name names.

"Genetics lab work," said Sam. "Sounds interesting." If he kept looking at

Andrea with those puppy love eyes, I was going to have to roll up a newspaper and stab him in the throat with it. Hopefully in all the pain, confusion and fear, he would wet himself, so I could then rub his nose in his own urine. It takes that sort of firm discipline to break a bad habit.

"I got your bag," I told Andrea. I stared at Sam. "To protect her papers from all the *snow*."

"Alright, alright," said Sam, "I'm going." He plucked the shovel from beside the door and ventured into the storm. Another couple inches had drifted against the door, and now fell on my floor.

"He seems like a good man to have around," said Andrea.

"He's alright. He's great, actually." I held the bag while Andrea dropped her papers inside. Legal documents. I saw the words "child custody". (I was going to preface that with *Before I could look away*, but I'm a bit of a snoop.) "I have a really good crew. I'm lucky."

"I could use a little of that," said Andrea. "A little luck would be nice." Her lower lip quivered.

I wanted to wish her all the luck and send her packing. But I'm a coffeeshop owner. I have professional obligations. "So," I forced myself, "you good?" Please don't cry, I silently begged. "Can I get you anything?"

Andrea gazed at the wall of white outside my big display window. Sam was just visible, carrying a shovelful of snow, looking for someplace to throw it. "Maybe a glass of water."

"I was going to make myself tea." I never touched the stuff. "Want one?"

"I'm fine."

"It's the best time to drink tea. When you're feeling fine." Actually there is no time that is right for tea, but I didn't like Andrea well enough to tell her so. I dangled and dipped tea bags while she drifted toward the counter stools.

"Why do you get to sit inside drinking tea while your employee shovels all that snow?" she wondered.

"We only have one shovel." I slid the cup of tea across the counter. "Your legal business must have been pretty important to come out on a day like this."

Andrea slipped out of her iridescent coat and carefully removed her stylish stocking cap. Her long hair was gently curled, a few hairs frizzy from the stocking cap. A full serving of makeup accentuated her doe eyes and cushioned her pointy chin. Her nails were long and manicured. She moved like a Southern belle, slow, deliberate, planned. "I might as well have stayed at the apartment, as it turns out," she said. A little grunt escaped her lips as she mounted the stool. That's why you don't see any five-foot tall barfly belles. "Rick and I are divorced, you know. I wasn't sure if you had heard."

Of course I had heard. Even though I had only seen Isabel twice since Thanksgiving, and repeatedly turned down invites to the McEwens' over the holidays, Mike and Valerie refused to admit I wasn't their natural-born son-in-law. I was in their inner circle whether I liked it or not. They would leave me voicemails detailing petty grievances with Andrea, juicy gossip about their construction company employees, and the latest touching maternal gesture Isabel had made toward Rick and Andrea's four-year-old son Tyler.

"I'm sure the McEwens have a lot to say about it," Andrea said bitterly. She crossed her arms, cupping her elbows so as not to cut her sleeve with one of her painted talons. "What did they tell you?" Her irises turned black and her chin grew another inch. I knew I was getting a taste of what Rick used to enjoy when he came home late from the construction site or after carousing with clients. Or, no doubt, when he accused her of sleeping with Kevin the Wells Fargo auditor. I had very little sympathy for this adulterous bitch.

"Word gets around," I said, to deflect her venom from the McEwens. And it was certainly no secret around Jamestown. Surely she had seen her face posted like a missing child on lightposts, billboards, and milk cartons, with the caption *Have you fucked me, too?* "Fifteen thousand people, and it's still a small town at heart."

"I hate it," said Andrea, just above a whisper. "Tyler and I were going to leave as soon as the custody agreement was final…but it hasn't worked out." She turned away from me, struggling to stay composed.

I knew, from a voicemail from Isabel's mom Valerie, that the McEwens were bringing serious legal resources to bear to keep Tyler with Rick in Jamestown. Andrea didn't have a chance in hell of moving away with that kid.

I had no idea what to say and no inspiration to think of anything.

"And now I'm in an apartment. Our house belonged to Rick's family, so I couldn't very well ask him to leave."

"So…you asked Rick for the divorce?" It was only fair that I asked for her side of the story, as I only knew the McEwen party line. Of course I had seen enough with my own eyes to draw a fairly objective conclusion.

She joggled the Herberger's bag. "According to this guy, when it comes to custody of the kids, it doesn't really matter who asked who."

"Chalk it up to a mutual decision then."

Andrea shrugged. "Everyone is so sure Rick is a saint. But what would you do if someone constantly…" She stopped and stared. With her heavy lids and a natural dark shading that haunted her eyes, it was a pretty effective stare. "I probably shouldn't say anything that's going to get back to them."

"I'm not much for keeping secrets, it's true."

Andrea was more than a little bitter. "I have to be careful what I say, but they can say anything they want about me, isn't that right?"

The McEwens were not the kind of family you screwed with, that was my impression. When the McEwens frowned upon you, so did Jamestown.

"But maybe you're not quite so tight with the McEwens anymore," Andrea fished. "If you're dumping Isabel."

"I'm sure I'll still have a good relationship with Iz's family, even if—"

"Are you? Dumping her?"

"I think we already declared that topic off-limits."

"You won't," Andrea decided. "You're afraid to make the McEwens angry, because then you couldn't get a coffeeshop in the Bluffs."

Like most things, Andrea had it all wrong. Not that I wanted Mike to think less of me, but if ignoring his daughter into breaking up with me prompted him to pull that sweetheart deal off the table and save me from a repeat of my impersonation of a train-wreck in California, it was for the best.

Because the temptation was there. Bill Hernandes was stealing my customers. He was printing coupons like funny money—everybody in town must have had a stack of them. You simply couldn't make money if every customer was cashing in a two-for-one. He had to be buying low-grade beans and watering down his milk, ensuring each batch of coupons that rolled off the press was worth less than the one before. Hernandes was a two-bit banana republic dictator running a hyperinflationary economy, gambling on winning the people's hearts before they realized they had lost their minds.

Andrea to take a sip of her tea. "Eeuu. God. Who drinks this?"

"Evil people. You should switch to coffee."

"No thanks. I should go."

"Probably for the best." It was impossible to have a relaxed time with this woman. The conversation vacillated between Andrea thinking I was too tight with the McEwens, and me thinking she was too much of a slut. And in between, things felt too familiar between us. I took back her cup. "Pretty soon you're going to need an avalanche beacon to find your car."

"I heard the snow was letting up," Andrea wished upon a star.

"Not until May."

"You're pessimistic."

"Realistic."

"But I suppose you love it this way."

"Nine months of winter and three months of pre- and post-winter? No, not particularly. I'm a California boy."

"Then why are you here?"

I started to answer, and hesitated, and then told her why. "Believe it or not, I moved here to start my coffee empire."

Andrea cackled. "Yeah, right. In North Dakota? Really. And?"

"Not so good."

"And now you hate North Dakota. I can tell."

"No. I don't hate it here. I love the people. I have a lot of great friends and customers. And there's a lot to be said for doing business in North Dakota."

"Name one."

"Okay. I won't get sued if someone gets hurt in my shop or spills hot coffee on her baby's head. I had a teenage customer break her ankle—five hundred pounds of poorly-stacked beans fell on her. Her dad came in the next day and called her a clumsy bastard for not getting out of the way in time. You won't find that philosophy of personal responsibility in California."

Andrea grimaced. "I'd say it's a lack of self-worth. People here would never sue you because they don't think they deserve any compensation. They don't think their lives are worth it."

"Oh. Nice. Thanks for knocking off my rose-colored glasses."

"My pleasure." Andrea was smug. "If you love it here so much, why did you spend the holidays in California?"

"How did you know that?"

"Like I can get Isabel to shut up about you."

"I hadn't been home to see my folks for a year. I actually cut the trip short by a week. Every time I sat down to relax and talk with Mom and Dad, all I could hear was the cash register not ringing here in my shop."

"One more week wouldn't have killed you," said Andrea.

"Another week and I might as well have stayed there for good, because there wouldn't be any customers waiting for me when I returned."

"You honestly don't think your staff can handle things without you?"

"No offense to my staff, they're hardworking kids. But they're kids. And kids attract other kids. Without an adult in charge, the next thing you know you got yourself a hangout full of kids with empty pockets, and not a paying customer in sight."

With a blast of cold air across my toes and the marimba music of coffee pails ricocheting off the walls, I deduced that my assistant manager Craig had come through the alley door. He stomped and staggered down the short hallway and paused at the storage room door, looking at the snow on his shoulders, looking at me. I nodded. Craig shook his head. We agreed to disagree.

"I should go," said Andrea.

"Okay lady. Stop in from time to time."

"Thanks, but I don't think so." She slid forward and dropped the last couple inches to the floor. "This isn't really my town, if you know what I mean."

I sure did. "I get a lot of moms coming in with their kids in the mornings. Especially when the weather's crummy. You might want to—"

"I wouldn't fit into their little stay-at-home-mom club," Andrea declared. "Tyler goes to preschool."

"You could carry a picture of him. Like a membership card."

Andrea gave me a sour smile as she buttoned her undersized coat.

"The Y has some great day-programs," I suggested. "Some singles stuff. I think I have a brochure around here somewhere."

"No thanks."

"You will be assimilated."

"No, I won't."

"Craig," I called into the storage room, "I need to run down the block. Will you watch the counter for me?"

"You planning on a big rush?" Craig wondered.

"No. In fact, I'm probably going to call it quits for the day."

"I'm not leaving."

"I appreciate that, homey." Like Charlotte, Craig was salaried, but he lived on a tight budget and operated under the suspicion that I would dock his pay if he ever went home early. I saw no reason to correct this misperception.

Andrea was going out the door. "Let me get my coat," I called after her.

"I didn't figure you wore coats," she referred to my shorts and loafers.

"I'm not crazy."

"Why are you coming with me?" Andrea demanded.

"I'll scrape your windows for you."

"I'll get your employee to do it. Looks like he's done shoveling."

"Are you sure? Just because Sam can stand on one side of the car and scrape the entire windshield, doesn't mean he'll do a good job."

"I'm sure."

Craig stood beside me as I watched Andrea step into the blizzard and hurry out of sight. "She has a nice pooper," he said.

"Yes she does, but I wish you wouldn't call it that."

"That's what it's for," said Craig. "Even girls' butts. For pooping. Does it make sense for us to look at their butts and start drooling? You should look at their vaginas. 'Nice vagina.'"

This was why I avoided conversations with Craig when others were around.

"I'm sure we would stare at it all day long," I said, "if it wasn't so hard to do it without getting caught."

"Just as long as you acknowledge that you're getting turned on by the place where poop comes out."

"Not Andrea's. But ordinarily, sure."

CRAIG ENDED UP leaving before I did. I planned on sitting in my tiny office and worrying over the three-year revenue numbers Charlotte prepared for me, as if data analysis would increase sales, instead of more customers. I resolved to work fast and get out of there before the sun went down, before my van was lost in a snowdrift at the townhall lot. Maybe call Jerry and Amber, see if they wanted to bowl.

Instead I sat in the front display window, safe from the whirling snow attacking the glass inches from my nose, and went back a little further in time. Andrea wasn't the only one having difficulty understanding my decision to move to North Dakota.

At my lowest point in California, when I laid awake in bed at night, I wasn't dreaming of greener pastures, of going back to college, of changing careers. I was reading coffee—journals and entrepreneurial how-to's and global field reports—and thinking coffee. I didn't know anything else—and didn't want to. If I was going to make money in this life, it would be in coffee. I was obsessed with discovering a new concept or product that would turn things around.

So when I received the last-chance it's-still-not-too-late reminder for the coffee retailers trade show to be held in Fargo—*Cool Trends in a Hot Market!* the postcard screamed the theme at me—I jumped on it.

I can't convey to you the excitement I felt. Like sly Fate had convinced the organizers to hold the conference in the great white no-man's land, hidden the Next Big Thing there amidst the booths and presentations, out on the frozen tundra where only the most committed or desperate would find it.

Which described me perfectly.

North Dakota in late October. Colder than I had anticipated. Cold drinks, said the speaker at the first session. Cold drinks are the future. And sandwiches. Everyone was gung-ho for cold drinks and sandwiches. The tone was infectiously upbeat, and why not? Three days to dream big and ignore the fact that most of the coffeeshop owners (and speakers) would be out of business in eighteen months.

The first night I found a bar with an acoustic guitarist on a small stage in the dusky backend, and conducted a one-man brainstorming session at a table halfway back. No ideas had come, just lots of questions, when a lanky brunette in a polo shirt and loose-fitting khakis stopped in front of me and said:

"I don't usually go for guys with high foreheads, but, I just had to say hi."

"There must be some mistake." I pulled my mop of hair back. "See?"

"Solid hairline," she admitted. "Then it must be your eyes. You have the sexiest eyes I've ever seen."

"Sexy," I said, like a parrot.

"I'm interrupting your work," she said. "I just wanted to say hi. I would have kicked myself otherwise." Before I could say "kicked", or ask her for a cracker, she sashayed away, melting into the patrons crowding the bar.

I was flattered of course—she was a pretty girl, in spite of the drab clothes—but actually didn't give her more than a couple fond thoughts over the next hour as I drank vodka tonics and continued to struggle between the need to expand my menu offerings, and my intense dislike for anyone who came into my shop and ordered something other than a coffee-based drink.

I will admit that I scanned the crowd as I headed for the door. Not to worry, she had the entrance staked out. We talked there, and then in the parking lot, huddling and using her car for a windbreak against the icy wind.

Isabel was from Jamestown, a quarter Fargo's size but still one of the state's big cities. She was in her mid-to-late twenties like me. Two months earlier she had lost her high school teaching job, and had been working for her father's construction company back in Jamestown since then. Construction wasn't her bag, so her pop had given her time off to come to Fargo and stay with her sister while she completed an eight-week independent seminar to become a certified financial planner. Which might be fun for awhile, Isabel thought; but what she really wanted to do was return to teaching.

"So tell me about you," Isabel said.

"I own three coffeeshops," I said.

"I'd like to get to know you," she said, like I was some kind of mogul, or solvent.

"I'm here for a seminar," I grudgingly disclosed. "I'm from California."

"I've heard that the world is shrinking, right? Geography is irrelevant." Isabel winked. "Brian Lawson, there is something special about you."

"It's probably my personality. I'm what you call an extra-introvert."

"I don't think that's a category."

"Either I'm special or I'm not."

Isabel had smiled. "Whatever you are, it's something I've never seen before. Fate brought you here, and I'm not going to let you go that easily."

Isabel was a blend of blunt forwardness and cool detachment. Her words hinted that she was teetering on the precipice of reckless abandon. Her body language suggested she wasn't even close.

We met for trick-or-treating the next evening. Isabel was saddled with her nephew for the night while her sister traveled to Minneapolis on business. Instead of his neighborhood, little Benjie wanted to hit the strip mall. Not the indoor kind. With the temperature in the teens and a thirty-mile-an-hour wind out of the north, Benjie and maybe fifteen other kids pounded the pavement in costumes masked with scarves, hats, mittens and heavy winter coats.

As we stood in line for bite-sized Bit-O-Honeys at Play It For Me Over And Over Again Sports, a tremor coursed through my shoulders. And then again, enough to make my teeth chatter. "Wow. What's happening to me?"

"You're shivering," said Isabel.

"I find that hard to believe."

"You're wearing shorts," said six-year-old Benjie, with a judgmental tone.

"It's my California costume. At least people can see my costume."

The kid stuck out his tongue at me.

"Your lips are turning blue," said Isabel. She crouched to rub life back into my bare legs. "I have an old coat in my trunk. We can cut off the sleeves and you can use them for leg warmers."

"I'm not that cold, honestly. I'll be fine, once this wind dies down."

Isabel stood and looked me in the eye, deadly serious. "This is North Dakota, Brian. That never happens."

Little Benjie couldn't have cared less about my suffering. The kid was focused on filling his candy bag, forcing us to make three passes up and down the row of retailers. Benjie was also not concerned in the least about this stranger sniffing around his auntie's skirts, or in this case, heavy woolen pants.

One of the participating businesses was a coffeeshop, The Java Hut, with red-checkered tablecloths and ruffled curtains. "Let's go in here," I suggested.

"You're freezing, aren't you?" Isabel accused.

"No, that's not why."

The place was packed, people at each of the five tables and another five customers in line. The matronly middle-aged woman behind the counter greeted us with a smile. "Welcome to The Java Hut. I'll be right with you."

The distinct stench of burnt coffee hung in the air. The woman worked the till and the bar, making one drink at a time. Slowly. I watched her scorch milk and consistently go long on her espresso pulls. Sure enough, my macchiato was watery and flavorless, except for the hint of boiled milk.

"You're smiling," said Isabel. "Must be good."

Not only wasn't it good, it was barely coffee. "I'm pleased," I said.

"This is the best coffeeshop in town," she said, dunking a gingersnap cookie.

"No kidding." My mind was whirling.

We returned to Isabel's sister's house and put Benjie and his candy bag to bed. Isabel put on New Age instrumental music, with a mellow but insistent drum beat. She lit candles at either side of the room and turned off the lights. The house was uncomfortably warm, making it natural for Isabel to strip down to a tanktop, me to a t-shirt.

And for the next hour we danced. Without touching each other. Rooted to one spot in the middle of the living room floor. Isabel called it mirroring. It was Star Trek alien love. Isabel would slowly stretch her right hand out to the side, and I would do the same with my left, mirroring her, maintaining a constant couple inches of separation. We would reach for the ceiling, and then bring our hands back to shoulder level. The whole circuit might take twenty seconds, and then we would repeat the movement on the other side, oh-so-slowly and never touching.

She's tall for a girl, so we were face to face, nose to nose, eye to eye. I could feel her warm breath, and smell the gingersnap cookie on it. Incense-scented perfume wafted from beneath her tanktop, enveloping my head. Eventually my only awareness of the music was the arrhythmic beat keeping time with the quiver in my chest. I began to anticipate her, sensing the coiling of her shoulder muscle, the energy load on one side of her body that initiated action. There was no perceptible delay between her lead and my follow.

And at some point it was no longer obvious who was leading. I was moving, she was moving, and by some magic, it was all synchronized, a choreography we had been practicing for months. It was extremely sensual without being in the least bit sexual. That's a puzzling statement, I know. Big turn-on without the boner, maybe that paints a clearer picture.

My head was swimming, detached from my free-floating body. I was so disoriented I couldn't have pointed to the floor, and yet capable of performing the mirror image of Isabel's modern dance routine while maintaining a constant half-inch buffer from toes to nose, hips to fingertips.

Our first physical contact was the brief goodbye hug at the door. There was no kissing, no opening to take things further. In retrospect Isabel really wasn't in the running for any chastity trophy, but at the time I was bowled over by her self-control, her respect for Benjie and her sister, and my near-psychotic desire for her. I had fallen in lusty love.

I didn't even beat off back at the room. If Isabel could wait, so would I. I would save myself, every last drop for that woman. Isabel was right. I swear I could feel the hand of fate, reached down from its ghostly shell between Earth and Heaven, patting me on the back to let me know life-changing events were in process.

Now, when Isabel stuck her tongue up my ass and jacked me off that next night, I did have a *Hold on there! What am I getting myself into?* moment. But it passed—doubt had no chance to take root, after another big-tent coffee revival day at the conference, and after all the excited talk at dinner that night with Isabel, about starting what would be the only coffeeshop in her hometown of Jamestown. Maybe the only real coffeeshop in North Dakota. Sounded like a no-brainer.

Six winters later and there I was, alone in a blizzard, my business's lights barely visible to would-be customers as they passed by. Felt that way.

T - 16

I intended to show up early for Testimonial #3 for the McEwens' deceased son Brent. Because for one thing, like my dad taught me, it's just as easy to be early as it is to be late. And for another, I knew that if I came late, I would probably end up staying even later, after everyone else had left, encouraging the McEwens to leap to the conclusion that I was back in their fold.

Of course, that's why I was there. To give it another chance. Isabel deserved it.

In my head I believed that. My heart was having a hard time with it. Or vice-versa. There was no doubt I had treated Isabel poorly. By this time, late April, we were another couple months without really being together. Getting my head on straight, getting my finances in order, getting my ass handed to me at work, getting caught up on my reading...excuses, excuses, I had used them all on her. I had even dusted off my lupus.

I wanted to be an honorable man, I wanted to treat her right. But I don't think I was being unreasonable, I also wanted a nausea-free relationship.

The head or the heart, which controlled the gag reflex?

Isabel's nearly perfect, I reminded myself for the umpteenth time as I pulled onto the McEwens' street. We connected beyond anything I had ever experienced. When Iz had visited my coffee stand that afternoon, tension I didn't know existed just melted away. Iz was a day-brightener, literally. Colors were brighter with her around—I think because only then did I relax enough to see them. She had a rangy frame that turned me on, and her burnt-brown hair framed her face in a starlet way. And she loved me more than I deserved, more than any woman ever had. Maybe even including my mom.

So what if right before I met her, Iz had made it with a student in her sophomore creative writing class. So what if it was a girl. So what if it wasn't just once.

Oof. There was that queasy feeling again.

I'm as superficially decadent as the next guy. You wanna talk ménage à trois, toys and aids, softcore S&M, I'm in. At least in theory. But if I dwelled too long on Isabel's sick act, if I let the thought and images sink in too far, I became ill.

Struggling to Saranwrap my soul before the degenerate taint of statutory lesbian rape soaked in, I drove around the block—then put the van on autopilot and drove around and around, debating skipping Testimonial #3.

Number Three, I griped. Brent was a fine young man, but how many wakes does one person get? At least three. A year had passed, and the McEwens weren't ready to let go. I'm not much for death talk. I'm not even comfortable reminiscing about the lives of dead people. Dying scares the ever-lovin' crap out of me—much more on that later, unfortunately.

But I was sucking it up, for Iz. She loved me like no other; she had loved me in ways like no other. Yes, she had a self-control issue. Who didn't? I had one—coffee. It had ahold of me. Others had food issues, gambling issues, money issues, porno issues, and worse. My girlfriend had kinky, creative sex issues. Was that so bad? Most guys would kill to be in my shoes.

She loved me and I loved her. To move forward simply took forgiveness. She had made a mistake, granted a big one, but it was still a mistake. An indiscretion. Yes, a criminal indiscretion, if the girl's parents had gone to the police. But when Isabel promised to quit her teaching job, they hadn't. If those parents could forgive her, so could I. And anyway, Isabel told me this youngster was very mature for her fifteen years, and for the most part it was just holding hands and talking about the future. Knowing Isabel, probably some tickling, and kissing, and light petting...

I could see her face, her chestnut eyes glowing with warm understanding as she laid hands upon that girl. Nausea rushed up my throat, carrying a mouthful of bile.

Don't think about it, I counseled as I pulled up to their house, threw open the van door and leaned out to spit in the grimy snow-clotted gutter. *I may not be able to control the gag reflex, but I can choose not to think about it.*

For crying out loud, it was six years ago, I reminded myself. *Isabel was younger then, only twenty-six, too young to know better.*

And she had a point, girls mature early.

Heck, if we're being honest here, Iz probably raised that girl's standards for finding a loving, considerate mate, which is all any father can hope for.

A couple more times around the block.

This wasn't a trust issue; the tryst happened before I met her, and as far as I knew, never since. Isabel was fairly upfront about it, willing to supply more details than I could handle. I believed she had been as honest as I would let her be. A little more remorse would have been nice, but the topic was tied so closely to the abrupt halt to the teaching career she loved, I could forgive the wistful look in her eye.

And who was I to complain about one flaw in an otherwise wonderful woman? Regardless what Isabel would tell you, I was not the world's best boyfriend and fiancé. Starting with my first job at the Davis Drip, I had always put my heart and soul in coffee. I gave everything to my customers and employees, fourteen hours a day, six or seven days a week. For any relationship that extended past business hours, I had nothing left to give.

An extra-introvert? That's not just a stupid phrase I made up to irk Isabel. It's the truth. After putting out all day long, after being "on" from six a.m. to close, I just wanted to go home and veg. I know television is bad for me. I know that watching me fall asleep to the boob tube is no one's idea of a good time. Yet there was Isabel, rubbing my feet while I watched SportsCenter, knowing full well it was only going to knock me out sooner. She never took offense; instead of stomping out and complaining later how we never talked, she would clip my toenails and put Brightstrips on my teeth while I snored.

And then there was me, pretending one little ancient episode disqualified her from consideration, when in fact I was the one who didn't deserve her. I wasn't Mr. Morality, doing the difficult but correct thing, holding her accountable for a rash act; I was simply being too lazy to make our relationship work, and rationalizing an escape. An escape I would regret one day.

And let's face it, I have an over-active gag reflex. One time I puked when I saw a runny-nosed baby lick his own snot.

I can make this work, I decided. *I really can.* There was nothing more Isabel should have to do to soothe my damaged sensibilities, to convince me of her goodness. It was on me, my effort, my heart, my ability to distinguish between old history and today's reality. She was the best person out there for me. And a different person, a changed woman from the girl who had made that mistake. Still loving, still crazy, and definitely still kinky—but different, in the right way. Could I truly expect to find a better person than Isabel? The answer was a definite, definitive No.

It took me twenty minutes of driving around the block to come to this conclusion. So of course in the end I was right on time.

"Right on time as usual," Mike welcomed me at the door wearing a dark blue suitcoat over a slightly lighter blue shirt. "That's one of the many things I love about you, Brian. Swear to God."

"I love the way you love me, Mike."

"Nice job today," said Mike. "Great warm-up for the real thing."

I ran a coffee stand at the groundbreaking ceremony for his retail center, the Bluffs. I had a coffeeshop on wheels. It was a honey, a laundry van retrofitted with a generator, water tanks for brewing, a coffee machine, and a swing-out counter, so we could serve our customers at ground level instead of looking down on them like from a county fair concession stand.

Charlotte told me I was too proud of that sweet ride. Maybe she was right, maybe it was another vanity, like renting an apartment instead of living out of the storage room behind the shop. As my credit card balances grew and the past-due notices piled up, no doubt fiscal prudence dictated that I sell the mobile shop before firing employees. Luckily Craig hadn't drawn that comparison when I let him go, two months prior. What can I say, Craig did things I could do myself, like roasting coffee and delivering beans to wholesale accounts in Valley City and Carrington. And the mobile shop treated my customers a lot better than Craig did.

Mike gave me a strong hug. "I'm glad you're here."

I raised my eyebrows to Isabel in greeting as Mike rocked me to and fro.

"Dad, give the rest of us a chance, huh?" Isabel rubbed her father's shoulder as he turned away to dry his tears. She kissed me friendly-like on the lips and then hugged me, a little friendlier yet, with more hip-to-hip contact than friends might normally enjoy. It felt good. It felt right.

I looked at Isabel's black dress. "I guess I'm not dressed appropriately."

"Floral shirts and shorts are never inappropriate for you, Brian," said Valerie, Isabel's mom. "It's not what you wear that counts. It's that you're *here*."

"Thanks Mrs. McEwen."

"Listen to him," said Valerie, owner of one sexy senior neck, smooth skin and ropy muscles feeding into a velvety crescent of collarbone exposed by the broad necklines she favored. I fantasized about that neck. But only the neck. Her brown hair was thin and bobbed; her eyes and mouth heavily creased; her breasts, until proven otherwise, presumed wrinkled. Her neck could only be an appetizer, a fantasy canapé to whet my appetite for something a little fresher.

Of course this was all moot now that I was getting back together with Isabel. No need and no spare energy for fantasy with a girlfriend like Isabel.

I am getting back with her, right? I verified. *Definitely*, I reassured myself.

Valerie kissed my cheek. "Brian's not even a local and he's one of the few people in this town who pronounces our name right."

They pronounced it "McCune". I wanted to call her Val or V or even Mrs. Robinson, but Valerie just loved it when I called her Mrs. McEwen. "I'm just one of the few who's willing to mispronounce it the way you like," I said.

Valerie beamed. "Oh you."

"It shows respect," said Mike. "A rare commodity these days."

Now I felt guilty for the Mrs. Robinson thing.

We were in the foyer, curved frescoed walls sporting tall unframed paintings of Italian vineyards and Euro-countryside, spindly trees in the corners, and Mike's collection of medieval pikes displayed vertically over the fireplace mantel. The foyer created the sensation of soaring open spaces, as if you might catch a summer's breeze and go floating about the house, free and unfettered.

Then you realized the air was a little stale, the ceilings weren't all that high, and there was only one way forward, through a narrow gap between the wall and the top of the basement stairs. Mike liked to stand at this pinch point.

He had designed the house himself. The foyer was his containment area, an attractive holding pen for milling and chatting while Mike debated whether to send you packing. If you passed his muster, it was on to a cozy lounge with a generous wet bar, and the huge deck beyond.

"Come on in," Mike ushered me forward. "I know it's a little chilly, but we're gathering on the deck. The heat lamps should keep us warm."

Like the Bluffs, the McEwen house sat at the edge of the modest James River valley. Their bluff sloped in a series of small earthen cliffs a quarter-mile to the river, which was mostly obstructed by cottonwoods. The long-range vista had a Lewis and Clark feel to it. Rolling prairie grass hills bordered the east bank of the river—after a string of unseasonable days in the fifties, only their northern sides had snow. A couple hundred yards further east the land flattened, and so of course it was farmed. Stubble fields not yet dry enough for the plow were the rule as far as the eye could see, making it more difficult to imagine roaming buffalo and camping Indians. But being the son of a crop insurance adjustor, I appreciate the hard work and economic impact that large-scale farming represents. Too bad for the Indians they didn't think of it first.

Five people dressed in their funeral best were gathered around Rick at the deck railing. Rick knifed between them, extending his hand. The shake was firm and brief. "Thanks for coming, man."

"No problem, homey."

"Let me introduce you."

Thirty or so people came to pay their respects over the next two hours. I suppose I knew half. To the others I was introduced as the local coffeeshop owner. Three of them told me how they almost opened their own coffeeshop, and another two let me know they were currently considering it. That's about the usual percentage.

Some of the stories were about Brent. I told the one about the woman, a recent transplant to Jamestown, who saw Brent walk into my shop and whispered to her friend how she would be all over that guy if she wasn't married, with no clue her friend was Brent's mom. A few of the guests seemed intent on ensuring we had ample tales to tell at their testimonials. More than once, Darin Erstad's name came up. Twice I had to listen to the story I had already heard a thousand times: small-town boy makes it to the big leagues as the center fielder for the Anaheim Angels. The details always changed, but the escape theme was constant. Considering my life had played out in exactly the opposite direction, I didn't care for the story.

All in all, the testimonial did its job. We fixed a little more permanently the distilled memory of Brent's goodness and popularity. And then it was just me and the McEwens, lounging at the wet bar inside the house. "This was great," I said. "I should get going."

Valerie beamed at me. "I can't tell you how happy it makes me to see you and Isabel back together."

Thinking about getting back together, is the way I would have phrased it. "Relationships are a crazy thing," I said.

"You belong in this family, Brian," said Mike. "No two ways about it. Welcome back, son."

"He never really left." Valerie held up Isabel's hand and pointed to her engagement ring. Isabel winked at me.

"This is a great family," I said. I couldn't be any more vague, and yet from the smiles on everyone's faces, you could have sworn Isabel and I had just announced our wedding date.

"Great families take care of their own," said Mike. "And they never forget their own," he added, voice cracking.

After a pause, Valerie said, "I can't believe Andrea didn't show up."

That was my cue to leave. Thanks to the latest voicemail update from Valerie, I had a good idea of the current friction between them. On Friday the judge had turned down Andrea's request to move Tyler back to Colorado. I'm sure the judge was impartial, but I also knew that McEwen Construction had built the judge's house, two doors down from Mike and Valerie. I guess Andrea had freaked out in court, going off on Rick, Mike, the judge, and the state, in that order, before breaking down sobbing. She had to be escorted from the judge's chambers.

Meanwhile, the McEwens' lawsuit against the hospital and the doctor was still in process. Mike had offered to drop the suit in exchange for a ruling forcing Dr. Bhani to cease all research and experimentation on the "miracle" cure he had used on Brent. But the judge refused to grant the injunction. Coincidentally, according to a customer of mine who clerks at the court, Mike had to be escorted howling and cursing from the judge's chambers. I don't believe that judge owned a McEwen home.

"Little Tyler should have been here to hear all the nice things people were saying about his uncle," said Mike.

"Except the shotgunning," I pointed out, backpedaling into the foyer.

"True," said Mike.

"And the part about peeping at the cheerleaders through the slit in the locker room window."

"Yes," said Valerie. Isabel shrugged.

I waved goodbye, one hand on the front door handle. I had done my duty to the McEwens, and was content with a baby step toward getting back together with Iz.

"Hold on, Brian," said Isabel. "Rick, didn't Andrea say she was coming? I wanted to see Tyler."

"He's slow to get ready and out the door," said Rick. He wasn't eager to fan the flames crackling in his family's eyes. I respected that. No one could blame him if he chose to join the crowd and badmouth his cheating ex. "They'll be here."

"What does she do all day?" Mike demanded. "People tell me she never leaves her apartment." 'People tell me' was a little passive. I'm sure Mike had her watched.

"I invite her to lunch every so often," said Isabel, "but she never accepts." She reached out her hand and beckoned me. I shuffled to her side, relinquishing the hard-fought ground.

"A person can't sit at home all day," Mike stated emphatically. "A person can't live that way. It's a terrible environment for Tyler. What the hell is she thinking? Does she have any clue how to be a good mother?" He worked himself into a lather. Before Brent's tragic ending, Mike's devotion to his family was fierce. Now it was maniacal.

Rick put up a lukewarm defense. "Andrea doesn't have any close friends here. She's feeling isolated."

"Of course she's isolated!" Mike erupted. "She's sitting home all day!"

"She might be depressed," I offered. "It can be debilitating."

"So are my hemorrhoids," Mike grumbled. "I don't let it stop me."

"I have been pretty worried about her," Rick confessed. "She's not the same person she used to be."

"I introduced her to some of my friends," said Isabel. She reached across her body to hold my left hand with hers. With her right hand she probed my armpit, pushing tendons aside, slipping between the muscle fibers. A little deeper all the time. I was being pit-fucked. Shouldn't have been erotic but it was. If she smelled her fingers, I'd probably cum in my pants. "They said Andrea refuses to participate in anything they invite her to," she reported.

"We've done all we can," said Valerie, exasperated.

"I'm worried about our grandson," said Mike. "That's a terrible environment."

"He's doing fine," said Rick, looking around the room, searching for some distraction, anything, maybe a grease fire. "Jamestown's not the easiest place in the world for an outsider to fit in."

"There are so many wonderful people here, son," Valerie corrected him. "You're being nice, which is admirable. But Andrea really has no excuse."

"You damn right," said Mike. "This town has a lot on the ball. Speaking of which, Brian, Kip is ready to map your store's interior. Let's get it done."

"Mike—uh," I grunted as Isabel hit a nerve. She pushed it aside and plunged further into the interior. Was anyone else seeing this? I cleared my throat. "I'm sorry. I don't know if I'm ready to move forward on this. Timing's pretty terrible."

"Timing's not optional, Brian. The Bluffs will open in two months. They can't have a vacancy—especially not the anchor. Gotta have someone in there. If not you…" Mike winked, making clear this wasn't a threat. "I arranged financing terms for you that are way below market. We're talking three points."

"I simply can't understand someone like Andrea," Valerie was saying. "Letting life pass her by."

"She's working, at the hospital," said Rick. "That's a start anyway."

"Someone with her attitude cannot make a good secretary," said Iz.

"Research assistant, isn't it?" I recalled.

"Listen, Brian." Mike held my elbow and lowered his voice. Hand, elbow and pit. The three points of contact were unnerving. "If startup costs are going to be a burden, you know we can work something out."

"That's very generous of you. Way too generous. Once again."

"You deserve success," Mike said earnestly. "You're a hard worker."

Valerie was frowning. "I didn't know they did research at the hospital, other than…"

That's when Andrea and Tyler walked through the door. Tyler ran forward to hug Rick's leg and receive an affectionate hair tousling. "Sorry I'm late," said Andrea. "I didn't want to miss this, but, you know how it goes." Oblivious to my presence and the stonefaced statues that were the McEwens, she unshouldered a backpack bigger than her torso and dropped it against the wall with a groan. She unzipped it to peek inside. "Tyler, did you bring in your toys and your books?" She looked up and saw me and pursed her lips. "Oh. Hi. How are you?"

"I'm good."

"Andrea." Valerie put her hand to her mouth. "Are you working for Dr. Bhani?"

Isabel gasped. Her hand fell out of my armpit. Mike's eyes bulged. The scientist's name sent a shockwave through the McEwen family.

Rick wiped a bad-looking taste from his mouth and followed his son downstairs to the playroom. Andrea was on her own. Oblivious to the bomb that was about to go off, she focused on Iz's and my interlaced fingers.

"Brian said you're working for a researcher at the hospital," said Valerie. "We don't know of any other researchers in Jamestown."

"Oh, that's what Brian said." Andrea crossed her arms and gave me an ice-cold glare. "That's right. I took a job with Dr. Bhani."

I can't even begin to tell you what a bad idea that was. Bhani was indeed the only federally-funded researcher in town, a fact trumpeted in a glowing article published in the *Sun* a few months before Brent died, an article that had made Bhani a local celebrity. Bhani was a Bangladeshi doc who had started his career as a North Dakota physician. Ten years ago he hit upon a potential cure for cancer, and was inspired to devote his life to research, moving to a lab at the University of Minnesota, his alma mater, and eventually relocating to Jamestown, putting the local hospital at the cutting edge of cancer research.

The day Brent died, Bhani went from the toast of the town, to toast in that town. He used to come into my shop regularly, probably just to soak up the rock star treatment. But after Mike tried to beat his face in at the Safeway store a month after Brent's death, Bhani went underground. If it weren't for Andrea's bombshell, I wouldn't have known he was still in town.

"You took a job with Dr. Bhani," Valerie mumbled, dumbfounded. "But why? Honey, we could have found you a job at Richford Homes or Madison Electric, or the Tool Crib…"

"Yeah, well," Andrea chuckled bitterly. "This was a little better match for my background. I had just started my dream job at a genetics lab in Denver when Rick made us move here, you know."

Wrong time to grind that ax, I thought to myself.

"Honey," Valerie pleaded. "Dr. Bhani…?"

"For Pete's sake, Andrea," said Mike. "That quack killed our son!"

"No." Andrea vehemently shook her head. "Dr. Bhani saved Brent. If you recall, Brent's regular oncologist told him his cancer was incurable. Dr. Bhani's treatment saved Brent. An infection killed him."

"An infection your boss gave him!" Red-faced, Mike stabbed his finger in the general direction of the hospital. "He *gave* it to our son! On purpose!"

Andrea trembled as she knelt again to rummage through the backpack.

"He *gave* him an infection!" Mike croaked. "That's what killed Brent! You can't deny it!"

"I'm not going to," said Andrea, digging vigorously in the backpack. "I could tell you why you're wrong, but you wouldn't listen anyway."

"I'm listening!" Mike's voice cracked. "I'm listening!"

Valerie put her arms around Mike and rubbed his neck. "Andrea," she said condescendingly, "we're listening."

Andrea talked into the backpack. "I don't want to talk about it."

"Neither does anyone here," said Isabel, using her teacher voice. Her classroom voice, not the statutory lesbian rape one. "We're struggling to get through this. Which is why hearing you're working for that doctor is so difficult to understand."

Rick returned to stand beside his sobbing mother. "Andrea," he appealed.

"You know Dr. Bhani feels bad about what happened," Andrea countered.

"He feels *bad?*" Mike exclaimed. He took a step forward. "That sonofabitch feels bad? How do you think we feel? After everything we went through, only to have Brent get sick and die from your doctor's bug."

"It wasn't his."

"Oh!" Valerie, Mike and Isabel exploded together. "Bhani *gave* Brent strep," Mike wailed, "and according to the coroner, Brent *died* of strep!"

That someone could die from strep was news to me, but this wasn't the time to ask for clarification. Didn't seem like the type of inquiry that was going to get me out of that house any faster.

I would have ganged up on Andrea too, except for two things. One, Bhani was hailed as the cancer messiah until Brent died, so chances are he wasn't a quack. And the McEwens weren't exactly unbiased observers.

Two, the day after Mike attacked Bhani in the Safeway cereal aisle, I got an earful from an irate customer, a local kid attending med school up in Grand Forks. His coffee was fine; it was the McEwens he badmouthed.

According to this kid, Bhani was a god in the cancer research community. He had already saved a few terminal cases, and his treatment was only coincidentally related to the infection that killed Brent—who, the kid pointed out, had only come to Bhani because the oncologists at the hospital had basically thrown in the towel and given Brent four months to live. The kid made a compelling argument.

Of course, it didn't change the fact that Andrea was an insensitive idiot.

Rick stood in front of his ex, shielding her from his family's venom. "This is going nowhere. That's enough for tonight," he said, like he was accustomed to people listening when he took charge. "We'll discuss this another time."

"There's no discussion," said Andrea, shaking her head when Rick fluttered a hand in her face, trying to shut her up. "I'm not quitting."

"You sure as hell will!" Mike shouted, stretching his neck to look around Rick, who shook his head in resignation and backed off.

"You have to, honey," said Valerie sharply. "For Tyler."

"How can you work for that evil bastard?" Mike demanded.

"I'd like to think I'm helping him make a difference—"

"You are disgracing this family!" Mike thundered. "You are disgracing this family by working for him!"

Andrea marched to the door. "Say goodbye to Tyler for me."

Instead of *goodbye*, Isabel said, "You are a selfish bitch."

Andrea turned around and shot a stunned, hurt look not at Isabel but at me, before slipping out the door.

I was a little stunned myself. Why did I get the look? I was at worst a negligent bystander to the verbal beating Andrea had taken. Isabel did have a husky voice—had Andrea mistaken hers for mine?

"Isabel," Valerie scolded, "you know I don't like that word."

"If the shoe fits," said Mike.

I was upset. "Did you see her look at me? I think she thought I said it."

"Don't be silly," said Isabel. "You're standing next to me, it just looked like she was looking at you."

"No. She looked directly at me."

"Maybe she mis-looked," said Valerie. "That happens."

"It's not like an errant golf shot, Val," said Mike. "Andrea understands that Brian is a member of the family. No, I think that look was no accident."

"You did the right thing to tell us about her job," Valerie assured me.

"It wasn't a secret," I noted. "You would have found out sooner or later. I really don't want to be in the middle of this."

Valerie nodded. "It's hard to fathom what that girl is thinking, isn't it?"

I shook my head. "I'd rather not try."

"Brian and I are going to take a drive together," said Isabel, plucking a black sweater-jacket off the coat hook and slipping it on.

"We're so glad you shared this time with us," said Valerie, forming a V with her hands, putting my face into that V, and kissing me, our first lip kiss.

Rick invaded my personal space to grip my hand. "Thanks for coming, man."

Mike was holding his arms apart, waiting for me to come get some. Then he hopped forward with alarming speed and hugged me good. "We'll talk to-morrow." This was an order, not a request. Mike was as hot for me as his daughter, ready to consecrate our business partnership.

Outside, Isabel said "brr" and clung to me as we walked to my van. The wind had picked up and the temperature had fallen, after what had been a fabulous spring day. "I'm so glad you were there."

"I really wish I hadn't been. For that last scene, at least."

"Oh you." She pinched my nipple. "Why?"

"It's none of my business, mostly." I held the passenger door for her. Isabel climbed up on the dirty hump of rotten snow caking the curb. She was not real strong in the arms, not real nimble in the feet, so I gave her a steadying boost into the van. "For another thing, I'm not sure Bhani is quite as satanic as your family makes him out to be. I feel sorry for Andrea. But..." I ran around the back of the van and jumped in the driver's seat. "...not enough to waste any more time thinking about her."

"Don't let Andrea fool you. She's a master at being a nasty bitch, and then making you feel guilty when you call her on it."

"I'll watch for that." I started the van. "Speaking of...actually, there's no good segue for this. What exactly were you doing to me in there? I've been, you know, interested, ever since. Is that weird? That doesn't seem right, does it? I mean, you were in my armpit."

"Sounds a little twisted, I agree," said Isabel, very pleased with herself.

"You wouldn't want to keep doing that, would you?"

"So bad I can taste it."

An inappropriate figure of speech for a discussion about the armpit; with

Iz, it was no figure of speech. "I'm going to drive very fast now, so hang on."

"Drive around the block," Iz instructed, "then turn off your lights when you come back around the corner."

This was my tenth time around the block that day—Iz might have wondered how I managed to avoid every shadowed ice rut and slush-filled pothole. As we idled toward her folks' house, she had me park in front of a rugged strip of no-man's land that drained the neighborhood down to the river. Isabel jumped out. "Follow me."

We picked our way hand-in-hand across the mucky open space before curling left toward the bluff. At the blunt edge of the cliff Isabel found a graveled gap through the ice-clotted weeds. We slide-stepped down and picked our way along a skinny catwalk that gradually descended until our heads were below the top of the bluff. We continued shuffling along.

"I think this is it," Isabel whispered. She let go of my hand to mount an assault on the ten feet of embankment above us.

She struggled and grunted up the muddy gravel slope, the shushing of her filmy dress and the glimpse of black lace high up her thigh compensating for her lack of grace. She scrambled over the edge before I could reach up to give her a boost. Stepping on upright clumps of grass and kicking in a toehold here and there, I followed.

We were behind the playhouse that Mike's construction team built for his grandson. "Here?" I hissed. "Won't Tyler come out here?"

"Too cold," Isabel whispered. She peeked around the corner, then held out her hand. Feeling as though I should be the mission leader, I swallowed my pride and allowed Iz to lead me to the front door. She keyed the lock and pulled me inside.

I pushed the door shut. "Hey, how convenient, a bed—"

Isabel was on me, kissing me, hands all over me, tongue way down my throat, pants unzipped, my schlong in both her hands, pulling hard enough to uproot it.

"What about the armpit?" I mumbled. "Do that armpit thing."

"Pull up your shirt," she ordered.

I grabbed my shirt down low with crossed hands the way I always practiced at home, and pulled up. When my shirt had almost cleared my head and my arms were at full extension, Isabel clamped her mouth on my left pit. "Whug," I groaned. I maintained this position, trying not to move a muscle, in no way wanting to dislodge her, this kinky crazy broad.

First her lips worked me over. She could have been a lip masseuse, such strength and multi-directional control.

Then the tongue. With every deep probe, concentric waves of delight fanned out across my chest, making my heart and lungs ripple.

Finally the teeth. Isabel was chewing my pit. I was crying out, something like, "Oh Goddie—mommy—ho-ho, oh my lordie—no—"

Isabel finished pulling off my shirt so she could put her fingers to my lips. She tossed the shirt onto the kiddie desk against the wall of the ten-by-ten playhouse, and went back to work. I wheezed, I giggled, I wept, I bestowed blessings upon her as best a layman could.

"You're hyperventilating," she approved.

"Sweet Song of the South, what have you done to me?"

"What you're experiencing is a flood of toxins into your system."

"That's what it feels like to be poisoned?" I gasped. "I always wondered."

"Sometimes hormones will be flushed along with the toxins," Isabel purred. "Your lymph nodes are filled with all kinds of goodies."

"You're diddling my lymph nodes." Uncontrollable quivers coursed through my private parts.

"We need to finish the flush," said Isabel. "Roll over."

"Roll over, roll over...and then the porcupine fell out." High on lymph goodies, I babbled nursery rhymes while Isabel flipped me over and worked my shorts off. "Ten in the bed and the little one said—holy shit!"

In a highly coordinate attack, Isabel fingered me in three places, under each butt cheek and in that soft spot below the scrotum. I bucked as she fingered. Isabel saddled up and rode me backwards, hot breath on my ass. Thighs clamped on the sides of my head, Iz buried her face in my crack, fingers fingering all the while. I grabbed her thighs and screamed into the pillow. My body spasmed and flopped as the demons of the immune system howled through my bloodstream.

For all that, my ejaculation was short and unnoticeable. I only knew it happened because my body went instantly to jelly. I lay underneath her, unable to breathe, unwilling to even try, and trying not to wonder how Isabel knew about such things. Hopefully she had read it in a picture book from India.

Through my delirium I had a notion to somehow attempt to return the favor. I threw a couple lame licks at her sweaty thighs.

"Shh," Isabel stopped me. She sat up and kneaded my butt and hamstrings. After working me over for awhile she said, "That was a fairly extreme reaction you had. I'm expecting the police in a few minutes." She slid down a little further and massaged my calves. It would have felt nice if I had had any muscle tone left. It must have been like massaging a bag of gel.

"That was the longest I've ever been insane," I mumbled into the pillow. "I touched the void, I'm sure of it." I struggled to rise, to breathe. Isabel dismounted and knelt beside me on the floor. I rolled onto my side, my head propped on the pillow, and blinked at her. "It was probably the best half-hour I've ever had."

"Five minutes, tops."

"Promise you won't do that to me more than once every couple years."

"That seems about right." Isabel drew spirals in the pubic hair that grew like ivy up my belly. And let me just say that if ivy looked like pubic hair, the Cubs wouldn't have nearly as many fans.

My belly was way too big. Isabel didn't seem to care, but I vowed then and there to start going to Taekwondo class more than once a week.

"Will I feel a difference now?" I asked my personal lymph system guru.

"Eventually. You might feel like you have a touch of the flu for a day or two. But once the toxins clear your system, you should feel the difference."

"Wow. This is great." I cocked my head and listened like a dog. "And no sirens. So, can I do the same for you? As soon as I can lift my head for more than a couple seconds at a time."

Isabel petted my face. Her hand smelled like my butt. "We each have roles to play in this relationship. You make me feel good in so many other ways."

"Good point."

"Brian, you've always been there for me, in ways you don't even understand. I don't need you to *do* things for me. I just need you. You are my rock, my anchor. I knew it as soon as I saw you in that bar in Fargo."

She was something else. And no matter what she claimed, she deserved a lot more than just my presence. I could no longer use the coffeeshop as a crutch. I could, I would give more to her.

The resolution made my brain as warm and fuzzy as my body. I rolled onto my back, became one with the mattress. "You are so good to me."

"I'm glad you feel that way, sweetie." Isabel stroked my stomach. I tried not to be self-conscious about the extra pounds. The muscles in my hips and lower back weren't worried about it; they sagged in blissful contentment. I sank deeper into the thin mattress. I couldn't get any more relaxed. Iz had the magic touch.

She cleared her throat. "I did notice a lump on the back of your thigh, right where it meets the buttocks."

"A lump?" I said dreamily. "What kind of lump?"

"Mm, I don't know. You should get it checked."

"Geez. Okay. I guess I could..."

"Tomorrow. I'd feel better if you went to the doctor tomorrow."

T - 15

The next day was crazy. Like usual I was at the shop by five, to open at six. We were busy, just not as busy as I would have liked. By eleven o'clock when Charlotte's shift ended, we had made five hundred twelve dollars.

I used to round to the nearest fifty or so. Nowadays that wasn't precise enough. "Around five hundred" didn't tell me whether I had covered Charlotte's salary with enough left to pay Dan the pastry man when he made his third and what I'm sure he hoped would be his final trip to collect the prior quarter's outstanding balance.

"We cleared sixty bucks in tips," Charlotte reported. She raked one of the divvied piles off the counter into her hand. "Not bad."

"Sixty even?" I prodded casually for more information.

"Fifty-eight, actually," Charlotte clarified.

"Oh," I said, trying not to sound too disappointed. "Why don't you take it all today." This was difficult to say. I made it a policy not to understand my employees' financial situations, or pretty soon I would be subconsciously favoring the poorer kid over the richer one, giving her more hours, better shifts, quicker raises. I preferred my discrimination to be conscious.

But I do hear things. Charlotte needed the money even more than I did.

"Nonsense," said Charlotte. "I know Dan's coming back again today. You *have* to pay him. I do not want to see him again this month. Eeu." She shivered. "He gives me the creeps. He leers at me." Most of our male customers did, some were just better at it.

I nodded to the only customer left in the store, Theresa, a forty-year-old homemaker enrolled full-time at JC, taking brain-melting classes like calculus and organic chemistry, hoping to be accepted into the Pharmacy program at NDSU. "Careful," I said. "Theresa probably finds Dan wildly attractive."

"Huh? Who?" Theresa looked up from her Biochem textbook, pretending not to be listening. Her eyes were glazed. Maybe she wasn't pretending.

"No one," said Charlotte. "Go back to studying." She leaned on the counter, looking down into the pastry case. "I don't know why we even bother with pastries. This case. Ugh."

Muffins and cookies were piled on one side of the far-from-spotless shelf, amidst crumbs and a few larger chunks from days gone by.

"I've been meaning to get to that."

"Brian, you hate selling pastries."

"But I really hate watching people leave Martin's bakery with a coffee." I pointed to the pile of dollars and coin. "Go ahead," I told Charlotte. "Take it."

"No, you're gonna need it to go get drunk after putting in a double shift. Sam called a few minutes ago. He can't make it in."

"What? When? Awww…. What about Sara? Can she come in early?"

"Nope. She has class until five. So it'll be five-fifteen at the earliest."

"Dana?"

"Out of town until Thursday."

"That's right. Crap. Did I know that?"

"Yes you did. I was standing right there when she told you."

"I have a lot on my mind," I complained. "She should know better than to tell me things and expect me to remember."

"Fire her. Wouldn't break my heart."

"And I need to run to Sam's Club. We're out of—"

"Just about everything?" said Charlotte. She sighed. "I can come back for an hour between three and four, so you can go shopping."

"You don't mind?"

Charlotte put her hands on her hips and stared at me.

"Stupid question. Forget I asked. I appreciate it. Alright, get out of here."

An hour later Isabel rang me, from Fargo. She had been calling all day. "Sweetie, finally," said Iz. "How did it go? What did the doctor say?"

"I didn't go in."

"Brian, you promised. That's it. I'm coming back tonight."

"Don't do that. Don't you have a meeting for your dad tomorrow?"

"He'll send someone else. I need to make sure you get your leg checked."

"I'm going in tomorrow, I promise. Today has been really busy."

"You better."

"I will. How's your sister?"

"She's good. Worried about you."

"Oh you told her about my lump?"

"She could tell something was bothering me."

"I don't want you to worry, okay?"

"Then you should have gone to the doctor today."

Isabel had a sixth sense about things. Could look at a woman and tell she was two weeks pregnant. Knew when I skipped a meal. Maybe three years ago I went home to see my parents. We drove to Sacramento to have dinner at this crappy little restaurant my dad loved, and happened to see a famous Californian. I had called Isabel during dessert. "Iz, guess who we just saw?"

"Where did you see this person?" she asked.

"We're in Sacramento, at this supposedly trendy restaurant."

"Oh, how are your mom and dad?" she asked.

"Come on, Iz, guess."

"Kato Kaelin," she said nonchalantly.

I paused. "How did you know that?"

"I just had a feeling."

Now she had a feeling about my lump. That night, I wished I had gone to the doctor. I lay in bed touching the lump and telling myself not to. This wasn't the first time I had touched it, of course. I had been feeling it all day. Every time as my fingers approached the site, I prayed the lump would feel smaller or softer.

Exhaustion from the playhouse romp had ensured a peaceful sleep Sunday night. But not now. I laid there for a couple hours, my hands all over that lump, worrying about what it might be, worrying about being exhausted when the alarm went off at four-forty-five, worrying that worrying was exactly the sort of negative energy a malignant lump would feed on. I was desperate to fall asleep.

Hey, I thought, a good self-servicing always does the trick.

I laughed at the ridiculous assumption that Iz had left anything in my tank—and then went pale with the fear that the cancer might perk up its ears at the rustling in my 'nads, and go have a look-see. Everyone needed to remain still and quiet and give the cancer no cause to leave the back of my leg.

I was sure that's what it was. I've always feared death, and cancer seemed the best bet. Nothing violent, like a car crash or terrorist attack where I would have a decent shot at cheating death with quick thinking or my cat-like reflexes. Instead, Death would be silent and sneaky and immune to my knack for landing on my feet.

I only thought it would be more patient, waiting until the worst possible time to gun me down—waiting until I was at my highest point, with stores in fifteen states, married to a wonderful wife, proud father to a newborn baby.

But when I thought about it, this was even sadder. Taking me before I had achieved any success whatsoever.

In the end, the only thing that allowed me to get a couple hours' sleep was to stop agonizing and accept as fact that I had cancer. I definitely had cancer. Let the battle begin. Being stalked by some anonymous killer was scary. A battle against a known enemy, on the other hand, was something I could handle. And what was one of the most powerful weapons in any battle? A good night's sleep. With one last shuddering sigh, I fell into a dreamless slumber.

THE NEXT MORNING I called Jackie, a nurse customer of mine.

"What kind of doctor do you need to see?" Jackie asked.

"I don't know. General practitioner, I suppose. To start with anyway."

"How long have you lived here, Brian?"

"Five years."

"And you haven't ever been to a doctor?"

"I was in the emergency room for a racing heart last year."

"A lot of people think regular checkups are a good idea," said Jackie.

"I thought that was for old people."

"Old people don't need checkups," said Jackie. "They bring a list." We shared a laugh on the elderly. "So why see a doctor now, after all these years?"

"I have a lump."

Joke time was over. "I'll make you an appointment with Dr. Bonilla. He has a strong background in, in things like that. Be at the hospital by nine."

I called my mom and dad on the way to the hospital. I haven't told you much about my parents. They haven't impacted this story, yet they're everything I am. If I differ from them in any way, it's only by conscious effort.

I hung up before they could wake up and answer. No need worrying them before the doctor took a look at me. Although I already knew I had it. Isabel wasn't a worrywart. She was damned near clairvoyant. If she was concerned, it was time to start shopping for wigs.

SITTING in the waiting room I couldn't get over the fact that the timing wasn't right. Death was supposed to strike later, after I had become the person I wanted to be, after I had seized the good life. For maximum effect, Death should arrive a split-second before I was ready to rest on my laurels, just as I prepared to sit back and survey my thriving business empire and enjoy my beautiful family. Death was patient; Death wrote the book on heartbreaking tragedy. Death was forfeiting the opportunity to drop a doozy of a bombshell twenty years down the road.

But of course the cancer had perfect timing. What's more tragic than a thirty-two year old with cancer? It wasn't the cancer's fault that after fifteen years in the biz, here I was in North Dakota, engaged to a sexual deviant and running one rinky-dink shop. Couldn't blame the cancer for assuming I was a guy with low expectations who had already achieved his mediocre goals. No matter what I was about to find out, I couldn't whine that life was unfair. It is fair. It was my own damn fault.

BEING my parents' child worried me, as the nurse sampled my blood. If I reacted to a bad diagnosis like my mother, I was going to say "oh well" and go about my business, no less kind or gentle. La-la, what are you going to do. I would cry myself to sleep most nights, but then get up the next morning as chipper as ever. La-la, don't you worry about me. "I'll say this for Brian," people would say after I died, "he sure dealt with his cancer well." La-la.

If on the other hand I took it like the old man, a fatalistic numbness was going to come over me. I would detach from myself, step back and watch, closely, the cancer's every inroad and progression. Take it like a man. I would neither say it was fine by me, nor would I complain. A man doesn't complain, and he doesn't struggle. He accepts his fate. He doesn't alter his routine, except to forfeit all the joy that life used to bring him. He doesn't miss a day of work. Never. Never ever.

After I died people would say, "That Brian sure didn't let cancer slow him down."

I flipped onto my stomach so the physician's assistant could deaden my backside for the biopsy. I decided right then and there to fight my genes and do things my way. I couldn't go la-la, and I couldn't go numb. I had to be fully in every moment. Ask a lot of questions, listen very carefully, record everything. Find somebody with a computer and go on-line and research every facet of my cancer. Get angry, get upset, get better. Laugh when I needed to, cry when appropriate.

I would take my healthcare into my own hands. A proactive ownership mentality—I would need to become the general contractor, subcontracting each research topic and procedure to various surgeons and specialists, coordinating them, holding them accountable, never worshipping them and by no means putting my life in their hands. I would listen, research, ask questions and question everything.

"Your shin looks pretty tough," said Cindy the physician's assistant. "What's going on here?"

"Taekwondo." I was working toward my black belt in Taekwondo. I had always wanted to become a deadly assassin, and figured I had the legs for it. "I assume you're talking about the bruises, on top of the bruises."

"Ouch," said Cindy. "Is that normal?"

"I hope not. Hopefully I'm doing something wrong, something that I can correct. I'm looking forward to not shrieking every time I kick somebody."

"You could stop kicking people," said Cindy.

"No thanks." I like to kick people.

Even as Cindy and a nurse, Nancy, quizzed me on my lifestyle and family history, my mind wandered. I was trying to figure out why Dad is who he is, so I could choose to be as different as necessary, so I could recognize that crucial moment *when* to make a conscious break from my genes.

I remembered him coming into my room late one night when I was twelve, in his hand one of the military history books he loved to read. Every year or so Dad would tuck me in, when he had something important to tell me.

"The key to being an effective soldier"—*man* and *soldier* were interchangeable as far as my dad was concerned—"the key to getting out of your foxhole as the shells scream overhead, the key to marching forward as men scream and fall ahead of you, is to assume you're already dead."

This was meant to steady my nerves for the MathCounts competition. Looking back, it was a tough sell for a kid who thought he was special, a chosen one, a little more self-aware and suffused with destiny than the next guy, and therefore too extraordinary to die, too valuable to lose.

Now the times when I felt that heroic certainty of a happy ending were fleeting and usually alcohol-related. I couldn't afford to buy enough comic books and booze to maintain that mindset. I was going to need a new outlook.

But let me tell you, that "I'm a dead soldier" crap really shook me up. I didn't sleep much the year Dad dropped that one on me, and there on the gurney it brought me close to tears. I believed in God until that very moment. Suddenly I couldn't envision an afterlife, only a void, a whole mess of nothingness, and it scared me senseless. I wanted nothing more than to be a firm believer. I craved Heaven's comfort; I labored to convince myself God was there and waiting to embrace me.

Maybe if I'd had a traditional religious upbringing. Dad grew up Methodist, but by the time I came along he was disillusioned with the dogma and what he called "religious people". "I'll worship my own way in the privacy of my house," Dad would say. As far as I knew he did, but I never saw him with a Bible in hand.

With Mom, any religious discussion invariably, somehow, turns to music. She would drive to the parsonage Saturday afternoon and pick up the playlist, and then spend the intervening waking hours on the piano, practicing. Mom's specialty was harmony. She knows the harmony part for at least a thousand church songs. The minister loved the way Mom filled out the congregation's sound. He didn't have to stand next to her and try to stay on melody.

Faith-based or otherwise, there had to be a way to deal with my cancer that wouldn't result in false bravado, stoic acceptance, or paralyzing fear. I wouldn't find it in Mom and Dad's brains—I was getting dizzy and melancholy in there, in too deep to step back and figure things out. I am them, they are in me. I tried to escape the biochemical entanglement, struggling through the jungle of my own mental fibers, glistening, pulsing, fated, fibrous…

I played word association against my will, moving at high speed from a network of neurons to a black writhing snarl of tumor. I threw up on the end of the gurney, soaking the crisp white paper and splattering Nurse Nancy's legs.

"Geez, I'm sorry."

Cindy and Nurse Nancy told me that puking all over their gurney, floor, clothes, and sterile instruments was no big deal, while simultaneously looking more shook up than medical personnel should at the sight of a patient's internal fluids.

I collapsed into a chair, embarrassed. "That really took me by surprise."

"It's okay," said Nurse Nancy, yellow-blonde with wide fluttering eyes.

"Not a problem at all," said Cindy, an elderly woman with mannish hands that stripped the paper roll so the arriving orderly could clean the gurney. "Really. You wouldn't believe how often that happens."

"When kids throw up in my shop, I always wish the parents would give them a good spanking," I said.

"That's funny," said Cindy. "Nancy honey, run down and order up an MRI and a CAT scan for us, would you please, dear?"

Nurse Nancy practically ran out of the room.

"CAT scans are for the brain, right?" I asked.

"Sometimes throwing up can be a symptom of broader issues." Cindy looked as though she may have said too much.

"It's all in my head. Thoughts, I mean. Not a tumor. Sometimes my mind gets a little carried away. I make mountains out of molehills. You know the type," I babbled, waiting for her to soothe me with something like, "Sugar, don't you fret, we're just going through the motions to keep our insurance company happy."

Cindy was washing her hands. "The best thing is to let us do the work and not worry about this."

Would have been easier without the worried look on her face. *Please just cure me.* "Can I put my clothes on?"

"Sure. You're going to need a clean gown anyway." Cindy put her man hand on my shoulder. "Your leg is probably a little numb—would you like some help with your underwear?"

I WAS DOING a poor job hiding my humiliation and black thoughts when Andrea spotted me in the hospital hallway. "There he is," she said.

"How are you, lady?"

"Let's see," Andrea mulled it over. "What would I like the McEwens to know?" She looked for the sting of her rapier wit, but I think my eyes remained dull. "What are you doing here?"

"Waiting to see an oncologist."

"Oh. I'm sorry. You have someone here? Someone with…" She lowered her voice for the C word. "…cancer?"

"Yeah. Me."

"You?" Andrea glanced at my street clothes. "No you don't."

"I just had an MRI and a CAT scan."

Andrea flinched. "I can't believe that."

"They let me wait out here as long as I promised not to sit on my biopsy hole. I can't stand being cooped up in the exam room."

"Well that's terrible."

"I don't think it's in my brain. I don't even know whether I have it. That's not true—I'm sure I do. It's in my leg. I found a lump."

I thought she was going to hug me. Then the cool detachment returned. "Do you have someone here waiting with you? I'm sure you do. Where's Isabel?" She made an exaggeration of looking up and down the hallway.

This was way too much work. "I don't know," I said.

"I'm sure she'll be along here any moment," said Andrea, snotty. "I'd like to avoid any more awkward moments like Sunday night."

"I don't know if awkward is the right word to describe an attempted lynching."

"You should know." She tossed her hair and struggled with a quivering lip. "You were part of the lynch mob."

"I wished I hadn't been, if that's any consolation."

"Not really," Andrea said softly, close to losing it. "I'm going to go now." She wanted me to stop her, I could tell.

But I had no capacity for sympathy. My head was jam-packed with *I don't want to die!* "Okay lady. We'll see you."

Andrea shook her head and hurried down the hallway.

I COULDN'T STAND the thought of sitting home alone, waiting for daybreak when I could start calling the hospital to learn the results of my tests. But no one was available on short-notice for dinner or drinks, so I went to Taekwondo class. I doubt it was on the list of approved post-biopsy activities.

Never felt so weak. My knees quivered as I descended to the basement of the strip mall where the dojang, the Taekwondo gym, was located. Was it the cancer already eating away at me, every ounce of my body's energy devoted to the fruitless task of stopping the voracious monster? No. It was my fear.

By no means am I a hypochondriac. I had seen a doctor maybe ten times my whole life, usually for a sports physical. But I had a feeling, an awful feeling I was doomed. The faces on the hospital workers hadn't helped. I could tell, they thought I was doomed, too.

"Ahn-yahn-hashmika, kyo-sah-nim," I greeted Instructor Garrett, a twenty-year-old kid with a quarterback's build and movie star good looks.

"Ahn-yahn-hashmika," Garrett greeted me, returning my bow and accepting my attendance card. "Ready for some action?" he asked quietly, as he bowed and received the next student's card.

"You know it." Taekwondo was all about conquering fear. Walk in the place and hear the kihaps, those peculiar shouts we were taught to belt out with every kick, meant to temporarily disorient and frighten your opponent the smallest bit. But the kihaps were also a way to manage your own fear. Kihap-triggered adrenaline hung like fog, secreted from one class to be reabsorbed by the next. Adrenaline to replace the fear, the fear of pulling a muscle, of getting kicked in the face.

"Break us down, sir," I requested.

"I'll do my best," said Instructor Garrett with a smile.

"What are you doing?" Genevieve demanded. She's a regular at my shop, a North Dakota farm girl, beefy shoulders, big knockers, muscular butt, a belly, blond hair and a gorgeous Ivory girl face. She backhanded my shoulder. "Did you tell Mr. Garrett to work us over?"

"No," I lied.

"Brian, I'm going to have to kick you."

I backpedaled toward my place in line, halfway down the front row. "Shouldn't you limber up first?"

"I don't need to stretch to kick your butt."

"Genevieve, you better save it for class," said Khalq, trimmed beard, feathery hair. He had a Middle Eastern porn star thing going, the only guy who made his uniform look like naughty pajamas. Khalq is a part-time physician for a few of the surrounding small towns, and the stiffest man I ever met. Genevieve, Khalq and I had started together two years prior, passed eleven belt tests and attended at least two hundred classes together, and Khalq was no more flexible now than he was on Day One. His hamstrings defied logic. They squeaked when he kicked. Fortunately for him, Master Kwan's philosophy was "each to the best of his abilities". Khalq bragged that he would be the first black belt in history who couldn't touch his toes.

There were six of us red executive belts scheduled to test for black belt in November. Genevieve, Khalq and I had bonded—the other red execs didn't seem to find life quite as funny as we three did. "We wouldn't want you running out of gas before the class is over," Khalq baited Genevieve.

"Are you kidding?" Genevieve shook her head in sadness. "I'm going to be exhausted before the warm-ups are over."

"Miss Genevieve," Instructor Garrett called from the office doorway, grinning, "will you lead the class in warm-ups?"

"Yes sir," Genevieve chirped in her little girl's voice. She stepped to the front and faced the class, now thirty strong. "Jumping jacks. Ready, begin."

Everybody followed orders except a tall athletic-looking white belt woman in the back of the room. She went on ignoring us and kicking the crap out of a training pylon. I had never seen a white belt kick like that.

Genevieve counted out the repetitions. "Ha-nah, duo, set, net, tossut, yossut...yossut..."

"Ilgup, hudool," Khalq finished for her, chortling. "That's Korean for seven and eight, Genevieve."

"Thanks, Khalq." Genevieve regularly screwed up the order of exercises and stretches, and slaughtered the Korean counting. It was great entertainment for the class, especially the upper belts who had known her for so long. Genevieve took it well, up to a point. Then she would snap and start kicking people. Khalq was usually first on her list, whether he deserved it or not.

The warm-up was a great distraction, my mind preoccupied with readying the body for the abuse it was about to receive.

Like usual, my arch nemesis Troy didn't show up until we had finished all the calisthenics and stretching and most of the basic warm-up kicks. The teenager claimed it was farm chores that made him late, but I think it was deliberate. I guess he had no need for warm-ups, since he barely moved during the kicking drills, didn't even work up a sweat. That lazy bastard. I had hated Troy from the moment I first tried to find his eyes behind those tinted photosensitive glasses.

"Nice of you to join us, Mr. Troy," Instructor Garrett verbally spanked him.

Troy nodded, inscrutable behind his smoked spectacles. My heart pounded, harder than the series of combo kicks called for. That's what it's like, to have an arch nemesis. My heart has never pounded for love. Just bloodlust.

"Alright," said Instructor Garrett, "everybody pair up."

"No Master Kwan today, sir?" Kenny Clews asked Garrett.

"He's in Valley City," Garrett answered.

"Doesn't he love us anymore?" asked Genevieve, playful, disappointed. Master Kwan was everyone's hero. A former national champion, he was a little guy with a Bruce Lee body and the ability to make your jaw drop with his speed and power.

"He's very focused on opening his new dojang over there," said Instructor Garrett. "Everyone have a partner?" He had had his fill of us griping about Master Kwan splitting time between his old and new gyms.

We paired up, me with Khalq, Genevieve with the new white belt. Genevieve was very quiet around this woman, almost shy. Everybody was casting wide-eyed looks in her direction—probably because this is an upper-belt class, I decided. White belt rookies, gorgeous or not, weren't welcome.

"Roundhouse back-kick combinations," Instructor Garrett ordered. "Ten reps, fast as you can, keeping the transitions under control."

Khalq held the padded, racquet-shaped paddle for me. "Do you know who that is?" he whispered, nodding to Genevieve's partner.

"Chuck Norris's wife?"

"Ready begin," Instructor Garrett barked.

"Tell you later," said Khalq.

Everyone's unique style of kihap filled the low-ceilinged room, "hai!" "sheeah!" "pa-chaaaa!", along with the thuds of dull contact and the occasional sharp crack of a well-struck paddle. After a few kicks, throbbing began in the ass-leg junction where the physician's assistant had taken a core sample.

"Full turn on the roundhouse," Instructor Garrett counseled. "Turn that hip over."

I probably should have told Garrett; should have said something like, "I'm pretty sure I have cancer, sir, and when I really turn that hip over and extend my leg, it hurts my biopsy hole." Instead I said "Yes sir."

But Karate Man only bleed on the inside. Karate Man he make no excuses.

Besides, I was dripping sweat and feeling better. I was an old dog who had never tried martial arts tricks until I joined Master Kwan's dojang. Even after two years of training, the first couple repetitions of each routine always seemed strange, always looked bad. Then the muscle memory would take over, the footwork, leg angles and balance would become second nature, and I could start zeroing in on the paddle until I was bringing it with everything I had, making the paddle crack and Khalq complain.

It was an adrenaline rush, and a rapid physical drain. Normally I recovered quickly. Not that day. We alternated holding the paddle, ten to twenty kicks per turn. I was still breathing hard when it was my turn to kick again.

Was it simply a bad day, just an anomaly? Or was this the beginning of my cancer decline—worse, the continuation of a trend? Had I been taking longer to recover lately, say maybe the last couple months, as the disease sprang to life and began to feed upon me? Worry gnawed at me, and in response I kicked even harder.

Genevieve apologized to the tall white belt for kicking her paddle so hard.

"Go easy on her, Genevieve," I called over. "You'll scare her away."

The white belt woman waved me off. "Honey," she told Genevieve, "you gotta throw it if you got it." I liked her attitude, and so would Master Kwan. Thank you ma'am, can I have another.

Instructor Garrett put us through three two-minute rounds of no-contact shadow sparring. Two minutes is an eternity, for those of us who don't subscribe to the concept of pacing. As the clock seemed to slow down so did our kicks, while the gasping and trash talking picked up.

"Time," Instructor Garrett finally announced.

"Sadist," Khalq muttered. "Sir." While I bent over, hands on knees, he clasped his hands behind his head and walked it off. Strutted it off, that porno king.

"Get a drink," said Garrett, "then we'll go light contact."

I stayed put, telling myself to swallow my pride and take a seat for the remainder of class. Garrett motioned for me to join him for a demonstration. He assumed the fighting stance and I did likewise, squaring off with him. He indicated that I should keep my guard up. "Just touch your opponent," Garrett instructed the class as they returned from the water fountain. His back leg drove forward, toes pointed, knee raised and turning parallel to the floor as his hips made a full pivot—all of this at lightning speed, popping me point-on the solar plexus, just a little slap with the top of his foot, enough to make me gasp against my will and tightened abs.

I launched a retaliatory kick that Garrett slapped away with a grin. "Sorry Mr. Brian, it's a one-way street."

At the whistle Khalq and I went at each other. Sometimes we were too careful, our kicks stopping short of each other's bodies. Other times we connected harder than recommended. Control wasn't our strong suit.

"Ow, you sonofabitch," I hissed when he kicked my thigh. "That's a bruise." Khalq's kicks rarely rose even to hip level, much less the solar plexus where we were taught to aim. On those rare days when he was feeling particularly limber, his feet would ricochet off my hips and butt, peppering my groin.

"Time," Instructor Garrett finally called out. "Switch partners."

Khalq selected Genevieve and the white belt hottie paired with another red executive belt, a domino effect ending with Troy standing before me.

Instructor Garrett came over to stand beside us. "I think you two better put on pads," he made light of our history.

"Go get him, Brian," said Khalq.

"Light touch, gentlemen," Instructor Garrett reminded us. "Ready, fight."

Things might have been different if he had said "Ready, begin". But no, he said *fight*. It was like throwing a switch. I came out smokin', launching a kick at Troy's thick midsection. It was perfectly controlled, would have thwapped his solar plexus like Garrett had thwapped mine. But the prick blocked it. Stuck out his two-by-four forearm, catching me flush on the shin.

White light blossomed in my head. I stifled a squeal and kicked with my other leg. Troy stepped in tight, preventing any extension, sapping the power from my kick—a textbook move in a real match, but not the point of this exercise. He planted a meaty fist in my chest and drove me backward.

I expected Garrett to chastise Troy. Not a word. Troy stood there with his blank smoked-glass face, waiting. So I kicked him again. Fast kick this time. Shuffle step, pick up the front foot and kick, in one smooth motion. I had planned to avoid any more kicking with my right leg—my pulse pounded in the biopsy hole and layers of bruised flesh coating my shin bone. But I got confused and used it, putting everything I had into the kick. And sure enough the bastard blocked me again.

The pain was so all-encompassing, it didn't really hurt. Took my breath away and brought tears to my eyes, but no discomfort of the standard sort.

"Follow it up," Instructor Garrett coached. "Combinations. Bang-bang-

bang."

First time I ever hated Garrett. I could barely see Troy through the starburst explosions across my eyes as I attacked again. I think my first roundhouse kick was with my right leg. It connected. Left leg roundhouse, connected. Fast kick, missed. Roundhouse, glancing blow. I was exhausted, out of adrenaline, unable to lift my leg for another kick, unable to pivot out of range as Troy stepped behind me and for the love of God kicked me below the butt, right in the biopsy hole.

Pain and terror shot up through my groin and lanced my heart. I crumpled to the floor and screamed, some horrible animal-in-a-bear trap wail.

"Brian!" Garrett ran to me. "Are you alright?"

"I have cancer!" I cried out. "He kicked me in the cancer!"

I RETREATED, FLED rather, to the bathroom, stopping along the way to grab a handful of mini band-aids from the first aid box. Best I could I pasted four of them around the edges of the weeping incision, and then sat on my other cheek on the toilet lid, wanting to do some weeping myself.

If there had been a window, I would have crawled out. But we were in the basement. I wanted to stay in the bathroom all night, until everyone left, even the night cleaning crew. "Hey," the Guatemalan wastebasket emptier would say, "I heered that you screamed and cried like a baby tonight."

I couldn't stay in the john forever without looking like an even bigger puss. Sure enough, everyone waited, milling about in the front room where parents watched their little martial artists through the plasti-glass window.

Instructor Garrett was pale. "Are you okay?"

"I'm fine. Really." I had tunnel vision centered on the hallway door.

"Because if there's anything I can do…"

"It sounded worse than it was." Please start laughing, I silently begged them. Give me a hard time, make it a joke, mock me, and then it'll be over.

Genevieve put her arm around me, slowing my flight. Khalq patted my shoulder. A few parents looked on, trying to be supportive while hugging the margins of the cramped room, leery of close contact with cancer or hysteria.

"Brian, why did you come to class?" Garrett fretted, pacing, debating whether to call Master Kwan and file some sort of incident report.

"You are such a warrior," said Carolyn, an orange belt, and a black belt groupie. In Carolyn's mind, anyone nearing black-belt ranking was a deadly killer. And so whatever made a deadly killer wail must be terrible indeed.

"I'm a gigantic puss," I said. "I can't believe I screamed like that."

"You think you were loud," said Khalq. "If that was me, I would have been calling for my mommy."

"Khalq's a much bigger pussy than you are," Genevieve confirmed.

"He is a big pussy," I agreed, desperate to escape, shuffling toward the door, shame pounding so loudly in my ears I couldn't hear myself talk.

A few of the kids from our class had remained in the workout room. They were watching me through the observation window. From their expressions I could see their worldview had been shattered. They realized now that there was no one out there to protect them, that adults were just as weak and scared as they were. *Yeah kids, you're all gonna die someday.*

And there was Troy standing behind them, staring at me (I think) through those brown lenses. He turned and kicked one of the heavy padded pylons, rocking it back and forth. I was too distraught at the time to hate him properly.

"You're going to the hospital, right?" Garrett urged. "Just in case...?"

"I will," I assured him, relieving some anxiety from his face.

"I'll drive you," Khalq volunteered.

"Thanks homey. But I'll be fine. I could use some alone time."

Everyone said goodbye and filed back into the workout room. I limped down the hallway and out to the parking lot and my van.

What came over me to cry out like that? In a heartbeat I went from a martial arts warrior—a warrior, period, who had played the second half of a JV football game with a separated shoulder; who had fallen fifteen feet off the side of a boulder while race-climbing his best friend, landed on his back, got up and still beat his buddy to the top; who had elk hunted in Montana with Joshua and a couple of his buddies, illegally shot a timber wolf, and carried the carcass on his back on a five-mile detour to avoid the ranger; who had played poker at Jerry's house till five a.m., gone directly to the shop to open, put in a ten-hour shift, broke the roaster and spent all night with Craig fixing it, in time to open the shop again—to an object of pity, and probably disgust. I had been proud of my ability to suffer through pain, to persevere through adversity. Now I had thrown away all that Spartan history in one pathetic moment of irrational hysteria.

If they couldn't laugh at me, why couldn't they have at least shunned me, turned their backs on me and walked away whispering to each other, "I thought Brian was a bad ass, guess I was mistaken." The last thing my subconscious needed was to be coddled, to have my self-pitying behavior condoned. But they had huddled around me making clucking sounds, tissues at the ready to wipe my nose and dry my tears.

I vowed this would be the last time anyone would see that kind of weakness from me, regardless how bad things were going to get.

...and then immediately realized this was my dad talking; or maybe it was my mom. Either way, I retreated from the vow as quickly as I had made it, and was left with no clue how to feel, what to think, or where to go from there.

When I reached the right turn toward the hospital, I kept driving straight, to my apartment, where I sat in the dark and cursed myself, envisioning improbable scenarios that would allow me the opportunity to publicly display my fearless manhood and prove this shameful episode was a fluke.

It didn't take long before my rage turned against the cancer that wanted me dead. I screamed for an hour. I cursed my folks, Taekwondo and North Dakota, Bill Hernandes and Starbucks. I flung couch pillows, punched the walls, and threw a tantrum in every room until I was spent, lying on the floor, chest heaving, with not an ounce of feeling or humanity left in me.

And then a *really* big wave of emotion hit, and I broke down, weeping and wailing and begging God to give me a second chance. Now it was everybody and everything I loved, parading through my mind. I had never felt such intense love, and I was desperate to hold onto them, Mom, Dad, Isabel, my friends, my business. My life. Oh God, I prayed, let me keep my life.

It was no longer a mystery why I had lost it at the dojang. I was beyond scared. I had never even wondered how I might react to a bad diagnosis. Poorly, as it turned out.

I fell in bed with my brain empty, full of hopelessness. My last conscious thought was how badly I didn't want to die.

T - 14

A pleasing hubbub came from the other side of the bar that Sunday morning. Men's voices bubbled below random shrieks from toddlers and a chorus of women seemingly competing with each other, one at a time ratcheting up the volume and sharpening the timbre until everyone was on the verge of yelling, a brassy crescendo climaxing in howls of laughter. Rising and falling, rising and falling, slight variations on a standard theme. Music to my ears.

Except the kids. I know a world without children would soon be nothing but abandoned buildings overgrown with weeds and prowled by scavenging animals. But still…. Children are generally rude. They spill more than they buy. After little Jeffy knocks his drink over, his mother cuts to the front of the line, demanding the mess be immediately cleaned up, and assuming that a free replacement drink is on the way, something else for Jeffy to spill. When a kid walks in my shop, it's basically a two-for-one. "Make sure you put extra whipped cream on that," the mother says as I'm putting the lid on the free refill. "And sprinkles. My little Lisa loves to look at the sprinkles."

"Yeah," I try to be sweet, sure that without sprinkles' temptation the lid would stay on and the drink wouldn't spill, for the third time. "Now be careful," I remind them, getting a look from little Lisa and her mother, as if it was comments like this that made them spill the Ghirardelli hot chocolate in the first place.

Ghirardelli chocolate for a three-year-old. A three-year-old doesn't appreciate Ghirardelli. I needed two cans of Ghirardelli, one filled with Nesquick for the children. The margins would be better and I wouldn't cry as much when it spilled.

"More milk!" Charlotte called to Sara, our runner that morning. Sam had the till and Charlotte and I ran the bar, me on cup prep, Charlotte on the wand, the two of us taking turns pulling shots.

"Kenny," I greeted the manager of the Wells Fargo branch where Kevin the auditor had planned his trysts with the former Mrs. Rick McEwen. "Lady," I greeted Kenny's wife, Laurie. They stood at the back of the four-deep line. They came in four or five times a week. Good, loyal customers.

"Brian, how's it hanging?" Laurie greeted me. For the wife of a bank manager who was also head of the Chamber of Commerce, she's a little rough around the edges. But for Jamestown, just right.

"So far so good," I responded. "I'm not sure how long that will last, though." I was to start chemo and radiation the next day. The biopsy had confirmed cancer.

Kenny and Laurie chortled. "Medium nonfat vanilla cappuccino and a caramel macchiato?" I verified.

"Yes sir," said Kenny, smiling that I remembered their drinks. Customers think I remember only their drinks, only their kids' names, only their latest golf score, only their hard amber durum yield. In fact, I know over three hundred drinks by heart, probably a thousand kids' names, ages and activities, a season's worth of golf scores, handicaps and memorable shots, a bushelful of crop yields. I don't have an exceptional memory. Just the will to memorize everything about my good customers. I hate nothing more than the customer service dogma that you have to treat every customer like a king. If I gave every customer the royal treatment, no matter whether they had just told me how much they love my coffee or how stupid I am for not selling Tazo berry cream frappuccinos like Starbucks, then I've lessened the experience for my good customers. If I treated every customer the same, how would the good ones know how much I appreciated them?

"We should probably be a little more spontaneous," said Laurie, "but we're too old to change now."

"We're in a rut," Kenny confessed.

I smiled. "Looks like a groove to me. Of course," I said to Laurie, "when you're not here, Kenny orders a chocolate espresso smoothie."

"He doesn't!" Laurie cackled, poking Kenny in the ribs. "Do you?"

"That Brian is such a joker," said Kenny, looking flushed.

"Okay, I guess he doesn't," I said, eyebrows raised.

"Sugar-free hazelnut latté," Sam relayed an order, for Genevieve from Taekwondo. She was studying me as she paid for her drink.

"Brian, how are you?" she asked.

"Oh, you know."

Genevieve was itching to ask about my health, but didn't know whether my condition was common knowledge. "Happy to see such a good crowd this morning?" she offered a reason to be thankful.

"I am happy about that." The shop was packed. Not a seat open, people filing in and out, standing waiting for a seat to open up. Nice day.

"I've been thinking a lot about you since class on Tuesday." She sidestepped to stand before me on the other side of the espresso machine.

"I wish you wouldn't," I said. "I'm trying to put it out of my mind. I'd like to delete that episode from everyone's memory banks." I fixed Genevieve with a mindbending stare and prayed hard for amnesia for her. Very limited brain damage. No such luck.

"It wasn't that bad, Brian," she said. "No one could blame you."

"What happened?" Charlotte asked.

"Master Kwan kicked one of his students so hard, his lung popped," I said. "Sounded like a balloon. I fainted."

"Who was it?" Charlotte was dying to hear. She really liked the idea of hurting people. Preferably by her own hand.

"That's not what happened. Brian got mad at Troy," said Genevieve, putting the best possible spin on my meltdown.

"That kid does get on my nerves. But I may have overreacted."

"I don't blame you," said Genevieve. "Troy pisses me off."

"Troy Becker?" Sam asked.

"Your classmate," I confirmed.

"I'd kick the crap out of him myself," said Genevieve, "if I wasn't such a fat ass."

Charlotte gasped. "You are not. You are so hard on yourself."

"Charlotte, you don't understand," said Genevieve, crestfallen. "I used to be really good looking. I'm ashamed you have to see me like this."

Sam and I could only laugh. "Just because you don't spend five hours a day working out like some people," Charlotte griped. "Some of us actually have a life. Unfortunately, our butts reflect that."

"You have a great body, Charlotte," said Genevieve.

"Fabulous body," I agreed. "It's incredible."

Charlotte whacked my shoulder. "Shut up."

That may bruise, I thought to myself. Can't have my body working on healing a bruise. Only the cancer.

"It's true," said Genevieve. "I always used to think I was too fat. Now I look back at pictures. I had a knockout body. I should have been wearing bikinis twenty-four hours a day. I was an idiot."

"Sam has taken that philosophy to heart." I jerked my head in his direction. "Thong and pasties. Under his everyday clothes."

Sam paused on his way to the refrigerator and lifted his shirt, treating us to his roly-poly belly. Charlotte yanked his shirt back down. "Thank goodness Brian has a dress code for us," she said.

"Whatever you do," said Genevieve, "don't stop Charlotte from wearing tanktops and short skirts. This is her time to shine."

"It's in her contract," I said.

This earned me another backhand, another bruise.

Charlotte sighed as she checked out her own figure. "If this is as good as it gets, that's depressing." It was an act. She knew what she had.

"Have a couple kids, get a full-time job. It's all downhill," said Genevieve.

My ex-manager Craig slipped in the door. If he wasn't carrying coffee beans, his hands were jammed into his coat pockets. To make forward progress in a world with doors, Craig had to turn sideways and slide through the cracks.

"Hey Craig," I called to him. After I let him go, Craig stayed away from the shop long enough that we never had to go through an awkward stage. For some of my customers it was a different story. With no clue why he was let go, and even after I assured them it was purely a financial decision, they assumed the worst and shunned him. Looked as if they might spit on his feet. How dare he show up at Brian's shop! Hell, Craig should move out of town!

"What can I get for you?" I asked Craig.

Craig stared at me. Or through me. Craig is a smoker. Smokers get a lot of practice staring while they drag on their sticks and wait for the nicotine to sink in. And beyond these mechanics of the addiction, smokers seem to have a natural soap opera style. Plus he had a mustache. I had time to pour mocha syrup in two cups and write "Jimmy" on a third and then look up to catch the tail end of Craig's stare.

"Small drip," he said.

He initiated a fresh stare, this time accompanied by a slow nod, so I knew he had more to say. I knocked spent grounds out of the portafilter bucket, re-filled it with fresh ground espresso roast, re-holstered the portafilter and hit the shot button, and then made eye contact again as he said, "I was hoping to get a moment alone with you."

"That can be arranged." I canvassed my team. "Okay if I step away?"

"Go, go," Charlotte urged. "Make Sara earn her pay this morning." She glanced over her shoulder in time to dodge Sara's half-hearted swipe. Sara knew better than to actually make contact with Charlotte. We all did.

Kenny and Laurie were in front of me by this point, awaiting their drinks. "So what's the weekend have in store for you?" Kenny asked.

"I figure I have two options," I said. I didn't know how else to announce it. "I can start fasting now to get the swing of things before my chemo tomor-row, or gorge myself all day, one last binge."

"Your what?"

"My chemo."

"Your what? Your chemo?"

"Yeah, I've got cancer."

"No you don't," said Laurie.

"Yes I do." I pulled shots while giving them the news. "Bone." My head was abuzz with turbulence—no real thoughts, only a constant chaotic panic since I had received the exam results. "They found it last week." My hands were shaking ever so slightly, and the espresso shot went too long; I had to toss it and start over. I wanted to scream.

Kenny and Laurie were horrified. People in line gaped. Activity around me came to a halt. I kept talking, glancing up from time to time, careful to make no eye contact. "I was so sure it was high up my leg, right under my butt. Turns out it's in my shin. Which probably doesn't matter either way, but at least it doesn't creep me out quite as much." An urgent murmur traveled around the room. *Brian has to be joking*, most of them thought. *Brian's such a kidder. Any second now he'll come clean.* Any second.

"The tibia or the fibula?" Laurie wanted to know.

I had to chuckle at that one. "That was my first question, too. I guess it doesn't really matter, since they won't amputate one without the other."

Kenny's eyes were huge. "You, uh, you must uh...how are you doing?"

"Oh I'm pretty upset."

"You wouldn't know it though, would you?" Charlotte shook her head as she filled Laurie's cup with steamed milk. "Same old Brian, joking about it. Pretending it's no big deal." She froze in mid-pour, then set the pitcher down.

"Keep it together, lady," I growled.

Charlotte lowered her head and breathed deep. "Brian, you're such an idiot." She choked on the last words. Waving an apology she backed away from the bar, wiping her eyes with her wrists.

"I've been crying ever since he told me," said Genevieve from the end of the counter, finally free to unleash her ample emotions. She sobbed and held open her arms, and Charlotte went to her for a hug. Sara was right behind her.

Now Laurie was crying, and Kenny's eyes were watery. "Come on," I complained. Now I had to look up at the ceiling and blink, blink, blink. "You people are really making me angry."

The line stagnated. I think a couple prospective customers turned around and left. Here I was announcing the most heartbreaking trauma of my relatively young life, in the midst of stunned friends and loyal customers about to cry their eyes out for me, ready to start weeping myself, and I couldn't take a break from worrying about my bottom line. It's all about volume, gotta get them their coffee quickly.

"You need a hug," said Laurie. She squeezed past the cluster of grappling women to meet me at the blender. "I am so sorry."

"Yeah," that's all I could say. Questions bounced around the shop, joyful hubbub reduced to a sea of nervous chirping. Some moans. More people crying. Would this hurt or help business?

Normal operations ceased. Everyone was studying me. Laurie didn't want to let go, finally did, heading for the bathroom to compose herself.

Should I make a formal announcement? I wondered. Blow my nose and go back to work? Get on the counter and yell? Didn't matter, it was now a matter of hours before the entire town knew I had the big C.

Andrea entered the shop from the hallway. She had lost more weight, and was now the daintiest thing I had ever seen. Ninety pounds? Eighty-five? Even with the cancer, my odds of survival were still better than hers.

Mark Knutter breezed through the front door. "Knutter boy!" I greeted him. Knutter Brothers Dairy is big in these parts.

"Mr. Brian," Mark responded. "What's shakin'?"

"Not much, not much." I jumped to the espresso machine and revved up the pressure for another shot. "Mocha?"

Mark gave me the pistol finger and pulled the trigger. "You know it."

Gradually everyone fell back into conversation, albeit muted and sans laughter. Kenny lingered. "Brian, I want you to know we're here for you."

"Thanks man," I said, giving him a knuckle-knock and what he probably really desired, the permission to walk away.

In the next ten minutes a number of customers stopped by to pay their respects to dead guy walkin' before leaving the shop, or in the case of Terrence the next great American novelist and Theresa the older than average pre-pharmacy student, before settling in for a couple hours of hardcore furthering of their dream careers.

Three older ladies each reached across the bar to squeeze my hand. Which was impressive. I would be hesitant to make firm contact with a cancer patient for fear of snapping a decayed bone or dislodging a chunk of withered muscle. I had great customers. I was going to miss this place, when I died.

Craig waited on the farthest stool. With a lull before the next wave of churchgoers, I gave him the nod and led the way into my cluttered office. I sat in the squeaky roller chair and waited out his stare.

Craig closed the door. "So you have cancer." A predictable pause. "That's a raw deal. When did you hear?"

"I got the results Wednesday. I just started telling people today. That's not true—I sort of told people at Taekwondo on Tuesday. So how's things for you? Can't be any worse than my life I hope."

Hands jammed in his coat pockets, Craig used his thigh to straighten a slumping pile of overdue bills. "This is bad timing, considering. But I wanted to give you a heads-up. You know I want to make my career in the coffee business, right?"

"Who friggin' doesn't? But yeah, I know you're serious about it. And you know coffee. If there had been any way to keep you, financially, I would have." Maybe not. Craig's knowledge was great, but it would be an understatement to say he had never really bonded with the customers.

Craig weighed the kind sentiments against my initial sarcasm. "I took a job at Uncommon Grounds. You know, the shop by the campus."

"It's nowhere near the campus..." *Now's not the time*, I counseled myself. "...but congratulations. You figure it'll be around long?" I asked this like I was concerned about Craig's job stability rather than my own shop's future.

As if he was smoking, and as if this phantom smoke was stinging his eyes, Craig squinted. "Bill is really committed to growing."

Aren't we all? I almost retorted. But was I? Not at the moment, that was for sure.

"He's going to start an aggressive marketing campaign," said Craig. "Happy hours, two-for-one deals, coupons. He's been asking me whether you can afford it."

"He wants me to pay for it? That hardly seems fair."

Craig squinted, smirked, nodded—his version of the belly laugh.

"What did you tell him?" I asked.

"Nothing. I didn't tell him anything about your financial condition or customer volume. That's none of his business," he said with conviction.

I didn't believe him. "I'm amazed Billy is going to throw more freebies out there. He's been printing coupons like funny money for months."

I got the long cool stare. "He'd really like to force you out of business."

"That's the name of the game, I guess."

"I just thought you might like to know what you're up against," said Craig. "So," he made conversation, "how's business?"

I decided Craig's visits to my shop weren't out of lingering allegiance—which I admit would have been surprising under the circumstances. He came at Billy's bidding, to gauge my financial condition, hoping to intimidate me.

"Speaking of business…" I squeezed past him and opened the door. "I better get back to it."

"Cool. Maybe I'll hang out here for awhile—"

"I wish you wouldn't," I cut him off. "I won't have time to talk. And it might be a little awkward for the employees."

Craig had a melancholy twinkle in his eye. "I'd ask for a coffee to go, but you'd probably be afraid I'd take it back and analyze it. Help Bill figure out all your secrets."

"Probably."

Craig fidgeted. "Brian, I uh…"

"Good luck with Billy-boy. I sincerely hope he treats you right."

Craig slipped out the alley door and I rejoined my crew as the next after-service rush hit us. Sara was at the register, Charlotte still on the bar, and Sam was our floater. I stepped into the cup-prep slot. "Where we at?"

"That's a skinny mocha," said Sara, pointing, "that's a cappuccino, that's a three-shot latté, and that's a caramel macchiato."

For the next half-hour I operated in a quiet, distracted state. Silence was rare for me. My employees' chatter stopped too, and pretty soon the whole shop mirrored my subdued mood. Customers left behind half-full cups. Prospective customers passed by, sensing the death-shroud hanging like filmy drapes over the windows. First time I ever felt like a liability.

At Charlotte's urging I left early to get some sleep. Picked up a pail of ice cream on the way, and ate a dish with crackers. Ice cream was the only thing that had sounded good the past few days, and crackers seemed like a prudent and palatable balance to my all-dairy diet. Then I crawled in bed, hoping for a few hours of dreamless slumber.

Throughout my sickness, I've gone back and forth on sleep. Should I get extra, to give my body the energy to combat the disease? Or is it during the sleeping hours, when my defenses are down, that the cancer makes its move? It was an agonizing debate. Truly a life or death question. Get extra rest and live; or sleep my life away while the cancer ran amok.

Same for working. Should I devote myself to the business, as a stimulant and to take my mind off the cancer? Become a dynamo of activity, taking on all challenges and muscling my way to good health? Or, do workaholics use up all their energy and die? It was all a question of optimizing my defenses.

Probably a moot debate. With any defenses to speak of, I wouldn't have cancer.

I wasn't sleeping much those days anyway. As soon as I shut out the external pressures, the internal world came to life. My conscience, my guilt, my despair over my failing business. Now it was the Bluffs nagging me. I owed Mike McEwen a call.

I dialed his ass up. "Mike. Brian."

"Brian," Mike sighed into his phone. "How—"

"Brian from the coffeeshop."

Mike chuckled. He always got a rise out of that one.

"I didn't want you confusing me with some other Brian."

"There's only one Brian, buddy."

"Thanks. Hey, I've been thinking about the Bluffs store, about—"

"Brian, listen buddy, come on over for awhile, and just take a load off."

"I can't Mike. I'd like to, but, you know. I will, as soon as I can."

"Yeah. Okay." Mike breathed heavily. He muttered a couple low-grade epithets. "We can't believe it, Brian. We can't…. You got the basket?"

I was staring at it, a vase of lilies bowing over assorted California almonds, two bananas speckled black and pushing bruises into ripe nectarines. "It's great."

"That's from that little gift store at the corner of 4th and Main. Gal does a great job. Ships baskets all over the country."

"Good for her."

"We're just really eager to see you around here," said Mike. "We've all been worried about you. Very worried."

"I apologize for not returning all your voicemails. They've been great."

"I know you've been busy. The last thing we want to do is make you feel obligated to come see us."

"I really appreciate the concern. I've been meaning to give you a call."

"We'd like to have you over for dinner tonight."

"That would be great. But I don't think I'm feeling up to it."

"I know," said Mike. "We know what you're going through…" His lips smacked as he struggled to keep it together. "This is…it's very hard to accept."

"I know. The timing's crummy, with the Bluffs and all—"

"It's not the timing, Brian." The spark of exasperation bucked him up. "We care about you, a lot. Isabel, you know, she thinks the world of you."

Iz and I had talked a couple times on the phone, about my diagnosis and upcoming treatments, but I hadn't seen her since the night in the playhouse, and I was sure it was driving the McEwens crazy. She should have been the first person I turned to. I could claim that the shock of being diagnosed with cancer had made me temporarily antisocial. But I had been to dinner at Joshua and Denise's, and had Jerry and Amber over, twice; and in fact I had never been lonelier. I had come that close to asking my folks to fly out and stay with me. *Mom, Dad, can you visit? For a year or so?*

Actually, I hadn't told them. Skip college, avoid marriage, move a thousand miles away; and then tell your folks you have cancer? I couldn't be a worse son. Dad couldn't vacation for more than a long weekend, couldn't sit through a whole movie or take a long crap, without worrying the office was falling apart without him. Even if he thought I was dying, he couldn't bring himself to turn his back on his insurance agency. But all the while he worked, the guilt would be killing him.

I couldn't do that to him. At most I would wait until I had some good news, until I had made progress. Otherwise, they were going to have to wait for the obituary.

If this had been twenty years down the road, at a more reasonable age for cancer to strike, with Dad long since retired, maybe I wouldn't have hesitated to ask them to come stay with me. What a nice picture. The fifty-year-old bachelor cared for in his waning days by his elderly parents.

"Brian, why don't you come by?" said Mike. "We'll talk."

"I'd love to. I will, soon."

"I shouldn't push."

"No, I want to see you guys, too. But I'm really not up to it right now."

"No-no, I understand. Valerie is cooking you some meals. About a month's worth, from the look of it. She's been driving us crazy with the smells all weekend. She's cooking all this fabulous grub for you, and making us order pizza. Can you believe that?"

"She doesn't need to do that for me."

I heard Valerie in the background: "When is he coming over?"

"We're going to take the food to him," Mike told her.

"Didn't you invite him for dinner?" she asked.

"He's not coming over," said Mike, irritated. I couldn't make out Valerie's response, just the inquisitive tone. "Val," Mike barked, "he's tired!"

"I could stop by," I bluffed.

"We're bringing the food. You rest. It's very important you don't overdo it. I'm sure Dr. Bonilla is telling you to take it easy. You listen to him. I know how many hours you put in. You're a workaholic like me. Like my boys. I remember how tired Brent was. But he wouldn't listen to us when we told him to take it easy…"

Silence on the line while Mike fought for control.

"I'm okay, Mike." It was time to change the subject. I had a feeling the McEwens were planning a fourth testimonial, for Brent and Brian, with a blurry line between the living and the dead. "I've been meaning to call you about the Bluffs."

"We'll talk about that when it's time," said Mike, voice hoarse with emotion. "You don't need anything else on your plate. Valerie, is that food ready? Sorry," he apologized for yelling in my ear. "Hang on, she's saying something…okay, honey. Yes! I'll ask him! Brian, are you going to be home?"

"I'm not going anywhere. If I don't come to the door right away, keep knocking. I might be napping."

"Unlock your door, so we don't have to disturb you. Hold on…what?" He was talking to Valerie again. "Criminy, how much are you cooking? … Are we going to have anything left in this house for us to eat?! … Well wrap it up! He's hungry!"

"You guys are too good to me. I appreciate it."

"You'll beat this, Brian. I know it. You just get better. Just get better."

Exactly the kind of desperate hopefulness I didn't need to hear.

I OPENED THE DOOR two hours later and there was Isabel. She was carrying a J.C. Penney's shopping bag and leaning backward to manage the weight of an insulated Sven's Pizza delivery container hanging from a strap slung around the back of her neck.

"Special delivery," she grunted.

"Sorry, I didn't order a pizza. Or ten."

Iz smiled, trying to be a good sport. I stepped aside and she staggered to the kitchen and heaved the pizza container onto the table.

"I worked for Sven's in college," she explained, unpacking casserole dishes, baking pans, stuff wrapped in tinfoil, paper plates and plastic utensils, and napkins. "Somehow I ended up with one of their heat bags. Two of them, actually. The other one is in the car. It's even heavier."

"Did you help cook all this?"

"It was all Mom. It was a labor of love, don't worry. And don't feel like you have to eat everything. I know what chemo does to your appetite. That's why I did a little shopping for you." Isabel slid a stack of shorts and silk shirts halfway out of the Penney's bag. "I bought everything a size smaller than what you're in now."

"Iz, that's very nice."

She moved toward me. "Brian, I have missed you so much."

"I'm sorry I've been avoiding you," I said while we hugged.

She snuggled into my neck. "All I know is, I'm glad to be with you now."

"After everything your family went through, I didn't want you suffering through these first few days with me. Until the docs get a better idea what I'm dealing with."

"You don't have to protect us." Iz kissed me. "We're a strong family."

"I was planning to see you once I had started treatments. I didn't want you to have to go through the 'why me' stage."

"I'm not a 'why me' girl, Brian." She kissed me again.

"I'm a big 'why me' guy."

"That's why you need me around." Another kiss. "As you well know, I've been through a lot, and that thought has never come to mind. I miss teaching every day, but I never ask 'why me?' Every morning I just wake up and dream about what it's going to be like, my first day back in the classroom."

"That's more of a 'why on earth did I do that' question."

Isabel shook her head. "There's no sense in that. There's a plan for us, with roadblocks along the way. If we spend precious time dwelling on the roadblocks, we'll never reach the destination God has in mind." She stroked my cheek, her eyes moving around my face, searching, for what, cancerous lesions? Perhaps I was a little paranoid.

And a little distressed by her viewpoint. "Was what you did part of God's plan?"

"I won't say there was a reason for what happened between me and Melissa," she said, "and I won't say there wasn't. I only know I'm destined to teach. So that's where my focus is. Your destiny is to live and do great things in the coffee world and raise a wonderful family with me. I've known it since we met, since our first dinner together in Fargo. Focus on that, and leave everything else to Dr. Bonilla."

Only Isabel could freak me out and soothe my soul in the span of a few sentences.

"Dr. Bonilla will focus on curing you, and you're going to focus on building your coffee empire, from the Bluffs to Valley City to Fargo. And I'll be beside you every step of the way, reminding you how blessed we are."

"Okay." Strange to say, but even with all my pedo-lesbo-phobia, I still accepted that we were destined to grow old together. Immense quantities of planning, managing and dreaming energies went into the business; I didn't have the time or will to do the same for my love life. Searching for Ms. Right wasn't a priority, it wasn't a goal, it wasn't even a nice-to-have. I love people in general, and I loved Iz—the concept of True Love didn't resonate. If the woman I was with was a good person, I was confident we could have a great life together.

Is Isabel a good person? Sure she is. Here's a woman who should be harboring a major demon in her skull. Yet Isabel was the most grounded, self-actualized, person-at-peace I ever knew. And all that tranquility gave her an extraordinary capacity for thoughtfulness. She regularly sent flowers to my apartment and chocolates to the shop; she never forgot my folks' birthdays or anniversary; and check out my new wardrobe in the Penney's bag.

"Iz, you're too good to me."

"You're someone who deserves the best life has to offer."

"I can't argue with that." I gave her waist a playful squeeze. "But what do you get in return from me? Nonstop worrying about my business. Extended absences. Cancer. You deserve better."

She kissed me. "I won't find better, because you're the best. Everything you described—your work challenges, your health, the times you need space to get your thoughts straight—those aren't the measure of you. It's who you *are* that I'm crazy about. You're beautiful. I knew it the first night, when you shadow danced with me. And I'm not the only one who sees it. In five years here, you have more people who love you than anyone I know. I'm just the lucky one who gets you."

I let my eyes linger on hers, taking in all her love and happiness. "I'm afraid at some point you'll get tired of waiting for me to get my life straight."

Iz smiled. "We're in the middle of an amazing love affair here. I'd be crazy to let this go. A romance like ours isn't smooth and linear. Without some curves and some heartache along the way, we wouldn't have any stories to tell our grandkids."

"I do like a good story."

"To be a good storyteller, you need to be a good story maker," she told me. "I want to be part of your story. I'm willing to wait for that opportunity, and I'm willing to suffer for it if I have to."

"And you have."

"Yes I have. And look—I'm still here. So next time you're feeling sick or confused or scared"—she unbuttoned my shorts with a quick expert twist of her fingers—"you're not going to hide from me, okay? You're not going to try to spare me the emotions, right?"

"Right."

"Now then. You know why I'm here, don't you? Dad said you sounded tense on the phone." She cupped my privates with both hands. "No more tension." As the last word left her mouth she clamped it, still open, over mine. The word *tension* buzzed my molars.

"Hey-hey," I broke it off, gently. I was feeling wonderful about everything Iz had said, about what it foretold for our future together. But in the here-and-now, the reference to her fifteen-year-old playmate was still too fresh. I know women's emotions can lead them to unfortunate entanglements, and I was sure Iz had cared deeply for young Melissa—and that was the problem. She cared deeply for me too, and I was having trouble differentiating the two of us. When Isabel yanked my control rod, I couldn't help imagining her doing the feminine equivalent to her little student. "I'm a cancer victim, remember."

"You were a cancer victim a week ago, too," Isabel reminded me. "It didn't stop you then." She sucked my Adam's apple.

"I'm feeling really sensitive."

"We can make that work to our advantage." She rubbed me down there, you know, down there where it counts. I knew myself well enough to predict that my lesbo-pedophile nausea would quickly be forgotten, and then we would have sex.

And the thought of sex with someone who made me queasy, made me ill. I buttoned my shorts and seized Isabel's hands. "Let's go get the rest of the food. Stay and eat dinner with me. Then I need to get some rest."

I WAS NERVOUS THE WHOLE MEAL, chicken cacciatore and garlic bread, still hot from Valerie's stove. Isabel was trying to seduce me. She was determined to take my mind off the cancer. She could hardly pay attention to the conversation, with all the plotting going on in the back of her mind. I thought women could multi-task.

I tried different topics, hoping to engage her. Really just hoping to talk.

"Joshua and Denise are planning a week-long fishing trip to Lake Sacagawea. They invited us to come along. Depending on how my treatments go, maybe I'll drive out there for a couple days."

"That would be fun. We could fool around while they fish."

"Yeah, yeah, good idea. I kind of like to fish, though. Hey, did I tell you, Craig's working for Hernandes now. He came into the shop this morning and told me Hernandes is starting an even bigger marketing push." When Isabel didn't react, I provided her the appropriate reaction: "That's not good."

"Mm, no, it's not."

"I think Craig wants to stay on my good side, hoping I'll hire him to manage the Bluffs shop, if it ends up going through. Craig's not the right kind of guy to manage a new shop. He's a hard worker, but he's not personable enough. But I may hire him just to piss Hernandes off."

"I always liked Craig."

"That's funny, because I'm pretty sure he hates women."

"No kidding."

"Get this. You know Khalq, the doc from Syria? He made a presentation at the last Chamber meeting, about how Jamestown can develop a thriving Middle Eastern community. I was surprised, everyone was pretty excited. And I guess Arabs love coffee."

"I've always wanted to try a Turkish coffee."

"Good, good. That's good. So, anyway, I'm wondering how bad this chemo will kick my ass. I really want to work on my golf game this summer."

"I know."

"And I don't want to fall behind Khalq and the rest of the black belt candidate class. Plus I'd like to kick Troy Becker in the nuts. But I'm sure his nuts are as solid as the rest of him, and my cancerous tibia would snap in half."

"I think it's great you want to stay active during your treatments." Isabel gave me a naughty wink. "It's good for your stamina."

Sex and food, neither had ever sounded so unappetizing. "So how about Andrea? What's her story? I ran into her at the hospital, and then she actually came into the shop a couple days ago. I got the feeling she cares about me, but she'd never come out and say it. She did ask whether I'd consider Dr. Bhani's treatment. Crazy, huh?"

"She's crazy all right," said Isabel, caressing my knee under the table. Not even the invitation to gossip about Andrea could derail her one-track mind. I had one hundred percent of Iz's focus, but none of her attention. Instead of taking a permanent chunk out of my fear and loneliness, our time together only pushed it back a couple hours. Isabel schemed and I fretted, trying to craft a plausible escape plan.

Of course escaping from one's own apartment is nearly impossible. We were stuck together. So I resorted to focusing on the positives, which had become a mantra-like checklist in my mind:

1. She loves me.
2. She treats me wonderfully, better than anyone else ever could.
3. She's great in bed.
4. She has a great family.
5. She loves coffee.
6. She doesn't hold grudges; she doesn't blame me for anything, not even holding her hostage in an indefinite, perpetual engagement.

7. She made a huge mistake, but she's batted a thousand since we met.

8. She's faithful—a bevy of nubile youngsters could throw themselves at her feet, and I was confident Isabel would stay true to me.

And she was beautiful, even demure in a white blouse and a soft red sweater. Her deep brown hair fell on her shoulders. It looked even softer than her sweater. Which was saying something.

At seven sharp I put down my fork. "I'm supposed to stop eating now."

Isabel's fork clattered to her plate. "Let me tuck you in."

"I'm going to sleep in my clothes on top of the bedding, so there's really no tucking necessary. Thank you for coming though. I'll have to find some way to let your mom know how much I appreciate all the food."

"Sorry I had to throw that pail of ice cream to make room in the freezer."

"It was getting old."

We cleared the dishes and secured the leftovers. "Okay Iz, thanks again."

"I wish there was something else I could do for you."

"You can be very satisfied with everything you've done for me."

"But I'm not satisfied." She stuck her tongue in my ear. Like a drunk prone to blackouts or William Hurt in a deprivation chamber, I was no longer responsible for or even aware of my actions. With a tongue in my ear, I wouldn't be surprised to learn I had run around town naked slaughtering pets and humping livestock. Isabel kept it in there long enough to get me hot and bothered and in bed.

I PRETENDED to fall asleep afterward, and pondered—was that charitable hospice sex, or was I simply irresistible? I couldn't be that good in bed. Could I? No, I wasn't.

Isabel left the bed, and over my gentle rhythmic breathing I heard her getting dressed. She left the room. I sighed with relief.

Whatever her motivation, the sex was great, definitely a tension reliever. Still I can't tell you how badly I wanted her gone, how much I wanted to be alone, even acknowledging the loneliness that was bound to return. Every second was excruciating, waiting to hear the front door open and close.

Isabel reentered the room. Almost caught me peeking. Might have. After some muffled rustling, a funny clicking sound, and a weird noise or two I couldn't identify and can't describe, the bed depressed under her weight. She reached under the covers to pat me on the butt. She lightly scratched my ass, then found the biopsy site and gently drug her fingernails around the healing wound. Felt good. Too good.

"Sleep well, Brian," Isabel whispered in my ear. It was still a little damp in there, making her breath cool, making me shiver. She scratched in the crease, that junction of leg and butt. I couldn't help but recall our time in the playhouse. Felt good. She ran her fingernails up and down the inside of my thighs. Couldn't help but separate my legs enough to accommodate her.

"I need you to lift your hips a bit," she instructed, like a nurse might.

I mumbled gibberish, my impression of a semi-conscious man, and obliged. Her greased finger slid inside me so fast and so far I dared not drop my hips. Her other hand took care of me in record time.

That this was my second time, in under ten minutes—I know this is stupid, but it made me feel virile and full of life and suddenly certain that anything was possible and that I could beat this thing. Cancer? What cancer?

Isabel wiped her hands on the sheets, patted my butt and left the building. She left me lying there spent on the bed. There's a lot to be said for a relationship like that.

T - 13

"Mr. Lawson. Mr. Lawson. Brian, I need you to wake up."

For a time the doctor's office and my head were on different coordinate planes. I wasn't sure how to bridge this gap. Finally with a little click the two planes joined together as one. Nurse Nancy stood before me.

"I think I dozed off."

"I think you fainted, honey." Nurse Nancy had a very white face under her cap. Her hair was pulled back into a thick yellow-blonde wad. Nurses aren't sexy, I don't understand that common misconception. Most of them are kind of mean. "I came in and you were slumped forward in the chair with your face blue," she said. "Gave me a little shock."

"Maybe you overdosed me."

"Mm, no." She was taking my pulse. "We give small doses of the chemo drugs these days, fractions of what we used to. Smaller doses, more often. It helps with the side effects."

I was oh-so-woozy and having difficulty breathing, like waking up too quickly from a deep sleep induced by strangulation. "Maybe I have a really low tolerance for chemo drugs."

"I don't think that's the problem." Nurse Nancy walked me to the exam bed. She helped me up and laid me down.

"You're saying I fainted."

"It happens. It doesn't mean you're afraid."

"I'm scared to death. I wish I wasn't."

She patted my foot. "We'll find someone for you to talk to. There are plenty of counselors here at the hospital to help with the process."

"What process?" Without lifting my head I could only see her nurse's cap as she rummaged through the supply cabinet. I wasn't in the mood to move my head. But it would be informative to see her face when she answered.

Who was I kidding, she wasn't going anywhere near that one. "Dr. Bonilla will be in to see you very soon," she said. "Will you be okay here? Not feeling nauseous?"

I hadn't been sure she remembered me from my last visit. "I'm fine."

I was exhausted, but I forced my eyes open, fixed on the ceiling vent, afraid to doze off, terrified of not waking up.

Not waking up. That was the world's most frightening phrase. *Now I lay me down to sleep...* I could never say that prayer, which I've heard is meant to comfort children before they fall asleep. Other children must see a gentle Lord carrying them up to the playgrounds of heaven, now that they had died before they waked. I only saw a gray-black void, and the world going on without me.

But of course that was the kicker. There would be no void, no world to see, because there would be no Brian to see it. How could I suddenly cease to exist? How could the world go on without me? (And with barely a record of me, which was a related but separate despair that would resume its mental assault later.) The idea terrorized and confused me. I didn't want to contemplate it. I was trapped in the adult version of one of Piaget's developmental stages, a man-baby who wants people and objects to cease to exist when he leaves the room. I've even had a hard time coming to grips with the idea that things happened here on earth before I came along. I think that's the reason I love history books. To become so familiar with the details of centuries past that I could almost believe I had played a part.

The incredible sadness of the nonexistence of Brian Lawson. That was the state Dr. Bonilla found me in.

"Hi Brian. Don't get up." When I remained on my back, Dr. Bonilla crossed the room to shake my hand. Bonilla rhymed with vanilla. Tall and thin with light brown close-cropped mildly curly hair. Very intelligent looking, the way I liked my doctors. "So we've worked you over already this morning. Radiation, chemo, the works."

"Ain't so bad." Didn't remember much of it.

"Don't get cocky, that's not all we've got." Dr. Bonilla looked at my shin, lightly probing the skin. "So do you have any questions for me?"

"Pretty much every question on the list. It might be easier to refer me to the FAQ section of your website."

Dr. Bonilla put aside his clipboard and sat on the roller stool. Our heads were at the same height. "Let me give you the lowdown on what we know, and what I think we should do. Then you can fire away. A lot depends on what you want to do."

"Fair enough. Go," I said like a game-show host.

Dr. Bonilla initially came off as a soft-spoken, cerebral, caring sort of guy. Now that we were going to talk cancer, he worked extra hard not to seem chatty, which probably wouldn't have been possible for him anyway. The result was a voice like a robot with the volume turned way down.

"You have a sarcoma, which is a cancer of the connective tissue, including bone. It appears you have bone cancer. I say 'appears' because it's rare for cancer to start in the bone. Usually it spreads there, from somewhere else. The lung, the prostate."

"I know you told me to hold my questions to the end."

"No, please, ask away."

I sat up and slid off the table and returned to the chair where I had fainted. I didn't really have a question, but Dr. Bonilla's robo-monologue was killing me. "Did I catch it at Taekwondo? I feel like I bruised my shin so many times, cancer was inevitable. In retrospect, anyway."

"That a common misperception," said Dr. Bonilla. "Someone bangs his elbow, it heals real slowly if at all, hurts more than it should, and turns out to be cancerous. Did the bruise cause the cancer? Probably not. Most likely a coincidence. A person bumps into things all the time, okay? Doesn't usually result in cancer. More likely, the bruise simply calls attention to the cancer."

"Then I guess I can't sue this Troy kid."

"Troy Becker?"

"Yes, as a matter of fact."

"Troy's father is a good friend of mine."

"Troy's a great kid, I'm sure. But he's murder in the ring."

Dr. Bonilla gave me a polite smile. "So we're pretty sure the cancer originated in the bone. As you know, we took a number of pictures. MRI, CAT scans, X-rays. We looked you over from top to bottom. You look clean everywhere else."

Clean everywhere else. I liked that.

"So what do we do next," Dr. Bonilla asked himself. "I propose to continue chemotherapy, in two- or three-week sessions, to stop the growth and the potential spread of any remaining cancer cells. A couple rounds could very well do the trick. But I don't like the wait-and-see approach. I want to take an aggressive stance with your cancer."

Boys are hypnotized as babies and told to act like rabid chipmunks whenever someone says *aggressive*. I slapped the arm of the chair and wiped foamy spittle off my lips. "You're talking amputation. I'm in. Let's do it."

"Not quite so extreme," said Dr. Bonilla without batting an eye. "I was thinking minor surgery to remove the tumor." He winked. "But I'm glad you're game for whatever I have in mind."

"Believe me, I'll take 'we have to amputate' over 'I'm afraid your cancer has spread', every time."

"My goal is to never have to deliver that line to you," said Dr. Bonilla. "So throughout the process we'll also be hitting the tumor with a couple different types of radiation therapy."

"That makes me nervous. I haven't gone forth and multiplied yet."

The doc smiled. "We'll target the tumor with a precise beam of radiation. The technology at our disposal these days allows us to pinpoint our attack."

"You're positive there's no cancer where you took the biopsy?"

"Not as far as we can tell," said Dr. Bonilla. "The swelling back there may have been a reaction to the cancer. Or to an infection. Or just because. Lymph nodes will do that. If it was the lymph system reacting to the cancer, I would take it as an encouraging sign—it probably means we caught the cancer about the same time your body did."

"So just the shin," I verified.

"Correct."

"Tibia or fibia?"

"It's fibula. But it's the tibia."

"The cancer?"

"Yes," said Dr. Bonilla.

"Which one?"

"Bone cancer."

"No, I mean which bone?"

"I told you." He sounded a little irritated. "The tibia."

"Not the fibia?"

"It's the fibula."

"Oh man, is it in both?"

"No, just the fibula. Dammit, I mean the tibia."

"Whichever," I said, done messing with him. I love Abbott & Costello. "So, Jared Caldwell." Caldwell was my radiologist and Sam my employee's father. "What do you think of his abilities?"

Dr. Bonilla frowned. I think he had a headache now.

"I'm just wondering if I shouldn't go to the Mayo Clinic, or Mt. Sinai. Or maybe to a hospital in a town of more than twenty thousand people."

"Dr. Caldwell has been running radiology for us for the past decade," said Dr. Bonilla. "He's had something like two thousand patients. This isn't a statistic that's available to patients, but when you compare Dr. Caldwell's success rate to the rest of the U.S., he's quite a bit better than the average."

"What about Canada?" I challenged, to loosen him up. "I've heard a lot of good things about Canada's healthcare system. And it's just up the road."

Dr. Bonilla pretended to take my request seriously. "Canada. Hm. Well, I think we could get you in for treatments sometime in the year 2010."

"Must be a quality product, with a waiting list that long."

Dr. Bonilla chuckled. He straightened up on his stool and slapped his knee and outright laughed. "I can tell you this, Dr. Caldwell has worked on quite a few Canadians in his career."

I could have cared less about Dr. Caldwell or Bonilla's success rates or how they stacked up internationally. I just wanted doctors who liked me enough to bust their asses to save my life. I had to believe that a doctor who cared, I mean really cared, would work harder for me. Put in extra hours, lose sleep—but not too much sleep. I wanted a doctor who was clear-headed. And single-minded. A doctor who focused on me at the expense of all else, other patients, dictation, family, everything. That was the doctor I wanted.

"Okay," I said, "let's stick with Jared."

"Good choice," said Dr. Bonilla. "Brian, you look like you're feeling pretty good so far."

"No. Not really."

Dr. Bonilla gave me a tight smile. "It's going to get worse. We soften the effects of the chemo drugs the best we can. But they're designed to do damage to your cancer, so the rest of you is going to take a beating, too."

"So long as my hair doesn't fall out."

"I'll note that." Dr. Bonilla pretended to scribble a note. "'Patient desires to keep his hair. Or at the very least, to grow it back later.'"

"Later? Doc, I don't know how this is going to work if you don't listen more carefully to my demands."

"Brian, with what we're going to give you, maybe one in a thousand patients doesn't lose a good deal of hair."

"Keep in mind that since most people have mediocre hair, they don't make it a priority. I have nice hair. I have to like my odds."

"We'll do what we can," said Dr. Bonilla, looking a little tired of my act. I thought he was going to stand up and bring our talk to a close. Instead he clasped a knee and leaned back on the stool. "Let's talk about anything else you have on your mind. How's your mental state?"

I would have said "fine" and let him be on his way, but Dr. Bonilla seemed like he truly wanted to know. And I was truly ready to tell somebody. "Terrible. I'm really afraid of dying. I mean really afraid. I've always believed in God—didn't really understand Him, you know, the mechanics of heaven and souls and that whole thing. But I believed He existed. Until a week or so ago. Now, now that I'm trying to visualize it, for the first time, really, it sounds a little farfetched. I really want to believe—that's my number two prayer. 'Help me believe.' Right after 'Save me.'"

Hunched on the stool and staring into the floor, Dr. Bonilla rubbed a knuckle across his lips.

"I know this isn't your area of expertise," I said. "But you did ask."

He broke out of his reverie. "I can tell you what I know, from my experience with similar situations."

"That would be great."

"I've seen people who were at peace with their faith, who went much faster than I thought they should have. Circumstances where I thought his or her prognosis was good. And then they passed away."

This statement rattled me. "If you're not comfortable talking about the deaths of your past patients, I completely understand."

"Are you comfortable hearing what I have to say?"

My feet lost contact with the floor. All the ambient sounds were vac-uumed from the room and the halls beyond. The future, the past, all gone. Dr. Bonilla's prominent cheekbones stood out in sharp definition against a blurry background. It was clear to me that nothing mattered but what he was about to say. It was crucial that I understand.

"I want to know."

Dr. Bonilla squeezed the blood out of his lips. "I've seen people lose their faith, and go kicking and screaming. Their last days are filled with anger and a sense of betrayal. By the end, they're exhausted, depressed, nothing like the people they used to be. It's a terrible last few days. Or weeks, or months."

His voice was soft and rich and touched with heavenly reverberation, fill-ing the room and enveloping my brain. A vise tightened around my chest. I could only nod.

"And then I've seen people who believed life was special. Maybe I read too much into it, but I'm pretty sure they thought they were special too. They were the patients our staff fell in love with. They had a glow."

Dr. Bonilla rolled closer. "And I don't know how they achieved it, but they had a balance. A certainty there was life after death. And a certainty they weren't going to need it quite yet. Even as the cancer progressed and they had setbacks, and all sorts of painful treatments and humiliating side effects, and reactions to the disease…they remained focused on getting better, and on go-ing about their lives. These were the people, no matter how bleak things got, they knew they were going to make it."

"Wow," I croaked. "That's how I want to be. I think, I hope, that maybe that's how I am."

Dr. Bonilla nodded. "They're the hardest to lose. Heartbreaking for every-one."

We nodded together for a time, while my bowels loosened.

"Anything else you're unsure of?" he asked. "Any other questions?"

Any way I could get you to be a lot less candid going forward? "I'm ready to go home now."

"So the plan is chemo and radiation, then surgery to remove any remain-ing tumor. Then another round of treatments. Sound good?"

I nodded. Dr. Bonilla shook my hand and excused himself. I ducked into the bathroom and threw up.

No, it wasn't the cancer.

But of course it was the cancer.

I do have a nervous stomach. Back in high school I always had to take a dump minutes before the basketball game started, but that was a treat, a clean-sing relief. This was a trip to the woodshed. I vomited again, whatever was left of Valerie's chicken cacciatore, and picked my head out of the bowl, thankful I had followed directions and fasted for the last twelve hours. This thankfulness lasted no more than thirty seconds, when my empty gut began to twist—fear wasn't done with me, treating my stomach like a wet towel and wringing out every last drop.

My legs were wobbly as I pulled on my shorts. My cellphone was vibrating in the pocket. I put it on speaker and listened to the message while I pulled off the gown, mopped up cold sweat, and put on my shirt.

"I heard you were coming in today for your treatments," said Andrea's voice message. "Give me a call when you're done, if you want. I'm going to be done early today, so I could give you a ride, if you need one."

Did she think I walked here, I wondered. Or had she rightly guessed I would be enfeebled from all the puking? I was two for two here. My new MO. "Remember Brian?" the hospital staff would recall me fondly. "The way he threw up every time he came into the hospital, it was so cute."

I went to find Andrea, to give body and brain time to recover before getting behind the wheel, and to see how good ol' Dr. Mengele was doing. I asked at the nurses' station for directions to Bhani's lab. The nurse frowned, wanted to know why. I wasn't sure whether she was shielding him from an agent of the McEwens, or protecting unsuspecting patients from his diabolical chamber of horrors.

"A friend of mine works for him," I told them.

"Oh. Lower level three."

I waited at the service elevator with an orderly and a corpse on a gurney. When the door opened the orderly waved me in. "After you," he said.

"I'll catch the next one, thanks."

The orderly grunted something derogatory as he wheeled the corpse into the elevator. I watched the indicator lights track to the bottom, to lower level three. I hit the Down button; the same car came to get me, smelling of formaldehyde. "I'll wait," I said to myself and punched the button again. This time the other car arrived, and I descended into the belly of the beast.

The hallway was wide with a cement floor, painted cinderblock walls, and asbestos ceiling. The lights swear-to-God flickered overhead. No sign of the corpse, no sound except the elevator as it left me. I walked the length of the long hall. Doors were staggered every ten yards, most unmarked. A few had misleading labels like Waste & Offal and Bacterial Contaminants, obviously intended to scare off the curious. I had no doubt there were Robin Cook atrocities taking place behind these doors, and I was content to let them continue.

Dr. Bhani's office was one door down from the elevator, in the opposite direction. I knocked and entered.

The lab was the size and shape of a boxcar, much smaller than I would have guessed, given the monumental research supposedly taking place. Andrea sat behind a desk stuffed into the corner to my right, facing me. "Hey there," she greeted me. "I'll be with you in a second."

The woman across from her didn't turn around to look at me, which I thought was strange. In this basement, with the morgue a few doors down? I'd be curious who just came in.

The lab reminded me of my barebones high school science classroom, the lab bench equipped with a sink and a microscope, and a piece of equipment that looked like a bread machine. No moaning delirious patients, no tanks bubbling with green goo, no Dr. Bhani—none of the stuff I expected to see.

I hummed Squeeze's *Black Coffee In Bed* so as not to eavesdrop on privileged doctor-patient or experimenter-experimentee communications. Although with the woman's back to me, I could only hear Andrea's side of the conversation. Here's a snotty sample: "These are all the records we have to show you. It's difficult to prove that we haven't received something. You're asking the impossible. How do we prove a negative? Hm?"

I finished *Coffee In Bed* and moved on to *Tempted*, feeling a little self-conscious, in need of a better way to kill time. But it didn't seem proper to browse a scientist's lab bench, even a mad scientist's lab bench. Especially a mad scientist's lab bench.

"That's something you'll have to ask Dr. Bhani when he returns," Andrea snapped at the woman.

I should go, I thought. Politely wave goodbye and go home. Or to the shop. I was behind on my paperwork. I was overdue prioritizing the nonpayment schedule of my past-due bills. But a catfight was coming. I would stick around to watch tiny Andrea claw this woman's eyes out.

In the meantime I felt stupid hovering and humming over the woman's shoulder. So I browsed the lab bench. A light layer of dust covered the black slate surface. How long had Dr. Bhani been gone? Was Andrea employed not as a research assistant but a smokescreen, to give Bhani time to elude the authorities? Or at least the McEwens' lawyers.

Next to the microscope stood a laminated placard titled Nonspecific Immune Response, a cartoonish rendition of our immune system doing its thing. Arrows led from one group of squiggly cells to a different group of squiggly cells. In the next frame the second group now bristled with antennae. A third species of amoeba-like cells lurked in the margins, looking as threatening as amoeba can. Judging by the zigzag urgency of their short bold-faced arrows, they had locked onto the frequency emitted by the antenna-sprouting squigglies, and were itching to descend upon them for some serious butt kicking. I put my eye to the microscope, hoping to see the bad-ass amoeba in action, but it was dark in there. I didn't have the guts to lift the lid on the bread machine.

"I've given you people everything we have," Andrea snarled at the woman. "This is a big waste of time."

The woman kept glancing to her left, when clearly she should have been contemplating the exit to her right. That's when I realized the wall facing me was a cheap partition, and that the woman was interested in what was happening on the other side.

"Ma'am, I have work to do," said Andrea. "You're going to have to leave. Come back with a warrant." She came briskly around the desk, her hip bumping the woman's head as she bent to grab her briefcase.

"Bitch," said the woman.

"Now that I heard," I said.

Andrea kept walking, shaking her head. I retreated with her, as far as that boxcar of a room allowed. We waited until the woman stomped out.

"I'm not really sure what was going on there," I told Andrea. "But if you had decided to kill her, the clean-up would have been a cinch." I pointed. "The morgue is right down the hall."

Tears sprang to Andrea's eyes. She wiped them away, careful not to smudge her mascara. "I'm sorry. She makes me so mad."

"I shouldn't joke about wanting to kill her. Unless you want to? We could probably still catch her."

"No. Well, maybe."

We remained tucked together in the corner, standing so close to each other that Andrea was more underneath than beside me. I fidgeted, paced in place like a tiger in a pet carrier. Andrea didn't notice my discomfort, preoccupied with using each finger in turn to ferry tears off her lashes.

"Who was she?" I asked. "If you're ready to talk about it."

Andrea tugged her oversized sweatshirt past her hips and shuddered as the frustration left her body. Her petiteness was on full display, hair pulled back and piled up on her head, exposing a thin neck and allowing a clear measurement of her small cranium. Smallness should have been irrelevant, but it was a factor, making her appear childlike and helpless against the adversity that swirled about her. Frail little Andrea obviously needed a hug, any gentleman could see it, and she was standing close enough to make it a simple act, just stretch out my arms and pull that little body to me. I could envelop her. It would be very comforting, from her perspective.

"She was from the state health department," Andrea told me. "They want proof we're not going to infect anyone else, the way Brent died."

"But I thought you said Bhani didn't infect Brent."

"He didn't."

"So you shouldn't say 'anyone else'. Leave off the 'else'."

"Her words, not mine," said Andrea. "You look terrible by the way."

"I threw up. A couple few times."

Her eyes darted to my shirt.

"Not on myself. I was pretty much naked."

"How convenient," she said, as if I had been doing a nurse at the time. "So I'm going to close shop early. Do you need a ride?"

"I'm good. But I appreciate the offer."

"Are you leaving now? Or do you have time for a coffee?"

"You're a coffee drinker now? I knew there was something different about you. Smarter, better looking, taller." Not true, she was the same old Andrea, but the more people who believed coffee was a miracle drug, the better.

"Let's say I can stomach it," said Andrea, "with a lot of cream and sugar."

"Whatever it takes to get it in you." I appreciated the excuse to postpone going into the shop. Everyone knew I had gone in for my first treatment. They would be looking for an upbeat report and a confident pronouncement of my invincibility, things I wasn't able to give. And returning to my apartment midmorning sounded depressing. I had never been in my apartment between the hours of seven a.m. and three p.m. I should have sublet it to a nightshift worker. "But you have to drink coffee, or I get up and walk out."

"Fine."

"So were you lying to the state health woman, or is Bhani really gone?"

"He's out of town," said Andrea.

"Do you mean out of the country?"

"Not as far as I know."

"The real lab is on the other side of the wall, right?"

Andrea nodded. "This room is for small demos, and interviews. This is where we discover whether the patient is serious about treatment—or really a health inspector pretending to have cancer."

"No way. That's happened?"

"We're pretty sure. Do you have time for a tour?"

Andrea hadn't budged during our conversation, and I had given up trying to escape, leaning back against the wall to create a small buffer between us. It struck me then how all alone we were, in that room and probably on the floor. Us and the corpses. Imagine if Isabel and the rest of the McEwens could see us cozy in the corner like this. I should have followed the state health woman out the door. Shouldn't have gone down there in the first place.

Yet now that I had, I felt guilty for not showing up sooner. It wasn't right for Dr. Bhani to leave Andrea alone down there. Righteous health workers, sex-starved orderlies not quite ready to try necrophilia, the McEwens— Andrea was ill-equipped to defend herself against any of them. At the same time I acknowledged—most likely Mike McEwen's voice echoing in my head—that Andrea was an adult and a parent, a woman who had survived many nights alone since the divorce, obviously more resilient than I was giving her credit for. The need to protect her was an irrational impulse.

Andrea's eyes were on my purple and green bruised shin, probably wondering how she ended up with a cancer victim for a guardian angel. "I want to show you why you should consider talking to Dr. Bhani."

"True story, there's an acupuncturist in town who swears he can cure me. We call him Asian Vince. You know him? He's equal parts wannabe Confucius, wannabe Bruce Lee, and wannabe ancient mystic healer. He heard about my meltdown at Taekwondo and called me the next day to offer his services. In addition to the obvious stuff like backache, impotence and male pattern baldness, Asian Vince is sure he can cure Lou Gehrig's disease, Alzheimer's, scurvy, and now cancer, if only I'd give his needles and herbs the chance."

"What does that have to do with Dr. Bhani?"

"I've decided to go with Western medicine."

Andrea sighed. "That's fine. Fine, fine. Thanks to the McEwens," she mispronounced their name on purpose, "you're going to just turn your back on your best chance for a cure."

"Should we go get that sweet creamy coffee now?"

"Fine. I'm sure the hospital cafeteria coffee will be right up your alley."

"I actually had another place in mind. I'll drive."

EVEN THROUGH THE SLEET we could see Hernandes's big blinking portable electronic sign from a block away.

Twofer Tuesdays!

On the other side of the entrance to the parking lot, a bigger sign with Vegas-style running lights announced *No Sleep Sundays!* This was the cheesiest shit I had seen in quite a while.

"No Monday Madness?" I wondered. I pulled a u-turn in the parking lot and parked on the curb in front of the Twofer sign, completely obstructing it.

"I can't get out," Andrea notified me. "The sign is blocking my door."

"Throw your door open. Maybe you can knock it over."

"No. You pull up."

"I really like this spot. Come out my side."

Andrea made unhappy sounds as she clambered over the console and dropped to the street beside me. "Happy?"

"Not until that sign says Going Out of Business."

"You have sign envy," Andrea cooed. "Get one of those for your shop."

I thought about it. "Maybe I will." Leaving my sign board out in the snow had ruined it, and Charlotte still hadn't made me a replacement. No doubt the sign nazi thought she had won. (Now I knew how the Jews felt...? No.) I wasn't prepared to go to my grave down one to the sign nazi.

We slopped along the sidewalk. Andrea stopped to study the new sign above the door. "Was this place always called the Campus Coffeehouse?"

"No." All I could think was, Billy, what took you so long?

The place was grungier than before. More dusty sofas, more crap hung on the walls—bad artwork, shelves of books no one in North Dakota was pretentious enough to read, and pictures. Three blue-haired ladies crowded around a tiny table underneath a print of Kerouac, and an old farmer in bib overalls drank coffee beneath a poster of Johnny Depp as Hunter S. Thompson.

I stopped to browse the inside of the front window, plastered with announcements: Future Farmers of America meeting (last Wednesday); Fellowship of Christian Athletes recruitment supper—last Tuesday; Wind Festival in Kulm; the Jamestown College Choir Spring Chorale; Van Halen, coming to Bismarck; three auction sales, and a flyer for Woodstock III in New York.

"The winds of revolution are blowing strong through this place."

"Who can tell, it's so dark in here," said Andrea.

Couldn't have said it better myself. What a joke. Hernandes had to be on his last legs. Come on Billy, give up the ghost and close already.

Kenny the Wells Fargo bank manager sat with his wife Laurie in easy chairs on either side of a lamp stand illuminating a framed enlarged photo of rough-looking Central American coffee pickers slouching around a pile of empty burlap coffee bean bags. "Hey you two," I greeted them in passing.

"Brian! Hey!" Kenny yelped and jumped up to shake my hand. "We were on our way to the college to drop off some student loan applications."

"Ah." I felt like pointing out that only one coffeeshop sat on a direct line between his bank and the college, and it wasn't this one.

"Brian, how are you?" Laurie used a caring tone reserved for those who gave a shit about me, which she obviously didn't, keeping Billy afloat another day to torment me and wean a few more customers off the taste of coffee.

"I had my first round of treatments this morning, so I've been better. Do you two know Andrea? Kenny and Laurie. They're customers of mine."

"Andrea," said Laurie. "You're Rick's ex-wife, right?"

"That's right," said Andrea, less than overjoyed to be identified as such.

Kenny fidgeted, wild-eyed. "So Brian, checking out the competition?"

"Andrea doesn't like coffee, so we came here."

"Oh, ha-ha-ha," Laurie laughed. She threw a quick look toward the counter. "Your coffee is *so* much better," she whispered.

"Speak up, I can't hear you," I urged.

They laughed nervously. "It's true," Laurie said, still whispering.

"Obviously not everyone thinks so," said Andrea.

"It's the free refills," said Kenny. He lowered his voice. "It attracts the older-than-average crowd."

"My refills are only a quarter." I tried not to sound defensive.

Kenny waved us forward until we huddled like a football team. "Old folks won't bank with us unless we give them free stuff," he whispered. "Even if it's only a balloon. I'm serious. If I put a 'Free, Hard Candies!' sign in the window, senior citizens show up in droves. They're not the most rational folks."

"One time," Laurie confided, "Kenny gave away plastic stagecoach piggy banks to new customers and picked up fifty retiree accounts."

"Brian throws coffee beans at his customers," said Andrea.

I broke the huddle. "And they're welcome to take those beans home with them." It was actually Sam's shtick to throw beans at customers—and given that Andrea hadn't spent more than a few minutes in my shop, I wasn't sure how she knew anything about the bean throwing—but that was neither here nor there. "I guess I'll have to consider free refills to win you two back."

"Oh not us," Laurie heehawed. "You still have us! But yes," she dropped her voice to a loud hiss, "do it for the senior citizens."

"I would, except we're not a Denny's. We'll let you two get back to your drinks." I wasn't in the mood to beat them up over their defection. Kenny and Laurie are good people; if they liked Hernandes's shop better, there wasn't much I could do about it. What worried me was the possibility they were staying away because of my cancer. If it was going to be bad for business, I'd rather it just kill me quick.

"We were leaving anyway," Kenny assured me. "You can have our table. Come on, honey, let's get those applications over to the campus."

"We'll see you down at your shop, Brian," said Laurie.

"Okay lady. Bye-bye." I turned to Andrea. "Do you want to get me a brevé Americano? I don't feel like going up there."

"Okay…." She looked put out. "What's a…whatever you asked for?"

"Brevé Americano. They'll know." Kenny and Laurie hadn't vacated their spot so I sat down heavily at a spindly-legged table in the middle of the floor. My bones ached. All of them, not just the shin. I knew chemo was rough on the body, but this seemed too soon. I had an awful feeling it was the cancer, everywhere. But it couldn't be, they had x-rayed me, MRI'd me, pumped me full of iodine and scanned me, and found nothing.

I was worried, and my customers weren't helping. Some tried to be supportive, some just wanted to show off their medical knowledge. Mary Kazler told me that swollen lymph glands could indeed mean my immune system was mounting a defense. Or, she said, it could be lymphoma. That's a bad cancer. If there was such a thing as a good cancer, lymphoma was definitely a bad one. I decided I wanted another CAT scan.

Andrea returned and plunked down a cup of milky-brown fluid topped with big bubble foam. "Well they had no clue. Or maybe I pronounced it wrong, I don't know."

A bubble popped in my cup. "What is this?" I asked.

"Hell if I know."

"What did you get?"

"Hot chocolate."

"Didn't I tell you I was going to leave if you didn't drink coffee? Come on," I complained. "You're putting me in an awkward position here. How are you ever going to take my threats seriously if I don't get up this second and walk out of here?" I faked a move to get up and leave.

Andrea smirked. "You can't leave such wonderful ambiance."

Instead of piped-in music, Hernandes had piped in poetry. Beat poetry, judging by the reader's outraged tone. The quality of the recording and the shop's acoustics were both poor, so it actually made for a mellow, inoffensive background babble. It irritated the hell out of me.

"Or such wonderful company," Andrea added, unable to muster a smile to go along with her sense of humor. Felt like we both had cancer.

Neither of us spoke, misery loving company. Andrea stared at me with a sour, suffering look. "This lady from the state really has you down, huh?"

"I shouldn't care what she thinks." Andrea pulled a clip off her head and her hair dropped to her shoulders. Not thick hair, but nice enough. "As long as we don't have any obvious health code violations, Dr. Bhani is sure they don't have jurisdiction. I guess I'm just not equipped to handle adversity any more."

"Good thing you took a job with a mad scientist then."

"First of all, Dr. Bhani was basically my only choice," said Andrea. "And secondly, he's doing unbelievable things. Honestly. The immune system is the key to fighting cancer. Your immune system doesn't think of cancer as an invader, for some reason. Some scientists are trying to figure out why. Dr. Bhani has found a way to make your white blood cells attack the cancer."

"By giving you a deadly infection."

Andrea gave an exasperated chirp. "It wasn't Dr. Bhani's infection that killed Brent. Do you have to believe everything the McEwens tell you?"

I shrugged. "I'd rather take my chances with the standard treatments."

"Chemo and radiation shouldn't be standards," Andrea said hotly. "They don't work."

"My doctor practically guaranteed me they would shrink my tumor."

"Shrinking isn't curing."

"I'll take what I can get."

"So it shrinks. Yeah, that's fine. But I'll bet they won't promise you the tumor won't come back."

"Promises are for suckers. There are no guarantees in life. Believe me. I've seen too many sure things go south overnight."

Andrea chuckled humorlessly. "You don't have to teach me that lesson."

One-upping each other's tales of woe and hardship didn't appeal to me. I took a sip and regretted it. Did brevé mean burned in Portuguese?

"I won't bug you anymore about your treatment," said Andrea. "But there's a book I want you to read. I have it in my car back at the hospital."

"Sounds good."

"You don't want to know what it's about?"

I doubted we shared the same literary tastes. And I couldn't imagine picking up another book until the cancer was gone. So I didn't pretend to be curious. "Sure."

Andrea's lips twisted into a disgusted configuration. "It's about a guy with cancer who didn't accept the *standard* treatment."

"What kind of cancer did he have?"

"Lymphoma."

My temperature plummeted. "Do you, uh, you think that's what I have?"

"The type of cancer isn't the point," said Andrea. "The point is that he went searching for alternative treatments, and found a cure."

"You're telling me I should go talk to Asian Vince."

"I'm telling you doctors aren't always open to the possibilities. And just because your doctor doesn't know any better than to pump you full of chemo and hope for the best, doesn't mean that's the best course for you."

"Okay, whatever, I'll read it."

"For having a fatal disease, you're not taking this very seriously."

"Let me tell you about a dream I had last night. I was floating up into the air. I kept rising, higher and higher. In my dream I realized I had died. I was in spirit form. And for some amazing reason, I wasn't too upset about it.

"I keep rising, and now I'm in space. I can see the Earth below me. It's nice. Now I'm looking out into space, and I see a white light, way out there. I'm heading toward it, this bright white light. I'm flying faster and faster, eager to see what's out there. But the light starts to dim. The closer I get, the dimmer the light gets. I'm hurtling toward it faster and faster, the light's getting dimmer and dimmer, and then *wham!* it's a black hole. That's when I woke up."

"Geez." Andrea blinked a few times. "That's a bad dream."

My heart pounded, reliving the black hole moment. That was the most positive dream I'd had in a week. "I take death seriously."

Andrea slowly stirred in her whipped cream. "You don't like your drink?"

"I should have had the hot chocolate."

"So I hear you're going to San Diego to woo Muslims."

"I don't know if they're all Muslim. Probably. How did you hear about the trip? Do you know Khalq?"

"Dr. Bhani told me. So you're Jamestown's envoy to the Muslim world?"

"The Chamber of Commerce is doing a road show. We're targeting the

Middle Eastern communities in a few cities, promoting everything Jamestown has to offer."

Andrea snorted, probably saved me from doing it.

"There are twenty or so businesses participating. I drew the long straw, San Diego. If I'm up for it. I haven't bounced the trip off my doctor."

"Your chemotherapist?"

"I think he prefers 'oncologist'."

"I suppose you'll take Isabel."

Weakened from the cancer and the chemo, at Isabel's mercy in a hotel room. I had an adverse physical reaction to this idea. A full-body cringe. "She wouldn't be able to get that much time off."

"Mike would pay her double-time to go with you."

"I'm not going to ask her," I said. "It's not a vacation."

"So you'll go alone?"

"It's just an overnight. I'm sure we'll be meeting nonstop, or else I'll be lying in my hotel bed moaning. Either way, it's best that I go alone."

Andrea was disgusted. "If you're so feeble, maybe you should hire a nurse to accompany you."

"I'm sure Mike would hire me one, if I asked for it. I shudder at the amount of money he's willing to throw down a hole for me."

"You could save him a few bucks and hire an illegal immigrant to take care of you," Andrea suggested. "You know, service you."

I wouldn't take that bait. Andrea and I had a short list of acceptable conversational topics, and sexual banter wasn't on it. "Next thing you know, my organs are being trafficked on eBay."

"That's a nice thought," said Andrea. She patted my hand. "If you need a chaperone you can trust, you let me know."

"You better not be talking about yourself."

"Why not?"

I watched Hernandes pop out of his office for the second time to stare at me with a troubled expression. "Taking you to San Diego would rank right up there with you going to work for Dr. Bhani."

"You care so much about what people think?"

"I care about what certain people think. Including friends and customers." I couldn't believe I had to defend my preference not to take the ex-wife of my future brother-in-law as my personal attendant on a business trip. "What about you? Having a son makes it a little tough to slip out of town on a lark."

"I don't know about that," Andrea challenged. "Maybe I would bring Tyler with me. I need a vacation from this town. A permanent vacation."

"Things haven't improved, even now that you're working?"

Andrea's jaw dropped. "Do you like living here? My God, you're from

California. Don't you miss it?" She came alive, lifting off her chair with each burst of emotion. "I've been to Davis. I love that town. The weather is fabulous. You're close to Napa Valley and San Francisco and Tahoe. The only thing we're close to here is freezing to death. How can you stand living here?"

"Is it the winters getting you down?" I deflected her. If she wanted to vent, fine. I expected as much. But it wasn't going to be about me. I had my own issues with North Dakota, always simmering under the surface. I didn't need Andrea fanning the flames.

"Sure, yes, it's the winters," Andrea was sarcastic. And loud. "Everybody here thinks they're so tough. No one else can survive the winters. If you don't like living here, it's because you're too soft to survive the winter."

"Locals do have a little bit of a superiority complex when it comes to surviving the elements," I admitted. Quietly.

"A little?" Andrea was incredulous, borderline yelling and oblivious to our attentive audience. "It's not a little. I can't tell you how many times I've heard someone say, 'Keeps the riffraff out.' Or 'Winters here aren't for the fainthearted.' The next person who says that to me is going to get their eyes clawed out." She crossed her arms, blood-red nails protruding from under each arm. Venom glistened on her lips. "It's not the weather. If the weather in Davis or Denver suddenly changed, no one would leave, because there's actually something to do in those places. Why does Jamestown even exist? I can't figure it out. It's for people who don't have any goals, who couldn't get a job anywhere else. It's not a place to live. It's a place to hide."

Andrea had jacked my eyebrows halfway up my forehead, and I couldn't get them to return to their resting position. The old ladies at the Kerouac table glared at us. "You might want to consider not saying that quite so loudly next time. If you survive long enough for there to be a next time."

"Oh, there'll be a next time."

Sometimes I felt like Andrea and I were taking turns playing the same part, the sassy wise-ass refusing to let the world get away with the nutty stuff. Except I didn't play it quite so sour and bitter, and people liked me. So far. She was a bad influence. "Maybe you should consider moving away."

"Oh, yeah, I'll tell the judge—who's a native North Dakotan, by the way—'Mr. Judge, I know you said Tyler couldn't be moved from Jamestown. But I respectfully disagree. Tyler and I are moving back to Colorado.'"

"I meant without Tyler."

"I've considered it, believe me."

Because you don't seem like the mothering type. "Because Tyler seems pretty happy here, from what I've seen. From what the McEwens tell me."

"What exactly have they told you?" Andrea demanded.

"In passing. In conversation. Nothing really." Except that you're a horrible mom, person and wife, and your existence in Jamestown, any town, is barely worth it. "Nothing in particular."

"Do they say he's happier with Rick than he is with me?"

Of course they did. "No." All the time.

"Because if they're saying things about me, and about the way I'm raising Tyler..." Andrea's little body trembled.

"You know what," I said, trying not to lie, or say anything that would find its way back to the McEwens, "they're worried about Tyler growing up with divorced parents. And they're worried about you, because they know you don't like it here."

I must have walked the tightrope effectively, because Andrea slumped back in her chair. "I've thought about leaving," she said. "But I can't. Every time I consider it, my heart breaks. I couldn't live without Tyler. I'd go crazy."

She didn't break down and weep. But it was obvious she was speaking from the heart. "You just seem so unhappy."

"How would you feel?" Andrea demanded. "I never agreed to this. I thought we were going to live in Colorado. The three of us. The next thing I know, we're here. I was told it's just temporary. But then it's not, it's permanent." Her voice cracked and warbled, but she pressed on. "And it was never the three of us. We basically lived with Rick's whole family. His family, his job, everything comes before me. And then he divorces me. Now I'm single, surrounded by people who hate me. All my friends and family are back in Colorado, and I'm living in the last place on earth I would have picked. Trapped here, for the next fifteen years."

Andrea was breathing hard and wiping away tears before they left her eyes. I saw a napkin on the next table and swiped it for her. "I'm sorry," I said. "I never really thought about it that way."

"How could you not?"

"I spend most of my time wallowing in my own self-pity."

Hernandes approached our table, his pear head bobbing, black hair shiny even in the dingy lighting, his tiny bulging eyeballs watering like a Chihuahua's. I made him wait. "No plans to appeal the judge's decision?"

"My lawyer doesn't think it's worth it," said Andrea. "I'm trapped."

I looked at Hernandes. "Billy."

"Brian Lawson!" Hernandes exclaimed. "This is your second visit to my humble shop! To what do I owe the pleasure?" He hesitated. "This is only twice, right?"

As if I hung out in his shop whenever he wasn't there, hoping to steal his coffee secrets. "I don't have the time to drive all the way out here very often."

"We got a great location," said Hernandes. "You love the décor? It's my son's idea. He fell in love with the West Coast coffeehouses."

"I'm from the coast, and they don't look like this." Not the good ones, anyway.

"I thought the incense-scented floor wax was a little much." Hernandes bent down and sniffed deeply. "But my son said it's what people expect from a coffeehouse. Especially college kids. And he's right. We've been going gang-busters. And now you're closing. Very sorry to hear that," Hernandes said solemnly, hands clasped at his waist.

"Closing what?"

"Your shop," said Hernandes. "At least until your cancer is cured."

"He's not looking for a cure," Andrea argued the wrong point.

It did give me couple extra seconds to reconsider the profanity-laced tirade yearning to be unleashed. "I'm not closing, Billy. Who told you that?"

"You're not closing?" Hernandes did a great job pretending to be shocked. "Really? Will you be able to work during your treatments?"

I drummed the tabletop. "I'd really like to know who told you I was closing." I was sure the rumor had started right there in Hernandes's shop. I wanted to shake him until he gurgled *I am a rumormonger, and a liar. I shot Kennedy, and J.R. And I hate the taste of coffee.*

"I get so many folks in here," said Hernandes, wiggling his fingers at the Kerouac ladies. "Martha, your drink is okay?"

"It's fine," said Martha, glaring at Andrea.

Fine, my ass. I couldn't choke mine down. Martha must have no fucking taste buds. I was raging inside.

"We aim to please," said Hernandes, spunky and in command. He gave our table a slap, and then had to steady the piece of shit before it toppled, on my fragile body. "I'll have to have Craig fix that. Speaking of former James River Valley Coffee folks, thanks for sending him my way. He's been a godsend. That kid knows his coffee."

"I didn't send him your way, I fired him. And the kid is thirty-one."

"He's a natural for the coffee business, at any age."

"A coffeeshop only needs one expert. But you're right, it does need at least one."

"You can never have enough expertise on board." The color had left the skin around Hernandes' thin stretched smile. I was getting to him. "That's something I learned in the business world."

"And of course the margins are so huge," I said with heavy sarcasm, "paying for that expertise is no problem."

"Oh I think I had a realistic understanding of the margins," said Hernandes. "I knew my business expertise was going to mean the difference between scraping by, and making a very comfortable living. I was a controller for a big company, you know. I had responsibility for purchasing."

"You told people you were a broker for a hotshot Wall Street firm."

"My company did have business on Wall Street, it's true. I'm really glad I wasn't a broker. It's almost like fate, how my purchasing background has helped me negotiate steep discounts and favorable terms with my suppliers."

"Of course it's long-term relationships and coffee knowledge that make all the difference," I said, as if this was nothing new to him. "Without the coffee knowledge, the bean brokers will have you paying a twenty percent premium for low-grade peaberries. And unless you're Starbucks, purchasing discounts don't get you too far. Isn't it amazing how coffee is such a unique industry?"

"Mm…" Hernandes scribbled mental notes. "Which reminds me…when you sell your shop, I want your inventory. And maybe your location."

"I'm not selling." I was now officially staying open forever, or until Hernandes went out of business, or I died. Whichever came first.

"You should sell," said Andrea. "Move back to Davis."

"Is that where you're from?" said Hernandes. "Davis—California, right? Quite a change. The winters had to be a shock. Not for the faint of heart."

I looked at Andrea and then nodded toward Hernandes. "Go ahead."

She pretended not to understand.

I gave her a disappointed look. "I had a feeling it might be cold here," I told Hernandes. "I own a globe."

"I'm Portuguese by blood," said Hernandes.

"I know, you told me last time."

"But my parents used to live—"

"I have to be leaving now," I interrupted his genealogical rambling, on my feet and immediately impatient for Andrea to do likewise.

"Thanks for stopping in, folks," Hernandes brayed. "Brian, we're pulling for you. This community wants you back on your feet."

"I've never been off my feet, Billy." I pulled Andrea to hers and propelled her toward the door.

"Whatever I can do, let me know," Hernandes called after me.

"Get a deadly cancer," I answered as we exited, probably out of earshot. I stalked a few paces down the sidewalk. "I think I really shook him up in there. Don't you think?"

"I wasn't really paying attention," Andrea said with perfect boredom.

"He's rattled." We reached the van. "Is that the word on the street? That I'm quitting? Have you heard anyone say that?"

Andrea shrugged.

"Why am I asking you? You don't talk to anybody. I need to call Mike." Wheels were turning. "I need some exposure. It's time to get the Bluffs shop moving forward." My mind was suddenly made up—Hernandes was going down. It felt great to have a plan, to have a goal. I helped Andrea into the driver's-side door. "Thanks for the coffee by the way."

"Uh-huh. You really enjoyed it."

"I would have," I said, "but it was terrible. And I was too upset about you ordering hot chocolate."

Andrea cracked a weary and not-so-amused smile. "Sure."

"You were going to claw the eyes out of the next person who told you the winters are too harsh."

"He said it to you, not to me."

"But I chew my fingernails." I held them up for inspection. "How am I supposed to claw anyone's eyes out?"

"Kick him in the balls," Andrea suggested.

"I am a good kicker," I mused.

Andrea frowned. "You shouldn't chew your nails. I've heard the chemo drugs settle in your nails and hair."

"Thanks for giving me one more thing to worry about."

"No problem," said Andrea, sounding genuine. Which any topnotch smart ass knows is the best form of sarcasm.

T - 12

"No you can't go with me to San Diego. Love to have you along, but it's not possible." This I said to Isabel.

"I'd like to think anything's possible." This was her reply.

"No spouses or significant others. Just the Chamber. Breakfast, dinner, and everything in between, we're either meeting with locals or each other. The Chamber is paying for everything. It wouldn't be right to bring you along."

"Dad says you need to treat this as fifty percent vacation."

We were out to eat at Jamestown's finest restaurant, the Grainery. We looked at each other past a prairie grass centerpiece. Country décor and haute homestyle cuisine was the Grainery's claim to fame.

"Extend your stay by a couple days," Iz problem-solved, "and I'll join you after your meetings have wrapped up. We'll turn it into a mini-vacation."

"I'm not in the mood for a vacation," I said.

"That's when you need a vacation the most," Isabel countered.

"Hi Ms. McEwen," said our waitress. All the waitstaff wore white tux-style shirts, bow ties and black slacks.

"Hi Tina. Do you know Brian?"

"I go to his coffee shop. Hi," the high schooler greeted me shyly.

"Hello lady."

Tina maintained her professional face. "I brought you some bread."

Isabel started cooing. "It looks wonderful," she said. The delicate fluted sleeve of her beige sweater-shirt scooped up a pat of butter as she reached for the misshapen loaf of bread. It was a full-size loaf, could have fed ten. She sawed two inches off the end, oohing and ahing. The pat of butter fell out of her sleeve and she used it on her bread, as if that was the way she always retrieved her butter. Tina took our order for drinks and an appetizer and left.

"I'll cut you a slice," Isabel offered.

"I'm saving room for the calamari."

"Ooh," she purred just before taking her first bite. "It's so good," she said while chewing. "Let me cut you a small slice."

"No thanks. It looks like it could have come from my grandmother's kitchen." I touched the lopsided loaf. "Warmed up in her microwave."

"It's homestyle. Bel and Delbert do all the baking from scratch."

"I like a professional, expensive-looking loaf."

"I didn't know you were such a presentation person," Isabel chided me.

"You need to get past the looks, because the food is unbelievable here."

"I've eaten here before. It's good for Jamestown."

Isabel nodded solemnly as if we agreed. "It's good for *anywhere*."

"No, it's good for Jamestown."

"Brian, this is the best food I've ever eaten!"

"That could very well be."

She stared at me, trying to decide whether the chemo had eaten away at the gourmet dining appreciation section of my brain.

"There's nothing to be ashamed of, being the best in Jamestown," I said.

"Of course there's not."

"This could very well be the best food in the entire state."

"Delbert and Bel lived in New York City," Iz explained. "They had their own restaurant there. It was very successful. But they realized how much they loved North Dakota, and how badly they missed Jamestown. So they decided to move back here. We are blessed they did."

"Maybe it wasn't by choice. Maybe they couldn't hack it in the big city."

Isabel swallowed her bolus of bread. "With food this good? I doubt it."

"I don't know why no one can admit that everyone and everything here aren't the best of all possible worlds," I muttered.

I knew deep down that unlike Bel and Delbert's situation, North Dakota didn't represent a retreat for me. My reasons for being there were entirely different. I was a special case, able to run a coffeeshop like no other, in any city.

But at that moment I couldn't put my finger on exactly how I knew this. Depression's dull appetite claimed another chunk of my consciousness.

"You must not be feeling too well," Isabel said with a mixture of defensiveness and concern, brightening when Tina brought our drinks. She touched the back of Tina's hand. "Thanks, sweetie."

"Are you ready to order?" Tina asked us.

"Give us a couple minutes, would you honey?" Isabel watched Tina walk away. "She's a sweetie," said Iz, perhaps loud enough for Tina to hear. "I watched her grow up in our neighborhood, a few houses down the street."

I frowned, ready to call Tina's parents to warn them. Probably too late.

"She was such a little fish. She was down at the pool every day, open till close. I could sit and watch her dive all day. The Draytons had a trampoline. I think that's where Tina learned her body control."

"Okay, you're starting to freak me out a little here."

For an instant Isabel was puzzled. Then came a sly knowing nod. She leaned forward. "All I'm thinking about is your body, naked and glistening with body oil."

I grunted from the convulsion in my esophagus. "That's just not right."

"What isn't?" Isabel purred. Her shirt sagged so I could see the tops of her breasts and low-cut beige satin bra. Pain like an ice cream brain freeze blossomed under my eyebrow ridges. Not the reaction I like to get from breasts.

I shook my head, refusing to speak. Isabel finally settled back in her chair, with no clue what was going on in my head. She took a drink of her Manhattan. "Mm, this is good. Manhattans are my new favorite drink. Taste it."

"No thanks."

"It's fabulous! It's ice cold, with a hint of cherry. Very smooth."

"I'm a clear booze drinker. I'm not much for whiskey or brandy."

"This is really good."

"I'm glad you like it."

"How did your treatments go today?"

This was Day Eighteen, my last day of the first of two chemo cycles. I had no doubt the cancer had been halted, because everything in my body seemed to have stopped growing. My innards felt numb. Everything in my belly and my brain had fallen silent, the gears and wiring melted by the chemo poisons. Even if Isabel's breasts did turn me on, I couldn't have pumped enough blood to raise my dick. I had lost fifteen pounds, and a similar percentage of hair.

My self image: a collection of inert organs, no pumping, no processing. I laid in bed at night, perfectly still, waiting to sense movement inside. Focus on it long enough and even your heartbeat seems to stop. Except for the constant stomach ache and the frequent sweating, I felt dead. I hadn't done a thing toward making the Bluffs a reality.

"They're taking another MRI tomorrow to see if the tumor shrank."

"I'm sure it has."

"I'm sure it has too. The chemo is killing me."

"It can be rough, I know."

"No, it's really killing me."

Isabel's face darkened. She stared vacantly at the cherry in the bottom of her glass. "When Brent was going through his chemo, it was so terrible to see what it did to him. He was vomiting, his hair fell out. He looked so weak."

She dangled sympathy, just out of reach. Brent was dead, and I was there in front of her, dying, needing something more than another exotic screw.

Isabel squeezed my hand, drawing precious strength from me. "Brent would barely recover from a round of chemo and then the cancer would come back, and the process would start all over again. When Dr. Bhani offered us a way to escape this cycle, we all jumped at it. And it was like magic—Brent only felt sick for a couple days after Bhani's treatments, and then the tumor disappeared. Brent was feeling great…and then suddenly he was gone."

"I know. I know." I nodded, trying to be compassionate or at least appear so. I had heard this story a hundred times. I had *been* there when it was going down. I had held Iz, listened to her, dried her tears and given her all of my understanding and compassion. It was her turn now.

"It was awful what the chemo did to Brent," Isabel lamented. "But he should have given it one more try. Instead of going to that witch doctor."

My opening for a topic change. "I see Andrea quite a bit, when I'm at the hospital for my treatments."

Isabel wiped away tears and blew her nose. "I hope she's doing well."

"I'd say no. She's the loneliest person I've ever met. When we talk, it's like we both have cancer."

Isabel tilted her glass and extracted the cherry by its stem. She let the alcohol drip off and ate it. "That would be too bad. Or she could catch an infection from her boss and die."

Here came Tina the teenage waitress with our calamari. "Have you two decided on entrees?"

Isabel looked up at Tina, reached out for her hand, received it, squeezed it, pulled Tina a step closer and gave her back a scratch or a rub, I couldn't tell which. Tina bent over and gave Isabel a quick one-armed hug.

It's harmless, I told myself. I'm reading too much into this. Women, girls, they hug and rub each other all the time.

Isabel kept Tina bent over so they could peer at the menu together. "What do you recommend, sweetie?"

"Well, the porkchop is a favorite." Tina straightened up. "Delbert infuses it with lemon and then braises it in his prairie sage sauce. He puts a little risotto and creamed swischard on the side."

"Ohmygod that sounds incredible." Isabel closed her menu and gazed into Tina's eyes. "Now tell me about the fresh fish."

MY SHIN THROBBED AS Dr. Bonilla sat me in front of a viewing screen in his office. He watched me fidget and grimace. "Are you ready for this?"

"As long as you're not going to say something like, 'We've never seen anything like this before.'"

"Deal."

"Then bring it."

"Here's what your tibia looked like, three weeks ago." Dr. Bonilla punched a button and an image like an x-ray filled the screen. "We're looking at an angle down the tibia, a diagonal cross-section of the interior of the bone. This is marrow." He pointed to a Rorschach blot that for all I knew could have been my pancreas. "And this is the bone. And here…" He indicated a small discolored patch lighter than the surrounding bone, a starburst blob with two extended arms suggesting the ability to creep and infiltrate. It made my skin crawl. "Here was the tumor."

My heart skipped a few beats. "Was. You said 'was'."

Dr. Bonilla smiled. "You're trying to steal my thunder." He produced calipers and measured the tumor in the three-week-old picture. "Diameter about three centimeters. Now, here's the shot from this morning, taken from the same distance and angle."

Caliper measurement—unnecessary. I could see the difference. The tumor was half the size.

"Diameter one centimeter. We did a more sophisticated computer analysis, and the volume has actually decreased about eighty percent."

"Oh boy." Tears came from nowhere. "You did it. You killed my cancer." The throbbing in my shin was an indication of healing. I was going to live.

"We're killing it," Dr. Bonilla cautioned, "but it's not dead. You see how the tumor is lighter in color than the surrounding tissue." He tapped the screen with the calipers. "That's because it's alive, compared to the bone cells. If we don't continue the treatments, it will come back, badder than ever." He was staring at my knee. "But it's working. We're on the right path."

"So I'll need another round of chemo and radiation?"

Dr. Bonilla nodded. "It'll be rough. And, I still want to run an arthroscopic laser in there to remove any fraction of the tumor that's still viable and accessible." He cocked an eyebrow. "Are you up for it?"

"You'll be amazed how much I can live through."

He patted my good leg and stood. "We'll give you a three-week break before the surgery and the next round of chemotherapy. Give your immune system time to bounce back. I'm putting you on some heavy-duty general purpose antibiotics to provide some backup for your immune system, since it's been fairly well compromised by the chemotherapy. Try to stay away from daycare centers and rock concert crowds in the meantime."

"Shoot, I had tickets to the Massive Metal Homicide concert Saturday."

"I'll tell you all about it Monday," said Dr. Bonilla, grinning.

"Actually I'm a soft pop fan. You know Kenny G? Small audiences with very little hepatitis."

"Perfect." He shook my hand. "Don't overdo it. I want you to rest."

"So rest is good? I should get more rest than usual? Not less?"

He looked a little perplexed. "That's right."

"That is very good to know." I wanted to hug him. One less internal debate to anguish over. I hugged him. "Thanks, Dr. Bonilla."

I trotted down the hall to the service elevator. My leg felt strong. I jumped into the empty car—no corpses, a great omen—and hit the LL3 button. I cocked my bad leg and held it, ready to throw a kick, maintaining my balance in the swaying elevator. A human weapon, that's what I was. Master Kwan ran an afternoon black-belt preparatory class. I was going. Then I would embrace Dr. Bonilla's advice and go home and sleep the clock around.

The door opened and I sprang into the hall. Same flickering halogen lights, but now it was obvious they crackled with excess energy, rather than straining from the power drain of unholy experimental apparatus. My stride was long and strong.

At the door to Dr. Bhani's greeting room I came face to face with some sort of Muppet man. He was tall with yellow-olive skin, a long thin face, recessed eyes and a mop of messy black acrylic hair.

"Excuse me." Then I realized it was Dr. Khaled Bhani. He had changed, and not for the better. Weight loss, hair loss, sickly skin tone.

"Brian. It's good to see you," said Bhani in his squeaky British accent.

"Same here. I haven't seen you down at the shop for awhile."

Bhani gave me a sad smile. "I've been traveling a lot lately. Are you..."

"I'm here to see Andrea McEwen. We're friends." This sounded really stupid. I couldn't remember the last person who made me nervous. I had been face to face with Bhani many times before; but not when he was Brent's killer.

"It's not McEwen," Andrea called from inside the office, sounding irked. "Did you forget I was divorced?"

"Yes I did," I called back. I heard her sigh.

"So Brian," said Bhani, "you are a cancer patient here?"

I cocked my head. "Did Andrea tell you?"

"No. I can tell. Skin tone. Hairline. Weight loss." Bhani pointed at my cheek, my hair, my waist.

Same to you. "I'm actually feeling good. My hair has been spunkier, I'll give you that. But I'm not exactly emaciated." I pinched an inch for his consideration. "And my skin tone hasn't been good since I moved here."

"Amen," Andrea called out.

Bhani grimaced. "I've been in the business a long time. Some things are apparent, unfortunately."

"Come on. Andrea must have told you I have cancer." *Had.*

Andrea appeared in the doorway. "Do you think I talk about you all day?" Her wry scratchy voice was growing on me.

"How long have you been in treatment?" asked Bhani.

You tell me, Nostradamus. "Three weeks or so."

"What was the diagnosis?"

"Sarcoma. Bone."

"Primary?"

"Yes."

"I told Brian he should have come to you," said Andrea, "instead of the chemotherapists upstairs."

Bhani looked like an alien race's best attempt at a human. In his recessed eyes I saw huge intelligence looking out at me—I would have bet the shop his

IQ was double mine—and a touching compassion for me and my species. "Enrolling anyone new in our trials would be difficult right now," he said. "But Andrea is right. Chemotherapy is not the right approach for you."

"Actually, I just found out my tumor shrunk by eighty percent. One more round and I should be cured."

"No wonder you're in such a good mood," said Andrea. I wouldn't say she sounded disgusted. I wouldn't say she sounded happy for me. Without misery, maybe I'd have no need for her company.

Bhani squinted, compassion gone. "Did your chemotherapist tell you that? That you would be cured?"

"You know how doctors play it close to the vest."

"Your cancer will come back," Bhani pronounced. E.T. the fortune teller.

"Let's hope not, huh?" I touched Andrea's shoulder. "I came down to see if you wanted to celebrate with me. Dinner or a drink. A high-five. Whatever."

"Sure."

I held out my hand. "It was good to see you again, Dr. Bhani. Good luck with your...experiments."

Bhani ignored my hand. "When you're through with chemo and radiation, come see me." His raging case of doctor ego was on full display. "Even if there is nothing I can do for you, I might be able to get you into another protocol. Some scientists are doing exciting things with the immune system."

"I don't think that's going to be necessary. But thank you."

"The key is not to destroy your immune system, like chemotherapy does, but to harness it. To boost it. Okay?" He turned to Andrea. "You will have my response to the California board ready for my signature before you leave?"

"I didn't know you wanted it done today," Andrea responded softly, looking back into the office.

"Can you?" Bhani willed her to say yes.

"Sure. It might not be by five o'clock, though."

"I won't be able to look at it until later tonight anyway." Bhani nodded at me and walked briskly down the hall, his soft-soled shoes making not a sound. He unlocked and ducked through the door at the end of the corridor, hopefully returning to his pod for some overdue rejuvenation.

Andrea and I stared at each other. I was grinning, she was looking slightly amused. "So," she said.

"Eighty percent shrinkage. How do you like them apples?"

"That's impressive." She continued to stare up at me, head cocked. Andrea was not uncomfortable with extended stares and drawn-out silences. Her patience was a challenge to perform, to say something interesting. Do a jig. Maybe the robot.

Luckily I am quite the talker. "I was so pumped when Dr. Bonilla gave me the good news. I wanted to share it with someone."

"And you thought of me."

"You were closest."

"Is that the only reason?"

"No. Not at all. I feel like we have a bond. A bond of misery and suffering. It's kind of nice."

"Uh-huh." Andrea checked up and down the hall, a magician's distraction enabling her to move a little closer. "You like misery and suffering?"

"Not usually. You want to get dinner and celebrate with me?"

"Sure. Except it might need to be late." She pouted. "I didn't know Dr. Bhani was going to need me to have his response ready to go today. He thinks it's easy to pull it together. It's not."

"That's fine. There's a lot of paperwork waiting for me at the shop. This will force me to get it done."

"Where should we go?" she asked. "I've heard the Grainery is good. Although I have a hard time believing it."

"It's not my favorite. Bad bread."

"I heard you cook. Why don't you cook me a meal."

"I could do that."

"Can you bring your paperwork here to work on?" Andrea suggested.

"You mean like, doing our homework together?"

"Kind of like that."

"Will Bhani be around, or are you going to be all alone down here?"

"I never know what he's going to do at any given moment."

If no one else was going to be there to protect her, I didn't see how I had any choice. "Why don't you call me if he leaves."

This pleased her. "I will."

"I'll let you get to work now."

Andrea swayed from side to side. I felt like we were saying goodnight at her folks' front door.

There would be no kiss goodnight. "Okay lady. I'll be in touch."

"HEY," I GREETED MY CREW as I hustled into the shop ninety minutes later. I pointed Charlotte toward the office. "Can I see you for a minute?"

"Ooh, Charlotte's in trouble," Sam taunted.

"What did I do now?" Charlotte played it up.

I closed the door after she squeezed into the closet-sized chute with me. "I was just at the dojang and I heard there's an open house at the new retail—"

"At the Bluffs!" Charlotte exploded. "Hernandes is running a stand—"

"Hernandes?" I squeaked.

"I found out about it this morning! I called Mike's assistant Margie and asked her what was going on. You're opening a store over there, and that old fool Hernandes gets to serve the coffee! What kind of deal is that?"

With Charlotte riled up, I was free to calm down. "What did Margie say?"

"She said I should talk to Mike."

"What did he say?"

Charlotte looked sheepish. "I thought you should talk to Mike. He kind of scares me. I know he shouldn't. He just does."

"I could really care less whether we serve the coffee at the open house," I growled, "except I really hate Hernandes."

"Someone needs to put that jerk in his place." Charlotte growled, too.

"It's not Hernandes's fault," I pointed out. "He has to try to compete for business." I only played the devil's advocate because it was nice to let someone else badmouth Hernandes for a change.

"He doesn't have to complain about our sign board," Charlotte accused.

"You should see the blinking neon signs at his place."

"Blinking neon signs!" Charlotte nearly popped a vessel. "Uhh!" she grunted her displeasure. "How does he get away with that?"

I sighed. "I don't want to have to call Mike. He wouldn't screw me over like this, would he?"

"You better call him," Charlotte insisted.

"I will. Alright…yeah, I better do it."

Charlotte could see that I was mentally frozen in place, temporarily out of gas. "I could send Sam over there to beat up Hernandes."

"Would you? That would be nice."

Charlotte's smile faded as she studied me. "You look like…a little tired. Wait a second—you said you were at the doe-whatever."

"The dojang. I hit the black belt prep session this afternoon."

"You didn't."

"Oh yes I did."

"Brian, no," Charlotte protested. "Don't be stupid."

"You can't stop me." I wished she had. Not for the exertion—Instructor Garrett went easy on us in my honor—but the embarrassment. We were supposed to be polishing the thirty-odd kicking and blocking sets learned during our progression through the first ten belt levels. After my clueless performance that afternoon, I was sure Garrett would recommend Master Kwan demote me back to white belt.

Which wouldn't be all bad, after getting another look at our dojang's exotic new white belt.

"You know what you need is a wife," said Charlotte. "To nag you, so I don't have to. Is that going to happen anytime soon?"

I reached past her to open the door. "Not unless I can convince some woman that I'm worth more dead than alive."

"You need a whopping big life insurance policy," Charlotte advised as we joined Sam behind the bar.

"I was holding off until I had a loved one to support. Now it looks like I'll need a policy in order to get a loved one."

"Make me your beneficiary and I'll be your loved one," Charlotte promised.

"What is going on here?" Sam asked, fairly certain he didn't want to know. He ducked under the hanging menu board, docked a pitcherful of ice and smoothie mix in the blender, and punched the button.

"Charlotte's willing to marry me," I shouted over the cacophony of crunching ice and the blender's wailing motor. "Only if I promise to die in the next six months."

"It would be worth it, don't you think?" Charlotte asked Sam. "You should do it. You could handle anything for six months and a million bucks."

Sam grinned and shook his head. "I don't think so."

"Brian's pretty old," Charlotte pointed out, starting to giggle. "Your needs change when you get to be his age. All you'd have to do is read to him and stir up a glass of Metamucil every so often. Sam, the worst thing you'd have to do is give him a sponge bath once a week."

"Promise you'd bathe me more than once a week," I requested.

"I'll hire my brother's scout troop to give the baths," Sam decided. "They're always looking for ways to raise money. One hundred thousand dollars to keep you smelling fresh."

"Their parents would be all for it," said Charlotte. "In case any of the boys had gay tendencies, this experience would scare them straight."

"Next thing you know," said Sam, "you'd have to earn your sponge bath badge to make Eagle Scout."

"Speaking of sponge-bath candidates, guess who I think I saw at Taekwondo this afternoon? Tall, blonde," I gave hints. "Homicidal."

"Edna Applejack?" said Charlotte.

"That's what they called her. I hate it when somebody else gets to coin the cool nickname."

"That's not a nickname," said Sam.

"No way. Edna Applejack. Wow."

"She's better looking than that name would imply," said Sam.

"Edna's gorgeous," said Charlotte. "I can't believe I haven't seen her yet." She shuddered with anticipation. To my curious look she responded, "It's not a sexual thing. It's just…Edna."

"The fact she's an ex-con doesn't bother you?"

"Sure," said Charlotte. "Sure it does. But…"

"You really haven't heard the stories about Edna Applejack?" Sam asked me. "The all-time leading high school basketball player in the state? Turned down offers from UConn and Stanford, not to mention NDSU and UND, to play hoops for Jamestown College? Led them to two national championships? Killed her husband ten years ago, with her bare hands?"

"Whoa. No she didn't."

"And it was a fair fight," said Sam, still in awe after all these years. "Hand to hand combat. She killed him with her bare hands. Edna was in Taekwondo at the time, two weeks away from passing her black belt test. If she had been a black belt, the judge would have had to tack on another ten years."

Jerilyn Givens left her two-year-old at a nearby table to pick up the story-line. "Kyle Micklejohn was her husband. He graduated with my older brother. Kyle was a short nerdy guy. Computer geek. He was already writing programs for a defense contractor in high school. He was talented. Really geeky."

"What an odd couple," I said.

"It was so cool, how such a huge star stayed in Jamestown *and* married a nerd," said Jerilyn. "For awhile, we all wanted to date one. It didn't last long." She wrinkled her nose. "Nerds just didn't smell right."

"That's why I won't eat cage-raised beef," I said. "All that sitting around, taints the flavor."

"Amen," said Sam.

"So she killed Kyle with her bare hands," I marveled.

"They say Edna strangled him and tore him up pretty good," Sam reported. "The death blow was a punch to the temple."

"So the warnings are true," I said, gingerly touching my temple.

"Apparently so," said Sam.

"So stay away from her," Charlotte advised.

"If she wants to spar, I'll tell her I'm a man of the mind, not the body."

"That will only turn her on all the more," Sam warned.

"What if she hears through the grapevine that I was a chess club champion in high school?" I said.

"You weren't really," Charlotte challenged.

"No, but Edna doesn't need to know that." I exchanged a knuckle knock with Sam. "Make sure that gets to her."

"That's why I bring Nathaniel in here," said Jerilyn with a grin as she walked to the display stand to pick up the *James River Valley* golf caps her kid knocked to the floor. "Great role models."

I was suddenly too sick to my stomach to keep up the banter. The anti-nausea drugs weren't working so well. Sweat ran down the back of my neck and I fought the urge to assume the fetal position on the milk-splattered safety mat. "Okay, I'm out of here. Has it been slow?"

"Not too bad," Sam reported. "A little over a hundred since ten o'clock. Where are you going?"

"The open house at the Bluffs."

"Thatta boy," said Charlotte. "Go bust some butt."

"Go bust some butt?" Sam pondered. "Don't you mean skulls?"

"That sounds too violent," said Charlotte.

"You bust your own butt, Charlotte," I explained. "You bust other people's skulls. It's just the way it works."

"Well I don't do either," said Charlotte. "But you go do whatever you want to that Hernandes fellow."

"It's true, you don't bust your butt, do you?" Sam asked Charlotte to confirm. Yelling followed me out onto the sidewalk, and through the big front window I saw Sam ducking and weaving to avoid Charlotte's blows.

Now was the perfect time to take Dr. Bonilla's advice and sleep. Lingering effects of the chemo drugs left me pleased but no longer euphoric over the encouraging MRI report. I could lay me down to nap, satisfied with how I had gutted it out at Taekwondo, hopeful about the prospect of a cancer-free future.

But I was way too angry. Hernandes and his coffee freebies were prying away my customers. Cutting Craig's position had only prolonged the inevitable, and what was happening at the Bluffs was no doubt speeding it up.

I should have been completely preoccupied with not dying. That's the way it works, I was told. A serious illness clarifies priorities and renders meaningless all petty grievances and stressful obsessions with career, money, bills, success. Smelling the flowers, laughing with the children, growing old with loved ones—you learn to cherish the gift of life. Being a big fan of living, I definitely don't disagree. But I couldn't stop worrying about my business.

Maybe because in my heart of hearts, even before Dr. Bonilla gave me the good news, I knew I was going to survive. The overall survival rate for bone cancer is seventy percent. Bonilla had rated my cancer Stage II / Substage A / Grade 2—small and contained, with no more than a twenty percent chance of spreading. High marks for a tumor, so I had figured my chances were ninety percent or better. Not only that, the cancer was sitting a long way from the heart, the brain, the important stuff, content to nibble away at a fairly minor bone. If the doctors couldn't save it—hey, I still had the fibula after all.

And that's what the logical, higher-order layers of my brain were thinking. Dig deeper, where caveman testosterone raged, and maybe there was still a functioning remnant of the childhood self-image of the invincible hero.

So even while wallowing in the injustice of being struck down by cancer in the prime of my life, I inevitably found myself assuming I would soon be cured, and then looking beyond, to the resumption of my former healthy life. That's when my stomach really ached. Cancer and capitalism, what a tag team. The second I decided I was going to beat the disease, I was slugged in the gut by the fearsome certainty my coffeeshop was going under.

I failed in California at my calling, my passion. Now I was failing in North Dakota. A goofball who didn't know a thing about coffee was kicking my ass. We were competing head to head, and he was beating me.

And for some reason Mike McEwen was helping him.

THE BLUFFS RETAIL CENTER was painted in adobe colors, red clay to golden sandstone and a few desert hues in between. The shops were aligned on a gentle curve, so that every storefront was visible at all times. I liked the sales psychology—why leave when everything you need is right there in front of you, lunch, videogames, clothes, tools, liquor, shoes, coffee. I liked having my sign in the shoppers' faces at all times, just in case the first glance at my stylized meadowlark emblem didn't make you uncontrollably thirsty.

I wasn't as crazy about my door opening directly onto the sidewalk. This was the three-season Upper Midwest, winter coming, winter, and winter leaving, birthplace of the enclosed mall. I had flashbacks to the miserable trick-or-treating with Isabel's nephew at the Fargo strip mall those many years ago.

"Architects experimented with setting the stores behind a long enclosed fronting hall," Mike had explained. "It was impossible to make the hall feel like anything other than empty space, a moat between the retailers and the customers." Mike's solution was heated awnings that created a hot zone buffer to stop the icy wind in its tracks before it crept up the pant leg and penetrated the window shoppers' longjohns.

"How about a glass-enclosed plaza instead," I had suggested. "With palm trees and a huge fountain."

"How about an extra five hundred a month rent?" Mike had shut me up.

The parking lot was three-quarters full. The same fraction of the tenants were open for business—Herberger's department store, ACE Hardware, Taco John's, Jordie's Drycleaning, Northern Harvest Bread, and J-Town Games & Such. Hernandes' Campus Coffeehouse cart was parked under the awning in front of my store. A very young girl filled customers' orders and worked the till while Mike McEwen and Billy-boy talked. Mike hurried to intercept me.

"Brian! I didn't know if you could make it. You got my message?"

"My message service is unreliable." I didn't let Mike stop my forward progress. Keep your feet moving, that's the key. "How's things here?"

"Fine, we had a little glitch in scheduling the coffee service—" Mike tried but couldn't get it all out before we were standing in front of Hernandes. Who now decided to lend a hand to the grade-school girl behind the coffee cart.

"Hey Billy," I said.

"Hello Brian." Hernandes could barely look up to give me a wink, he was suddenly so busy. "How are the treatments coming? Any progress?"

Mike tugged me down the sidewalk before I could respond. "My office wasn't involved in scheduling this," he explained. "The management company handled it. Let me tell you," he griped, "I'm gonna kick some ass."

I took a few steps back and gazed at the vacant endcap storefront, at the sign in the window that Charlotte had made—*Coming Soon, James River Valley Coffee!* "Did they have to park him in front of my shop?"

Mike finger-combed his thick salt-n-pepper hair. "Criminy I feel terrible. I asked Bill the same thing. He says this is where they put him."

I listened hard for sounds of true remorse. I didn't want to believe he had orchestrated this in retaliation for the way I had been treating Isabel. "So I should be chewing the management company's ass. Who is it?"

Mike grimaced. "You don't look like you're ready to chew anyone's ass."

"I chew ass better when I'm dead-dog tired."

Mike put his arm around my shoulder. "Are you okay?"

"Just sick about my future, that's all."

"Isabel tells me you had another MRI."

"My tumor has shrunk quite a bit."

"That's fabulous, Brian! I am so happy to hear that!"

During Mike's hug I stared at two of my regular customers, Vince and Angelika, in line to buy a cup of Bill's swill. They were smiling and bantering with the couple behind them—I didn't know their names, but they had been in my shop once or twice. "Next step is surgery, after I get back from San Diego. Unless the Chamber decides to send Billy-boy instead."

Mike tipped his head back. "You're killing me." He held me at arms' length and forced eye contact. "Accept my apology, alright? And trust me, you're the man the Chamber wants in front of a crowd." His face darkened. "Not that I'm in favor of opening up our town to an Islamic infestation."

"Probably a moot point, with me as the Jamestown poster boy."

"Are you physically up for the trip? Because I think it's a great idea for Isabel to go along and keep you well-fed and cared for."

"I'm actually looking forward to some alone time."

"You're alone all the time!"

"Maybe by your standards. I'm an extra-introvert."

Mike eyeballed me. "What kind of psychobabble is that?"

"Brian!" Joshua Grunden hollered from the other side of the parking lot. "Hey! What's up?!" Joshua was packed so full of energy that he skipped toward us, between the parked cars and around a cluster of senior citizens studying Hernandes's price list, the most masculine skipping you can imagine, a bowlegged hopping, bowlegged because he wore his jeans so tight I could make out his religion.

"Hey buddy." We exchanged a violent handclasp. I had knuckle-knocked Joshua once, and only once, two years ago during a basketball game. Two knuckles were still swollen. "Tell me you're not here for the coffee."

"Why?" Joshua barked. "Isn't this your coffee stand? It's your store—what the heck is Campus Coffee doing in front of your store? Huh?"

"That's what I was asking Mike."

"Serving it up hot and fresh," Hernandes called out as he pumped his pot. He did an abbreviated dance step, the hot'n'fresh jig I suppose.

Mike ignored Hernandes and threw a phantom punch at Joshua. "Just like this guy. Causing trouble. Everywhere you go, eh?"

Joshua works part-time for Mike while he attends JC—also part-time, from what I can gather, despite the fact he plays football for them. Joshua spends a lot of time helping out on the family farm, and fishing, and hunting, and playing hoops and golf, and doing handyman jobs for anyone in need.

"I thought you had class Wednesday afternoons?" said Mike.

"I had to help Shep move his lathe and rewire a section of his machine shop," said Joshua. He giggled like a madman and then gave us a pained look. "Don't tell Denise. But gosh darn it, I have to find the time to make a little money here and there."

"I keep telling Joshua that if he wants to make some real dough, quit school and work for me full time," said Mike.

"That's good commonsense advice," I said.

"Denise won't let me quit school though," said Joshua, dejected.

"Women," I said.

Mike gave me his father-in-law face. "Keeping them happy is the most important job a man has."

I cocked my head. "I guess I've never heard you prioritize things before, Mike. I would have guessed you might have ranked work a little higher."

"It's a close number two. So I hear you two play a little hoop together?"

"Speaking of which..." Joshua squared off with me. "When are you going to start showing up? We need you back out there, runnin' and gunnin'."

"Soon. Need to get this cancer licked first."

"Yah, you don't look so good." Joshua's German accent thickened depending on the sentence.

Next to him I probably looked awful even without cancer. Joshua had been chiseled from a block of tan granite and then sandblasted smooth. He had thick curly brown hair, and muscles. They bulged in the backs of his hands and so you just knew they were bulging elsewhere—and they were, I could confirm from our hoops and locker room time together, and watching him level would-be tacklers on the JC football field. He was Achilles with blue eyes and a high-pitched giggle.

"Maybe a little golf would put color back in your cheeks," said Joshua.

"I am really anxious to get out there."

Mike gave Joshua a stern look. "There's no need to rush things."

Billy left his cart to join us. "Brian, how fantastic, to have so many people worrying about you. That's the mark of a truly blessed man." He wiped his hands on the towel tucked in his belt and then he touched me, patted me on the back. "You better get better, so you don't disappoint everyone."

In order to kick Billy in the face with my good leg, I would need to take a shuffle step to the left—and maybe stretch the hamstring a little first. "I was thinking of getting better for myself, actually."

"Bill does have a point there, Brian," said Mike. "Sometimes we need something a little bigger to live for. My daughter is crazy about Brian," he shared with Billy. "She would stop working for me and go to work caring for Brian full time, if he gave the word." He looked at me, waiting, hoping.

I had teenage girls working for me. Iz would never pass my background check.

"So that's who you were with in my shop the other day," said Billy. He didn't phrase it in the form of a question, so I didn't answer.

"That reminds me," said Joshua. "Denise wanted me to ask you two over for dinner tonight. Can you make it?"

"I'm a little whipped today."

"Tomorrow night then? Okay it's a deal. I'll pick you up."

"I'm still able to drive, you bastard."

"It's on my way home from work," Joshua protested, as if he wasn't doing me any favors.

"Alright homey, it's a date. See," I told Mike, "I'm plenty busy."

Mike grinned against his will. "I'll let Isabel know about dinner," he said.

"Thanks. Joshua, I was wondering, you wouldn't happen to have any more of those trout you caught up in Canada this summer?"

"I do have a few filets left from last weekend at Sacagawea."

"Can you spare a couple?"

"Sure. I'll have them ready for you tomorrow night."

"Actually I need them for tonight. I have a hankering for trout," I explained. "It's like pregnancy cravings, only that's no baby growing inside me."

Mike winced and I regretted the joke.

"Stop by the house," said Joshua. "I'll have Denise pull them out of the deep freeze." The deep freeze took up half the living room of their trailer house. "You just need one, right?"

"Two," I said.

"They're big filets," said Joshua.

"I know a lot of people feel differently, but I really like leftover fish." I almost gagged saying it.

Hernandes whistled. "Look at that line. We're already running low on milk."

"It's not that the line is so long," I said, watching ten-year-old Betsy frowning down at a pile of change sitting in her palm. "It's just not moving. But don't worry, I won't be putting you any further behind."

"I had coffee at home," said Mike. "All coffee'd out."

"I'm heading over to James River Coffee," Joshua announced to everyone in line, in the parking lot, inside the stores. "Their coffee is unbelievable!"

"Thanks man." We knuckle-knocked. It was worth the pain.

"So I'll pick you up tomorrow at your apartment at six?" Joshua verified.

"Sounds good," I said, backpedaling toward the parking lot.

"I'll have Isabel call you," said Mike.

"That's okay," I said, refusing to solve the puzzled look that came over Mike's face.

"Thanks for stopping, Brian," Hernandes called to me.

"Sorry you're all out of milk," I called back, loudly.

And I'll be darned if people didn't step out of line and head for their vehicles.

I HAD A FOOT on the bottom step leading to my second floor apartment, toting the cooler Joshua's wife Denise gave me, when the door to apartment #1 opened beside me.

"Hey Brian," Dennis hailed me. Dennis Rearden, short and powerful with a thick neck. He came into my shop most days. I've never figured out what he does for a living, because he's vague when I ask him. "A little here and a little there, a little of this and a little of that" was his standard reply. From listening in on his conversations I knew he was an extreme fighter. I don't believe he fought in a sanctioned league. I do think a lot of money changed hands. Which was at least a partial answer to my question.

"What've you got there?" he asked me.

"Trout. A buddy of mine, Joshua Grunden—"

"I know Joshua," said Dennis.

"I shouldn't be surprised. But I guess I still am, since he's only been going to school here for a couple years."

"I pheasant hunted with him down by the South Dakota border." Dennis indicated the cooler. "Throwing a party?"

"Just a couple filets."

"A couple. Who are you cooking for?"

Dennis wore his long straight hair parted right down the middle. That's not an unusual style around here, but it was still distracting.

In fact, I was becoming obsessed with hair, hairlines, hair thickness. Dennis's hair probably wasn't as thin as it appeared, more fine than thin, I'm sure that's how he would have described it. Did mine look that thin? I wondered. The first round of chemo was surprisingly gentle on my scalp. I didn't notice hair on my pillow or clogging my drain. But it was preying on my mind. I don't comb or brush my hair, ever, not once in all my thirty-two years, yet I kept having visual flashes of a yellow long-handled comb with clumps of my hair clotting the teeth.

"It's only a couple trout," I dodged his question. "A lot of ice, though. Getting heavy." I plodded up the stairs, embellishing the effort with grunts. "I'll catch you down at the shop."

"We should get together sometime," Dennis called after me. "Maybe do dinner. Your place or mine. Either way."

"Sounds good."

I ducked into the apartment, aware that I had a problem. Andrea was going to come prancing up that sidewalk and inside the building and up those stairs, under Dennis's watchful eye and keen ear. When she stopped at the first door on the second floor and knocked, I was busted. Dennis was our neighborhood little old lady, sitting at the front window in his rocker, keeping an eye on the comings and goings.

When I first moved in, Dennis knocked on my door with mail in his hand. "Look," he said, "my key opens your box too. Cool, huh?"

"Yeah, cool," I answered, looking at my mail in his hand.

After a couple weeks of this hand-delivery service from my non-government-sanctioned mail carrier, I started to get perturbed. Dennis would call out "Mail!" as he knocked on my door. "Whoops, looks like someone's late with his phone bill!"

Finally I had Vern from the post office stake out our lobby. I didn't know he would bring backup. Dennis was hauled away in handcuffs and spent four hours in a police interrogation room. The cops made me come down to the station, where I declined to press charges. I gave Dennis a ride home, apologizing all the way. He said the worst part was getting his ass chewed by Vern.

Dennis never touched my mail again, but I think the whole episode only heightened his commitment to watch over me. Every couple months he asked whether Iz and I had set a date. Isabel was his high school classmate, one of his favorite people in the world, and part of our apartment building's natural rhythms. Andrea was not.

"James River Valley Coffee," Sara answered the phone. Sara is always smiling, and it came across over the line. It was a good feeling, when Sara answered your call.

"Hey. It's Brian. From the coffeeshop."

"I know," said Sara. "Where are you?"

"I'm home, why?"

"No reason," said Sara, cheerfully, always. "What are you doing?"

"Preparing a coffee soy ginger marinade for my two trout filets, why?"

"No reason." And this was true. "What's up?"

"Did Dennis ever fix the drain catch under the sink?"

"You mean that thing that keeps backing up, with all the disgusting stuff?"

"That's the one."

"I don't think so."

"You want to give him a call and ask him to come down and do it?" Dennis was a decent handyman. He helped me out all the time with the little mechanical stuff that otherwise would drive me crazy. Maybe his handyman skills actually made him some money. Just not from me.

"Right now?" said Sara.

"Yeah, it's really bugging me."

"Okay."

"Don't tell him I asked you to do it. If it comes from you, he'll be down there right away. He likes you."

"Eeeuu."

"Not that way. Like a little sister."

"Eeeuu."

"Not in the West Virginia sister way. Will you do it for me?"

"Of course. Right now?"

"I'd prefer it."

"Okay. Was that it?"

"That's it, lady. I'll see you tomorrow?"

"Sure."

The floor and ceilings and walls weren't so thin that I could hear Dennis's phone ring, but I did hear a door thud shut a few minutes later, and sure enough there was Dennis hustling toward the detached garage with a little skip in his step. I had lied, he liked Sara in the Biblical way. Hopefully I wouldn't burn in hell for that.

That was no longer a throwaway line. The more I thought about it, the more nervous I got.

"James River Valley Coffee," Sara answered cheerfully.

"Hey. It's me again. Brian, from the coffeeshop."

"Brian, what's up?"

"Don't tell Dennis this was your idea. Tell him I told you to call him. Tell him I asked you a week ago, but that you had forgotten to call him until now."

"Why?"

"I don't want him getting the wrong idea."

"Thanks," Sara said with a smile in her voice. She has a smile on her face all the time. I mean, all the time. A customer had come in a few days earlier. "My drink yesterday was cold," the pudgy-faced lady said to Sara.

Sara smiled. "I'll get you a free drink today, and I'll make sure it's hot," she assured the lady. "Vanilla latté?"

"Yes," the lady replied. I was off to the side reading the paper, eavesdropping. Sara finished the drink and handed it to the lady. The lady took a sip.

"Is it okay?" Sara asked, smiling even wider.

The lady winced. "A bit hot," she said. I held back a chuckle. She looked at Sara suspiciously. "Decaf, right?"

Sara smiled. "Oh, I didn't hear you say decaf." That's because she didn't say decaf, I said in my head. "Would you like a new drink?" Sara asked, smile as big as ever.

"Yes. I always get decaf," said the lady, disgusted with Sara.

"I'll remember that," said Sara with a smile. After the lady left, Sara looked at me, smiling. "I could kill that bitch," she said.

I wandered about the apartment looking for something to clean, until there was a light, crisp knock at my door. Small and sharp, Andrea's knuckles.

She greeted me with an impish smile, short and plump in her puffy iridescent winter jacket. "I'm a little early," she said. "Hope you don't mind."

"As long as you don't mind dinner's not ready. Can I take your coat?" I wanted her out of that coat, pronto. I hated that puffy coat, especially in April.

From the pillowy depths Andrea produced a bottle of white wine. "Something told me you wouldn't have anything to drink around here."

"That's pretty intuitive." I had beer, I had wine, and I had booze, a lot of it, but planned on keeping it hidden. If inviting Andrea over for a cozy quiet dinner for two was a bad idea, and it was, then serving alcohol was downright insane. "I honestly don't even know if I have a corkscrew," I said as I tossed her coat on the floor of the empty spare bedroom.

"I have one in my car."

I couldn't help but be impressed.

"It's my winter emergency survival kit, in its entirety. Should I go get it?"

"No, you stay put." I didn't need her parading back and forth for all eyes to see. I rummaged in the miscellany kitchen drawer. "Here we go. I'll leave it here on the counter, whenever you're ready."

"That would be now." Andrea made short work of the cork. "You're having a glass, aren't you? Of course you are," she said firmly.

I stood staring at the fish filets soaking in my marinade. Flustered or retarded, I couldn't remember what to do next. "I don't know that I should be mixing alcohol and chemo drugs."

"Don't tell me you haven't had a drop to drink the past month."

"No, that would be a lie."

"Don't lie to me any more. Or any less. Ha ha." Andrea found the cupboard with the wine glasses. And the wine did look good. Every so very often I had a deep parched thirst that only white wine could slake. This was one of those times, unfortunately. "Here you go." Andrea handed me a glass and stood facing me, pretty close. "Should we toast?"

"What would we toast?" My voice croaked. I jumped the gun and took a sip. "Oops, sorry. I blew the toast. Dry throat. Probably catching what will become a fatal cold, with my depleted immune system."

"You don't want to toast, that's fine. I had a good one all ready to go, but…" Andrea turned away. I think she was truly put out. "Aren't the fish getting soggy?"

"Maybe. I've never tried this recipe with trout. I'm a salmon guy originally." I couldn't take her pouting. "Okay, what was your toast?"

"Mm…"

I felt like I was back in high school. "Come on. I'm sorry. I should have waited." My throat was cracking again, dried out by the chemo. Possibly the excessive vomiting. I needed more of that sweet nectar in the worst way. "Give me the toast. Quickly."

Andrea cupped the bowl of the glass in both her fine-fingered hands, staring down at the shimmering swaying surface of her chardonnay. "I was going to toast to being stranded together on a frozen, deserted island." She raised her eyes to me. "And to finding a way off."

I let that one sink in.

"Speechless, huh?" Andrea clinked my glass. "Take a big drink."

I did.

"Did that loosen up your vocal chords? They must have been stuck."

"You just have me worried about the trout, that's all," I lied. "I'm going to throw them on the grill. Be back in a sec."

"On the grill? It's freezing outside."

"If it's worth cooking, it's worth grilling. Even if it really was freezing."

"Then you go do that," said Andrea, savoring the toast in her mouthful of wine. "Is that all we're having? Wine and fish?"

"I'm pretty sure I asked you to bring a side dish."

"Nice try. Don't worry about it, I'm fine with a limited menu. So. What did Isabel say when you told her about this?"

"I'm not planning on telling her."

"Oh is this a secret?" Andrea was positively purring. "Hm, I wonder what Rick would say."

"It's up to you, of course, but I'd rather you didn't tell him."

"Why?" Andrea wondered. "Do you think he would assume there's something going on between us?"

That would have been an interesting topic if I was trying to seduce Andrea. I escaped to the tiny deck, and dawdled there, fiddling with the grill, brooding, and not just about Dennis eventually returning home to notice Andrea's car—but that too, because holy shit of course everybody knew everybody in this town of fifteen thousand, as well as what he or she drove, which seemed to be more important than what he or she did for a living.

Andrea had made a terrible toast. Maybe I was stranded in North Dakota. But the island wasn't deserted. Literally hundreds of people in Jamestown had taken me into their hearts—not to mention the substantial number who had taken me into their homes—and cared about me, and trusted me; and vice-versa to all of that. I wasn't a huge fan of the town itself, the weather, or the proximity to Canada; and I hated the *mood*, that seemed to condone aspiring to nothing more than barely scraping by as the owner of a couple little coffeeshops. But I liked the people. Talking to Andrea was like plotting with a conspirator, against everyone in Jamestown, all their affection, all their trust.

"I guess you were thirsty." Andrea looked askance at my empty glass when I stepped back into the dining room. "Can I refill that for you? We are celebrating, right?" She tried to perk me up. "You're on you way to being cancer free. That's wonderful."

"I'm pretty excited about it."

"You look excited," Andrea said sarcastically. "What are you thinking right now? That your fish are soggy and you're embarrassed you can't offer me a salad, and you wish we had gone out to eat?"

"No, that's not it."

The sarcasm left her voice. "So what is it?" she asked softly. "That you don't want me here?"

"That's not it either." I discovered my hand reaching for my head, and stopped it. I was terrified of running my fingers through my hair and coming away with a handful. "Not exactly."

"I won't tell Rick," Andrea assured me, sourly.

"I figure he's going to know sooner or later anyway."

"Oh, do you envision this being a regular thing?"

"No. Maybe. I mean, I do things on a regular basis with a lot of people. I have people over for dinner all the time."

"Single women? You have a lot of single women here? Maybe I should have asked around, before I accepted your invitation."

I poured more wine for both of us. "Who are you kidding, you don't know anybody to ask about me."

"Lucky for you."

"Why don't you come down to the shop? Spend some time down there.

You'll get to know a lot of people in a hurry."

"Yeah, well, I don't want to know anybody."

"Why would you say that? This is where you live."

"Not really."

"You're here until Tyler graduates. That's thirteen, fourteen years. That's a long time to be a recluse."

Andrea shrugged. "If you don't belong someplace…. And what do you care whether I fit in? Maybe you'll be my only friend."

"If we're going to be friends, then I want you to get to know a few people and try to fit in, at least a little bit. You can be nicer than people think."

"Gee, thanks." Andrea acted put out, but I could tell I had scored a couple points. She strolled to the deck window. Other than my primo Beefeater grill, it's not a memorable view—more apartment buildings across the street, an empty lot on one corner, a sliver of a neighborhood visible in the other direction, one-story starter homes hiding behind big cottonwood trees. "Maybe," she said, "we'll have to be secret friends."

"I'm no good at secrets. I don't keep other people's secrets. I doubt I can keep my own."

Andrea faced me. "Then I guess it won't be a secret."

"Shouldn't we have something in common? Besides misery and contempt, I mean."

Andrea grinned, I think. The sun was backlighting her as it set between the apartment buildings across the street, wiping out her features. "I'll bet we both love sunny beaches."

"There's that, I guess."

"I want you to take me with you."

"With me? To San Diego? With me, to San Diego?"

Andrea chortled. "Don't you think we'd have fun?"

"Uh. I'm sorry. I can't."

"Well I'm going. And then I'm going to follow you, to your hotel." She moved toward me with careful, graceful steps. A bride moving down the aisle cradling a wine glass instead of a bouquet. "I guess you'll have to turn me away at the door."

I stared her down. "If I have to."

"How come I doubt that?" She rubbed my arm, gently enough not to slosh my wine or irritate my chemo-tenderized skin, and then strolled into the living room. "I've decided I'm going, so you're going to have to deal with it."

"I'm going to clean the cooler," I announced, determined to pretend this conversation hadn't occurred, couldn't occur, not in the world of the rational and the sane.

I cleaned the kitchen and tended to the grill, a little rattled that Andrea gravitated to my favorite band amidst four towers of CDs. Squeeze had a story-song for every major event in my relationship history. It was hard not to like a band who had written your dating soundtrack.

"How's it coming?" Andrea called out while Squeeze sang about that time I cheated on my girlfriend with the state jobs development intern in Sacramento. "Every time you open that door, it smells great. I'm starved. Do we have to eat at the table, or can I stay here on the couch? I'd like to sit in here and soak up the fabulous ambiance you've created."

Total smartass. I spared no expense on my grill. My CD collection was amazing. Otherwise, all my money went to my shop. A secondhand couch, a threadbare recliner with a busted footrest and two bean bag chairs in my living room, that's all. No artwork or framed family pictures on the bare off-white walls. Four place settings and a few pots and pans. A king-size bed from the previous dweller, and all my clothes in neatly stacked milk crates that doubled as packing boxes. My friends, folks and the Salvation Army were going to have it easy if I died suddenly.

"Couch is fine," I said.

"Good, because I'm very comfortable."

Isabel would have been doing the cooking. She would have had me propped up on the couch, feet up and rubbed. A hand-job for an appetizer and a blow job for dessert—*mmm, was there soy in that marinade?* Andrea lounged while I waited on her. Nice for a change.

I presented her filet, all alone on the plate. "Can I get you anything else?"

"More wine. Unless you finished it off already."

"I may have refilled my glass once or twice." I retrieved the bottle and emptied it in Andrea's glass. "I think you bought alcohol-free wine by mistake. It's not doing anything for me."

"Maybe you're an alcoholic."

"I'm really thirsty tonight, for some reason."

"Let me try this fish." Andrea flaked off a small wedge of trout and slipped it in her mouth. Her lips weren't big, but the surrounding flesh was, causing her lips to protrude. Her lips were active as she chewed, drawn in to be licked clean, then popping out again to proclaim the fish tasty. As an old lady those lips would be frightening. Her grandkids would be afraid of them, radiating deep wrinkles and bristling with prickly hairs. But for the time being they weren't half bad.

"So you don't need anything else before I sit? Salt, pepper? A side dish?"

"You never told me to bring a side dish," said Andrea.

"You don't have to feel guilty."

"Oh I'm not." She thought for a second while daintily separating another morsel. "Honestly, I don't think I've felt guilty for anything I've ever done."

"I doubt that." I stabbed a bite from my plate and ate it on my way out to the grill. "The fish is good, huh?"

"It's great. Why don't you believe me?"

"It's my own special marinade," I called from the deck.

"Uh-huh. It's wonderful. What do I have to feel guilty about?"

"Didn't you ever steal candy from the grocery store?"

"Yeah. But I didn't feel guilty. What's this?" Andrea asked as I stood above her with a steaming tinfoil pouch of grilled potatoes and veggies. "No way—a side dish?"

"You didn't strike me as dependable, so I had a backup plan. Didn't you ever get caught lying to your mom and dad?"

Andrea held the glass to her mouth like an oxygen mask. "I'm a really good liar."

"But don't you feel guilty about lying to your folks?"

"No. By the time I was in high school, my mom and dad were so old, they didn't want to know what I was doing."

No guilt. An admirable quality, I suppose. All I know is, if I'm ten seconds late for work or an appointment, or if a cop car approaches, I feel guilty. A life without guilt would be nice. Sometimes. Maybe just a break from guilty feelings, every other week. I'd be a dangerous character without a little guilt.

I sat down in the recliner, at a right angle to the couch. "And were you a bad girl back then?"

"I was bad enough."

"How about during your marriage?"

"Aha." She held up her fork and examined a chunk of fish, losing and not replacing a drip of marinade. It made me a little angry. Maybe I was too proud of that marinade. "Well. We finally come to the real reason you had me over."

"It was to celebrate my cancer-free future, remember?"

"I'll tell you about my marriage to Rick, if you want you want to hear."

"I'd be glad to stick with the smart-ass banter."

"Because he treated me bad," she said. "He really did." Andrea must have had a bad memory at the ready, because she instantly looked miserable. "I had an affair with a college boyfriend." News flash. "The guy you met, who came into your shop while he was auditing here in town."

"Vaguely, I remember."

"But I don't regret it. Not at all." Definitely no remorse in her voice. "So." Andrea set her plate on the floor and wiped her lips and put her hands in her lap. "What do you have to say? Are you mad? Do you understand? ...do you care? What? Tell me."

"I was right about not wanting to know."

"Then you shouldn't have kept pouring us more wine. Why don't you want to know?"

"I would like to say it's none of my business. But that's the problem, of course. I date Isabel. I'm going to be in business with her father."

"What do you mean, you date her?" Andrea sought clarity. "You're not engaged anymore, are you?"

"Technically, yes."

"For God's sake, why don't you call it off? Or do you still love her?"

"I have very strong feelings for Isabel—"

"Pity?" Andrea suggested.

"No. I care about her. It's probably love. We just can't be together."

"Why?" Andrea pressed.

"I know too much."

"Too much…about what?"

"I'm sure you probably know already. About Isabel having sex with one of her students."

"No I didn't know. Wow. I guess you can't keep secrets."

"I can't believe you didn't know."

"It's not surprising," Andrea said bitterly. "The McEwens never really considered me part of their family. When did it happen?"

"Six years or so ago. Nothing like it has happened since."

"As far as you know."

"I'm pretty sure it hasn't. So it wouldn't bother me so much, I don't think, if the student hadn't been a girl."

"Whoa." Andrea gaped, then threw her head back and laughed. Cackled. "My. Now that's a naughty girl."

"Can you match that one?"

"I've never been that naughty, I can honestly say."

"Isabel is the naughtiest I've ever met. Of course occasionally that's a good thing."

Andrea was disgusted. "Whatever floats your boat." She polished off her wine. "So that's why Isabel quit teaching."

"She made a deal with the girl's parents. Iz promised to never teach again, and the parents agreed not to prosecute her. She plans to start lobbying them soon, to let her teach again. Or else rig their brakes to fail."

"If I were them," said Andrea, "I'd put the agreement in my will. Or do you think Isabel is no longer a threat to Jamestown's young girls?" Andrea's opinion was obvious; this question was really a test of my ability to objectively assess Isabel's character.

"I don't know," I said honestly. "I'm pretty sure she's decided she loves teaching more than statutory rape."

Andrea grimaced. "How noble. Where are you going?"

"To open another bottle of wine."

"I thought you didn't have any."

"Oh no. I have plenty." I opened the tall pantry door and crouched, ignoring the burning down my shin to reach way back and feel around and pull out a bottle of California chardonnay.

"So you can't get past what she did," Andrea prompted as I opened the bottle.

"If she had messed around with a male student, I think I'd just be happy for him. Making it with the teacher, that's a guy's high school fantasy stuff. But girls are different. That could really mess with a young girl's head. I know it's messing with mine. Every so often, the image of Iz kissing that girl, Iz's hand between her legs—"

"Okay. That's good. That's an image I don't need."

"Me neither. Looks like I'm stuck with it, though."

"I know a good way to get rid of it," said Andrea. "Break it off. Completely this time."

I leaned heavily on the island counter separating the two rooms. "The McEwens are such a good family, it's hard. They've been great to me. I love Mike and everything he's done for me. If I could be his son-in-law without getting married to Isabel…that would be perfect." I rubbed my forehead, careful not to harass the hairline. "I should break it off, I suppose. I'm having a hard time because Iz really is a great person. I think I'm a little afraid of making a mistake I'll regret. She's always there for me. She dotes on me. She waits on me hand and foot whenever I let her."

"Maybe you need someone a little less smothering," Andrea said with a smirk. "More detached, less caring. Not quite as sexually deviant."

"I'd settle for a happy medium," I said, making sure not to look at Andrea, so that the discussion of my ideal mate would stay hypothetical.

"Hm." Andrea held up her glass. "I think that wine has breathed enough."

I refilled her glass and bused her plate. Andrea finished her trout, and I came close, the most I had eaten in quite a while. I aimed my butt for the chair but Andrea patted the couch, so I sat there, wedging my back into the well-padded corner, getting comfortable. She swung her legs up and said her feet were cold, so I let her push them under my leg. She wanted to talk about Rick, so I listened.

Standard marital strife stuff. He ignored her. His family came first. Every time they went out, it turned into a greater McEwen function. Andrea would often end up driving home alone. She's a sexual creature (a conventional one, she made sure to point out); Rick would come home exhausted after working late and doze off in the middle of her attempts to rouse his interest.

"Hey." Andrea nudged me with her feet. "Wake up, for crying out loud."

"Whoops." I had fallen asleep. Didn't spill any wine, I was proud to see. "Playing the part of your ex-husband Rick, will be Brian Lawson."

"God. I must be really boring." There was no self-pity in her voice. She was disgusted with me. "Are you awake now?"

"I don't know for how long. It's been a long day. I was up at five to open the shop. The final chemo treatment. Taekwondo." I sat up straight and blinked. My head was spinning. "Cooking this big meal for you."

"Yeah, yeah. Wake up." Andrea grabbed my arm and yanked me back and forth. "Come on. Surely you can think of something better to do than sleep."

My mouth tasted like chemical. My throat hurt. "I have to get up early again tomorrow. I need to get some shut-eye."

"Fine." Andrea set her glass on the coffee table and hopped to her feet.

"I'm sorry."

"No," she said curtly. "It's no big deal."

"If you're too drunk to drive, you can crash on my couch."

"I'm fine."

I retrieved her puffy coat and caught her at the door. "Thanks for coming."

"Yeah, well." She put on her soap bubble costume and stood there, facing me. She expected me to kiss her goodnight.

If there was going to be a first kiss, it wasn't going to be with chemo breath and dried eau-de-trout spit on my lips. "I'll walk you to your car."

"You don't need to do that. I doubt North Dakota has muggers."

She was being a martyr. I was prepared to let her. "Okay lady. Drive safe."

"Okay…"

"How about a hug?" While Andrea debated whether this would suffice, I hugged her, a solid one, cheek to cheek. I had the door open before it was over. I gave her a final squeeze. "Good night."

She shuffled into the hall. She was so darn tiny. "I'm going to walk you out," I decided.

Andrea followed me, excruciatingly slowly, down the stairs. I waited, holding the front door for her. "Are you parked on the street or in the lot?"

"Maybe I'll let you figure that out."

"That's a fun game."

Andrea didn't like my tone. "Heaven forbid we should have any fun." She hurried to her pickup, parked front and center on the street, and opened the door. "Well," she was snotty, "thanks for a nice evening."

"Sorry I'm such a party pooper. Sorry I'm such a cancer patient."

"Yeah well." She was pausing again, shivering, stamping her feet against the chill, overdoing it a little.

I kissed her on the lips to get it over with.

"There. That wasn't so hard, was it?" she asked. "It didn't take too much out of you, did it?"

"I hope you didn't give me any germs. I have a compromised immune system, you know."

Andrea dropped into the driver's seat. "Just remember, you kissed me."

"I promise not to blame you if I get sick and die."

"Good. Good night." She drove off, looking satisfied.

Things were stranger by the day. I felt like I was blindly blundering through a series of unfortunate situations. A walk to clear my head and collect my thoughts seemed like the right thing to do. Even the romantic thing to do. Imagine if I really did have a soul mate, right here in Jamestown, and she happened to see me, the solitary man walking the silent streets as the fateful prairie winds swirled around him. She wouldn't even have to be my soul mate. Just a woman who was actually good for me, driving about aimlessly, wrestling with her own assorted crises. Her heart would be mine forever.

But without knowing my context—the struggle to achieve my coffeeshop dreams, the battle against cancer, the procession of crazy women—my dream girl wouldn't see the romantic glow about me. She would shiver and drive on and we would both go to our graves sooner or later without knowing how close we had been to true love.

Besides I was beat. I trudged up the walk. Dennis waved from his chair by the window.

T - 11

I was up at five and at the shop by five-thirty. Jerry Evans liked to help me open. He was a day trader who found he had better luck wiping his mind clean before the exchanges opened. Jerry used to cram for an hour prior to the opening bell, studying historical charts and trend lines and poring over the after-hours trading data. Now he took down chairs and unrolled the floor mats and kept me company while I filled the till and revved up the espresso machine and brewed the coffee. Either way I don't think he made much money. But I appreciated the company.

And his baldness. I still had a ton more hair than Jerry.

"Brian," he called from the front door, "I can't put the sign outside."

"Why not?"

"She won't let me." Jerry stood aside to let a woman enter the store.

"We're closed," I told her. "We open at six...oh, hi Frannie."

"It's Francesca," said the sign nazi. She raised her eyebrows and stared at the counter, two feet below my face. "I wanted to catch you before you opened. You know you can't put a sandwich board on the sidewalk. It's against the law." Law versus ordinance, an irrelevant distinction for Frannie. She held up a stapled booklet. "I brought you a copy of the municipal code."

"You brought me one last time, Frannie."

"I'll leave it for you." Frannie dusted off her booklet, smoothed it, petted it, and set it on the nearest table. Parting was such sweet sorrow.

"What's wrong with having a sign on your sidewalk?" Jerry asked. Jerry almost always smiled, so you couldn't tell how big he was. He was the son of a former NFL linebacker and a pro prospect himself before participating in a multi-car pileup fifteen years ago. Jerry was heading back to college after a weekend visiting his folks in Jamestown. His was the last vehicle to join the accident, on an icy stretch of Minnesota interstate. Jerry hit the brakes and ended up coming in backwards. There were significant injuries, but probably none as costly, from a career earnings perspective, as Jerry's ruptured discs.

Still, he smiled. Rare times like these when he didn't, he was an intimidating presence.

"There's nothing wrong with a little sign on the sidewalk," I said.

"That's not for you to decide," said Frannie. She wisely kept her eyes averted as she moved past Jerry. "Since this is your second warning in the last six months, the next violation will result in a penalty."

"Penalize me now, because it'll be out there all summer long."

From the doorway Frannie pointed her hooked finger at the booklet. "The appeals process is spelled out in there. Page seventeen, I believe."

"Frannie, if Billy-boy Hernandes can call his place Campus Coffee, I can put a little sign on my sidewalk."

"What does that have to do with anything?" Frannie demanded.

"False advertising," I replied. "I'm pretty sure it's against the law."

"Is that who complained?" Jerry demanded. "Bill Hernandes?"

"We're not at liberty to discuss that," said Frannie. "If Mr. Lawson wishes to stop down at our office, we can show him a copy of the complaint."

"Frannie, save yourself another trip and go ahead and fine me."

She paused in the doorway, wringing her hands. "We'd really prefer you didn't put that sign on your sidewalk."

"I'd really prefer you quit letting Bill Hernandes call all the shots."

Frannie fled without responding. I stocked the cash register, stewing, until Jerry spoke. "What do I do with this sign?"

"Put it out there. I'll make John and Carolyn come collect the fine in person." I knew all the council members and considered John and Carolyn to be good friends. "If John pushes it, I'll kick his ass on the golf course and take the money right back from him." I slammed the register drawer. "Have you seen the flashing neon billboards Hernandes has in front of his shop? Whether he's breaking any ordinances or not, how about a little common sense? Hernandes must be sleeping with Frannie, that's all I can figure. I gotta talk to Mark the town manager again. I don't want to interfere with Frannie's only way to get nookie, but this is crazy."

"She enjoys this role," said Jerry. "She tried to stop Amber from hosting Longaberger basket parties because our house isn't zoned commercial."

"Did somebody complain?"

Jerry hemmed and hawed. "Aaa...yeah...yeah...probably one of our neighbors. Amber started selling Longaberger right after another woman in the neighborhood. I'm pretty sure Amber took some of her customers."

"Stole them. That's what we call it in the commercial world."

"Thanks. I'll tell Amber."

"Didn't the same thing happen with Amway?"

"Just a coincidence," said Jerry.

I loved Jerry and Amber and would defend them to the end. But I doubted it was a coincidence. They had two kids, a big mortgage (for Jamestown), and shaky income production from Jerry. They had tried every pyramid scheme out there over the past couple years, from phone cards to juice pills. If they saw someone making money, they wanted a piece of the action. Talked about opening a coffeeshop once.

When Jerry came back inside, the relaxed smile was back on his face. "I saw your sign in the window at the new strip mall on the bluff."

"It's a retail center. I guess that's different from a strip mall. Unroll that mat over there, would you?"

"It's not strictly retail." Jerry drug the mat in front of the cash register and looked for my approval before unfolding and unrolling it. "I'm looking at leasing a little space. Just a cube. They've been working on me to commit. But..."

Jerry paused. I waited. Jerry was prone to pauses. I had known him since my first week in Jamestown, and had watched the pauses lengthen. These weren't the smokers' sort. Jerry didn't use the pause to read you or to gauge the effect of his words upon you—if that were the case, his pause length would have decreased as he got to know you better. Instead, it was taking him longer and longer to form the next sentence.

The easy correlation to pause length was responsibilities—in the past four years Jerry had married, had kids One and Two, and quit his accounting job to day trade, all the while becoming more involved in his church and his kids' daycare and the business community. The coup de grace was taking up golf. Jerry had a lot on his mind, more every year, so some amount of distraction was understandable.

But my theory was that he was choosing his sentences more and more carefully. Jerry was a smart guy. He could lead a full life and carry on normal-paced conversations, if he wanted to. I think he was gun-shy, with an acquired taste for vague chit-chat. Like a chess master he worked three or four moves ahead, trying out sentences and the likely ensuing conversational give and take before choosing one that didn't lead to trouble.

He made his selection. "I'd be in the midst of other traders. Probably a couple eBay brokers. Not sure how that would go."

I never hesitated to hold up my end of a conversation. If I didn't have a fully-formed thought, I just threw out the fragment. "High-speed connection?"

"High-speed connection. Yeah. Probably. No doubt it would be a lot faster than my home setup."

"Bloomberg terminal? I've heard they're nice to have."

Jerry grinned. "I'll demand one from Jennifer."

"Getting out of the house wouldn't be so bad, huh?"

Jerry obviously didn't like the looks of the future that a straightforward answer would bring. I had time to fill three pitchers with milk. "Speaking of growing households," he said, "I hear you've expanded yours by one."

"Oh?"

"Andrea McEwen."

"Huh?"

"Or whatever her name is now."

"What are you talking about?"

"You had her over for dinner last night," said Jerry. "Dennis told me." No pauses here. "I saw him at the gas station this morning."

My counter was low enough that I could lean on it with my hands spread wide and my elbows locked. This brought my shoulders up beside my head like a turtle shell.

"We're both early fillers," Jerry explained.

"Huh," I grunted. *Repercussions.* Repercussions, repercussions..... I wasn't envisioning anything specific, just the word, over and over.

"We both like to keep our tanks topped off," said Mr. Conversationalist.

Oscar George walked in. I usually have a handful of customers before we officially open. Oscar is a retired farmer, two cups of regular and a cup of decaf before heading out to the farm to harass his son. "Gentlemen," he greeted us. Born and raised in North Dakota, and he still had a thick German accent.

"Oscar," said Jerry.

"Oscar." I handed him his first cup.

Oscar frowned at the tall bumblebee-decorated mug in his gnarled chapped hand. "Is my favorite cup dirty already then?"

"Oh, shoot, give me that." I took the bumblebee mug and poured the coffee into his favorite, a deep purple Lake Tahoe mug.

If the bumblebee mug held eleven ounces, then the Tahoe mug held ten. Roughly one ounce of freshly-brewed coffee curled like a surfer's dream wave out of the Tahoe mug and broke over my crotch. The sound of the surf roared in my ears.

"Ouch, oh, man!" I thrust the mugs onto the espresso machine shelf. The Tahoe mug tipped over and splattered my legs with more steaming coffee. "Son of a..." I pulled my corduroy shorts away from my private parts and strutted up and down behind the bar. "Ahhhh..."

"You alright there, Brian?" Oscar leaned over the bar, craning his neck. "Uh-oh. You didn't break my Tahoe cup, did you?"

"I hope so," I groaned.

Jerry moved up for a better look. "What happened back there?"

"Brian's a little clumsy this morning," said Oscar.

"Oscar just has to have his favorite mug," I said, sopping at my shorts with the bar rag. "No matter who gets hurt."

"I hope you didn't break my cup," said Oscar.

"You bring your own mug from home?" Jerry questioned Oscar.

"No-no. It's Brian's. I just love it. Coffee tastes better in it, you know."

I wiped off the Tahoe mug, refilled it with nine or so ounces, and handed it to Oscar. "That'll be a buck-fifty plus tax."

"I didn't bring my coffee card today," said Oscar. "Put it on my tab."

I nodded, wincing. My left nut was aflame. "Jerry, watch the bar for me, would you? Charlotte should be here any minute."

"You need a 'Warning: Hot Coffee' label on your cups," Oscar suggested.

"I'll carve it into your fucking Tahoe mug," I threatened.

"No need to do that," said Oscar. "Just be more careful next time. I hope you're not burned too bad," he called out.

"I'm sure Brian has someone who can kiss it and make it all better," I heard Jerry say as I stared at the stain in the bathroom mirror.

"That's not happening," I hollered. "No intimacy until my cancer treatments are through. Doctor's orders."

Oscar hooted and Jerry asked, "Why's that?"

"My sperm's radioactive," I yelled. "Someone could get hurt. That's why Superman never has sex."

"What about Lois Lane?" Jerry asked.

"He always pulls out. Of course now that I've boiled my balls," I called out as I left the bathroom, "my jizm's probably no longer a health threat."

Oscar, a seventy year old Korean War vet, was blushing in the deep creases of his weather-beaten face. He directed my attention to the register, where Donna Erlingmayer stood.

"Oh hey Donna. I didn't hear you come in."

"I'm going to sneak in every time now," said Donna, a middle-aged Sun Country flight attendant, stewardess, waitress in the sky. "I had a feeling all the good conversation stops as soon as I show up."

"I try to tailor my stories to the customer," I said.

"I like 'em dirty," said Donna.

"Now I know."

"It isn't every day that Brian spills a cup of hot coffee on his lap," said Jerry, accurately.

"Oh no," said Donna. "Oh no," she repeated when she caught sight of my wet crotch. "Are you alright?"

"Maybe. I'll find out for sure tonight when I take my shorts off."

Oscar hoisted the Tahoe mug. "My cup is fine, you see."

"Good for you, Oscar," said Donna.

"Hey," I said to Jerry, "how about golf this afternoon? It's a beautiful day. Supposed to hit sixty."

Jerry stared at me for five seconds. "You can golf? It's fine for the leg?"

"The leg's fine. My back, though, that's another matter."

Jerry blinked a couple times. "The cancer moved into your back?"

Oscar and Donna froze. Flash-frozen. "No," I said, flash-thawing them. "I just have a sore back."

"Probably from the other night," Jerry said to no one in particular.

"God help me, my back kills me most mornings," Oscar growled as he sat at his favorite table closest to the counter.

"Maybe it's cancer," I said. "You should get it checked."

Oscar shook his head, gazing at the little pine tree on his Lake Tahoe mug. "You can't joke about that kind of thing now."

"I know," I said. "But I still do."

"You have to joke about it," said Donna. "It's all you can do sometimes."

"That's for sure," said Oscar. "My cousin died of cancer when he was thirty-eight."

There was a moment of silence for Oscar's cousin, for cancer patients in general, for me. I turned to Jerry. "Golf?"

He had mapped out a safe, acceptable conversation. "You're jumping the gun, Brian. The courses aren't open yet. Not until May."

"Are you serious? Not one? No matter how nice the weather is?"

"How long have you lived here that you don't know that?" Donna asked.

Jerry smiled and shook his head. There was no doubt he intended to speak. So we waited. He cleared his throat. "I go through this with Brian every spring. He forgets he's not in California anymore."

"It was Sacramento, right?" asked Donna.

"Davis," said Charlotte, breezing in from the alley door. "That's all I hear from Brian, how *wonderful* Davis was."

"Just the weather," I said, moving into high gear, pulling shots and cranking up the frother, matching Charlotte's crisp movements at the cash register as a host of regulars converged on the front door, six o'clock sharp.

"Tom," I greeted the middle school science teacher. His skull was knobby, his hair was long and stringy, his drink was the depth charge.

"Brian, hey there," said Tom, "good morning. I was afraid I was early. Thanks for being open, not making me stand out there in the cold."

"It's beautiful out there, what are you talking about." I held up a shot of espresso in one hand, rearranging milk pitchers with the other; Charlotte held out a large coffee in a to-go cup; I dumped in the shot, the depth charge. I could have poured it without looking, we were such a well-oiled machine.

"Brian's California dreaming," Charlotte told Tom as she fitted on a lid. "That'll be one-eighty-five."

"C'mon," I complained. "It's a warm, beautiful day. It's a crime the golf courses aren't open. A crime! Melissa," I called out to the elementary school principal coming through the door. "Tell them it's a crime!"

"Whatever happened, I think Brian's guilty," Melissa testified.

"That's a pretty good rule of thumb," said Charlotte. "Brian's guilty, guilty until proven innocent. Adam, XL latté?" she verified with the auto mechanic standing quietly in line.

"You know it," said Adam. He already had a grease smudge on his cheek.

"I'm getting crucified here," I announced. "Feel free to step in at any time and defend me," I told Adam.

"Oh I will," he said, eyes on Charlotte's chest.

I banged out the used grounds and refilled and holstered the espresso bucket. I gave Adam a strong look as I handed him his drink. "When you finally get around to it, it'll probably be too late. Just so you know."

Adam grinned. "Charlotte, thanks for the drink."

"I'm the one who made the drink," I grumbled. "I make the drink, while getting pounded, and you get the thank you."

Charlotte laughed. "What can I say, Adam likes me better."

"Maybe it's the string tanktops," said Tom the hippy science teacher, sitting at the counter.

"I don't have any choice," Charlotte pouted. "It's at least one hundred degrees back here." She turned to the next customer, a new face in the store, and turned on the charm. "What can I get for you?"

"I count on those tanktops to deliver the tips," I told Tom. "Don't make her feel self-conscious."

"Skin equals tips?" Tom wondered.

"Don't go there," said Charlotte, blushing ever-so-slightly. The new face at the till happened to be a handsome one.

"What do you recommend?" the new face asked.

"I personally like our mochas," said Charlotte. "They're not so sweet, but the chocolate flavor is intense. If you're looking for a cold drink, the mocha smoothie is our most popular."

"I'll take a mocha," the young man decided.

"Do you want it hot?"

"I do."

"Would you like whipped cream on that?" Charlotte asked, and then bowed her head and started to giggle as Tom and Donna and Melissa all laughed. Now it was the young man's turn to blush.

"Brian." Jerry stood at the front door. I got the feeling he had been there awhile, scripting. "I may have an alternative golf plan for us."

"Do what you can, homey. I'm itching to swing the clubs."

PRIOR TO GETTING TO KNOW the Grundens, I could pretend I was living as frugally as possible. My apartment, basic cable, half-price appetizers before six at Lucky's—what are Things That Are Affordable. A trailer house hauled from the family farm, network television with tinfoil rabbit ears, a side of beef from a cow you butchered yourself, what are Free Things.

After golf, it was back to Joshua and Denise's trailer house for dinner. We drank Jerry's beer as we waited for the oven timer to buzz. Joshua, Denise and I lounged on a calico couch, the fabric worn but clean. Jerry sat in a reupholstered chair with JG '93 carved in the wood below the curved claw arm.

I could picture both pieces of furniture sitting twenty years ago in Joshua's folks' living room. (And I could picture the stuffed timberwolf on the wall mount, striking the same pose against the Montana skyline right before Joshua plugged him.) Earlier that day, Joshua, Jerry and I had detoured to the Grunden farm outside the little town of Kulm, to drop off a rebuilt lawnmower motor on the way to the local golf course. We ended up staying for lunch. The Grundens had a classic farmstead, a two-story house with a broad porch, a red barn, a steel Quonset, two stuffed-sausage dogs halfheartedly chasing the chickens and avoiding the goose. Cats, lots of them. An old pickup and a newer one, both really muddy. A smiling mom who fed us schnitzel and potatoes and gravy and green beans in butter sauce, before we hit the links.

Long day, lots of walking, much sun. Devoted the last of my energy on the drive home to suavely swapping Jerry for Isabel as my dinner date, when I should have been laboring to beg out of it. Not that I wouldn't have been in the exact same position at home, slouched into the corner of the couch with a beer in hand; except my eyes would be closed. I was by no means unhappy hanging with Joshua, Denise and Jerry; in fact, surrounded by a few of my favorite people sounded like the perfect venue for a nap.

"The pizza smells great," I told Denise. My end of the couch was next to the deep freeze. Denise sat at the other end, with Joshua in the middle. "But I don't know how much I can eat. I'm still stuffed from lunch."

"That was a pretty big meal," Jerry agreed, stretching his long legs and patting his stomach. "How did your mom know we were coming for lunch?"

"She didn't," said Joshua. "She always cooks that much."

"What did your mom cook?" Denise quizzed him. Denise was tall, full-figured, with strong almost mannish features. She was a good-looking woman. A handsome woman, perhaps. She carried herself very erect, and she moved with a fluid grace. She was regal, with her first-rate posture.

"Schnitzel and knepfla."

"Oh for crying out loud," said Denise.

"What?" Joshua exclaimed.

Denise slapped his thigh. "Your mom makes too much for lunch."

"It's not a bad thing," I said. "The food was unbelievable."

"See!?" said Joshua.

"I'd hate to see what your dad's cholesterol level is," said Denise. "If he ever got it checked."

"I'd hate to see mine!" Joshua countered. "Look at what you're feeding me! Pizza, strudel, cheesy hotdishes!" He laughed his crazy cackle.

Denise raised her eyebrows and tapped Joshua's knee. "What did I feed you last night? Hm? Tell Brian and Jerry what I fed you."

Joshua shook his head. "I don't remember." He grinned at me.

"It was fish, wasn't it?" Denise made her point in a controlled soothing manner. "Baked fish. How many nights a week do we have fish?"

"Not enough." Joshua laughed and slapped his own thighs and sprang to his feet. "Who's thirsty?"

"I could drink one more," I said.

"I'll take another, just to keep Brian company," said Jerry.

"So how did you like the golf course today?" Denise asked us.

"Those synthetic greens are wild, man," I said.

"They take some getting used to," said Jerry.

"You think *you* have a tough adjustment," said Joshua, returning with four beers. "I don't think there's a huge difference between grass greens and Kulm's greens. But try going from sand greens to synthetic. Man!"

Jerry's brow furrowed. "Sand?" Jerry had a great head, the perfect head for baldness. Prominent round forehead with perfectly spaced creases. My forehead was smooth and sloped.

"Kulm used to have sand greens," said Denise.

Joshua took a toot from his Moosehead. "The oil was seeping into the ground. The EPA was going to fine the town, so we replaced them."

"Oil?" said Jerry.

"If you don't oil the sand," said Joshua, "it blows away."

"Makes sense," I said.

"In the old days you could really attack the flag," Joshua said wistfully. "I got really good at lofting my chip shots. Now the ball bounces right off."

"That happened to me once or twice out there today," I said.

"I remember it *not* happening once or twice," said Jerry.

"I'm so tired of Joshua complaining about those greens," said Denise.

"But at least we're out there playing when every other course is still shut down!" Joshua reminded us.

"Amen," I said to the clink of the beer bottle toast.

"Did your mom send any more deer steaks with you?" Denise asked.

Joshua glanced at Jerry and me. He shook his head. "No deer."

Actually, there had been. We first spotted the beast sauntering across the fifth green out in the far southeast corner of the course. Joshua had joked that he should shoot it, not an idle threat, because he had a .22 rifle in his golf bag.

As we approached the seventh green, the deer reappeared on the adjacent tee box. It struck a Hartford elk pose on the elevated mound. Without saying a word Joshua drew his .22 and sighted the beast. I caught his toppling golf bag as he fired. The deer's legs buckled. By then the temperature had fallen so that we could see our breath, and I never saw another puff of steam exit the nostrils of the deer, truly dead before it hit the ground.

"Holy Hannah!" Joshua had run forward, and then stopped. He turned and looked back at us. He was wide-eyed.

"You killed a deer with a .22," I observed. "That really shouldn't happen."

"I took a head shot," said Joshua. "I didn't think I'd hit him."

"That's over a hundred yards without a scope," said Jerry. "Not bad."

"Yeah," said Joshua, with no satisfaction.

"I don't believe it's deer season," I said.

"No," said Joshua, shaking his head. He looked dizzy.

"Maybe Fish & Wildlife has an exemption for lucky shots," said Jerry.

"I don't think so," said Joshua. "Let's not tell Denise about this, okay? She hates it when I do this."

We were still standing there, seventy-five yards from the green, twenty feet from Joshua's ball. I had hit a beautiful approach shot and would have been on if it weren't for those Astroturf greens. My ball had caromed away and was waiting for me over by the deer.

I caddied Joshua's bag to his ball. He marched up, pulled out an iron and hit his chip shot without taking any practice swings. It was a pretty fair shot.

The three of us dragged the dead deer with the hole for an eye into the tall grass, atop a steep slope above a slough far below. I had envisioned the deer tumbling all the way to the frozen waterline, swallowed up by the cattails. Instead, we were barely able to shove the carcass below the ridgeline and out of sight. After the round Joshua drove his pickup through the planted fields and grasslands bordering the course, all the way back to the eighth teebox. We loaded the deer into the bed and dropped it off at Joshua's parents' house. Mrs. Grunden promised not to tell Denise. I had played terrible golf but was consoled by the prospect of a couple pounds of jerky and sausage.

"...Brian? Brian? Hey buddy, are you still with us?"

I had dozed off, thinking and then dreaming about the deer. Denise leaned across Joshua, looking down on me with a mixture of humor, anxiety and pity.

I straightened up and wiped away drool. "Did I miss anything?"

"It's that deep freeze." Denise nodded unhappily at the big top-loader beside me. "You can't hear a thing at that end of the couch."

"That's why we can't have it in the spare bedroom," Joshua countered. "Guests can't sleep with all that noise."

"Clearly that's not true," said Jerry, nodding to me.

"And that's not the real reason," said Denise. "The real reason is that Joshua has to have his precious deep freeze where he can see it and fantasize about the next deer he's going to kill."

Joshua sat there with a weird, faraway look. Jerry and I exchanged a glance and then took a long pull from our beers. "Now that I took that trout off your hands," I said, "you should have room in the freezer for some deer meat." I felt a huge case of the giggles coming on. Joshua saw it and shook his head, one quick barely-noticeable back and forth twitch.

"Was the trout good?" Denise asked.

"Excellent."

"What trout?" said Jerry.

"I gave Brian a couple trout filets from when I went fishing at the Garrison dam last weekend."

Now it was my turn to squirm. I could see into the conversational future as well as Jerry.

"I had twelve filets in there." Joshua looked forlornly at the humming freezer. "I only have two left. Man they were good." I could feel him looking at me. I had a faraway look in my eye. "When are you going to eat the other one?" he asked.

"Hm? Other one?"

"The other filet."

"If I knew you were in love with those trout, I never would have asked."

"Come on," Joshua prodded. "I give a guy two of the most beautiful filets you'll ever see. The least you can do is tell me what you did with them."

"Were there two?" I debated. "I'm not sure. There were no leftovers."

"They were good-size trout." Joshua held his hands twenty-four inches apart. "I gave you two."

"Actually *I* gave Brian the fish," Denise clarified.

"Yes it was Denise," I said.

"And it was two," said Denise.

"Does Brian always borrow food from you?" Jerry wondered.

"I do," I said. "Sometimes I'll even cook them a meal. It all evens out."

"Who were you cooking for last night?" Joshua asked.

"My cancer therapist," I said. "Denise, do you have any Tylenol? My bone cancer is really hurting all of a sudden."

Denise reached across Joshua to squeeze my hand. She rose gracefully and glided into the kitchen.

"I'm sorry if you're hurting, buddy." Joshua mirrored Denise's compassion. Then it was gone. "So who was your date last night?"

Jerry's eyes gleamed. "It wasn't a date," I said.

"I don't care what you call it," said Joshua. He was relentless. "Who was at your place?"

"I'd rather not say, I guess."

"Well I'd rather you did," said Joshua. "We'd like to know." Jerry nodded.

If I hadn't been engaged, this would have been fun—I pretend that I want to keep my new conquest a secret; Joshua, Denise and Jerry persist; I finally give in, outwardly embarrassed and uncomfortable about kissing and telling, proud as hell on the inside.

And maybe Joshua's digging was good-natured. As seldom as Iz and I were together anymore, our friends could have assumed our relationship was over. But regardless whether his intent was innocent, the results would not be.

Here came Denise with my Tylenol. "If Brian doesn't want to tell you, Joshua, he doesn't have to."

"I don't want people getting the wrong idea, that's all." I washed down the pills while Jerry studied me. I decided he had put Joshua on the hunt. Jerry wanted to scare me, shame me, tattoo a temporary scarlet letter on my forehead. I expected my friends to come equipped with strong moral judgment; it was an attractive quality, except when they started using it on me.

I swallowed. "Tell you the truth, I'm realizing right now that it was bad judgment. It doesn't look good. I haven't been thinking things through lately. You know, the cancer diagnosis and all."

Joshua nodded and waited. I was a treed raccoon and no one was going to call off the dogs.

"Of course, in the long run I don't know if it even matters." I sighed, letting them know I was reluctant to continue.

"Why?" Denise prompted.

"Well...how much do you guys know about Isabel's background?"

"I know her a little bit," said Jerry.

"I see her down at Mike's office," said Joshua.

"I don't know her at all," said Denise. "So go ahead."

"Let's see, how do I put this? Isabel has had what some might call an experimental past. Others might call it illegal."

"Others might call it what?" Denise poked her head in closer. She slapped Joshua's arm. "I hate that deep freeze! We should unplug it when we have company! I swear I miss half of what's said."

"It's not the freezer. You're going deaf, woman," Joshua said pitilessly.

Denise laughed. "That could be."

They all three leaned closer to hear me, three coon dogs confused about what exactly was up in that tree. "Isabel had sex with a minor," I told them. "Back when she was a teacher."

"That's statutory rape," Denise charged.

I nodded solemnly. "I don't know about North Dakota law, but I understand homosexual sex can be illegal, too, regardless of age."

"What do you...?" Denise put her hand to her mouth. "Oh my."

Joshua giggled high and crazy. "Oh boy. You're saying that she...oh boy." He shook his head and groaned.

"Maybe this is something you shouldn't be spreading around," said Jerry, looking upset, perhaps regretting he had tabloided my ass.

"Maybe you're right." If I was about to get slammed for being unfaithful to Isabel, they were going to know the whole story. "But I've been struggling with my feelings for Isabel. It happened six years ago, before I met her. What she did is in the past, I'm pretty sure. I should probably forget about it. But I can't. Am I being unreasonable? I could use some help sorting out my feelings on this, and I know I can trust the three of you not to spread this around."

Denise was aghast, Joshua stunned, Jerry ill. *Hey homey, I can relate.* While we talked over homemade pizza, Denise became more and more indignant over Isabel's behavior. Joshua withdrew into his own thoughts. Jerry was stuck in pause mode, unable to model an acceptable conversational path.

At the end of the meal, at the point where Denise was ready to call Isabel or the police, I changed the subject, to my upcoming San Diego trip. Everyone agreed Muslims are scary. The mood brightened. Pretty soon Joshua jumped up and grabbed a deck of cards. Everyone had had enough of the heavy stuff for one night. We played spoons, hearts and then whist for the next three hours. After Denise and I set Joshua and Jerry for the third straight hand, Jerry threw his cards at Joshua in disgust and stretched.

"I'm tired."

"Yeah," I agree. "It's time to hit the road."

Denise cleared coffee cups and beer bottles while Joshua escorted us to the door. We were a couple steps down the sidewalk when Joshua asked me to stick around.

"Just me?"

"Do you have a few minutes?"

"Sure. Yeah. I shouldn't get to bed too late tonight, but okay. Sure."

"Goodnight," said Jerry. It looked like he was running away.

We went back inside and sat down. Denise turned off the kitchen lights, kissed us both goodnight, and excused herself. Joshua sat on the edge of the couch, elbows propped on his knees, wearing for him a serious face. "So I'll bet your cancer has you really shook up."

"Not right at this moment so much. But if I think about it long enough…"

He scooted forward until the couch contributed minimal support. "I can't imagine what you're going through. You and I, we're too young to be expected to deal with this."

"Don't tell me you have cancer too?"

"No. No." Joshua chortled softly.

Too bad. For that instant I had my hopes up—I could have used a buddy, charging into battle with me against this fucking ridiculous disease.

"But I'm suffering for you," said Joshua.

"I know. I hate to put all my friends through this. Almost more than I hate going through it myself. Part of me wants to have all my friends and family envelop me. We'd all move into a commune together and kumbaya the crap out of 'our' cancer. Another part wants me to run away, far far away. Nova Scotia, Kenai Alaska, the Congo, Fargo. Just disappear. Deal with life, death, and everything in between, all by myself."

"No no, you belong here, that's for sure." Joshua was humorless and solemn like I had never seen him. "You've been in Jamestown for what, just a few years, right? I've only known you for three years, and I don't think I know anybody with more friends than you. It's amazing how many lives you've touched. So many people are pulling for you."

"I'm blessed. I've been pleasantly surprised at all the people stopping by to say hi. Even if they don't buy a drink. Which makes me a little angry. I mean, as long as you're in the shop, right? Why not buy a drink? Just a drip coffee, that's all I ask."

"I know, I know." Joshua chuckled.

"I notice you don't buy a drink every time you stop in."

Joshua giggled. "I'm a poor college student, what can I say."

I nodded knowingly like the Dalai Lama.

Joshua struck his own zen pose, fingers pressed to his temples, rocking back and forth on the bit of his ass cheeks clinging to the couch, seeking to return to his serious place. I had thought his brow was too smooth and tight to furrow. "Friends are great," he said. "Friends are very important. We have to have friends." It was a laborious segue. "But there's something else we need to consider. It's something we should already have squared away. But sometimes it takes a crisis like this to push us in the right direction."

"I don't know if I'm in crisis mode anymore," I said. "The chemo and radiation seem to have helped quite a bit."

"I think it's definitely a crisis." Joshua was resting his face against steepled fingers, concentrating on my beltline, occasionally looking into my eyes. His were very alive and excited. "Sometimes God uses something like this to send us a signal. To tell us it's time to make a change."

"A little wake-up call," I confirmed.

Joshua nodded. "Or a big one. Brian, I don't know what you believe, about God, and Jesus Christ. But—"

"I do—" We both talked at once.

"Go ahead." Joshua was eager to hear what I had to say.

"I was going to say that it's a private thing for me. Partly because I have to be very careful not to bring politics or religion into the shop."

"It is private and you do have a business to consider," Joshua agreed.

Next topic, I thought to myself.

"But if you had to describe your relationship with God..."

How to give him just enough comfort in my spirituality without opening the door to any long-winded theological discussions. "It's pretty straightforward. I believe in God. I go to church on an irregular basis. I'm very non-denominational about it. I just want to do what it takes to make it to heaven."

"Exactly!" Joshua clapped his hands. "You wanna do whatever it takes to get to heaven! I am amazed you realize that. Most people would say that they want to be good people, or serve other people, or do what God asks of them. But the whole goal is to get to heaven. And we never know when we're going to die. I mean, you got cancer, but I could go first."

"I hope you do. But I hope you live to be a hundred."

"I'll go first, gladly. You know what? Dying doesn't scare me."

"Me neither. It terrifies me."

"Is that because you're afraid of not going to heaven?"

"That, sure. And the lack of being alive. I got a lot of living to do. I have a big to-do list, and I can't seem to get to any of it."

Joshua used my own Dalai Lama nod on me. "What if I told you that you could guarantee getting into heaven?" He reclined into the couch, eyes wide.

"I'd say, wow, that's great. Then I'd wonder what's the trade-off? Do I have to sell all my worldly possessions and become a missionary?"

"It's a lot easier than that."

"Because I owe so much money, I really don't own anything. If God wants me to drop everything today and move to Costa Rica, I'm ready."

Joshua shook his head vehemently. "There's no need for that. God wants you to keep working."

"But should I stay in coffee? I'm having a hard time figuring that out. If I am, why would He send Bill Hernandes here to sell coffee too, and eat into my volume?" That's me being funny, without joking.

"Maybe it's a test."

"If I pass this one, I suppose He'll send in Starbucks next."

"I don't think you have anything to worry about. Everyone loves you so much, I don't think a Starbucks could compete."

"I hope God knows the coffee business better than you do."

"I'm sure He does." Joshua never cracked a smile. "You know, we're talking about going to Heaven. But what I'm going to tell you will have an impact on this life, too. It can make every part of your life better. Your job. Your relationships. Especially your relationship with Isabel."

"Either I need to get a hankering for fifteen-year-old girls, or Isabel needs to lose hers. Either way, it might take a miracle."

"You need to have grace," Joshua ministered. "Grace for those around you and grace for yourself. As far as Isabel is concerned, it might just take forgiveness. But that'll be between the two of you. Or three of you."

Joshua could have been including Andrea or God in this threesome.

"Brian, you can't believe the changes that are possible, when you take Jesus into your heart. It's unbelievable." Joshua was momentarily at a loss. "I have a hard time describing the feeling. Denise does a much better job. But I wanted this talk to be just the two of us. You and I get along so well together."

For now at least.

"Has anyone asked you to accept Jesus Christ as your personal savior?"

The silence inside the trailer house was deafening. Denise made no sound in the back bedroom. I felt like the rest of the world had gone to bed or ceased to exist. Glimpses out the trailer's windows revealed no lights, no life. Absolutely nothing to distract from our conversation, just that damn deep freeze.

If I didn't like Joshua so much—if he wasn't so earnest about this—I would have thanked him for dinner and walked out. "Not that I recall."

Joshua took a deep breath. "I was really skeptical when it happened to me. It seemed like it was out of the blue. I was definitely not searching for anything. I believed in God, in a vague way. I believed, but I didn't really know why, or what I believed. I thought simply believing was enough."

"But I'm assuming it wasn't."

Joshua giggled in amazement, shaking his head. "It wasn't even close. I was so confident that I knew everything there was to know about God. I didn't know how close I was to dying and not going where I thought I was going."

"Heaven, you mean."

Joshua nodded slowly. "I should have been searching for more. I should have been searching for salvation. Luckily God was searching for me. He's always searching, reaching, moving toward you. I see that now."

"How do you see that?" If I didn't comment, if I didn't ask questions, if I just let Joshua drill me with what felt like a prepared but no less passionate speech, my brain was going to swell with frustration until I dropped an F-bomb and stormed out of there. Plus I was a little curious.

"I just feel it," said Joshua. "I used to love to smoke and drink and have sex. Now I have absolutely no urge to do any of that."

"You and Denise…you don't…"

"Oh we do."

"Good. That's good. So you were quite the party animal, huh?"

"I was terrible, Brian." Joshua was shocked by his own behavior. "I was out partying every night, starting in eighth grade."

"I think we all go through that phase."

"This was more than a phase. That's why Pastor Frontius came to me. He wasn't even my pastor. He's Assembly of God at our church in Kulm. I was Baptist. He says God spoke to him every night for a week in his dreams, tell-

ing him to save me. Maybe He did," Joshua mused. "I know it saved my life."
He looked at me sideways. We stared at each other, taking turns nodding.

"What?" I said.

Joshua was reluctant to say. "You're not going to believe it."

"Maybe I won't. But that's okay. Did God tell you to save me?"

Joshua nodded. "It wasn't in a dream. I was wide awake. It was after I saw
you at the new retail center yesterday."

"Retail center. Not 'strip mall'. Mike would be so proud of you."

Joshua popped to his feet and crouched beside my chair. "This is *really*
strange. I was sitting in my Econ class taking a test. I was supposed to answer
a fill-in-the-blank question about the demand curve. I think the answer was
increasing. Instead I wrote *Save Brian.*"

The hair stood up on my shin, cancer leg. "How many points did that cost
you?"

"I'm getting a D anyway," said Joshua, trying to stay on task. He bowed
his head for a moment. "Does talking about religion make you nervous?"

"Not religion in general. But this topic, about accepting Jesus as my personal savior…yep. Very uncomfortable."

"Don't be." He gripped the arm of my chair, flexing the frame beneath me
and making it creak. "There's nothing difficult about the process. There's
nothing to be afraid of. Maybe nothing will change, not right away anyway.
But maybe you'll feel something happen immediately."

"Is that the way it was for you?"

"Oh yeah. I felt …I can't describe it, but it was unbelievable. I knew immediately I had done the right thing. I could feel Jesus." Joshua thumped
knuckles to his chest. "I could feel Him in there, Brian. And in here," he
added, pointing at his skull.

"You know, sometimes I definitely think I can feel Him, you know, in my
heart or whatever." These sorts of words were never spoken in my family or
even my church. These words did not flow easily from my mouth. "Sometimes it's more difficult to feel it. You know, to feel…Him."

Joshua was nodding in agreement.

"I suppose it's the same for you."

"Actually, I feel Him all the time now. When I'm playing football or basketball, when I'm on the tractor. Today playing golf."

"We invented a new sport, by the way. The Dakota Biathlon."

"Can you believe that shot?" Joshua cackled, a wary eye on the hallway.

There were moments in the next half-hour that I was talking to Joshua,
just Joshua, and it was great. Most of the time I was one-on-one with an info-
mercial pitchman, dealing in my everlasting soul instead of my flabby abs, and
I couldn't wait to get out of there. I tried making the case for the equal merits

of the Christian community's varying Biblical interpretations, for my fuzzy notion that good people and good dogs—or was it all dogs?—go to heaven.

And then Joshua would scare the shit out of me with his vivid depiction of a torture-chamber Hell, and I would come that close to repeating after him.

I believe Jesus Christ was crucified and died for my sins. I believe he rose from the dead and ascended into heaven. I believe the only way to get to heaven is through Him, to accept Jesus Christ as my personal savior...

I wasn't incapable of believing in dramatic faith conversions. In fact I always assumed sooner or later it would happen to me. I just felt like it would be a bolt of lightning, an epiphany. Something poetic, something dramatic, something by myself. Not in a trailer.

Joshua was up and down, never seated for more than a couple minutes, quick to realize his frenetic pacing was a distraction and return to the couch. When he sat down, his jeans stretched tight across his thighs, outlining perfect quads. Sitting was like cocking a crossbow. He should have smacked his head on the ceiling when he released the catch.

"Before you're saved," said Joshua, "you can feel God, sometimes. You know He's watching you. But then the feeling leaves, and you go about your business, and you kind of forget that He's there. These are the times we do things we shouldn't. When we give in to temptation. Believe me, I know. I know how weak we can be."

"Whether I feel God watching over me or not, I constantly challenge myself to make the right decision."

"We all do," Joshua agreed, "and we usually fail. We can't make the right decision without God's guidance. And we don't have his guidance without Jesus. Jesus is our go-between. We need him in our hearts, to hear his voice at those crucial moments. Should I take this beer someone is offering me? Or this girl, offering herself? Or snort this line of coke? Right? How many times do you make the right decision in these moments?"

"Joshua, you've never done coke, admit it."

"No, but I did smoke a marijuana joint once. I hated it. I could hardly walk. But I love beer. No matter how much I drank, I could walk straight. And run and jump, and other things. I felt like Superman when I drank."

"I just think everything's funny when I tie one on."

"It's the devil at work."

"Amen, suckah."

Joshua sat down again on the edge of the couch, cocking those quads, shrugging off my attempt to lighten him up. "But you know, as important as it is to have Jesus in your heart to help you make the right choices, that's not the biggest reason. You know what I'm going to say, don't you?"

"No, not really." At this point I was putty in his hands, numb and exhausted from the day, the treatments, the sales pitch.

"I almost don't want to talk about it," he said, "because it's so serious. I think about all the people I know, good people, who aren't going to heaven when they die. No matter how good a person you are. No matter how many good deeds you do."

My throat went dry. Dri*er*.

"It doesn't even matter if you make all the right choices in life. There's only one way to get to heaven. It's through Jesus Christ."

This would have scared the bejesus out of me even without the potentially terminal disease. Since I was a teenager, I've laid awake far too many nights for way too long, trying to imagine and then trying not to imagine the feeling when I died. The lack of feeling.

Trying to Believe, solely to gain comfort in the existence of an afterlife. Trying to believe that even if I didn't Believe, there was indeed an afterlife, and thanks to my innate goodness and strong work ethic and plentiful close friendships, there was no way I wasn't a strong candidate for admission, regardless my lack of faith.

Whether Joshua knew it or not, his pitch was tailored to my fears. What a deal: an irrevocable ticket to Heaven, no fussing with faith in God, Jesus will take care of that, just say the magic words and climb aboard.

"I'm afraid for you, Brian." Joshua curled in on himself, clenching his hands together and drawing his elbows tighter to his body. "I will always be grateful for Pastor Frontius taking the time to have this talk with me. He saved me. He saved me from not going to heaven. He saved me from going to Hell. I can save you Brian. Sorry, scratch that, Jesus can save you. But I can help."

Hell I could handle. It was Nothingness that scared me. In Hell, no matter how terrible, at least I would be feeling something. I can take an awful lot of pain. At least I would be alive, conscious, still Brian. Put me in Hell, and I'll never give up. I'll escape, if there is any conceivable way. I'm a single-minded purpose kind of guy. Give me a task, a goal, and I like my odds.

"He's made it so easy for us," Joshua referred to God. "I remember thinking it can't be that easy—"

"That's where I'm at right now," I said. "It seems like your actions should be the most important test of your worthiness to get into Heaven. Actions should speak louder than words."

Joshua laughed, the contrarian mocking the absurdity of conventional wisdom, reveling in the secret inside information he was sharing with me. "That's what you would have thought, right?" he exclaimed, nodding.

"You know the adage, if it seems too good to be true, don't be an idiot."

Joshua chuckled, shook his head, lost his smile. "Not in this case. If there was ever somebody for whom the normal rules don't apply, it's Jesus, right?"

"I suppose so."

"So what do you think? Do you want to do this?"

"Right now?"

"Right now! I'll tell you what to say, we'll ask Jesus to come into your life right now." Joshua ran to the little bookcase and retrieved his Bible. He had the spot bookmarked. No, the bookmark was what he was after; on it was the paragraph password to Heaven. He left the Bible lying open on the couch. "You just have to repeat after me."

"Joshua, man…" I grimaced and sank back into the chair. "I don't know. This is really fast. I need time to think about it."

"But what's to think about? It's clear cut. You have to accept Jesus Christ as your personal savior, or you don't go to Heaven. It's as simple as that."

"I know you fully believe what you're saying, and I know you put a lot of thought into it, and I respect that, very much. But I'm not an impulsive guy."

"Okay. I understand that. I am an impulsive guy, but I know not everyone moves as fast as I do. It drives Denise crazy sometimes."

"I've never seen a woman who loves her husband as much as Denise loves you. It's very impressive."

"I have a great thing going," said Joshua. "But I wouldn't, if I hadn't made the choice I'm offering you. And that's the beautiful thing—it's not really even a choice. You don't even have to believe that what I'm saying is true. You just have to ask Jesus into your life. He'll do the rest."

I pondered this one for awhile. Joshua stared at me the whole time. He is the most earnest honest forthright person I have ever known. His stare carried great weight. I was going to shrink in his eyes if I refused him.

"I need time to think about it."

This troubled him. "I know that's usually the right approach. But this is one of those times, maybe the only one, where you might not get another chance. He's watching us right now, Brian. I don't know how to say this, but…this might be your only invitation."

"That's a scary thought."

"Very scary. It scares me. I have goosebumps right now. Look at that." Joshua stuck out his arm and pulled back his sleeve. His forearm was lightly tanned and hairless. All the veins and bands of muscle were prickled with gooseflesh. "I know I shouldn't be so worried about you. But I am."

"I appreciate that. I really really do. I just don't know…"

And so it went for another few minutes. When the clock struck midnight, I was ready to say anything, nearly anything, to get out of there.

"Joshua, thank you, for everything you've done and said. I know it's not easy to do what you've done for me tonight."

"It's incredibly easy," said Joshua, as fresh as ever. "It's life or death."

"I know." I rose, for the first time in a long time. "But I can't do it tonight. You've made a big impression. No matter what the outcome, I'm very impressed with everything you told me."

Joshua was distraught about letting me leave, unsaved.

"I know what you're saying, that all I need to do is say the words, and Jesus will do the rest, but..." I loved the feel of the doorknob. I twisted it and pulled and bathed in the fresh cold air sweeping over me. "It doesn't feel right for me to say it, yet."

Joshua put his hand on the edge of the door; it slid off and fell to his side. His mouth moved, searching for some other combination of the same words that would finally get through to me.

I was on the bottom step when I had a change of heart. "Joshua, I'm sorry. This isn't for me. I can't do it. Ever. I have all the respect in the world for you and your belief. But it's not for me. I'll take the risk I'm wrong. I'm sorry."

I backpedaled down the gravelly sidewalk. "Tell Denise thanks for dinner. It was excellent. I'll have you guys over soon."

Joshua nodded dumbly.

"Good night."

I drove home with the window rolled down, laughing in big gasps and cursing the pressure Life had put on me, the injustice of having to fly blind and the horrifying downside of making the wrong choice.

T - 10

"We should have driven together," said Andrea after she had settled in beside me at the gate for our shuttle flight to Denver.

"I don't think that would have been a good idea."

She ribbed me cheerfully. "Come on, who would have seen anything?"

I could say she followed me. Stalked me. I could say it was a coincidence. No one would believe me. Even though no one else from the Chamber was on our flight, I was resigned to being busted. I was prepared to simply tell the truth and let the chips fall, let them fall where they may. "I guarantee you somebody here at the airport is going to recognize me and see us together."

"Oh and that's so bad why?" Andrea wondered. It wasn't an act. Andrea genuinely felt innocent. Or at least not guilty.

I gave her a sidelong look. "I can't believe you bought a ticket to San Diego."

"I can't tell you how bad I need a vacation."

She did. I did. We didn't.

"Okay everyone." A United Express attendant whisked through the waiting area, ten seats back-to-back in the middle of the floor and five seats by the window. "We'll board the flight to Denver now. Please follow me. We'll take your boarding passes at the aircraft door."

Thirteen of us filed down the stairs and outside, across the tarmac to the fired-up turbo prop. The pilot was waiting to welcome us at the door. "I saw it's supposed to be eighty degrees in San Diego today," said Andrea. The buzz of the plane's engine grew exponentially louder with each step. "I can't wait to get there." She kept talking, but that was the last thing I could hear.

Mercifully it wasn't much quieter on board. I fell instantly asleep, didn't even wake up for the take-off.

THE LEG to San Diego was on a much bigger, quieter plane. Andrea had again booked the seat next to me. She made a comment how she hated the middle seat, but I didn't offer her the aisle.

In the Denver airport during the two-hour layover, we dined at a restaurant close to our gate. Andrea had been so smug and content with our elopement of sorts as we climbed down from the little plane and strolled across the Denver tarmac, soaking up the view of the white mountains shimmering in the west, that I had decided to put her on the spot for leaving her kid behind, on a lark, on a junket. If I couldn't shame her, I could at least let her know how I felt.

But then she spent most of our breakfast time talking about Tyler. How he couldn't go to bed until she read him at least three picture books. I found myself visualizing the two of them cuddled up in a big easy chair—I could hear the tone of Andrea's voice, motherly and happy, the cynical edge missing. She talked about how Tyler loved to go to the playground, even in the winter, forcing his mom to freeze her ass off on a snowy bench while he played on the equipment. I'll be damned if she didn't love her kid.

Andrea was easy to hang with. She rambled on about working at the hospital, about how messed up Rick was, about daily life with her son. She even asked a couple questions—not about me, really, but my relationship with Isabel and Rick and the rest of the McEwens. I didn't give her much information or insight. She recognized the stonewall and accepted it with a sly smile.

On the flight to San Diego I tried to nap while Andrea planned her vacation from a book called *Choose San Diego*.

"Your meetings are close to Old Town, right? It says that's a fun area to visit, but that all the nightlife is downtown in the Gaslamp Quarter."

I kept my eyes closed. "I've never been to San Diego."

"It says they have a great mass transit system, so we shouldn't need to rent a car. But I've also heard they have an illegal immigrant problem."

"Makes sense."

"So I'm thinking we should rent a car anyway."

"I told you, I'm going to be with the Chamber group, pretty much the entire time. So you do what you want."

Andrea let the book flop shut on her lap. "Do you think it's safe for me to go out at night on my own?"

"If I had to make a recommendation? I'd avoid hitting the clubs alone."

Andrea crossed her arms. "You're making me angry."

"I wish I could make this the vacation you're dreaming of. I just can't."

Andrea shifted to face me. "Would you *let* me go out alone?"

I started to say, wanted to say, *sure, it's a free country, do whatever you want, that's your credo anyway, regardless how inappropriate*. But she was so tiny in that seat. Her feet barely reached the floor, for God's sake. "No," I had to say, feeling more than anything fatherly, like Denzel Washington as a burned-out bodyguard for the little American girl. "I wouldn't let you."

"Well okay then." Satisfied, Andrea went back to reading.

WE RENTED A CAR. As we drove to the Old Town district, our mayor, our delegation's leader, called to tell me we were meeting for breakfast for a final strategy meeting. The night, what was left of it, was ours, mine and Andrea's.

"Do you know where you're going?" Andrea asked.

"You asked me that already," I replied.

"Because we're still not there."

"Don't you think I know where we're going? Old Town. I think what you meant to ask was, do I know how to get there."

"Clearly the answer is No."

It was eight-thirty when we finally rolled into the Old Town district. It took me another twenty minutes to find the Clarion, an adobe-style hotel with the only lit-up sign on the ground behind a big yucca plant. I might have gone on a little rant, but I was just so glad to park the car and stand up.

I really hate to complain, to anyone, in any forum. If people ask me how I'm doing, I'll tell them truthfully, good or bad. But I won't volunteer my pain.

But let me tell you, I was in agony. The pain in my shin circled up the back of my thigh and filled my right butt cheek with fire. At this point, this *stage* I suppose, I was feeling it whenever I sat too long. All I had done that day was sit. I couldn't stand the thought of sitting down for dinner.

After checking in we stood at the foot of the stairs leading to our second floor rooms. I described my pain and finished with, "I can't go to dinner."

"Why not?" Andrea was crestfallen and angry.

Here was a nice reaffirmation of my conviction not to share my pain. I had been afraid of people pitying me, but when they didn't, that was worse. Although I guess I couldn't blame her. I had already convinced Andrea that walking the streets of San Diego alone was a death sentence. And the Clarion felt more like a motor inn than a full-service hotel. Room service was unlikely. If I didn't eat, Andrea didn't eat.

"I don't want to go to a restaurant," I said.

"So…" She stared at the floor like a child.

"I was thinking," at that very moment, "of ordering something to be delivered to my room. Should I order for two?"

"Yeah, well." She was softening. I had already learned to read her. Andrea was an easy read. "What are you going to order?"

"Are you a picky eater?"

"I ate your fish the other night."

"Hey now."

"A lot of girls wouldn't eat fish like that."

"I don't know about that. Meet me in my room in an hour?"

She pouted. "What am I going to do for an hour?"

"Half an hour? That's my lowest offer."

"Fine. You better have alcohol for us, that's all I'm going to tell you."

"Deal." I huffed her mammoth suitcase upstairs, pretending to be a porter hoping for a big tip, feeling more like her husband. She opened her room door for me to bull through and heave her load onto the bed, then followed me in, the door closing behind her. With raised eyebrows and an expectant grin she stood clogging the narrow passageway between the bed and television console. One of us was looking for a big tip indeed.

"Okay lady, give me thirty minutes. I'm going to squeeze past you now."

After a pause Andrea stepped back and aside, wearing a smirk and a sleeveless pink smock.

I ventured outside and down the nearly deserted street until I found a restaurant that was still open, returning to the hotel precisely a half-hour later with a box of pulled pork and rice, and a pitcher of mojitos. By the time I set the pitcher down on Andrea's dresser top, my leg was no longer in pain, just tired, a much better feeling.

We sat cross-legged on her bed facing each other over the food, plastic bathroom glasses filled with mojitos. "I'm impressed," said Andrea. "This isn't room service?"

"It's Brian service."

"Is this what I could expect on a regular basis?"

I shrugged. "We gotta eat, right?"

"And drink. San Diego is making me thirsty."

My cellphone rang. I checked the readout. "It's my folks. I better take it. Hey, this is Brian."

"Well hey there," my mom cooed, "we found you."

"Aren't cellphones nice?"

"Where are you?" The way she said it, somehow Mom could tell I wasn't in North Dakota.

I decided to lie; even though I was still a half-continent away, they'd be hurt to hear I was in the state and hadn't bothered to stop by. "Miami."

"No! Why?" With absolutely no basis, Mom was sure I was on the lam. Too many cop shows. She loved Harrison Ford in *The Fugitive*. Always had an alibi at the ready for me, in case things got dicey.

"A bunch of us from the chamber of commerce are doing road shows, to convince folks that North Dakota ain't so bad."

"You're in the chamber of commerce? Did we know that?"

"I've been in the Chamber for a few years. I'm pretty sure I told you."

Mom conferred with Dad who always lurked in the background. Dad liked his phone conversations filtered through Mom. "We're proud of you," said Mom. "The Chamber is lucky to have you. Honey, are you feeling okay?"

"I'm great." My self-assessment prompted Andrea to nod with smug satisfaction, so I downgraded myself. "I'm doing okay. How's things?"

"We're doing good. Your father pulled a muscle this morning climbing on a forklift to inspect some avocados." I heard Dad correcting her. "You father says it was a front-end loader and almond trees." Dad added clarification.

Mom sighed. "I guess he'll have to tell you himself. But he didn't stretch this morning, that's for sure." More kibitzing from the peanut gallery. "I know your body," Mom told him, ending his heckling. "Brian, I have to tell you it worries me to hear they have you traveling, and to Miami of all places."

After receiving the good news from Dr. Bonilla, I had finally told my folks about the cancer, as an afterthought, painted as a nuisance, like kidney stones or a yard fungus. Mom had still cried, and I could hear her lips quivering now. "I'm doing good," I assured her, watching Andrea propped against the headboard, bored, neglected. "I really should run here—"

"When is your surgery?" Mom asked, full of dread.

"In two weeks. I'm sure it'll go fine."

"We want you to come home to recuperate."

"To Davis? I'd like to…I just can't, Mom. I really appreciate the offer."

"Brian, I could take care of you."

"Mom, it's a minor surgery. A little clean-up, that's all. There probably won't even be anything left by then." I avoided words like *tumor* and *cancer* and *stage* and *disease* when I talked to my folks.

"You're not going to be able to walk, are you?" Mom was sure I would be a paraplegic.

"It could be a couple days on crutches, depending how much bone they need to remove. Don't worry, I'll still have the fibula." My new favorite bone, the fibula. Instead of counting sheep I could just say *fibula* over and over, and drift into pleasant slumber. Fibula. Fib-u-la.

"Let me take care of you," said Mom. "I really want to." She started to cry. Dad took the phone.

"Hi Dad."

"Come home for a few days and let your mother take care of you." Dad's bark was hard on the ear after Mom's honeyed pleadings. "I told her she doesn't have time to take care of two needy men, but she says she does."

"I can't, Dad. I can't afford to take that much time off from work."

"But I hear you're in Miami for a few days," Dad questioned my logic.

"So now I really can't take any more time off."

"So you pay an extra salary for a few days. That won't break you."

"It's more than that. I can't afford to lose any more business right now. Things are pretty tight." I would never tell Dad how dire my financial situation really was. The amount of debt I had rung up on credit cards and past-due payables to suppliers—it would kill him to know. Like everyone else in the world, Dad believed I should be making money hand over fist—hire teenagers at minimum wage to froth ten cents worth of milk, toss in espresso brewed from five cents' worth of beans, and charge three-fifty—how could you not make a killing on margins like that? The coffee biz was almost criminal.

And so I was clearly doing something wrong. A decade after launching my so-called coffee career, I was running one single solitary store. Dad never said it out loud, but I was a disappointment.

"I suppose your market is shrinking," he provided me an excuse, to soothe my pride and probably his own. "I read something the other day how all those North Dakota farmsteads are being abandoned while everyone moves to Minneapolis. You can't make a living in a dying state."

"Jamestown is actually growing, Dad." No lie, we went from 15,085 to 15,101 last year.

"Growing old, maybe," said Andrea, able to fill in the other side of the conversation. "Your dad's right."

"Who was that?" Dad asked.

"The mayor. I should probably get going."

"Oh, I'm the mayor now?" Andrea cackled. Not loud enough for Dad to make out the words, but I had a feeling she was only going to get louder.

"So why don't you have the surgery here?" said Dad. "We have a great hospital, you know."

"Jamestown has a great hospital too." That may have been an overstatement. "It'll go fine."

"Huh. Okay, well, your mom's saying she's going to fly there then. She'll stay with you for awhile."

"Dad, no. I would love to have you two visit, but that sounds really depressing. Like I'm a queer fifty-year-old bachelor dying of AIDS."

Dad coughed out a serious chuckle. "Bone cancer is nothing to joke around with. A lot of people don't recover too well from it," he said gravely.

"I know. But I'm doing great. It's almost gone, and this surgery will clean out anything that's left. I'll try to get out there soon—I was planning on driving out for a week this summer, when everything settles down around here."

"Naw, you gotta fly. It's too far to drive."

"By the way, I've been getting quite a few calls lately, Ryan, Jered, Tammie. And Mrs. Van Rosen. I had to listen for an hour while she cried and prayed for me. I told you not to tell anyone."

"People ask about you," said Dad. "What are we going to do, lie?"

"Don't tell anybody else. I mean it this time. I better run."

Andrea seconded this, muttering as she picked through our dinner for the perfect piece of pork.

"Your mom and I have been doing a lot of thinking." Dad wasn't through with me. "And I've been doing some poking around. There are a few opportunities that don't look too bad. Stuff you might be interested in."

"I appreciate you looking into jobs out there, but this isn't a good time. We can talk more later."

Dad reluctantly agreed and I hung up before Mom could take back the phone. I wasted no time catching up on the pork. I hadn't fallen behind on the mojitos. I gave Andrea a suffering smile. "Aren't cellphones great?"

"Great. Yeah." Andrea wiped the corners of her protruding lips with a hotel washcloth. She wasn't a dainty eater, but she cleaned up well. "So." She put me under her microscope. "Your mom and dad want you to move back home. Why don't you?"

"Because I couldn't make enough money out there. Not that North Dakota is any different."

"Why don't you do something else?"

"I really like coffee. I think I'm good at it."

Andrea polished off her mojito. I divvied up what was left in the pitcher. "That went down pretty well," she said. "Looks like you'll have to make another run." She readjusted, from crosslegged to sidesaddle, legs drawn up under her hip. Long thighs for a short girl. Shapely. "So why can't you make money with your coffeeshop?"

"It's volume. I can't do enough volume with one shop."

"So open another one. What about the Bluffs?"

"It scares me to death. I branched out in California, and it went poorly."

"Why?"

"You don't really want to hear this, do you?"

"Did I ask?"

She actually seemed interested, so I told her. She let me talk uninterrupted.

"…and if customers don't think they're going to see me, they'll go wherever's closest." I wrapped up the condensed version of my business history, edited for most of the tears, profanity and self-pity. "Just the other day, Genevieve from Taekwondo told me she loves my coffee, that it's the best she's ever tasted—but that she wouldn't go out of her way to come to my shop if she didn't think she was going to see me. It sounds vain—in fact, it sounds really stupid to say it out loud, but I've come to the conclusion that a lot of my business comes because people like me."

"I don't find that hard to believe," said Andrea.

"That's a compliment, and the kiss of death." I stabbed and offered up the last piece of pork, ate it when Andrea declined.

"So when you open a new store," she summarized nicely, "you put in less time at the first store, and so you start to lose customers."

"Exactly. It's a competitive business. You constantly have to outlive new competitors. And then there's Starbucks. They won't be outlived."

"People would go to Starbucks instead of a local coffeeshop?"

"It's the place to see and be seen. Regardless how crappy the coffee is."

"So you need someone to run your first store, someone everyone likes."

"But I can only afford to pay high school or college kids. They just don't have what it takes to attract customers older than thirty-five. You know, customers with money."

"So get a partner."

"A partner would be nice. Somebody who would work his butt off and get along with the customers as well as I do. And not give me orders. I've been calling the shots for so long now, good or bad, I couldn't let somebody else call them for me."

"Just make sure you clearly divide the decision-making responsibilities."

"But we'd also be halving the profits. So we'd have to open six stores in order to make any money, and then we'd have the same problem I have now."

"Hm." Andrea was actually working on this. I was flattered. "Why can't you spend a lot of time at both stores? Not really working, but making your customers happy."

"Somebody would have to do the real work, and I don't think I could support the increased payroll."

"But your volume would increase. You said volume is the key."

"It is. It is."

"It seems to me," said Andrea, "the only way you're going to make it is to open lots of branches. Then everybody knows your name. In your region you become as well-known as Starbucks. And it becomes a habit for people to go to your shops." She propped pillows and leaned back against the headboard. I caught a glimpse of a small roll of stomach fat before she readjusted her loose-fitting shirt. "You need a strong manager, who can handle the employees and the business side of things, and free you to do customer service."

I gathered the empty pork box and the washcloth-napkins and bussed them into the hall. "I'll be right back," I called and jogged downstairs. Talking about ways to salvage my business, the ideas Andrea was throwing out, the fact that she seemed excited about it—my brain was firing with positive energy for the first time in weeks. I didn't want the conversation to end.

I hailed the desk clerk, a gentleman about my age with a nice mustache and a little extra flesh on his cheeks. "I've got a little get-together going upstairs, and we're out of alcohol. I was wondering if you had anything."

"There's a bar down the street, señor."

"I don't want to go out this late. I was hoping you might have something on hand." I pulled out a very thin wad of bills and peeled off a ten.

The clerk debated the wisdom of leaving his post, then ducked into the office. Bottles clanked. He returned with a half-bottle of Patron tequila, two shot glasses, a lime, a knife and a salt shaker shaped like a volcano. He put it all in a cloth bag and dangled it before me. "You know how to use this?"

"That's beautiful. What do I owe you?"

"It's on the house."

I peeled off another ten-spot and slid the bills across the counter. "I really appreciate this."

"Thank you, señor. Let me know what else you need for your party."

"I will."

"Girls?" The clerk nodded like he was reading my mind.

"We're good. Thanks again." I hustled the bag of goodies upstairs.

Andrea had made herself cozy. Shoes off and curled up amongst the pillows. If I had found her pacing or perched at the edge of the bed, second thoughts would have rushed in and I might have ended the evening.

Instead I got all excited. "Look what we have here." I knelt on the floor beside her and unpacked the drinking paraphernalia, the bed as our table. Andrea purred in approval, watching me pour shots and slice thin lime wedges.

"Looks like you know what you're doing."

"Basic skills." I licked the crook of my thumb and forefinger, shook salt from the volcano into the wet spot, licked again, threw down a shot and took a quick suck of lime. Andrea followed suit, heavier on the salt and with a longer suck of the lime.

"Good?" I asked as she let everything settle down. "One more?"

She nodded. I was severely buzzed, so I couldn't imagine how drunk this woman half my size must be.

"So your mom and dad want you to move home," she said.

"I'm their only kid. They have too much time to worry about me."

"I'm an only child too," said Andrea. "But my parents don't worry about me. They love Rick. They think he's still taking care of me."

"He doesn't?"

Andrea soured. "He's fine to me. Considering his family hates me, he treats me pretty well."

"The McEwens hate you?" I said innocently.

"Like you didn't know that."

"I don't see them much these days."

"What do you say to them, when my name comes up?"

"If your name ever comes up, I change the subject."

"You don't want to know anything about me?"

"I'd rather hear it from you."

She liked this answer. "When are you going to tell Isabel about…this?"

"I doubt I'll have to. She probably knows already."

"Small towns," Andrea griped. "Everybody knows everything."

I was thinking more specifically of the McEwens. They did have connections. By now we had a bug in our rental and a camera in the headboard.

"Don't you want to move back to California," Andrea asked me, "where there's some life? Some people, besides a bunch of farmers?"

"Sometimes."

Sometimes, most times, all the time, because honestly who gives a shit if you become a North Dakota coffee mogul? Put a shop on every rural Midwestern street corner, and so what? Even if I could solve the riddle of The Man Who Killed His Business By Duplicating A Good Thing and actually turn a profit, would that coin spend on the coasts? I'd still be the guy who couldn't hack it in a sophisticated, competitive market, carrying around a pocketful of plugged nickels.

But if I said that out loud, we might as well slit our wrists and blood-seal our unholy pact. "Dad would love me to take over the agency eventually. It's crop insurance," I told her. "California is the nation's biggest agricultural state, and far and away the biggest purchaser of crop insurance."

She faked a yawn and followed up with a real one. "Sounds boring."

"It is. I worked in the agency when I was in high school, until I got a job at a coffeeshop. Dad always hoped I would come back. But it would feel like a huge failure. I've tried to tell him—without hurting his feelings, that crop insurance isn't my thing. I've always seen myself doing something big. I don't know about being famous...but successful. Exceptionally good at what I do. I've always believed I'm capable of great things. So it gets to me that Dad doesn't see that in me. He thinks I would be satisfied running the agency."

I gazed at the last two inches of tequila in the square bottle. "It didn't require a degree, so in Dad's eyes owning a coffeeshop can't be a real job. It's an immature lark, a fun hobby. Dad never got a degree either, but he's convinced that you can't succeed without one these days. If I don't turn this into a real business, a chain of stores, he's going to consider me a failure."

"I can tell you're going to succeed." Andrea was matter-of-fact. Her eyes were calm and cool. And sober, I swear. "It feels like you're famous already. I don't know how to explain it, but there's that...that aura, I guess. I'd say it's obvious to everybody that you're going to make it big."

"I don't know about that..."

"Well it's obvious to me. I can tell you're going to be rich and famous."

"Right now I'd settle for solvent and cancer-free. But here's to rich and famous." We salted and licked, swallowed and sucked.

Andrea patted the pillows, and stacked a couple beside her. "Why don't you get up off the floor and make yourself a little more comfortable?"

The bed had already been calling to me. My knee ached, even through the alcohol anesthetic. I moved the tequila apparatus to the nightstand and lay beside her. Andrea scooted down and nestled into my chest and shoulder. Was this how it went down with Kevin the Wells Fargo auditor? My turn to play the dangerous game.

"Comfy?" she asked.

"You're a pretty good fit. You good?"

"My God. I can't tell you how good it feels to be out of Jamestown. I don't think I'm going to want to go back on Friday."

I started playing with the hem of her smock, high on the shoulder where a sleeve would attach.

"Maybe we'll just have to stay here, hm?" Andrea purred.

"Yeah, maybe," I said to the shirt.

"You like that shirt, I take it."

"It's a great shirt," I said.

"You can have it," said Andrea with a short soft laugh.

"I'm sure it looks better on you. But I did pack a little light, so I might have to take you up on it." I let the back of my fingers move against her skin as I handled the coarse cotton. "So what are you going to do tomorrow while we have our meetings?"

"You're not going to be up for a long day so soon after your chemo treatments. Maybe we can go to the beach together in the afternoon."

"I probably should take it a little easy." I don't know if there had been air conditioning and now it shut off, or if the outside temperature was rising, but I started to sweat. Andrea too, from the way her shirt caught against her skin as my hand drifted down her side. "But the Chamber is paying for this trip, so I have to hang in there as long as I can."

"Then maybe we'll just have to extend our stay through the weekend," said Andrea, a dreamy quality to her voice.

"Maybe the Chamber would pay for us to stay and observe Muslims in their daily lives." Andrea's shirt rode high and I was touching skin. I slid a finger across her belly and into a small crease, slick with sweat. "Do they drink coffee after sundown? That's a question we need answered."

"Do you really expect a bunch of Muslim people to move to Jamestown?" Andrea wondered in a semi-hypnotic state.

"Good question. I'm not sure what to expect." Our conversation moved as slowly as my hand. I dawdled at her belly, getting an enormous amount of pleasure from simply touching a woman's skin. Somebody's flesh that didn't make my skin crawl. Andrea wasn't the best person in the world, or Jamestown, or her block for that matter. But as far as I knew she wasn't a pedophile. And if she was, I wanted her to keep that to herself.

Andrea cleared her throat after failing in her first attempt to speak. "Mike and Rick think it's crazy to recruit Muslims to come to Jamestown."

"You should tell Mike that not all of them live in tents, so there might be some business in it for him. And they never bomb where they live. The more of them that move to Jamestown, the better our odds of survival."

For a few frantic moments I thought I was going to cum in my pants, from nothing more than a couple minutes of belly rubbing. Now the urgency subsided—probably thanks to images of sweaty disaffected Islamic radicals. I shifted my attention a little higher, stroking Andrea's ribs, bumping up against the bottom ridge of her bra, before retreating back to her stomach creases.

"Do you now," said Andrea, apropos nothing, perhaps an escaped snippet of her inner monologue. I was back up at her bra, dizzy from the alcohol and the heat and the perfume of her hair. Her skin was wet enough that I could slide my fingers underneath the tight fit.

Andrea didn't speak coherently until I pulled them back out. "You're not afraid someone from the Chamber is going to find out I'm here?"

"Not at the moment, no. I'm sure I'll regret it next week."

"But you're not regretting it right now, are you?"

"No I'm not." I took a roundabout route to her breast, moving up her side, coming at it from the armpit, lifting the edge of the bra with two fingers, stroking her flesh with the free digits. I was flying blind, Andrea's head tucked under my chin and blocking my view—from what I could tell, the bra seemed to have slid up over her small breast. I stroked her gently, crawling my fingers forward, getting more excited the closer I got to paydirt. It was freshman year in high school all over again.

"Is it hot in here?" Andrea said quietly, unable to muster any inflection. She squirmed ever-so-slightly, and I lost my way. Everything was wet and soft and undefined; my dizzy skull couldn't form a mental map to guide me the last couple inches to my destination. I backed up, fingers retreating outside the bra and sliding down below her ribs, to start the process over again.

"The air conditioning must be broke."

"I don't mind it hot," said Andrea.

"It's good to sweat," I agreed. I went back up for another try. The bottom of her breast was outside the confines of the bra. I lingered there for a few moments before working my way under the rigid frame, searching, searching. Was that it? Had I touched it? I retraced my path. I moved left, I moved right, hindered by the bra, slipping and sliding across her skin.

"You're driving me crazy, you know that?" Andrea tried to sound conversational, having a hard time breathing.

"Me too." I had been searching for fifteen minutes. This was record-length foreplay. I didn't know whether I was touching her breast or a fold of skin. I needed to get that bra out of the way. I followed the ridgeline to the midpoint, but the garment wasn't equipped with a front release feature.

I killed time in the very shallow valley of her breasts, expecting Andrea to make the next move, turning into me or even away from me, depending on her style. There was some urgency, we were both losing fluids fast, lying in a pool of our own humidity. She lay motionless, except for an almost imperceptible undulation to an internal rhythm. So instead of backing off to the belly and then heading up again, I continued down, fingering her waistband, almost reluctantly sliding my fingers underneath, an inch or two, pausing when she moaned, and then retreating. And back up top.

This time I found the nipple, I'm almost certain. Immediately I reversed course and dropped back down, a little further this time. Andrea turned her face up to me and I kissed her.

THINGS ACCELERATED from that point—even though I did my darnedest to make it last all night. It was up to me to initiate each step, move to the next base, remove another piece of clothing. My commitment to patience was tested and ultimately thwarted by Andrea's moans—it had been a long time since a woman was writhing in response to my actions.

I apologized after, for the quick ending.

"My God," said Andrea. "That was incredible. I've never experienced anything like that. How can you last that long?"

"One word," I replied. "Alcohol."

Andrea shook her head. "No. You are incredible. That was incredible. I can't…" She shivered. "I can't even put it into words."

"It was pretty good, huh?" I said, starting to believe it was me.

"Pretty good? I think that's an understatement." Her clipped, jaded style returned. It was endearing now. Life was ridiculous and unfair, we both saw it—we were cynical together, and so it couldn't touch us. We were impervious to Fate's cruel twists and turns.

ONE NIGHT of blissful ignorance, that was all I got. Nothing had changed. We were both trapped in North Dakota, Andrea with no way out, me with nowhere to go, and San Diego simply a temporary escape. I made the most of that night; and felt terrible the next morning, lying in bed contemplating blowing off breakfast, in the end unable to disappoint my peers.

Andrea's spirits were bright. She was content to spend Thursday solo shopping and sightseeing and soaking up the sun, beating me back to the room by a couple hours to prep for our night together. The day was draining—Khalq and the Chamber had been efficient scheduling meetings and presentations, to get the biggest bang for the bucks we had shelled out for this trip. The night was wonderful. Faced with another half-day jam-packed schedule on Friday, I was all for Andrea's offer to extend our hotel stay and rebook our return flights for Sunday evening.

Friday afternoon we hit the beach together. Andrea was in heaven. Each day away from Jamestown she became more animated, smiling and talking, hugging me and making suggestive comments. Assumptions, really.

"So, what should we do tonight?" she asked.

"I don't know." We lay on beach blankets Andrea had packed. "We could drive to the Gaslamp district and check out the nightlife."

Andrea was propped up on one elbow, looking down on me, her head no more than an inch from shielding my eyes from the vicious sun. "You think you're going to want to leave the hotel room? I wonder. I don't think so."

"Shouldn't we do a little exploring, as long as we have the chance?"

"Yeah. You'll be doing some exploring, I'm pretty sure of that."

"I'll tell you, the way I'm feeling right now, sleeping might be all I have in me. I'm serious."

Andrea gave me a sex smack smile. "We'll see." She stretched out on her back with a contented chuckle.

I lay there trying to convince myself I was enjoying the sun boiling my flesh, the hairy German prancing around in the Speedo, the three little kids running back and forth above my head and screaming at each other in Canadian. I had a stomach ache, from the chemo or the guilt, whatever, I needed to get used to the pain, as they would both be with me for awhile.

"We're going to have to go back a day early," I announced.

"What? No. A day early would be tomorrow. No. Why? We just got here."

"I don't have a reason to be here any longer."

"*I'm* not a good reason to stay?" Andrea was back up on one elbow.

I mirrored her. "You're a great reason. But…"

"Do you know how much I paid for my ticket?"

"I have an idea."

"Fifteen hundred bucks, for two days?" She worked up a good lather.

"I'm feeling guilty. My business is tanking, and meanwhile Mike is helping me get set up at the Bluffs. And I'm lying on the beach, with his ex-daughter in law." I was suddenly obsessed with getting home, back to my shop. My crime against Iz and her family was still in process and I was already anxious to get back and face the music.

"Why did you come down here?" Andrea demanded.

I sat up. "To sell Jamestown and help the community."

"I mean why did you come here with me."

I had no clue how to process that question.

"Do you really think Mike or anyone else cares whether you spend a weekend lying on the beach?"

"With you? Yeah, he does. A lot of people would. Don't you think—"

"I think it's a good thing at least one of us doesn't worry about what people think." Andrea stood and dusted off her legs and shook out her towel in my face. "You have a good thing going here and you don't care if you mess it up, fine. Do whatever you need to do." She was going to cry.

I hate to argue, so I usually just keep talking. "I don't know what I'm going to do. I think you and I did some great brainstorming on my business. Now I need to figure out what my next steps are."

"And I could have taken those next steps with you," said Andrea, losing volume. "We could have had a good time together. But no. You're going to ruin it." She turned away to stuff her beach supplies in her drawstring bag.

I kept providing support for my decision, as if this was a rational conversation. "We had a great time, Andrea. And I'm glad we're staying an extra night. But if I extend it another day, while Mike's back in Jamestown spending money on me, my heart isn't going to be in it." I folded the blanket while Andrea waited impatiently in her half-length terry cloth hoodie and Jackie O. sunglasses. "I know myself too well. All I'd be thinking about is how much money I'm losing every day I'm away."

"I think you set this up," she accused, "to ruin my vacation."

"Whoa. Really? I mean, you invited yourself along—"

"And you really seemed to hate having me in your hotel room!"

The three grubby little Canadian kids stopped their pointless chase game and stared.

"I had a good time," I soothed.

"Oh I know you did."

It wasn't that good, I wanted to say, but Andrea was already powering up the sand hill toward the parking lot. The little Canadians stared as we marched past. "Watch out for the Pacific sand sharks," I told them.

Andrea ran out of gas, allowing me to pull abreast. "Andrea, I'm sorry."

"I can't believe you're ruining this," said Andrea. We threaded our way through the busy, packed parking lot. "I shouldn't have come with you."

"My leg is really hurting," I said. "God I hope the cancer isn't coming back."

It was a cheap card to play. I don't know if it worked, maybe she had already run out of tears and complaints. Either way, we spent the drive to the hotel and the rest of the day and night in silence. We scored the last two standby seats on the Saturday morning flight to Denver. Andrea avoided me during our three-hour layover. By the time I limped into my apartment that night, my leg really was killing me.

T - 9

I regained consciousness in gentle stages, on a cot in a big white hall, one of many cots, one of many patients. Nurses were moving from bed to bed. One came to mine, a big one.

"You're awake a little early," she said. "Is everything okay?"

"Not sure," I croaked.

The hulking nurse pulled up the sheet and appraised my lower half.

"You didn't…" I made a nasty smacking sound, looking for spit to swallow. The nurse let me sip from a straw, from a styrofoam cup of ice water she was carrying around. I nodded my thanks. "Is my leg okay?" Lying in what felt like an Army hospital, sipping from the communal cup, in the hands of a nurse who looked like she'd be equally comfortable wielding a thermometer or a hacksaw, I wouldn't have been shocked to hear I had lost the leg.

"Everything went well," said the nurse. "I'll let the doctor give you all the details. Do you feel like you need to sleep some more?"

"I could." I struggled to free my arms from the bedding or maybe it was restraining straps, in order to sit up to get a look at my leg. That's the last thing I remember from that high-ceilinged hall. When I opened my eyes again I was in a semi-private hospital room and my mother was sitting there looking at me. I mean she was on the edge of the chair, leaning forward, examining me.

"Whoo," Mom said. "You looked so white and peaceful, I thought you might be dead."

My childhood buddy and best friend from Davis moved into view. Things had to be bad, for Ryan to be there. "Hey bud," he said, stepping forward to clasp my hand. "It's good to see you awake."

With my free hand I reached down under the blanket. "Still have both legs. That's a good sign." Flexed some muscles and saw my feet move. "And everything's still connected."

"The doctor stopped by an hour ago," said Ryan. He's a half-breed, Chinese and white. His sisters look Chinese, he looks South American. "Dr. Bianci, or Chinchilla…"

"It was Brillo," Mom corrected him.

"Bonilla," I corrected her. "I hate his name. I feel like a little kid with a lisp who can't say vanilla."

Ryan grinned. "Dr. Vanilla didn't have time for questions. But he said everything looked good."

"Really? He wasn't just saying that?"

"I didn't sense any sugar coating."

Mom stroked my hair, tearing up. "You pulled through."

"It wasn't brain surgery, Mom." Now I could be brave. "How embarrassing would it be if I couldn't survive tibia surgery?"

"You have cancer," Mom scolded me.

I waved my hand in her direction until she snared it, so I could squeeze it. "I'm just acting all tough for Ryan. When did you guys get here?"

"Early this afternoon," said Ryan. "I was surprised how easy it was to get here. Just one connection."

"Now you'll be popping in on a regular basis," I complained. "You two flew together? Dad didn't come, did he?"

"He wanted to." Mom daubed her eyes with a used tissue. "He has a big meeting Monday to prepare for. But he would have come—"

"If I had died on the operating table?" I finished her sentence with a wink.

Mom turned white. "Please don't say that."

"It's funny now that I survived."

"Not for your mother," said Mom.

"I'm pinch-hitting for your dad," said Ryan. "Team Lawson has a great bench."

"You could be a starter on any other team," I said.

"Thanks, bud." Knuckle knock.

I got emotional, knowing my buddy was willing to pay for a ticket and jump on a plane to come see me. "Mom, tissue." My vision was too blurry to see whether she gave me a fresh one. "Salty discharge is a normal post-op event," I explained.

"I've heard that," said Ryan with a wink.

"How do you like Jamestown so far?" I asked while I collected myself.

"I think your father and I should move here," said Mom. "Everyone's heavier here. I fit right in."

Ryan chortled. "Mrs. Lawson, you're not what I would call heavy."

"Are you kidding? I have the biggest white hips in California." She stretched her floral shirt to her thighs and sat on it.

"No way," I said. "Ryan, what about that Eileen Henderson, the girl you dated from Dixon?"

"She was white," Ryan agreed. "And her hips were definitely bigger than yours, Mrs. Lawson."

"And you didn't seem to mind," I said.

Ryan sighed a happy little sigh and gazed dreamily into the distance.

"Alright you two," said Mom. "Time to change the subject."

A big wave of noise and air and finally people swept into the room.

"Hey!" Joshua bellered, running around Ryan to attack me on the other side of the bed. Denise trailed him. Filing in and crowding behind her were Charlotte, Genevieve and Khalq from Taekwondo, and a crowd of regulars from my shop, Jerry, Dennis, Carolyn, Donna, and Mitch and Kelsea Carlson, who owned the sporting goods store at the other end of our block. Andrea too, peeking around the room's dividing curtain.

Joshua pulled me half out of bed to hug me. "You survived!"

"Joshua!" Denise wrestled him off me. "What are you doing? You're going to hurt him! You'll rip out his IV!" She was embarrassed and proud.

"He's in a hospital!" Joshua countered. "They'll put it all back in!"

"There's no better place to have a medical emergency," Ryan agreed.

"See?" Joshua demanded an apology from his wife. Denise shook her head, mortified and beaming.

"Joshua, Ryan. Ryan's my best friend from back home. And this is my mom. This is Joshua's wife Denise…alright, there's no way I can handle all these introductions in my weakened state. Can someone else take over?"

Joshua started pointing and naming people, even those he didn't know. Everyone collapsed toward the middle to shake hands.

He missed one. "And behind the curtain," I said, "is my friend Andrea."

The conversational hubbub died on cue. Andrea got a 'hi' and a 'hey', and that's it. Even Mom seemed aware that this woman was to be shunned.

Andrea appeared willing to take on the whole room. She opened her mouth to speak, but lost out to Khalq. "Don't you feel sick to your stomach?" he asked me. "I always get viciously sick from the anesthesia."

"No, I feel pretty good."

"I felt pretty good after arthroscopic surgery a couple years ago," said Khalq. "So I ordered a pizza when I got home. I threw up nonstop for the next twenty-four hours."

"You're used to that," I said. "I know they taught you in modeling school to purge before a big shoot. To get that sunken cheek look."

Mom turned around to get a better look at Khalq. "Oh, you're a model? That's wonderful. I didn't know they had models out here."

"I'm not a model, Mrs. Lawson," said Khalq.

"Well you are a very handsome young man," said Mom, looking him up and down. "I love your Arabic features."

"He's a dreamboat," I said.

"When do you come back to Taekwondo?" Khalq asked me politely. "So I can kick your ass."

"That may be a little while," said Dr. Bonilla, squeezing through the crowd. "We had to replace a little bone below the knee, so I'd recommend keeping your kick-fighting to a minimum for a few weeks."

"There's gotta be a way for them to settle the score," said Dennis

"Anything but a fashion runway walk-off," I said. "Khalq would annihilate me."

"Doctor, do you need to talk to Brian alone?" Mom asked. She was all business, ready to clear the room.

"If that wouldn't be too much trouble," said Dr. Bonilla, and Mom sprang to her feet, shooing my friends away from the bed. "Only for a minute," the doc apologized. "And then everybody can come back in."

"Brian," said Kelsea, backpedaling out of Mom's reach. "Mitch and I just wanted to say hi and let you know we're thinking about you. We'll stop back when you're not so busy."

"Sounds good. Thanks for stopping."

"We left some flowers for you," said Kelsea, pointing at the rolling table under the television set, crowded with flower pots.

"I'll plant them as soon as I get home," I promised.

Mom poked my shoulder. "You don't plant them, son."

"No. Okay. I promise not to plant them."

"Thank goodness your mom is here," said Kelsea.

Dennis, Jerry and Carolyn begged out in similar fashion. Andrea gave me a long look before disappearing. I obtained a special exemption for Ryan, sparing him from being swept along in Mom's bum rush. He hovered at the edge of the curtain. "So," I said, "shoot me straight, Dr. B."

"I would classify your surgery as successful," said Dr. Bonilla in a quiet voice from his anchorage at the foot of the bed. "Under the kneecap we did find some cancerous growth, high up on the tibia—"

Mom gasped.

"...right under the knee, as well as in the kneecap itself. We replaced a little more bone than we had anticipated, but that part of the procedure went fine. We used a new technique...lightweight polymer..."

Mom's moaning was distracting.

"...bone mold...injected—"

"What about bone mold?" I interrupted. "Is that bad?"

Dr. Bonilla waited for Mom to settle down. "It's a biodegradable injection molding of your tibia," he explained. "We inject the polymer into this mold, after dissolving the bone that contains the cancerous tissue. As we inject the liquid polymer, the old dissolved material is extruded, replaced by the polymer. When it dries, the polymer is very lightweight and strong. Stronger than the original bone."

"What about the cancer you found in Brian's kneecap?" Mom's voice quavered. "You said there was more cancer than you expected...?"

"We really didn't know what to expect until we got in there," said Dr.

Bonilla calmly. "Even the best MRIs and X-rays don't tell you everything. We hoped to find the area completely clean. Because it wasn't—do we do anything different now? No. We still go forward with another round of chemo and radiation, like we planned."

This was terrible news to Mom. "I was hoping it was gone."

"Me too," I said.

"Was that a realistic expectation?" Ryan asked.

"Realistic?" Dr. Bonilla pondered. "Cancers of this type are rare enough that each case is its own animal. We have a standard approach, but we know going in we'll have to tailor it to the specific circumstances."

Mom reached for my hand. I gave it to her. She gripped it in both of hers. "How would you rank Brian's cancer with others you've seen?"

Dr. Bonilla frowned. I looked at Ryan. "What's my weight class?"

Ryan bent to read my chart at the foot of the bed. "One-seventy-two. I believe you're a super-middleweight."

"I'm not sure how cancer rankings work." I looked at Dr. Bonilla. "Do I want to be a contender?"

"Ah, well," Dr. Bonilla fumbled for a way to not answer the question. "That's not the way we normally like to think about disease management. I guess if I had to—"

"I'd actually rather hear about the polymer you used," I said.

Dr. Bonilla patted my foot to show his gratitude. "The polymer serves two nice purposes. Enhanced structure for your leg, and a barrier to the cancer. It's coated in immune blockers to avoid rejection, and it's an inorganic material, so cancer cells can't proliferate any further up or down your leg. Assuming we've excised or killed all the cells in the tibia and the kneecap, we can expect the growth of the cancer to have ended."

"But I'll still need another round of chemo."

"We think it's best."

"I was really hoping to avoid any more chemo."

"I've heard there are a few experimental treatments out there," said Ryan. "Alternatives to chemotherapy."

Dr. Bonilla nodded. "There are quite a few experimental treatments out there." He was ready to let it go at that.

"Do you provide info on the more promising ones?" Ryan persisted.

"We let the institutional review boards or the FDA decide whether any given treatment has promise," said Dr. Bonilla, making notes on his pad. "That saves physicians from having to separate true results from the hype."

Ryan stared at the doc. "I'd like to know whether you recommend Brian look into any particularly promising new treatments."

Dr. Bonilla was oblivious to the bulldog tearing at his pant leg. "Brian could look into getting himself into a protocol, if he felt like it was an avenue he needed to take."

Mom's head was swiveling between Ryan and the doc. She turned to me. "Well, what do you think? Should you?"

"Maybe I should."

"I don't recommend it," said Dr. Bonilla, irritated at being forced to go on record. "These treatments are unproven. They haven't received regulatory approval. They're experimental."

"Experimental," Mom whispered the word. "That sounds dangerous."

"It can be," said Dr. Bonilla ominously.

Mom put a death grip on my hand. "I think you should stick with the traditional approach."

"Okay," I said. I hadn't been seriously debating it. "When do I start my chemo treatments again?"

"As long as we have you here for a couple days," said Dr. Bonilla, "we'll begin tomorrow, if you're feeling up to it. Now that we've had a look inside, I'd rather be too aggressive than not enough. He drifted away from my bedside. "Any other questions? No?" He couldn't get out of there fast enough. "Rest easy. Keep the visitors to a minimum"—he twitched his head in Ryan's direction, but it could have been a muscle spasm—"and give your body a chance to recuperate. Mrs. Lawson, it was good to meet you."

"I'm not going anywhere," said Mom, sniffling.

"I'm sure Brian appreciates you being here." Ryan the medical gadfly was clearly excluded from this sentiment. "I'll see you tomorrow."

The remnants of my visitors filed back in, Joshua and Denise, the Taekwondo crew, Charlotte. Mom was wiping a steady stream of tears. "Mom, you're supposed to be cheering me up," I said for everyone's benefit. "Come on lady, lighten up a little!"

Mom swatted at me and excused herself.

"So what'd he say?" Joshua demanded over Mom's honks from the bathroom. "Are you cured?"

I held my hands a foot apart, so that Joshua would picture a medium-sized trout. "Close."

"Your mom didn't seem to think so," said Charlotte. "What's up?"

"More chemo," said Ryan darkly, recruiting conspiracy theorists.

"But, I am now the proud owner of a space-age super-strong tibia," I bragged.

"They had to replace your bone?" Charlotte gagged. "God."

"I told you what they were doing."

"I know but…" Charlotte shuddered. "Eeuu."

Time for another topic change. "How's things?"

Charlotte knew what I meant. She sighed. "It's fine. We ran out of Sumatran yesterday. And of course the next three customers all wanted a pound of Sumatran. We're running low on Colombian, too. Craig thinks we might have a week or so."

Sam had left for Alaska the week prior, and I never made it into the roasting room after San Diego. Ten minutes before they put me under, Charlotte had called to tell me we had a bean crisis on our hands. I held off the gas mask with one hand and called Craig with the other, to ask him to roast for me. He was reluctant, so I had begged. He made me promise not to tell Hernandes. I offered him time-and-a-half, but he wouldn't accept more than his current hourly rate. Which was about fifty percent higher than what I used to pay him.

"Craig has been there a lot," said Charlotte. "He did a ton of roasting. And he pitched in behind the bar this morning when things got busy."

"Make sure he logs all his hours."

"I'll make sure his time sheet checks out," Charlotte assured me.

"I'm not worried about him overbilling me. Just the opposite. I really appreciate him working double-time to help me out. I am worried about being able to afford to pay him, but that's another story."

"Craig's a great guy," said Joshua.

"He goes to our church," said Denise. "Craig has been an inspiration to a lot of the younger kids in the congregation. A year ago he was..."

Saved? I wanted to finish for her.

"He was definitely searching," Joshua chose an alternate ending.

"Craig is a little bit of a misfit," said Charlotte affectionately.

Craig was tightlipped about his past, but the same couldn't be said for everyone. I had heard a few stories, not flattering. And now I was discouraged to realize that of the two of us, Craig was the one going to heaven.

The conversation lost energy. Joshua and Denise made me promise to let them cook my meals for the next month, and hustled out.

"We should be going, too," said Khalq, including Genevieve.

"Did you two come together?" I insinuated hanky-panky.

"We agreed to drive together after class," said Genevieve. "That's the last time I ride with Khalq. He drives like a madman."

"Did you get to ride in the Viper?" I asked. "That's worth the risk."

"No it's not," said Genevieve. "I'm not one of those floozies who put up with assholes just because they drive a nice car."

"I am," said Ryan. "You have a Viper?"

"It's an unbelievable machine," said Khalq. "Want to take it for a spin?"

I shook my head violently at Khalq, *no-no-no*, until Ryan turned to look at me. "Sure," I said, smiling and nodding. "Ryan's a great driver."

"I've improved since high school," Ryan defended himself.

"You wrecked three cars in six weeks. You couldn't get any worse."

Ryan turned his back on me. "I promise not to break anything."

"Are you a…you know," said Khalq, "a U.S. citizen?"

"Ryan only looks Colombian," I explained. "He's half-breed grade-A U.S. Chink."

"And damn proud of it," said Ryan.

Genevieve kissed me on the forehead and the three of them walked out. Mom returned from the bathroom in time to say goodbye, and then pulled a chair close to my bedside. "You had quite a crowd in here. You should have seen all the people who came by while you were sleeping."

"I see all the flowers."

"They wouldn't all fit in here. You have flowers in the hallway and at the nurses' station."

"I'm lucky. I have some great friends."

"I liked that blonde girl," said Mom. "I feel small next to her."

"Her size comes in handy."

"Should I let you rest for awhile?"

"You don't have to go, but I might be ready for another nap."

Andrea peeked around the curtain. "Are you finally almost alone?"

"Andrea, this is my mom."

"We met," said Mom, coolly.

"Right. Andrea works in the basement of this hospital."

"Oh, how nice. In the morgue, or are you a janitor?"

Andrea sneered. For a woman who seemed to have designs on a future with me, this was a helluva first impression on my mom. I made no attempt to act as a buffer. Even in her preliminary stage of the grieving process, Mom was more than capable of handling anything Andrea could dish out, leaving me free to enjoy the show.

"I have a form for you to sign," said Andrea. "Will you?"

"Definitely." I positioned the document's signature line over the top of the bed's railing. "Grab me a pen over there, Mom."

Mom hesitated. "What is this form?"

"I have no idea," I said, snapping my fingers for the pen.

Mom clucked disapprovingly as she scooted her chair to the nightstand, intent on retrieving the pen without getting up.

"I have a pen," said Andrea. She held it a few inches beyond my reach. "Dr. Bhani wants permission to use a sample of the bone they removed."

"Dr. Bhani?" Mom frowned. "That's not your doctor's name, is it?"

"It's the mad scientist Andrea works for in the basement."

Mom covered her mouth. "Oh my goodness."

I sat up and snatched the pen out of Andrea's hand. "Sure, Bhani can have my leftovers. I'm working on a stool sample as we speak."

Andrea crossed her arms. "I don't think that will be necessary."

"Anything for mad research."

"Brian," Mom snapped, panicked. "You don't mean that."

"He's not a mad scientist, Mrs. Lawson," said Andrea, frustrated by the both of us. "Dr. Bhani is a cancer researcher. He could have probably cured your son by now, if Brian had let him."

"Or killed me, like Isabel's brother."

While Mom moaned, I authorized the release form. Andrea yanked it away before I could put the final flourish on my signature.

"What's he going to do with your...leftovers?" Mom fretted.

"Clone me."

Andrea folded the form and tucked it in her handbag. "He's going to design a vaccine targeted to your cancer." While her tone was abrupt, she remained hovering over me, perhaps a touch of compassion in her eyes. "Not that you'll ever give him the opportunity to use it."

"Vaccines prevent you from catching a disease," Mom pointed out. "Even I know that. Brian already has cancer."

"Spot on, Mom." I requested a high five.

"I'll make sure I tell him that," said Andrea, rolling her eyes.

"Thanks for stopping by," I said. And then, when she didn't leave my side: "Stop in again if you get the chance. I have to spend two nights here."

"I'm sure you'll have plenty of visitors. Has Isabel been here yet?" Andrea had to ask.

Mom was hopping and wiggling her chair forward, creeping closer, wedging her way back in. The metal casters squawked on the tile floor.

"Haven't seen any McEwens yet," I said. "They may have been by while I was sleeping off the anesthesia. Careful, Mom's going to run you over."

"I see that." Andrea debated whether to dig like a tick or cut bait and run.

"I hate not being close to Brian," said Mom. "You know how moms get."

"Yeah well." Andrea didn't. "I better be going. Maybe I'll stop by later. If you're ever able to talk."

"It could happen."

T - 8

The chemo didn't beat around the bush this time. It started kicking my butt on Day One. By Day Fifteen my gums were blistered, my joints crackled when I moved, and I pooped blood. Ordinarily pooping blood would have alarmed me. Now red poop in the bowl wasn't a big deal. As long as my eyes opened when the alarm went off, it was a good day.

"How are you feeling today?" Jerilyn Givens asked me at eight-thirty that morning. I had eight customers at the bar and tables and two more in line, maybe forty dollars of revenue. Taking into account the twenty dollar-a-day fine for the sign board on the sidewalk, I was fifty-eight customers from breaking even for the day.

"Crappy. Really crappy. I'm miserable. The good news is that the fake bone in my leg is actually feeling pretty good. I'm not even limping any more. Otherwise, everything feels awful."

Charlotte worked next to me, running the register, pumping brewed coffee, prepping cups, costing me seven-fifty an hour. Whether she was sick of hearing me whine or too emotional to speak, she said nothing.

Jerilyn clucked. "I'm sorry." I wasn't getting the same degree of sympathy during Round Two. No more tears. What did they take me for, a career cancer patient? Brian has cancer, we're reconciled to that. He'll take treatments for a few months and the cancer will go away. In a few years it will probably return, in his liver this time, and he'll go through treatments again. And so on.

A few years' remission with a guaranteed recurrence was a deal I would have taken. I was frightened the cancer had climbed my leg, even after everything they had thrown at it. What was the chance the treatments and the surgery had cleaned out every last cancer cell? And the cells that had outlived the chemo and radiation, wouldn't they be more malignant and resilient than ever? Like germs that survived a round of antibiotics.

This I had asked Dr. Bonilla. "It's possible," he said. I think even my doctor was getting tired of all my downer cancer talk.

I wasn't confident I could survive this second round. The chemo was killing things inside me, useful things, things I was betting I couldn't do without.

And my hair. The fallout began in earnest. I'm not a vain man, but I definitely like to look good. I'll accept a few extra pounds and wrinkles. The slow decay of time I'm comfortable with. But there is no evidence of balding in my family picture album; I've never felt the need to reconcile myself to hair loss. I could—if the doc told me I had recently acquired the male pattern baldness gene, accidentally or by some inappropriate choice, and that beginning today the hair would start melting off my crown, my hairline receding gradually over many years' time, I would be fine with it. I would start cutting it shorter. I would thank God every day for the hair I had left. I would quick get married before the pool of willing candidates thinned in lockstep with my hair.

Out of spite or panic or unrealistic expectations of a Bruce Willis or Vin Diesel cranium waiting to be unveiled, I had shaved my head two nights before. No such luck, I looked like a cancer patient. Now I wore a ballcap.

"You hang in there," Jerilyn counseled me.

"Queen don't want me to try suicide."

"See you tomorrow," Jerilyn chirped on her way out.

"If I'm still alive." This got a chuckle, like a decent joke, but I would not have been shocked to have died that night. Terribly sad, but not surprised.

Jerry walked in. "You're late," I chastised.

"I overslept." Jerry was embarrassed. He handed Charlotte his prepaid coffee card. "I don't remember turning off the alarm clock."

"That's your brain saying you need a break," Charlotte comforted him.

"At least now I get to see what this place looks like after the sun comes up," said Jerry, staring down at the pastries.

"I think it looks better in the dark," Charlotte decided. "The pastry case, for sure."

I lured Jerry to the pickup platform with his latté. "Back to work?"

"Naw." Jerry stuffed his hands in his pockets and kicked at the floor.

"If you can't make a killing in the market before eight, you're not into it?"

Jerry studied me during the ensuing pause. "Why are you looking at me like that?" he asked.

I peered up from under the brim of my ballcap. "Like how?"

"Like that. Like a gangsta. You wear your hat too low."

"It's because I don't have a friggin' forehead." I ripped off the cap and chucked it to the floor.

"Whoa," said Charlotte, eyeballing my head and sidestepping away.

"I hate hats," I bitched. "I quit baseball when I was thirteen because our coach made us wear hats. I loved playing the outfield, but because I don't have a forehead I couldn't see out from under my cap well enough to catch fly balls. So he moved me to the infield. When there was a pop-up, I had to rip off my cap like a catcher's helmet." I stifled a curse word and kicked the hat into the storage shelf under the bar.

The rest of my customers waited for a funny follow-up quip. I had nothing. I was feeling slow-witted, as if the chemo was eating my brain right along with the hair.

"Nice kick," said Jerry. "You should have played soccer. No hats," he pointed out, demonstrating a seldom-used quick wit and probably topping my belated *I'd love to shove that hat up my baseball coach's ass.*

I made drinks. Jerry stood with his coffee mug tucked against his chest. "Let me know when you have a few minutes to talk," he said.

I got worried. "Did you ask me that already?"

Jerry paused. "No."

"Good. I've been forgetting things lately. I don't know if it's the chemo or the restless nightmare sleep. I don't want my mental disability to hurt our friendship."

"I'll hang in there with you." Jerry paused. "So..."

Katrina Thielges my self-appointed realtor marched from her Lexus toward my front door. Katrina can't rest at night knowing an important businessman like myself rents an apartment. Meanwhile I was wondering if I could live out of the roaster room across the alley and save the five-fifty monthly rent. I whistled to get Charlotte's attention, jerked my head at the door, shook it, and made for the hallway. "Now is good," I told Jerry. He tracked me along the other side of the bar, into the hallway and all the way back to the alley door. "So what's on your mind, homey?"

"We didn't need this much privacy," said Jerry.

"I like to give you one hundred percent of my attention," I told him. "That having been said, if I hear Katrina's heels in the hallway, I'm outta here."

"I better say my piece quick," said Jerry.

I knew this wasn't possible, so I didn't pressure him.

"I don't want to pry," said Jerry. "You know that."

"I know you don't *want* to pry."

He grinned. "Only when it's for your own good."

"I know you're there for me, homey."

"That's why you should know what I heard about Andrea," said Jerry. "Maybe you already know."

"I doubt it. We haven't talked much lately."

"I guess she was dating Sam, your employee."

"That's a new one. When?"

"Before he left for Alaska."

"Before, as in a few months before? I need to get the dates straight, for the timeline of important milestones I'm building in my mind. Were they 'dating' right before Sam left for Alaska?"

"So I hear." Jerry studied me as I tipped my head against the wall and closed my eyes. "You would have rather not known?"

"I'm a little shocked, but not completely surprised. Andrea and I aren't dating, you know."

"Hey." Jerry held up his hands. "I'm not one to pry."

I grinned, and groaned. "I'm glad you told me. I just don't know if it matters, or what I'm going to do with that information."

"I was afraid to tell you. I didn't want you to be angry with Sam."

"How could I? That's a decent coup for a college boy."

"Depends who you ask," said Jerry.

"Andrea has her pluses and minuses." I rubbed my face with both hands, normally a very enjoyable feeling. "Ow, Jeez."

"You okay?" Jerry was ready to call 9-1-1.

"I feel like I tore the skin off my forehead." I blinked at him. "Did I?"

Jerry inspected me from several feet away. "Looks okay to me."

"It feels like I'm being boiled on the inside. I'm sure it's crazy, but I have this sensation that the chemo is killing everything but the cancer."

Jerry cocked his head; we drifted through time together. "That's probably a common complaint, for people going through what you're going through."

"Hope so."

"How much longer do your treatments last? Ten days?"

"Ten? Holy shit, I'd never make it. Seven. Seven seems like forever."

Jerry raised his hand to pat my shoulder and then thought better of it. Catch my cancer or break my brittle bones.

"Do me a favor? See if Katrina's still here."

Jerry strolled down the hallway, disappeared around the corner, and then reappeared. "All clear."

A small middle-aged woman squeezed past him en route to the bathroom. She stopped in the doorway and stared at me with her head cocked like a puppy. "Are you undergoing treatment?"

"For a few issues, unfortunately," I said.

She moved closer. She was short, her black hair glimmering with silver like tinsel. "I mean cancer treatment. Chemo."

"As a matter of fact I am." I was sure she had overheard me or someone in the shop discussing it.

"You shouldn't." She held out her hand—when I didn't give her mine, she took it. She waved her free hand over the back of my hand, brushing my knuckles. "Mm-hm. I can definitely tell there is some damage going on." She gazed up into my eyes. "You know that chemo drugs are poison?"

"My doctor's the only one who doesn't seem to think so," I said. "I told him that all I need is a motive, and he'll be doing hard time."

"You should stop taking those drugs," said the woman. "I'd recommend stopping immediately. You're suppressing your immune system." She wasn't telling me these things as much as relaying what she was receiving from the astral plane. "That's the key to holding this disease in check." Reluctantly she released my hand to dig in the purse hanging under her arm. She pulled out a pen and a business card, and wrote her name and phone number on the back.

I read the front of the card. "Merle's Meats."

"That's not me," she said. "I picked up that card a few months ago. I was exploring the medicinal effects of animal connective tissues. Gristle, that sort of thing. Nothing came of it. Good meat though." She forced me to turn the card over and tapped it. "I'm Suzanne. You'll call me? We can map out a better treatment plan for you."

She entered the bathroom and I continued on to Jerry. "Interesting gal," he said. "I'd recommend sticking with your medical doctor's advice."

I pocketed her card. "Probably a good idea. I don't know what's worse though. Dying of cancer or dying of chemo."

"It's that bad, huh?"

"Can't sleep, can't stay awake, pooping blood, vomiting…"

"Brian," Charlotte called with an edge to her voice. A line had formed.

"Damn customers, interrupting my laundry list of complaints. Homey, thanks for messing with my mind." I returned to the bar, and retrieved my hat.

Charlotte was a blur of activity, making change and queuing cups and bagging a muffin all at the same time. "I need a tall caramel macchiato—"

"Tall caramel macchiato, stat!" I yelled. Heads swung my way.

Charlotte shook her head, deafer in the left ear. "And a skinny white mocha—"

"Skinny white mocha, coming up!"

Charlotte sighed and glanced down the line. "Ma'am, what can I get you? Oh, Valerie, hi. It's been awhile. The usual?"

I hadn't seen any of the McEwens since before the San Diego trip. That's not true, a week prior I had seen Rick from a distance at Sam's Club and ducked and scuttled into the pet supplies aisle, pretty sure he didn't own a dog, until the coast was clear. And I had clipped an article on the growing demand for teachers out of the hospital's *North Dakota Trails* magazine and sent it to Iz with a note: *They need you back / Hope things are good / Chemo again, no fun, laying low.*

I wanted a long rehearsed speech at the ready when the inevitable confrontation came, to let them all know how much I cared for them and appreciated them, especially the Bluffs site, even if they were bribing me to take junior muff diver off their hands with a gift I couldn't afford to receive. But I hadn't found the energy to write said speech.

Valerie watched me, shaking her head in response to an internal rhetoric that went a little sumthin' like this: *Haven't we done everything for this boy? Yes we have. Did we not take him under our wing, provide him with a golden business investment opportunity at very little down, treat him like a son, serve his coffee at all the meetings and industry symposiums that we host, and bless his proposal to marry our daughter? Yes indeed we did. Then what kind of monster could do this to us?* Of all the McEwens, Valerie was the one I least wanted to face, and without a prepared speech.

"Hey lady," I said. "Two percent chai latté with honey, coming up."

"Well that was pleasant for a change," said Charlotte. "What do you know, maybe you don't need to shout."

She was right, I could taste blood in the back of my throat. Out of the corner of my eye I watched Valerie glide forward like an avenging specter, to pay for her drink before taking a bite out of my everlasting soul.

"Hey Jerry." I tried to make eye contact with my big bald buddy as he stood at the bar polishing off his drink. "I forgot to tell you about my latest run-in with the town."

"I want to hear about it, but I'm running late." Jerry carefully stacked his cup in the heaping dirty dishes bin and made for the door. No doubt Mr. Morality knew why Valerie was there, and approved of what was about to happen, but cared about me too much to stay and watch. "Tell me tomorrow."

"Tomorrow will be too late, but whatever, homey. Whatever." I was casing the crowd for someone in need of a mediocre story.

Valerie floated from the cash register to stand before me. "Hello, Brian."

"Hey lady, how's the McEwen household today?" I talked without looking up, clanking cups and rattling the metal frothing pitcher against the wand, making the sounds of very busy. "Charlotte, what was this?" I nodded at a to-go cup marked SM-LW.

Charlotte stopped to stare at me. "The same thing that particular arrangement of symbols always means. Skinny mocha, light whip."

"Oh. Looked like you slipped a couple Chinese characters in there."

Charlotte grabbed the cup. "Where?"

I snatched the cup back. "It was the angle." I glanced over the espresso machine at Valerie. "I'm sorry, I didn't hear your answer."

"I didn't say anything."

"Mike is good? Rick? Isabel? I haven't seen you guys." I announced the skinny white mocha's presence on the receiving platform like a debutante arriving to the ball. "And you?" I asked Valerie. "You good?"

"I was hoping to speak to you," said Valerie. "Will you have time?"

"Uh, yeah, I should be able to sneak away for a few minutes. As soon as we get this rush taken care of."

"Go," said Charlotte. "You'd probably just mess up the drinks anyway. Since you seem to be having trouble with my handwriting all of a sudden."

"Your penmanship is definitely deteriorating," I said. Valerie drifted to the end of the bar and bobbed there, waiting for me. "Call me if it gets busy. Call me pronto."

"Yes Brian. I will call you." Nothing irritated Charlotte more than pretending we weren't a well-oiled machine able to read each other's thoughts and anticipate each other's next move.

Valerie preceded me into my little office and waited for me to squeeze past before taking a seat, crossing her legs and carefully adjusting her coat over her kneecap. "So."

"I've missed you guys. I feel like we're due for another game night. Or maybe the first ultimate Frisbee game of the season. Are Monica and Gene coming back for a visit any time soon?"

Valerie scowled. "Brian, we're very confused. I was hoping you could shed some light on what you're thinking."

"You mean lately? The past couple weeks? Let's see…I've been focused on trying to keep a meal down. Trying not to think about whether they're going to have to amputate my leg. Wondering whether I need to fire another couple employees to avoid bankruptcy." I hit her with everything I had, to knock her senseless with pity. "Debating moving back to Davis to live with my folks. Just trying to survive."

There was a loosening of the drawstring puckering Valerie's face. "Well…I'm sad to hear all that. We've been worried about you. I really hate not seeing you and hearing how you're doing. Isabel is…" Valerie tugged on the drawstring. "Rick said he saw you at Sam's Club the other day."

"Wish I had seen him. I wanted to tell him I'm impressed with the warehouse his team is putting up on the north side of town."

Valerie nodded. "Isabel wants to call you, to see how you're doing."

"That would be nice. I dropped her a note, not sure if she got it…"

"You wouldn't mind if she called you?"

"No, no. I'd appreciate it." I started entertaining the glorious impossibility that the McEwens were unaware of my San Diego bunkmate.

"Mike hasn't heard from you lately on the Bluffs site."

"I know. Apologize for me. I've been so busy here. And at the hospital."

"You're still planning on going forward with the store?" Valerie pressed.

I started rearranging the stack of bills, slipping the past-due notices to the bottom. "I suppose."

"Brian, if you're not committed to this store, we have to know."

Valerie was Mike's strong arm. Mike had been known to let bad employees run roughshod over him and destroy morale. He would let customers' bad debts ride for months and years and finally fall off the books. I was a case in point. For a construction guy, Mike was a softie. Valerie wasn't.

"We developed the Bluffs," Valerie continued. "It will live or die based on that anchor spot. We owe the other tenants a quality, committed store. It can't sit idle, and it can't move at half speed. We need you at your best."

"I understand that. I do."

Valerie sat forward and tapped my knee. Her plucked eyebrows were raised for the entire ultimatum. "We want you to be part of our family. You're one of us, in everything but name. We don't want a partnership with you. We want a union. You are a leader in this community. Everyone thinks the world of you. Mike loves you, and so does Isabel. You two love each other. So let's do the right thing."

She nodded, slowly, until my head started bobbing too. "I feel like I've been roughed up a little bit," I said. In fact I was borderline giddy, to have escaped scot-free. Now I could write that speech and break up with Isabel on my own terms. Gradually.

"I'm sorry, honey. I can be a little short." Valerie caressed my cheek. "We're so worried about you. The chemotherapy is harsh, isn't it? I remember Brent at this point."

Charlotte was calling, sounding harried, but I couldn't break away from Valerie's gaze. Her hand found mine and squeezed my fingers, turning the tips white. "You have to hang in there and make it through your treatments. We felt so terrible for Brent..." Valerie's eyes glistened. "We didn't want him to suffer any more. So we took the easy way, with Dr. Bhani. It's hard to forgive ourselves for that."

"I'm sure it seemed like the best option at the time."

"We anguished over it," said Valerie. "You remember. That bastard Bhani was so persuasive. He was so confident." The bitterness tugged at Valerie's skin, adding weight to the bags under her eyes and causing her wonderful throat to sag. "I'll never forgive him for what he did to our boy. He experimented on us, when we felt like we had nowhere else to turn."

"Desperate times, I suppose," I said, standing up, a little brusque but feeling like I was the wrong person to sympathize with her son's tragic cancer-related demise.

"We're going to get through this with you, Brian. We'll fight it together. No shortcuts. We'll do things the right way this time." Valerie produced a tissue from her coat pocket and soaked up her tears. She kissed me on the cheek and walked out of the office. "Edna!" she exclaimed. "Edna Applejack!"

Edna Applejack. The murderer was in my shop. I hurried to see.

A little crowd encircled her. I thought she was going to be beaten by a mob of my customers. How many could she kill before they took her down?

Mary Quill the wife of Pastor Brad was shaking her hand. Bart Schock the husband of the local pediatrician was patting her on the back. Suzanne the lady on the back of the Merle's Meats card was touching her sleeve. Valerie ploughed through the group and hugged the tall beautiful ex-con.

"I thought we had an emergency out here, from the sound of your voice," I said to Charlotte.

"Well, sort of, we do," said Charlotte, gazing star-struck at Edna.

"Because she's a killer?" I said below the roomful of excited chatter.

"No because I think I'm going to faint," said Charlotte.

Charlotte was pale, a little wobbly. "Because you're afraid?"

"Because she's a legend," Charlotte hissed. "She's just so...so amazing."

You'd have thought Darin Erstad was in the house. I let loose a blast of air from the frothing wand, claiming everyone's attention for an instant. No reason people couldn't buy drinks while they fawned. "Lady, can I get you something?" I asked Edna.

"It's on the house," Charlotte blurted.

I looked at her.

"I'll pay for it," said Charlotte, heading for her purse.

"No employee discount," I yelled after her, half-joking.

"That's fine," she hollered back. "We have a celebrity in our midst."

"Wow." I punched buttons and shuffled cups, for effect, as Edna moved toward me. "Will I get this treatment too when I get my black belt?"

"Edna's a black belt?" Charlotte gushed as she came hurrying back from the office waving a five-dollar bill. She locked eyes with her favorite killer in the world and blushed. "Oh, hi. I didn't mean to interrupt you."

Edna smiled. She had luxurious blonde hair, almond-shaped eyes, and a long delicate pointed jaw. "Actually I never quite made black belt. And now Master Kwan demoted me back to white after my extended absence." Sharp chin, mellow voice. "And you can interrupt me for espresso any time."

"And ice cream, don't you think?" I said.

"When are we going to get a Cold Stone here, huh?" Edna was a couple inches taller than me. It was an unusual view, the underside of a woman's chin. The skin was stretched taut, a flying buttress from her chin to the midpoint of her throat. If we got into a fight, I would put a death grip on that buttress and ride her like a bucking bronco.

"I love Cold Stone," Charlotte chirped, eager to be included.

"If we don't get one soon," said Edna, "I'll have to start one myself. Until then, thank the Lord for Ben & Jerry's."

"You love Ben & Jerry's too?" Mary Quill squeaked, desperate to be included. "The Funky Monkey. I love the Funky Monkey."

"It's Chunky Monkey," I said.

"No, it's Chunky Hubby," said Mary, laughing a little too loudly while she hyperventilated. "Chunky Hubby. I should know, believe me."

Edna admired Mary's petite frame. "I doubt you overdo the ice cream."

"No, I mean my husband is fat," said Mary.

"Pastor Brad could stand to shed a few pounds," I said. "I don't know if I'd call him fat. Or even Chubby."

"Well I would," said Mary, staring up at Edna, forgetting all about her porky husband.

"I'd recommend the bone cancer diet, but it's expensive. Something like five thousand bucks a pound." No laughs. All the men in the shop, and a few others in attendance, were fantasizing about sleeping with Edna. 'Sleep with Edna' held little allure for me. 'Sleep and wake up' was good enough. "What am I making for you?" I asked Edna's buttress. "Go nuts, Charlotte's buying."

"It's Charlotte?" Edna reached across the bar to shake Charlotte's hand and make her knees wobble. "Edna Applejack."

"Oh I know." Billy Ray Cyrus had stopped in for a coffee on his way to the state fair and hadn't affected Charlotte like this.

"Can Charlotte get the employee discount back if I make the drink myself?" Edna asked me.

"Are you qualified?"

"Eminently."

I turned off the frother, set down the pitcher of milk and wiped my hands on my apron as I stepped away from the espresso machine.

Edna clapped her hands. "Honestly? You'll let me pull a few shots?"

"If you make it yourself, and maybe a couple other drinks, it's on the house."

Edna squealed with pleasure and rounded the counter in four long strides. I retreated to the till as she punched the hot water button to rinse the little metal espresso carafe, pounded the spent grounds from the portafilter, refilled it with fresh ground coffee, and seated it in the machine with authority. She stuck her cute little sorority girl nose in my milk pitchers until she found the one she wanted, then shoved it under the wand and cranked the steam knob.

"The lady's got style, Brian," said Cal Brisbee from the Ford dealership.

I nodded. "I'd say she's done time behind the bar. The espresso bar."

I tensed for a palm-strike to the temple, but Edna grinned. "Hey there," she greeted my part-timer Spence Johnson as he walked in the door. The college boy did a double-take and adjusted his hair so it hung just right over his eyebrows. "Step right up and state your pleasure."

Spence's shift was due to start five minutes ago, but he obediently walked to the till like a customer.

"I've never worked in a coffeeshop," Edna told us. "But I was taught how to do this by Douglas Fosseton."

"No way," I said.

"What can I get you?" Edna asked Spence.

Spence gaped. "Are you working here now?"

"Charlotte's making Edna fix her own drink," I told him.

Charlotte swatted me with a towel. Very politely to Edna she said, "You don't have to make your own drink."

"You're going to have to pry me off this bar," said Edna.

"Soy latté," Spence ordered.

"I was at the Junior National All-Star game at UC-Davis, a long time ago," said Edna, to me, to all twenty-some people in the shop. "I scored forty-three points but missed a shot at the buzzer, and we lost. Coach took us to a coffeeshop after the game. Being a North Dakota farm girl, it was the first one I had ever been in."

I touched my fingers to my temples and closed my eyes like a psychic. "Dougie Fosseton. The Davis Drip."

Edna was shocked. "You know it?"

"I used to work there."

"No kidding! You worked for Douglas Fosseton? We learned from the same master?" Edna finished the frothing and kicked off the espresso switch in what seemed like a single move. She selected the bumblebee mug and poured in a shot, at the same time adding the steamed milk, starting and stopping, alternating espresso and milk. This was wrong.

"It looks beautiful," Charlotte gushed, admiring the creamy chocolate butterfly pattern that had risen from the depths of the drink.

"Try it," said Edna.

"Oh I couldn't," said Charlotte.

"I insist." Edna pushed the mug at Charlotte.

Charlotte's eyes fluttered at Edna over the rim of the cup as she sipped. "It's incredible," she breathed.

Edna took a sip. "Mm. That's the way I remember it."

"Brian," Charlotte reprimanded me, "it's better than yours."

"Craig did roast a heckuva batch of beans."

"No." Charlotte shook her head vehemently. "The drink. There's something about it. It's the best I've ever tasted."

"Sipsies," said Bart, motioning for the cup.

"Bart, girl cooties," I warned.

He shook me off and slurped Edna's latté. "Ohmygosh. That's good. What did you put in there? Is that cream?"

"Skim," said Edna.

Had to be half-and-half, I thought. Two percent at the very least.

"Cocaine?" Bart asked.

"None," said Edna, completing Spence's soy latté. This time the rising crema pattern resembled a miller moth more than a butterfly, in my opinion.

But Spence's reaction was the same. He raved about the drink.

"Come on, Brian, try this." Charlotte stuck the communal cup in my face.

"I have a cold," I said. "I'll never taste it."

"Brian could catch a bug from one of you and die," said Valerie gravely.

"Thank you," I said.

"But I'd like to try it," said Valerie, sparkly-eyed.

"I'll make you a drink," Edna told Valerie. "Then we can have our chat."

She had taken over the bar. I didn't know where to stand. Charlotte hovered at the cash register, not to run it, just to be close to Edna. I'm pretty sure Valerie and the next five customers got their drinks for free.

Edna finally strolled back out onto the floor, to cheers. I told Spence to get his butt behind the bar, told Charlotte I was feeling ill—this was not a lie—and went home.

MY APARTMENT LOOKED LIKE it was for rent, furnished. Mom cleaned before she left, four days' prior, and the place remained immaculate. Cancer didn't make me neat—my van was trashed, stray fries, empty cups, bills, newspapers. I just couldn't stomach cooking for myself. And if I wasn't cooking or eating or cleaning up afterwards, my existence left little trace.

Nothing sounded good. I only agreed to eat if someone else cooked it. I wouldn't even warm leftovers in the microwave. My freezer was still half-full of Valerie's dinners.

I sat in the corner of the couch, desperate for deep sleep. Obviously I was overtired, otherwise getting publicly bitch-slapped by Edna Applejack wouldn't have bothered me so much.

Couldn't force myself to crawl into bed, to disrupt the tight corners Mom left behind, so I had been sleeping on the couch. Despite Dr. Bonilla's assurance that plenty of rest was a good idea, I was afraid to turn my back on the cancer. So I would sit up for the first couple hours, intent on staying awake or at least alert while I rested.

I hadn't adjusted to being alone again, after Ryan and then Mom left. As I had feared, Mom's visit turned me into a sissy, a bachelor mama's boy. I pictured myself dying alone in a sterile room. Tears stung my eyes—the start of a big weeping meltdown if the entrance buzzer hadn't squawked. I sucked it up and asked who was there.

"It's me," came the electronically garbled reply. I hit the buzzer. It could have been Lizzie Borden or Charles Manson, I would have let them up.

Andrea stepped into the apartment and gaped. "Oh my. Your hair. What happened?" Looked like she might turn around and leave.

"It fell out." I gave her a hug. Her body was an undetectable nugget in the center of the puffy packing material of her down coat. Made me feel big, even though I had fast become a shell of my former self.

Andrea wandered through the living room and kitchen, eyeing my place like a prospective renter. "I've been really lonely the past two weeks. Not that you probably care."

I perched on the sofa arm, hands stuffed in my pockets. "Oh I care."

"Do you." She picked up a candle on the window ledge like she was thinking of purchasing it. "Are you ready to apologize to me for ruining my trip to San Diego?"

"I didn't know there was anything to apologize for."

"Oh?" Andrea stood in front of me for a moment before seeking out the easy chair backed up to the window. She huddled on the edge of the seat. "Well, I spent almost two grand on a plane ticket for a two-night stay. That sounds like a problem, doesn't it? When I was expecting a long weekend?"

"Your room was free the second night," I reminded her. Andrea looked down at the floor and started to cry. "Hey now, I'm sorry. I didn't know it hit you that hard." I retrieved the box of tissues Mom left behind. "Come on now," I coaxed as she dried her face. "Let's talk this out. You know I had to get back to work, don't you?"

"All I know is it hurt," Andrea snapped. "It was like you couldn't wait to get away from me after the first night." She choked out a gurgly sob.

"I was so worried about the shop," I groveled half-heartedly. "Although I guess I could have stayed a couple extra days, since I'm going to lose business anyway, when word gets out that you were with me."

This cheered her up. "Has anyone said anything? Does Mike know?"

"Not unless he's keeping it on the down-low while he lines up the hit. Which might not be so bad." I groaned as I lowered my withered butt into the couch. "I talked to Valerie today and she never brought you up."

"Hmm. Maybe I need to say something."

I shrugged, bluffing. "If you have to."

"I'm assuming you broke it off with Isabel."

"I haven't talked to her since we've been back, so..."

"God," Andrea snorted.

"It's going to happen. It was going to happen regardless what happened in San Diego. But I'd prefer to do it with a little class. Isabel deserves it."

"Does she?"

"Hey." That was the sharpest tone I had used on Andrea. On most anyone. She looked like she had been slapped. "Isabel deserves my respect. And so does her family. Plus," I exposed my seamy underbelly, the part Andrea liked, "I need to stay on Mike's good side if I want to do business in this town."

"Mm. Well then." Andrea's demeanor softened. She removed her coat, exposing a lot of skin in a sleeveless skintight white shirt. "Have you missed me these last two weeks?"

"I have. But my leg has been keeping me busy. How'd my vaccine sample turn out for your boss?"

"I don't know. I don't think Dr. Bhani has much time for research. He has three state health labs requesting information and interviews. And of course the McEwens are suing him for malicious negligence."

"Mean *and* sloppy. I don't know if there's a worse combination."

Out of the blue—I can only assume by the cosmic coincidence of pairing "mean" with "sloppy" while being within a couple yards of that translucent shirt—I got horny. And horny begat bravado. I was suddenly horny and confident. Confident I was sexy no matter how hairless and emaciated. And confident I didn't need to put up with a girl like Andrea to make it through the night. I could stand on my own two feet. I could brave the howling winds of fate alone. Right after some sex. I would seduce her, complete our sexual liaison in the next fifteen minutes, and send her packing.

I patted the couch. "Why don't you come sit over here with me?"

Andrea gave me a suspicious smile. "You're feeling lonely over there?"

I rubbed the seat cushion. "Uh-huh."

She sat primly next to me. I leaned on her and kissed her. I had the angle this time, there would be no confusion about the location of her nipples. In fact, I could see a hint of them through that shirt, which was tucked into her jeans. I took hold of the lowest exposed button and tugged.

"You, uh, you don't like this shirt?" Andrea wondered.

"It's a beautiful shirt." A gut cramp doubled me over; I went with it, kissing her stomach through the filmy fabric. I felt like shit but very much alive. "Is this a deep tuck?"

"I don't know." Andrea sat back and let her hands flop to her sides. "I guess you'll have to find out."

"I intend to." I tugged and tugged, lifting her hips off the couch. The shirttails cleared her jeans. I popped the bottom button and worked my way up. In very little time her shirt was open, exposing a lacy bra. "You have a beautiful body," I told her. "I've been dreaming about it since San Diego."

"Really." Some heat was brewing beneath her cool demeanor. "Have you." She looked me in the eye while I reached around to unhook her bra. "Do you think this is fair? Hm? Well, goodbye shirt," she bid the garment adieu. I was manhandling her, stripping her, pressing against her, kissing her. She broke it off. "Do you think this is fair?" she repeated, reprimanding me. "Shouldn't your shirt come off about now? Uh, goodbye bra. Are you going to *strip* me bare and *have* your way with me?"

I yanked my shirt off. "Both."

Knock-knock.

God help me, I said, "Who's there?"

"It's Isabel," came the reply.

I wanted to holler, "How'd you get up here?" Instead, "Give me a second," while I put my shirt on. Andrea just laid there. "Go-go-go," I hissed.

She arched an eyebrow and smacked gum I hadn't known she was chewing. "Are we done?" She kept her voice down, not quite low enough.

"Can I get you to wait in the bedroom?" I whispered. "I'll take Isabel out of here, and then you can leave."

"Or maybe I'll stay." Andrea took her time gathering her shirt and bra, and strutted her stuff across the apartment. She had a high butt and a short back. "Good luck," she said.

I put on my baseball cap and waited for Andrea to be safely hidden, before opening the door. Iz stood like a zombie. A bag of groceries slipped from her fingers. I caught it an inch above the floor and leaned the bag against the jam.

Isabel stared into the apartment. "Is someone here?"

I deflated. Even though I didn't have my speech written, I could have marshaled the courage to usher Iz out of there and spend the next five hours parked on the bluff, extemporaneously explaining how this had nothing to do with her and everything to do with me. I wasn't prepared to lie to her face. I peeked at her from under the brim of my cap. "Someone's in the bedroom."

Isabel bit her lip and nodded. "Who is it?"

"Oh man." This was unbelievably terrible. My heart was sinking rapidly. "I'd rather not say. I'm sorry…"

Isabel bent to pick up the groceries, couldn't make sense of her opposable thumbs and abandoned the bag with an anguished squeak. She hurried for the stairs with her hands on her face. I stood in the doorway, holding onto the door handle for support, head drooping, eyes squeezed shut. When I looked up, Isabel was back in front of me.

"I forgot to give you this." She held up the engagement ring I purchased four years ago on credit. I owned approximately sixty percent of it.

"Can we please postpone this discussion, for a little while anyway?"

Iz grabbed my wrist and jammed the ring into my palm. She closed my fingers around it, her hand lingering on mine for a moment. "No," she told herself and dropped my hand. "It's definitely over."

I shivered as we stared at each other. "Iz, I'm sorry."

She drew a shuddering breath and stopped searching my eyes for clues. "I'm obviously not satisfying you, so there's nothing to be sorry about." She looked beyond me, toward my bedroom. "Except for handling it like this." Isabel stumbled backward toward the stairs, turning at the last second and clutching the banister to aid her descent.

I tiptoed to my living room window, without shutting the apartment door, not ready to signal Andrea's release from the bedroom. Iz had collapsed on the front walk. I was about to go to her when Dennis hurried out of the building and helped her up. He put his arm around Isabel and guided her inside. I felt the door to apartment number one thud shut. Dennis's dream moment.

There was a certain amount of relief, surrounding a gaping hole that should have been filled with the speech I never wrote and never gave.

Andrea left the bedroom without authorization. "Is she gone?"

I held up the engagement ring. "Made it official." As if I had ended it. In a way I did.

Andrea put her hands on her hips. "It's about time."

"That's what Dennis thought too," I complained.

"Who's Dennis?"

"My downstairs neighbor. He and Iz were high school classmates. Dennis always had a thing for her. She's in his apartment right now." I suddenly pictured the two of them in the Kama Sutra commiseration position. "I'd like to get out of here for awhile. You wanna go to a movie?"

She put her hands on my hips. "If I recall, what you had in mind wasn't legal in a movie theater."

I removed Andrea's hands. Her face fell. "I don't have it in me. I hate to use my cancer as an excuse, but it's hitting me hard right now." The stomach cramp was still there, and me without a boner.

"Maybe you should just go to bed," Andrea suggested, disgusted.

"I have to eat something so I can take my next round of pills. Of course I'm pretty sure I'll puke up anything I eat. And these pills are eating a hole through my stomach even with food in there, judging by the excruciating pain and the blood in my poop."

"Maybe you should quit the chemo and let Dr. Bhani cure you."

"Has he ever cured anyone?" I shot back.

Andrea was indignant. "A lot of people. He cured Rick's brother."

"Cured him dead."

"A lot of people catch an infection in the hospital. A lot."

"Most people aren't *given* an infection to cure their disease," I pointed out. "A lot of doctors frown on it. It's on the list with leeches and bloodletting."

Andrea went on defending Bhani, but I wasn't into the argument. The more we talked about cancer and disease, the worse I felt. "I have to lie down for a bit." I started for the bedroom. "Will you tuck me in?"

Andrea soured. "That sounds like loads of fun."

"It was more like a favor." I imagined Tyler asking for a kiss goodnight and Andrea snarling, *Again? You got one last week.* "You don't have to."

"Go climb in bed, and I'll kiss you goodnight. Good afternoon, I guess. Let's not make a habit of this, okay?"

"You're right, I need to commit myself to making it through an entire day without napping or puking." I dropped my shorts and crawled into bed while Andrea loitered outside the door. My stomach was twisting and my thighs vibrated. The blood left my head, left it cold and ringing. "Could I get you to bring me a warm washcloth for my forehead?" I called.

I heard her sigh. "Warm? With water?"

Maybe I could call Iz back up. "If you could."

"You want it wet then."

"I guess so. Not dripping," I was hesitant to request.

Andrea worked soundlessly. Or I passed out. Whichever, there she stood above me with a damp washcloth draped over her hand.

My teeth chattered. "Hurry before it cools down."

"My God." She stared down at me, not liking what she saw. "Aren't you pathetic."

"I know." I nodded at the cloth.

Andrea folded it and again the long way and laid it on my forehead. "There." She patted it condescendingly, careful not to touch my skin.

The last tremors worked their way out of my ribcage and my body relaxed. Andrea stood over me with her arms crossed. "Is this it for you today?"

"Could be. I hope not. But it's possible. I feel like crap."

"I couldn't tell." She weighed leaving. "I had something to tell you, but now I don't know."

"Now's the time to bare your soul. All the terrible things you've done. Chances are I won't remember it when I wake up."

"It's about your work. I've been thinking a lot about it since San Diego."

I shifted a few inches inland to make room. "Have a seat." Twenty minutes ago Andrea had been high maintenance and I couldn't wait to get physical and get rid of her. Now I was needy, and all I wanted was to be babied.

She looked around for a chair. "I'll stand."

No doubt I had become repulsive to her. "It's not contagious."

"I'll just tell you what I'm thinking, and then you can mull it over and get back to me when you're feeling a better."

"Give it to me fast. Gauging by what's going on in my gut right now, I have about ten minutes before I puke again."

"Wonderful. Well…you said you want to open another shop, but you can't, because you can't be in two places at once. I have a solution."

"If it's cloning, I'm all for it. I would absolutely love another me. Without the cancer."

"Yeah. No. That's not it. It doesn't involve cloning."

"Can your boss do it, though? And I'm not talking about a Baby Brian that I have to raise and wait for him to grow up. For all I know, by the time he becomes an adult he wouldn't even want to run a coffeeshop. And it would be too late by then anyway. I can't hang in there financially for another eighteen years. Two is probably a better estimate. He needs to come out of the cloning tank an adult, with my exact brain."

"Are you done?" Andrea sat on the very edge of the bed, and rested her hand unnaturally on my hip. "No. What I'm thinking is, *I* could be your partner. I received a nice settlement from Rick. So cash isn't an issue. I could manage the workers, and work a shift here and there. *You* could just flit back and forth between the stores, working the crowd, doing whatever you do to make the customers happy and keep them coming in the door. We could run three or four stores like that, at least. You're nodding."

Nodding as a substitute for responding. I turned on my side and cuddled into my pillow. "Did you know that when I was young, I would call my mom into my bedroom at night to flip my pillow over when it got too warm?"

Andrea crossed her arms. "You had your mom flip your pillow over."

"I like a cool pillowcase," I cooed with a dreamy smile and drowsy eyes, willing myself to fall into a coma-like slumber.

"I'm not surprised, now that I had to place a warm cloth on your head."

"Same kind of thing, huh?"

Andrea rested her hands in her lap. "So what do you think?"

I was wide awake, forced to respond. "I didn't know you were spending time thinking about my business dilemma."

"It occurred to me that this is a solution that helps both of us."

"How would this help you? Other than partnering with a coffee kingpin."

"Because…" Here was her *ta-da!* moment. "…our stores would be in Colorado. Or California."

I blinked at her for awhile. I might have looked pretty cute, curled up and looking up at her sideways, blinking, still the owner of most of my eyelashes. The shaved head and pale skin probably ruined the effect. And the scraggly beard. It hurt to shave.

"You can't leave the state," I reminded her.

"I'm pretty sure this would be enough reason for the judge to let me go."

"What about Tyler?"

"We'd have to work out a sharing arrangement. Rick can afford to fly him back and forth. Or, I'd get sole custody."

"What would Rick say?"

"What would Rick say?" Andrea pondered. She was having fun shooting down one objection after another. She seemed to think I was playing devil's advocate. "Hm. He should say, 'Gosh, I guess I shouldn't have treated you quite so badly. Then maybe I'd still be married to you, and I could move with you back to Colorado.'"

"I think Mike would hire a team of cutthroat East Coast lawyers to get full custody of Tyler and have you declared mentally incompetent, lobotomized, and tossed in a dark hole with a pound of coffee and your favorite slippers."

Andrea shook her head. "That's not like Rick. It's not that he doesn't love Tyler. He does. He just wouldn't fight it if the judge okayed it. I think in the end he would move wherever Tyler and I moved."

"And leave his business here?"

"His dad isn't going to retire for a few years—he's having too much fun working with Rick. And they have a guy working for them that Rick thinks would make a good partner eventually."

"It's not Joshua Grunden by any chance?"

"You know him?"

"I do. Joshua knows we had a date, by the way."

"When I came for dinner? I wouldn't call it a date," said Andrea. "I remember you saying you had friends over for dinner all the time."

"But I don't have sex with them a week later. Usually."

"Let's get back to the topic at hand, shall we?"

"You want me to abandon my shop here and run away to Colorado."

"We could have a transition phase," said Andrea. "You would stay here, and I would run the shop in Colorado. You'd have to make quite a few trips the first couple months. You'd have to stay with me when you were in Denver. I'm sure you'd hate that." Andrea smoothed her jeans atop her thighs, certain that I couldn't wait to get my dirty paws all over her silky drawers. The way I was feeling, the aborted attempt on the couch might have been my last hurrah.

"We could get along for a few days at a time," I played along with her fantasy.

"What if you traveled all that way, and then I made you late for work?"

"I'm never late for work. I hate being late. I still remember the one time my dad chewed my ass for being late. He told me that being late is disrespectful to the people waiting for you, and to yourself. He laid into me for a good ten minutes. I was never late for dinner again. Or anything else."

"Well." Andrea sat up straighter and pulled her shirt down tighter against her chest. "We'll see who wins that discussion."

"Have you ever managed a retail store?"

"I worked at the Gap in high school and college," said Andrea. "I was assistant manager when I left. I know how to manage people, believe me." Gestapo Andrea. *Ve have vays of making you vork.*

"Coffeeshop employees are different." I rolled onto my back, hoping to untie the knot in my intestine. "If we were going to do something like this, the two of us would need to be within shouting distance while you learned the business. Contrary to popular belief, it takes some skill. You could manage the Bluffs store. Then I could—"

"No. We're not doing it here. I have no desire to stay in Jamestown. Or anywhere in North Dakota. Neither do you. You can't make any money here. North Dakotans don't appreciate good coffee."

"Neither do you."

"I thought you wanted to be big," Andrea challenged.

"I do." I sat up in bed. My stomach didn't want me standing up, it didn't want me lying down. This was the last realistic position to try. "But I already tried to make it in a bigger market. A very sophisticated coffee market. I got my ass handed to me."

"That was before you met me."

"Talking smack before you even get behind the bar. I like that. Here, I might as well get up." Andrea stood aside and I shuffled to the kitchen. "I have to eat something so I can get some more of that freaking poison in me."

"Wow," said Andrea when I opened the fridge, surveying my condiments and fruit. "That's pathetic. Why do you have all that fruit in there?"

"They were going bad on the countertop."

"Now they're going bad in the refrigerator."

"I can't bring myself to eat fruit lately." I swung the door shut and sighed. "What am I going to eat?"

"Don't you have anything in this place?" Andrea opened and quickly closed one cupboard door after another. "I guess not."

The phone rang. "Probably the shop. I've been neglecting it the past few days. I can't afford to be paying so much in wages, but…this is Brian."

"Brian, it's Mike."

My pulse quickened. "Mike. How are you? I'm glad you found me. I suppose you tried the shop. I went home early," I felt the need to apologize. "The chemo has been stomping me lately."

"That's what I heard," said Mike, voice flat.

"Valerie said you'd be calling about the new location." I heard Mike breathing through his nose. "She said it's put-up or shut-up time at the Bluffs."

"That's not really why I'm calling, but you should know that the finishing crew is coming in Monday." Sounded like Mike was holding the phone a foot from his face. "They need fifteen grand in hand Monday morning."

"Fifteen. Ouch."

"I guess that's what it takes if you're serious about this store."

"You've been great to me, Mike. Really great. You've never asked for a dime until now. But fifteen grand is doubtful." Mental picture of my checking account. "Make that impossible."

"There's something I need to ask you. When you were in San Diego, was there a woman with you?"

"There was."

"Was it Andrea? Was it Rick's ex?"

"It was. She needed a vacation," I spoke conversationally, just telling another story, "and when she heard I was going someplace warm.... I ended up coming back early. The Chamber meetings went well—"

"Stop it. Don't...don't..." Mike cleared his throat, for ten seconds. "I need to say this before I lose control of my emotions. You have until Monday morning at nine to deposit fifteen thousand in the Bluffs operating account. Otherwise I'm moving forward with an alternate tenant."

"Alright, I'll do what I can. About San Diego—"

"I'm not going to tell Val or Isabel," Mike talked over me. "Neither of them needs to know. As far as I'm concerned..."

Silence. I couldn't tell whether Mike was choking up or losing cell coverage. Andrea smirked as she gazed out the window, enjoying the crap out of this conversation.

"This needs to be face to face," said Mike.

And I thought the phone was perfect for this. "I have to run out for some lunch. I guess we could meet somewhere." I sounded nonchalant but my hands shook. "I was thinking Maggie's by the Buffalo Mall." Public place, lots of people, hopefully a few good Samaritans and plenty of witnesses.

"Meet me at the Bluffs," Mike instructed. "I'll pick you up something from Taco Johns. I'll be there in fifteen minutes."

"Alright. Get me a Taco Bravo and—"

Mike hung up. I stared at the ceiling until Andrea said, "I gather you're in trouble."

"You could say that." If I had felt stronger I would have thrown the phone through the window. I let it clatter to the table instead. "Fuck."

"Okay, tell me what's wrong." Andrea couldn't keep the satisfaction off her lips. "Hm?"

"First of all...naw, I gotta get ready to go. You can hang out here if you like." I applied fresh pit stick and pulled a clean polo shirt off the hanger. Andrea watched me from the dining room. "I want to smell nice for the emergency personnel, after Mike shoots me," I explained.

"He's angry?" she asked, as if this was unreasonable of Mike. "Does he expect you to marry Isabel, even if you don't love her?"

"The point, Andrea," I was sharp with her, "is why don't I? Why don't I love Iz? That's the way it was supposed to work. And I honestly can't say I don't love her. Part of me wants to go bust down Dennis's door..." My voice rose, they could probably hear me through the cheap-ass floor. "...and kick his ass for consoling my fiancée! That's the least Mike should be able to expect from me! It's the least I should expect from myself. Where's my hat?!" I had no clutter, where the hell could it hide? "We spent a long time together, and Iz deserves better than Dennis. I really like the idea of being with her."

"Why don't you then?" Andrea snapped.

"You didn't let me finish. I said I liked the *idea*. When I picture Iz, what she looks like, her sense of humor, the way she looks at me..." I tucked in my shirt for a change. "I like everything I see. Isabel in theory is a great gal. In actual practice, there's something missing."

"Oh. And that missing *something*...do you find it with anyone else?" Andrea was certain-sure she possessed it and I wanted it, couldn't contain my desire for it, couldn't stop myself from all manner of destructive acts to get my hands on it.

I hustled past her, looking for my keys. "This is something we should discuss when I'm not worried about a couple of Mike's construction thugs sending me down the James River in a trunk. I'm really doubting my sanity right now, for the things I've done lately...where the hell are my keys?" I spotted a key and part of the ring sticking out from between the couch cushions, where I had been trying to diddle Andrea.

"With me, you mean?" Andrea demanded. "You're doubting your sanity being with me?"

I stopped at the door. "We might be having two different conversations here. Let's pick this up later. In the meantime, if you have fifteen grand ready to invest by Monday morning, that would be good."

"I won't spend a dime in North Dakota," Andrea crabbed.

"You staying or leaving?"

"Oh, can I come with you to lunch? Since you didn't feed me here?"

"There's plenty here if you're resourceful. Why don't you stay and see if there's a recipe in my Betty Crocker cookbook that involves squishy nectarines, moldy bananas and a variety of condiments. Penicillin porridge."

"I have to go pick up Tyler."

"Then let's go. I don't want to keep Mike waiting."

"Sure, rush me, kick me out. Isabel's family still comes first."

I shook my head at her. "You are extremely high maintenance."

"Yeah. But I'm worth it."

I wasn't so sure.

MIKE WAS LOOKING out the door of the vacant coffeeshop space, his eyes an inch above my *Coming Soon* sign. He saw me and turned away, then as an afterthought twisted the deadbolt to let me in.

"Thanks." I paused in the doorway. "Did you get us lunch, or—"

Mike pointed at Subway bags and fountain drinks on the window sill.

Subway. He had promised Taco Johns. I bit back a complaint and picked up a sub. "What'd you get me?"

"You got what I get. Italian."

After a month of yogurt shakes, 'Nilla Wafers and Cream of Wheat, I had no business getting friendly with a bunch of salami, pepperoni, oil and cheese. But, it was free, and the fear of indigestion was no match for the thought of the chemo drugs sloshing unchaperoned in my stomach. I grabbed our subs and our drinks and followed Mike across the empty room, walking over the future location of the espresso bar and the long counter that the morning crowd was going to love. Mike stopped at the back wall.

"We're not going to sit in the office?"

"This will be fine," said Mike.

"For sure. We get spoiled by chairs and tables." I held up his sandwich bag. When he grabbed it I lost control of the drinks. One of them only left my hand for a moment, but the other did a complete flip in the air. I caught it a foot off the floor and set both drinks down without spilling a drop. I spread my arms. Ta-da! Mike ignored all this.

He stood staring at the wall while I sat crosslegged on the floor, obsessed with food, unbagging and unwrapping my sandwich. I took a big bite, got a cramp in the cancer leg, straightened it, and knocked over Mike's drink. The lid popped off. "Oopsies. Can you grab a rag?"

Mike scowled at the puddle expanding over the concrete floor. I think this was to be my Last Supper, out of the goodness of his heart, and now he regretted the distraction. While I threw down napkins he laid into me.

"What you did was wrong, Brian. Worse than wrong."

"You're right. I screwed up. I'm sorry, Mike. I apologized to Iz, and I want to apologize to you and Valerie."

Mike paced to the window and back. I did the best I could on the spill, then scooted away from the wet spot and got after my sandwich, staring at the floor to camouflage my chewing—I didn't want to be disrespectful, Mike had every right to a good rant.

"I would have staked my reputation that you were incapable of doing this to anyone," Mike barked. "Certainly not to Isabel. I still can't believe it. Am I missing something?" He spread his arms, waiting. Thinking Mike would blow steam for awhile, I had taken a big bite. His blood pressure rose while I chewed. "There is no excuse for this!" Mike yelled. "I want to know exactly what you were thinking when you took Andrea to San Diego!"

I'm capable of groveling. I'd do it without hesitation, if the need ever arose, if the situation called for it. What that situation could possibly be, I don't know. But when it arises, my pride will not get in the way, I promise you that.

When I screw over a good person, someone I like and respect, someone who feels likewise about me, I'm not going to beg their forgiveness. I shouldn't have to. That's friendship—it isn't a guarantee of future performance, it's a credit balance to carry you through the rare deficits.

One of my good friends in high school was built exactly like Mike. Frightening head and a drill sergeant face atop a wrestler's stunted body, starved and dehydrated down to high-strung muscle and bone. Seth was a year older than me. I made out with his girlfriend after a basketball game—a game Seth starred in while I sat on the bench. Substitutes and role players, cancer victims and failing businessmen, there's no accounting for some girls' tastes.

When Seth confronted me at a party at Ryan's house the next night, I admitted it. No rationalizing, no excuses, no lying about being drunk. No explanation, period. "Yes, Seth, I made out with Paige. I fucked up, and I'm sorry." Seth slugged me in the face, and so began what we all still remember as The Fight. It started upstairs, continued downstairs, and moved back upstairs. We broke a desk, a chair, the law, a door, and a wall. When it was over, and even though we took a rest break in the middle during an extended headlock, I've never been so tired.

I don't know if Seth was thinking something like: *Brian's the same guy I've always known, this doesn't change that. I've known him a long time and he's always treated me right. He's due one screw-up, and I know I can trust him never to do it again.* But after the fight he looked me in the eye, clapped me on the shoulder, and said "Good brawl, dude," as we were escorted to the back seat of the police car waiting out front. We've remained good friends.

When I said "sorry" to Seth and now to Mike, a lot was obviously left unsaid. It's not *Caveat emptor, let the buyer beware;* and it's not *Humans are weak in general and we men in particular are pigs.* It's not *I'm flawed, you're flawed, and so you can't be surprised this happened; and no matter how bad I feel and how strongly I vow to be good, starting* now, *remember that we are all flawed creatures, and so you can't be one hundred percent confident it'll never happen again.*

But of course it's a little of all of that. Mostly it's trust that has grown out of our friendship. Trust that I'm morally bright enough to recognize and lament my mistake, and morally strong enough not to do it again. It all goes without saying; so don't make me say it. Haven't I proven to you repeatedly in years' past that I'm a good guy, a caring guy, a thoughtful guy, a trustworthy guy? Haven't I done you favors without you asking? Haven't I gone out of my way to be good to you? If I grovel now and make all sorts of excuses, I'm cheapening everything that's come before.

And if you're going to demand that I get down on my knees and beg your forgiveness, you're throwing back in my face everything I've ever done right. And then maybe it is go time.

(By the way, I think in the end Seth believed I let him burn off his aggression, that for our friendship I risked my face and brain and organs to let him take his warrior's vengeance on me and thereby reclaim his honor. He'll never know how at a certain point in the fight something snapped in me and I was hoping to knock him out or worse.)

Mike stood above me, fists clenched, waiting. I swallowed before the recommended minimum number of chews, and said as heartfelt as possible, "Mike, I'm sorry. Here." I poured half my Dr. Pepper in his cup and securely sealed the lid.

Mike loomed above me. "That can't be all you have to say."

I leaned against the wall and cocked my head to make eye contact. "Mike, I fucked up. I'm sorry. I don't know what else there is to say."

"God d-" Mike choked on taking the Lord's name in vain and headbutted the wall, a nasty but calculated blow, aimed at the middle of the unfinished sheetrock, equidistant between two studs. I put my sandwich down and wished for a clean napkin for the oil and vinegar on my chin.

Mike lurched toward the big plate-glass window, hands opening and clenching, yearning for something to throw in the empty room. "You're engaged to my daughter!"

"She gave me the ring back today."

Mike chugged back to where I was sitting and held out his square hand. "Do you have it? I'm gonna shove it up your ass."

"I left it at home," I lied. I was going to pawn it right after the meeting.

"Do you think this is funny?"

"Not at all."

Mike fumed at my knack for remaining outwardly calm in a crisis. "Why don't you stand up," he growled.

I did. "We have company."

Joshua Grunden and Edna Applejack came in through the storage room entrance. "Hey boss!" Joshua greeted Mike, and then me, "Hey, Brian," with less gusto. He wore a tight paint-splattered t-shirt bulging with muscles. Same for the tight worn-out blue jeans. Edna had on a tanktop and red sweatpants. She sure had nice shoulders.

"Brian!" Edna exclaimed. "You're still in this thing?" She threw a trim arm around my neck and beamed at Mike and Joshua. "What a team!"

"We're a team?" I asked.

"Brian has decided not to invest in this store," said Mike. If a team was forming, Mike didn't want me on it.

Joshua was disoriented, trying to figure out what he had stumbled into. Edna—so much for women's intuition—kept on babbling. "No way! Why? This is a great location! Brian, why aren't you pumped?"

"It's not that I'm not pumped. I am. I'm also broke. Or less than broke, as far as my creditors are concerned. I'm definitely in the hole."

"And you still owe me a dinner," Joshua piled on with a weak smile.

I managed the same. "You catch 'em, I'll cook 'em."

Someone was giving the front door a good shake. "They're not open yet!" Mike yelled, failing to recognize the alien form of Dr. Bhani.

Edna hustled to the door. I imagined her darting across the lane to receive a pass from her point guard. She twisted the bolt lock and threw open the door and ushered Dr. Bhani inside. "Congratulations, you're our first customer!" Edna had her arm threaded inside Bhani's, so that he appeared to be escorting her, right toward Mike. "Of course we're not quite open yet," she cooed.

"Are you a member of the set of 'we'?" I asked Edna, confused. "Hi Dr. Bhani. This is quite the surprise."

"I heard you were opening soon," said Dr. Bhani. "We're desperate for coffee over there. Oh." He finally noticed Mike. "Hello there…"

Mike growled and seized Bhani by the suit coat lapels, driving the mad scientist backward. Neither of them said anything, but there was grunting, surprised grunting, angry grunting. Bhani's dress shoes made tap-dancing sounds as they skimmed the floor. Caught off guard, Edna still beat them to the door and pushed it open as Mike propelled Bhani through the opening. I could easily see her providing weak-side defensive help, crossing the lane to swat away a back-door layup in the nick of time.

Dr. Bhani was inside the shop for twenty seconds. Now he was back on the sidewalk and Mike was locking the door. A dust devil sprang up in the empty end of the parking lot and twisted for Bhani, peppering him with salted grit. He walked away rubbing his eyes like he was crying.

"Holy shit, Mike," said Edna. "I guess we're not open yet."

"It's 'we'?" I asked again. "Because not too long ago, it was just 'me'."

Mike roared and charged me.

When you get your black belt, the government registers you as a deadly weapon. To avoid prosecution, you have to announce your ranking three times before kicking someone's ass. At least that's what we were told. Although I was not yet a black belt, I had been preparing for that moment.

"I'm a black belt I'm a black belt I'm a black belt!"

I think I deep-down hoped that after attending a hundred or so classes, doing a couple thousand air kicks, and memorizing ten choreographed routines, I would now be equipped with instinctive and debilitating counterstrikes for every occasion. But with Mike bearing down I backpedaled, keeping my bad leg behind me, tucking my elbows tight to my body to protect my soft underbelly. Not exactly Bruce Lee. Maybe Sara Lee.

Joshua picked off Mike with a slick under-and-up blocking maneuver that ended with Mike against the wall. Edna with her catlike quickness jumped between us, standing tall and waving her arms. "Whoa, whoa, easy there guys," she refereed.

Mike suddenly dropped, going from standing to sitting in a split-second. His teeth clacked when he hit the floor.

"Joshua!" Edna yelped. "Did you have to hit him?" She seemed prepared to accept a pop to Mike's jaw, as long as it was deemed necessary.

"He slipped," said Joshua. "The floor's all wet." He bent over to help Mike to his feet. Edna was checking out his goods, the muscles rippling across his back and bulging in his arms. Joshua told me once he hadn't pumped iron, ever, except to see how much he could lift. He didn't do pushups or sit-ups or chin-ups, unless it was a contest, which he always won. I accused him of being developed in a governmental lab, and he had just smiled at me.

Mike refused assistance. His pants squished like a diarrhea diaper as he rolled away from Joshua. He struggled to hands and knees and then his feet.

"You alright Mike?" Edna asked.

Face white as a sheet, Mike swatted at his butt, splattering Joshua and the wall with Dr. Pepper, and advanced on me.

I moved out of Edna's shadow. *Now* I was ready. While not quite second nature, the Taekwondo skills were available. This time when Mike charged me, I would snap a front kick under his chin and follow that up with a jab to the nose. Then a sidekick to send that crazy old bastard through the drywall. I was getting angrier by the second. It was message time for Mike.

"You don't want a piece of this, Mike. If we're gonna go, we're gonna go for real. I won't stop until one of us is dead." I hated being dead more than anything in the world. But I meant what I said. "I fucking mean it."

"You sonofabitch." Mike's legs were wobbly. Edna could have held him off with one hand. I didn't care. I was ready to take him apart. "You dishonored my daughter," Mike growled. "With that slut."

"Mike, come on now," Joshua reprimanded. "Brian's not that kind of guy. Brian and Isabel weren't right for each other."

Mike turned on him. "What do you mean? That's crap. Don't you dare make excuses for him."

Joshua was painfully earnest. "That's not an excuse. That's the truth."

"You're ready to collapse," said Edna, maneuvering Mike to the low windowsill. "Did you hurt something when you fell?"

"I slipped," Mike muttered. "Brian spilled my drink all over."

"I did ask you for a rag."

Mike twisted out of Edna's light touch and shook a finger at me. "Instead of smart-mouthing me, you need to apologize." He winced and bent forward, reaching for his lower back.

"I already apologized. To you and Isabel. And I meant it. I am sorry. If that's not enough, then I guess we can keep talking. But right now you need to get out of my face and go see a doctor."

"Don't tell me what to do," Mike snarled. This time he let Edna lead him to the windowsill. He yelped when his butt touched down, and toppled onto his side. "Oh, good gravy, I think I broke something."

"Coccyx," said Edna, kneeling to cradle Mike's head until he was resting in an awkward fetal position. "I saw a girl do exactly what you did, in a game. Came down right on her butt. Broke her coccyx. Too bad you kicked that doctor out of the store. We could use him about now."

Mike's jaw worked furiously. "I'll go get a real doctor," I volunteered.

"I'll go with you," said Joshua, following me outside. He squinted into the wind. "Sorry about what happened in there. From the way Mike was talking, I didn't know you were still planning to own this shop."

"I wasn't," I admitted. "Not really. Mike handed me the location, and then pushed me hard to get in there. I kept stalling him, and now lately he's had a change of heart. But I thought it was still officially mine. He gave me until Monday to get fifteen grand together for the finishing work."

The hospital was walking distance, but the parking lots were separated by a mucky ditch. I wanted to drive, but wasn't going to wimp out in front of Joshua. We leaped the trench as one. I landed almost as high up the opposite bank as Joshua. And that was with a cancer leg.

"I suppose that fifteen grand is for you," I said.

"A tiny piece of it," said Joshua. "I'm doing the taping and texturizing. And the painting."

"What color?"

"Dark cherry and deep amber."

"It's Bill Hernandes, isn't it?"

Joshua frowned. "I didn't know you were still involved," he repeated.

"It's not your fault." I wondered how long Mike had Bill waiting in the wings. Even though I had been stringing Mike along, I felt betrayed. "How about Edna? Do you know her pretty well?"

Joshua was reanimated. "Oh yeah. She's the only girls' basketball player I've ever met who might be able to beat me. She could dunk."

"Nice."

"I think she's investing in the coffeeshop with Bill. Mike's been talking with them for a month now."

I stopped to look back lovingly at the JRV shop that could have been.

"Sorry," said Joshua.

"Forget about it, homey. I couldn't have managed it." This I tried to convince myself, while a part of me screamed that the site was mine. "So what's with this Edna? Is she out on parole, or did she break out of prison?"

Joshua chortled. We entered the hospital. "She served her time, I guess.

Her husband was a scumbag. Too bad she had to do any time at all."

"I heard he was a harmless computer nerd."

Joshua shrugged. "Maybe. Edna's a great woman."

"So I've heard." Her dead husband's mother probably blamed him too.

"They're going to retire her number at a ceremony Monday. The College waited for her to get out."

"The first felon to have her number retired at JC?" I wondered.

Joshua pondered my question. "I don't know."

"Excuse me," I interrupted a nurse's paperwork. "I need two orderlies and a stretcher."

The nurse jumped to her feet. "Sir, grab one of those chairs, and I'll get someone to help you, right away."

"It's not for me."

She did a double-take and studied me with a frown that said *It's only a matter of time.*

T - 7

"I heard you had a little trouble at the new coffeeshop this weekend," said Charlotte as she swapped out an empty pump pot after the Monday morning rush. I called it the morning rush, but it was *the* rush, no other rush in sight.

"It was Thursday, actually. But yeah. It got a little ugly."

"What happened?" Like a mother Charlotte sighed and crossed her arms and waited for the ugly details.

"In a nutshell? Mike McEwen wanted to beat me up."

"No! Why?"

"Various reasons. I was about to kick his ass when he slipped on some Dr. Pepper. It was his own Dr. Pepper, incidentally. He broke his coccyx."

Charlotte giggled. "I think it's pronounced cock-six."

"I'm pretty sure it's *cock*-icks."

She had the giggles. "Brian, I don't think so."

"Let's ask Terrence. Terrence."

He looked up from his journal. Terrence wrote all his novels in journals, typed them into the computer at home, and then returned to my shop to hand-edit the printout. Not the most efficient process. "Eh?" he said.

"C-o-c-c-y-x. Did you get that? The medical term for the tailbone. Is it pronounced cock-six or *cock*-icks?"

"I don't know," said Terrence.

"Come on man, you're a writer for God's sake." Ordinarily Terrence would have known the answer. I don't think his brain was working too well. Earlier he had shown me a rejection letter from the agent he was counting on, the only agent who had shown an interest in his latest novel.

Terrence apologized for his ignorance.

"Okay. Theresa."

At the other end of the shop, at the table in the front window, Theresa had her nose buried in a big fat textbook. She looked up with a punchdrunk face.

"Is it cock-six or *cock*-icks." I really punched the cock on option two.

"Cock-six."

"But either way is acceptable, right?"

"No."

"You alright over there?" Charlotte asked her.

Theresa started crying. I felt bad, the coccyx question really broke her up.

Charlotte took off around the bar. "Theresa, what's wrong?"

Theresa held up her Blackberry. Her head drooped to the table.

Charlotte read the screen. "Oh Theresa, I'm sorry. Theresa didn't get an interview for pharmacy school," she announced.

"Theresa, geez, that's a big bummer."

Theresa wiped away tears and took a deep shuddering breath. "Two people in my organic chemistry class applied to NDSU, too. They got rejection letters a week ago." She had to breathe some more before she could continue. "I was telling myself that no news was good news, that they were checking my references and scheduling interviews. I finally e-mailed the program director to see if they had made their decision. The way her e-mail sounds, they made their choices two weeks ago, but forgot to notify me." Theresa sobbed and Charlotte hugged her to her stomach.

"Those bastards," I said, and I hated them, like I hated the agents and editors rejecting Terrence, the way I hated the anonymous power keeping me from building a successful franchise. Why couldn't someone I know catch a break? It would have been reassuring to know it was even possible.

Charlotte was indignant. "How could they do that? I'm furious." I still think 'indignant' was more accurate.

Theresa patted Charlotte and dried her face for a second time. "That's okay. I probably didn't have any right to think they'd accept me."

Charlotte put her hands on her hips and stamped her foot. "But your grades have been fabulous!"

Theresa nodded. "They weren't so great my first time around, twenty years ago. That probably hurt me."

"Theresa, you are smart!" Charlotte declared. "You got an A in calculus, an A in neuroanatomy, an A in statistics...what more do they want?"

Theresa's tears were bubbling up again. "I don't know."

Charlotte retrieved the box of Kleenex from the bar and tore out a chunk for Theresa. "What are you going to do now?"

Theresa shook her head. "I don't know. Try again, I suppose. I really, really want to get into pharmacy school. I've never had a goal like this. Now I want it so badly..."

Terrence walked to Theresa. "This probably doesn't help, but I know what you're going through. I just received a big rejection letter today too."

Theresa used the whole wad of tissues to clean off her face. It was very wasteful. I was going to stuff a few back in the box if they weren't too badly creased. "You're a writer, aren't you?" Theresa asked.

Terrence nodded. "We've never officially met. Terrence." Misery looking for company. "I finished my fourth novel a month ago," said Terrence. "Just like every other time, I did a ton of research to find the right publishing houses or agencies for my type of fiction. Just like every other time, I sent out a ton of book proposals. This time I even had my first chapter recorded by a professional voice man. You know, like a book on CD."

"Wow," Theresa sniffled, "that's a great idea."

"Isn't it though?" I chimed in. "I listened to it. It was great. And Terrence's books are excellent. When you get started, you can't stop. I chew through them in a couple sittings."

Terrence smiled faintly at the compliment. "And just like every other time, I was rejected soundly by every agent and publisher."

"I'm sorry," said Theresa.

"One agent asked to see the entire book. She sounded really interested. That was two weeks ago. I got her rejection letter today. Nice letter, not like the form letters I usually get. It was meant to be uplifting, I'm sure—'keep trying, you'll get there, just not with me'. It depressed me more than ever."

"It's just like my situation," said Theresa. "I'm ready and willing to go back to school, for an advanced degree. My science and math grades are great. But I can't get in. There are so few slots, and the competition is so intense. I know I'd be good at it, and so do my teachers. I never thought I'd be denied the opportunity to go to school."

We all nodded at each other. "Doesn't seem fair," said Charlotte.

"What does it take?" I wondered.

"It's all connections," said a bitter Terrence.

"Brian," Theresa sniffed, "you had another MRI today, didn't you?"

"I did. It went well. Very well. The cancer appears to be almost completely gone. This last round of chemo and radiation, along with the surgery, seems to have done the trick."

"That is beautiful," said Theresa. "I am so happy to hear that."

"That's beautiful, man," Terrence echoed, trudging back to his chair. "Is that the end of the chemo?"

I sighed, happy and weary. "Three more days."

Terrence was back in his corner. Theresa stayed in hers. They were both hunched over, slumped over their work. I was slumped behind the bar while Charlotte toasted a bagel for herself. Jamestown was slumped at the edge of a muddy little river. No one cared whether any of us existed. Terrence was right, it was connections, and if any of us had them, we wouldn't be there.

Terrence was a traffic engineer who wanted to be a published author, just enough to make a good living. He wrote every day in my shop for at least two hours. Every day. He was talented. Theresa was a homemaker and a former nurse who wanted to be a pharmacist. She had been busting her ass for the past three years, acing difficult classes. She was smart.

I wanted to run a chain of coffeeshops and make people happy, horny, creative. I had been preparing for fourteen years. I was good. But I couldn't make it. And compared to Terrence and Theresa, I had nothing to complain about. At least no one was preventing me from opening new stores, from trying. Not only couldn't Terrence get a publisher to give him a shot, he couldn't get an agent to even *try* to peddle his work. Theresa had proven her abilities, and yet there simply weren't enough slots to go around.

The world was going to be deprived of our talents and our passion; the world was willing to relegate us to lesser roles and settle for lesser output. It didn't seem right, didn't seem American. No matter how much we knew, no matter how hard we worked, we would not be allowed the chance to realize our dreams. Finances wouldn't even permit us to pursue them much longer.

"I have to run an errand," I announced all of a sudden to Charlotte, when I was already halfway down the back hallway.

"Dana comes on at noon today," she called after me. "You know she freaks when she's alone and more than two customers show up."

"I'll try to get back by two."

All weekend I had replayed and rehashed the fiasco with Mike, becoming increasingly obsessed with owning that store. Mostly out of spite. If I couldn't kick Mike in the throat, at least I could ruin his little scheme to squeeze me out. Forget that it was Bill Hernandes. I was livid he had gone to anybody behind my back, at least a week before anything with Andrea had transpired.

Yes, Mike was the only reason I even had a shot at that store. Yes he had treated me like a son or at least a favorite son-in-law for years. Yes, a father's protectiveness for his daughter is righteous and beautiful. Yes Mike had been through a lot. I still wanted to punch his lights out.

After witnessing Terrence and Theresa's despair over their rejections, the Bluffs became my lifeline, my last chance, the figurative and literal commanding position on the hilltop. If Bill Hernandes got a foothold on the Bluffs, backed by Edna Mankiller Applejack, I was going to be wiped out. It was time to swallow some pride, to do what it takes. It was time to turn on the charm.

ANDREA WAS BEHIND HER DESK, in the little office separated from the laboratory by the false wall and the mock lab bench marketing the notion this was just another boutique clinic selling laser eye surgery or supervised weight loss, rather than germ warfare on cancer. There should have been HazMat warning signs plastered up and down the hall and next to the LL3 elevator button.

That was my thought as I listened to Andrea argue with the state epidemiologist.

"But we don't have any live bacteria here," Andrea was saying, in her snotty condescending way. "You obviously didn't believe me the first time I told you. The s. pyogenes is attenuated. We're only using the immune response-triggering endotoxins, not the entire bacteria."

I whistled. "Attenuated. Endotoxins. Wow."

Andrea had no difficulty ignoring me. "We know the statute," she sassed the caller from the state lab. "We are familiar with the biological agent classifications. Dr. Bhani had the state of Minnesota review his work. The CDC is aware of his research. ...hm? That's not relevant. ...no. No. If you want to discuss Dr. Bhani's history, you'll have to talk to him personally. ...no, he's out this week. ...no I don't. I'll let him know you called. ...that would be fine. ...okay. ...uh-huh. ...fine." She hung up with authority. "What assholes."

I plopped into her guest chair. "Are they ready to quarantine the basement and send in the guys in the white biohazard suits?"

"Practically." Andrea was jotting notes from her conversation. "God I get sick of dealing with these people. They don't have a clue what they're talking about. But does that stop them?"

"Nope. Luckily, I'm here to take you away from all this."

"Oh?" Andrea cocked her head. "Where are you taking me?"

"To the bank. We're going to buy the new store at the Bluffs."

"We? You must have a turd in your pocket."

"No turds. Just you. And me. We're going to be partners, like you said."

An old lady knocked on the jam and entered the office with a young boy. The lady was haggard, and the kid looked worse. Pale, super skinny, with a few sores on his chin and neck, like zits repeatedly scratched open.

"Hi Mrs. Price," said Andrea. "Hi Thor," she sweetly greeted the boy, who was maybe twelve years old. "How are you today?"

"Fine," he mumbled. The kid was obviously a cancer patient, except that he had all his hair. He had better hair by far than the old lady. Hers was permed into see-through loops and waves. His was long and blonde, in his eyes, snagging on his eyelashes until he flipped it to the side.

"Are you ready to see Dr. Bhani?" Andrea asked Thor. "Your grandma is taking off work to bring you here. That's a pretty good grandma." She received a quick nod. "I don't know if anyone has told you this, but my God," said Andrea, "you have the most beautiful eyes."

Thor fought back a grin while he examined the floor.

"Too bad no one gets to see them anymore," said his grandma. She tried to push Thor's hair out of his eyes but he slipped her swipe with a practiced head turn. Grandma settled for smoothing the shoulder seam of his shirt. "We're a little nervous about our visit today."

"Dr. Bhani is looking forward to seeing you," said Andrea. "He's reviewed all your history and notes. The hospital wasn't exactly forthcoming with your records," she said to the grandma.

"If you need someone to break into the records room upstairs, I'd be glad to," I volunteered.

"We're from Indiana," said the grandma. "We're staying at the Ronald McDonald House for a couple weeks while Dr. Bhani helps Thor."

"All the way from Indiana," I marveled.

"Dr. Bhani is famous in the small circle of bone cancer patients," said Grandma. "And infamous in others. We like what we've heard though, don't we?" She laid a wrinkled hand on top of Thor's head. He didn't have a problem with this. He nodded.

"This is Brian," Andrea introduced me. "He has bone cancer too."

Thor gave me a good look for the first time. The kid had big blue suspicious eyes. "Oh," Grandma exclaimed. "Are you seeing Dr. Bhani too?"

"He's seeing me," said Andrea.

"I have it in my leg," I told Thor. I hiked up my shorts, an unnecessary move, and pointed to my scarred, puffy, discolored shin. "How about you?"

Thor glanced at his grandma. He gave a quick up-and-down flick of his hands. "All over."

My throat closed up. I nodded.

"That's usually when people come to us," said Andrea quietly. "After a lot of chemo and radiation, and the cancer continues to spread. At some point maybe we'll be able to convince doctors to send their patients to us earlier. So they don't have to go through all the misery caused by the chemotherapy. So we can cure them early on." She gave Thor a sweet soft-core flirt face, until he smiled and blushed, apparent on his white cheeks. His grandma's eyes were swimming in tears. I had to look away.

"Dr. Bhani is ready for you," said Andrea. "It's the first door on the right, just past the elevator."

"Are you ready?" Grandma asked Thor.

"Bye," said Thor. Grandma nodded at me and they shuffled away.

"Phew." I took a couple deep pulls of basement air. Seems I had been holding my breath. "That's gut wrenching."

"Dr. Bhani will cure him," said Andrea.

"Most doctors don't use the C word," I said.

"Most doctors are too afraid to try to cure their patients," she retorted.

"You were sure nice to Thor," I observed.

She smirked at me. "What, you think I should be that nice to you?"

"You could compliment me on my eyes. Or my hair. That would be nice." I removed my cap and waited.

Andrea raised her eyebrows. "You want me to lie?"

"If you can do it convincingly."

"You've lost more weight."

I put the cap back on. "Maybe I'm fine without the compliments. So are you ready to go?"

"For one thing," she said, "I can't go anywhere until five o'clock."

"But that's too late, the bank will be closed," I whined.

"For another thing," Andrea continued, "I already told you, I'm not investing a dime in North Dakota."

"You are made for the coffee business, lady," I buttered her up. "I wasn't sure until I saw you turn up the heat with young Thor."

Andrea made notes while she talked. "I adore that boy. He'd rather not have all this attention, but he doesn't have much choice. He's been through every treatment you can imagine, but the cancer keeps spreading."

I can't tell you how thankful I was for that morning's good MRI results.

"There's a writer who wants to follow Thor's story," said Andrea. "He wanted to sit in on their visit with Dr. Bhani today." She stood to access the file cabinet behind her, on her tippytoes peering into the top drawer until she found the right file. "His grandma wouldn't let it happen. I think she doesn't want Thor to know how serious this is."

"But it's pretty bad."

Andrea stared at me for awhile before answering. "Dr. Bhani thinks he has a few months at most."

"Oh." My stomach did a flip. "Jeez."

"You should see his MRIs." Andrea's voice went hoarse. "The cancer is everywhere. It's everywhere, really."

Neither of us spoke for a little while. Changing the subject was inappropriate, but at least the desperation theme was consistent. "So can I pick you up at four-thirty to go to the bank?"

Andrea's face twisted. "I'm not buying a coffeeshop in North Dakota."

"This is the only way to go," I stated. "You need the training before we move on to the big time in California."

"I'm a very quick learner. And I say we should start with Colorado."

"Andrea." I cleared my throat, and frowned. Felt like I tore off and swallowed my epiglottis. "If I don't get this store, there isn't going to be any Colorado or California. And I really really want to shove this thing down Mike McEwen's frigging throat. I don't mind him covering his bases," I said bitterly, "but he should have told me he was talking to Hernandes."

Andrea grew smug. "The McEwens aren't as holy as you thought, huh?"

"You were right."

I don't do sheepish very well, but it worked. Andrea was vindicated. And apparently that meant more to her than escaping North Dakota. We agreed to meet at the bank at four-thirty.

DANA'S FACE LIT UP when I walked into the shop a little after noon. I was on my cell with Kenny the Wells Fargo branch manager, confirming my ability to deposit funds to the Bluffs construction account.

Business that afternoon was terrible. I wished I could send Dana home, or at least not pay her for being there. She broke character and volunteered to scrub the floors, and I took her up on it.

'Round about two o'clock I forgot Bart Shock's name. It didn't bother him a bit—it's not unusual for me to call you Lady or What's-His-Face. When I greeted him with, "Hey...you", Bart figured it was part of my schtick. But I had no clue what his name was. Couldn't even put his face into context; felt like a big black gap where a whole lot of memories should be. I had a small nervous breakdown.

I DIDN'T SEE ANDREA'S PICKUP when I pulled into the bank parking lot at four-twenty-five, so I waited in my pickup. Time passed slowly. Even though I was tense, I had to struggle to stay awake. Getting up at four-thirty every morning, with or without cancer, meant that I couldn't sit down to read a book or watch television, or eat, for that matter. I got drowsy taking a dump, fell asleep jacking off. Coffeeshop owners do it on their feet.

At four-forty I left the van, sucked chilly air to dissolve the mental fog, and started across the lot. Mike McEwen fell into step beside me.

"What a coincidence," he said sarcastically. I kept walking, not looking at him. "Kenny told me you were coming," he said. "What are you doing?" He was bumping me, jostling me. I was ready to send him flying into the shrubbery when I realized he was limping badly and struggling to keep up.

I stopped. "Your ass broken?"

"Tailbone fracture," Mike grunted. Sweat beaded on his forehead.

"That's your coccyx." No clue whether my pronunciation was right. "I asked you for a rag. I hope you remember that."

Mike grimaced as he tried to stand comfortably. "I'm here to talk money. You have no business trying to get back into this thing. It's too late."

"Mike, we have a signed contract that calls for me to open a James River Valley shop at that site and reimburse you for all your upfront costs over the next ten years. I shouldn't even have to put any money down."

This wasn't exactly a bluff—it was technically true—but it was bold. I had grown emboldened the past few days, as word spread about our confrontation. I was surprised how much support I appeared to have. People sought me out at the shop, on the street and over the phone, to grumble—quietly, concerned their voices might carry—about the McEwens' past strong-arm tactics.

Turned out the McEwens weren't universally loved, and crossing them wouldn't be curtains for me. I wouldn't go so far as to say the townsfolk were starved for someone to finally stand up to the McEwens. But I definitely was seeing an uptick in business.

"That's a hell of an attitude." Mike kept a careful eye on the customers coming and going from the bank, timing his remarks, worried about making a scene. "I would have expected a little more gratitude from you."

"Mike, I am grateful. But I would have expected—"

"Save it. And forget about that contract." He chewed the inside of his cheek as he glared at me. "No money changed hands. It's not valid."

"The contract doesn't call for any money up front," I pointed out. "But that's a moot point, because I'm funding the account right now." I was getting giddy. Me against goliath. I was my own Trojan horse with fifteen grand of Andrea's money inside.

"Where are you getting the money?" Mike demanded.

On cue, Andrea pulled into the lot. "I have a partner."

"This deal was with you, exclusively."

"My partner is investing the money in me. The contract to run the shop is still exclusively between you and me."

Andrea parked in the spot right in front of us. The bumper of her pickup stopped a foot from Mike's knee. Mike was choking on his own angry bile, oblivious to his surroundings. "Who the hell would loan you fifteen grand?"

A fair question, but with a week or two I could have pulled together that and more. Quite a few of my friends and acquaintances in Jamestown and back home had a naïve amount of faith in me and the coffee business. I just liked and respected them too much to lose their money. (Sorry, Andrea.)

I made for the door as Andrea climbed out of her pickup. "I need to get inside before the bank closes."

"I already promised Edna Applejack this store," Mike barked at me.

I opened the vestibule door. "I'm seeing Edna tonight at the College ceremony. I'll explain everything to her."

Mike shook his finger at me. "She doesn't…" He wheeled as Andrea stepped onto the sidewalk behind him. Mike's leg gave out and he had to use the bug guard of her pickup for support. He thrust himself back to an awkward standing position. "What are you doing here?" From ten yards away I saw a globule of what could only be angry bile glistening at the corner of his lips.

"What?" snapped the Woman Without Fear. "I can't bank here?"

I hurried inside and jogged across the lobby into the warren of cubicles where the business bankers lived. Matt my banker was on the phone. He held up his hand, asking for a couple minutes' privacy. I plopped down in his guest chair and started massaging my cancer leg, grimacing.

Matt talked quietly into the phone with his back to me. I climbed on my chair to periscope my head above the cube partitions. There was Andrea, filling out a form at the customer workstand. And there was Mike under a big potted tree in the corner, on his cellphone and steaming. I ducked back down.

Matt didn't notice a thing. I wondered if I shouldn't find a more observant banker. No, a clueless lender was probably the right choice for me.

I pulled out my checkbook and filled out a deposit slip. Wandering the alleyways between the cubes, I flagged down an unoccupied employee and asked her to take the deposit slip to Andrea. I described her vividly.

Darlene was a tall business banker with huge cheekbones and a bouffant hairstyle. She was puzzled by my request.

"I don't want Mike McEwen to see me," I explained. "He's very angry with me."

Darlene nodded as if that was the norm with Mike. Maybe Andrea and I weren't the only ones with a price on our heads. Maybe once I got to know Edna better, I could take up a collection to pay her to strangle Mike.

Standing on Matt's chair again and peeking over the tops of the cubes, I watched Darlene do my bidding. When Matt finally hung up the phone, he told me it had been a private customer call.

"Bull," I said. "That was Nancy," his wife. "You're just talking about what you're having for dinner tonight."

"It's still private, Brian," said Matt, smiling reluctantly.

"I won't tell anyone you're ordering pizza again tonight."

"I wish that was a joke," said Matt. "So what can I do you for?"

"I need to move fifteen grand from my James River Valley account into Mike McEwen's Bluffs construction account. Maybe Kenny told you?"

"I don't recall." Matt swiveled to his computer and started clicking. "For the new coffeeshop? I heard at roundtable—the business bankers have a roundtable every morning at seven—so much for banker's hours, huh?" he joked. Matt's a small guy with red-blonde hair and fuzzy sideburns. He has a wry style and a fatalistic outlook. Maybe he's taken too many corporate spankings for extending bad credit to struggling little businesses like mine. "I heard at the roundtable this morning—we always compare notes, you'd be surprised how many businesses have overlapping transactions or needs. I heard Bill Hernandes was going in there." He stopped clicking and got this faraway look in his eye. "And Edna Applejack."

It was amazing the spell she had on this town. She wasn't Salk or Gandhi. She wasn't even Darin Erstad. "She's a sweetheart, huh?"

Matt clicked through what must be an e-labyrinth, judging by his intense concentration. "Brian, you don't have the funds…oop, something just popped in. A cash deposit, for fifteen thousand. Coincidentally."

"It's no coincidence. I have my own private genie."

"That's the fifteen grand you want to move, huh."

"Think of this as legal money laundering."

Matt had a limited range of facial expressions. He inclined his head a couple degrees to indicate he got the joke and that it was a good one, and scratched his cheek real slow-like to suggest that I never utter that phrase again. All with the same weary cynical look. "It can take up to two days for deposited funds to become available."

"Andrea Goldine—my genie—has an account here. You can see she has the funds to make the transaction."

Matt eyed me. I sounded and probably looked desperate. "I'll need to get manager approval."

"Kenny knows I'm doing it."

"Actually"—Matt checked his watch—"my manager is in Fargo."

"It has to be today, or I don't want to do it. And if I don't do it, we might as well work out a plan to liquidate my shop and pay off as much of my loan as possible. Ten cents on the dollar is my guess."

Matt winked at me. "We'll make sure you stay in business long enough to pay it off, with interest."

"Then we need to move this money today."

Matt excused himself. I slumped in the chair to conserve energy. Maybe I wouldn't attend the Edna ceremony tonight. I was exhausted. I closed my eyes for a moment.

It was 4:58 when Matt breezed back into his cube, into his chair, onto his computer, clickety-click-click. He stabbed a key with finality. "Done deal. You're no richer or poorer than you were a half-hour ago. Free money—that's a pretty fair way to capitalize a business."

I shook his hand. "It's not free, not by a long shot. I appreciate the quick action."

"I'm looking forward to that first cup of coffee from your new shop."

"I wish I could give it to you for free, but I know it's against your code of ethics."

Matt shook his head. "It's de minimis."

"Not to me."

The lobby was empty of customers. Darlene the business banker waited for me at the door, unlocking and then locking it behind me. No sign of Mike in the parking lot, but there was Andrea in her pickup, making busy with her checkbook. I rapped on her window. She did not startle.

"Thanks," I said when she rolled down the window.

"Sure." She smacked her gum and looked at me like I owed her something. "So we need to get together and talk business."

I wanted to bask in the glow of owning a new shop before starting to worry about how I was going to keep Andrea from driving away my customers. "I'm going to the Jamestown College basketball game tonight. They're retiring Edna Applejack's number."

"What's an enda applejack?"

"That's a basketball star who murdered her man with her bare hands."

"How nice." Andrea seemed impressed, intrigued.

"You wanna come? It would be good for you to start meeting people."

Andrea considered this the worst idea she had heard all day. "No, I don't think so. Why don't you swing by afterward."

"It'll be pretty late."

"Maybe some things are worth losing sleep over."

"We'll see. Did you talk to Mike? Does he know you're helping me?"

Andrea smiled, smug and satisfied. "He was back and forth, in and out of the bank manager's office. And then he stormed out of there just before they closed. Yeah, I think he knows we're working together."

"You might want to get in the habit of checking your brakes before you get in the car. I gotta run. Sure you don't want to come tonight?"

"Why are you going?" Andrea wanted to know.

"Edna might kill someone. I don't want to miss it."

ON THE WAY TO THE GAME I got a call from the hospital. "Brian, it's Dr. Bonilla. How are you?"

"Feeling pretty good, considering."

"That's good. Good to hear. Hey, so, I was taking another look at your MRIs this afternoon, and there are a couple things I want to follow up on. Can you come in for additional pictures?"

"Follow up on…" I let that sink in. *Follow up on…* Anymore, my body was primed to overreact. I broke into a cold sweat and lost my peripheral vision. I had to pull over, into the Hardees parking lot at the busiest intersection in town, at the main bridge over the James. "How soon do you need to, uh, follow up on…"

"Are you available to come in first thing tomorrow morning?"

My fingers tingled. My arms went numb. My automatic life-support system was shutting down. I switched over to Manual, rocking back and forth to pump oxygen and blood. "'First thing' definitely has an urgent ring to it."

"You know how we operate with this kind of stuff," said Dr. Bonilla. "We want to set everyone's mind at ease as quickly as possible."

"Dr. Bonilla, my mind hasn't been at ease since I met you. If you really care about my peace of mind, cure me already."

"You know we're doing everything we can…" He blathered his malpractice insurer's mandatory CYA spiel while Jeanie McDonald, a regular customer, pulled into the adjacent parking spot and jumped out of her car to say hi. I waved and let my head droop, questioning whether I had the energy or the pride to lean out of the van to puke. When I looked up, Jeanie was gone.

"…and sometimes additional tests turn out to be unnecessary," Dr. Bonilla wrapped up the required disclosure. "But it's always better safe than sorry."

"Why don't I come in tonight? Since I won't be sleeping anyway."

"I could probably make that work," said Dr. Bonilla after a short pause. "Let me make a couple calls."

"No." If eight a.m. was early enough for Dr. Bonilla and his malpractice insurer, it must be fine. "I really should attend the JC exhibition game tonight."

"They're retiring Edna Applejack's number," Dr. Bonilla gushed. "I'll be there too. She was incredible."

"It doesn't bother you she murdered her husband? With her bare hands?"

"I can't imagine what she must have endured up to that point. It must have been a horrible environment."

"How terrible could it be, living with a computer geek? Boring maybe."

Dr. Bonilla's voice flattened. "I didn't really know much about him."

"If it turns out that…"

"Mm? Brian?"

I was going to make a joke about how if it turned out I was terminal, I wanted to marry Edna and then bore her so badly she felt compelled to tear me apart with those beautiful hands of hers. But my lungs failed to provide enough oxygen to weave the scenario. "The MRI?" I managed to say. "You think it's bad?"

Dr. Bonilla paused. "I can't speculate, Brian. Come in tomorrow and let's get a good, all-over look at you."

"If it is—say it is bad. What then?"

"We have a couple different options, other therapeutics we haven't tried yet. Or we can get more aggressive with our current treatment plan."

I no longer salivated at the word aggressive. "Most of my organs were already dissolved by the chemo. If you get any more aggressive, the cancer won't have anything left to eat. Which is a form of a cure, I guess."

"We'll try to strike the right balance, whichever way we decide to go. How's your appetite lately?"

"What appetite? I look like Twiggy."

"We have you on the chemo weight-loss program, do we?"

I know he was trying to joke along, but it wasn't his forte. "'Fraid so."

"Let's see if we can't fix that a little bit, too."

"What about alternative treatments?" I revisited the topic. I didn't want to be a guinea pig for a scientist like Bhani. It would have felt desperate, a panic move. I wanted Dr. Bonilla to take care of me. I was comfortable with him. He was so calm and cool and professional, ninety percent of the time, and he was dedicated to curing me, within the bounds of reason if not my expectations. I wanted him to reassure me I was making the right choice.

"Yes, of course, other options do exist, as we discussed with your mother and your friend a couple weeks ago." Dr. Bonilla labored through his least favorite subject. "There are many scientists, some reputable, others not as much, who are working hard to solve various forms of cancer. I monitor the journals closely, for treatments that have been confirmed effective over an extended period of time. And I think that's the key. If there were any miracle cures out there, I would have heard about it."

"I guess the pharmaceutical industry would be all over a real cure."

"There would definitely be some people ready to profit by any new treatments that are proven effective. And safe. Of course nothing moves very quickly in the world of drug development."

"Damned feds."

"Mm." Dr. Bonilla had no room for banter, he was working too hard forming his next thought. This was the one I would bank on. "I would feel professionally negligent, if I encouraged you to spend time chasing treatments that are still in the unverified stage. I have seen, unfortunately, patients who dropped everything, their jobs, their relationships, everything that gave their lives meaning, to pursue a cure. It's admirable to take your health into your own hands. I'm an advocate of patients feeling responsible for their well-being. But there's a cost. Potentially a great one. Cancer research is incredibly complex and confusing. It makes physicians' heads spin. I feel sorry for laymen who feel compelled to enter that thicket."

"That's what I thought." My vision returned to normal, my grip strengthened on the wheel. The sweat had stunk up my clothing but cleansed my pores. I rolled down the window and gave a "Hey lady" to Jeanie returning to her car, waving as she munched French fries.

"If you want," said Dr. Bonilla, "I'll refer you to a website that publishes information on studies that might be looking for volunteers."

"I don't think that's necessary. I'd rather stay the tried and true course. I'll see you tomorrow morning."

"I may not be around. But Dr. Caldwell will be ready for you. Then we'll get together to talk about what we see."

"Sounds good. Maybe I'll see you tonight?"

"I'll be there cheering for Edna." My doctor was in love. "Goodbye Brian."

I'd rather have my doctor hang up on me, I decided, instead of telling me "goodbye". Just say "fuck you, Brian" and hang up. Doctors can't help but sound sinister when they say goodbye.

I PLAYED FOR DAVIS HIGH, so I was familiar with the sound of a crowd that loves its team. I was too short and not quick enough to consistently get my shot off, which limited my playing time and meant I didn't get near enough opportunity to feed off the crowd's energy. I was envious to see the JC men doing just that, firing passes more crisply than usual, getting extra lift on their jump shots, aggressively driving to the hoop, looking more athletic than their norm. Holding their own against the superior Pan-Am team.

In the waning moments of the first half, the excitement level in the civic center peaked. And then rose higher above that false summit, until the roar became the frenzied single-note scream that only comes in the final seconds of a tight, meaningful game. With two ticks remaining on the clock, JC's Danny Bernstein came up with a loose ball in the corner and the fans erupted; when he launched a three-pointer as the horn blasted, the scream strangled silent while the ball looped to the hoop, and then resumed times ten when it went in.

The aural blast continued for some seconds, everyone's arms thrust in the air, delirious to the point of insanity. The public address man knew exactly why it was so and before the teams had even left the floor announced, "Ladies and gentlemen, I give you the greatest basketball player in North Dakota history, Edna Applejack!" The screaming went ultrasonic.

"Nice," I shouted to Joshua. "Now I have cancer and I'm deaf. I heard there's an eclipse next week. Think I'll look at the sun."

Joshua couldn't respond because of his fingers in his mouth, folding his tongue to channel a shrieking whistle. We were crowded into the runway between the bleachers with Joshua's wife Denise and their hometown friend Allison and Mike's employee Wally, and fifty other maniacs.

Edna took a few long strides to reach center court, beating the man with the microphone. With that kind of speed in heels and a tight knee-length dress in the shape of the state of North Dakota with a neckline star representing not the capital but Jamestown, how could anyone have stayed with her as she filled the lane on a fast break and jammed down another two of her twenty-five thousand three hundred eighty-one points?

"Thank you," said Edna, and then into the tardy microphone, "North Dakota, God bless you." The cheering couldn't get any louder, people must have been spitting throat blood. I know I was. "Jamestown, God bless you!"

A man carrying a glass-framed jersey strolled out to join her. "That's Jim Adelson," Allison told me. "He's the most famous sportscaster in North Dakota. Ever." She had to lean in close to make herself heard. She had to rise up on her tippytoes to speak into my ear. She had to be one of the sweetest little numbers I had seen in a long time, glossy hair framing dark flashing eyes and a beautiful smile, with a body that was alive and fidgety with energy. Allison would have turned heads in any other crowd; she was unfortunate to be standing in the one state where Edna Applejack walked free.

I nodded and elbowed her chest to get a better vantage point.

"We're here tonight to honor this woman," bellowed Adelson, sixtyish, silver-haired and ruddy in a checkered sport coat. The crowd never took a breath and neither did he. "The greatest basketball player of either sex in the history of our state!" Banshee cries of group ecstasy punctuated each phrase. "Number twenty-one at Jamestown High and number twenty-one for the Jamestown College Jimmies, Edna Applejack, it was my honor to watch you then and retire your number now!"

I'm not kidding, people were dancing in the bleachers, they were falling off the ends, they were jumping and screaming and losing their minds. Edna hoisted the framed jersey, making the North Dakota plains shimmer and roll.

"Thank you North Dakota!" she shouted. "I love you!"

She came right for us with Adelson jogging to keep up. Like relay racers our little group started moving backward so that by the time Edna reached us we were at top speed and walking alongside her—Allison had to skip on her stubby legs—while Security sealed off the runway and kept at bay the surging screaming horde, gawking, clapping and shedding tears, whiffing in their attempts to pat Edna's back like defenders swiping futilely at the ball as Edna broke down their double team.

In no time we were inside the athletic director's office. The closing of the door vacuumed out the crowd sound. I stood there like everyone else coping with my deaf buzz. Adelson opened his arms and embraced Edna, his face nestled into the sharp crook of her neck.

Edna doled out hugs, six of them counting the athletic director, tall and crane-necked with acne scars on his jowls. He shook our hands, introducing himself as AD Guldseth. "Edna, that is unprecedented," he said. "Never before—not even when you were playing—has our house rocked like that."

"I don't know," said sportscaster Adelson. He had a puffy chest. "I remember a few games...the state class A high school tournament final against Bismarck Century in eighty-eight."

"That was some game," said AD Guldseth. ADG struck a relaxed pose, one hand in his pocket and the other picking at his throat; but he was watching Edna like a hawk, every fiber tensioned to leap into service, if he could only anticipate what she might need. "Edna, you went off, if I remember right. Fifty-three points."

"It was only forty-eight," said Adelson. "Only. Phew."

"I was watching with the other Shanley varsity ballplayers," said ADG. "We had a great team that year..."

Adelson clapped him on the back, making ADG jab himself in the Adam's apple. "You were a fine ballplayer in your own right, Bobby. Edna, are you a little overwhelmed by all this?"

"A lot." Edna perused ADG's photo gallery. She was in half the pictures, either in action with her hair flying or posing smiling with various Most Valuable Player plaques. She had a real jumpshot, not a girlie push-from-the-chest, judging by one framed photo prominently displayed to the left and ahead of ADG's desk where he could glance at it on a regular basis whenever he got tired of looking at the framed picture of his wife and kids beside his computer. Edna's release was high above and a little in front of her head. The ball was resting lightly on her finger pads, like it had been placed there. She had long tapered creamy white thighs.

Edna tapped the glass of one of her action photos. "Joshua, I forgot that I played with a girl from Kulm. I know she's a little older, but did you know Sandy Schuldtheis? She was a great baller."

Denise snorted gaily. "It doesn't matter who you were going to say, we would know her. Kulm's so small, there's a good chance we're related."

"Denise and Joshua are cousins," I told everyone.

"We are *not*." Denise slapped my arm while Joshua chortled.

First, I mouthed to Adelson while absorbing increasingly firm slaps. Denise was a sizeable gal, a Farm Girl, and I had a bolt of fear she would bruise my bone and start fresh cancer. And she was scandalized over nothing, no one seemed the least bit disturbed.

We watched Edna stroll down memory lane. Adelson stood slowly shaking his head. Wally was drooling. Allison had shrunk, into the corner. Denise waited for me to say something else smart ass.

"You look fabulous tonight, Edna," said ADG. "Not many people can pull off wearing the state of North Dakota."

Joshua stared at Edna's dress, the kind of blatant ogling that is illegal on some campuses. Denise started palm-striking his shoulder but couldn't dislodge his puzzled gaze.

Finally the light came on. "Ohh," said Joshua. He slapped his forehead and cackled like a crazy man. "That's North Dakota." And sure enough his gaze went straight to Lake Sacagawea, a reservoir stretching from Edna's lower abdomen to her upper thigh, a cool blue patch tastefully blended with the green prairie grass shoreline.

Denise moved to stand beside Edna and began pointing out areas of interest. "Do you see this, Joshua?" She indicated the sharp-pointed neckline. "This star is Jamestown. Here's Kulm," a couple inches below Edna's left breast, "and *that* is Lake Sacagawea." She was the geography instructor of every horny teenage boy's fantasy.

"I see, I see." Joshua's laughter was high-pitched and high speed. "Where's the state capitol building?" he asked innocently, and then cackled again. I'm no expert in North Dakota landmarks, but I was pretty sure it would be a little south of the lake.

Denise threw up her hands and pleaded with the rest of us for sympathy, before putting her husband in an affectionate bear hug. "I can't believe you sometimes."

"You better believe it," said Joshua as they rocked back and forth.

ADG clapped once and hugged Edna with one ropy arm. "I am so pleased to give you this evening. It is so well deserved. You have meant so much to the state, to this town, to the College," ADG carried on. "And to me personally. If there is anything I can do for you—"

Adelson broke in before Guldseth could propose something unprofessional. "I know the administration here would love to have your name associated with the College, Edna. You might want to ask for a building to be named after you, while all this euphoria is still hanging in the air."

And that's when a particularly wonderful, a dreadfully perfect idea hit me. While Edna mulled over which building would be best suited to bear the name Applejack, I plotted. And realized I had stumbled upon the answer to my prayers. It involved stepping on more toes and breaking more promises, so I had to be careful.

I needed a way to get Edna Applejack alone, without starting any more rumors and soiling my reputation so dirty it would never come clean.

"Edna, you wanna get a beer with me? I have a proposition for you."

T - 6

Edna took a raincheck in favor of a party the McEwens threw for her back at their pad. Maybe that's why everyone craved her, she was so good at playing hard to get. Or maybe it was because she was gorgeous and athletic and sexy and dangerous and convinced that North Dakota was paradise.

Edna was the thirty-six year old bomb. I wanted to picture her while they slid me shivering into the MRI tube the next morning. Instead I kept envisioning my cancer hiding from the camera, escaping detection by ducking behind my spleen, holding still in a kidney-like clump, masquerading as organs, playing dead, buying time until it could creep up my spine and infect my brain.

Then the MRI machine started clacking, not clickety-clack but CLACK-CLACK, bone-jarring attack clacks meant to stun the cancer, disorient it while the computer took a good picture of the horde I feared was swarming my testicles and gobbling up the soft tissues in my gut.

Then again maybe it was the chemo doing the swarming and gobbling. In which case the MRI tech would present the incriminating photos of chemo molecules shredding my testes to confetti, pancreatic gore dripping off their chins—my doctors would nod and knuckle-knock each other and tell me everything was going according to plan.

Very soon I had to focus on pretending I wasn't stuffed in a small tube, like being shoved backwards into a zipped-up sleeping bag, which my best friend Ryan and I used to do to each other, the torturer holding the open end closed until the torturee had a panic attack. Which I didn't want to do there in the MRI tube, because we'd only have to start the whole process over again, meanwhile giving the cancer extra heads-up time to hide.

So I imagined myself lying in a grassy meadow, the non-itchy type of grass, gazing at the high clear blue sky, a gentle breeze caressing my face. This was fairly effective, although I had no explanation for the CLACKs.

After taking my picture, they pumped me full of my daily dose of poison and sent me packing. Driving to the shop I tried not to dwell on what the MRI results might reveal. That was the tough thing about having cancer—always working hard not to think about it. Any other problem, I would obsess on it until an action plan came to mind, and then attack it. Here there was nothing to attack. I could ponder my cancer all day every day, and no action plan was going to take shape.

The same could be said for my descent into bankruptcy, of course. Look how long I agonized over that one, and what good it did me. In the end it wasn't brainstorming that materialized a solution out of thin air, it was being in the right place (next to Edna Applejack) at the right time.

Should have been focusing on driving. We were having a late May storm, rain changing to sleet changing to ice on the streets as the temperature plummeted. North-facing street signs were caked white. The Y-shaped Hardees intersection just past the bridge was a five-vehicle accident scene, so I bypassed Main and crawled through the backstreets into downtown.

The shop was spunky for ten-thirty on a weekday. The bar chairs were all full, three of the six tables occupied, and Terrence in his corner writing. I stopped to chat with Tony Silver and his wife, who were meeting her brother and his wife, visiting from New York.

"Where have you been?" Charlotte chastised me as I continued across the floor. "Jerry has wanted to talk to you all morning."

"I have an offer you can't refuse," said Jerry.

"Oh no, I can refuse it," I said. I always did. Every few weeks I would get an offer, to partner with someone on their business idea, or to sell for them, flowers, fresh fruit, oil and gas rights, greeting cards, Amway, Mary Kay. I always turned them down point-blank, holding out for coffee to come around and start treating me right, but knowing that at some point I was going to have to start taking these offers seriously.

And then Edna had come along, and maybe I wasn't so foolish to hold out for a miracle.

"What's the offer?" my downstairs neighbor Dennis asked. I wanted to know if he was dating Iz, but I didn't know how to approach it. *Hey fucknut! Are you dating everybody's favorite pedophile?* I couldn't figure out how to make that come off well.

"Some cockamamie idea about me being his salesman, that's my guess," I said, stopping beside Terrence.

"Don't you think Brian would make a great salesman?" said Jerry.

"He gets us to drink this swill," Dennis agreed.

I waited out the chortles. "That's easy compared to convincing people to let Jerry be their portfolio manager." While everyone laughed, I turned to Terrence. "So how's it going?"

He had a lot of scribbled-out slashed-out sentences on the journal page in front of him. "Not bad," he lied. "Yourself?"

"Oh, you know. Could be better." I thought about this for a couple seconds. "Could be worse." I rubbed my face, gently. Probably psychological, but I was sure the powerful MRI magnets had further scrambled my decaying epidermis. I imagined my fingers knocking loose some of the corrupted underlying layers—they would fall in chunks and collect under my chin, leaving behind the outer skin like a sheet of cellophane. I took my hand away from my face. "It's bill collecting day today. I'm not looking forward to lying to all my suppliers. I'm really not looking forward to them not believing me."

"That's crazy," said Terrence, surveying the temporarily-packed joint. "I can't see how this place isn't profitable. Everyone loves your shop."

"I know. But there's love, and then there's volume." I shifted my weight off the cancer leg and crunched coffee beans. I looked down at the beans scattered on the floor around Terrence.

"Spence was throwing beans at me," Terrence explained.

"You see beans. I see pennies."

Terrence got the giggles.

I knuckle-knocked him and joined Charlotte and Spence behind the bar. "Grande skinny mocha," Charlotte told me.

Spence stepped away from the machine and started tidying up the bean buckets. I popped out the portafilter and knocked the old grounds into the trash hole, with authority. "How's things?"

"We had a fairly good morning," said Charlotte. "Maybe five hundred." Under her breath she asked, "Did you see Mr. and Mrs. Adultery?"

"Hard to miss them."

Bob Macafee is a State Farm insurance agent. He's been selling insurance for years, a highly visible face in the community—he smiles at you from a billboard at the south end of town, and seriously contemplates your insurance needs in one of the silent still-shot ads that run before every movie at the Buffalo Cinema Seven. Bob was recently divorced, again. Everyone knows he's a letch, except those to whom it matters most, his ladyfriend targets.

Greta Church had worked for the county for twenty years. Also very visible. But still married. They stood whispering by the Culligan water dispenser. Their lips were inches apart. Bob was stroking Greta's arm. Greta's forty-five year old hips were doing slow gyrations, tempting Bob's forty-eight year old penis. They pretended to be conducting confidential business—from time to time Bob would throw out an insurance term—but their puppy lust was obvious to anyone watching.

And we were all watching. Our little public peep show. Sometimes they would park in a secluded spot by the shop. (There wasn't really such a spot.) Then the gawking began, a constant parade of my customers and employees past their car. We were forced to walk closer and closer as the windows fogged over from all the dry humping.

Times like this, we were treated to an in-store heavy petting show. They would squeeze themselves into a corner. Thinking that their Klingon cloaking device was working, they would go to town. Bob was an unbelievable salesman, able to talk himself and his newest squeeze into precarious, ridiculous, adulterous situations.

"You know," I grumbled, "if they gotta be adulterers, then I guess they gotta be. But do they have to do it in my shop?"

"I overheard a little bit of the conversation," said Spence. "I think they're debating which hotel to check into."

"I hope they don't choose the Motel 6 again," Charlotte complained. "My sister hates it when she has to listen to Bob tell her the room is for an out-of-town client."

"That's where I conduct my insurance business," I said. "Out of town in a room at the Motel 6. Grande skinny mocha," I announced.

"Thanks Brian," said Cat Jefferies.

"Any time, lady."

"Oh yeah," said Charlotte, "and Liza is using all our paper again."

Liza sat at the display window table, scribbling furiously on my paper. I bought tower blocks of three-by-three inch scrap paper, for us or our customers to jot down notes or reminders. "Liza", this woman with plastered black hair and clown makeup who reminded us of Liza Minelli, would peel off big hunks of my paper, write for a couple hours, plowing through sheet after sheet and mumbling to herself all the while, and then push the heap of paper into her handbag and hurry out. Each tower cost me ten bucks. I was betting Liza had gone through three of them.

"That really burns me," I said. "Can't she bring her own paper? Charlotte, go tell her to stop."

Charlotte shook her head vehemently. "She's psycho. It's your shop. You go do something about it."

Where was Craig when I needed him? "How much did she take?"

"About two inches." Charlotte spread her thumb and forefinger to demonstrate. The gap was more like three. She raised her eyebrows, as fed up with my gutlessness as I was with Liza stealing my paper.

"Alright, I better go say something." I shuddered. "I wonder if I could write her a note and throw it on her table as I run by."

"It would just get lost in her pile," Charlotte pointed out. "Uh-oh." She nodded at the door. In walked Mr. Greta (Trent) Church, like a gunslinger into the saloon. "Ooh, this is going to be good."

Trent stood like he was a customer in line. I nudged Charlotte. "Ask him if he wants something to drink."

"Do we have whiskey?" she whispered.

That reminded me of the Kenny Rogers song where the big farmer—and Trent Church was big, he was a mountain of a man—begs his wife Lucille not to leave. Trent's massive heart was breaking. I actually had that song in the random CD loop. If we had a particularly rowdy morning crowd, I could lead a honky-tonk sing-along when it popped up. I hoped it wouldn't happen now.

Trent started forward and Bob Macafee saw him. He actually gave Greta a little shove to create space between them. She had a hurt puzzled look on her face as her big husband bore down on them. Without the hard-on I'm sure Bob would have wet himself.

Seems Trent wasn't so much heartbroken as insanely angry. "What are you doing?!" he asked his wife. I think he was trying to keep his voice down, but it boomed through the shop. Cat Jefferies jumped a foot in the air.

Greta shook her head, looking at the floor. Bob raised a shaking hand and stepped forward. "Let's talk about this—"

Trent swatted his hand away. "Shut up Bob, and stay out of this."

"I think this concerns me," said Bob in a quavering voice.

Charlotte and I glanced at each other. Her eyebrows were way up there. Considering the weather I was wondering whether I should preemptively call 911 to give the ambulance a head start.

Into my shop walked Frannie the sign nazi, removing her hair scarf and shaking sleet on my floor. I decided I truly hated that woman. More than the city and its inconsistent rules. More than Bill Hernandes and his quest to put me out of business. More than ticks and crushing injuries.

Trent towered over Bob. "Step away from me. Right now."

"I can't do that." Bob mumbled, because his balls cuddled his larynx.

Nazi Frannie slithered toward me. As luck would have it, John Jones from the city council was in the house, having coffee with Pastor Kyle. They were scooting their chairs to clear space for big Trent Church to operate. PK bumped Cat Jefferies, who spilled her drink and called for a rag. It was a busy day at the shop, my kind of atmosphere, minus the nazi.

Trent's hands were balled into fists the size of boxing gloves. He was leaning forward while Greta burrowed into his stomach, pushing him back. "You don't know what you're messing with," he snarled at Bob.

"You don't know what you've been doing to her," Bob squeaked.

As I came around the bar my cellphone was playing *Funkytown* on the counter. "Could you get that for me?" I asked Charlotte, doubting she could hear me over Trent and Bob.

"What I do with my wife is none of your damn business!"

"I'm making it my business…"

I tried to catch somebody's eye as I approached. "Hey you guys."

"…you need to listen to your wife."

"You don't tell me a sonofabitchin' thing about my wife!"

"Guys," I whispered like they were not yet making a scene.

"Gentlemen," said PK.

"Mr. Lawson," said nazi Frannie. The crazy hag was right behind me.

"Trent, Bob, Greta," I said sharply, getting their attention and pointing toward the door. "I like a good scrum as much as the next guy, but you have to take this outside."

"Brian, I apologize for this," said Bob, playing the grownup's role.

I wanted to punch him in the nose. I wished Trent would just get it over with. Maybe strike Frannie a glancing death blow. "Let's go." I ushered Trent into an about-face. He crossed the floor in five giant strides and blasted the door open. Greta hurried after him, looking at no one, while Bob apologized on behalf of Trent to anyone who made eye contact.

I kept him moving, out the door and into the blizzard. When I turned around there was Frannie, sticking a piece of paper in my face. "Lady." I looked past the paper to see Charlotte beckoning me with my phone.

"Mr. Lawson—"

"Excuse me Frannie." I ducked around the nazi and caught a glimpse of Liza tearing a fresh sheet off the stack. My stack. "Hey." I leaned over the table and lowered my voice. "I'm really sorry, but I'm going to have to ask you not to use all our paper."

She blinked at me. Her mascara was clumped on her eyelashes, a little clinging to her pencil eyebrows. I wish I could say she didn't look like Liza Minelli up close. "I'm writing letters," she said.

"I know." The shouting outside was distracting. "But it's expensive for me to supply you with paper all the time."

Liza laid her arms across the scattered pile of used sheets. "I have my own paper, you know."

"Then you should use it." I resisted grabbing my depleted stack of paper as I left her table. I held a finger to the nazi's face before she could speak. "Frannie, I have a phone call."

Frannie stayed right on my tail. Her thin raspy voice made my neck hair stand up. "It's Francesca, Mr. Lawson. And this bill is past due."

"If it makes you feel any better, that's not my only one."

"The fine is set to double tomorrow. I wanted to give you a grace period."

At least I think that's what she said. The argument outside my front door was loud. I admit that I was straining to hear what they were saying, which shouldn't count as eavesdropping. My customers looked uncomfortable. "PK," I said, "can't you break it up and counsel them through this?"

"Well I thought about it," said Pastor Kyle. "But I don't want to get punched out."

"Me neither," said Councilman Jones. "Brian, it is your shop."

"That's what Charlotte tells me." I looked down at Councilman Jones. "John, I'd really like you to see what you can do about this sandwich board fine." I put my arm in the small of Frannie's skeletal back and nudged her forward. "Otherwise I'm going to mount big blinking neon signs on each side of the building. Really."

Councilman Jones tipped his chair back and looked at Frannie like she was a dentist with a big whirring drill.

"Can I call them back?" I asked Charlotte as I backpedaled toward the door and the cockfight cacophony outside.

Charlotte pointed at the phone. "It's your doctor."

I made a face and stuck my head outside. "Guys." Trent and Bob stopped in mid-argument, face to face tucked against the side of the building under my little awning. Why hadn't Trent killed him yet? "We can hear you in here. It's distracting for my customers." The sports fan in me wanted to watch, the business person knew better. Not much better, but a little. "You're going to have to take it further away."

Both men looked at the wall of sleet coming down sideways. Greta was already standing in it, white on one side. She took off walking across the street and Trent followed her. Bob started after them and then hesitated.

"Bob, I wouldn't." Not waiting to see his fateful decision, I hustled back across the floor. Councilman Jones and Frannie now occupied Macafee's make-out corner, John receiving a verbatim reading from the city code book. Conversational buzz resumed. I took the phone from Charlotte. "Hey doc."

Liza walked up to the bar across from me. She had a handful of loose three-by-three sheets. She waited until I looked at her and then threw them at me, pushing the little paper snowstorm right in my face.

"Wow." I stifled a chuckle.

"Brian, are you there?" said Dr. Bonilla. "I wanted to talk to you about..."

"I'm never coming back in here," said Liza.

"Good, because you can't," I told her. Liza sashayed out the door, with a certain savoir faire, a certain practiced grace, a touch of star quality. Holy cow, I thought, could it be?

I had to re-start Dr. Bonilla again. "I'm sorry doc, could you say that again? I'll listen this time."

"I'd like to have you come down and discuss your MRI results. Are you available..." He did his best to strip the urgency from his voice. "...now?"

"Right now?" I did my best not to sound scared shitless. "No. But I could be there in fifteen minutes."

"That's reasonable," said Dr. Bonilla. "Come up to my office on three."

I disconnected the call and set my hat on the counter so I could wipe away the sweat. "Aw cripes."

"What?" Charlotte was prepared for the worst. "What did he say?"

"He wants to see me. Now. Not tomorrow. Not this afternoon. Now." I bent over the counter and looked at the ghostly reflection of my great big shiny forehead. "You know, sometimes I get a glimpse of myself and I just go, 'What am I thinking? How could I have left the house looking like this? Am I serious?' You know what I mean?"

"So you're strange looking," said Charlotte. "Nothing's changed."

"Yeah? Yeah, I suppose you're right. How do I get friends then? Why do people seem to like me?"

"It's your personality," Charlotte said definitively.

Edna Applejack walked in. She was wearing a woolen scarf over her head, sunglasses, and a short denim jacket over a form-fitting lacy pink dress. Everyone stopped what they were doing and stared. Only when Edna peeled back the scarf and removed the sunglasses did the greetings fly and excitement buzz through the shop.

"That was a good disguise," I said. I was ignored. Charlotte forgot I had cancer and ran to the till.

"What can I get for you?" she asked before Edna was anywhere near the counter. She was talking and laughing gaily with Pastor Kyle. Councilman Jones practically threw Frannie aside to get back to the table before Edna moved on. Too late. She bypassed Charlotte and came to me.

"Lady."

"Mr. Brian. I've been thinking about your proposition all morning."

"What proposition?" Charlotte demanded.

"Edna can't answer that, because I haven't made it yet," I said.

"What is it?" Charlotte demanded.

"It's secret," I said. "I guess I have two propositions for you," I told Edna. "The first one is, you wanna come to the hospital with me?"

"Sure," she said, and quite a few people in the shop groaned. The crowd sank into a sullen state as I made two double-tall cappuccinos, some of my best work, and then slipped out the back with their precious Edna in tow.

My precious. "So here's the deal." I maneuvered the van out of the lot behind my building. Cancer privileges, I had started taking a spot. A spot-and-a-half, because I am a poor perpendicular parker. "There's only one place in this town where a coffeeshop is an automatic moneymaker," I told Edna. "The campus. And there's only one person in town or in the world who would be allowed to open a shop on campus."

"You," said Edna.

"No. Whoopsies, look out." Almost flattened a pedestrian crossing the alley with her head bowed against the storm. "But hold that thought for the next statement of fact. Which is, there's only one person in this town who knows how to run a successful coffeeshop."

"Bill Hernandes," said Edna.

While I was pretending to be offended while Edna pretended to be serious, I took a quick glance at her smooth egg-shaped kneecap. I could imagine the temporary paralysis when that kneecap speared my thigh as Edna took a power hop-step into the lane to establish position for a short deadly jumper. "The campus is the only sure thing I've ever seen. I've coveted it since the day I arrived. It's the best spot in town. Maybe the only spot."

Not only was the JC campus a retail goldmine, but it's a Christian college. I used to be pretty confident in my relationship with God, until cancer and Joshua screwed with my head. Seemed straightforward that you believe in God and go to church and feel bad for your bad deeds, and you get into heaven in the end. Now I wasn't sure at all whether my everlasting soul was in good hands. Assuming Jesus was a capitalist in favor of his minions making a fair profit off each other on sales of a quality product, partnering with a Christian school had to burnish my eternal résumé.

"Bill says the endcap at the Bluffs is the best place in town," Edna parroted with authority. "He says it's the hard corner."

"The hard corner, huh?" I steadied my cappuccino as we fishtailed onto Main. Brought the cup to my lips; but after fasting for the MRI, after the call from Dr. Bonilla, my stomach wasn't prepared to receive the tasty offering. "Bill's got the lingo down. But he doesn't know what he's talking about. For one thing, it's not a corner. It's a strip mall along a highway. And even if it was on a corner, there would need to be another couple thousand homes up there to make it a desirable location. Hard corner. Come on."

"Then why did you work so hard to steal it from him?"

"Technically, it never was Bill's location. I made the required payment before Mike's deadline."

"But you only agreed to put a store up here"—we were cresting the hill leading to the Bluffs and the hospital—"because Mike was financing the whole thing."

"If you want to get technical, yes."

"And when you cheated on his daughter, he offered it to Bill."

"Well for one thing, I'm pretty sure he went to Hernandes before I schtupped Andrea. For another, his daughter is a lesbian pedophile."

I put gossip in three categories. There's the kind where you're a disinterested bystander who simply gets off on brokering info and acquiring a reputation for being in the know. Or you're a nasty bitch with scores to settle against your enemies or womankind in general. And then there are instances like this where it's him or me, a zero-sum winner-take-all game of he-said she-said. The Heavenly Scales might be blind to these distinctions and Hell the price for gossip, period, but I can't sit idly by while the most powerful family in Jamestown tramples my reputation into the tundra.

And eternal suffering still sounds better than Nothingness.

Edna fell silent while I pulled into a spot on the south edge of the hospital parking lot, closest to the Bluffs. "Crap," I said, counting at least five construction workers scurrying in and out of the new shop. "They're already spending my money over there."

"Mike is eager to get it done, whether it's you or Bill," said Edna, monotone, eyes fixed on the van's temperature gauge, which read 28°F—and then warmed up two degrees under her intense stare. Her knee pistoned a couple strokes a second.

I steeled myself to be a big boy and not make a scene if Edna was ready to nip our potentially beautiful relationship in the bud. "I completely understand Mike's motivation," I told her. "I know the Bluffs needs its anchor stores up and running. But I never asked to be in there. I couldn't afford it, I tried to tell Mike. Dating his daughter only made it more complicated. Complicated is also a good way to describe my relationship with Isabel. There's so much about her I love, but in the end I couldn't get past her, uh, her little problem. And all the while her dad, it's like he's bribing me with this coffeeshop.... I'm talking way too much." I was nervous, unable to read her. "I don't want to poison you against Mike and the McEwens."

"Don't worry, you can't." Edna's leg stopped jimmying. She turned her big blue eyes on me. "And you don't have to worry about my opinion of you. Did you know that a friend of mine at the state pen used to get your coffee and share it with me?"

"Kerry Bjornson."

"That's right," said Edna.

"She robbed a farmhouse outside of town, and then burned it down."

"The McGoogans. Snowbirds who were gone nine months a year. They tried to recruit me to play for Arizona State. I never cared for them. Kerry burned their house down by accident. She was a basket case in prison."

"Did you make her your bitch?"

"No."

"Good, because I slipped her a shiv in a pound of Guatemalan."

"Did you really?"

"No, but I always wanted to try, to see if I could get away with it."

With a smile Edna reached over and turned off my van. "I like you, Brian. Jamestown is lucky to have a guy like you. Let's get you healed."

WE EXITED THE ELEVATOR ON THE THIRD FLOOR. "You don't mind doing this with me?" I asked.

"I'm not squeamish about cancer," said Edna.

"Me neither." We stopped outside Dr. Bonilla's open door. "I do have a big issue with dying though."

"It happens," said Edna. I had a flash vision of her long white fingers around my throat. There were worse ways to go. She linked her arm with mine, took my hand in both of hers, and we crossed the threshold together.

"Edna Applejack! What a surprise! Hi Brian," said Dr. Bonilla as an afterthought.

"Hello doc. You two know each other?"

"Not exactly. I'm Paul doctor—Doctor Paul—I'm Paul. Bonilla. I'm a doctor." He wanted to shake Edna's hand, which meant she had to let go of mine, which I was reluctant to allow. "I'm an Edgeley boy," Dr. Bonilla plowed forward, mastering his tongue, "but I followed your career closely."

"Where did you go to college, Paul?"

"UND. Both my undergrad and med school."

"You stayed in-state to get your MD," Edna approved. "I've heard the med school in Grand Forks does a fabulous job."

"I like to think so," said Dr. Bonilla.

"I like to hope so," I said.

"So..." Dr. Bonilla was uncertain what came next.

"Edna's not afraid of cancer," I told him, and became weak in the knees. "I am though. I'd like to sit down."

Dr. Bonilla guided Edna into the hall. "We'll be a little while, if you want to wait in the lounge." He stepped back into the room and closed the door. "That's pretty special that Edna came with you," he complimented, probably puzzling how a bald scarecrow like me pulled it off.

I wondered the same thing. "It's just business," was the only explanation.

"Ah," said Dr. Bonilla, not comprehending. "So, your results."

"I didn't expect to hear anything until tomorrow."

Dr. Bonilla perched on the corner of his desk, hands tucked under his armpits. "Unfortunately they didn't turn out as good as we had hoped. You have a more aggressive cancer than we thought. I've discussed—"

"It moved?" I croaked, trembling.

"It spread," Dr. Bonilla qualified, and the room tilted. "We're seeing signs of malignancy in the abdomen, and the pelvic area." He used his own body as a demonstration device, waving his hand over the areas where the cancer was currently going about killing me.

I had to stand up. I was compressing the cancer, squishing it, squirting it all over inside. I would never sit down again.

Dr. Bonilla realized I was falling before I did. He slipped his arm around me while the floor tilted like the deck of the Titanic. I managed to turn away from him and threw up on his small gray filing cabinet. One of the drawers was partially open. My brain decided I was vomiting up my own cancer-ravaged stomach lining, which really freaked me out. I hurled with a vengeance, gasping and choking and trying to identify the chunks I was filing. An orderly put a towel to my face and we marched out of the office and down the hall, me coughing and crying and retching all the way.

I was in the bathroom so long that Bonilla probably tried to slip out for a drink with Edna. The brave young orderly stayed with me for the duration. I made a lot of noise in there. I should have been embarrassed to limp out and climb in the waiting wheelchair while nurses, doctors and Edna watched. But I was empty, no shame or Cream of Wheat or thoughts of seeing June.

I apologized to the orderly and then the nurse who helped me into a bed, and then Bonilla when he stood over me, not because I was sorry, only because it was the polite thing to do. I didn't want anyone thinking I went peacefully or willingly. I'd rather go down making a scene, kicking and screaming and spewing my guts everywhere. I wanted the spectators traumatized. Disturbed. Devastated, if I could help it.

I couldn't believe what I had heard. I didn't want to say a thing, or move a muscle; I wanted to listen and feel for the cancer inside, make self-confirmation that the doctors' interpretations of my MRI were correct. This was denial. It lasted a couple minutes. Then I started to cry.

"I want you to take some deep breaths," said Bonilla. "This is not out of the ordinary. I've been through similar developments before, and it is not as bleak as it sounds. We have more weapons we can use..."

Blah blah blah. I was a dead man. I looked past Bonilla—I would no longer call him doctor, unless it was Kevorkian, because doctors saved lives, and Bonilla was only hastening my demise, but then again it was my own fault, for putting my life and my livelihood in the hands of a state best-known for its declining population. Edna stood in the doorway. I pulled the van keys out of my pocket. "Here you go. I shouldn't have dragged you down here."

Edna gave my hand a nice squeeze as she took the keys. "What should I do with your van?"

"Keep it."

She bent closer, assuming I hadn't the strength to finish my sentence. "Keep it where?"

"At your house. Or sell it if it's not your style. Whatever." Brian Lawson, master thespian of the overly dramatic, or the king of understatement. But this was no act. "I'm not going to need it any more."

"Brian, you need to slow down a little here." Bonilla sat on the bed and rested his hand on my good knee. "You are going to die someday, but it might be a few decades. What's happening inside you right now isn't good. But it isn't a death sentence."

"It spread," I filled Edna in. "All over me." I wept softly.

Bonilla continued addressing me. "We can see two nodules, one below the stomach and the other in your groin. Neither was big enough to detect during the physical exam I gave you prior to the MRI. That's a good thing. There are a few very small shadows in the surrounding digestive cavity that we'll need to follow up on—"

"Great," I sobbed. "More follow-up."

Bonilla raised his voice and talked over me. "—but that might or might not be anything. We get blips."

Blips and shadows, things a doctor doesn't have to take seriously. Never mind they always turned into tumors. Bonilla was more shook up by my despair than my cancer. Regardless the outcome, I got the feeling he would sleep well at night knowing he had followed standard procedure. Under Bonilla's interpretation of the Hippocratic Oath, the physician was graded not on healing but on strict adherence to the latest guidelines.

"Wherever it is, Brian, you have to fight it." Edna dropped into a crouch and rested her pointy chin on the mattress. "You're a lucky guy, actually. You have yourself a partner who can pick up the slack while you're in treatment."

Andrea? I was thinking, wanting to cry more.

"You and I will carry each other through the tough times," said Edna.

She was talking about herself. I sniffled and dried my tears.

"Did I miss the engagement notice?" Bonilla asked. A married man, he still seemed crestfallen Edna might be off the market. Another reason for him not to risk pulling a mental muscle straining to find a way to beat my cancer.

Edna kissed my forehead and stood. "It's a business partnership. But that doesn't mean we aren't going to break some hearts." She left the room, with my keys. Bonilla stared after her, thinking about me, thinking about Edna, I don't know.

He sighed. "Brian, the way I see it, you have two treatment options." I didn't want choices. I wanted Bonilla to tell me how he was going to cure me. "I could point you to a grief counseling group. We have ten or so terminal patients and their loved ones that get together regularly."

"Ten, or so?"

"The membership fluctuates."

"Nice to see you haven't lost your sense of humor."

"I got that one from one of the members of the group. You'd be amazed at how they come to grips with their mortality. It can be a little shocking at first."

I closed my eyes. "Maybe I should attend. I should probably get to the point where I'm not so afraid of dying that I go out crying and puking."

"It's a helluva deal, isn't it?" Bonilla studied me. "You can pretend there's nothing wrong, nothing to be afraid of, and then get blindsided at the end. Or you can spend all your time adjusting to the possibility you could die, preparing for death and beyond. Either seems like a strange way to live."

"What's my second option?"

"You can decide you're going to live, and we can hit this thing even harder." Bonilla climbed all the way onto the bed. His thin arm was beside my head, his skin radiating a powerful clean, like he had scrubbed, dried and deodorized each hair individually. "We'll use a different chemotherapy cocktail, at a more aggressive dosage. We'll go after anything living. We'll knock out what's left of your hair, stop your fingernails from growing, make everything inside and out sore. And kill the cancer."

"I like that part." Sniffing a man's arm, feeling comforted by the heat of his hand on my stomach. Only in a hospital. "And you could spend the next couple weeks researching what's out there, in case other doctors are having luck with new treatments or new breakthrough drugs."

"I know exactly what to use. It's well documented in the literature." Bonilla rubbed my tummy and slid off the bed. "We'll discontinue the last two days of this cycle and start the new dose Monday. Ordinarily I'd wait a couple weeks for your body to recover. But that means the cancer recovers too. We're not going to allow that."

He threw a right hook to my jaw to affirm his tenacity. Bonilla was going to cure me by the force of his determination. The chemo was nothing but a backup. Probably a placebo. Might have worked if I had any faith left in him.

"I'll still point you to the grief group if you'd like."

"I'd have us drinking Guyana-flavored Kool-Aid by the third meeting."

Two candy stripers came in and scrubbed the vomit off my shirt sleeve. Bonilla winked at me. "You hang in there Brian. I'll see you Monday."

THE SHIRT WAS DAMP, clinging to my chest and making me shiver as Edna drove me back to the shop. "Maybe you should wear pants," she suggested.

"It's almost June. I can't wear pants in the summer." My teeth chattered. "Even if it is snowing."

"You feeling better?"

"I'm not going to throw up again anyway."

"Was it the chemo drugs that made you toss your cookies?"

"And bawl? No, it was fear. I'm pretty sure I'm going to die soon."

"I think you're in great hands. Dr. Bonilla seems very talented."

"You only think so because he got his MD in North Dakota," I said. Edna's face clouded and I received a displeased look. I decided to move along. "I don't think Bonilla likes my chances. He's been hitting it with surgery and radiation and every chemo drug in the book, and the cancer keeps coming."

"You seem like the kind of guy who can beat long odds." Edna squeezed my knee. The other knee. "How are your parents handling it?"

"Not great. They keep asking me to move home. I don't plan on telling them about today."

"You have to be honest with your folks, and trust they can handle it," said Edna. "If they're anything like you, they can."

"If they're like me, they'll throw up on the phone and start wailing. Actually," I admitted, "they're a couple of the toughest people I know. And you're right. When this wave of despair wears off, I'll be ready to beat this thing."

Edna gave me what looked like a flirtatious smile. That couldn't have been Evolution talking. Guys riddled with cancer and full of pluck were inspirational, but didn't offer the best odds at perpetuating your bloodline. "While you were recuperating I talked to Bobby Guldseth, the AD at the College." Edna drove with one hand down the slick slushy hill into downtown. The brake lights of the cars ahead flashed, trying to warn us. "He's going to set up a meeting with Terry Lovold, the head of Student Affairs."

"Did you get a sense whether Bobby thinks a campus shop is possible?"

Edna laughed. "I got a sense alright."

A little pickup fishtailed and then lost it, occupying most of both lanes as it drifted sideways downhill. I felt the thump and heard the frictional whirr of brakes locking all around us. Edna slipped the van into Neutral and guided us to the left, squeezing between the meridian and the bumper of the pickup. I nodded to the driver, Kip Carlson, who was looking over his shoulder, pretending to steer. We eased past him. I looked back and watched Kip spin another ninety degrees to face downhill again, and then drive straight into the steep ditch, taking a little Honda economy car with him. No need to call 911; we glided through a bottleneck created by a tow truck, an ambulance and two police cars already assisting at another accident scene at the bottom of the hill.

Edna shifted back into Drive and tucked a loose tendril of kinky blonde hair behind her ear. "That's a tricky hill." North Dakota was right. This woman was special. She would be good at anything. NASCAR, B-ball, tiddly-winks...coffee. "By the time I was done talking to Bobby," she continued her story, "he was begging me to put a coffeeshop on campus."

I was dazed, unable to comprehend the speed with which we had become partners. One thing was for sure—Edna was my goldmine. I had struck it rich; assuming I lived to see the new year, I was going to get a shop in the promised land. "So when's the meeting with Terry Lovold?"

"I don't know yet. Do me a favor though. We need to swing a good deal on rent, so don't seem too eager when we talk to Terry."

"I don't think that'll be a problem."

I had dealt with Terry Lovold when I first moved to Jamestown. With five thousand students rich enough to afford the pricey tuition, stranded on a campus isolated by the river, I knew where I needed to be.

When I couldn't get an appointment with Terry, I drove onto campus, admiring the old New England style buildings with fresh paint on the wood and ivy clinging to the brick, and pretty coeds strolling along the riverwalk under some of the only trees in the state. The administration building had a clock tower and a spire with a cross.

I had walked up to Terry Lovold's secretary and asked to see her. Terry heard my voice and walked out of her office. "Mr. Lawson, I was going to return your calls. There was no need to come in."

"Hi. I'm Brian." I had turned on the charm, until it became obvious it would get me nowhere.

"You're interested in putting one of your shops on campus."

"I thought it might be a win-win—"

"The College has a strict policy against allowing commercial interests to locate on campus. So I'm sorry."

"Is that a religious decision? Because I know…"

Terry shook her head so hard I couldn't keep talking. "It's campus policy."

"How about right next to campus?" At this point I already hated her. "I mean right next door. With a big sign the kids can see from the other side of campus. I could call it God's Brew."

"You'll find out that the College owns most of the land adjacent to the campus." Terry is structurally attractive, thick glossy hair and smooth golden skin, with the face and style of television's 1950's mom. But with every word she looked more like Disney's wicked stepmother. "I'll give you a tip. There's a retail development in process across the river. A company owned by a gentleman by the name of Mike McEwen is refurbishing an old newspaper building. You should look into opening a shop there. Okay?"

"Thanks for the tip."

Terry Lovold then turned her back on me and started giving her secretary orders for the rest of the day, with a tone that was even more condescending than the one she used on me.

"Alright," I said, the conductor announcing the last chance to jump on the money train. "I'm out of here." Terry threw me an irritated glance and continued to rag on her secretary. I loitered in the doorway. "I'm thinking about taking a class. Maybe I'll even get an MBA. It doubles your earning potential, that's the figure I've heard thrown out there. Bandied about. Do you have an extension program?"

Terry jerked a thumb at the hallway. "There's a brochure out there."

My wicked stepmom wouldn't let me go to the ball. But everyone knows what happened when Cinderella got herself a powerful goddess.

T - 5

Thursday night Edna cooked for me. She lived in a brick house in the ritzy end of town, north of the Bluffs retail center and with approximately the same square footage. In her marble kitchen, in her Wolf oven, Edna broiled a herb-crusted flank steak that I couldn't stop eating, because of a certain spice that drove me wild, until it was gone, at least a pound of meat, by far the most I'd eaten since Joshua's mom stuffed us full of lard-fried veal, German dough and buttered vegetables before our Dakota biathlon on Kulm's funky links.

I chased the steak with a cup of green tea and two shots of ouzo, which aided my digestion as the Greeks promised, a miracle given that yogurt shakes were the only protein my stomach had been contending with during the current round of chemo.

It came as quite a surprise, that Edna might be hot for me. My head was shaved but my hair was still obviously thin, and patchy, my skin pasty. I limped from the pain in my leg, which made me appear not two but three inches shorter than her. And I had cyclophosphamide breath. And yet she stood close to me. She squeezed my thigh a good six inches above the knee when she left the couch to grab the ouzo bottle. She said suggestive things, like, "How drunk do I have to be to get you to put me to bed before you leave?" Like Charlotte said, I must have a helluva personality.

We didn't really talk strategy for the next day's meeting. Edna just went on about how excited she was to work with me, how she was looking forward to being back on campus again, how we were going to make a boatload of money—and would we be able to turn the shops over to our employees for a week at a time so we could take vacations together? Listening to her I could believe I had a long life ahead of me.

She was different at home, just the two of us. She spoke more softly. She looked me in the eye for extended periods. She operated inside my personal space, the space many men dreamed of sharing with Edna Applejack. I was touched by the care she put into cooking and making me comfortable; and I was surprised at the sad shadow across her face when she made an offhand reference to the time lost in prison. Had I assumed she lived life to the fullest in the slammer? That life was good for Edna Applejack regardless whether fate put her behind bars, or burka-bagged her for some Taliban freak, or decreed a windswept rural existence? Yes. So I might have overreacted to her vulnerability that night, and I was probably overly flattered that she allowed me to see it, hoping that she couldn't help it because she was so deeply smitten with me. I wanted Edna in deep smit, because I sure was.

WHEN WE MET FRIDAY afternoon in the JC parking lot, Edna hurried over to me and grabbed my hand and pressed against me. When my first girlfriend on our first date slid across the bench seat of my folks' Cutlass Sierra to sit hip to hip with me, that's what it felt like.

"Pants and everything," Edna approved, giving me the once-over.

"Are you ready for this?" I could talk quietly, the only way my throat liked it anymore, because she walked so close to me.

"Let's go get us a campus coffeeshop," said Edna. This was the trigger for a rapid transformation back to her public persona. She was calling out to administration old-timers from her glory days and smiling at star-struck students practically creaming in their pants as we crossed the lobby and walked into the office of the VP of Student Affairs without knocking.

Terry Lovold hurried around her desk. "Edna! It's so good to see you again!" A sizeable gentleman with dark Brylcreemed hair abandoned his guest chair in time to avoid a midget's-eye view of Terry's breast as she hugged Edna. Terry wore her blouse and skirt tight, but it didn't feel like a bid for sex appeal. From my impression of her, she was punishing her big tits and sweet childbearing hips for making her look soft and feminine and would have worn a suit and tie like Mr. Brylcreem if she could have gotten away with it. Maybe the answer was simpler, she was ready to move up a size.

"You know Brian Lawson?" Edna introduced me.

Terry pretended not to as she shook my hand. "Hi. Terry Lovold."

"We've met," I said.

"Glen." Edna saved up a big hug and kiss for Mr. Glen Brylcreem. "Long time no see."

"Edna," Glen purred. "You are a sight for sore eyes." He hugged her like he meant it, enveloping her, bending her backward, getting grease on her face. If he hadn't been the president of the College, I would have had to challenge him. Snap my depleted twig of an arm on his square jaw.

"Brian Lawson," I announced. "I own James River Valley Coffee."

"Great little establishment you have there," said Glen. He must have been talking about the exterior because I knew for a fact he had never set foot in my shop. "Jamestown is lucky to have you."

"Isn't there another coffeeshop," Terry wondered, "closer to campus?"

"There is a coffeeshop across the river," I said. "And he calls it Campus Coffee. But it's actually a little further."

Terry frowned and nodded in the general direction of Hernandes' shop. "But it's right across the river."

"It would be closer, you're right," I said, "if you had a boat. It is closer as the crow flies. Supposing you were a crow."

"I still think it's closer," said Terry.

"Excluding sailors and crows, I'm closer by almost two hundred yards."

"Sounds like you've already stepped off the distances," Glen joked.

"I get upset when a competitor resorts to false advertising. That's all."

Edna threw me a warning look and indicated that everyone should take their seats. "So let's talk about a real campus coffeeshop." She remained standing, waiting for everyone else to sit. Gentleman Glen was determined to wait for Edna. They ended up sitting down together, synchronized sitters, foreplay for Glen from the way he licked his lips as he gazed upon her.

I worried whether they had something going on. A steamy affair would guarantee us a campus shop; I was ready to give up coffee and sell Mary Kay to keep Edna to myself.

"Bobby tells us you'd like to open a coffeeshop here." Glen spoke to Edna. He had to lean forward and look past me to do so. His voice was deep and confident. The hair on his temple was a vividly etched curve sprinkled with a touch of gray, perfect sidewalls. He crossed his legs like a girl and still looked like a man. "Terry and I have discussed it. It's an interesting concept."

"It's a concept we can make a reality before the leaves start to fall," I said. "Which is early August around here, am I right?"

Glen humored me with a polite smile, and then got back to ignoring me. "We feel you're the key to this idea, Edna. You would be the draw. The reason why kids come into the shop."

"I've never done a study to back this up," I said, "but the key to a successful coffeeshop has to be the quality of the coffee. You bring in Bill Hernandes to run things, and you'll be out of business in two years. No offense to Bill; but he doesn't know jack about coffee."

Edna eyeballed me like I was dangerous. To avoid having you draw any more unflattering conclusions about me, I probably should have skipped this detailed description of the meeting and just reported to you that everything went fine and we got the shop. But I'm not ashamed to say I'm a little competitive. I'm accustomed to being the first and last one talking. Not an easy transition to fourth wheel on the trike.

And my mental state, it wasn't all that stable. I was three days gone from a death sentence, three days away from starting a *really* aggressive round of chemo that Bonilla promised would destroy every living thing inside me. And still leave me alive? Only if I was somehow more than the sum of my dead parts. If I had any dependents to provide for, I would have started trafficking my innards on e-bay while they were still functioning. Do some self-surgery. Start a bidding war among universities specializing in deformed organs.

"Edna is an important part of this deal," I said. "But you need to know that I have a great track record running coffeeshops here and in California."

"We'll be sure to check your references before we decide on anything," Glen promised. "So Edna, tell me." He uncrossed his legs and shifted onto one buttock, tilting toward Edna, getting intimate with her through me. "Can we expect to see you here morning, noon and night?"

"Do you think you could keep me away?" Edna rose and spun around her chair, gliding behind me. She was taking over the meeting and I had no ability to contain her. I could imagine similar frustration from defenders back in the day when Edna made an unexpected backdoor cut to the hoop for an alley-oop slam. She gave me a disciplinary pat on the back, continuing on behind Glen, laying a softer hand on him. She perched on the corner of the desk. "I have missed our school so much. Having the opportunity to come back is so exciting for me. I have many opportunities in Jamestown, as I'm sure you can imagine. But I want to be here with you. At the College." Edna clasped her hands to her chest. "It's where my heart is."

"We are so excited to have you," said Terry. "The students would be thrilled to have a living legend on campus."

"You would be a powerful recruiting tool," said Glen. "And not just for athletics."

"Your name means excellence," said Terry. "Period."

"That's why I believe Edna is the perfect partner for James River Valley Coffee," I said. "We both stand for excellence."

"Brian's coffee is wonderful," Edna testified, staring at me, a frozen smile on her face, willing me to shut up. "He has a great reputation in the community that will carry over to our campus shop. Brian could go anywhere in town—anywhere, period. And he chose me and the College."

"The town has any number of very fine retailers," said Terry. "I can't tell you how many times we've had to regretfully reject proposals to partner with the College. Everyone wants to be on our campus."

"It's your students," I said. "They're rich."

Edna cleared her throat to reclaim Glen and Terry's attention. "The sophistication of the JC student base makes this an attractive coffeehouse market. This is really win-win, you guys." She got chatty, and Glen and Terry ate it up. "The shop will be profitable. And you get to offer an amenity that a lot of the top schools are providing to their students."

"Which brings us to our preferred plan," said Terry. "We'll own the shop, so that the College retains control over the hours, the menu, the staffing. Edna, you'll manage the store. Brian, we'll pay you a licensing and consulting fee for your business model and expertise." She was unaffected by my head wagging back and forth. "The name will have to be closely linked to the College, with a possible religious theme. Eternal Brew, something along those lines."

"No, no, no," I said.

This was mild compared to Edna's reaction. She blew past Glen, picked up her handbag, and said sharply, "We're singing from different hymnals. Brian has no interest in selling his management style, and I don't care to be your figurehead." She gave me a nod and I jumped to my feet. "Thank you for your time, Glen. Good luck here. I hope you can come up with a workable plan to give these students a quality coffeeshop."

Glen clutched Edna's hand. "We want you in here." Belatedly he took a step back and spread his arms. "We want you both. Brian," he said solemnly, sincerely, "we know you have a great product. And Edna…you know how much we love you. How much you mean to the College. We'll work this out."

"I love what you're saying," said Edna. "But the only things to work out are where we're going to build it and when we can start."

"Agreed," said Glen.

AND THAT WAS THAT. Ten minutes later we walked out with a handshake deal to open a James River Valley coffeeshop next to the student union.

"That went unbelievably well," I said at Edna's car. "I can't wait to get together to start mapping out the steps to opening day."

"We'll start now, by breaking the good news to Bill," said Edna.

"Mm?"

"Let's go tell Bill he gets the Bluffs site after all."

"I guess…yeah, I guess that is good news." I'm not a procrastinator. I like to move at high speed. My speed. Edna's pace made my head spin. "We're sure this is a done deal?"

"I can guarantee it, sweetie." Edna hugged me hard. A lesser man would have yelped, because I had a severe neck ache, like a knife in the spine. When Edna hugged me that knife jabbed up into my brain. I was already convinced that chunks of my cancer could be jarred loose from their relatively harmless locations and end up sticking somewhere vital. This knife-in-the-noggin sensation only fed my compulsion to remain perfectly still at all times.

Edna tipped her head back and soaked up the weak sun. "I can't wait to tell that SOB we have a campus location."

Just like that, Bill Hernandes was Edna's enemy too. "We should wait a little longer to tell him," I cautioned. Man I hated being the conservative one, the passenger along for the ride. "Just in case."

"Glen won't dare back out on me." Edna waved to a group of girls loitering on the front walk of the library in the distance, watching us. You know how sometimes it seems like your life is being recorded, how even when you're alone you're under observation, maybe by God, maybe by some other monitoring committee, and this keeps you from being completely uninhibited or gross or uncool? For Edna the sensation would be accurate.

"This is an earthquaking development for Jamestown. We shouldn't waste our big announcement on Hernandes."

"We won't mention this shop," she acquiesced. "But I'm going to let him know his partnership with me is over. And you need to sell him your investment in the Bluffs."

This did sound more enjoyable than getting a refund from Mike. "Alright. You want to ride with me?"

"No," said Edna. "I'll race you there."

EDNA TURNED INTO THE PARKING LOT FIRST, but I beat her to the door. I pointed up at the Campus Coffeehouse sign. "I see another name change in Billy-boy's future."

"He can just cover the sign with a Going Out of Business banner."

Bill must have had a video surveillance camera out front, because he was jogging toward us before we were through the front door. "Edna Applejack!" Everyone in the shop stopped what they were doing, even the dude playing folk guitar on the temporary stage under the velvet Dylan poster. Bill hugged Edna and rubbed her back. "What a pleasant…pleasure. And Brian. Looking for a good cup of joe? Ha-ha! Come on in." With Edna pinned to his hip, Bill walked the aisle waving like a star at a world premier. A few people clapped.

Bill gave a high sign to one of his employees sitting with her girlfriends. They all jumped up, grabbed their drinks and swept crumbs off the table, and retreated to stand against the wall. We sat down. "I really pack them in with this music," said Bill. "Brian, you ought to try it."

"My customers are obligated to laugh at my jokes. That's enough punishment."

Edna laughed, loud and sparkly. Only great athletes have the natural ability to sound good whooping. She gave me a high-five. She was out of the loop, didn't know about the knuckle-knock. Felt good to have something to teach her. Edna needed me. "I knew we were going to make a great team," she said. Hernandes's face fell, and I gave her a sharp look. She patted me on the chest, not too hard thank goodness. "Bill, I'm pulling out of the Bluffs. Sorry. But there's good news. Brian is here to sell you his interest in the site." She turned a blind eye to Bill's state of alarm. "How much, Brian?"

"Maybe we should give Bill a minute to absorb."

Edna took Bill's hand and placed it atop the table, under hers. "Bill can absorb the dollar figure at the same time."

"I put down fifteen thousand." I crossed my legs and tapped the table, my best high-roller impersonation.

Bill nodded. He probably knew that already. Good thing I hadn't tried to turn a quick profit. He squirmed and scowled at the folk singer. When he finally spoke, his accent returned so thick I thought I could understand Portuguese. "Well that is good news. What a good site. So close to the hospital."

"In case your customers have a reaction," I said. "Milk allergies and whatnot."

Bill's upper lip trembled. "I, I guess I'll need to think about your offer."

"There's no time," said Edna. She pinched the inside of Bill's elbow, claiming his attention. He looked at her with touching sadness. Edna smiled, and over time Bill's expression mirrored hers. "I know you had financing lined up before Brian decided to invest in the Bluffs. You need to tap it and get in that store ASAP." She was mesmerizing. "I've heard Starbucks has been scouting Jamestown. And you know Mike is the guy they would be talking to. The Bluffs is a natural fit for Starbucks. Or for you. Everything needs to be in place by the end of day tomorrow."

"Tomorrow," said Bill with sluggish tongue, "that could be difficult."

Edna shook her head. "Brian starts another round of chemo Monday. I don't want him burdened financially. You and I will sit down tomorrow morning with Mike and work this out. If you're not sure about the Bluffs, Brian will just revert his interest back to Mike, to be resold to the highest bidder."

"Let's not loop in Mike yet," said Bill. "I do want to be there. We can get this done. I'm ninety percent certain…I'm sure I can get you the money tomorrow morning. I'd…yeah, I'd like to get this done. Today, if possible."

"Great," said Edna. The woman possessed Jedi mind-control powers. Why was I surprised? She released Bill from her grip, if not her spell. "I'm going to act as Brian's proxy. Finances get him all worked up." She winked at me. "What he really needs to concentrate on is getting well."

"He looks like hell." Bill willed me to keel over dead. Bill was not a Jedi.

"Brian's a warrior," said Edna. "He'll be back." She said this with such authority I straightened up and believed it.

"Edna…" Bill's eyes got misty. "I was looking forward to working with you."

"I know," she said sweetly, sadly.

"That's what you're saying isn't it? That we can't work together? That you won't be my partner?" He reached his manicured hand toward her.

Edna's hand was no longer on the table. "Timing is everything, honey. We were that close." She held up a tightly-spaced thumb and forefinger.

We walked away. I looked back and Bill still hadn't blinked, the image of that narrow gap burned on his retinas. "So that's that," said Edna, outside. She gave me a kiss on the cheek that sent warm tingles down my side. "I'll have your money in hand by tomorrow noon."

"You're like Sherman marching to the sea. Nothing stands in your way."

"Aren't you glad you're Union?"

"Yep. Wow. This is really going to happen. Assuming I stay alive."

"It'll happen anyway." Edna laughed gaily. "But that would be best."

"Let's get a celebratory beer somewhere."

"Can't. I'm having cocktails with Glen."

"Oh. Wow. Excellent. Good business move, huh? You can make sure we're all on the same page. That's a good idea. Well then, let's talk tomorrow."

"Could I interest you in stopping by later?" Edna invited. "Say eight-ish?"

"Can't. I have a dinner date."

"You're right, you're tired," said Edna. "I'll let you get your rest."

I guess both of us heard what we wanted to.

ANDREA HAD INVITED ME to dinner. Clearly I should have backed out. But she had sounded lonely and needy and maybe a little too small to survive on her own. I couldn't help wanting to protect her. I didn't know how Rick had been able to abandon her. I, a man who could physically protect no one, had stepped into the role of her guardian.

Andrea opened the door in a light pink camisole and calf-length pants, a defenseless outfit if there ever was one. Her childlike arms dangled from the loose sleeves. How could those arms push a lawnmower or shovel snow or even tighten a loose screw on the toilet paper holder? Andrea would be an apartment dweller until someone married her.

Which seemed like contributing to the delinquency of a minor. Maybe that was part of her appeal, forbidden jailbait fruit. Maybe it was that smug look that told me how highly she thought of herself and how confident she was I was going to kiss her hello and hope for more later. I wasn't sure if I was attracted to her for the child she wasn't, or the woman she thought she was. I threw my ballcap to the floor, stepped in close and lowered a kiss to her up-turned lips.

"Mm. Well. That was nice."

"Likewise." I produced a bouquet of wildflowers from behind my back. "You have a vase for these?"

"Sure. Flowers. Very nice." We strolled into the kitchen. "Vases are in the top cupboard."

On tiptoes I selected a glazed earthen vase decorated with Aztec symbols. "You couldn't have reached this with a step ladder on top of the counter."

"Rick put them up there when he helped me move in."

"Has he no respect for your dwarfism?"

"Ha ha. What made you decide to bring me flowers?"

Because I felt like celebrating.

I was high on the adrenaline rush of success. Gone was all the frustration—eight years in Davis, five in Jamestown, each time growing the business for three years and then watching sales flatten and expenses fatten, knowing I had a great product with a sweet delivery and yet no way to serve more than a couple thousand customers a year. Dried up was the puddle of blood, sweat and tears that had reflected the heartbreaking fact that success was impossible no matter how hard I worked—that the golden confluence of passion, decent (not great) margins, rising disposable incomes, and an addictive product meant absolutely nothing.

Success—I was one of the last to figure it out, so I'm sure this is no new news to report: it isn't *what* but *who* you know. Terrence yearning to get published, and Theresa desperate to get into pharmacy school—like me they had talent and a great product. We had all three labored under the false assumption that while success may be far off in the distance, we were building toward it, each failure a stepping stone to eventual triumph. In fact the gap had never shrunk. Like me, Terrence and Theresa were worshipping the false idol of perseverance. Unlike me, they didn't have Edna Applejack.

This campus shop was going to be huge. We were going to crush Bill Hernandes within the year, and likely scare off Starbucks. Edna was the biggest name in North Dakota. There was no reason we couldn't set up shop on every campus in the state. I had stumbled onto a frigging franchise.

I ran water in the vase and arranged the flowers to the best of my ability. "I bought these flowers, because they're pretty like you."

"Yeah, well." Andrea pretended not to buy this line, then spent a little extra time arranging the flowers. They weren't the prettiest flowers in the world, so I moved the conversation forward.

"Thanks for having me over. I smell something, in the oven."

"It's lasagna. I hope you like lasagna."

I'm snobbish about a few things, most involving coffee, most of the rest involving food, lasagna being one of them. Please, please don't boil the noodles first. Layer them in the pan right out of the box, and I promise you the noodles are going to bake in the juices from the sauce and the tomatoes and peppers and zucchini, to al dente perfection. I'm the only one in the world who knows this, for which I take no pride, only anger.

"I'm probably not going to do your meal justice. My stomach is all messed up." Along with my mouth, my throat, my intestine and my anus. I believe that's the alimentary canal, and mine must have looked like a four-thousand year old pockmarked Venetian street.

"Fine." Andrea was girlishly snitty. "I don't need you to eat like a real man." She put four place settings on the table. "We're having extra company."

"I'd rather not."

Andrea stuck her tongue out like a third-grader. "Too bad."

I pouted until company arrived. "Brian," Andrea re-introduced us, "you remember Thor and his grandmother Rebecca."

"Sure do." The cancer kid from Bhani's lab. Skinny and reserved with blonde hair in his eyes. "That's 'Tor' with a 'Th-', right? How are you?"

"Fine," Thor mumbled.

"You little bastard, you haven't lost any hair."

Thor grinned like he was getting away with something.

"How can that be fair?"

"You haven't lost much either," Granny Rebecca lied to me.

"I wouldn't go that far," said Andrea, eyeing my sparsely stubbled head. "The lasagna's ready, so come sit down. We can mock Brian while we eat."

"Why should dinner be any different than usual?" I sat next to Thor, with his granny to his left. He fumbled with the napkin tented on his plate, sneaking a peek while I spread it on my lap, and then doing likewise. "So I heard you spent a little time at the Mayo Clinic in Minnesota." I got puzzled looks all around. "To receive Dr. Bhani's treatment," I explained. "Andrea told me North Dakota was making it hard for Dr. Bhani to do his thing, so you had to go to the Mayo."

"Oh," said Granny, exchanging a look with Thor.

"It turns out we didn't need to travel quite that far," said Andrea. She maneuvered the lasagna pan to the edge of the oven rack, preparing to lift it.

I jumped up. "Here, let me help you with that. So you didn't have to leave the state?"

Andrea gladly relinquished the potholders. "We technically left North Dakota without crossing the border."

"Now there's a riddle for you." I hefted the pan and set it on a hot pad on the table. Grease bubbled at the corners, further browning the noodles. Crispy top and soggy bottom. I should have done everyone a favor and chucked it in the garbage can. We still had garlic bread and salad. "What's the answer?"

"Well, we drove a couple hours south and west of here," said Granny, sounding defensive. "To a hospital on a Native American reservation."

"You had the operation on the rez?" I exclaimed.

"It's not really an operation," said Thor in his monodrone. "They just like inject you with bacteria, or, uh, like parts of the bacteria, so that it can't reproduce inside you. Then like your body does the rest."

"Not so many 'likes'," Granny quietly reminded Thor.

"I know," he said, a little put out.

"We're trying to break a bad habit," Granny told me, patting Thor's hand.

"Speaking of bad habits," I reinforced Granny's guidance while smoothly segueing back to the topic at hand, "you didn't really have the operation on the rez?" Unless you were unconscious and unchaperoned, I couldn't imagine submitting to a medical procedure on the reservation. I had driven through a couple, including one in North Dakota. Everyone walked, or would be doing so soon as they rattled around trash-strewn streets in severely neglected vehicles. Every house needed at least one window replaced. And a paint job, except that would be like sugar coating dog crap and calling it candy. Speaking of dogs, the rez breed was missing fur and legs and faithfulness. "An experimental medical procedure on the rez," I marveled. "Holy Toledo. You're a brave young man. So, how did your body handle it?"

"Thor got real sick," said Granny. "I don't know if I've ever seen a boy that sick, since my brother had measles, back in 1933."

"It was bad," Thor admitted. "I felt awful." His eyes were big and gentle, when he let me see them. "But I wasn't like sick from the bacteria that Dr. Bhani used. It was like my own immune system, fighting the bacteria."

"You do say 'like' a lot," I told him.

He frowned. "I didn't just say it there."

"I'm pretty sure you did."

Granny nodded appreciatively to me. "Dr. Bhani tricks your immune system, I guess," she said. Granny seemed the kind of person who might still have doubts whether we walked on the moon, until she got there herself and saw the footprints. "While it tries to wipe out Dr. Bhani's bug, it destroys the cancer at the same time."

I used their story as an opportunity not to eat the block of lasagna on my plate. "And?"

"And it worked," said Granny, nodding, eyes watering as she looked at her grandson. Her arm trembled as she reached for Thor's hand, which he awkwardly gave to her. "We're so thankful."

I gave Thor a pat on the back. "That's beautiful. I'm very happy for you."

Thor was embarrassed by the attention. "So, how's your...yours?"

"My, mine, thing, the cancer, deal? Oh..." I leaned back like I was full, and sighed. "Not great."

Andrea put down her fork and retrieved a manila envelope from the counter. "Brian, you need to see these." She handed me an MRI negative and said somberly, "This is Thor's scapula before the treatment."

I held the negative up to the light. We were in the presence of a demon, a shocking photo of the bogeyman, a glimpse of a child-eating monster at the margin of the videotape that prickles the pores on your back. Andrea pointed unnecessarily at the cottony amoeba mold growing on the bone.

"Fuck. Sorry." I pushed the picture back at Andrea. "Quick show me the good news."

Like those before-and-after weight loss photos, I swear the lighting was better in this one; Thor must have been standing straighter; he had been drinking his milk. The bone was bigger and brighter, knock your socks off better. Maybe it was the lack of a thunderstorm-gray cottonball creature that improved the subject's attractiveness the way a few missing pounds never could.

"Come on. This is someone else's scapula."

"No," Thor assured me, "that's mine."

"Mr. Lawson, you can't believe the difference," said Granny. "Before, I couldn't even touch his shoulder. Now he's asking for backrubs all the time."

This statement hurt Thor more than the cancer.

I winced for a different reason. "Are you sure you want to rub the cancer around, and break it into lots of pieces?"

"Brian," said Andrea, "Thor's cancer is dead. It's melted away."

"Doesn't that seem a little too good to be true? Sorry, that's not a very nice thing to say. But maybe it's still too early to celebrate...?"

Thor flipped the hair out of his eyes. "I might not believe it either, but like I feel so much better."

Andrea stared at me, hands on her hips. "After all this time, you still don't believe it works, do you? How many cures have I told you about?"

"True, true." I wouldn't bring up Brent McEwen's non-cure in front of Thor and Granny. "I guess I should actually pay attention when you talk."

Andrea whacked me on the back. I really wished she wouldn't do that. "Hey," she said, "I have a surprise for you."

"I don't think you can top Thor's MRI results."

"No, but look what I bought." From the pantry she produced a copper-plated la Pavoni espresso machine and set it carefully on the countertop.

I left the table to caress the sleek Italian beauty. "This is topnotch, lady. You shouldn't have."

"Shouldn't have what?"

"Bought it for me."

"Yeah, right. This is for me. I need to become an espresso connoisseur."

"How come?"

She frowned at me. "So I can run the new store with you."

"Right, right."

"I need you to teach me how to use this thing. But not tonight. Right now I just want you to make us a cappuccino."

"Us, including you? You're part of 'us'?"

"I'm going to learn to tolerate coffee."

If our partnership wasn't already caput, that statement would have done the trick. "For one thing, we're going to make espresso, not coffee. It's the difference between Canadian whiskey and a single malt scotch. For another, nobody *tolerates* my espresso. I'm going to make you fall in love with it."

"We'll see about that. You need to finish your lasagna first."

"I'm too excited to fire up this bad boy. Thor? Granny? Two double espressos coming up."

Thor wrinkled his nose. "I've never had straight espresso," said Granny.

"You'll never go back to coffee," I promised.

"That's a bold statement," said Granny. "I'm Norwegian."

I filled the reservoir and switched on the pressurizer. "Oh, so you normally drink coffee-flavored water."

"That's right," said Granny, chortling.

"This is going to be a bigger challenge than I thought." I opened the freezer. "Coffee beans?"

"Over here." Andrea spun the corner lazy susan and pulled out a pound of James River Valley beans.

"First lesson: always keep your beans in the freezer." I had little choice but to pretend she and I were still going to be partners. She wasn't going to be any less angry, whether I gave her the bad news that night or the next day when Hernandes bought her out. Of course there was always the happy possibility she'd be relieved. "Even Folgers, Granny."

"You're not proud I bought your beans?" Andrea demanded.

"Very proud. Check this out. Built-in burr grinder." I poured three scoops of beans into the back of the espresso machine. "Thor and Granny, stay calm over there. I'm going to mellow your espresso with a little cream and sugar."

"I'm not having any."

"Thor," I warned. "This is a celebration. I don't want any trouble from you. If you don't like it, just dump it down the sink when I'm not looking."

"Okay, I'll do that," Thor promised.

"But you're going to give it a fair try."

"Maybe."

"Granny, your grandson is making me angry."

"To tell you the truth," said Granny, "I'm not sure I won't be dumping it down the sink too."

"Come on!" I barked. "Yes, wasting perfectly good drinks is a sign of appreciation in most cultures. But this is America, baby!"

I got a smile out of Thor. "What cultures?" he asked.

"Oh, I don't know, take Canada, for one. Milk," I ordered Andrea around. "Do you have any heavy cream? Blenderize a few ounces for me, with sugar. About halfway to whipped cream. So yeah, Thor, if you're dining in the home of one of our Great White North neighbors, when you're done licking your plate clean, you throw it like a Frisbee against the nearest wall. And then you dump your milk down the drain and grab a beer."

Thor picked up his plate and cocked it like a Frisbee. "Hey," said Andrea.

"Of course everybody eats off paper plates in Canada," I said.

In no time I had four double-shots of espresso lined up, two of them Turkish dessert-style. "Get 'em while they're hot."

Andrea warily accepted her cup. "No cream and sugar for me?"

"You must be sweet enough already," said Granny.

I shook my head. I sipped. "Oh yeah," I cooed. "That's a good machine."

Andrea sniffed her espresso and wrinkled her nose. "Maybe you'll own it after all."

Thor and Granny dipped their lips. "My," said Granny, "that's good."

"Thor?"

He shrugged. "It's okay."

I clenched a fist, shaking with rage. "I am so angry at you right now."

Andrea sipped once, and again. "It's different than I thought."

"Different...?"

"In a good way. That's not the way I remember coffee tasting."

"That's because it's *not* coffee," I said through clenched teeth. "Gol. Gee."

"Calm down over there." Andrea drank some more. And repeat. She finished hers before I did. The first sign of trouble.

"Mr. Lawson, have we convinced you to try Dr. Bhani's treatment yet?"

I sighed. "Granny, I don't know."

Andrea licked her lips. "You'd be crazy not to. Hey, since we're just standing around talking," she said like a jittery junkie, "why don't you make us another one. They're so small."

"They pack a wallop though, sweetie." Granny was practically tonguing her cup. "I won't be falling asleep early tonight."

"I'm not a coffee drinker," said Andrea, "so I don't think it'll affect me the same way."

Unless Granny became a horny devil-cat on the drive to the Ronald McDonald House, she was right about that.

I filled the portafilter. "So what are my chances of being cured by Bhani? Or of even surviving the treatment? I'm not as young and hardy as Thor."

"Your chances of survival are almost one hundred percent," said Andrea.

"It's the 'almost' that gets me."

Granny got serious on me. "Brian, what are the mortality statistics of your cancer, when they use the standard chemo treatment?"

"Honestly, I don't know. I really haven't wanted to look it up."

Andrea caressed my back as I pulled another couple shots. "Brian has basically the same cancer as Thor did. In every study we've seen, these types of sarcomas have very little long-term response to chemotherapy and radiation." She slipped under my shirt and scraped the waistband of my underwear with what I knew to be a long shapely fingernail.

"So there isn't really any debate," said Granny. "I'm going to feel awful if we don't convince you to take Dr. Bhani's treatment."

"The standard treatments give false hope," said Andrea. "They trick you into thinking that some reduction in tumor size or slowing in the growth rate means progress. It doesn't. It only delays the inevitable." She explored my back, stabbing me with a fingernail, producing a blossom of electrical currents and possibly drawing blood. Sort of a cross between S&M and necrophilia, she was seductively abusing me while discussing my certain demise. "And in the meantime chemotherapy causes permanent damage to just about everything except the cancer." She caressed the base of my spine while I lovingly worked the la Pavoni. I had an erection, but I wasn't sure which one of them deserved the credit.

"You should take the treatment," said Thor. "It really works."

"Is Bhani's procedure covered by insurance?" I asked over the roar of the espresso machine bludgeoning the ground coffee with hot water. "Because the chemo is fully covered by my—"

"It's free," said Andrea, irritated as always by everyone else's lack of knowledge. There were plenty of stupid questions as far as Andrea was concerned. At the same time, she was stroking the front ridge of my hip. "Dr. Bhani is still working off a couple grants, so he doesn't need your money. He needs your data to submit to the regulators."

"We weren't charged a dime," Granny confirmed as she dashed around the table with the dishrag, wiping up some bread crumbs, sending others flying. Thor was flipping the hair out of his eyes every five seconds. The caffeine was kicking in.

"I'm not looking forward to more chemo," I admitted. "I'm still feeling the effects of the last round. I start another three-week protocol on Monday."

"How soon could Mr. Lawson start with Dr. Bhani?" Granny explored my options.

Andrea pounded her shot of espresso. "A strong immune response is crucial. Because Brian's immune system is depressed from the chemo, Dr. Bhani would wait at least a couple weeks." She beamed up at me, a weird light in her dark eyes. I heard Sumatran natives whisper-chanting to a primitive drumbeat somewhere in the far reaches of her caffeine-addled brain.

"You should do the treatment," Thor urged.

"Would the health department be ready to allow Dr. Bhani to administer his treatments in the U.S. by then? Not that I'm afraid to have a medical procedure on the rez. Actually I am."

"Not likely," said Andrea. She hooked a finger through a belt loop on either hip and pulled me into a quick simulated penetration. "Don't be afraid."

"But I am though." Of many things. Dying from chemo, dying from not doing chemo. Dying from Bhani's "cure". Dying from not trying every method of destroying cancer known to man. Also afraid of being dry-humped in front of Granny.

"It's time for Thor and me to get going," said Granny. She gave me a hug, with Andrea still partially attached to me. "You take care of yourself, okay?" She started sniffling.

"I will, Granny. Thor, it's been nice to meet you. Congratulations on your cure." It felt really wrong to call it that. "Let's stay in contact. I can let you know what I decide to do." *And you can alert me to any relapses or horrible fatal infections before I do anything stupid.*

We said our final goodbyes. I did not want that kid to die. Their footsteps were still echoing down the hall when Andrea pulled me onto the couch.

"So I'm seriously thinking about Bhani's treatment."

"I think it's time for you to stop thinking," Andrea rasped, leaning into the sloped armrest. "You might have something better to do right now. Hm?"

I was more than a little ready myself. All night I had been feeling like a playa, breaking one girl's heart and toying with another, while being pursued by the official state goddess. Being the playa I was, it was too early in the relationship to feel guilty for stepping out on Edna.

Although I was a little jealous that she was sipping cocktails with Glen.

You're a playa, I had to remind myself. *Pleasure the one you're with.*

Twenty seconds into kissing and Andrea was already moaning, more like grumbling, as our heads sank into the corner of the couch. Submerged in grumbles and slobber, I lost track of time and space. Visual snippets of the sweat on her stomach and the wetness between her legs flashed into our secluded world. When she put her hand on me, an aggressive act for Andrea, I realized I was way ahead of my San Diego pace, too far along to slow things down. In a hurry I shucked our pants.

The orgasm came soon after. It was troubling. I'm accustomed to a seemingly infinite flood of energy and what-not leaving my body. This one never really got going. It kind of jammed inside me. I kept thrusting, hoping I was about to be blessed with a mystical, multi-stage, escalating orgasm.

My penis squished out. I smushed it up against her a couple times, got no response from either of us, and laid still.

"Well," said Andrea. "That was something."

I grabbed my pants and made for the bathroom. Tough luck for Andrea, but my psyche was in no condition to pick up with my fingers where my limp dick had left off. My plumbing had me worried.

In the bathroom mirror my once-impressive legs were skinnier than ever. Thin legs did make my dick look fatter, anyway.

Pride in my relatively impressive penis evaporated as I examined my body. My ribs showed, but I still had a bike tire of fat low on my stomach. My skin was mottled—from the sex or the chemo or the cancer? I touched around my belly button and regretted it—tenderness on the outside, pain on the inside. My forehead was slimed with cold sweat. Not the way a healthy body looked and felt. Not even a sick body putting up a good fight. I was dying.

The gray specter of death shadowing my face confirmed it. Maybe that was the effect of two burned-out light bulbs above the mirror, I don't know.

It was all I could do to kiss Andrea goodbye and pretend I was basking in the afterglow of great sex. I had to fend her off, she was wired and ready for more. I should have kindly informed her that if she did have the insatiable caffeine-driven urge to go out and get a little more, I hadn't much polluted her with jizm. Too bad for her that Sam was in Alaska, assuming Jerry's rumor of her debauching that young man was true.

I drove home agonizing over what had gone wrong. Either my tank had been empty from the get-go, or I had a blockage. Even though it would entail more medications, more procedures, more pain, I preferred the blockage explanation.

I really would rather not analyze my semen, here or in general. But sex and semen are so central to what it means to be alive. That's not just my personal credo. From what I understand, once the genes realize your seed-spreading days are over, the body's defense systems give up. Everything's geared toward copying oneself into the next generation. Once that's no longer possible, once the sperm-manufacturing process is mothballed, the body sees no sense continuing to take up earthly space.

Back home I attempted to jack off, unsuccessfully. I selected Edna, which was a big mistake. Even with complete fantasy control, I was intimidated by her. First I made her sex-starved and begging for it, which turned out to be too implausible. Frustrated in fantasy and reality, I forced myself on her, staying just on the bad-boy side of the rapist line. Edna punched me in the face and threw me out of the toilet stall. Finally I was the one pleading for it, all the while my dick begged me to stop.

I stunk of desperation. I went from trying to trick my body to trying to motivate it, to convince it there was a reason to put up a fight and live, even if it was in the sad state of the eunuch.

"Body, goddammit, sex isn't everything. Does it really matter whether I can get jiggy with it right now? I'm not married, so it's not even appropriate. Jesus frowns on it, and for crying out loud, let's hope Darwin did too. I'm staying busy in the meantime, contributing to building a rich and vibrant society—as I'm sure you're aware, Body, it's tough to propagate the species if society is breaking down. And honestly, and don't ask me why this is so, but currently at least three women seem ready to pay for my sperm, if it comes to that. Thanks to medical technology, I don't have to copulate to reproduce. The final five-to-eight inches of piping are irrelevant. Get with the times, will you? And p.s., please don't give up on those final five-to-eight inches."

Was my body paying attention? Who knows. Andrea called while I was indisposed, and left a message:

"I just want you to know you made a big mistake leaving early tonight. The thoughts running through my mind, well," she had chuckled, "they're probably not even legal, I don't know. If this is what caffeine does to me, I'd say you're going to be in for a treat when we're working late together at our coffeeshop in Denver. Of course, if you decide to go home early like tonight, it'll have to be some lucky customer or employee. Let's hire a lot of cute young boys, just in case. If you get this and decide you're not really that tired, I'll be up for awhile yet. Quite awhile. Feel free to come over. Okay then, I guess I'll hang up. Bye."

With this still fresh in your mind, let's skip ahead twenty hours, to Saturday night. It explains a lot of what would happen in the weeks to come.

"You're back so soon," Andrea greeted me at the door to her apartment. "So soon, but way too late. Unfortunately for you, the caffeine has worn off. And I won't be drinking any in the near future, because it left me with a really bad headache that I'm just now getting over."

"Can I come in?"

"Sure," she said, like she was being magnanimous after the way I had treated her. Like I was there for one thing and one thing only, and she wanted to make sure I knew she knew it. I think psychologists call that projecting. "Can I get you something to drink? Something decaffeinated?"

"Naw. I should get to the point, since we'll probably be discussing it for awhile. Hopefully discussing, and not arguing."

"Wow." Andrea stood behind the couch and crossed her arms. "What?"

I dug a bank receipt out of my pocket. "Bill Hernandes wired fifteen grand into your account today."

"Why?" Andrea asked with a sharp, suspicious edge.

"I had him buy out your investment in the Bluffs shop."

"Why did you do…" Andrea couldn't finish the sentence, her voice mechanisms collapsed.

I set the receipt on the end table. "I'm backing out. That location is a loser." This had nothing to do with the Bluffs and everything to do with Edna and the campus location; but the more I thought about that site, the more I believed what I was saying. "We would have lost our money, sooner than later. Don't ask me why Bill is so eager to get in there. Well, I do know. He's an idiot." Andrea shrank while I talked. She uncrossed her arms, searched for something for her hands to do, and finally let them dangle at her sides. "You can find a much more profitable way to invest your money," I told her.

Andrea's head quivered like she had Parkinson's. "So we're not going to run a coffeeshop together?"

"Nope." I wanted to be blasé, but I'm pretty sure I was brusque. Maybe downright rude. I'm not the most patient person. Plus, I could be dead in twenty-four hours, and how disappointing would it be to have spent two of them coddling Andrea's fragile psyche? I knew from San Diego there was no letting her down easy. "It won't work."

"Not anywhere? Colorado or California?"

"I don't plan to move any time soon."

"Suddenly you like it here?" she snapped. If she were any bigger I would have been scared. "Suddenly North Dakota is the greatest place in the world?"

"That might be stretching it." I gave her a little chuckle, to convince her we were still on the same team. At least until I was out that door. "But the prospects have definitely improved over the past couple weeks."

"Oh. Oh. And me?" She wanted to give me a snotty look, but couldn't bring her eyes up to mine. They hovered off my left elbow. "You don't give a crap about me, is that right?"

"No. I mean it's not right."

"You don't care about me, and what my plans are."

"If they coincided with mine it would be great—"

"No." Andrea did me a favor cutting me off—that explanation was heading in an exceptionally tactless direction. "You don't give a shit about me. It's all about you, isn't it? Are you thinking about me at all? No." It didn't really matter what I had to say, she was perfectly capable of conducting both sides of the conversation. "Who are you thinking of? Isabel? I'm sure that's it. Did she ask you to back out, for her daddy?"

"That doesn't make any sense."

"Then why?" Andrea's voice cracked. "Why?"

"Andrea, don't over-think this. A different opportunity came up, that's all. A different opportunity that makes the Bluffs unworkable. I wish I could have thought of a gentler way to tell you this. But we know each other well enough, we can be honest with each other and avoid spending a lot of time—"

"Are you opening a different shop?"

"It's way too soon to tell."

"Who is it?"

"I don't feel comfortable discussing it. From a business perspective, I mean. It's just that there are confidentiality issues, and nothing's for certain."

"You're working with someone else. Why?" Now Andrea looked me in the eye, pleading with me, not for an explanation but for a change of heart.

I needed to calm her down, she was borderline hyperventilating. "It's not

about you—it's about a unique opportunity that only works with this person."
I kept my voice low, purring the way I would like to hear from my mother if I
was a lion cub and men with guns were hunting nearby. Actually I would want
to hear the men screaming as my father tore them to shreds. Andrea was going
to have to settle for motherly purring. "The Bluffs would have dragged us all
under. By switching gears to this new opportunity, I'm actually looking out for
everyone's best interests."

"Who is it?"

"Edna Applejack."

For a second Andrea seemed to be thinking, *Oh, that makes sense.* Then
her body quivered. "You are a bastard. I can't believe you're doing this to me."

"I'm not doing anything to you."

"*No.* No. Yes you are. *Yes* you are. You are and you don't care."

"Come on now." I moved forward and she turned her back on me.

"Go." She pointed at the door. "I want you to leave. You don't care
enough about me to treat me with respect, so I don't want you here. Go."

If I was the sort of guy who's comfortable walking up behind an angry
woman and wrapping her in his arms, this would have been the perfect opportunity. There must be dairy farming in my genes, because approaching an agitated female from behind was instinctively wrong. Plus there was nothing I
was going to whisper in Andrea's ear that would improve her disposition.

"I'll call you. Later." For no one's benefit I pointed at the receipt curled up
on the end table. "Don't forget to verify that the wire went through."

Andrea was crying. It was real hard to leave her like that. She looked so
defenseless. She looked so small, even in that little apartment. I would have
felt a lot less guilty leaving her crying in an efficiency.

T - 4

On Tuesday Edna came to the shop at the right time, minutes after the morning rush became the midday lull. We talked at a table while Charlotte ogled her and wiped down the bar in preparation for what would hopefully be a busy afternoon.

Business had picked up. Whether it was Edna's constant presence or community support for my stand against the McEwens, the past week we had averaged an additional $125 a day. That's close to four grand a month—not striking it rich, but a nice start.

"We're looking good at JC," said Edna. She was looking good, slacks and a soft blazer over a silky blouse that exposed a sweet V of breastbone. She was skinny, wow. Her crossed legs were off to the side, but that didn't mean she sat sideways. In my book that's flexibility. I've heard that world-class athletes excel at keeping their core centered. That's what was happening there—her core remained comfortably balanced on the chair while her legs played over there. How do you defend against that? You don't.

Edna knocked on the table, accustomed to corralling a man's straying attention. "We're going to be kicking Bill's ass by September first. I want to have our grand opening on the Saturday after the first week of classes."

"Pretty aggressive."

"I've already cleared it with Rick."

I choked on my coffee. "McEwen?"

"They'll be ready to start whenever we say Go."

I held a napkin to my mouth and coughed coffee out of my lungs. "That's not such a good idea. My relationship with the McEwens has been rocky."

"Rocky" was being positive. I heard through the grapevine they were saying uncharitable things about me. I was getting a lot of hang-up calls—which was actually a relief, when it wasn't the hospital with more "follow-up" items. If I didn't pick up, someone was leaving messages. The first few were heavy breathing, Iz, I assumed, trying to get me to come join them in Dennis's apartment. Then there was the occasional muttered slander like "ingrate" and "bad beans". At least that's what it sounded like through all the clicking and static I was getting on my cellphone, which led me to believe it was tapped. Also, Dennis was watching me all the time, either sitting at my counter or in the rocking chair at his front window. I knew if I challenged him, he'd claim that was the way he always behaved, and I couldn't argue with that.

"There's nothing like putting fifty grand in the McEwens' pockets to smooth over the past," said Edna.

"Family comes before money with Mike. I had a bad breakup with Iz."

"I don't want you to give this another thought," said Edna. "I can deliver Rick. And whatever ill will Mike might be harboring for you, he loves me." Edna never showed any curiosity about my relationship with Iz, or my dalliance with Andrea. We weren't exactly going steady, but Edna seemed to dig me. What woman didn't show a little jealousy over past girlfriends? "Leave all the construction negotiations to me."

"I think you're underestimating Mike's ability to hold and avenge a grudge. I'd really like to explore other options."

"Brian." Charlotte was standing right beside me with the phone in her hand. "Phone for you."

I looked up at her, keeping my hands on my coffee mug. "Are you sure? I didn't hear it ring."

"You didn't even hear me walk over here."

"Of course I did. What, you want me to say hello every time our paths cross?" I waited for Charlotte to sass me, but she was watching Edna stroking the back of my hand with a finger. Charlotte forced the phone on me. She was still staring at that finger as she left our table. "Hello?"

"Brian? This is Tami down at Dr. Bonilla's office."

"Shoot, I was hoping it was a crank call. Or a bill collector."

"Oh, ha-ha. Dr. Bonilla was wondering whether you were planning to come in today?"

"Tami, I'm sorry. I'm not. I forgot to call you."

"That's okay. Should we set up an appointment for tomorrow? We could squeeze you in the afternoon. I know afternoons are better for you."

"No."

"No good? Let's try Thursday. Friday at the very latest. We really need to get you in here." You would have thought Tami was working on commission.

"I'm going to explore another option. I honestly don't know if I could survive any more chemo."

"Dr. Bonilla would be happy to talk about modifying your treatment plan," said Tami. "This decision shouldn't be made hastily."

I waved to Mitchell Glast, the foreman at the Stutsman County Stockyard, as he clomped into the shop. He did a double-take when he saw Edna, and hovered in no-man's land between our table and the till. "Hi Edna," he said like he loved her. He received her finger-wiggle wave and floated the rest of the way to the counter. "I'm sorry," I told Tami. "I've decided to go in a different direction."

"I'm going to have to let Dr. Bonilla know," said Tami with the same tone the playground monitor had used as she headed into the school to tell my 4th-grade teacher I had kicked dog crap into Michelle Bazzalla's hair. "I'm sure he'll want to talk to you."

"If you have to. Do me a favor? I need a refill prescription for the immune system booster I've been taking. Can you have the doc write it for me?"

"I'll see what I can do." If I was unwilling to let Bonilla keep shrinking my testes with his chemo ray gun, Tami didn't sound inclined to do me any favors.

Edna had waited impatiently. "What other option are you exploring?"

The smart person would have played something this controversial close to the vest. Don't think for a second that I don't know what smart persons do. "I'm sure you heard about Brent McEwen while you were in the slammer. He had a similar cancer to mine. He received this experimental treatment from a researcher named Dr. Bhani, and it sounds like it cured his cancer."

Edna was up to speed. "Brent died of an infection from the treatment."

"Per the McEwens. Dr. Bhani says his treatment had nothing to do with it. He says it was an infection a lot of people get in the hospital."

"What else was he going to say? My bad?"

"Good point. But he's had some amazing successes. I met one of them, a young kid who had bone cancer, too. Dr. Bhani's treatment completely wiped out his tumors. I know there's some risk, but right now I'd try a witch doctor's potion instead of going through another round of chemo. I wasn't kidding on the phone. The drugs are killing me faster than the cancer."

Edna pushed my coffee cup aside and slipped her hands inside mine. "I'm sure a miracle like Bhani is promising is attractive. But honestly, isn't chemo the only tried and true weapon against cancer?"

"Get this. I was reading a book someone gave me. Alright, it was my ex-girlfriend, Andrea. I didn't think I'd like it, but I read the whole thing this weekend. I couldn't put it down, it had me so excited. It was written by a guy named Neil Ruzic, who was diagnosed with cancer. He was encouraged by his doctor to start aggressive chemo and radiation therapy immediately. He knew what chemo was going to do to his body, so he went looking for other opinions. He's a rich guy, he could afford to fly all over the country and consult topnotch oncologists. He heard the same thing from every other doctor he talked to—chemo is the recommended treatment."

My voice quavered. In the span of a weekend I had grown attached to Neil Ruzic and his battle. His incredible research effort—years' worth—was stunning to read, and the heroic lengths he went to, to beat cancer and then write the book to educate the rest of us, put me to shame. The deeper I read into the book, the more I was pulling for him. The more I listened to his optimism and love of life (and unpreparedness for the afterlife), the harder it became to separate our stories. After the first few chapters I stopped trying.

Neil's cure came from an experimental cocktail that starved his tumors of their blood supply. This is what drugs like Celebrex do for a living. Neil recommended them highly. Gerry Olson the pharmacist had slipped me two weeks' worth of Celebrex samples, and in a couple days I would be begging him for more.

To my chagrin, Neil never explored the idea of using deadly bacteria to stimulate the immune system. But Dr. Bhani was exactly the type of maverick researcher Neil worshipped and recommended.

"Instead of blindly following his doctor's orders, Neil did a ton of research on the effectiveness of chemo," I told Edna. "And he discovered it does a lot more harm than good. A lot more. Chemo does postpone death—but only for a few years. Five-year survival rates are basically the same with or without chemo, for most cancers. Including his and including mine."

"Then why do all the doctors recommend it?"

"Maybe they're too busy to read the journals about the new research out there. And a lot of them specialize in chemo. They know it well, so that's what they prescribe. And, it's what insurance companies pay for."

"But chemo really doesn't work?"

"No." I was getting worked up. "And it's insane what it does to your body. Worse than I thought. The effects Neil described, I'm experiencing them all. Organ damage, ulcers, gum bleeding…" And loss of mental abilities? I was pretty sure. But I couldn't bring myself to tell Edna that her business partner was in mid-stage senility. I guess I could keep a secret. "Neil had friends die on chemo, friends he made after he was diagnosed. Friends he couldn't convince to stop the chemo and try one of the new therapies. It tore him apart, and it was awful to read. His book convinced me to stop the chemo. If I'm going to die anyway, I would like it to be without a shriveled penis."

Edna's big football-shaped eyes glowed. "Do you feel like Dr. Bhani's treatment is your last chance?"

"I haven't explored every avenue out there. No avenues, really. Mostly because Bonilla frowned on it. But I would imagine that if this fails, with all the time it would take to figure out what else is out there, and get signed up for a different protocol…" I was hip to the vernacular after reading Neil's book. "…it would be too late."

"I want to hear more about this."

"I have write-ups on Dr. Bhani's treatment results, and descriptions of the procedure, back at my apartment."

"We'll go get them when we're done here," said Edna. "If it looks good, we're going to get your treatment started immediately."

"Well, okay, I guess. I mean, I'm—"

"If it looks promising, we're not waiting," said Edna. "We're going to assault your cancer. Massive counter-attack. You are being attacked, right?"

"Sure feels that way."

"Then you have to return fire." It was halftime of the conference championship and Edna was not going to allow her team to lose. "You have to *know* you can beat it." Edna tapped her forehead. Then she picked up my hand and pulled it to her lips. She kissed two of my knuckles, individually; I heard Charlotte moan and then cover it with a cough. "We'll beat it together," said Edna, lips brushing my knuckles.

"I get the feeling you could beat my cancer without my help," I said.

Edna winked. "Okay, let's finish our discussion on the campus shop. I have some ideas about hiring. Even though we won't be open for a couple months, I want our team on board as soon as possible, so they can hit the ground at full steam on Day One."

It was a momentary struggle to switch gears. "We'll have to post for applicants soon," I said. "There are four or five kids who periodically check with me about a job. We can start—"

"Hold that thought." Edna rose as Jolene Crause and Butch Johonson chugged to our table, and laid hugs on both of them.

"We heard you were back in town!" Jolene was sixtyish. She rubbed Edna's upper arms fast enough to throw sparks. "You are looking so good!"

"Thank you," Edna said sincerely.

"I'm Jolene. This is Butch," she introduced the beaming retired farmer.

"Butch and Jolene are an item," I informed Edna. "Everybody's waiting for them to set a date."

Butch pointed the toe of his boot to the sky and swayed back and forth, his burnt brown cheeks reddening. Jolene spared me a polite smile. "So, Edna, we were just talking about what a thrill it was to watch you play basketball!"

"Well thank you. I loved playing in front of Jamestown crowds. No one appreciates basketball like North Dakota fans."

"It's so true," gushed Jolene.

"I've heard Indiana has the second-best fans," I said.

This was ignored. "So, you got any eligibility left?" farmer Butch asked with a tobacco-stained leer.

"I'm afraid not." Edna leaned in and spoke very close to Butch's grizzled face. "And then there's that little matter of my murder conviction that the NCAA might have trouble with."

Butch hooted until he choked and coughed and produced a hanky to catch a grain dust lung biscuit. My dad runs a crop insurance agency, I might have mentioned. I had worked autumns adjusting crop losses and yields. I knew what grain dust smelled like.

"What are you doing now then?" Jolene inquired, gripping Edna's hand and staring up into her face, head cocked like a puppy at its master.

"Believe it or not..." Edna put a finger to her lips. "...opening a coffeeshop on the JC campus."

"Oh, my! No! You are? Well that will be our new favorite coffeeshop," Jolene pretty much screamed. She remembered me. "Oh, Brian, I'm sorry."

"We're going to own it together," I said.

"Oh wonderful!" Jolene squealed. "Then we won't have to feel guilty!"

"You still should," I said. Guilty that they were ready to choose a famous personality over the best coffee they'd ever had (not to mention an equally compelling personality). I was bitter over this flaw of human nature, and excited to start exploiting it.

"We'll be open September first," Edna proclaimed.

"We'll be your first customers!" Jolene yelled.

"Yep," Butch agreed.

"It's still sort of a secret, though," I cautioned.

Charlotte cleared her throat. I excused myself and met her at the end of the counter. "What's going on? Are you opening a new store?"

"With Edna," I confirmed.

"Ohhh..."

"Breathe, Charlotte. Breathe, girl!"

Charlotte warded off my hands. "I don't need chest compressions. Ohmygosh. You're serious. You and Edna.... That is going to be huge. Where?"

"On campus. It's still a secret, though. Sort of."

Charlotte shivered with anticipation. "I'm so excited I can't tell you."

"So I see."

"I want to work in that store," said Charlotte as she returned to her post.

I sat down again with Edna and nodded toward Jolene and Butch, whispering excitedly to each other. "Looks like we have our first two lifetime customers. Not that it's a huge commitment at their age."

"I can pull 'em in," said Edna, bringing her famous face close to mine. Her skin showed some age, a few lines and a slight loss of suppleness. But it still wasn't normal skin. Those weren't mortal muscles moving her mouth, not mortal bones underneath it all. Her head didn't glow and it didn't crackle with electricity, but it was something like that. Her face was inches away and simultaneously projected on the big screen. A thousand pairs of eyes looked on Edna's face with mine. "But I can't keep 'em all by myself. Neither can you. We need great employees."

"It's crucial," I agreed. "It was my biggest challenge when I opened a second shop in the past. We need to hire employees who really want to work. Kids who need money more than they need to party. Kids who show up when they're scheduled, and take pride in—"

"We need older employees," said Edna. "We need mature, professional retail salespeople who thrive on commissions and dream of opening their own coffeeshops. We need adults."

I blinked at her. Given that I had fifteen years behind the bar, compared to her fifteen minutes, I was dumbfounded Edna felt comfortable running the show and instructing me on the perfect coffeeshop employee.

But what was I going to argue? *No, I'm a firm believer that scantily-clad girls are the key to success.* I could see how one might draw that conclusion, but the truth, Edna would soon learn, was no one older than twenty-five would work for what we could pay them. And removing sleeves and shedding a layer was the only way for youngsters to make a decent wage. Sex might not sell coffee, but it did increase the tips. For the females. The male employees were left with having to be friendly to the customers.

"We'll put out a statewide casting call," said Edna. "Newspapers, the Internet, flyers. We'll hold auditions and hire them as soon as possible, and then have them hit the streets and work the community and the campus to drum up anticipation. We'll teach them to pull the best shots this town or any other has ever seen. Our customer service is going to blow everyone away."

"It's a crock."

"Ouch." Edna laid her fingers to my neck. "That sounded rough."

"I wasn't clearing my throat, I was commenting on customer service. I hate it."

Edna withdrew her hand. "Most people would agree customer service is the key to business success," she suggested.

With hiring, I could afford to let Edna live and learn. On the topic of customer service, there must be no mistake. "The concept of customer service has single-handedly set American business back twenty years," I informed her. "It's been translated to mean 'The customer is always right.' 'Serve the customer when they want, where they want, how they want.' Nails on the chalkboard. Who's the expert here, me or the customer? I've never asked a customer how she wants to be served in my life. I'm betting you never asked the crowd how you should play defense, or whether you should pull up for the J or drive the lane."

"Don't believe I did," said Edna.

Across the room Butch toasted that sentiment with hoisted cup.

I leaned forward and lowered my voice. "Every suggestion a customer has ever made was bunk. 'You need to stay open later.' 'You need to turn down your music.' 'You need to stop serving me regular when I ask for decaf.' 'You need to clean your pastry case.' 'You need to sell soup and sandwiches.' I will never sell a sandwich or an appetizing pastry as long as I live. It might please the customer, but I'm not in business to please customers. I'm here to make money, pure and simple."

"Amen, brother," said Edna.

"Some of my customers would be pleased if I offered waffles in the morning and sandwiches at lunch. And pastries that are fresh, and attractively displayed. But I don't want to buy waffle equipment. I don't want to clean syrup off my chairs. I don't want to contract with a prepackaged sandwich company and pretend to be grateful for the pathetic margin and hold my temper at the spoilage I have to eat. I don't like food, and I'm not selling it. I can picture the scene, a customer walking back up to the counter. 'My cappuccino tastes *weird*.' 'That's because you just ate a smoked turkey sandwich with horseradish mayo on tomato'n'herb focaccia.'"

I took a breath. "I don't want to have to hurt anyone. I'm here to make money. To serve the best damn mug of coffee and itty-bitty cup of espresso I can. With a story thrown in here and there."

"That's beautiful," said Edna.

"Our business plan should be to charge each customer individually based on whether we like them or not. 'I'll have a brewed coffee.' 'That'll be a buck.' Next customer. 'Brewed coffee, if you please. And could you clean off that table over there? It's got crumbs on it.' 'Six dollars.' 'What? But that guy only paid a dollar.' 'I like that guy. I don't care much for you. Six-fifty.'"

Edna beamed. "Our coffee is so good, and our shop is going to be so kick-ass, he'd pay it."

It's usually the women customers. But I let Edna's gender error go uncorrected. "It would cut down on all those helpful suggestions real quick. Don't you ever take a customer survey," I told her. "I haven't met a customer who knows better than I do. The great retail chains don't ask customers what they want. They tell them. And then it becomes true. What the customer thought he wanted is irrelevant." I sipped my coffee. "Just my opinion."

"No," said Edna, "it's our business model. It's also going to be the make-or-break question for our prospective employees." Edna laughed. I entertained her, if nothing else. I wouldn't get much fulfillment out of being a full-time comic, but I do like to put a smile on your coffee-drinking lips.

"I can't tell you how excited I am for these interviews," said Edna. "We're going to have such a strong team by Opening Day, we'll already be planning our next campus shops in Bismarck and Valley City." She was staring at the bar—at Charlotte or the espresso machine, I couldn't tell. "We're going to rock this world, Brian."

For the first time in quite a while, I felt like a rocker.

Edna stood. "Let's go have a look at Dr. Bhani's credentials, shall we?"

Charlotte stretched across the counter to hand me two standard envelopes

and a large manila one. "You got some personal mail here." I cringed at Charlotte's farm girl vernacular, as Edna seemed to size her up.

The wind beat on us as we stepped outside. "I'll drive so you can open
your mail," Edna volunteered. I eagerly accepted. She had a Talon. I was smitten with those cars, knowing full well that in ten years it would be considered
the mullet and the mesh tanktop of its generation.

Jamestown had been without rain or snow long enough to dry out the
street grime, powder it to a fine grit, and send it airborne. We crossed Main
with heads bowed, squinting, lips pressed tight. In North Dakota, which way
does the wind blow? In your face.

"Hey Brian," Mitch the Hometown Café owner called from his doorway,
carrying a box of supplies and blinking the dirt from his eyes.

"Mitchell." It felt good to get the props over Edna for a change.

"Is that Edna Applejack?" he asked. Edna was already in the car, so I pretended not to hear him.

I settled into the passenger seat and groaned. "Something wrong?" Edna
asked.

"No, that's normal." I tucked the bills beside the seat in hopes I would
forget them there, and opened the manila envelope. "Huh. Pictures..."

I thought they were of torture victims, shot from above and from low angles, the victims lying on their backs and on their stomachs. Perhaps closeups
of Saddam's disloyal citizens. "Disturbing stuff. Jeez." Naked, bloated,
bruised all over. Open sores on the groin and in the armpits. Gaping oozing
wounds with blackened pus-crusted edges.

And then I realized the pictures were of the same person; and the person,
even with his face swollen, and his throat and cheek...*eaten*, was Brent McE-
wen. "Oh man."

Edna tried to look while she drove us through downtown's noon rush. I
held one of the pics for her to see. She blanched and put her eyes back on the
street. "No. I don't want to see that."

Comprehension continued to come in stages. "Holy hell." Comprehension, accompanied by chills. "It's the infection," I realized. "It's Bhani's cure."

"What? What do you mean?"

The pictures lay on my lap. I didn't want them touching me, the filthy
fucking scary things. I piled them together with the back of my hand and
pushed the lot onto the floor. "Maybe you should find a place to pull over. I
may have to get a refund on that breakfast burrito."

I ate too much that morning, a whole burrito and a carton of yogurt, excited about Neil Ruzic's cure, about seeing Edna, about believing that in the
near future I was going to have money to spend. Now the odds of being alive
to love Edna and make and enjoy that money were miniscule. The bottom had

dropped out and I was falling.

Edna stopped the Talon on the gravel bed beside the railroad tracks. While the car rocked in the wind, I sat breathing and already missing my life so much it tied my ribs in knots. Edna was patient, and I was finally able to return to the moment. I tried to unkink my ribcage without really moving, willing the muscles to relax so I could speak without gasping. "I guess I don't have to puke. That's a first. But thanks for pulling over."

"Give me the story on those pictures."

"It's Brent McEwen. Probably in the morgue. Somebody wanted me to see what he looked like when he died."

Edna grabbed the envelope. "There's no return address. Who sent this?"

I swiveled my eyes to look at the envelope, careful not to let my better-than-average peripheral vision catch sight of the pictures. "I don't recognize the handwriting."

"Why did someone want you to see those?"

I thought talking about it might do me good. "It wasn't cancer that killed Brent. He died of an infection. I knew that, but...I had no idea." His purple and green face was contorted in a terrified snarl. Brent did not go quietly. "Maybe I should throw up." I opened the door and tumbled out. Tears streamed from my eyes and I gagged out a couple coughs before tossing creamed burrito in a yogurt sauce into the sharp gray rocks. Edna's door opened and I hollered, "I'm okay. It's over. Maybe a Kleenex?"

She reached across and through the passenger door to hand me a moist towelette. I wiped my mouth and buried the soiled cloth in the rocks, and climbed back into the Talon. Edna squeezed the nape of my neck while examining the pictures, careful not to let me see. "It's like he was tortured to death. What kind of infection could do this?"

I closed my eyes. "A bad one? Ebola? Typhoid, black plague?"

"I have never seen anything like that." Now Edna couldn't get enough of the grim pics. "Dr. Bhani said it was an ordinary hospital infection? That doesn't look ordinary."

"No. Huh-uh. Nope."

"I want to see Dr. Bhani's treatment results," said Edna. We peeled out of there, throwing jagged rocks at the deserted Burlington Northern shed. "Then we're going to pay him a visit."

BEST I COULD GATHER while lying face down on my couch, Edna was impressed by what she read. She called Bhani but couldn't reach him or Andrea. So she went looking for him, and mercifully took the pictures with her.

I'm not going to belabor the dread I felt. Chemo was out of the question, but there was no way I was going to die like Brent. Bhani would not be taking me to the rez and filling me full of his bugs. And seeing as how Neil Ruzic and I had very different cancers, it was a very long longshot to expect the researcher who had cured him to do the same for me—not that it would even be possible to get accepted into what was now undoubtedly an extremely popular protocol. Even for Neil, it had taken all his time, energy, money and connections. I was a little short on all those. So I would continue the over-the-counter version of his miracle cure. And that's about it.

I planned to remain face down all evening and night, wallowing in the depths of self-pity and trying my best to sink ever lower. But around five o'clock it really hit me: when the secret formula for coffeeshop success had finally become known to me—perhaps in the form of the girl of my dreams, who could say?—I was going to die. That's the kind of irony that makes a man thirsty. I decided to go buy something expensive to drink.

Watching me function at a high level the rest of the evening, you might draw the conclusion I had somehow come to grips with the fatal nature of my disease. Not at all. Death and Nothingness and the disappearance of Brian Lawson from the face of the earth and from people's thoughts and my parents' lives—the utter lack of me in the future and how it really didn't impact anyone or anything in terms of their ability to carry on and laugh and love and vacation and work, how it didn't interfere with Time's ability to simply move on and cause all kinds of amazing things to happen without me ever knowing it—these were my constant companions then and in the coming days.

You forget that for the past five years I had operated under the near-certainty of business failure, or breakeven mediocrity at best. All that time no one could say I was depressed or lacking in vitality. Brother, that's why they come to my shop. I'm a happy person. I laugh, and I like to make others do the same. This night was no different. I'm intrigued by people and the amazing and unexpected events they cause to happen. I can't get enough of it all. That's why I don't want to die.

"Oh, so Brian, you're one of those people who live life to the fullest. You treat every moment of every day like it's your last. You Just Do It. You recognize the cosmic truth that by simply being alive, you're a success, and—"

Shut up, Tony Robbins. First of all, have you noticed that the mantra "live each day like it's your last" is only tossed around by those who have already cheated death? They're in the clear. They're not the ones facing imminent annihilation. Each day *could* be my last, and if I dwelled too long on that concept, I was a bedridden wreck.

Second of all, don't kid yourself that I experience more than a small fraction of the life of the rich guy raking in daily dividends greater than my net worth. If he's living life to the fullest, vacationing and going to major sports events and eating and drinking the best that life has to offer, mating with a woman of similar caliber, investing his money in worthwhile businesses, giving his mom and dad and siblings and friends wonderful gifts, and every so often kicking back to bask in the glow of the achievements that brought him to this point—if he's living life to the fullest, then I'm at five percent, tops.

Five percent. Honestly, without some actual success, that's the ceiling.

Maybe you're different. Maybe none of those things increases your quality of life. Maybe you don't enjoy having people call you a star. Maybe you get no inner peace knowing your retirement is going to be fun and stress-free, knowing your kids are getting the best schooling possible and that every woman out there wishes you had impregnated and maybe even married her. Then you're not like me, that's for damn sure.

Yes I do take pride in the fact that I work harder and put in more hours than most people. I am proud to be exceptional at what I do. My pride is a thin blanket that cuddles me each night as I fade off to sleep; but I have to leave my security blankie at the door when I step outside the house.

There's being good at what you do, and then there's being a success, two completely different things. The carpenter in Bangladesh might be a pro at hovel remodels, but no one calls him a success when he dies from dysentery at age fifty, missing half his teeth and lying in a sewage puddle. The whole fucking Bangladeshi nation might be filled with the world's hardest workers, but no economist is labeling that country a success story. Please don't confuse hard work with success.

I'm the piano man, surrounded by all these people who have topped out in life, maxed out at mediocre, looking enviably at me and wondering what I'm doing here. Why do you think, dumb ass? Wise up. I wouldn't be here if I wasn't just like you.

So when you see me having a good time, don't think I've accepted my fate. Don't suppose I'm fine with dying. And don't pretend for a second that what you and I are doing is as good as life can get.

At the liquor store I bumped into Bobby Guldseth, the College's athletic director. I asked him what made Edna Applejack such a cult figure in the state, and he offered to show me.

We drove to the deserted Administration building. Bobby brought me to his dark office and had me pull up a chair in front of a fifteen-inch TV. He opened his desk drawer and took a couple seconds to select the right videocassette, from fifteen years ago, and then popped it in a player that was ten years older yet. "This game is just what you're looking for…" He was slipping back in time, under Edna's spell, like in the old days when he sat in the stands and fantasized about coming across Edna alone in the locker room after a big game, her undies and even her uniform soaked through with sweat and that rare combo-smell of victory and womanness—I'm taking liberties with

Bobby's fantasy life, but I'll bet it's pretty close. "Let me show you why Edna is a goddess around here," he said.

Here's what we saw. Bobby had the tape queued to the third quarter of a game against the University of North Dakota Fighting Sioux. UND is five times the size of JC, a NCAA Division II university versus a backwater NAIA college. The score is tied. Edna is gorgeous. Her long hair bounces and misbehaves as she floats across the lane. She's fluidly athletic and heterosexy at the same time. She's quick, oh-so-quick catching the ball in the high post and twisting past her bigger, thicker defender to score on a layup or short jump-shot. I want to say she plays like a man, but it's more otherworldly, one of those hot alien chicks Captain Kirk would fall for on Star Trek.

"You're right," I said. "I can see why she's famous."

"There's more to it. It's coming up..."

The Sioux girls were bigger, faster, stronger—better, except for Edna, who outclassed them all. UND scored at will, and so did Edna, keeping the score close. The JC Jimmies had a talented point guard. Little Number Ten would pretend to look for another girl and then feed Edna, who would put the ball in the hoop. Every so often when the entire UND team collapsed on her, Edna would toss it back out, and Ten would drain the eighteen footer.

"Okay, watch this," said Bobby.

The Jimmies were on defense. The Sioux's beefy six-foot-three-inch center was working hard to establish position down low, but Edna, two inches shorter and fifty pounds lighter, kept beating her to the mark and then somehow muscling the big girl away from the hoop. Unable to throw the ball inside, UND's point guard dribbled back out front.

The Sioux's top scorer was a wiry redhead with an explosive first step. Red liked to drive the lane and nail short pull-up jumpers. Now she set a screen for her point guard. When JC's Little Number Ten tried to squeeze past, Red drove her shoulder into Ten's face. Her head snapped back and she went down hard.

The crowd gasped. No foul was called. Edna froze, and the Sioux point guard whipped the ball inside to her center for an easy bucket. As the UND players congratulated each other and headed downcourt, Li'l Ten got to her feet, shaken but okay.

"She shouldn't'a oughta done that," Bobby drawled, transfixed on the screen.

Edna looked lost on the Jimmies' ensuring possession. A teammate forced a bad shot; the Sioux rebounded the ball and brought it the other way. Edna grabbed her shorter teammate who had been guarding Red, and shoved her toward the UND center. Reading the mismatch, the Sioux point guard threw the ball inside—but somehow Edna intercepted it. She fired the ball to Li'l

Ten to start a fast break, which concluded with a layup for Edna.

Next time down the court, Edna once again redirected her teammate to guard the UND center. This time it was Red who sensed a mismatch, and called for the ball. I could see that Edna let her receive it, and then swarmed her, a one-woman swarm. Red was not allowed to dribble, not allowed to pass. She feinted left and tried to bust Edna to the right. Edna's quickness was incredible. A shuffle-step by Edna and Red ran right over her—except that as they fell, both of them gripping the ball, Edna twisted and came down on top, hard, the ball between them and knocking the wind out of Red. The ref called a jump ball and the crowd went wild for Edna.

"Goodness."

Edna easily won the tip, and JC scored. Red was angry. She ran Edna off a couple screens and received the ball on the wing again. This time Edna let her drive, into the lane, for her patented pull-up jumpshot. Edna seemed to be beaten, and then rose up and tomahawked the ball back in Red's face.

"Son of a gun."

At Jamestown's end Edna staggered Red with a hard screen. The Jimmies scored and led by six. On defense Edna packed the middle, preventing an interior pass and baiting the Sioux point guard to throw the ball to Red, who now looked confused. She thought about shooting, decided to drive, and was cut off by Edna, who hounded her until Red threw the ball up for grabs. Another layup for JC, and now the lead was eight.

Red's face was contorted with a mixture of rage and frustration. She did not want the ball, but Edna left her so wide open the Sioux point guard had no other choice. Red actually backed up as Edna came at her.

Edna seemed to swallow the girl up. The ball popped free and Edna was racing downcourt, with Red in pursuit, possibly crying. Edna slowed down; Red caught her, and then Edna exploded to the hoop. They jumped together, Edna effortlessly and Red in desperation, flailing at the ball. With her forearm Edna used the girl's face to boost her skyward the last few inches and throw down a rim-rattling dunk, the ball ricocheting off Red's upturned face. She hit the floor, bounced and rolled into the basket stanchion. The Sioux trainer and a teammate helped the sobbing Red to the bench and then to the locker room, while the crowd went berserk.

The cameraman treated us to a close-up of Edna. I swear there was a breeze blowing her blonde hair back. Her cheeks were flushed and her eyes alight with a heroic flame. Man, her breasts heaved.

"I have goosebumps." I didn't mention the hard-on, which probably went without saying.

Bobby's breathing was shallow. "God that woman is something else."

"I'd say Edna has a strong allegiance to her teammates."

Bobby clicked off the TV and rewound the tape, watching the counter closely and stabbing the stop button at the right moment. "Edna was fiercely loyal to her teammates, and to the state of North Dakota. She truly thinks it's the best place to live, in the whole wide world."

"With her in it, maybe it is."

"She was recruited heavily by the top Division I schools," Bobby told me. "But there was no way she was leaving the state. When UND realized it, they went after her, full throttle. They're a class program, had just won the Division II national championship two years' running." Bobby stood; it was time for me to leave. I think he wanted to be alone with his memories and videotapes. "Edna asked them to promise to stop recruiting out of state. She was passionate that North Dakota had enough quality players to field strong teams at all the colleges. UND and NDSU wouldn't agree. We did. The rest is history. All-time leading scorer, for the NAIA and for North Dakota. The most famous basketball player in our state's history. Bigger than Phil Jackson."

"Phil never gave me goosebumps." Or a sports-related erection.

Bobby nodded, real slow like. "So now you understand."

"I think this coffeeshop is going to do okay."

"It's going to become a mecca."

"All those thirsty pilgrims lining up outside my door."

"I'll be there every day, I'll tell you what."

"You're looking forward to having Edna on your campus, aren't you?"

"Fuckin-A right."

T - 3

It had been three weeks since my last chemo treatment, since Edna and I made our pact to take the coffee world by storm. We were holding interviews, in one of the College's conference rooms. By the time I arrived, Edna had arranged the space to her liking. The fifteen-foot marble table with its supporting pedestals was somehow pushed into the corner. Four chairs formed a tight square in the middle of the floor, with tablets and pens for Edna and me. We had interviewed twenty-some candidates, and I hadn't taken many notes.

I was distracted, though no fault of my own. I had tried to find spiritual peace beforehand, before I polluted our prospective employees with my fear of dying.

The night before had been the worst yet. I hadn't slept a wink—that's a lie whenever someone claims it, but it's as good as true in this case. Every time I woke up from dozing off, the silent oppression of my empty apartment and the vastly unpopulated state of North Dakota beat down on me, a low bass wobble of the funeral organ, long shallow sound waves without the sound, a sample of what death would feel like.

Of course death might have *no* feel, not even the dull hopelessness of eternal silence. That thought smacked me so hard I lost a few degrees' body heat—I would have gone insane except for some mental deficiency that prevented me from grasping and holding the Nothingness concept for very long.

Edna had been encouraging me to stay over. If she persisted, eventually I'd get over my reluctance to spend the night in her bed blubbering with fears of death, or blubbering in her extra bedroom after she spurned my unwanted advances. Me with one foot in the grave, pawing at Edna's boobs. Pretty sad.

I spent two hours that morning enduring full-body MRI and CAT scans. I would hear the results Monday and they would not be good. I wanted to be ready and reconciled to my ending, that I might die sad but at least not shrieking. Better yet of course would be a reason to believe in the afterlife.

So I had visited Pastor Kyle in his office in an aging strip mall on the east side, sandwiched between Domino's Pizza and H&R Block. PK didn't have his own church—his congregation met in an abandoned Our Own Hardware. He had labored for years to grow membership to the point where a building fund was feasible. In advance of my visit, I had given PK an executive summary of what I was looking for, sort of a road map to heaven. But he spent the first twenty minutes talking about his own challenges, hoping to route my heavenly journey through a permanent home for his ministry.

I have pastors, priests and the like in my shop every day, and I think there's a good-natured but intense competition to sign me up. As PK complained how hardware store architects didn't know squat about acoustics, I was tempted to officially designate him my pastor, to get his highest quality counseling. But I didn't want him resting on his laurels. I wanted to keep PK's competitive fires stoked. Clergymen are the most competitive people I know. Far more than doctors, let me tell you. If preachers could earn credits for every soul saved, Hell's volume would slow to a trickle.

Unfortunately, they have to earn money instead. While I went on about how badly I wanted to be saved, PK keyed on the *how*. Next thing I knew he was talking customer service pledges and spitballing a new faith-series of books, while an unearthly fire burned in my knee and now my hip.

As I left, PK begged me to schedule a follow-up visit, practically clinging to my pant leg or whatever they call the shorts' version. Even though I had the feeling a lot was riding on keeping my butt in his chair and committing myself to the painstaking process of coming to grips with the means to salvation, I wasn't in the mood to brainstorm the lecture series that would make PK a Christian-secular crossover sensation. I figured if I walked out his door, shamed him a little and put the pressure on him, maybe he'd come up with the answer I needed, before it was too late. Pardon me for dying, but I needed a little personalized attention.

What I needed was a bolt of lightning. Burning bush, flood, pestilence. Something to make me believe. Not canned phrases; not customer service pledges. I needed answers. I needed Faith. Faith is hard. I understand that. But professionals should have the tools to make me believe. The doctors couldn't make me believe in their cures, and PK couldn't convince me it didn't matter.

I had a sinking feeling that if I hadn't yet developed a full-fledged case of Faith, regardless whether PK rose to the challenge and showed me The Way, it was too late. I was that pathetic soul desperate for a deathbed conversion; and God's no sucker, that much I know. 'You didn't come to me when you had a good day at the office, or when your credit score hit 775. Now you're gasping your last breath, and suddenly you got religion? I don't think so.'

That's where my head was, as Edna gave the bum's rush to our latest pair of interviewees. We saw them two by two. Contestants, Edna called them. They had come in all shapes and sizes, and truth be told, I would have hired most of them, even if my brain was calm enough to listen to what they said. Edna was cold to anyone under the age of thirty—and, I'm proud to say, anyone who used the term 'customer service' in a positive fashion.

Edna had been visually assessing my vitals for the past half-hour. Now she knelt beside me. "How you doing?"

"Oh, not good. How many more do we have waiting out there?" Edna had turned the adjoining conference room into a holding pen.

"A few. But I think we already found our managers." She was referring to a guy named Dennis and a gal named Patti, both well north of twenty-five, and coincidentally, both bankers, Dennis local and Patti from nearby Valley City. Not so coincidentally, not at all surprisingly, both were huge fans of Edna Applejack. "It's you I'm worried about."

"Yeah, I'm going downhill here." I was hungry, for calories to arrest the slow shutdown of my engine, and queasy, knowing that the digestive system would need to move fast to extract nutrients before my stomach sent the food back up the pipe.

Edna treated me to her incredibly expressive eyes, studying me while mulling something behind the scenes. "You should take Dr. Bhani's treatment," she finally said.

I shook my head. "I'm going to stick with the Neil Ruzic route. Popping Celebrex to reduce the blood flow to the tumors."

"And did Celebrex cure him? All by itself?"

"He was on heavier, experimental stuff, too. Same theory, though."

"Your doctor actually prescribed Celebrex for your cancer?"

"Not exactly."

"Then how did you get it?"

"I have my connections." Gerry the pharmacist had run out of free samples, but Charlotte's mom works for an orthodontist, and somehow she's able to get any meds I've ever needed, in exchange for free drinks. Lucky for me she's not into pricey specialty drinks—she's a traditional brewed coffee drinker, and not a heavy one at that. My kind of prescription drug plan.

"Why stop with Celebrex?" Edna challenged. "Why not take the experimental drugs this Neil guy did?"

"I would actually need a doctor's recommendation for the heavy artillery. Bonilla has more faith in chemo than experimental procedures. I could start shopping my cancer around, try to get onto a protocol, but it doesn't sound like my chances are good. And I'd have to do a lot of research to find a promising protocol."

"You're not being very proactive," Edna scolded.

I got defensive. "I thought I was. I don't have the time or money to devote my life to a cure."

"Sure, it's only your life. No time to save it."

"Wouldn't be much of a life to save if all I did was work on saving it."

"Then you should have taken Dr. Bhani's treatment a long time ago," said Edna. "And if you're so worried about money, we'll find a way to get more."

"I don't think I can raise any more money in good conscience. But I really did appreciate the golf tournament."

Edna smiled. "Eleven thousand bucks for your treatments."

"I wouldn't be feeling so guilty if my foursome hadn't won. And it felt strange calling it the First Annual Brian Lawson Memorial Golf Tournament."

"I'm already thinking about the First Annual Brian Lawson Memorial Bowling Tournament."

"So you can pop out of another cake in that Wonder Woman costume."

"You should see me as Catwoman."

I squirmed in the chair. "Not to be a party planner pooper, but..."

Edna rested her cool hand on my forehead. "You have a fever, honey."

I suddenly felt like crying. "I don't want to continually lay my troubles on you...but I have a bad feeling about what's going on inside me. This past week I've been having pain I've never felt before. It's scaring the shit out of me. I'm dreading the results of my tests from this morning."

"From now on, I want you to stay away from the hospital," said Edna. "From what Dr. Bhani told me—"

"You talked to him?"

"I told him I'm researching alternative treatments for you. He gave me copies of all his research publications and excerpts from his case files. I've called him a few times since then to get clarification on a few things. We're pretty chummy."

"You're amazing."

Edna winked. "He's certain Brent McEwen died from an infection he caught in the hospital. The bacterial strain Dr. Bhani uses is very similar to what Brent caught—that's what makes it so hard to prove it wasn't his."

I fought back images of Brent's death photos. "So what killed Brent?"

"S. pyogenes."

"What does that mean?"

"That's the bacteria that killed Brent."

"I know, but what the hell is S. pyogenes?"

"S. pyogenes." Edna's voice sharpened. "That's what it's called."

"Alright, sorry, I guess neither of us are doctors."

"That's true, but at least *one* of us has spent the time to do some research."

"And I really appreciate it."

"I don't want your gratitude, honey. I want you cured. And I've studied Dr. Bhani's materials long enough that you need to believe what I'm telling you. I've also spent time surveying other alternative treatments out there, and the reactions from the medical community. I wanted to know how Dr. Bhani stacks up, and what his peers have said about him." Edna's long fingers played with the hairs on my arm. Felt good. "Dr. Bhani's method is extreme. That's why he's not getting any favorable press. And other doctors have had some trouble replicating his results."

"Why?"

Edna shook her head. "I'm only guessing, but I don't think other doctors are willing to apply his treatment to the extreme that Dr. Bhani recommends. Making you violently sick in order to make you better sounds medieval. Suffice it to say a lot of people think he's a crackpot."

"That's why I'm more afraid of his treatment than I am of the cancer."

Edna dropped her head. "Who sent those God-damn pictures to you?"

"I'd tell you if I knew. I'd have to guess one of the McEwens. They're the only ones who would have had access to the pictures. And hate me."

"Rick and Mike said it wasn't them. I have to believe them." Edna's nostrils flared and her eyes grew wider, from footballs to rugby balls. She gave me her hand, and together we stood. "We're wrapping this up," she decided, "and you're going home to get some rest. Then you're coming with me tonight, to the July Chicken Fry at the Assembly of God church. I was invited to go with the McEwens, but I want you to be my date. We're going to find out tonight who sent you those pictures."

"I'm not sure it matters—"

"It matters," said Edna. "It matters to me."

I nodded at the door to the adjoining conference room where the rest of our applicants waited. "What about them?"

"They'll have to come back later. We're worth it."

EDNA PICKED ME UP at six in the Talon. Yeah, she was the man in this relationship. Edna had a way of taking charge without making me feel threatened. Besides Charlotte, she was the only person I felt comfortable talking for me. And I didn't even agree with a lot of what she said. "I was thinking," Edna told me as I dropped into the Talon, "maybe that heavy-set guy, the one getting his MBA from UND by correspondence, wouldn't be a bad choice. He had some interesting marketing ideas."

"Wasn't his name Brian?"

"That's the one."

"We can't have two Brians."

Edna laughed. "He couldn't tell whether you were joking about that."

"That's because I was pretending to be pretending to be serious."

"It's not the name," said Edna, "it's the way that you use it. When people say 'Brian', it'll be obvious who they're talking about."

"Did you mean me or him?"

"Well, both."

"See?" I said. "Confusion already."

Edna frowned. "Okay," she decided. "He's out."

Felt good. So maybe I wasn't completely ready to hand over the reins.

"Did you get some rest?" Edna asked.

"Yes," I lied. I had gone into work, to will my customers to choose me over Hernandes's first day at the Bluffs.

"You look good," said Edna.

Probably also a lie. Although some of my hair had grown out a half-inch. If my medicine cabinet and handheld mirrors could be trusted, an illusion of decent coverage had been created, allowing me to shuck the ballcap. "I am ready to party all night."

From Edna's tight smile, she could tell this was a bluff, thankfully.

"We probably shouldn't make a scene tonight," I recommended. "No matter what we find out about the pictures."

Edna put her hand on my leg. "There's no occasion so sacrosanct that evildoers should enjoy immunity from prosecution."

"Sure, that's one of my rules of thumb, too. I just thought tonight, a community event, in a church…"

"Complacency kills. Churches understand that better than anyone. Life without strife and struggle is empty of significance."

I was dating a revolutionary. "Speaking of struggles…I drove through the campus yesterday, and there is absolutely nothing happening at our site. It's going to be a struggle to be open by September first, don't you think?"

Edna shook her head. "Rick has committed to me. But if it makes you feel better, we'll corner Mike and get him to do the same."

"Before or after we accuse his family of using their son's horrific death to scare me away from a potential cure?"

There was the grim smile again.

"The pictures really aren't the deciding factor in my decision not to use Bhani's treatment," I assured her. I was in no mood for a confrontation with the McEwens. "I was freaked out by the idea already. And I want to give Celebrex a chance to work. Honestly. I'm not foolin'. You're not listening to me. At least not closely. Hey, look, the Bluffs is almost deserted." I spotted no more than ten cars in the lot as we drove by. "That's a shame."

"Bill closed early for the July Chicken Fry," said Edna.

"Oh. How, uh, how did you know that?"

"I stopped in after our interviews."

"Checking out the competition?"

"That's right."

"You didn't make a cameo appearance behind Billy's bar, did you?"

"No."

"Was he busy?"

"Fairly."

"How many customers would you say he had? Ten? Less than twenty?"

"Doesn't matter," said Edna. The Assembly of God church parking lot was full, and yet she drove to the front row and found an open spot. "Things will be different the day we open."

I had no doubt that was true. But I wanted to be kicking Hernandes's ass all by myself, without Edna's star power.

Bill Hernandes, the first person we saw as we descended into the church basement. The air was heavy with chicken-flavored carbon dioxide, a hundred people laughing and chewing and talking, crammed onto folding chairs at long tables. A couple guys yelled my name, and a few more shouted for Edna. My vision was blurry, I couldn't make out who was calling to me, so I smiled and waved like a float queen. It must have been a hundred degrees in there.

A puff of air down the stairwell parted what felt like some longer-than-acceptable strands of hair on the back of my head. As I reached up to pat down my scraggly 'do, Hernandes grabbed for my hand, so I gripped his right hand with my left.

"Pleased to meet you, Bob Dole," Hernandes quipped, holding our un-conventional handshake aloft for everyone to see. "And Edna!" He was on top of the world. He ruled the joint. He owned the town. "*Thank* you for stopping by at our grand opening today, Edna. That meant so much to me." The room rapidly quieted down. Parents shushed their kids in order to tune in their con-versation. Hernandes clung to Edna's arm. "It stamps your seal of approval on the new location, do you know?"

Edna wiggled fingers at her admirers. "Was business good then?"

"It was crazy," said Hernandes. "The place was buzzing after you and Rick left. I swear they must have been calling their friends and telling them to come down. We became even busier."

"You went with Rick?" I asked her. "McEwen?"

"And speak of the devil," said Hernandes.

Rick sauntered over from the line to join us. "Brian." He stood uncom-fortably close and gave me a serious, caring stare. "How are you, man?"

Rick hadn't been in my shop for months. Maybe it was the fatigue, but seeing him brought on a melancholy nostalgia. "I'm good. You know. It's really good to see you."

He gave me a quick head bob and gripped my shoulder. "I know I haven't stopped in lately, but we've been thinking about you a lot."

Considering how much I respected Rick, and everything that had hap-pened with his sister and his father, this gesture meant a lot to me. Tears filled my eyes. I nodded to Tyler, following his dad and towing his mother with him. "Hey kiddo. Hey lady."

Andrea wouldn't look at me. "Tyler had his last basketball game today and scored ten points," Rick reported.

I tousled that young-un's hair. "I think he's grown a couple inches since I saw him last. Is he as tall for his age as you are?" Rick was around six-three with broad shoulders that carried a couple more pounds each time I saw him, experience adding gravitas to his frame, making it easier and easier to picture him stepping into Mike's shoes to run the company.

"A couple girls on his team are taller than he is," said Rick.

"What, cheerleaders?" Hernandes blurted. And then he looked at Edna and almost started crying.

Rick was a space invader as it was. But he was really standing in Hernandes's wheelhouse when he said, "It's coed. Nerf league. They started it when Edna was playing at JC. Because every kid in diapers wanted to be like her."

"Now they'll all want to be coffeeshop owners," I said.

With Hernandes frowning over that one, Jerry Evans left his table to join us. I knuckle-knocked him. "You getting fed over there?"

Jerry smiled and looked over at his wife and toddler twins. Looked back at me and raised his eyebrows. Lowered them. "Good stuff."

"Glad to hear it."

Edna was stonefaced throughout. She took hold of Rick's forearm. "After we're done eating, Brian and I want to talk about the construction schedule. Among other things." She let go and left fingernail imprints.

Hernandes was slight and small-boned. He looked up at Rick and then Edna, back and forth, a child trying to catch Daddy's and Mommy's eyes. "What construction schedule?"

"You haven't heard?" I said nonchalantly. "Edna and I are opening a coffeeshop on campus."

"Whoa," said Hernandes. "Really. Wow. The two of you? That's great!" He pumped Edna's hand. "Congratulations!"

Not the reaction I was hoping for. I wanted tears. "We're not sure what we'll name it, since 'Campus Coffee' is already taken. Maybe 'On Campus Coffee', huh?"

"That's a good one, man," said Rick.

Pastor Kyle had been eyeballing us since we walked in. He was pinned against the dirty dishes cart by an older lady attempting to lay her heavy burden upon him. "Looky there, it's Brian and Edna!" He pretended to notice us for the first time. "Excuse me for a moment, Agnes." PK broke her grip and fled. "Two of our biggest stars! I am so glad you came!" He shook everyone's hand, some for the second time I'm sure.

The minor commotion inspired Joshua to stand at the farthest table and beller, "Hey! Get yourselves over here!" He pointed in a commanding way at two empty seats.

"No!" I yelled back.

"Lawson," Joshua growled. He headed for us while Denise shielded her eyes in embarrassment, peeking to enjoy the spectacle her husband loved to create.

"That Joshua," PK said with affection. "What are we going to do with him?" He put a hand on my shoulder. "Listen Brian, I feel terrible about how our conversation ended this morning. Maybe we can sit down and eat together? Did you bring a big appetite?"

"I think I can do a little damage."

PK surveyed the masses. "For our inaugural year I'd say we're doing all right, don't you think?"

Joshua plowed into us and shook PK like a rag doll, making his Charlie Brown head float side-to-side like a Macy's Thanksgiving Day parade balloon. "Joshua," said PK, "I've been having back problems, and I promised my wife I wouldn't overdo it tonight, carrying around the big tubs of chicken." He arched his back and groaned. "Now she's going to think I lied to her."

Joshua just grinned.

"Still, I'm glad you're here. I was telling Brian how pleased I am by the turnout. It's a combined effort of four churches," PK told me, "and Joshua volunteered a lot of his time distributing flyers."

"Almost as busy as the Catholic fish fry," I congratulated them.

PK leaned into our group and said in a conspiratorial whisper, "That's what we're aiming for. We're considering going head to head next year."

"Throw in a raffle, and you could put the Catholics out of business."

"I thought it was the Jews you were after," said Jerry. "Jew-Lie Chicken Fry...? July and Jew-Lie can't be a coincidence."

So that's why Jerry always paused, I thought.

PK's eyes got big. He pointed at Hernandes. "Bill, you're Jewish, right?"

Hernandes nodded, frowning at Jerry.

I covered for him as best I could. "Bill, I didn't know you were Israeli."

Hernandes's expression changed from stony to puzzled. "I'm not."

"What are we going to do about those Palestinians, huh?"

"I've heard it gets hot there in the summer," said Joshua. He giggled as he examined the floor and scuffed the tile with his Sunday-best shoes.

"I better get back to my meal." Jerry went slinking back to his table, cursing himself under his breath.

"No I don't want to be your day trader salesman," I hollered after him. "You damned anti-Semite! So yeah," I said to everyone who remained, "Edna and I are opening a new shop on campus."

PK nodded approvingly. "Let me tell you, I think that could be a real moneymaker."

"You think so?" I stole a glance at Hernandes. Were those teardrops forming in the corners of his bulging chinchilla eyeballs? They always glistened so it was hard to be sure. I urged PK to go on. "You think people will dig us?"

"I would think that between the two of you," PK obliged me, "you'll land every coffee drinker in town. And create a few new coffee lovers on campus."

"Coffee is a great study aid," I said. "Huh, Edna?"

She smiled politely. PK endeavored to engage her with follow-up questions, while Hernandes withdrew a step, muttering to himself.

"Hey everybody," said my downstairs neighbor Dennis, materializing out of the coat closet corner. And then came Iz.

"What were you two doing hiding back there?" Joshua demanded. "Necking in the closet? At a church dinner?"

Isabel smiled wickedly. "Come on, Joshua," said Dennis, blushing, uncomfortable to have Iz draped over his thick shoulders. "I'm a God-fearing man, you know that."

"God doesn't frown upon a little necking," said PK.

"That's what I told Denise when we were dating," said Joshua. "She bought it." He giggled like a crazy man.

"I used the same line on my wife, if I remember right," said PK.

The heat and the nostril-clogging grease were getting to me. I wanted Edna to take me home, but she was grilling Rick about the construction schedule. Hernandes drifted near them, pretending to be included, downcast and probably wondering whether it was too late to get his old job back. It served the dumb sonofabitch right, thinking he could waltz into my town and start a shop. Who did he think he was? Hernandes could build a bridge to the campus and it wouldn't matter. Hire an Edna Applejack impersonator— "Watch the North Dakota legend throttle a city boy with one hand and whip up a skim-milk latté with the other!"—and we'd still be kicking his ass…

My mind stumbled down its own ranting road. And then I realized I really had stumbled. I suddenly had a fever, a few thousand BTUs escaping out the top of my head, leaving me dizzy and weak and covered in a sheen of cold sweat. I looked for a nearby chair, empty or otherwise.

"I'm going to get Brian's sign-off on our store plans," Edna told Rick, the sound ebbing and flowing, "and then we'll want you to start pronto." Her voice was hypnotic like the ocean. I wished for seasickness pills.

Rick rubbed at his jaw, as if his sparse blonde stubble was a genuine five o'clock shadow. "I was taking a look at our schedule today. It's going to be tough to get started until after Labor Day."

"Maybe we should be working with Redd Vapp," I named the McEwens' only competitor, playing the part of the tough negotiator while pawing for the wall. I slid for a few feet along the circa 1970s paneling before getting my sea legs under me. No one seemed to notice, or care, that I was fading fast.

"Rick will handle this," said Edna, deciding the issue.

I was wrong, my slow fainting spell hadn't gone unnoticed. Iz was beside me, her warm hands in the small of my back. "Brian, you need to sit down."

"Or I could just fall down here." I teetered, knees shaking. It was going to take more than Iz to keep me on my feet.

"I wasn't aware Dad made a couple late season commitments," Rick explained to Edna. "They're rigid."

"That's something for you to work out internally," Edna said firmly.

Rick shook his head. "I'd like to…"

"Andrea," Iz called. "Andrea," she snapped, "could you help me?"

Andrea debated coming to my aid, slowly approaching, disgusted.

"As long as you're in the mood to disappoint me," said Edna sharply, glaring at Rick and pointing at me, "why don't you tell us why your family sent Brian those pictures?"

"Oh boy," I said as the room faded.

"What are you talking about?" I heard Rick ask.

"You know damn well," said Edna. "The pictures of Brent."

My sparkles cleared in time to see the color drain from Rick's face. "What pictures?" he said.

Edna had the decency to tone down her reply. "His autopsy shots."

Rick wasn't an expressive man. He had two faces, a police interrogation face and a softer hint-of-a-smile police interrogation face. Nothing new now, except he fixed his no-nonsense stare on an imaginary block of wood that he chopped with an axe-like hand. "I never saw any pictures." Air whistled through Rick's nose. "After Brent got sick, I never saw him, period."

Mike and Valerie wandered into the conversation like dazed accident victims. Mike's tailbone must not have been healing properly, because he walked with a limp and a cane. "What did you see?" he hissed at Edna. Valerie reached out and clung to Edna's arm. Isabel bridged the gap between her mom and me, a hand on her mom's waist, a hand on mine. Dennis put his hands on Isabel's waist.

My tall gorgeous partner dared the McEwens to meet her fierce gaze. "Someone used the pictures as a scare tactic to frighten Brian away from Dr. Bhani's treatment. It was a cheap, sniveling, gutless—"

"What pictures?" Mike demanded.

"I did it," said Andrea. She had left my side a long time ago to stand beside her ex, hugging Tyler in front of her.

"What pictures?" Mike demanded, this time of Andrea. He had chicken grease smeared on his chin. It was really obvious. Pastor Kyle was looking at it. We were the highlight of the dinner now, bigger than Jesus, and more than a couple folks were staring at Mike's greasy chin. Jerry was transfixed by it from his nearby table. I was pissed at Valerie for not wiping it off. Mike was going to need all the dignity he could get. "You have pictures?" He advanced on Andrea. Valerie closed from the other side, until I could no longer see the little woman. "I want to see them. I never saw him. I never saw my son."

So it was Andrea. Maybe she was looking out for me, I theorized. Maybe she was having second thoughts about Bhani's treatment—she was too ethical to publicly criticize her boss, but determined to do the right thing and warn me of the danger.

Man I'm a good person, I decided, unable to control my meandering brain. *Look at me giving Andrea the benefit of the doubt, when everyone knows she's nothing more than a vindictive bitch.*

Rick wedged between his parents and Andrea. I thought his folks were the least of his worries. Edna was circling behind Andrea, who was clueless, counting on that old adage, that Jesus looks out for the child-like, the self-righteous, the smug, the guilt-free.

"The hospital wouldn't let us into the room." Mike was having a reminiscence of sorts as he struggled pathetically to get past Rick. "They said it was too contagious. They wouldn't let us see his body."

Edna had Andrea in her sights. She and Mike would simultaneously lay hands on the little woman and a tug of war would ensue, until someone got the lion's share of the wishbone.

They say there's never a cop around when you need one, but we had the next best thing, pastors, four of them. PK, Pastor Brad, John the Baptist minister, and Reverend Sergio converged on the scene. If everyone had ducked, I think they would have banged heads.

"I want to see those pictures," Mike babbled. Valerie was clawing at her son, going to claw right through him to get to Andrea.

Who was now in Edna's possession. As long as I wasn't going to pass out, I needed to save her. I lurched from the wall and was bumped by PK. Yes he's a solid guy, but at my normal weight and without a fast-moving fever playing havoc with my professional-grade equilibrium, I wouldn't have gone down.

I fought it—shouldn't have—and careened forward. Looked like I dove, Jerry told me later, into Mike McEwen's knees. His cane snapped like a twig and he buckled. I looked up to see Valerie's sexy but tasteful underwear, and Edna lifting Andrea off the ground so abruptly that Andrea's head snapped back. "God!" Her yelp had a Doppler effect, like she was whipping past on a roller coaster. Instead of pleading for her life, or even struggling a little, Andrea was indignant and inert, confident justice would prevail and the men in her life would soon have this maniac in restraints.

"You nasty little bitch." Edna put Andrea down and squeezed her cheeks, no doubt infuriated by the smug look that would not come off. "What you did was goddamned wicked." Any second now Edna was going to pop Andrea's head like a grape, and Rick knew it, working quickly to pry away Edna's fingers, assisted by Joshua and John the Baptist minister. A rush of diners left their seats and overran PK and Pastor Brad's peacekeeping positions. The first few were careful not to step on me and Mike, but chaos was building in the shouting, jostling rugby scrum above us.

"You need to knock this shit off right now!"

"Some son of a bitch just bit me!"

"You are fucking psycho."

"Everyone now…hey, hey, hey…God damn it, you need to settle down!"

Don't worry about the tender ears of the men of God. They're the most intense guys I know. Besides golfers out on the course, preachers in casual conversation are the most likely folks to let fly with a cuss word. They get credit for two of the quotes above.

We needed to get off the floor. I crawled to Mike and helped him to his feet. He lurched past me before I could ask him if he was okay. Edna was screaming, and everyone was shouting for her to settle down, except Andrea, who was scowling and checking her puffy blouse for damage, tucked under Isabel's loosely-jointed wing and being led away from the fray. "You are screwing with Brian's life!" Edna raged after her.

"If Andrea managed to scare Brian away from that fruitcake Bhani," Valerie said with a quavering voice, "then she saved his life!"

"Valerie, listen to me." Edna shook off John the Baptist minister. She was free for the moment. "What happened to Brent was just a terrible misfortune."

Mike waved his hands to ward off what he saw as Edna's temporary demonic possession. "You don't know, Edna, you weren't there to see what that man did to my boy. How sick Brent got when Bhani injected him with those toxins. Even though he seemed like he was getting better afterward, we should have known. We should have seen that he wasn't okay…"

While PK and John the Baptist minister were captivated by the family drama, this was too public for Pastor Brad. "Mike, Mike," he said in an urgent hush, "come on, let's take this somewhere private."

But Mike only had eyes for Edna, and now they were locked up, gripping each other's forearms and speaking, loudly, face to face.

"It wasn't Bhani's treatment!" Edna insisted.

"You weren't there!" said Mike.

"I've done the research!" said Edna. "What Bhani is doing is right!"

"No-no-no! He's experimenting, on helpless people! It is not right!"

"He is *curing* people! Terribly sick people who would die without him!"

It was whips-and-chains sensuous, the way they were arguing right into each other's mouths. Valerie must have thought so too, because she wormed her way into the middle, forcing them apart. I almost pulled her back.

"Don't you tell me what I'm supposed to feel about my son," Mike pleaded with Edna.

"And don't you presume to know what's right for Brian," Edna retorted.

Morris Nelson, retired city policeman and part-time security guard at the high school, abandoned his plate of fried chicken and waded through the crowd. "Come on now, break this up!" he ordered. The combatants were now a good four feet apart and looking spent, but Morris stuck a hand in both their chests for good measure.

"Edna!" Bobby Guldseth the College's athletic director barreled down the stairs and grabbed Edna from behind, wrapping her up tightly and pulling her backward. Because they were the same height and because of Bobby's crane neck, their heads were side by side like Siamese twins. This combined entity rocked back and forth, the Edna head growling and the Bobby head saying, "Take it easy, baby," in a soothing purr.

"Bobby, it's okay," said PK, as uncomfortable as the rest of us with this scene. "Edna's okay."

Looking perplexed, Bobby disentangled from Edna. "I didn't want you to do anything to jeopardize your parole."

"I'm not on parole," said Edna.

"Probation," Bobby corrected.

"Nope," said Edna.

Mike turned on me, wincing and unsteady on his feet. "Whatever you do, don't let that Bhani bastard get ahold of you."

We agreed on this, but I still wanted to be standing in Edna's camp. Progress toward her was slowed by all the peacekeepers. I tried to get her attention, but she was glaring at Andrea, who was being tended to by Rick, leaving Iz with no one to mother and coming for me. I grabbed a napkin from the condiments table and handed it to Mike, indicating his chin. When he didn't understand, I took the napkin back and wiped up the chicken grease myself.

"That is such a beautiful sight," said Isabel.

"That grease was driving me crazy."

"The bastard almost killed me," said Mike, clutching at his back and limping away.

"I'm glad I have a chance to talk to you," said Isabel.

Joshua joined us, shaking his head and chuckling ruefully. "That was almost a full-scale brawl."

"I hope you and I would have been on the same side," I said.

"Joshua's a pushover," said Denise, a late arrival to the melee.

"For you, maybe," I said. "I would want you both on my side."

"We're always on your side, Brian," Denise assured me.

"That makes three of us," said Iz, trying to hold my hand.

I kept my hands busy, pretending to wave to someone across the room, checking for overgrown hairs on my chia pet head. "I want to get Edna out of here before another brouhaha erupts."

Joshua agreed. "She still has a fire in her eyes."

"Maybe Bobby was right to hold her tight and whisper sweet nothings in her ear."

"And butt-hump her," said Joshua. Denise raised her eyebrows and a hand to slap him. "Well?" Joshua argued his accurate appraisal of the coupling. "Wasn't he?"

"I have a feeling that girl takes it from any angle," said Iz.

Now Joshua was scandalized. "I like Edna."

That was my cue. "We'll see you-all later," I said, heading for the noisy knot of people clumped around Edna.

Iz shadowed me. "I know you were dating Andrea—"

"I wouldn't call it dating."

"And you're with Edna now."

"I wouldn't say that either, necessarily. Iz, I don't want to talk about this."

"They won't be true to you," she whispered. "Believe me, I've seen them. I don't think you understand what it's worth, to find someone loving and faithful. It doesn't come around more than once in a lifetime."

"In my condition, I honestly couldn't blame a woman if she wasn't faithful. But that's—"

"You deserve better," Isabel insisted. "No matter what condition you're in. Don't forget that."

Edna knifed through the crowd and took me by the arm. "Excuse us sweetie. It's time to leave." That was supposed to be my line.

"Oh, pardon me," said Iz icily. Icy wasn't her style, though. She melted. "Brian, I just wanted to make sure you're okay."

"He's going to be fine," said Edna defiantly, challenging anyone to try to stop my healing. I threw a goodbye wave at the crowd and was marched upstairs.

"Elvis has let the building!" I heard Joshua announce.

Edna was silent en route to our front-row parking spot. I jabbered, riding an adrenaline boost. "I'd be worried that little scuffle tarnished our rep and ruined our chances with the campus location, except I think Bobby gets turned on when you get feisty. Jeez, I broke Mike's cane. And maybe his back. He didn't look good after. I'm killing him, one day at a time."

We dropped into the Talon and Edna turned to me. She tucked gossamer hair behind her ear and took my hand. "I want you to move in with me. Right away. When Dr. Bhani administers his treatment…I know it's going to be rough, and I want to be there to pull you through."

"I appreciate the offer, but…" It was hard to disagree with Edna. And hard not to be suspicious that she fully expected major complications from Bhani's treatment, hoped for them almost, so that she could be my savior. It wouldn't be Dr. Bhani proving the McEwens wrong, it would be Edna. "I'm not planning to go to Dr. Bhani."

She shook her head. "I know it's a big decision, and you need more time to prepare yourself, mentally." Edna touched my cheek. "Either way, you and I are partners. I want us to be as close as possible."

"You really want me to live with you?"

"I do."

"Well…" This was obviously a big decision, but I skipped right past the pros and cons list. "…okay." What Edna wants, Edna gets. Who was I kidding, there was no need for her to waste time arguing with me over Bhani's treatment. She knew she would get her way.

Something whacked my window, making me spasm so hard my seatbelt locked. Andrea stood beside the Talon, fuming. Edna made to jump out but I grabbed her wrist and held her in place. Andrea's men had now saved her life twice that night. I pushed the door open. "What's up?" I said casually.

Andrea's voice was snottier than ever. "I wanted to tell you something. That book I gave you? The guy who found his own cure for cancer?"

"Neil Ruzic," I said.

"Yeah, well, it turns out he died last year. Of cancer."

"What?"

Andrea soaked in the shock registering on my face. "Just wanted to let you know." She turned on her heel and marched off.

"Holy…shit." I let the door pinch against my cancer leg.

"What's going on?" Edna demanded.

Tears ran down my face, and I didn't know how to tell her why. Why I was crying for a complete stranger, who had died a year ago.

EDNA COULDN'T UNDERSTAND, and didn't really try. She was still boiling over Andrea's manipulation. At least she didn't argue when I said I needed to be alone. She left me on her couch and went to bed. First night living together and we slept alone. I could marry a woman like that.

I wouldn't have been able to find the composure or the words to explain my grief over Neil's passing. As I read his saga, his battle had become a proxy for mine. I had been pulling for him, because I knew deep down that if he could figure out a way to win, I would too—his way, my way, some way, the cancer didn't stand a chance. No matter how bleak things got, I would be holding this certainty as my ace in the hole.

And so maybe my depression over the cancer's relentlessness had been some sort of affectation—a lot of reality, sure, but perhaps a fair amount of subconscious theater, acting the way a terminal patient should, looking for sympathy, all the while just as subconsciously certain I was going to win the battle. All that existential gnashing of the teeth and beating on my breast over the existence of God, convinced I had sunk into uncharted depths of despair— to a certain extent, I had been fooling myself.

Because this was deeper, this was worse. Underneath the depression was now a gaping hole where that ace must have been. Three years ago Neil Ruzic had declared himself cured. Two years later he was dead. I was dead. Cancer didn't give a shit who I was or what I had done, how much time and effort I spent on a cure, or how passionately I wanted to live. Cancer was unstoppable.

I cried some more, a mess on Edna's couch. Take away the future, and your past disappears too. I had truly become meaningless. The sounds of the grandfather clock ticking and car engines running outside, the feel of my pulse in my shin, the vague memories of happier times…all of this floated in the black goo swirling around me, all of it equivalent, random bits of meaningless data embedded in the vortex.

My mind must have finally grasped the certainty of my pending annihilation, for a virtual PK appeared, floating above me, soothingly reciting a touched-up timeline of my life, reminding me Jesus was waiting, administering a last rites home version. I choked and wailed at the utter lack of comfort and almost died right then and there. I think I came that close.

T - 2

Sunday morning Edna treated me like I had a hangover. Gave me a lot of space, kept the chitchat to a minimum, didn't push anything more than a cup of coffee on me. The first sip burned my tongue so I took another, bereft of the self-preservation instinct.

I'm sure it bothered Edna that I didn't shower, that day or Monday morning before she drove me to my apartment building to retrieve my van. "I really wish I could be there," she said, referring to my doctor's appointment, "but I'm going to Rick's office to lay down the law on our construction schedule. If he's not going to guarantee what we're looking for, Vapp's will give it to us."

"I came to the conclusion last night that if you have the strength to tell people you're depressed, you're not really depressed." The words tumbled out because I didn't have the energy to talk.

After a couple blocks' pause Edna said, "Then you must not really be depressed."

I bobbed my head to create a grunting sound.

We pulled up to my van. While I willed my hand to open the door, Edna stretched into the backseat to rummage through her handbag, coming away with a fat legal document. She unclipped and shuffled through the papers. I pushed myself to a protohuman standing position. "I guess I'll see you later."

She tore her attention away from the papers. "Are you going to tell Bonilla about Dr. Bhani's treatment?"

"Hadn't planned on it, no."

"Good. That could lead to more scrutiny than Dr. Bhani needs. I'm going to make sure he fires Andrea," said Edna, businesslike, "so you don't need to worry about that."

I shrugged. It hurt. I peered in at her handbag. The pictures were in there. "You're not going to show Brent's pictures to the McEwens."

"They need to understand," said Edna. "They need to come to grips with the real reason Brent died. And Andrea's true nature."

I didn't want to cause the McEwens any more suffering, seeing as how they were just wrapping up a year's worth of grief that no thanks to me was as fresh as ever. I should have argued with Edna, but it so drastically paled in comparison to my problem, I said nothing, said goodbye, and played some minor role in guiding my van to the hospital.

THE NOTHINGNESS IN MY HEAD left me open to detailed observations I don't normally make, as I sat in the exam room. The sanitary paper was crinkled where it stretched over the end of the padded exam table, creased by someone's sweaty behind. The stirrups' mounting rods were coated with dirty grease, a schmear of active cultures. The *Danger—Explosives!* sign was two-thirds missing on the oxygen tank, which leaned heavily against the flimsy cart's restraining strap.

The healthcare profession has done a helluva sales job convincing us they have it all under control. American hospitals are viewed as sanctuaries of healing and revitalization, and we trust American doctors to give us the best treatments. Yet here were all these warts, these signs of harried, overworked staff too tired or careless to keep the germs away. I wished for a rag and a jug of bleach so I could do a quick disinfect.

What did it say about the doctors? Were they too taking shortcuts in the interest of time, choosing whatever the pharmaceutical companies told them was best and pretending to be experts? After a long day studying charts and listening to endless complaints, were they willing to spend a couple hours at home absorbing the latest research reports and treatment efficacy studies?

Some. That was as good as it ever got. Some aides and orderlies disinfected all the way into the corners and the crevices, and some doctors picked up the Journal of the American Medical Association at ten p.m. Some.

"Brian." Bonilla was inside with the door closed before I registered his presence. He reached down to shake my hand. "How are you today?" His eyes were on my leg. I hiked my shorts to give him a clear view up to my knee. "Hm." Bonilla lowered his roller stool to put him more on level with my knee. He didn't ask me to hop up on the table, because he probably doubted I could. He squished the puffy bruised area below the knee, exactly like I wished he wouldn't. "You didn't bump this over the weekend?"

"It's gotten worse, hasn't it?"

"Since Saturday." Bonilla rolled to the countertop to retrieve my file, pretending to study it while he perfected the message he had to deliver. He closed the file, crossed his legs, and hooked a knee. "From what we see on your scans, the cancer is aggressive." Remember when I used to like that word? "We would now type it Stage Four. There is some movement into your abdomen and possibly your chest. Small enough that we feel confident we can have success with another round of chemo and targeted radiation. These past three weeks we lost some time and some of the advantage we had gained, to be honest with you. I fully respect your decision not to have undergone another round so soon after the last one. I appreciate what you're going through. But if we're going to stop these nodes from further proliferation...."

I nodded through the whole spiel, first trying to recall what had possessed me to have stopped my treatments for three weeks, then reminding myself it wouldn't have mattered anyway. "You know what, doc, I don't care one way or the other. I'm ready to do whatever you recommend."

Bonilla frowned. "You need to hear the rest before you make any decisions. I've been struggling with this...but seeing your leg now..."

I was amazed he could even look at my leg. But he leaned forward and continued to examine it, probing above the knee. I have sweet quads, teardrops on both sides of the kneecap, thighs made for the short-shorts I had always done my best to keep in style. So he had to get past some muscle, just not as much as a few months ago.

"I don't have confidence that chemo and radiation can reduce this tumor or even stop it from growing," said Bonilla.

I was suddenly sure he was going to refer me to Dr. Bhani.

"This is tough to say and much tougher to hear," said Bonilla.

"It's okay, doc. I can handle it."

"We need to remove your leg at the hip."

I stood and then fell back into the chair, making it slide and squeal. Bonilla reached out to steady me. I started to convulse across my midsection, shaking hard and losing control of my arms and legs.

"Come here." Bonilla bent me forward into his lap and rubbed my back, telling me to breathe. Obviously I know implicitly the importance of breathing, yet it helped to be coached.

"Oh no," I said, and then repeated it, again and again, slower and more softly until Bonilla made me stop.

He sat me up straight and scooted in tight, putting stabilizing hands on my hips. "Brian, you're right, this is serious and it's traumatic. But it isn't the end of the world. It isn't the end of anything."

I nodded. He probably thought I was agreeing with him. I rocked back and forth, fighting back the rising bile. There was no hurl pail at the ready, quite an oversight given my history.

"I want you to calm yourself," said Bonilla. "Don't think of anything but a future without cancer. Okay? Stay in this room as long as you like. In fact I'd like you to stay here for a couple hours. I have other patients to see, and then I'll stop back in. In the meantime I'm going to ask one of our counselors to come see you." He gave me a final steadying squeeze before rolling away to stand. "Dr. Carter is a psy-D with a lot of experience with folks who have made it through similar circumstances. And you will make it through."

"Brian, this sounds a little more mystical than I'm comfortable with..." Bonilla waited for me to look up. "...but you possess a very striking lifeforce. Something that few have." He patted his own chest in a soothing way. "The nurses, they've noticed it too. We've talked about you. We all know you're going to beat this thing. If you can stay relaxed long enough, that lifeforce is going to kick in." He watched to see if this was sinking in. "Remember: life without cancer is going to be wonderful."

I waited long enough for Bonilla to move down the hall to his next patient, and then abandoned the room and ran limping to the elevator. I escaped the hospital without being challenged and drove to Edna's. Maybe I wouldn't even go back to my apartment, ever again. I didn't want to die there.

I WAS SHOCKED TO WAKE UP and find I had slept, curled up at the foot of Edna's bed. It was dark, after ten. There was no sign Edna had been home. With numb lips I ate a handful of mixed nuts and a package of ramen. I sat there for awhile, at Edna's kitchen bar, doing my best not to think of anything. And then all of a sudden I was ready to call Mom and Dad.

No answer. What a message to leave—but I had to say it, I couldn't wait any longer for them to know. "Had another doctor's appointment today. A follow-up from the tests on Saturday. Not good news. It's spreading. They think they can wipe out the new spots with more chemo and radiation, but the leg with the original tumor really worries them. My doctor wants to amputate my leg. All the way up to my hip." My throat tightened; only by picturing my mom sobbing as she listened could I act brave. "I'm not a big fan of that idea. I'll let you guys know as soon as I decide. So…I don't know, maybe I'll even fly back home. Let Charlotte run the shop for awhile. Edna would probably be happy to do it, too. We'll see. Not sure of anything right now.

"Hey Dad, I just remembered you're having that dinner meeting with the ASCS office tonight. You'll have to let me know how it went. I'm up late tonight—I think I've done all the sleeping I'm going to for awhile. So give me a call when you get home. I'm at Edna's. She's been great...."

I wrapped it up before the warning beep, not bad considering how comforting it was to talk to my parents' machine.

I sat, I walked around the house. I bounced up and down. I did the stairs, three times. Sometimes the leg didn't hurt at all. There was still a lot of good left in that leg.

When Edna wasn't home by midnight, I sat in her den under the main staircase, numb all over and just wasting time, unable to think, waiting for Edna to come home, feeling so not myself that I even contemplated surfing the Web. I hate e-mail and the Internet, computers in general. Every second spent in front of one of the soul-suckers causes exponential portions of life to slip away, never to be recovered no matter what interesting tidbits or great online deals or inspirational chain e-mails you might come across. But that's just me, I know a lot of you seem to enjoy it.

I brought up the Internet. Yahoo's top story of the hour was about a giant anaconda found slithering the halls of the Corn Palace in Mitchell, South Dakota, with a baby panda bear in its stomach. Authorities were doubly baffled. It was a great article, maybe I had been wrong about the Internet. The next story was about a twenty-two year old entrepreneur who had struck it rich with a chain of herbal supplement stores.

I turned off the computer and decided to surf Edna's desk instead. Sitting atop the leather-inlaid surface was an unmarked binder full of letters, printed e-mails to and from Edna, handwritten notes and news clippings off the Internet. It was all about me. All about Dr. Bhani.

I read a letter from Edna to a Dr. Vance Hotchkiss at the Mayo Clinic. She told him she was researching Dr. Bhani's treatment—a.k.a. "Bhani's Toxins", as quoted from Bhani's own research report, which proves scientists are the last remaining Americans to grasp the importance of marketing.

"I understand you were one of the participating scientists tasked with trying to replicate Dr. Bhani's results," Edna wrote to Dr. Hotchkiss. "While I have seen a summary of these independent studies, I'm interested in hearing specifics and any feedback you could offer." She went on to explain that a good friend has a serious case of Ewing's sarcoma and has been offered Dr. Bhani's treatment. Probably a little pathetic that I got the biggest charge out of Edna referring to me as her good friend. "How good?" I wondered aloud.

The letter was copied to three scientists at various research institutions. As they were all dated five days prior, I didn't expect or find replies in the binder.

Next was the summary Edna had referenced. *S. pyogenes-Triggered Non-Specific Immune Response As Treatment For Certain Sarcomas, Submitted For Peer Review By Dr. Khaled Bhani.* I was prepared to wade through a ream of technical jargon to get the gist, but the one-paragraph Executive Summary spoke loud and clear.

"Dr. Bhani's treatment, coupled with standard doses of chemotherapy and radiation therapy, was given to a random selection of cancer patients (the 'Experimental' group). As compared to a Control group subjected only to chemotherapy and radiation therapy, the efficacy of Bhani's Toxins was not proven beyond statistical error.

"For both the Experimental and Control groups, sixty to seventy-five percent of subjects experienced substantial reduction in tumor size in the first eighteen months after treatment, while five to ten percent of these subjects experienced sustained or continued improvement past eighteen months. No additional benefits accrued to the recipients of Bhani's Toxins. However, subjects in the Experimental group were fifty percent more likely to experience complications or what could be termed side effects from Dr. Bhani's treatment, in one case so as to be life threatening.

"To summarize, the results of our peer review are inconclusive at best, and at worst, adverse."

Go ahead and kick me when I'm down, cuz it doesn't hurt. You're telling me Bhani is a potentially dangerous quack? And therefore I'm all out of options, beyond physician-approved dismemberment? Thought so. Now I understood why he had to go to the rez to administer his "treatment".

And how did this square with Thor's miracle results? For one thing, he's the young Norse god, and the rest of us aren't. For another, and this made me even sicker to my stomach—how permanent was Thor's "cure"? The peer review, performed by real scientists, used two time periods to measure success: a relatively meaningless *eighteen months*, and the bigger enchilada, *more than eighteen months*. Thor was less than eighteen **days**. That fucking Bhani. Some cure.

I skimmed two articles, from the Online Cancer Journal and the Washington Post, in which Bhani touted his results. "I have seen substantial shrinkage or complete disappearance of tumors in seventy-two percent of all cases," said Bhani. "Judging by irregular and occasional follow-up treatments months or years later, eighty-eight percent of my patients were for all intents and purposes cancer-free three years later. My first two patients were treated long enough ago to have now passed the gold standard of cancer treatment—seven years of remission."

"Bhani's Toxins should be hailed as a major breakthrough," the Post reporter concluded, and reported that Bhani had recently received a grant from the National Cancer Institute.

I got madder the more I read. How the hell could he get away with this lie, when no one else could replicate his miracle results? Who was I kidding, Bhani must be a master marketer.

And yet with all Bhani's deception, I was convinced the biggest fraud was being perpetrated by the mainstream research and medical communities. Forget Bhani's small-scale scam; where was the Online Cancer Journal's outrage over the fact that every other doctor's preferred treatment—chemotherapy—only kept five percent of their patients cancer-free for longer than a year and a half? Why wasn't this common knowledge? How could they get away with pumping us full of radiation and torturing us with chemotherapy, when it flat-out didn't work?

Neil Ruzic had been right about one thing, the chemo culture had an unfortunate, baseless hold on us. What he didn't understand when he wrote his book, was that there wasn't anything better. Cancer simply wins in the end. My heart ached for him, mourned for how he must have felt in his last days, when he realized the truth.

Edna had collected a few of Bhani's case histories, and I was hungry for more disappointment, more support for my dark conclusions. The first was a fifty-eight year old "John Doe" with recurring cancer in his elbow. He had gone through four (!) rounds of chemo and radiation, each time showing improvement—but each time a little less encouraging. They had amputated first at the elbow and then the rest of his arm. "Three weeks later, abdominal pain" said the file notes. "3/11—lump in right pectoral"; March twelfth, "two lumps in left pectoral"; a week later, "lymph glands swollen under armpit, more chest lumps, ache in left thigh"; "anorexic and too weak to walk" by Easter, and "taking abundant pain killers". April first, surrounded by fools, "jaundiced, losing cranial sensation".

And then the cancer had surged with a vengeance, growing fat and hideous on the empty shoulder socket. A Polaroid was taped to the page, showing mottled cauliflower bubbles growing under skin hanging loose in the absence of pectoral and deltoid muscles. "Hardened lymph nodes, nodules cropping up everywhere. Ingesting liquids causes abdominal pain." April 15th: "...tumor the size of a baby's head attached to the esophagus near the stomach."

John Doe and his doctor agreed to end treatments. Reading between the lines, JD was going to be left to die with his dignity and a couple heads of bruised cauliflower. For the next two months they did nothing and the cancer spread, to his lungs and his throat. *That's what's happening to me.* "From head to toe patient is covered in small tumors like BBs." Three years after being diagnosed, JD went to see Bhani.

There was another Polaroid coming up, and I couldn't wait to see the movie before I read the book. JD's shoulder was now a pleasant-looking chicken wing, with no discolored cauliflower. I backed up and read the preceding two pages, reluctant to listen to Bhani taking the credit.

"We initiated the treatment on June 14 with an injection of the toxins directly into the tumor growing on the scapula and clavicle. Patient experienced a mild reaction, elevated temperature (100.5°), chills, some muscle ache. After ten days the tumor showed signs of necropsy, and no new tumor activity was found elsewhere in the patient, his first quiescent period of any length since December. After twenty days the tumor showed new signs of 'life', and we endeavored to apply a more concentrated dosage of the toxins.

"This time the patient's temperature spiked to 103° and remained above 102° for thirty-six hours. Patient experienced extreme physical discomfort—severe chills and occasional convulsions, debilitating headache, nausea, and two violent vomiting spells, hallucinating at one point—and a raging angry red case of rash-like erysipelas from head to toe.

"Beginning the middle of Day 2, the fever gradually subsided and the patient recovered enough to take liquids orally, retaining a small quantity of solid food by nightfall. By the morning of Day 3 the tumors were noticeably smaller and softer to the touch. Constant discharge of broken-down tumor material. MRIs on Days 5, 8 and 9 confirmed what became an accelerated death of the cancerous tissues. BB-sized tumors and the nodules in the chest and abdomen had disappeared by the 9th day.

"One month later—the original tumor and the abdominal tumor are completely gone. No new growth has been found. Patient's self-reported energy levels are consistent with pre-cancer period.

"Six months later—no cancer activity noted.

"Two years later—no cancer activity noted. Patient recently ran the Boston Marathon (time unknown).

"Five years later—no cancer activity noted."

"Seven years later—ditto."

Yeah, well, I thought, how come no other scientist could replicate this kind of magic? I was sure Bhani was lying. Had anyone verified what he was reporting, what he claimed to be seeing? Why wasn't he either exposed as a fraud or lauded as the next coming? *I'm sorry*, Bhani must have told the scientific community, *but my results cannot be duplicated. I will now raise Lazarus and turn water into wine.*

The second case study was an eighteen-year-old girl. The same tale of heartbreak and salvation—again with some nauseating similarity to my story. Jane Doe got herself a deep bruise when she was struck on the shin by a winch on an Alaskan fishing boat. (Hundred pound steel winch and Troy Becker's roundhouse kick, interchangeable agents of destruction.) The doctors poisoned her repeatedly with chemo drugs, killing most everything but the cancer. Like me, Jane D. opted out of the tourniquet, bullet bite-down, and hacksaw route; unlike me, she paid Bhani a visit.

His approach was the same: give her a moderate dose of his toxins, and when that didn't work, sock it to her good. Her immune system reacted with a vengeance, waging war against what Bhani described as his "toothless invader", the S. pyogenes bacteria, able to trigger an immune response but stripped of its replicating mechanism and thus lacking the capability to cause a true infection. Jane became terribly ill; she recovered; she relapsed; she recovered again, fully; she went on to live a cancer-free life with all her limbs attached and fully functioning.

Maybe functioning better than ever. Bhani wanted us to know that a year later Jane anchored the winning four-hundred meter medley team at the NCAA championships. Bhani was a fan of testimonials of this sort. "...after which Jimmy Doe starred as first baseman on the Dubuque, Iowa city league softball championship team..."

I got so mad I couldn't read another case study, another lie, the names fictionalized to protect the guilty Dr. Bhani from the light of truth. I thumbed forward, to an article from the Minneapolis Star-Tribune, from six months ago.

ago. *Herald of Change, or Hoaxster?* it asked, and then proceeded to give no satisfying answer. The reporter rehashed the same jaw-dropping, false results previously reported in the Cancer Journal and the Washington Post. It came across loud and clear how badly the reporter wanted these fictional case studies to be true. He was able to track down and talk to two of these "miracle survivors", heard them confirm their tales of cancerous damnation and then blessed salvation at Bhani's hand.

Unfortunately the reporter didn't ask these "survivors" how much Bhani was paying them to lie. He didn't mention just how wealthy Bhani stood to become, if he could con a pharmaceutical firm to buy his toxins.

The reporter spent half as much time detailing the inability of other researchers to verify Bhani's miracles on their own terminal patients, and claimed to be unable to reach any of these scientists for an interview. In which case he shouldn't have written the article.

He did allow Bhani to conjecture why he alone had the magic toxic touch. An ample serving of toxins was necessary to trigger a massive-enough immune response. Other researchers were reluctant to inject their patients with *any* deadly bacteria, much less scads of them. And because each patient seemed to tolerate / respond to / die from different concentration levels, Bhani hadn't set recommended minimum dosages.

The strength of any given patient's immune system was also a key success factor, needing to be peppy enough to rise up and rage against the medicinal bacteria, and in the process wipe out the cancer as a sort of fortuitous byproduct. But depending how much and how recently chemo drugs had been administered, the patient's immune system might be sicker'n a dog.

Toward the end of the article, the Star Tribune's propagandist had asked Bhani, "Is it possible other researchers would have any motivation to flunk your toxin treatment, because it contradicts or outshines their own research?" Bhani demurred from making such a heinous accusation, and then noted that some researchers do have investments in profitable mobile radiation labs, or "business relationships" with the pharmaceutical companies that made billions manufacturing the chemo drugs. The reader was left to conclude Bhani was the nation's last ethical researcher.

Edna had written in the margin: "No wonder this treatment isn't getting the recognition it deserves!"

Maybe because I'm morbid; maybe because deep-down I'm a borderline illiterate who prefers pictures; maybe I wanted Edna to come home and find me like a movie hero still "researching" at two-thirty a.m.; but I thumbed through the other case studies looking for more Polaroids.

Only one had any, and this one had three of them, and one of these was familiar, of Brent McEwen's lifeless and infected body, lying on a stainless steel table. The stark image hadn't lost its shock value. The second picture was of Brent's shoulder, where the cancer must have lived. The third picture was not a Polaroid but a printed MRI shot—Edna's caption identified this as Brent's cancer-free shoulder, two weeks after receiving Bhani's treatment.

I read his case study, some of it a rehash of what I already knew. Rick and Isabel's brother was diagnosed with bone cancer two years ago. Ewing's sarcoma, just like mine, a small early-stage tumor. They hit it with everything modern medicine had to offer, that is, chemo and radiation. Thought they beat it. It came back. Slugged it harder. Never really went away this time. And then the spreading began, into various sensitive areas, including his 'nads, which I considered gratuitous information Bhani could easily have left out.

Bhani was recently arrived from the University of Minnesota hospital, and came highly recommended, I remembered Mike telling me, prideful at how one of his many powerful connections had paid off. Bhani treated Brent at the Jamestown Hospital, and with the benefit of past experience made Brent violently ill on the first try.

The youngest McEwen, baby of the family and truly the apple of his parents' eye, the hottest, the studliest, the most likely of the four kids to have hot and studly children with a hot and studly mate, made an amazing comeback.

I can add an aside, something not in the file, something Bhani's attorneys defending against the McEwens' wrongful death suit might be interested to know should they depose me. While the McEwens painted themselves as a tight-knit family desperate for a cure and therefore easy targets for a snake-oil charlatan like Bhani, they might be more accurately depicted as a tight-knit pack of powerbrokers eager to be mentioned in the same breath with a budding scientist superstar. The McEwens never truly accepted the fact that Brent had cancer. They simply couldn't believe their young Achilles could be sick, especially not fatally, and by no stretch of the imagination with something like bone cancer that suggested a flawed, rotten core. So they had chalked up Brent's recovery to Brent—it had only been a matter of time for his hero's immune system to wake up and get busy—not to Bhani. In their minds, doctors weren't so much healers as threats to mess up Brent's supernatural constitution.

And boy did Bhani mess up, it would appear. According to the file notes, twenty days after the treatment and five days after the MRI photo proclaimed him cured, Brent wandered into the emergency room, incoherent, fever spiking into the brain-death range, his body bruised and oozing pus from head to toe. He received a massive infusion of antibiotics, far too late; before his family could arrive he was dead, and his body disposed of in the name of disease control. The McEwens never really knew how—how awfully, how agonizingly Brent died.

In Bhani's own hand, I read that Brent must have holed up when he got sick, in the days after recuperating from the toxin-inspired fever and being pronounced cured of cancer. He probably didn't want to alarm his folks, after everything they had gone through. Bhani described how Iz told the hospital investigators that Brent left an urgent message on her landline voicemail the day before his death, his voice weak and frightened, telling his big sister he felt terrible, that he kept throwing up until it was nothing but blood and mucous. That his body was covered with blisters that grew by the hour. Iz had been vacationing with girlfriends and had to listen to the voicemail posthumously. Why Brent hadn't called her cellphone, she didn't know.

Reading Bhani's account, information he must have pieced together secondhand, was like listening to the outpourings of a tortured soul. In the increasingly jagged and cramped script I sensed that he had difficulty finishing the file note. And yet his signature at the end was long, the loops full of ink, as if he wanted to leave no question of his role in Brent's death. It felt like the voluntary signature on a miserable confession.

Was Bhani to blame? There was no way the McEwens could conclude anything but. According to the autopsy, the final document in the file, Brent had died from streptococcus pyogenes. S. pyogenes. Flesh-eating bacteria.

I should probably be embarrassed to admit that I always considered flesh-eating bacteria to be a novelty, sort of a junior bogeyman, something that got under the skin of hillbillies and NASCAR fans, consumed a goodly chunk of their tissue, and then went away, leaving behind a few good pics for the National Enquirer. In the coming days I did a little research. Turns out each year it killed a couple thousand people, from all walks of life. Scientists suspected the bug was usually picked up in hospitals, where strep was prevalent, rampant even, and probably increasingly drug-resistant. What they didn't know was why only a small proportion of the populace seemed susceptible.

And now for everyone waiting anxiously for the smoking gun, I quote the coroner: "Interviews with Dr. Khaled Bhani and review of his research notes indicate that the treatment he generally uses and in fact did use to treat Brent McEwen nineteen days prior to his death, was a form of the S. pyogenes bacteria. Various guises of this bacteria case strep throat, impetigo, cellulitis—and flesh-eating disease, the cause of Brent McEwen's death.

"Dr. Bhani vociferously maintains that his attenuated form—endotoxins stripped of their infectious genetic material—cannot be implicated in this death. In my professional opinion, his claim cannot be 100% certain."

The understatement of the year, I wrote in the margin.

Iz told me the coroner's report formed the backbone of their wrongful death claim against Bhani. Now I understood why—he had basically come out and pronounced Bhani guilty.

At that moment I couldn't grasp why Bhani would hire the McEwens' daughter-in-law, after killing off their son. But I was glad he did. Andrea's job had provided her unfettered access to Bhani's patient files. Whether she sent me the pictures out of spite or some residue of affection[1], Andrea had saved me from a similar horrendous fate.

I jotted down the names of Dr. Vance Hotchkiss and the other peer researchers Edna had contacted. And then I was tired. The binder also contained various informational articles on revving the immune system to fight cancer, using interferon, tumor necrosis factor, vaccines. It could wait, maybe forever.

I curled up on Edna's couch, staring through the big front window at the night air drifting down the street and eddying through the trees, keeping the few remaining houselights at bay. I savored the memory of walking through that air. When I was in it, I didn't need alcohol; the smell of it was enough to make me giddy and horny and deliriously happy to be alive. Not creative, not inspired to do great things. I'll work from sun-up until the sun goes down, but not a second later. Night is the time to spend a little money and convince her to stay out past a responsible bedtime, to enjoy the fruits of my hard work, to take pride in all those great accomplishments and hope she felt it too. I prayed to be allowed to experience the night again; and not just one last time.

WEDNESDAY MORNING behind the bar I wore my grungiest look in a long time. Ball cap. A bad bum's scraggly beard. A pair of worn gray sweats that fit easily and comfortably over my knee, and under my apron an old long-sleeve Cal-Davis practice jersey I've had since I was sixteen, when Ryan and I conned homely little Bev Dalrymple to violate her sacred student manager duties and cop a couple for us. Now it fit me again.

We were midway through the morning rush, the shop crowded, Charlotte and Sara by my side, Jerry and the regulars at the counter. While making drinks I told Charlotte and Jerry about my night spent digging through Edna's files. Everyone else was free to listen in.

"So yesterday I called this Dr. Hotchkiss. At the Mayo Clinic. I couldn't believe he took my call. I told his secretary who I was and why I was calling, and she put me right through to him."

"Maybe he heard you're dating Edna Applejack," Jerry suggested.

I wasn't sure I liked him with a quick wit. Charlotte didn't, judging by her unhappy snort. "I told his secretary I was dying. Next thing I know, I'm talking to him. From what I hear, mostly from reading Edna's research file, this

---

[1] {Note to file regarding *Lawson, Brian*'s application to Heaven: candidate repeatedly demonstrates charitable assumption of Andrea Goldine's benevolence, all evidence to the contrary.}

Hotchkiss is well-known for his research, on the immune system, whether it's immune system deficiencies, or things like cancer…"

"What'd he say?" Jerry prompted.

I smiled the way storytellers do. "You don't think I know how to tell a story, do you?"

"I could tell you were stumbling," said Jerry.

"Whatever, man." I put a drink on the pickup shelf. "Skinny no-foam latté." Being around my favorite customers, and my favorite employee Charlotte, almost, almost was enough to make me enjoy the morning or at least the minute without sinking into a mental coma. "So I told him about my situation…" I stopped, drawing a blank on the drink I was preparing. I looked at Charlotte.

"Decaf americano, room for cream," she said.

"Thanks. I told Dr. Hotchkiss I was contemplating going with Dr. Bhani's treatment, and the next thing I know he goes into a rant."

"He wasn't encouraging?" Charlotte asked as she retrieved another gallon of whole milk.

"You could say that. He said he tried it on five patients, and none responded. 'Flat-out', that's the phrase he used. 'Those goddamn toxins flat-out don't work.' Hotchkiss said Bhani has no credibility in the research community. So there."

"Did you believe him?" asked Bart Schock, sitting beside Jerry.

"Jerry threw off my rhythm, so I'm not sure if I mentioned that Dr. Hotchkiss is a world-renowned cancer researcher. So yeah, seems like a good idea to listen to what he has to say."

"Maybe he's in competition with Dr. Bhani," Bart countered. "Working on a similar cancer cure."

"I wasn't really looking for anyone to play devil's advocate, Bart."

"That's the only reason this Hotchkiss would have been chosen to verify Dr. Bhani's results," said Bart. "Because he's familiar with the field, and probably doing similar things."

"From what I've heard, Bhani is off on his own rogue path," I said.

"The peer review system is flawed," Bart declared, a little put-out I wasn't agreeing with everything he said, because his wife is a pediatrician after all.

"Flat-out doesn't work," Jerry quoted my quote. "It would be hard to imagine…" He paused, humped over in his chair. "It would be hard to imagine a peer feeling comfortable making that sort of allegation, unless…" Jerry gave a slothlike look toward the front door. Everyone waited. We were a patient audience that day. "…unless he had rock-solid proof to back it up." He looked for agreement with a raised eyebrow. Jerry has thick, expressive eyebrows, with plenty of room on his forehead for those beetles to run.

I knuckleknocked him above Bart's coffee cup. "That's what I'm saying."

"What did Edna say?" Sara asked, smiling. I was surprised, not about the smile, about the fact that she was paying attention earlier when I related how high Edna was on Bhani and his toxins. Not to brag, but when I told a story, people listened. Not to be a downer, but when I was gone someone would no doubt step into my role, or not, and life would easily go on without me.

"I haven't told her yet. Decaf americano on the bar. Cal, Marvin," I greeted the Ford dealership owner and his service manager. "I don't feel like arguing about it with Edna," I told Sara. "I'd rather—"

Charlotte interrupted. "You and Edna are like an old married couple now? Arguing with each other, reading the paper over breakfast without saying a word to each other, that sort of thing?"

Through the door waltzed Kenny, the Wells Fargo manager. "Well, look who's back," I greeted him.

Kenny gave me a goofy smile. "What? Brian, I haven't seen you for awhile. We must be on different schedules. Work has been crazy lately. Going gangbusters, can't even draw a breath. You probably don't even remember my regular drink anymore," he babbled on.

"I remember."

"Brian has a long memory," Charlotte informed him. I had told her about finding Kenny and Laurie in Hernandes's shop, twice, and seeing his car parked at the wrong end of the Bluffs strip mall, more than a couple times.

"A good memory comes in handy," said Kenny. "Wish I had a better one."

"So you could remember where my shop is?"

Kenny stood awkwardly in front of the bar while the regulars looked him up and down. "I'd never forget the best coffee in town," he said.

I let him believe he was off the hook. "I was just telling these guys about my conversation with Edna the other night. She came home—"

"I heard Edna's your new partner here," said Kenny, all sparkly-eyed. "Is she in on a regular basis?"

"Here?" I played dumb. The sonofabitch was here to see Edna, not patronize my establishment. He was counting out his money. "That'll be six-fifty," I told him. It didn't register. "Six-fifty for your drink, Kenny."

He gave me a blank stupid smile.

"I raised the price today. For you."

"But…" He mumbled a few words. Charlotte stared at him with outstretched hand. "Ha-ha," said Kenny, digging in his pocket. He pulled out three more dollars and gave them to Charlotte. "It's worth it for your coffee."

"Good, because that's your minimum price from now on."

I was feeling eyes on me, and now I spotted their owner, Liza Minelli, standing forlornly beside what used to be her usual table in the window, before

I banned her.

"So," said Kenny, "is Edna—"

"Edna doesn't have anything to do with this shop," I cut him off. "She and I are partnering on a new store on the campus that will be open with or without me on September first."

"You should know that, Kenny," said Bart, still prickly. "You're probably financing the construction loan."

"Maybe Kenny can only lend to one coffeeshop at a time," I suggested. "That would be Bill Hernandes's shop at the Bluffs."

"Ha-ha," said Kenny, an onomatopoeia of a laugh.

"Is Bill making enough money to stay current on his payments?" I asked. "I figured that's why I see your car in his parking lot all the time. You're keeping an eye on your bad debt."

"Ho-ho!" said Kenny, startling the Red Hat ladies at the big table. "Not all the time. You don't see me there all the time. It's just very convenient to our branch on the north end."

Charlotte breezed past. "I drive by his shop." She was back and forth, doing it all, ringing up and chatting up the customers, filling bean orders, swapping out the empty pots, and keeping close tabs on the conversation. "I've even peeked my head in the door. That's all the closer I can stand to be. He's not very busy. Craig says the same thing." When Craig still worked for me, I always figured Charlotte hung out with him out of convenience. It was a relationship I couldn't fathom. Beauty and the Misogynist.

Liza inched toward the counter, on pace to arrive early that afternoon.

"Don't worry," said Kenny, "our loans are always collateralized."

"Careful not to divulge confidential information," Bart cautioned him. "You'll get a reputation for loose lips, and pretty soon Wells Fargo won't have any customers." He and Jerry looked ready to escort Kenny to the woodshed. My customers were a loyal bunch. I was a lucky man. Kind of.

"If Hernandes isn't going under yet," I said, "he will be soon. So anyway," I resumed my story, "I waited up all night for Edna, and then she stumbles in around six a.m. Turns out she was wining and dining Rick McEwen."

Cal was goggle-eyed. "Rick is making it with Edna?"

"It's business," I explained. "No, really. This woman is all business."

"Listen to this guy," said Charlotte. "A month ago he didn't even know who Edna was. And now he's the Edna expert."

"Are you jealous?" Cal asked.

"Hell no."

"I think you're jealous," said Jerry.

"Bye Kenny," I called as he tried to slip away unnoticed. He raised his cup and ducked out the door.

"Maybe we're all a little jealous about Edna," said Cal. "But who should we be jealous of?" he asked me. "You or Rick?"

"Since Rick's got more than a year to live, I'd pick him."

"Get outta here," said Cal. "You ain't goin' nowhere. I don't know a lot—I never finished high school, d'I ever tell you that? Started at the Massey Ferguson shop as a mechanic."

Everyone got restless. "You may have mentioned it," said Bart with a grin.

"Alright, alright," said Cal. "I won't bore you fine gentlemen with all the details." I handed him a coffee spiked with espresso. "Thanks. I'm just here to tell you, I wouldn't be where I am today without knowing how to read people. And let me tell you, Brian Lawson, you'll be around after most of these fellas here are long gone."

"I wouldn't bet the dealership on it."

"You're gonna die an old grandpa," said Cal.

"I guess we'll see about that."

"Yes we will."

"Yes we will." This was a stupid argument.

Liza Minelli cleared her throat.

"So what was Edna's business purpose for screwing Rick all night?" Bart asked, quietly enough to be considered discreet. "And can she take a deduction for that?"

"Honestly, it's not that sort of thing," I said.

"Maybe you don't get Edna all to yourself after all," said Charlotte.

I wanted to slap her. Where was Craig when I needed him. "Go take care of Liza," I ordered under my breath. Charlotte gave me a cold look but did as told. "Rick's building our campus shop," I finally neared the end of my story. "We need the shop finished by late August. Which I guess would be speedy."

"Supersonic," said Cal. "Brian, this is North Dakota. Construction firms have six months to make a year's worth of income. I know for a fact McEwen has two huge projects to finish before the snow flies. One down in Kulm, the other outside of town here. If Rick's taking time from those moneymakers to build your little shop…"

"She slept with him," Bart decided.

"No way," I scoffed. "You know what, Edna is Edna. She doesn't need to resort to sex to get her way."

"Maybe she even likes it," Cal suggested.

"Brian," Charlotte called me over.

"One way or the other," I told them as I backed toward the till, "we'll be up and running by September first."

"Are you closing this store then?" Bart asked.

"No," I whined, exasperated. "No, Bart. No. That's not the plan." I was ready to explain how this was finally my opportunity to grow, to expand and prove I was ambitious and capable of bigger things—California or North Dakota, it didn't matter, I could make money, I could be a success by any measure. But then I remembered it didn't really matter anymore. "This shop will stay open." I turned on Liza. "Lady. I told you September first."

The elfin woman with the plastered black hair shifted foot to foot like she had to pee. She cocked her head, staring at the countertop. "I'm sorry for throwing the papers at you."

"I know. You already apologized on the phone. Twice."

"So I'm forgiven?" She made a half-turn toward her table. "I can come back...now?"

"September first."

Charlotte huffed and walked off. "Oh, oh," Liza squeaked, "I can't take not coming in here. I haven't written a letter, not since you kicked me out. I'm so far behind. I need to be in here." She presented a loose stack of papers and then yanked them back. "I brought my own paper."

I sighed. "Okay."

"Oh good! Coffee, large, please." Liza ran to the table to drop off her pen and all that paper, then hurried back.

I had her coffee ready. "That'll be five dollars."

"Hm? Huh? No. It's one dollar fifty-eight cents." She reached for the steaming cup of coffee.

I pulled it back. "Until September first, five dollars."

"*Brian*," Charlotte hissed.

I sighed. "Okay. Two dollars."

Liza counted change in her palm, mumbling and shaking her head.

"Look out." Charlotte was about to hip-check me out of the way, then gave me a gentle push toward the counter crowd. "I'll ring her up."

Cal and Marvin had left. Bart was chuckling. Jerry smiled uncomfortably. Sara shook her head, almost not smiling, unwilling to look at me. "Tomorrow I'm going to charge Kenny seven bucks for his drink," I declared.

This cheered Jerry. "So your campus shop will be open by Labor Day?"

"A week earlier, hopefully."

Bart whistled. "She's good."

"Brian," said Charlotte, on her way to the little office, "can you come in here when you get a minute?"

Bart shook his head. "She's not supposed to be able to order you in there."

I acted disgusted. Jerry stopped me as I headed for the office. "Amber and I want to have you over for dinner. Can you make it tonight?"

"Sure. Can I bring something?"

"Like Edna you mean?" said Bart.

"Let me know," I told Jerry.

"Shut the door," Charlotte ordered when I entered. I did so. "Brian…" She was going to cry. I had found that if I pretended she wasn't, she wouldn't. "I'm really upset about your hiring for the new store. Isn't it going to be James River Valley Coffee?"

"It is." I sensed where she was going with this, and I was embarrassed I hadn't addressed it proactively. "It'll probably be called The Blessed Cup or something like that. But it's going to be part of our chain."

"It's going to be a chain." This was worse news for Charlotte. "Great. So…how come I'm not interviewing for store manager?"

"Who says you're not?"

"Brian, I know you already hired a manager. I talked to Theresa, my friend at First Bank, and she said you hired her boss, Dennis. She said he told her you're only hiring 'adults'."

"I don't know if that's necessarily true," I said. "And you're twenty-two."

"Obviously you don't consider me an adult."

"Aw, come on," I said gently. "You're the best employee I've ever had."

"Well? Then why didn't you…" She angrily swabbed at the tears sparkling in her eyes. Before I could respond she said, "Craig is pissed, too. He doesn't understand why you didn't offer him a job. Assistant manager or whatever."

"He shouldn't have gone to work for Hernandes."

"You fired him."

"I'd call it laid off."

"Brian, don't be an ass right now."

"It's hard to turn it on and off."

"Just turn it off and leave it off."

"You didn't like what I did to Liza out there?" I giggled to myself.

"No, I did not. Brian, she's mentally…retarded. Just give her some coffee and paper if she needs it, and let her be."

"Okay. Fine. Anything else? Besides manager at the new store, I mean."

Charlotte growled in frustration. She was going to cry again.

"Char-lotte!" I bellowed so that everyone in the shop could hear. That always got a chuckle. This time it got me a sore throat and a disappointed scowl from Charlotte. I shook her shoulders and when her body relaxed, hugged her. Slapped her hard on the back. "Come on now! Here's what I can tell you," I used my indoor voice. "Edna has a firm opinion of the hires we need to make. I don't know if she's right, I don't know if she's wrong. I haven't taken the time to think about it. She wants a strong sales background. She wants people who have a long-term goal to manage multiple stores."

"That's me. That's me, Brian."

"I know. And older. She wants you to be older."

"See! I knew it! Brian, that's age discrimination."

"I don't believe North Dakota has laws against it."

"I'm not talking about suing you." Charlotte sounded too weary to sue anyone. She was weary for her age. "I'm talking about what's right."

"Maybe you're right. Time will tell. But for now, this is the direction we're going. Plus," I tried to soften the blow, "I need you here."

She held her arms tight to her body and lowered her head, composing herself. "So what about this shop? Will you eventually go the same direction?"

"No. This is my shop, and mine alone. I'm very happy with the staff I have. Everyone does a great job. Everyone except Dana."

This prompted a weak smile. "Every store has to have someone to pick on and talk about behind their back," she said.

"I tried to tell Edna that. Come on now, cheer up. I love the job you do for me. You know I'd pay you more if I could. We would have gone under a couple months ago without you."

"What will the manager make at the campus shop?" Charlotte demanded.

Both our eyes went to the leaning tower of bills. "Let's just say this: they're going to be sorely disappointed if they expect to make as much as they did at the bank. Or the zoo, or the convenience store, or wherever they're coming from. This is a gamble on their part."

Charlotte waited for a better answer. For all I knew, Edna was paying them six figures with full bennies, bonus and profit-sharing. I wasn't going to admit how little control I had over the process. Charlotte left the office unhappy, and left work early complaining of a migraine.

I LEFT WORK AT THREE AND CAUGHT Edna on her cell. I invited her to Jerry and Amber's for dinner, but she was on her way to a meeting with Rick and the College's facilities manager, and didn't know how long it would last. They were coming to final agreement on the exact site location, the square footage, the orientation of the front door. They would decide on the number and location of parking spots. Architectural style and color. Signage.

Things were moving forward. All I had to do was stay out of the way, stay alive, and Edna would take care of everything. I would have loved to oversee the construction, planning the design and layout from scratch, but there was no portion of my mind available for future thought. I would try to plan something—creative new drink names for the campus shop, a round of golf, what to eat for lunch—and suddenly the gears would stop turning with an audible clunk, and a gray blanket would descend, a heavy numbing shroud laying upon my brain, unfurling to cover more and more of my body. Maybe it was a mental representation of my cancer. Maybe it was the cancer itself.

My cancer. The cancer. When the pronouns became interchangeable, when the cancer lost its foreignness and became mine, that would be the beginning of the end, when I started giving up the battle.

Edna wanted me to move all of my things to her house, and make it official. Her motivation was unclear. But whether it was affection or infatuation, to help me fight for life or to be my hospice caregiver, any rationale was fine with me. I liked the attention, and I had no guilt over subjecting her to the mental toll of living with a terminal patient—without a doubt, Edna was strong enough to watch me die and then move on.

When I mentally traveled down this road, the word legacy came to mind. If anyone could guarantee my legacy, it was Edna. I believed she would be committed to ensuring the Brian Lawson Coffeeshop Experience lived on. Maybe even a Brian Lawson, Jr., if I could get her drunk enough. I guess I was still capable of some future thought.

An older gentleman was sitting on the stoop of my apartment building. He rose as I shuffled along the sidewalk, and became my dad.

"So I did have the right building," he called out. My dad has a ragged, airy voice. Even before my own diagnosis, I was always afraid he was developing throat cancer. "There aren't any names on the mailboxes. And I've only been here once, when you first moved out here. How long has it been?"

"Six years," I said, legs weakening as I moved up the walk.

"Why the hell haven't you bought a house? Paying rent is just throwing money down a rat hole."

"I know." I stopped a couple feet in front of him. "Dad, wow…"

"Well here then." Dad stepped forward and hugged me. I got two quick pats on the back. And then as we separated, he hugged me some more. Dad is short, but that's not how I'm going to describe him. He has an enormous center of gravity—it covers his entire torso and extends halfway out his limbs, generating amazing leverage. Dad could have picked me off the ground and carried me inside, even thirty pounds ago.

After the hug he kept his hand on my shoulder. His eyes darted down to my leg. "Are you doing okay then?"

"Yeah. You know. You want to come inside?"

"Sure. I should grab my stuff."

"You flew here by yourself?" This I knew because grabbing his stuff was Mom's job.

"Your mother and I figured we could take turns staying with you for awhile. Till you get over it."

"You'd leave and then come back? You'd fly here more than once?"

"That's what we were thinking."

"Wow. I suppose I should tell you that you don't need to do that. But I'm glad you're here. I would have dressed nicer if I knew you were coming."

Dad fingered my sleeve. "I remember this shirt." He cocked his head and squinted up at me. "I really want to be here with you, Brian."

I looked into his eyes and nodded. "We better get your stuff and get inside before my waterworks start."

Dad chuckled and squeezed my shoulder. "You have room for me?"

"Sure. You're going to stay with me, for...?" I didn't want to assume; knowing Dad, he could have a return flight booked for that night.

"I thought two or three days, if you'll have me."

We cut across the lawn to the parking lot. "By tomorrow afternoon you're going to be going crazy thinking about work."

"Probably. But that's okay. Work can wait."

I wished he would stop saying things like that. The lump in my throat kept thickening. There was never any doubt Dad loved me and would do anything for me. But he is totally devoted to his job. He thinks about his crop insurance office every waking minute. This dedication is a little overboard—crop insurance isn't an emergency ward, it isn't the NORAD situation room—but his workaholism isn't an escape mechanism. It's the way he was raised to be. It's just the way he is. Dad loves his family, but unless there's an emergency, work has to come first. This was the first emergency.

"Our financial guys are really worked up about our capital levels right now," Dad was saying as he carried his suitcase into the building's foyer. "It shouldn't have anything to do with me. But I'm constantly answering their questions about the expected losses in California this year. I keep telling them they're going to be next-to-nothing. I don't think that's what they want to hear. I get the feeling they think we have surplus capital. But the way I understand it, we need it for the regulatory rating for our insurance company."

"You have your own insurance company, in addition to the agency? I never knew that." We talked about his job while he dropped his suitcase in the spare room, while I made us coffee.

"Coffee? No fancy lattés?"

"My espresso machine is at Edna's. I've never seen you drink anything but coffee."

"I just like to give you a hard time. This place looks deserted," Dad commented accurately. "Where's all your stuff?"

"I'm moving in with Edna."

"Is she a nurse?"

"A nurse...?" He got a chuckle out of me. "I don't look so good, do I?"

"Naw, you look fine. You have lost a lot of weight."

"I had some to lose. Not the muscle, though. That really bums me out. I haven't been active at all. No Taekwondo. No basketball. Not even golfing much this summer. I did play a course south of here a couple months ago. We got our buck." I sat down and started telling him the story.

"You told me about shooting the deer on the golf course. Pretty funny."

"I already told you that story...? Sorry about that. They say the chemo messes with your brain. It might have taken my IQ down a notch. I probably don't want to know."

Dad ran his fingers through his curly silver hair. "So this Edna wants to live with you even without muscles and a fully functioning brain." He winked. "She must really like you."

"I think so. You'll have to meet her. Edna is unique. She's a basketball legend in North Dakota."

"Right up your alley. I always thought you could have been really good if you had grown a few more inches."

"I tried, but your genes wouldn't let me."

"We should have moved here. You could have been a North Dakota legend too."

"The hoops quality isn't as bad as you'd think. They take their b-ball pretty seriously around here."

Dad wasn't buying it. "You were fun to watch. I never saw anyone go for the ball like you did. I remember that time you stole the rebound from the center for Sacramento East and put it back in to send the game into overtime."

"I loved doing that to the big guys."

"I know you did." Dad stared at me. "So. They want to take away your leg, huh?"

"Yeah."

"You thinking about letting them?"

"I don't know. It feels really permanent."

"Yep."

"Permanent things scare me right now."

"Everything's permanent, you know. Getting older, losing abilities. Just make a decision one way or the other. Things'll work out the way they're supposed to. In the grand scheme of things, losing a leg's not really a big deal."

"I know. I know it's true. I'd probably approach it that way, if I thought...I mean, I'm feeling like, either way..." *I'm fucked, Dad*, I wanted to say. "Edna wants me to try an experimental therapy."

"So?"

"It's experimental. Edna's been researching it, and she thinks it's a miracle cure. But it's the same treatment Isabel's brother received, and that didn't end so well."

"Mm," Dad vibrated his grim lips. "I remember. But there's nothing fool-proof and safe out there. Maybe you should do it."

I was startled. Dad's a conventional guy. I wondered if Edna had been talking to him, brainwashing him. Maybe she threatened to kill him.

"You can't wait around until they get it all figured out," Dad said, "because it'll never happen. I've seen people die from cancer. I've seen a few live. You have a pretty bad one it sounds like." He cocked his head and squinted at me. "But you always struck me as the kind of guy who would try the risky thing if you thought it was worth it."

"I wouldn't say I'm a big risk-taker."

Dad chuckled. "I remember you about twelve years old, climbing that crack at Yosemite so you could see the bighorn sheep babies."

"Oh man, I had forgotten about that…"

"That was way up there. Scared your mother to death. Your buddy Ryan wouldn't do it. He was scared shitless. You never bragged about climbing that crack. But you talked about those baby sheep. For a month."

"I can't believe you remember that."

"I remember the important things," said Dad.

He has unforgiving gray eyes, but I like them. "Those crazy little babies," I recalled, "they let me pet them, touch their little horns. I stayed up there with them for a long time. I knew I was worrying Mom, but I didn't want to come down. That's what started me rock climbing. That feeling of being in a place no one else could reach."

"Of course I did have to go get the park rangers to get you down."

"Sorry about that."

Dad winked. "It was worth it."

"If I hadn't torn my bicep climbing at the indoor gym, I think I would have been pretty good. Quite a few of the kids I climbed with went on to do competitions. They got their pictures in the climbing magazines."

"You had a job," said Dad. "They didn't. You were always a hardworking kid. I was pretty proud of that. I probably never told you that."

"Naw, you know…I knew it."

"Your mom and I were very impressed. Always have been."

That would sound great in my eulogy, but Dad wasn't naïve about the world or blinded by his love for me. He knew better, and I couldn't let him think that I didn't know better too. "I'm a hardworking risk-taker who topped out at age twenty-five."

"Huh? You have a good thing going here."

"One little shop. In North Dakota. That's not much." I was going to choke up if my sentences were any longer.

"Let me tell you something. Mom and I were surprised that you left the Davis area. You're kind of a home boy. But you saw an opportunity, and even though it meant moving half the country away, you took it." Dad tapped his chest. "Pretty gutsy. Let me tell you something else." He reached across the corner of the table and put his gnarled bony hand on mine. "It's tough to run a business. Working for a company, that's the easy way out. You're a risk taker. You never even consider working for somebody else."

"It's just one shop," I pushed the words through my constricting throat. "It's not that impressive. I'm not working as hard as I could. But I want you to know..."

"Hey, Brian..."

"I'm not a slacker. I was always trying." My chest heaved as I swallowed back the breakdown.

Dad was having a tough time as well. He pulled my hand across the table. "You're worrying about the wrong things, Brian. Don't think about what you haven't accomplished. Think about what you're going to do. Plan your next move, and then do it. Then plan the next one. And just keep doing things. That's the only way it works. If you keep looking at the negative, that's what you'll get. Keep looking ahead. Keep planning."

I knew how badly Dad wanted to see gritty determination on my face. I wished he was right about all this. I wished I was successful and had truly made him proud. I wished he could either teach me to be fatalistic, or convince me I had a fighting chance. I looked down at my coffee cup, which I suddenly hated along with the coffee in it. "You know what my favorite movie used to be?" I asked him. "Groundhog Day."

"Yeah?" Dad had no clue where the conversation had turned. "It's good? I think I might have seen it."

"It's got Bill Murray in it. He's stuck in a loop, every day the same, for infinity. He's the only one in this tiny town who knows it, the only one whose memory of the day isn't wiped out while they sleep each night." Telling this story calmed me down. "When Bill Murray figures out what's going on, he realizes he has a chance to exploit people, by learning all about them and then using that info to play pranks on them, or seduce them. Then when that gets old and he realizes he's really actually trapped in a single, awful, repeating day in a godforsaken podunk town, he wants to die. He tries to kill himself. He commits suicide, every day for something like a month straight. But he keeps waking up every morning, as good as new, on the same exact day."

Dad was grim. "Is that what this feels like for you?"

I shook my head. "One day he realizes he's been given the ultimate gift. By being stuck in an infinite loop, he has the time to do all the things a person never has time for. He can become a kung fu master. He can get a college degree. He can become an excellent musician. Seemingly overnight, for those around him. He can help people. He can help himself. He realizes he can improve himself. He has a chance to gain ten lifetimes' worth of abilities in a single day. He learns to play the piano, practicing every day. He takes dance lessons. He reads all the great literature. He trains himself in basic medical procedures. And after this goes on and on, for years, he's become an incredible, multi-talented person. Women want to sleep with him not because he knows what they like, but because he's *become* what they like."

Dad nodded solemnly. "I like the premise. There's a great moral there."

I nodded. "Most people think they have absolutely no time to improve themselves. They think there's never enough time in a day or the week to exercise or learn a language or a new skill. The thought of making big improvements in their lives is too intimidating. But the moral of the movie is that life lasts a long time, basically forever, and if you start now and work on improving yourself every day, the years go by and pretty soon you've accomplished something big. You're a broader person, and a better person."

Dad was impressed but still confused. "Why do you say it *used* to be your favorite movie?"

"Because it turns out it's not true for me. For me it's the opposite. My life is short. I don't have any more time to accomplish things." It was painful for Dad to hear this. "I know I'm not the only one in the world to have this happen to them. I know it happens way too often. But I'm unbelievably bitter. Every plan or idea I had in progress is now meaningless and useless."

Dad stared at the table. After a while he said, "Maybe that's the way Bill Murray felt, too. When he was trying to commit suicide. Or maybe," Dad labored to come up with something good, "maybe the moral is to live life to the fullest, because you don't know how long or short it may be."

"Except I do know, Dad, and I'm not good at accepting it, or lying to myself. But thanks for the Nike ad."

"Aw, that's bullshit." He got up and grabbed the coffee pot, refilling our cups. "I'm not going to listen to that. Let's change the topic a little here. Let's talk about work. Tell me what you've been doing at your shop lately."

Dad didn't get it. He was never understanding enough to let me feel sorry for myself, even when it was perfectly appropriate. I considered tipping my cup and spilling coffee all over the table, to see if it mattered. "Mostly I've been talking to pastors and friends with strong faith. Trying to convince myself there's an afterlife, some kind of heaven where I'm still me. I think that'll go a long way toward settling me down. I don't want to be afraid, you know?"

Dad squirmed in his chair, readjusting his jeans. "Maybe..." He cleared his throat. "Maybe we should get something to eat."

I had pushed beyond Dad's ability to cope, and it was time to let him off the hook. I had set the record straight, accomplished what I needed to, and felt awful for it. "I'm not hungry," I said. "But we can go get you something. I don't have any food here. I might have some 'Nilla Wafers left."

The phone rang. It was Jerry. "I'm making sure you're still coming to dinner."

"Whoops. Holy crow. My dad just got into town, unexpectedly. So…"

"Bring him along," said Jerry. "He's not completely like you, is he?"

"He's a little smarter than me," I reported. "Maybe not quite as funny. A lot nicer."

"Then yeah, bring him. Amber is making plenty."

"That won't be an issue. Dad's not a big eater. We'll be lucky to eat a full serving between us."

"Even better," said Jerry. "We'll see you in a few minutes?"

"Okay homey." I hung up. "You're okay with eating over at a friend's house? Jerry and Amber are really good people."

"Sounds fine," said Dad. His voice had degraded from raspy to hoarse with fatigue. Probably the last thing he wanted to do, but he agreed.

HE WAS QUIET AS we climbed in my van. Silent as we skirted downtown, other than a couple wheezy replies to my inquiries about Mom, her housecleaning business, her hammer toe. Dinner guest etiquette demanded I draw him out of his moodiness before we went inside. Get his mind off me.

"Jerry and Amber are struggling to pull in enough income to make their house payments," I said as we pulled up in front of their house. "Jerry quit his job a year ago to start his own day-trading investment business. He's having a tough time finding enough clients. He wants me to be his salesman."

When Dad spoke, it wasn't in reply to my gossipy dossier on our dinner hosts. "I was thinking," he said, "how I never had to tell you that life is hard." He sat small on the seat, hands folded in his lap. "I never had to use that concept to motivate you. I've given that speech to your mother from time to time, to remind her why I have to work so much. And I've given it to your Uncle Verlyle, more than once." He looked over at me. "But I never gave it to you. Sometimes I thought I should give you the opposite speech. Your mom was always afraid you took life too seriously. That you worked too much."

It dawned on me that Dad was doing a very difficult thing. He was trying to admit he had been wrong about his core philosophy. Hard work doesn't always pay off. It clearly hadn't for me. I wanted to make it easy on him.

"There's a guy named Terrence who comes into the shop and writes every day for two hours," I told him. "He's been doing it for years and he can't get his novels published." I shut off the van. The cessation of the engine's vibration beneath us was a punctuation between my examples. "Another customer, a housewife who's maybe forty, has been taking science and math classes for three years, prepping to get into a pharmacy program. She gets almost all A's. And yet her application was rejected."

I pulled the keys from the ignition and unbuckled. "And then of course there's Jerry here. He is an amazingly smart guy and great at what he does. And yet they might lose their house. He's probably going to have to go back to work for a company he hates. It's not much consolation—none, actually—but I'm definitely not the only one who's basically failed at his dream. Life is freaking hard. And then you can die."

Dad pinched his brow and shook his head. "I don't know about these other people you're talking about." Dad pinched harder, and then his voice cracked, became smoother somehow, as the tears came. "But you are not a failure. You're only thirty-two years old and you own a business. That's incredible. Most people are too afraid to even try to start their own business, and a lot of those that do try, fail. Okay?"

The high-pitched note of anguish in his voice made me choke up. "I didn't know you felt that way."

"I didn't understand that you didn't know it," he said. "Everybody that you've met, you've touched. Mom and I saw it in you as you grew up. Everybody wanted to be around you. People are drawn to you. We hear it all the time. We think you're incredibly successful."

And now some real blubbering began. Not many tears, maybe due to the desiccating effects of age, but Dad's body shook. I started bawling right along with him...while simultaneously, implausibly, a little magically, experiencing a strong current of electricity coursing through my brain. It was weird, and wonderful, crying and feeling excited at the same time.

Jerry knocked on the window. I keyed the ignition to lower the window, not bothering to wipe away the tears. "I'm sorry man," I told him. "We got talking out here, and the next thing you know, we're weeping."

Jerry was solemn. "Take your time."

"Jerry," I snuffled, "this is my dad."

"Hi Mr. Lawson. You both take your time out here. No rush." Jerry walked back inside. He paused to look up at the backyard cottonwood towering above his house. I stared at it too. I was struck by the soothing rustle of the leaves in the evening breeze. North Dakota trees huddle close to the few rivers that struggle across the windblown prairie in hopes of making it to tranquil Minnesota. The town has a number of big mature trees, providing the only shade for a hundred miles, beckoning to travelers and field-weary farmers, blocking the wind. Jamestown was an oasis, I realized.

Jerry called from his stoop. "Brian, don't feel like you're obligated..."

"I'm actually feeling better," I called to him. "Dad and I'll be in soon."

T - 1

"So thanks for dinner last night," I told Jerry. He was on his stool at the counter, flanked by regulars, Oscar, Cal, Bart and Donna, and my dad. I nodded at him. "Dad enjoyed it. It was good, wasn't it Dad?"

"It was," said Dad.

"I'm making an announcement this morning," I told the counter crowd. The zest in my voice kept startling people. "Two of them, actually."

"Oh Lord," said Charlotte. She was running around, doing whatever it was she did. Agitated. "I don't think I'm ready to hear this."

"It's good stuff," I assured her.

"Oh I'm sure it is. Dana, could you please clean up the corner table? It's been messy for awhile now."

Dana studied the table, trying to decide if messy was the right description.

"Or not," said Charlotte.

"I got it," said Dana. She hummed sinister organ music on her way to the table. Working in a coffeeshop for Dana means making drinks, and nothing else. She's clueless as soon as she steps away from the espresso machine. With her black-rimmed eyes and S&M wardrobe, I expected my customers to scatter whenever she came near. But more than a few consider Dana my best employee. She makes great drinks; and they figure that anybody dressed that way is surely headed for stardom. Conservative, Christian North Dakota has so few celebrities, they're ready to embrace the second coming of Ozzy Osbourne as long as the world acknowledges which state spawned her.

"You might need a rag," Charlotte called from her crouch behind the bar while rummaging for a fresh bottle of vanilla syrup.

"Oh yeah," Dana chirped. Charlotte growled softly into the low cupboard.

"What a team I have!" I bellowed. "I have a couple announcements to make, don't I Dad?"

"I guess so."

"Why don't you just tell us?" Charlotte suggested, no longer sure my insanity was an act.

"PK!" I called to Pastor Kyle before both his feet were in the shop. "You're just in time for my announcement." I had seen him coming, already had his americano ready.

"Have you ever considered Pastor Kyle might not like to be called PK?" Charlotte asked me. It never crossed my mind.

"I don't mind it," said PK. He has the strong, serene voice you look for in a pastor. Although I was also partial to Reverend Murray's quiet intensity. And I loved John the Baptist minister's spunk and whacked-out humor. I have a thing for men of the cloth, there's no doubt. "Coming from someone else, well I might take offense," said PK, like a cowboy without the drawl. "Coming from Brian, it's clearly a sign of affection."

"See?" I said to Charlotte.

"Whatever." Charlotte started to quote PK his price, then turned to me. "How much am I charging Pastor Kyle for his americano today?"

"Normal price," I said.

PK looked back and forth. "You mean I could have had a discount?"

"Not likely," I said. Maybe if he was working harder to save my soul. "I've implemented a flexible pricing structure. But rarely does it flex down."

"So I guess I better start minding my p's and q's," said PK.

"You gotta take risks."

"So what's the announcement?" PK asked.

I turned up my volume. "Okay everybody—do you want the big news first, or the really big news?"

I heard "big" and I heard "really big". "I'm going with the big news," I decided. Everyone in the place had stopped talking except for Judy Wellstone at the table directly across from me. Her current man-friend Tommy pinched her, but Judy kept on talking. "Okay, here it is. I'm opening a new store."

It was big, but not exactly news. Once everyone realized that was it, I received a nice round of applause. Someone said the actual word "hurrah". Judy Wellstone looked around, mouth open in mid-word, and then continued her story. I pointed at Dad. I gave credit to my number one homey, laying a stone cold rapper-pose cocked-bow straight-arm point on his ass. Dad nodded.

"Congratulations, Brian," said Oscar. To humor me he asked, "Where's the new shop going to be?"

"On the campus."

"Hey, that's wonderful."

"Thank you. I'm really excited about it."

"You left out the biggest part of your big news," said Charlotte.

"No I didn't."

Charlotte was irritated by my omission. Either her irritation was part of our standard act, or it was real. "Tell them the rest," she ordered.

"I already *told* them the important part."

"Brian."

"Okay." Everybody quieted down again. Judy was not a member of the set of Everybody. Judy was Judy, and she was cackling over something she had just told her soon-to-be-former man-friend Tommy. "I left out one small

piece of information. I'm opening the store September first...with a partner...whose name is...Edna Applejack. That's it."

The applause was louder this time, it's true. There was some actual cheering. Also some horny hooting from Bart.

"Unfortunately none of you can go to that store," I killed their joy. "It's
going to get plenty of new customers, so I need you all to keep coming here."

There were grumbles and there was muttering amongst the assembled.

"Will Edna work here too?" Cal asked.

"She'll make an occasional appearance," I conceded, to appease the people.

"That's not good enough," Jerry tried to throw his voice.

"How about if I let you see her right now?" I offered.

"It's a start," said Bart.

I motioned toward the back hallway. "There she is." On perfect cue Edna
appeared. Chairs squealed and banged to the floor as everyone jumped to their
feet and clapped and cheered. Edna walked to me and kissed me on the lips.
We faced the crowd together, her arm around my shoulders instead of my
waist where I believe the woman's arm belongs. I saw that Dad noticed.

Edna thrust her fist in the air, clipping the menu board hanging above us,
rocking the hundred-pound slab of lumber and glass on its little bitty hooks.
"Don't you think it's about time we had a coffeeshop on that campus?!"

The crowd roared its approval.

"Alright," I shouted, disconnecting from Edna, "are you ready for my next
announcement?" Customers walked in. I turned to Charlotte. "Fix Bruce and
Lydia their drinks, would you?" I would have asked Dana, but she had taken a
seat at the table she was cleaning.

"This is my favorite of the two announcements," said Edna.

"Mine too," I agreed. "Although I'm not sure I'd be as excited about this
one, without the first one. Okay, so I think everyone knows by now that I have
bone cancer."

"Yeah," everyone said, real soft like, soft murmurs, soft eyes.

"And I've taken two rounds of chemo and radiation, and it's killed everything but the cancer."

Everyone acknowledged this unfortunate fact.

"Fucking chemo," I grunted.

"Why do they even recommend it?" Charlotte wanted to know.

"We won't get into that," I said. "But it's because the doctors own shares
in mobile radiation labs, and because they receive free trips to Hawaii from the
pharmaceutical companies that make the chemo drugs, and because they're
too lazy to research other options that definitely exist."

The crowd was mine now, laughing a little, cringing a little, looking around to see whether any docs were in the room, but in all cases very attuned to what came next.

"So I've decided to stop the chemo and radiation, and go with a radical treatment that should cure me."

This started a hubbub. I heard "Brent" and "McEwen" on more than a couple lips. Good guess. "Dr. Bhani," Edna confirmed, loud enough for everyone's benefit. "It's Dr. Bhani's treatment."

"Good for Brian," said Bart emphatically.

"It's dangerous," I announced, in case anyone thought they could stop pitying me, and to stop Edna from taking over both of my announcements. "It's painful. It's not guaranteed. I hope it's free. And if it doesn't cure me, and assuming I don't die from it, they're going to have to saw my leg off."

Gasps were exactly what I was going for. I limped around the counter, out onto the floor. It was the Chernobyl version of the Willy Wonka scene: pity builds as Brian Wonka Lawson hobbles front and center; then instead of relieving the tension with a backflip, I lift my pajama pantleg and point to my tibia tumor.

"Oh Brian, good Lord," said PK. With everyone else recoiling, he bent to touch the knobby misshapen mass growing like a black tree fungus under my knee. Bruce and Lydia's little girl started crying, and then shrieking.

"My God, Brian, I had no clue," said Donna, recovering to step around PK and stroke my cheek. Oscar couldn't look; he turned away, cuddling his Lake Tahoe mug. Jerry couldn't speak—this was no pause, there was absolutely nothing going on behind the scenes.

"Dr. Bhani's toxins can cure even that," Edna pitched some snake oil. "You are not going to be able to believe the difference."

She was generally ignored. A first. "Brian I am so sorry," said Lydia.

"Don't be. If I have to lose the leg, I'm okay with it. I realized I'll be like any other war veteran. Damned lucky to have a good leg, and to be alive." I winked at Dad; not sure if he knew I was paying watered-down homage to the dead soldier mindset, but he winked back.

LATER I WALKED EDNA TO THE TALON. "You were fabulous in there," she said. "You are such a showman."

"Even when I'm dying. I can't stop it."

"Can you stop playing with yourself?"

"Sorry. The inseam on these pajama pants is goofy. It's chafing me."

At the Talon Edna gave my hands something better to do, placing them on her hips. We kissed. She angled her head and pressed her lips into mine. Instant hard-on. A mutually-acceptable configuration for the pj's and my crotch. We kissed a while. Edna's eyes opened. "Would you marry me?" she asked.

"Yes I would."

"*Will* you marry me," she clarified.

"Yes I will."

"Will you marry me soon?"

"I guess." So this is how movie stars did it. "After the treatment. But if I end up going with the amputation, we should probably wait awhile, to make sure I'm cured."

"People like us don't have to be pragmatic," said Edna. "We own this town. Who besides us owns this town?"

"The McEwens have a good-sized chunk."

"But I own them, so…" Edna was haughty and sexy, staring down into my face. I was pinned against the Talon with my legs spread wide and Edna's knees pressing uncomfortably against the inside of my thigh. Oh yeah, she had her hand on my dick, so I didn't care.

"So I guess when you consolidate everything up, we own it all."

"Brian, since the first time I heard about you, and then saw you, I knew this was inevitable."

"I wish I could say the same. I mean I hoped, but I didn't sense the inevitability."

"We're going to do special things together. The *Sun* will have to start a gossip column to keep track of us."

"For those 'tweener pieces that aren't business and aren't news."

"I can't wait," said Edna, with a delightful sparkle in her eye. "So let's get you cured. I'll bet Dr. Bhani can make a trip to Fort Yates this weekend."

"I'm not having it done on the rez," I said.

"Our hospital won't let him perform the procedure, because of the injunction request from the McEwens," Edna explained. "So it has to be the rez."

"The cancer, the toxins, rabies—something would get me there. We'll have to find someplace that hasn't heard about the injunction. How about—"

"The Fort Yates clinic is perfect," Edna snapped. "Don't make this harder than it needs to be."

"Sorry, but I have reservation reservations. Don't make me a reservation reservation."

Edna let out a screech.

"Hey." I held up my hands in a defensive position. "Don't kill me."

A smile took over Edna's mouth and the anger seeped from her shoulders. "That's not funny."

"I've been waiting to use that one."

Edna bit at her cheeks, her striking features all the more like a supermodel's. "Do you understand how far this could delay your procedure?" Over Edna's shoulder I saw Bart leave the shop. He spotted us and started to cross the street. Then he took a second look at Edna's posture and made an abrupt about-face. "Do you have a clue," Edna harangued, "how long it would take to convince another hospital to let Dr. Bhani administer his toxins?"

"I'm just saying…"

Edna settled back on her heels and scrutinized me. "You're not really serious about this, are you?"

"I'm not *being* serious, but I *am* serious."

"Then I guess it's your sanity I'm questioning. Don't you realize what's going to happen to you if you don't get Dr. Bhani's treatment?"

"Sounds like dismemberment for sure."

"Doesn't that bother you?"

"It does. I'll cry if you make me think about it for too long. Probably puke. But I have to take the long view. If receiving Bhani's treatment just isn't feasible, then I'm okay with giving up my leg."

"The war veteran analogy," said Edna sourly.

"It's a good one."

"What if the one-legged war veteran had also contracted malaria overseas, but refused treatment? Wouldn't be a very smart vet, would he? Because you're still going to die, Brian, even with the amputation."

Dad wandered out of the shop, looking for me. "Hey, there's Dad—"

"Don't look away from me!" Edna grabbed my jaw and adjusted the alignment of my head to ensure she had my full attention. "Chemo patients die! Chemo won't cure you! Do you understand that?"

I removed her hand. "I'm not going to die," I said without any hint of humor. "We'll talk about this later."

Dad joined us, giving no indication whether his angle of approach had permitted a view of our low-key physical exchange. "I thought you left without me," he said.

"I wanted to walk Edna to her Talon."

Dad gazed at the Talon. "I always did like the look of these cars."

"I want to convince your son to let Dr. Bhani cure him," said Edna.

"I thought that's what you were going to do," said Dad.

"I am," I said. "But I'm not going to do it on an Indian reservation."

"I don't blame you."

"I'm afraid he doesn't have any choice," said Edna.

"The hospital here is afraid of more of their patients dying from Bhani's treatment," I explained to Dad. "Their insurance company probably won't let them. I figure there's somewhere else we could go."

"Except you'll be dead by the time we can arrange it," said Edna. "Mr. Lawson, three-fourths of Dr. Bhani's patients have a favorable response. Ninety percent of those people are cancer-free after three years."

"I already gave Dad the stats. I read the same article. When I was snooping through your files."

Dad thought this was funny. Edna showed no reaction. "Dr. Bhani's success rate is night and day compared to chemo," she stated. "After taking chemo, less than ten percent of patients are cancer-free seven years later."

"Bhani's success rates are self-reported," I countered. "When they did an independent study, his method was no better than chemo."

Edna clenched her lips. "For one thing, the doctors in charge of the study didn't administer the right dosage level of his toxins. They were afraid to give patients a high dose of the bacteria. And they were also giving them chemo and radiation at the same time. Dr. Bhani pleaded with them not to do it."

"Bhani is right," I said, "and every other doctor and researcher is wrong."

"I'm giving you the reasons why they're wrong," Edna said sharply.

"I know. But it's a little strange."

"He's not the only one doing this," said Edna. "Other researchers are having good results with similar treatments. But it's too radical for most doctors."

"They haven't invented the approach that's too radical for Brian," said Dad. That was a little over the top, but I let it stand.

Edna patted my cheek, a firm love-tap to suggest the earlier contact was likewise. "Then Brian needs to put his money where his mouth is," she said.

"It's not that Bhani's Poisons are too radical for me."

"Toxins," said Edna. "Not poisons."

"It's that I'm afraid of Indians."

"They make me nervous too," said Dad.

Edna smiled. She left me to put an arm around Dad. "Now I know I picked the right family."

"It's a pretty good family," Dad agreed, shifting nervously under Edna's arm, scent and presence.

She gave each of us a nice kiss and climbed in her Talon. "I'm going to get your treatment set up in the next few days."

I pretended I hadn't heard this. "We'll see you at the house later?"

Edna pretended not to have heard this. "Goodbye Mr. Lawson."

"Call me Pete," said Dad as she pulled away. We walked back across the street. Dad said to me, "She's a strong-willed woman, huh?"

"You think so? I'll have to let you see video of her basketball days."

"She was pretty tough?"

"She's a killer, pop."

Abort

I can't spring this on you any faster than it was sprung on me. I woke six days ago with a lump in my crotch, in the hollow between my balls and my thigh. I touched it as soon as I came to, like my hand had been waiting for me to wake up, watching for my eyes to open, and then going straight to the lump. It's why my pants had been so uncomfortable. It's another tumor.

Each day it's grown bigger. Now I'd call it tennis ball size. I don't want to walk, for the physical pain and much worse the psychic terror of bursting or dislodging it. Don't ask me why this is what terrorizes me. Maybe it's because I don't truly comprehend how cancer works. The tumors just sit there and kill me. I'm so revolted and horrified to have them inside me. I can't believe I'm allowing them to sit there, and do whatever they want.

Three days ago, a lump formed in my lower back. On Wednesday it was a tightness, Thursday a thickness, Friday a lump. Now it's bigger too. Dr. Bonilla thinks it's pressing on my stomach, because now it hurts to eat. It hurts like unbelievable hell to swallow, and it's excruciating when food reaches my stomach. I haven't eaten solid food for two days.

My shin and my knee and my crotch ache and ache and ache. Maybe I can find a position that pleases one, but not all three.

This is the end. Each stage in the cancer's progression over the past few months must have been preparing me, because the sickening fear of death is no longer with me. Maybe it's the pain—I can't catch a breath big enough to relax long enough to worry. It's hitting me so hard and so fast, I only picture one thought over and over. Misery.

I'm in Edna's house, her bed. When Dr. Bonilla was here yesterday and Edna stepped out of the room, I told him I was ready for the amputation. Partly I just wanted to be anesthetized against the pain.

Bonilla knelt beside the bed. I smelled my own stink, my rancid breath and sour body reflecting off his freshness. He put his hand on my stomach and pushed around gently while telling me that I was probably too weak to handle the surgery. My cancer is spreading too fast for the amputation to do any good, he said. He said "not now" to the surgery, when he meant "not any longer."

He ratcheted up the pain meds. I don't think they've reduced the pain, I think I just don't care as much now. Still that one word, when Edna asks me how I'm feeling, and when I ask myself the same question. Misery.

Edna spent time in here this morning, talking about the new shop. My head throbbed when I tried to consider what she was saying. I couldn't do any more than listen. She hasn't mentioned marriage again.

Groundbreaking took place at a small ceremony involving only the college administration and a few special invitees, including the Jamestown College music director and his senior leaders singing chorals. The College's music program is nationally recognized. Edna and the administration want to discourage the perception that the shop will be a jock hangout.

They've poured the foundation. The skeletal structure will be up in a week. Edna and Rick are debating whether customers should queue from the right or the left when they enter the store. I'm sure it's a great question. Edna is conducting evening training sessions for new employees, after-hours at my shop. She started them Thursday. She's not asking Charlotte to assist her. Charlotte was in to see me yesterday, but she didn't bring it up.

"Tell me about the shop," I had croaked to her. The scans on Wednesday didn't show it, but I know I have a tumor growing in my throat too.

Charlotte sat there, swallowing.

"You're terrible at one-sided conversations," I told her. In normal circumstances she's great at them. She can go for an hour on nothing but nods and mm-hm's. She just couldn't do it with me in Edna's bed looking like a corpse. She cussed some, cried some, and hugged me goodbye. She left behind flowers and a giant get-well card from all my employees and regular customers.

Edna pokes her head in. "Are you up for company?" Sure. In walks Kenny and Laurie, Steve and Melissa, Tim, Caitlyn, Jerry and Amber.

"Looking forward to having you back on your feet," says Steve. Pretty stupid fucking thing to say, I suppose, but I tell him I appreciate it.

"You're looking pretty good," says Melissa, topping her husband. She wiggles my big toe under the sheet. She's a sweetheart.

"Thanks," I rasp.

"The shop's not the same without you down there," says Tim.

There's a long pause, everyone struggling to come up with something uplifting. This is perfect conversational rhythm for Jerry. "You're losing customers like crazy," he jokes with a sad smile. "You better get back down there."

"I will, homey."

"I see they broke ground on your new place," says Kenny. "When will you open?"

Edna tells him. She has the McEwens on task, on time, on budget. Everyone discusses the new shop for awhile. I do nothing more than nod at the appropriate times, and it still wears me out. Edna sees it. "I'd like Brian to get some rest now, if you all don't mind."

I get a knuckle-knock from Jerry, a quick hug from Amber, another toe wiggle from Melissa, and waves from everyone else. I'd be afraid to get too close to me, too.

Edna comes back in after they've gone, with a fresh glass of water and a hot cup of tea. "God-dammit, I can't get ahold of that sonofabitch," she rages, referring to Dr. Bhani. "I had to talk to Andrea again. I don't know why he didn't fire that bitch after I told him about her scheme to scare you away," she rants. "She's worthless. She's not sure where Bhani is. Sounds like he caught wind of a JAMA article coming out, that doesn't sound favorable. Here, drink this, it might help your throat."

"I hate tea."

"Drink it."

"Okay." The tea hurts like everything else I pour down there. Drinking is no longer accompanied by mental pictures of the coffee or Mountain Dew or water. Now it's silver razor blades.

"Do you want to take a walk with me? It's beautiful outside."

"Maybe later."

"I'll be gone most of the evening," says Edna. "We have a construction progress meeting. I really wish you could be there." She sounds sincere, but she really doesn't need me there, sick or healthy.

"You have it under control," I whisper. I don't want to talk anymore.

And so Edna leaves me alone, and I do my best to sleep. I thrash in slow motion for a long time.

"I'll go to Fort Yates," I say when it's dark, to an empty house. "I'll go to the rez."

I'M IN A LAZY FETAL POSITION with the sheet knotted around my good leg, face down into the mattress but no drool pooled, mouth so dry I can't wet my tongue to speak, to say "Fort Yates" when Edna kisses my cheek. She undresses in the dark, down to nothing, a beautiful silhouette to go along with the perfume lingering on my cheek. She pulls on a long sleeping shirt and leaves the room, and now I can't tell if it's perfume or cologne I'm smelling.

TWO DAYS LATER. I'm having a good period, the painkillers doing the trick. It's possible the tumors are doing the trick—all three are bigger, with what seems to be a new one in my armpit. I imagine that at some point the brain gets tired of receiving pain signals, sticks its fingers in its ears and says la-la-la-la-la real loud. It's giving me a window of opportunity to concentrate, so I call the shop. "It's Brian. Brian Lawson. The owner of that coffeeshop."

"I know," says Dana. "Hi Brian."

"I'm calling to see how things are going down there."

"Here, I'll let you talk to Charlotte."

Dana couldn't wait to get off the phone. Now I'm feeling the same way. I try to think of a reason for my call other than to tell Charlotte I'm dying.

"Hi Brian."

"Hey." I like to put the emphasis on the last syllable.

"Things are fine here," says Charlotte. "Everyone's asking how you're doing. I think Edna is telling people you're too sick for visitors."

"It's probably true. I like the sound of the espresso machine running and people talking in the background. Sounds busy."

"It's not too bad. For as hot as it's been, business has been okay."

"I was thinking about our bean inventory, and how the checking account is probably pretty low."

"Kenny increased our credit limit. I didn't even ask him."

"Wow. I didn't know he still cared. Normal price for his drinks from now on. Oh yeah, some credit card company with no business acumen sent me another card we can max out, too."

"Okay. Should I…do you want me to stop by and get it?"

"I'll have Edna drop it off."

Charlotte tells Dana to take the till. I can tell she's walking to the office, for privacy. "So…when do you think you'll be back?"

A knot of sadness clogs my throat. "I don't know how to answer that," I finally say. She has almost asked if I'm dying. I've almost told her. "Edna's trying to get a treatment scheduled for me down at Fort Yates."

"That's good. Is it that same treatment you were talking about when you made your big announcements? I wasn't sure you were going to do it."

"Same one. Edna's having trouble setting it up."

"She's been in here a couple times lately. We've been trying to figure out how much coffee she'll need for her first week."

"Probably twice our average, to be safe."

"That's what we thought." Charlotte has shifted to business mode. It's a good thing I called, she needs me, to make a few decisions. "Do you mind if I ask Craig to come in after hours and roast?"

"That's a good idea." All of a sudden it's difficult to focus again. I feel like my blood pressure and temperature suddenly plummeted. "Let him know that with two shops, you'll probably need a full-time roaster in the near future."

"Yeah but, so will that spic."

"He'll be out of business soon."

"Good. I hate him."

"Me too." I can conjure up no such feeling. "You like working with Edna?"

"Sure."

"Make yourself indispensable," I tell her. "I have a list started on my desk, with all the things she'll need to think about in the couple weeks before and after she opens. You should finish it and make it your own, and take it to her."

"Okay." Long pause while Charlotte fights her emotions. "You don't plan on coming back any time soon, do you?"

"Not soon. I told Edna you're a smart, organized, hardworking person."

"You told her I'm smart?"

"Aren't you?"

"Well, sometimes."

"You're smarter than me, that's all I know for sure. You should aim for being Edna's personal business manager. She's going to have a lot of irons in the fire, knowing her."

"Yeah?" Charlotte gets excited. "You think I could do it, with no degree?"

"Definitely. It wouldn't hurt for you to start taking classes, though."

"At JC? Do you know what tuition is there?"

"I'll talk to Edna. I'll bet she could get you enrolled for free."

"No way. You think so? It wouldn't have to be free."

"Maybe Edna could create the Edna Applejack Scholarship program for James River Valley Coffee employees." Or the Brian Lawson Memorial Scholarship. "Make you the first full-ride recipient."

"God would that be wonderful." Weary cynicism won't let her be too hopeful.

I wish I had treated Charlotte better. If it's the last thing I do, I'd like to accomplish this much for her. "I'll see what I can do. Anything else? Otherwise I think I'll stop talking for awhile."

"That's it. There's nothing to worry about down here. Get better, okay? Is your dad still there?"

"No. But he and Mom are flying here Friday."

"Both of them. Oh. That's good. Everybody says hi. And we want to come see you, as soon as you're ready."

"I'll let you know. Talk to you later."

Edna steps into the bedroom. "Strong enough for a visitor?"

My head is swimming and my lips are numb. I feel like I'm sinking deeper into the mattress. It's a comfortable feeling, actually. "Okay."

Edna stands aside and in walks Andrea. Half Edna's height. Homely in comparison. Maybe it's the sneer. "God," says Andrea.

"That bad?" I ask.

"It's not good," she says, maintaining the haughty look until her upper lip trembles. "It's not good. God." She forces herself to my bedside. "How are you feeling?" After resting her hand on the blanket, she folds her arms. "Not good, I suppose."

"This has been a helluva week."

"Yeah, well…. I haven't seen you for awhile."

"How's work?"

Edna interrupts. "I wanted Andrea to see you. I want her to understand we need to move forward with Dr. Bhani's treatment. Soon."

"Sooner is better," I agree. I imagine that Edna picked Andrea up and carried her here, complaining all the way. "I'm probably down to my last option."

"Okay," says Andrea without sounding like she's agreeing to anything. Edna leaves, closing the door behind her. "So." The knowing, sarcastic touch returns. "How are you?"

"Dying."

"Really."

"Want to see?" I pull the blankets aside to expose my leg. Andrea only glances. "I won't show you my groin. Or my back. Or my armpit."

She nods, looking at the headboard. "I'm sorry, okay? I'm sorry."

"It's okay."

Andrea uses the length of her finger to wipe away her tears, trying not to smudge her mascara. "No it's not. We should have got you in."

"You tried to convince me, for the first few months."

"Yes I did. So why didn't you tell me things are getting so much worse?"

"It's been all of a sudden."

"Mm." Andrea does a good job keeping her composure. "I'll do what I can. Dr. Bhani's research assistant is in town for a few days. His name is Dr. Sawyer. He's great. Maybe he can do it. Dr. Bhani has been going crazy defending himself from the state and federal regulators. I guess I have been too, pulling his results for everyone, trying to prove what they don't want to hear. I don't get it at all. He's cured so many people."

"Are they cures, or a postponement of the inevitable?"

"Whatever you want to call it," says Andrea. "He has patients who have been cancer-free for years. That's a lot better than anything else out there."

"Then I appreciate anything you can do for me."

"I'll try." Andrea brightens. "I have some news. I probably won't be around to see you recuperate. Rick and I are moving back to Colorado."

"Together?"

"We're going to get married again. This weekend. We're not going to tell anybody until it's done. I guess he hasn't been happy since we divorced. His dad wants Joshua to take a bigger role in the business. That way Rick can start a company in Denver, the way we planned before his brother got sick."

"Congratulations."

"Since you weren't available."

"Right."

She puts her hand where my arm is under the blanket. "I'm glad I got to know you." A goodbye on two levels.

"Anything you can do for me before you leave, I'd really appreciate it."

"Okay. Bye." Andrea crawls halfway onto the bed to kiss me on the forehead, then leaves. I wait for Edna to come back in. I should get up and go tell her the news, such juicy gossip, but I haven't felt this comfortable and pain-free in quite awhile. I think I'll sleep.

"GET UP BRIAN. WE'RE GOING TO FORT YATES."

Edna is at her dresser pulling out underwear, a tanktop, shorts, jeans. "We'll have to spend a couple days at least, so pack accordingly."

"You got it scheduled? What time is it?"

"Andrea made it happen." Now she's in the closet, gathering more clothes. "We're driving there now with Dr. Bhani's assistant. Dr. Bhani is going to fly into Bismarck and meet us there."

"Wow. Okay. I'm so freaking tired."

"I guess you'll get moving if you want to live."

It's a major debate. A car ride sounds awful. Lying in bed, wonderful. Not sure I can sit up.

I wrench myself out of bed and shuffle to the can. I won't describe what my dick feels like, what peeing is all about now, but it makes me whimper.

Edna has left the bedroom. I stand staring at my clothes; I own the right half of Edna's dresser. I take a few items out; put a couple back in; take out a few more, some of them for the second time. Shove them in a duffel bag Edna left on the bed for me. I really have no idea what I grabbed—some blue stuff, a yellow...something else, and a hat?

Edna's in the doorway. "Ready? I asked Bobby Guldseth and Rick to come with us."

"Why?"

"Extra security. The rez isn't known for law and order. Which is why we're going there, of course."

"I'd rather bring Jerry then."

Edna mulls it over. "Okay. I can ask one of them to stay behind."

"Both. One Jerry is all we need." I don't want Bobby or Rick along. Bobby Guldseth tonguing Edna's ear to help her through the grief, that's not going to be the last thing I see before I die. And Rick...he's probably married and living in Colorado by now. What day is it?

"Fine," says Edna. "Call Jerry. Right now, Brian. We need to get going."

I SIT SIDEWAYS IN THE Talon's passenger seat, so I don't put pressure on the tumor in my back. Every bump and shimmy makes me moan. Every muscle in my body feels torn, the ruptured fibers pushing their way through my skin. My gut is on fire, like I've been swallowing batteries and chasing them with

Easy-Off oven cleaner. I'm sweating from the exertion, of not dying.

"You okay?" Edna asks as we swing into the hospital parking lot.

"I just want to get to Fort Yates."

"It's at least two hours away. And we have to stop here first." She senses my reluctance. "We'll get you something stronger for the pain."

"Sleeping pills would be great. A bear tranquilizer, if they have one."

Edna parks in a visitor space. "I'll wait in the car," I say.

"Marvcus wants you to come down to the lab," says Edna. I stare blankly. "Marvcus is Dr. Bhani's assistant. Dr. Sawyer."

"Why do I have to come? Do you know why? Go ask him, I'll wait here."

Edna comes around to my side of the car, opens my door, holds out her hand. "You can do it." I rally the energy and commit to reaching the front entrance. Our progress is slow. Then Edna redirects me, and making the course correction, overcoming the inertia, is overwhelming. I stop until the shaking in my leg subsides. The pace is again Slow.

An orderly is waiting at a side door. He's about my age, stocky with a shaved bullet head. He stares lovingly at Edna.

"Hi Curtis. This is Brian."

"Hey," says Curtis without looking at me. "Dr. Sawyer is waiting for you. I found an exam room you can use."

"We don't have to go to the basement?" I ask.

"Dr. Bhani was evicted," says Edna.

"Bad press," says Curtis. We follow him way too fast down the hall.

"It's not far I hope. It's not upstairs I hope."

"Brian's not feeling too well," Edna explains.

"Dying, really," I clarify.

"Hence Dr. Sawyer," says Curtis. He looks where he's going only often enough to avoid dinner carts and wheelchairs and slow-moving patients, otherwise trying to maintain eye contact with Edna. "So have you been playing any hoops since, you know, lately?"

"No time for basketball," says Edna. "Brian and I are starting a coffeeshop on campus. You'll have to come."

"I'm not a coffee drinker. Will you have anything else? Like fountain drinks or sandwiches or smoothies?"

"No," I say.

"I'll still come," Curtis tells Edna. "Here we are." They stand aside so I can go in first. I nod my thanks to Curtis. "Some of us get together to play ball every Sunday night at the high school," he says quietly to Edna. "If you want to come down, around seven, that would be cool. I know Grimke, the girls' head coach," he name-drops.

A petite man in a starched gray button shirt and slacks waves me forward.

"Come on in. You're Brian, I'm betting. I'm Dr. Sawyer." He shakes my hand and beckons me to the exam table. He would be good looking except for his stature. Unfortunately there is a size threshold men have to exceed in order to be attractive. I feel bad for him. I mean, he is damned handsome, Rob Lowe-like. But no woman is going to want a mini Rob Lowe.

I climb up on the paper sheet. "I have to warn you, I have a bad habit of throwing up in exam rooms."

"If you blow chunks, we'll just call Curtis back," says Dr. Sawyer.

"There won't be any chunks," I tell him.

Edna strides in. "Marvcus."

"The v is silent," says Dr. Sawyer. "You're Edna. Thanks," he dismisses Curtis, who is watching the movements of Edna's skirt. "We'll call you if Brian pukes." He shuts the door in Curtis's face, proving that boners don't make good door-stops. "Let's have a look at you." Dr. Sawyer helps me take off my shirt. "Edna, it's up to you if you want to stay."

"It's naughty," says Edna, "but I'm enjoying watching you undress him."

"Dr. Sawyer is aggressive but surprisingly gentle," I tell her, my pajama pants around my ankles.

"You have a lot of activity here," says Dr. Sawyer, poking and measuring my "activity", recording the data in a little black book. "I don't have access to your file, so I can't get a feel for the progression rate of your cancer."

"I'd call it fast. I'd call it fucking fast, if I wasn't afraid of offending you. Given that you're my last hope and all." Dr. Sawyer continues feeling me up, so I keep talking. "I didn't have the tumor on my back or the one between my legs a week or so ago. I'm pretty sure a new one's coming in my armpit."

Dr. Sawyer prods me there. "Definitely." He's a tiny, crisp-talking Rob Lowe. "So you're metastasizing rapidly. I understand the original diagnosis was Ewing's sarcoma. When was it made?"

"April eighth at eleven-forty-three a.m. Approximately."

"Other symptoms?"

"I feel like shit."

"Can you be more specific?"

"Really shitty. And exhausted, if I forgot to mention that."

"Brian has had a headache since yesterday," Edna reports. "He can't eat, because of pain in his throat and stomach. He's lost at least ten pounds in the past few days, on top of the thirty he says he lost over the last few months. He didn't want to get out of bed to come here, and then he didn't want to get out of the car in the parking lot."

"I'm going downhill fast."

"Fucking fast," says Dr. Sawyer. We stare at each other. He's pondering whether I'm worth the effort.

"Where's Dr. Bhani?" I ask.

"He'll be meeting us in Fort Yates."

"Oh yeah. Edna told me."

Dr. Sawyer moves in tight and pushes two fingers against the inside of my thigh. He nods rhythmically.

"How's this for you?" I ask Edna.

Edna smiles. "Not bad."

"We'll need an ambulance to transport Brian to Fort Yates," says Dr. Sawyer, stepping back and looking me over. "I don't want to take any chances. Your vitals aren't great."

I'm not upset to hear this. More vindicated—I'm a little p.o.'d at Edna for dragging me out of bed.

"Maybe we should talk outside," says Edna to Dr. Sawyer.

"He's not telling me anything I don't already know," I tell her. "There's really not much you can do at this point, is there Doc?"

"Sure there is. But I am concerned about the stress of the trip."

"My mom and dad are flying here Friday. I don't want to go to Fort Yates unless you're sure we can be back by tomorrow afternoon. At the latest."

Edna frowns at me. "Brian..." She turns to Dr. Sawyer. "He's been saying things like that today. I feel like he's suddenly giving up."

"It happens to some people," says Dr. Sawyer.

Not me, I'm a warrior, I say to myself, at the same time thinking how beautiful it would be to take a long, pain-free nap in Edna's bed. Or here on the exam table.

Pain is a great motivator, I remind myself. No pain no gain. Pain means I'm alive. And if nothing else, I gotta remember that pain is something that can be controlled. It's not real, it's just the brain's representation of the information it's receiving from the body. An information representation, that's all pain is.

Feels like my bones are liquefying. A moan escapes my lips, turns into a sob. "I'm really hurting..."

"We'll see if we can get you something additional for the pain," says Dr. Sawyer. He pulls out his cellphone, talking to Edna while he pushes buttons. "Any way we can rustle up an ambulance?"

"Curtis will do it for me," says Edna.

"Tell him to make it snappy. I'm going to update Dr. Bhani."

I should clothe my hideous body, but the best I can do is use my shirt like a blanket and curl up on my side on the table.

I HAVE ONLY A VAGUE UNDERSTANDING that we're leaving...

...semi-conscious glimpses of a gurney and the back of an ambulance...

...turning corners at high speed with Edna's hand on me. An occasional bump in the road.

"EDNA." MY VOICE rattles through the dried-out flesh inside my mouth and the corridor of pus-spewing sores that is my throat. "Where are we?"

"Halfway there," says Edna, looking down on me. She's sitting on a folding chair. I'm lying on a mattress on the floor. Edna steadies an IV bag lurching over my head on a flimsy stand. An oxygen tank is bungeed to the wall, clanking metal on metal.

"This is a horseshit ambulance."

"It's your van," says Edna, distracted, listening to Dr. Sawyer, on the phone behind me. Edna doesn't seem to like what she's hearing. She makes an effort to give me her full attention. "We couldn't get an ambulance. Curtis went to the trouble to outfit your van for us."

"That Curtis is all right," I whisper.

Edna presses her lips to my forehead and forgets them there while eavesdropping on Dr. Sawyer. Fine by me. "Jerry's here," she tells me. "He's up front with Curtis."

"They should hit it off pretty well, huh?" I gently clear my throat, bringing up bloody pus to wet my mouth. "What's up with the doc?"

"I'm here, Brian." Dr. Sawyer scoots a folding chair into view and pockets his phone.

"Hey doc. I feel really dehydrated."

"We have an IV going, so you'll be okay."

"Could I just drink it instead?"

Dr. Sawyer pats my chest. "We have some powerful painkillers mixed in. You wouldn't like the taste. It might be best if you napped a while more."

"Sounds like a plan. How's Dr. Bhani?"

"That's a great question," says Edna, scowling.

Dr. Sawyer is uncomfortable. "That was him. A few things happened while you slept," he tells me. "I'm going to handle your treatment. No big deal. I've done a couple myself, and assisted on many more. It's not a complicated procedure, as you'll see. So not to worry."

Edna stares at Dr. Sawyer so fiercely the hairs on his temple curl. I prop myself up on an elbow. "What happened?"

"Dr. Bhani got cold feet," Edna alleges, daring Dr. Sawyer to dispute it.

"Considering everything he's been through, that's not fair," says Dr. Sawyer. "You have to understand the pressure Dr. Bhani is getting from all sides."

"And that's why he needs a successful treatment," Edna argues, voice rising. "Brian is perfect timing."

"Dr. Bhani doesn't see it that way. But," Dr. Sawyer cuts off Edna's protest, "I'm going to be honest with you. I'm a little surprised at his decision."

"A *little* surprised?" says Edna. "You sounded floored on the phone. I could hear both sides of the argument."

"There was yelling?" I ask.

"Dr. Bhani yelled," Edna reports, "and Marvcus took it."

"Dr. Bhani doesn't want me to have his treatment, huh?"

Dr. Sawyer grimaces. "We'll be okay." He turns away from Edna, trying to keep this between the two of us. "Dr. Bhani has hit upon an incredible cure. But he's feeling a little picked on. Most of the patients he receives, especially lately, are very far along."

"Their cancer, you mean."

Dr. Sawyer nods. "And they've already been subjected to months, or years, of chemotherapy and radiation. Their immune systems are compromised. Sounds like you've gone through a fair amount of chemotherapy."

Seeing as how I'm just snapping out of a dreamlike haze, I have no real ability to read the situation or gauge Dr. Sawyer's mindset. But I'd say he's on the fence, considering calling it off. Could be wrong, maybe it's solely Edna's agitation creating tension. She seems ready to hijack my van and put a gun to the doc's head and demand treatment for me.

I do know for certain-sure that I want the treatment. In my stupor I think I dreamed about dying. It left a very unpleasant sensation in my brain. "I haven't had any treatments for a month," I tell him. "They wanted to put me through another round of chemo, but I wouldn't let them."

"That's to your benefit," says Dr. Sawyer. Responding to my desperation, he scoots closer. "You have to understand I owe everything to Dr. Bhani. He's brilliant, and one of the bravest researchers out there. Few people have the strength and conviction to persevere with everyone aligned against them. But unfortunately I think he's been reduced to calculating the impact of any given treatment on his career. He's afraid to make a mistake with you."

Now I see it in his eyes. Marvcus is going to save me. "You're not afraid."

"To be fair," says Marvcus, "I have nothing to lose. I'm still free to operate the way Dr. Bhani used to. I can make every decision based on what's best for the patient."

"And this treatment is definitely the best thing for me?"

"Without a doubt. Dr. Bhani hasn't made you a convert?"

"I tried my best to convince Brian," says Edna.

"It sounds a little crazy, you have to admit."

"The concept of germ-inspired healing isn't out of the blue," says Marvcus. "The healing power of pus has been noted and exploited since the 1800s. Way back when," he slows his cadence, shifting from clinician to lecturer, "doctors noticed that pus around a wound—an infection, in other words, speeds the healing, and amazingly enough even bestows future immunity. Before medicine became the structured, regulated business it is today, doctors were known to infect their patients with a deadly disease in order to cure them of a deadlier one. They used malaria and gangrene to cure cancer. And syphilis to keep it from coming back."

"That one might be a toss-up," I say.

Marvcus flashes a tight smile. "If a patient had an open wound or sore, doctors would deliberately soil the dressing. Make sure it was thick with infectious agents."

I'm skeptical. "That was standard treatment back then?"

"Just the radicals. It's fascinating the lengths they went to, without a clear understanding of what causes diseases or how the immune system works."

"Now we understand it all, but Dr. Bhani is using the same old methods."

"There's still a lot we don't understand. And our methods are much more sophisticated now," says Marvcus a little defensively. "Dr. Bhani's toxins are finely tuned to maximize the immune system response—both non-specific and specific, antigen- and T-cell-based—without exposing you to any risk of infectious disease."

"That sounds good in the marketing literature anyway."

"Only because it's true."

I won't argue any more with Marvcus. Since he has officially become my last resort and all. Not too long ago I was certain I had long since passed the point of no return. Now I'm getting excited about the possibility of living some more. Amazing what good drugs can do for your mood. "Hey, I remember Andrea requesting a sample of the original tumor that they removed from my tibia. She said Dr. Bhani wanted to make a personalized vaccine for me."

Marvcus wrinkles his nose. "That was for show. Cancer vaccines are all the rage, so Dr. Bhani throws one in to placate the medical review boards."

"So you didn't bring my personal vaccine."

"Nope."

"Okay. No big deal."

Marvcus slaps his knees and rises, like he's going somewhere. Sorry doc, there aren't any other patients in the van for you to run to. "I wonder how much longer until we get there," he muses. "I'm going to call the hospital and make sure they're ready for us."

"With all this equipment and supplies, it doesn't look like you even need the Injun hospital." The monitors jouncing against the walls are dark, but presumably could leap into service if necessary.

"The hospital will be better equipped." Marvcus touches the wall to steady himself through the van's arrhythmic swaying; takes a look at his hand and wipes it on his pants. "And sterile. This was just a contingency."

"In case I start dying on the way there."

"In case we get evicted before you're ready to travel. I don't know if anyone's told you"—Marvcus smiles pitilessly—"but you're going to be a very sick man, real soon."

"So I've read." Now I'm afraid of violent gut-wrenching illness. I'm enjoying my current lack of pain. I really, really want to get this over with. One way or the other.

No, only one way. I want to live. At any cost. I like bumping along a choppy state road, lurching around when Curtis floors it into the passing lane. I like talking to people and making them laugh. I like Edna. Maybe I really like her. She's bizarre like a movie star, but I could be a movie star's man. Mom and Dad are showing up soon. I love sitting around and shooting the shit with them. I love making coffee for people, making them happy. There would be a hole in the world if I was gone—mostly a hole in my own life, admittedly, but in other people's too.

And I want to golf more. Jerry's been golfing his whole life, but I know I can beat him eventually.

Wow do I like the concept of *eventually*. Eventually, with all its anticipation; and all the life that comes between now and then. I love eventually.

Marvcus fiddles with his cellphone. Looks at me and Edna. Stops pushing buttons. Makes a sour face. "In the interest of full disclosure, and to give you more insight into Dr. Bhani's state of mind, you should know that the JAMA editorial came out today. It's not favorable. It's going to make it impossible for Dr. Bhani to get funding, or lab space."

"What did it say?" Edna demands.

"I happen to have a copy." Marvcus pulls out a faxed page from his briefcase and hands it to Edna. "Pleasant reading."

I stare at the corrugated ceiling. "Read me excerpts."

It takes Edna time to comply. Her teeth grind until she reads aloud. "'Now that so many eminent researchers have put Bhani's Toxins to the test, we can finally, unequivocally pronounce judgment on this extreme approach that many consider a direct violation of the Hippocratic oath, to first do no harm. The Toxins do not work. They are just that—toxins. Not a single case demonstrates enough improvement to warrant further pursuit of Dr. Khaled Bhani's Frankenstein vision. To harness the agents of Death itself in pursuit of Life…this sort of scientific madness we can do without.'"

"That's probably enough," says Marvcus, reaching for the paper.

Edna rebuffs him. "'Dr. Bhani is only the latest in a rash of borderline charlatans','" she continues, not to frighten me I'm sure, but because she's determined to build up a big head of steam, "'pushing pseudo-science backed only by laymen's commonsense and poetic sales pitches. These shrewd men and women understand the power of advertising and the eager supply of capital to be thrown at the next miracle cure. Publicity-mongers like Dr. Bhani prey on the fervent hopes of terminal patients and their loved ones, and then climb in bed with savvy stock marketeers expert in the game of exploiting investment bubbles. We cannot too strongly implore patients searching desperately for a cure—and individual investors looking for the next big thing—to stop looking in Dr. Bhani's direction."

Edna lets the paper drift to the floor. Thank goodness Marvcus doesn't try to pick it up, Edna would stomp on his delicate fingers.

"Congratulations on being Dr. Bhani's last patient," says Marvcus. The van lurches and he tumbles out of his chair. We bump heads and sort-of kiss. I look past his shoulder to see Edna's beautiful calf, her foot planted against the wall to steady herself. What body control. "For crying out loud," Marvcus complains as he crawls off me. "What are they doing up there?"

I rap on the wall and holler, "Lay off the hard drinking up there!" More of a hoarse whisper, really.

Marvcus apologizes for the mushy head-butt. I rub my forehead. "What's one more cancer hot spot?"

Edna crouches in the back corner beside a cabinet on wheels, her head bowed. Marvcus returns to his chair. "I'm sorry you had to hear that. But let me assure you—"

"Nothing I haven't heard before," I tell him, thinking of the McEwens. "I've seen proof that the toxins work. I figure if I can survive the immune response, I'm home free. It's your state of mind I'm worried about. Still willing to go through with this?"

"I'm in the business of saving lives," says Marvcus, "not pleasing the ignorant masses."

I like this little man.

His cell rings. "There's the hospital... Hello, Dr. Sawyer speaking. ...yes...yes—yes I saw it. ...yes. ...uh-huh. We're almost there...uh-huh....yes. ...yes. ...okay." He snaps his phone shut and disconnects the call. "Fort Yates read the JAMA editorial."

"I wouldn't have guessed they had a subscription," I say.

"They're turning us away," says Marvcus. "We lost our hospital."

Edna screeches and starts pounding the back door. We grind to a stop on the graveled roadside. Marvcus tips over, this time in the other direction. Fast-moving feet crunch outside, and the back doors open. Curtis jumps in and gives me the once-over. "You okay?"

"I'm good. Hey Jerry."

Jerry hovers in the doorway. "Brian. How are you?"

"Been better I suppose. I really appreciate you coming. Looks like our trip is being cancelled, though."

"The goddamn reservation won't take us!" Edna yells.

"We lost our reservation reservation," I say.

"It's not funny!" Edna yells at me. "It's not fucking funny! Who do these punks at the Journal of Medicine think they are?" This is directed more at Marvcus. "They're messing with people's lives! How dare they? God dammit!" She hurdles Jerry and bounds down into the ditch to throw curses at the amber field of grain waving in the wind. No one else says a word. She returns to lean against the bumper, swearing under her breath and resting her forehead on the van's rubber floor runner.

Curtis looks to Marvcus for direction. Jerry stares at me. He actually speaks first. "You look pretty relaxed, considering."

Marvcus and Curtis look at me. Edna lifts her head, grooves pressed into her forehead. "Brian, I'm sorry. I don't know what to do."

It's obvious to me. "We go back to your place, and Marvcus here gives me the treatment."

Marvcus harrumphs. "That's just not going to be possible."

"Oh you're going to give me the toxins alright. Curtis, turn this mother around."

Jerry claps his hands. "Let's move."

NOW WE'RE HUMMING ALONG in the opposite direction, back home. "The shop's been running smooth the past few days," Jerry reports. He gave up his front seat to Marvcus, who jammed his wrist on his last tumble and was looking a little pale.

"Charlotte is good."

Jerry spends some time on his next statement. "She misses you." He puts his hand on my stomach, preparing to say something nice and comforting. Nothing comes out of his mouth, his hand remains on my stomach, and it's nice and comforting.

We ride like this for a few minutes. I use Jerry's ample biceps for leverage to shift onto my side, to take pressure off my aching back. The pressure doesn't change one bit. If I was being more accurate in my descriptions, I'd call it excruciating pain. The IV drip is no longer doing the trick. It's time to jab a straw into a major artery and empty that bag. "By the way," I say, "did you hear Andrea and Rick are back together?"

Jerry stares at me, expressionless. Maybe this is old news. I'm a little fuzzy on timelines at the moment. Maybe they're already remarried.

Edna rustles in the corner where she crouches. "What did you say?"

"Rick and Andrea are remarrying and moving back to Colorado."

"No they're not," Edna vetoes the idea.

"I'm just going by what Andrea told me."

Edna's feet slip out from under her, plopping her into a sitting position.

"I dated Andrea for awhile, you know."

"I'm aware of that," says Jerry.

"She's a bizarre human."

"We all thought the same thing about you," says Jerry.

"I can't imagine marrying her, to be honest."

"Rick must know something you don't," says Jerry. That's the kind of charitable assumption that gets a guy into heaven.

"It's the small woman syndrome," I inform him.

"What do you mean?"

"Men are compelled to take care of small women. We're hardwired to protect them." I'm waiting for Edna to join the debate, but she's slumped with her head hanging in her lap.

"I doubt their size is a factor," says Jerry.

"It's an irresistible compulsion. I felt it. It was hard to overcome. I still felt guilty for abandoning her. Until she told me about Rick."

"Certain women just have a hold over certain men," says Jerry. "It doesn't have anything to do with size."

"Size matters," I say. "You married a non-small woman. You can't judge."

"I'm telling Amber you don't think she's small."

"Don't do that."

Edna sits silent and crumpled while we banter. I realize now she's crying. I don't say anything, because Jerry is oblivious.

After a few minutes the crying stops. For the rest of the ride Edna rocks back and forth, knees tight to her chest, silent even when Jerry and I discuss the new campus coffeeshop. Edna is in full-out anguish, and it takes my plodding brain a while to come up with the obvious answer. Damn chemo.

I'M PLEASANTLY surprised. Marvcus was a busy beaver during the drive to Edna's house. A home-health crew is already loading their truck, having finished a quick sterilization of Edna's bedroom.

We enter Edna's expansive foyer. I'm the only one not carrying anything. "Smells hospital-fresh in here. I thought I was trying to catch an infection."

"Nope," says Marvcus, following Edna into the main floor guest bedroom, pointing Curtis where to set up the monitoring equipment. "We only want your immune system to *think* you have an infection. In the state you'll be in, a real infection could do damage—or at least distract from your immune system's real mission, destroying the cancer. By the way Edna, besides taking the liberty of having your bedroom disinfected, without your permission..." Marvcus stops talking when it's obvious Edna isn't paying attention.

"How did you know the address?" Jerry wants to know.

"The home health crew didn't need any direction. When I said Edna, they said 'Applejack? We'll be right over.'"

I take a seat on the bed. "They probably drive past this house a couple times a day. Hoping to catch a glimpse of Edna."

"I know I do," says Curtis.

Maybe he's hoping that remark scores points, but Edna is in her own world, absentmindedly shuffling the few items the cleanup crew left sitting on her dresser, a bag of cotton balls, a tissue box, a picture of Edna in her JC uniform flanked by her proud parents. She stares at herself in the mirror, becoming more distraught.

"I have a nurse showing up soon," says Marvcus. "Glenda's helped us out in the past. She had to fly in from Minneapolis, so we need to give her a little extra time. Edna, I hope you don't mind me taking over your house."

"You can have it," says Edna. She leaves the room. I watch Curtis's eyes follow her progress up the staircase.

Jerry and I exchange looks. "What do you make of that?" I ask him. He shrugs, no intention of going on record. I'm not so reluctant. "I think she has a thing for Rick McEwen. I don't doubt they've been meeting every night to discuss coffeeshop construction, like Edna claims. I'm just saying they adjourn each meeting with a kiss. A long wet one."

Marvcus ignores me, laying out syringes and needles and little bottles of what I assume are the toxins, on a white cloth on Edna's vanity on the other side of the bed. Curtis is all ears as he sets up the IV station left behind by the home health crew.

Jerry stares blankly at me, as if unaware I've already spoken. Finally, "How does that make you feel?"

"Either I'm feeling too shitty to care, or I'm going to be the perfect movie starlet's spouse. What am I going to do, throw a tantrum and lay down an ultimatum? 'Dammit Edna, no more men or we're through! Personally and professionally!' Probably not in my best interest. If I live through this treatment, I'll throw a hissy fit. Then we'll get back to planning our glorious nuptials."

"Keep your mouth shut and count you blessings, dog," says Curtis.

"I'm with you, dog."

"You are on the in*side*, Holmes. It's where we all long to be, dog."

"Doggie gotta lay down now." I'm trembling through a hot flash of gut-sizzling nausea. I do a half-ass job of propping Edna's pillows before collapsing into the soft comforter. My heart races; at the same time I can feel a pulse in my shin, beating slow and steady. The tumor is in great shape.

I can't remember whether it's today or tomorrow. I lay still, trying to reconstruct the day's, or days' events. How long were we in my van? "Are Mom and Dad here?"

Jerry blinks. "I thought you said they're coming Friday?"

"Yeah, that's right. Sorry." Nobody says anything for awhile. They all assume (correctly) that I'm losing my mind. "I'm really feeling like shit." I feel like crying about it, a mixture of extreme discomfort and hopelessness. The cancer is taking over my general operations. Taking me over and doing a horrible job running things. I'm trying to teach myself how to swallow, before I choke on the saliva pooling in my mouth. I should just spit it on the floor, because I think the cancer is now running the show in my stomach and there's no sense making its life any easier.

"Time for me to fly," says Curtis. "You're all ready to rumble, doc."

"Thanks for everything." Marvcus pats my foot. "As soon as Glenda gets here, we'll start."

"Okay. Where's…" Holy shit, I was going to ask for my mom again. "…uh, where's…Edna?"

"Still upstairs," says Curtis, gazing up at the ceiling. "Probably in her bedroom." He loses himself in thought for a moment, and then leaves.

WE WAIT. ME IN MISERY. I smack my lips, a horrible awful deathbed sound. "How long has it been? Maybe we should just do it."

"It's only been an hour," says Jerry, sitting beside me. "You okay?"

"I've been better. You know."

"I guess we could get this party started," says Marvcus, checking his watch, eyeballing my vital signs. "Okay, let's do it. Shit, didn't Curtis get the IV going? Crap. I guess…I guess I can do it."

"You're a doctor, right?" Jerry verifies.

"It's just been awhile," says Marvcus. "And tapping veins was never my strong suit." He hesitates, looking at my arm. It's covered by the sleeve of one of my all-time favorite shirts, an Arkansas Razorbacks jersey a friend sent me after his family moved to Fayetteville. I was never a Razorbacks fan, but I loved the shirt, up until my sophomore year when I grew out of it. "Glenda was going to bring a gown for you," says Marvcus.

"I can take this off." I do so. Jerry backs up, stricken by what he sees. "Hey, I'm sorry you have to be here for this. Why don't you go get something to eat, and we'll call you when it's over."

Jerry shakes his head. "I'm not going anywhere."

If Jerry was a painting, the doorway would an inadequate frame. "Thanks homey," I said. "I really appreciate it." Good friends are priceless; at crunch time, big friends are even better.

Marvcus keeps an ear cocked for Glenda's arrival while rubber-strapping my upper arm and doing eeny-meeny-miny-moe to select a vein. He punctures it. "Hope that wasn't too bad. I almost didn't make it through residency for botching these things." Marvcus adjusts the drip rate on my bag of juices.

"What's in there? Good drugs, I hope."

"Sorry. Saline. I want you lucid and all systems fully functional. We need you hydrated, because before too long you'll be bringing up a lot of liquid."

"You mean he'll be puking his guts out," Jerry confirms. "'Bringing up a lot of liquid', that's a good euphemism. I like that. I think I'll use it."

"When everybody asks you how this went, tell them I was bringing it. 'You should have seen it. Brian was bringing it for hours.' I'll come off sounding pretty good."

"I'll make you look good, don't worry." Jerry nods toward the front door. "There's our nurse."

A chill spreads across my back.

After everything I've gone through, this is it. I've held wildly varying opinions about Bhani's toxins. For the longest time it was a vague medical procedure possibly implicated in Brent McEwen's death. Even when I was diagnosed with cancer, I never seriously contemplated Bhani and his miracle bacteria, preferring what turned out to be the real sideshow barker, Bonilla and his chemo 'treatment', choosing to join him in his delusional world, content to be poisoned, feeling no need to consider any other option.

And then I had read Edna's research file, and Bhani's Toxins became a cruel farce, no different than chemotherapy, just another way to give patients unfounded peace of mind in the months before their death.

Only recently did I begin to see Bhani's invention as a cure, made more precious with every detractor and every roadblock the world has thrown up.

Now I suddenly don't know what to think. I'm scared of the toxins killing me. I'm scared they won't do a thing. I'm scared to get any sicker than I am.

"Hi everyone," says Glenda, short and stout with chopped blonde hair, gliding into the bedroom and immediately going to work. She unpacks supplies from her bag, including a gown. "Brian? It's a pleasure to meet you. Throw this on." She checks my IV drip as she talks, momentarily unhooking it to allow me to don the gown. "You have the dosage ready?" she asks Marvcus in a singsong undertone. "I'm going to wash up, and then we'll begin." To the bathroom with her, her own pump bottle of cleanser in hand.

"Can I leave my pj pants on? Edna cut them off special for this."

"You think maybe it's time to retire those bad boys?" Jerry wonders.

"At the very least they can be washed." My voice is small and airy, like I'm talking through a straw.

Glenda breezes back into the room. "The shorts are fine. Dr. Sawyer, have you scarified the sites yet?"

"I was hoping you'd do that," Marvcus practically begs her.

"No idea what scarifying is," I say, "and it sounds pretty painful."

"We just rough up the skin a bit," says Glenda. "It's the optimal way to apply the treatment. Don't you worry, honey." She pats my cheek. "We'll be through with this and have you fixed up in a jiffy."

And now I relax. I'm completely in Nurse Glenda's hands. I climb back into bed while Glenda and Marvcus plan their attack. "We'll inoculate into the original tumor and three additional lymph sites, behind the knee, the lower back, and the right armpit," says Marvcus. "Fifty cc's each, with another twenty-five-cc booster in five hours. And then we'll play it by ear."

Glenda pokes around below my knee. From his bundle of tools Marvcus hands her a cheese grater. "The scaryfier?" I ask.

"Scarifier," says Glenda. "We scuff the surface to get a clean interface with the solution. We'll give you a topical first, to numb the sites."

"Doctor Sawyer said Brian has been a bad patient and doesn't deserve any anesthetic," says Jerry.

"Shut up, Jerry," I tell him. Glenda has already swabbed and stabbed my shin, keeps stabbing it with an anesthetic needle projecting from a paper packet. "You just let Nurse Glenda do what she thinks is best."

"That's good advice," says Marvcus, reduced to a spectator role, craning his neck to see. Glenda taps my arm and I raise it, and she swabs at my pit hair before deciding to grab a scissor and a razor. After cleaning out the under-growth she repeatedly stabs my armpit. Hurts. I hope it feels the same for the tumor. Raise its pulse a bit.

"Flip over," says Glenda. Jerry plays orderly and helps me roll over onto my stomach. Nurse Glenda gives it to me in the back. Each stab of the needle prickles my scalp. A whole lot of weariness pushes down on me. "How does this feel?" I'm asked.

How does what feel? I wonder....

I'm pretty sure I dozed off, because I open my eyes to find that I'm lying on my back again.

"I'd say we're ready," says Glenda. Out comes the cheese grater. The scaryfier.

"Someone's at the front door, calling for Edna," Jerry reports, while Glenda grates away on my shin like a prep cook.

Preceded by a wave of huffing and rustling, Mike McEwen bursts into the bedroom and beelines to my bedside. "That's enough," says Mike. "Stop what you're doing." He grabs Nurse Glenda's arm. She slaps his hand away.

"Mike." I shake my head at him.

He's ready to cry. "I can't let you do this, Brian. I'm sorry."

I know why he's here. I see the grief—for himself, for his son, for me. He's being tortured by a terrible case of déjà vu—with a rare hero's opportu-nity to change the past.

Empathy passes quickly. Hero my ass. Mike's a meddler, here to salve his soul. By derailing my treatment, he'll finally be able to lay Brent to rest, to leave Edna's house content that this time he did the right thing. My fate is really irrelevant to him.

I've kicked his ass before, and I'll do it again. I'm going to tear out my IV needle and stick it in one of the veins bulging in his neck. Time for Mike to turn his attention inward and save himself, the arrogant s.o.b.

Marvcus comes around the foot of the bed, yapping in staccato bursts. "Excuse me, what's going on here? Where's Edna? You have no business here. This is a private residence."

Mike jabs his finger at Marvcus, menacingly enough to stop the doc in his tracks. "This is an illegal operation."

Glenda has resumed roughing up my already raw shin. "Get your hand away!" she squeals when Mike tries to grab the grating tool. "You need to move back right now!" She reinforces her order with her chest, backing Mike up. "This is a sterile site. You are jeopardizing this man's health."

"No, you are!" Mike must have worked himself into a lather on the way here, because he's already at full steam. "You're the ones killing Brian! And I won't allow it!" He tries to pull Glenda away from me.

"Mike!" I produce enough volume to make him pause. "Come on," I cajole. "You can't decide for me. I want this."

Mike leans past Glenda, holding his ground while she bodies him away from the bed. "It's illegal, Brian. There's an injunction against Bhani."

"Mike, please."

"I'm sorry, Brian."

Glenda's combativeness stiffens Marvcus's spine. He takes hold of Mike's shoulders. "Mike, is it? Please step back from Mr. Lawson. Let's move out into the hall to discuss this."

"There's nothing to discuss." Mike twists away from Marvcus and stumbles against the bed, betrayed by his effed-up coccyx.

"Honey," says Valerie, standing in the doorway, with Iz. Valerie is already cringing, pretty sure her husband will be on his ass again soon. When trouble starts, Mike's the first guy to go down. "Mike," she implores, "honey, let Dennis handle this."

I didn't see him come in—why didn't someone lock the front door?—but sure enough Dennis is now guiding Mike back to the safety of his womenfolk. Valerie and Isabel latch onto their man.

Dennis ambles toward Glenda. He's stocky, with a helmet head and a stout neck under his long silky middle-parted hair. Dennis was a wrestler in college, and travels around the region in search of ultimate fighting tournaments. Like I've said, I'm not sure how he earns a living. (Rule number one, no one talks about Fight Club.) The only topic I've ever heard him get excited about is hunting.

Maybe I should warn Glenda and Marvcus that I'm suddenly ninety-nine percent certain he's an assassin.

"I'm sorry," says Dennis, "but you're going to have to stop what you're doing. He spreads his arms. Glenda and Marvcus are his flock. They're about to get herded.

"Dennis." Until now, Jerry watched quietly, pushed into the corner by all the latecomers to my bacteria party. Jerry is the funhouse mirror version of Dennis. He moves with a similar easy style. His voice is just as calm. He has the same blunt projectile head, except it rides a foot higher off the floor. His shoulders are as broad if not as deep as Dennis's. Jerry actually has a waist. "You need to let these people do their thing. Brian needs this treatment. He has a real chance at a cure, if you'll stand aside." Jerry must have spent his time in the corner scripting this speech, because there are no pauses.

They square off. "I'm afraid I can't do that," says Dennis. "Jerry, you know the Hippocratic Oath. First do no harm." Dennis takes hold of Jerry's shoulder. "C'mon, think about it. Do you think Dr. Bhani and his little helper are following that creed?"

Jerry removes Dennis's hand. He doesn't let go, because that hand plans on returning to his shoulder. Jerry twists that hand a bit. Dennis acts as if it doesn't hurt. Neither shows it on his face or in his voice, but they are Indian wrestling. "The doctors who put Brian through chemo are the ones who broke the Hippocratic Oath," says Jerry. "Dr. Bhani's cure is Brian's only hope." Whether he believes it or not, Jerry has the company line down pat.

"That's the wrong way to look at it," Dennis advises, lip quivering from the exertion.

"There is no other way to look at it." Jerry throws Dennis's hand down. It stays down. Jerry's hands are fists at his waist. "I'm getting angry," says Jerry, this so calmly that I think Dennis misses the significance. Jerry doesn't like to share his feelings. It takes an extreme situation for him to self-report what's going on inside. "I'm getting angry thinking about what you and the McE-wens will be saying when Brian dies. You'll be telling everyone that at least his suffering is over. And at least he died with his friends around him."

This is a little hard to hear, but I still like Jerry better without the pauses.

"Maybe you think you're doing the right thing," Jerry says quietly. Marvcus, Glenda, the McEwens, they're all leaning forward to listen. "But this isn't a question of right or wrong. This is life or death. And Brian doesn't want to die."

Dennis widens his stance and puts some flex in his knees. "We don't always get the choice. It's not easy to accept."

"*You* don't get the choice," says Jerry, eerily calm. "This is Edna's house. She calls the shots, not you." Jerry points at Mike. "Not him."

"Murder's still murder," says Dennis. "Can't let it happen."

"'Fraid you're gonna have to."

They're using gunfighter stances and syntax now. Things are about to get crazy. I sit up and swing my legs over the bed. "Guys—"

Glenda pushes me back down and holds me there. She picks up my bad leg and grates some more cheese. Blood seeps through the tool's perforations.

Dennis does a double-take. "Hey now, I told you to stop." He lays his hands on Glenda, and Jerry lays his hands on Dennis.

Dennis backhands Jerry's palm. Jerry takes a half-step closer and glares down at Dennis. His shirt is more like second skin now.

"Folks, break it up." Officer Pilsson pushes past the McEwens and squeezes between Jerry and Dennis. Officer Pilsson is five-ten and a hundred eighty pounds, so it's a brave move even with a gun. "No-no, move back, both of you," he barks an order, enforced by two other officers, one wearing a hazmat suit complete with helmet, which he tosses to the floor. He shadows Jerry while his partner, Zach, I think, beckons Dennis to join him at the door.

Jerry and Dennis reluctantly give ground. Through it all Glenda and Marvcus are trying to do their job. She's mopping blood off my knee, beckoning for the syringe Marvcus is preparing on the other side of the bed. Officer Pilsson notices. "That means you two as well."

"Thank God," says Mike.

"Are you Dr. Sawyer?" Officer Pilsson asks Marvcus.

"I am."

"You should know there's an injunction issued to stop these treatments."

"I believe the injunction only applies to Dr. Bhani," says Marvcus.

"No sir," says Officer Pilsson. "That's not the way it works. Please put everything down. We'll need to put everything here under our control."

"Well, officer," says Marvcus, flustered, "I would need to see some paperwork before I allow you to do that."

Officer Pilsson shrugs this off. "You'll see the paperwork soon enough."

Mr. Hazmat appraises Jerry's threat to interfere. He decides the possibility exists and points him into the corner. Jerry's Superman act only goes so far. He complies, and Mr. Hazmat heads for Marvcus.

I'm going to be denied. "Officer Pilsson, let them treat me." My voice quavers. "Honestly man, this is my only chance."

"I'm sorry, Brian."

I've always loved having Officer Pilsson come into my shop. Everyone says great things about him, that he's fair, that he listens before jumping into a confrontation, and that he's a brave guy. Two years before the Columbine shootings in Colorado, Jamestown high school had a similar situation. A kid with an assault rifle took the basketball team hostage during an after-school practice. Officer Pilsson was the first to arrive. Before backup could get there, a shot was fired. Officer Pilsson ran inside, hurried downstairs to the weight room, ordered everyone down on the floor and charged the snot-nosed punk with the gun. The kid took a shot at one of the basketball players and missed, and then it was lights out for him. From the disturbing writings they found after, the kid definitely meant to off a few jocks. Officer Pilsson was a hero.

When I was in school, I called my teachers by their first names. I use acronyms for pastors. Doctors variously earn and lose their titles of respect. But it'll always be Officer Pilsson, for everything he's done for Jamestown.

Still I hate him. I hate him with everything I have left.

"I don't have any choice on this," he says.

I let out a howl. This can't be happening, when I am this close, when the cure is right there in Marvcus's hand.

"It's the right thing, Brian," says Valerie, making me growl.

"That's enough, Mrs. McEwen," Officer Pilsson warns. "Clear this room," he tells Officer Zach, who steers Dennis and Glenda to the door and beckons Jerry to precede him into the hall.

Edna wanders into the room, stumbling into Zach's dragnet. She looks terrible, like she's been weeping. "What's going on?" She moves quickly around Zach, bringing Mr. Hazmat back to alert mode.

"They're trying to stop Marvcus from curing me," I tell her. "Please, Officer Pilsson," I beg. "This is my only chance."

"Edna, right there, stop." Officer Pilsson's voice cracks like a whip but Edna ignores him. She bears down on Mr. Hazmat, takes him by the arms, and drags him away from Marvcus.

"No one else comes in," Officer Pilsson barks at Zach and comes to Mr. Hazmat's rescue. "Edna, right now, this is over." He taps her shoulder, gets no response, and then peels her hand off his officer and puts it behind her back. Edna is flexible, he has to put it way up between her shoulder blades, her hand disappearing under her messy hair.

"No, no, no!" Edna screams, making Officer Pilsson's job difficult. Mr. Hazmat turns around and bumps into Marvcus, right behind him. Marvcus drops the syringe—it hits the tile floor and he says, "Uh-oh."

Mr. Hazmat runs up his commanding officer's back in his haste to get to his helmet. "Move!"

Officer Pilsson does, propelling Edna out of the room, yelling, "We got a spill!" Officer Zach ducks out and slams the door behind him, leaving just the three of us. Mr. Hazmat is on his knees, fumbling to secure the helmet's seal.

"I got it," says Marvcus, also on his hands and knees on the far side of the bed. He comes up with a damp cloth. "I need a disposal bag, pronto."

Mr. Hazmat in his stiff gloves fumbles with the old-fashioned doorknob and then bolts from the room, slamming the door behind him. He's back in less than a minute with two canisters bearing the hazardous materials emblem. Marvcus holds the cloth at arm's length and deposits it in the smaller canister. Mr. Hazmat screws down the lid, twist after twist through a half-foot of threads. He drops this canister into the bigger one, likewise screws it down, and runs three revolutions of tape around the junction.

"Clear!" comes his modulated voice as he leaves the room.

Officer Pilsson pokes his head in the room, hand over his nose and mouth. "I need you both into the hazmat vehicle."

"It's not an airborne bacteria," Marvcus dismisses him. "There's absolutely no threat."

"We have to be sure."

"Even if it were communicable," Marvcus lectures while attending to my shin, "even if we were 'carriers', which we're not, the best option would be to stay in here and not spread it all over the house and neighborhood."

Officer Pilsson reluctantly enters the bedroom. "What are you doing?"

"I need to bandage Mr. Lawson's open wound." Marvcus folds a cloth across my scarified shin and secures it with a shiny bandage. "We had the tumor site prepared for the treatment. If you haven't noticed, this isn't exactly a sterile environment. I don't want Brian to catch something truly dangerous."

Officer Pilsson is beside himself. "What were you thinking?" he berates Marvcus. "Performing an illegal procedure in a private home? You'll have your license revoked."

"Oh I'm not a practicing physician." Marvcus is talking and acting a good game, but he's sweating.

Officer Pilsson sees it. "Dr. Sawyer, I'm going to see if I can't find a reason to take you in. I don't like what I've seen here one bit."

"Go ahead," Marvcus sasses. "I haven't done anything wrong."

"Do we live in the land of the free?" I mutter at Officer Pilsson. My head is ringing. I'm on the road to throwing up. "Can you really do this to me? If I want to try something that could save my life, and he wants to give it to me, why can you stop me? I don't get it. I don't fucking get it."

Officer Pilsson—let's just call him Pilsson from now on—puts his hand on my shoulder. He squeezes hard, to snap me out of my growing hysteria, I'm sure. It works, but he's only postponing the coming freak-out. "The judge issued an injunction for a reason, Brian. The McEwens have been down this road before, as you well know. It may not be obvious right now, but they did you a favor."

"Please don't say that."

The son of a bitch squeezes my shoulder like he's some sort of father figure, father knows best, this is a good lesson for you son, life is full of these tough lessons and you'll be a better man for it, of course you'll be dead soon, but that's beside the point.

"And please stop touching me."

At the bedroom door he responds to a buzz on his shoulder walkie-talkie. "This is Pilsson." While he waits for a reply he says to me, "The McEwens are still here. I think they'd like to talk to you, if you're up for it."

I'm up for leaving everything behind, my shop, my friends, my van, Edna and North Dakota, hopping the next flight to Davis and lying down in my old bed. "Can you unhook me?" I ask Marvcus.

Marvcus extracts the IV needle and tapes a cottonball to the hole. "You're feeling up to being on your feet?" He eyeballs my shin. "How's your leg?"

"Fine except for the cancer." I ditch the gown and pull on my Razorbacks shirt, glaring at Pilsson. He looks away as his walkie-talkie squawks, "...Dr. Marv-cus Sawyer..." I shuffle into the showcase foyer. Officer Zach stands at the open front door, monitoring Jerry and Dennis as they argue on the front lawn. Mr. Hazmat, helmet on, reenters the bedroom to confiscate any remaining toxins, probably the last batch in existence, to be flushed down the toilet or shot into space or locked and forgotten in a hazmat vault at the CDC.

Edna sits at the bottom of the winding staircase. legs splayed and her head bowed. Somehow I thought she'd be able to make this happen. She's Edna Applejack, Queen of North Dakota, and yet she can't lay down the law in her own home.

Isabel runs at me, face filled with awful pity. "Brian, I'm so sorry." She holds my cheeks in her hands, obstructing my oxygen intake channels. I turn my head and she pulls me into a hug.

"Okay. Okay lady." I break free and now I have to take a hug from Valerie. I'm dizzy and nauseous and this close to screaming. Mr. Hazmat passes by with the goods in a cooler equipped with a handy carrying strap.

"Brian, my boy," says Mike, hands in his pockets, looking mournful. "I am so sorry. This has been a terrible day. I can't imagine how you're feeling. I'm sure Bhani had you thinking it was a cure. We understand, we've been through this before. The worst thing is to be misled..."

He's choked up; he's remembering his son, and I could care less about that prick. Brent was a cocky motherfucker. Mike wants to commiserate and pretend we're in the same boat. I've got news for him. There's a difference between losing a loved one, and dying yourself. One of us gets to wake up tomorrow to a brand new sparkling clear day, the other's a dead man walking.

Mike is so emotional, poor poor Mike, that Valerie has to hold and comfort him and be the one to tell me about a Fargo doctor running an FDA-approved cancer drug trial. Being such important North Dakotans with such powerful North Dakota connections, maybe they can get me in.

"It's too late, but I appreciate the info."

"No, no, Brian honey, it's never too late, please don't think that way."

"Okay, whatever the McEwens think is best, right? The McEwens have it all figured out."

"That's uncalled for," says Valerie. "You know that isn't fair."

"Everybody needs to leave," Edna orders. "Leave Brian alone."

Iz shakes a finger at Edna, her face slick with tears. She must have been smearing tears all over her face. Even her forehead glistens. "Where do you get off? I've loved Brian for years. You don't love him and you damn well know it," Iz sprays us all with spit and tears before collapsing into her father's arms. "We all know it."

"She's right, Edna, only the McEwens love me, to death."

Isabel sobs as Mike towels off her face with his sleeve. "How can you say that, Brian? Why can't you see what this is doing to me and our family?"

Edna advances on Isabel and Mike. "Are you insane? You just signed Brian's death warrant!"

"There's an *injunction*," Isabel moans, jittery as Edna draws near, unsure whether to protect Mike or hide behind him.

"And who had everything to do with that injunction?" Edna shouts in Isabel's face, making her quiver. "Don't pretend that you-all are upholding the law. The law is serving you."

"The law is right," Isabel blubbers. If Edna takes a swing, Iz will faint before the punch connects.

"Don't push me," Edna hisses. Her eyes are red-rimmed, the normally brilliant blue streaked black as if her pupils were leaking. "You don't know what I've been through today."

I should let that go, but I can't. "Sorry to put you through this. Don't worry, I'll be out of your way soon."

Edna tips her head back and squeezes her eyes shut, teeth grinding. Iz and Valerie rush to my side, cooing that everything will be all right. Edna reaches for my hand. I reject it, and she screams in frustration.

"Don't pretend that you've been there for Brian," says Iz.

"I'm sick of hearing from you!" Edna shrieks. When Edna shrieks, people stop breathing. Iz gasps for oxygen, lets loose a pitiful sob. Pilsson stops thumbing through his notepad and catches Officer Zach's eye, silently putting them on red alert. Edna screams again and storms upstairs; the officers downgrade the threat condition to orange.

"Excuse me, Brian, can I see you?" It's Marvcus, exiting the bedroom, lugging his oversized supply case, doing his best to look dignified. Mr.

Hazmat follows, carrying my rolled-up bedding and still wearing his helmet. They both instinctively give wide berth to the smoldering heat trace Edna left behind in the middle of her grand foyer.

Mike maneuvers between me and Marvcus. "There's nothing more for you to do or say here. Tell your boss this will be included in our lawsuit. If I have my way, there'll be criminal charges filed against both of you." Mike looks to Pilsson for validation, but he's engrossed in notetaking.

Marvcus doesn't react to Mike. "I want you within shouting distance of the hospital," he tells me. "If you have any issues, get there pronto. Have them find me—the officer here has requested that I stay in town for awhile."

"Maybe you should rent a room," says Mike. "Could be a long stay."

"My leg burns," I tell Marvcus. "I think the bandage is irritating my skin."

"Leave it on," says Marvcus. "It's important. We really scraped you up, and I'm afraid of infection. We shouldn't have done this outside an antiseptic environment."

"You stupid bastards, you just don't get it," says Mike, spoiling for a fight. "You shouldn't have done it, period."

Marvcus stares at my leg, something like wistfulness on his face. He heads for the door. "Just promise me you'll get to the hospital if you get sick."

"Sure." The Davis hospital.

"Tell your boss he screwed up big time!" Mike yells after him.

"Shh, Mike." Valerie puts her hands on his blotchy cheeks—this must be a McEwen female trait. Watching it makes me claustrophobic. I draw a deep breath but my chest aches too much to hold it. Which makes me even more desperate for air. I'm burning up.

Iz sees it. "You're looking flushed. Come here." She guides me to sit at the base of the staircase. "Mom, can you help me collect Brian's things and move him back to his apartment? I'm going to stay with him for awhile." She silences my weak protest. "I won't take no for an answer this time. It doesn't have to mean anything about us, sweetie, I'm not pressuring you. But you need someone you can trust right now."

"So am I right in assuming Edna and Rick were seeing each other?"

Valerie gives me a pitying look. "They've loved each other for a long time. Since high school. We were so sure they were finally going to be a couple. And now, suddenly, Rick is remarrying Andrea. We begged him to reconsider."

"Rick is fucking insane," says Mike. "Just completely off his rocker. I'm going out of my mind about it."

"We're wondering if Andrea got herself pregnant," Valerie hisses. "She might be blackmailing him."

"Andrea," Iz clucks. "I told you, sweetie. I tried to warn you." She casts a wicked look upstairs. "About both of them."

"Poor Edna," says Valerie. "I think she's devastated."

"We *hate* Andrea," says Mike.

"It's terrible to say," says Valerie.

"But it's true." Mike grunts and wheezes, close to stroking out. "I wish there was something I could do to stop them."

"Write Rick out of the will," I suggest.

"Brian honey, don't give that mess another thought," says Valerie, joining us on the stairs, bookending me with Isabel, who clutches my arm between her legs. With a straight-shot view from the front lawn, Dennis watches and nods, bestowing his blessing. I'm squirming, sweating, a big case of the heaves coming my way. "We'll get you set up with Dr. Osman in Fargo. His research sounds very promising. Mike, first thing tomorrow morning I want you to call Dr. Osman's office and get an appointment set up for Brian."

"Yeah," says Mike, stalking back and forth. "Yeah, I'll do it tomorrow. We'll get you fixed up, Brian. That's going to be our number one priority. Regardless what Rick decides to do with Andrea." This thought distracts him. "Yeah, we'll have to see…"

"Mike," says Valerie, looking expectantly at her husband while she rubs my back.

"Sorry," says Mike. "Brian, what time are you free, to drive to Fargo?"

A response would require diversion of resources I'm employing to keep from crying and collapsing into what will soon be a puddle of vomit. Oh shit I feel terrible. "I think I'm crashing."

No one responds. I said it too quietly, maybe no one heard. Maybe no one believes I can actually die. I focus on the center of a marble tile, everything a kaleidoscope around this square of fudge revel swirl.

Isabel's hand is on my cheek. "You're burning up. Do you want to lie down? Dad, we need to get Brian to bed."

"Maybe we need to get Brian to the hospital," Pilsson suggests, from far far away. "Zach, is the doctor still here?"

"Mike, help Isabel get Brian out to the car," says Valerie. "I'm going to make sure Edna's okay, and let her know we're leaving." She heads upstairs.

Pilsson crouches beside me. "Brian, you okay? You don't look so good, buddy. Any idea what's going on? Is this normal?"

"I'm going to throw up. That's not unusual."

They have me on my feet and into Edna's guest bathroom in the nick of time. I retch into the toilet while someone wipes down my neck with a cool cloth. I stand up with a pounding headache. The pain fills my head, my eyes, my skull, my teeth. I'm shivering, my teeth actually chattering.

"Let's get you back to your apartment," says Iz.

"I think the hospital is a better place," Pilsson advises.

"Let Isabel take care of him," Mike tells Pilsson.

"No, Dennis is waiting for her," I mumble.

"Mike," Valerie calls from above, sounding concerned. "I can't find Edna anywhere. I think she left down the back staircase."

Mike deserts me, but Jerry's powerful arm is there to support me as I rinse my face in the sink. I look into the mirror. Jerry shakes his head. "You look rough, brother."

"Feel rough. I don't care whether it's Edna's bed, or mine, or the hospital's, I need to lie down." We shuffle together into the front entryway.

Mike hobbles from the kitchen. "Edna's car is gone."

From out of the blue I have a vivid, fever-enhanced, Technicolor image of the indigo hatred in Edna's eyes. "Uh-oh." I've never seen that much darkness in someone's face. I'll bet Edna was wearing the same look fifteen years ago, right before she killed her husband. "I think Edna is going to murder Andrea."

Takes a moment for this to sink in. Pilsson touches his shoulder walkie-talkie and clears his throat. He looks at Mike and Valerie. "Does that sound possible to you?"

Valerie moans. She holds her own cheeks with trembling hands. "Yes. Yes it's possible."

"Do you know where Andrea is?" Pilsson asks.

Valerie stammers. "She said, Andrea said, she was going to get things ready to move today." Her eyes flutter wider. "I think she's already had the phone disconnected."

Pilsson talks into his shoulder. "Kerry, I need a car, ready to move." He releases the Send button. "Do we have a last name and an address for Andrea?"

"Goldine," I tell him when no one speaks up. "The Briarcourt apartments on Fifteenth Street. Number sixteen." Everyone stares. I shrug.

Pilsson relays the info to Officer Kerry. "I'm going to run over there," he tells us. "Please everybody, stay put. Or take Brian to the hospital. Call 911 if there's an emergency."

"Holy hell," says Mike as Pilsson hustles out the door. Valerie is on her cellphone, Mike hovering. "Are you calling Rick? Good..." We all stand here, waiting. There must be adrenaline in my veins, keeping me on my feet. "You can't get him?" A bit of panic in Mike's voice. "No answer?"

"He *always* has his cellphone with him," Valerie frets.

"That boy is a good cellphone user," says Mike. "Call our house. I asked him to level the new pool table for me today."

With a shaking finger Valerie quick-dials her house. No answer.

"Let's go," says Dennis. "I'll drive you to Andrea's place."

"You should go with them," I tell Iz. "Dennis, take Isabel."

Iz puts a boa constrictor grip on my arm. "It's right that she's with you," Dennis decides solemnly, giving us each a pat on the shoulder.

"I am dying, though," I point out.

"Come with us?" Dennis asks Jerry. "We might need you, buddy." A horde of cops, a gaggle of family members, an assassin, and still they need additional backup to bring down Edna. Seems prudent.

Jerry looks at me as he backpedals. He's in crisis mode and loving it. "Will you be okay? Isabel, you'll stay with Brian?"

"I'm not leaving him," says Iz.

I wave Jerry out the door. "Go, go."

Isabel presses the door closed. "Okay handsome, let's get you to bed."

Unbelievable. I truly think I'm dying, right here and now—I have never ever felt this terrible. Things are shutting down inside me. And Iz might be screwing me when I go. I shudder and gasp on another surge of vomit. I only mostly make it to the john this time. Me and the rug hug the porcelain crapper together.

My head is diving and dancing. My lips are hot and cracked, with no saliva left to swallow. "You gotta get me there. Hospital. Dehydrated."

"Did they leave the IV equipment behind?" Iz wonders. "I could—"

"No. Hospital now. Please God, Isabel. Please God." Don't know if that request was directed at God or Isabel, but the prayer is answered, she leads me out the front door.

We stop halfway down the walk. "I should call an ambulance," says Iz.

"Too slow. Come on. I'll drive."

Isabel cackles into the sky. "I miss that humor. You're hilarious."

She's insane. We make it to her car and Iz helps lower me into the passenger seat. She gasps. "Your leg! What's going on?"

I straighten my leg enough to see my shin. I have to blink rapidly, recruiting my last micro-ounce of moisture to melt the blur coating my eyeballs. My shin and knee are flame red around the bandage. The flesh is raised with what look like infected goosebumps, throbbing with my heartbeat.

I hike up my pajama shorts. The inflamed pulsing rash runs up my thigh to my crotch. There's my shriveled scared penis. Isabel's reaching again, for what I'm not sure. I yank the pantleg back down as far as it will go.

And then it hits me. "Oh boy."

"What?"

I point at the rash. "It's not the cancer. That's not what's happening." Hard to talk while Isabel strokes my cheek. "It's the treatment. It's Bhani's toxins. Marvcus put them on my bandage."

"No!" Isabel yelps. "Oh God. . ." She claws at the bandage.

"Let go! No Iz, stop! Leave it!"

"Get it *off*, Brian!" Iz kneels into the gutter, wailing, as we struggle. "It's killing you!"

"Yes! *Yes!* That's a good thing! God-dammit, stop!" I grab her wrists and pull her into the car on top of me, face to face. "Isabel, listen. You have to get me to the hospital."

Iz is senseless, not comprehending, near hysterics, committed to me dying on the McEwens' terms. "Get it off, Brian, please…"

"I'm going to be okay, Iz. This is the way it's supposed to work…"

"No, no, no…"

"…but I'm going to die of dehydration if you don't get me to the hospital fast. Move." I shove her and she lands hard on her butt. I try not to take pride in my power display. She sobs there on the berm. "Isabel. Iz, come on. Come on! I will die—Iz, no!" She was looking at the bandage again. "Leave it. I'm a goner if you don't get me to the hospital. Look, the neighbors are coming over here…" My mouth makes hideous crackling noises when I talk, a dual stream of English and African clicks.

Iz struggles clumsily to her feet and cries her way around to the driver's seat. We take off with a short squeal of rubber on the hot asphalt. I can't take my eyes off the bandage. "This is the cloth Marvcus used to wipe up the spill. He pulled the old switcheroo on Pilsson. Unbelievable. Marvcus told me how doctors in the early days would deliberately soil a patient's dressing to cause an infection. The infection is a good thing." I work to convince both of us as my leg grows more inflamed by the second. "It's a good thing. It's the only way to get my immune system to attack the tumors…"

I suddenly have my third consecutive moment of crisis-inspired clarity. "Uh-oh."

"What?" Isabel jerks the wheel. We nick a parked car and carom left.

"It's Edna." Ordinarily, even with a raging fever caused by a mad scientist's medieval medicine, I would have reacted to Iz's bumper car routine. "Oh boy. Edna. Oh fuck."

"Brian, what?!" Isabel gets control of the car in time to avoid a head-on with a gravel truck. She overcorrects to the right. We buzz the curb along an empty stretch of the street.

"Brake."

Firmly, Isabel does. We screech to a stop, straddling the yellow center line. "Drive, slower."

She's like the computer prototype of a voice-controlled car, not yet fully debugged. After weaving back and forth for another twenty yards the car straightens out. "What's wrong?" she asks, rightly full of dread.

"Don't freak out, okay?"

Deep breath, shuddering release. "Okay," she says.

"Let's drive to your folks' house," I suggest.

"Why?" Isabel shrieks this question.

"That's it. Pull over. I'll drive. I mean it. I'm feeling better." And I am, thanks to a triple-shot of adrenaline.

Isabel obeys. I drag my sorry ass around the front of the Camry while Iz scoots over and collapses into the passenger seat. I accelerate away from the curb and we're nearly bashed by a pickup I didn't have the time to look for. It's a soundless near-accident. No one uses their horns in North Dakota, except to say hello.

"Brian," Iz moans, "what is it? What's wrong?"

"Edna's not going to kill Andrea. She's going to kill your brother. I'd bet on it."

"What? *What?* Rick?" Isabel's shrieking, now with rage. "Go! Go! Go!"

She calls Rick's cell and then her folks' house, again with no luck. As we round the corner squealing onto the McEwens' street, she reaches Valerie. "Mom, what happened at Andrea's? Did you find Edna?"

Long pause. "What, what?" I hiss at her.

Iz shakes her head while struggling to hear her mom. "Andrea's there...? She's okay? Edna—no Edna? Is Rick there? Mom—Mom, listen, Brian thinks—oh no," she moans, "there's Edna's car. Mom, she's here," Iz gurgles, her voicebox turned to jello. "Get the police over here to your house now!"

We run up the sidewalk and Isabel trips over her flip-flops. I have to catch her. Something in my cancer knee pops as I support the extra buck-fifty. No pain, but now the leg doesn't work so well.

Front door's locked. Isabel kicks it, not like SWAT, and then we retreat and hurry down the embankment along the side of the house. My downhill leg (cancer, possible ACL rupture) buckles repeatedly. I'm still as fast as Isabel, who puts a lot of shoulders into it, runs like a doll with a few pins missing.

Under the deck she tries the sliding walk-out basement door. It joggles back and forth with some play in the locking mechanism. Isabel pounds the glass with the heel of her hand.

"Here." One, two, I rock the door back and forth and then yank hard and the lock snaps. The rollers are sticky so the door doesn't open all the way before Isabel barges through and knocks the door half off the runner.

"Careful," I try to caution, but there are screams from upstairs and Iz charges forward and up the basement stairs. She puts some distance between us...I'm half the flight behind her, and now she's screaming.

When my head clears the top step I see Isabel, clutching her mouth, knees stuck in the buckled position. I exit the stairwell door, to a grotesque freeze frame. Rick stands beside the wet bar, legs spread wide and making a broad triangle against the bright bay window. Edna is astride his back, atop his shoulders, wrapped around his head. She's looking at us. Her fingernails are sunk into Rick's bloody shredded face. Can't tell with the gore, looks like he's missing his eyes and crying at the same time.

Isabel lurches forward. "Oh God…"

Edna slides off Rick and points a knife at Iz, stopping her. I limp forward, fixated on the hunting knife's serrated edge. Rick wavers on his feet, a zombie.

"The police are coming!" Isabel screams. "You drop it! You *stop* it!"

And there are sirens, sure enough. "Edna, come on," I cajole. "Let's talk. Leave him. You've done enough."

"He's evil. You don't let evil live." Edna pastes her hair to the side with blood. "Rick is an evil piece of shit. I'm killing him."

"Edna, Edna…he's just a guy. Don't do this. Let me—*fuck*." She swipes at me, almost gets me. Could have, if she had wanted to.

Sirens are much closer, turning onto the McEwens' street, almost here. Isabel hyperventilates, working up the nerve to charge.

"Edna," I sharpen my tone, "don't. Our coffeeshop—come on, think about it—what about our partnership?"

"Sorry." Edna blinks. A droplet of blood bubbles on her eyelid where a chunk of eyelashes have been torn off.

"You're the biggest thing in North Dakota," I tell her. "Let's enjoy it. We can enjoy everything we've both earned. We can enjoy it, together."

"Life without conflict isn't life at all," Edna murmurs, grabbing ahold of Rick's fine blonde hair and shifting the knife to a backhand clutch grip.

"Edna, no, no." She's gathering herself to strike. "Hey—I thought you were a barehands killer."

Edna pauses. I freeze. Rather not charge her if I don't have to. Isabel is frozen like her brother. The cops break down the front door.

"This still counts," says Edna, and jams the knife into Rick's face.

"Get down!" a policeman yells, and we do; we all four head for the floor.

Rick had thrown up his hand to block the attack. On his knees now, his severed ring finger falls off and his maimed hand drops to his side. The knife is buried to the hilt, at an angle through his nose. Gotta be dead when he hits the floor, crashing against his sister who I think fainted. Edna sits down and the cops still tackle her. I crumple to my side and start vomiting again.

Post Mortem

Not dead. Not even close, far as I can tell. It's the other definition: the after-the-fact analysis of what went wrong, what was good; what did we learn from our experience?

Before we get into all that, let me say that my new shop is a beauty. Edna and Rick did a great job designing it without me. Two hundred seventy degrees of curved bar with windows to match, like a space-age diner. As I stand at the espresso machine, the sink, freezer and refrigerator are right there, all the essentials at my fingertips. I've put back fifteen of the pounds I lost to cancer, thanks in part to this efficient setup.

"Kayla, Miranda, hey." I'm having to learn the new generation of names. "Kip. What can I get you three?"

"Iced javas," says Kayla, including Miranda in the order, "half-decaf, with a shot of sugar-free vanilla syrup and a dollop of whipped cream." She leers. "How's that for an order?"

"It's still rock'n'roll to me, sister."

The girls laugh. Kip grows more serious, frowning at the menu board. He's definitely the grownup here.

"Brian, your hair's hot today," says Kayla, nineteen, devilishly cute, tank-top.

"Imagine if I combed it." It's not a hair-care strategy I endorse, but something, either the chemo or the radiation or the cancer or the toxins, something inspired epic hair growth. I wasn't bad before, but I don't mind looking better.

"How do you get a comb through that 'do?" asks Miranda, leggy and freckly.

"Oh I could."

"It's so thick."

"It's luscious," I agree. I tilt my head to give them a better look.

"I'll take the grande-sized mattina," Kip orders.

"Grande mattina!" I yell, to me. I sing along a few bars with Squeeze. "Now she's gone, and I'm out with a friend, with lips full of passion, and coffee-not-decaf-baby in bed."

"Who is that?" Miranda asks.

"That is Squeeze."

"God I like their stuff."

"Squeeze got it goin' on."

"Yeah," says Kip, laying down two seconds of a two-finger percussion track on my pickup shelf. "We put a lot more work into our hair than they'll ever know, don't we Brian?"

"They'll never know," I concur. "You'll never know," I tell the girls.

"Brian hasn't looked in a mirror once since I've known him," Charlotte reports, lugging a tray of dirty cups from upstairs. We have an upstairs, where couches and easy chairs await the customer, along with a view through the curved two-story windows, of the chapel and the river beyond. It's early October and the snow is flying, right on schedule. "He doesn't even own a mirror," says Charlotte. "Not that I blame him."

"You can't blame me, can you?"

"No," says Charlotte.

"Anybody left up there?"

"Nope."

"How'd they leave it?"

"Trashed again."

"Damn college kids," Kip assumes.

"Mothers with their little kid," says Charlotte. "They're the worst. First to complain, last to clean up after themselves."

"Why do mothers even come in here?" Kip tries to strike up a conversation with the ever-elusive Charlotte.

"Because it's close?" Charlotte suggests. The kid will get no play with her. Charlotte shows no interest in the JC boys because she knows there are no boyfriends among them, only casual partners. She's working full-time with a dream of being a coffeeshop manager, while these boys pay thirty grand a year tuition and hope not to work for a living. Charlotte isn't looking for an angle, unless it's how to inspire my other employees to work as hard as she does.

She's better looking than either Kayla or Miranda, but most people can't tell. Charlotte shows a lot of skin but doesn't flaunt it. She never laughs if it isn't funny. Charlotte and Kip move in different orbits, intersecting at only one point—me.

"Ladies, your drinks. And Kip."

A forty-year-old guy in dress shirt and slacks has been staring at the menu board and wandering around the shop. He leaves without ordering. "What was up with him?" says Charlotte.

"Another pilgrim visiting the shrine. It's going to take more than two murders for Edna to fall completely off her pedestal."

"I'm telling you, we need to serve an Applejack latté or a White Edna Mocha," says Charlotte. "At least then the pilgrims would buy something."

"Bye, Brian," the girls bid me adieu.

"Later my man," says Kip. "Have a good one."

"You can't stop me."

The girls laugh. Charlotte puts her hands on her hips and stares at me. "Doesn't that ever get old for you?"

"I'm pretty sure it gets better with age."

Charlotte nods at a tall shaggy-haired dude walking in and asks me, "Pilgrim or paying customer...Sam!" Charlotte abandons our central command post to run to hug our ex-employee, squealing all the way.

"Hey," I greet Sam. "Your dad said we might see you today."

Charlotte wheels and gapes at me. "You knew?! And you didn't tell me?"

"You never asked."

She growls and then squeals and hugs Sam again. "You've changed! Oh my gosh! Sam used to work for us," Charlotte tells Professor Adams, working at a nearby window chair and surreptitiously plugging his ears. "He went to Alaska for the summer to work."

"I know Sam," says the Prof. "Welcome back. I've heard working in Alaska can be lucrative."

"Now he's going to blow it all on one semester at JC," I lament. "Maybe you could get him a basketball scholarship. The Jimmies could use a tall guy like Sam, huh?"

"I'm sure they could," says the Prof.

Sam gives us his big goofy grin. Correction: now that he's thirty pounds lighter, I'm betting it's a sexy grin. "I don't play basketball."

"Can you believe it?" I ask the Prof. "What a shame, huh?"

"Maybe he has a brain instead," says the Prof, suggesting an inverse relationship between athletic ability and IQ level.

"You have changed!" Charlotte repeats herself.

"The lack of a haircut, you mean?" I say. "Any fool can grow hair."

"I can do it in my sleep," Sam says with a grin.

Charlotte links arms with Sam and escorts him around the bar. "It's more than that. But your hair does look great. And I think you're taller."

"How tall now?" I demand.

"Uh, I don't know, six-eight."

"No way. That's a lie. Don't lie about your height, okay? Okay? Jeez."

"Sorry." Sam grins. So sexy. "So how are things here?"

"Oh, same ol' same old," I say. "You know about Edna Applejack, right?"

Sam gives me a quizzical look.

"No? Your folks never told you?"

"I just got into town," says Sam. "I wanted to see you guys and your new shop before I saw anybody else."

"Didn't you talk to your parents the whole time?" Charlotte demands.

"We were on the boat or the island all summer," Sam defends himself.

"There's no phone out there. We didn't get mail until the last day. I have a whole pack of letters I need to read."

"Let's see if we can get you caught up." A throng of coeds stream into my shop. "Damn customers," I mutter. "Hang on."

"You want some help back there?" Sam volunteers.

"I think Charlotte and I can—"

"Of course we do," says Charlotte. "You're going to work here for the school year, aren't you?"

Sam ambles around the end of the bar, admiring our setup. "I'm transferring to NDSU. I leave for Fargo tomorrow." The richest kid in town is going to a state school.

"Isn't it too late?" Charlotte hopes. "It's at least a month into the semester. Hi," she greets the girls. "What can we get for you?"

"The salmon season went long," says Sam. "I was pretty much trapped on the boat for the last two weeks. It's definitely later than I was hoping. But it's NDSU; how hard can it be?"

"It's not where you are, it's what you make of it," I provide sage wisdom. The drink orders trickle my way. "If you were really committed to your education, if you wanted it bad enough, you could have found a way back to the mainland, am I right?"

"I could have swam," Sam agrees. "The water was a little chilly though."

"We all make choices. We all make choices."

"So...?"

"So...let's see, where did you leave off? I had cancer when you left for Alaska, right?"

"Had?"

"Had. Two-shot two-percent soy vanilla cappuccino on the bar!" I yell, way too loud for the circumstances.

The young coed customer doesn't notice, like her friends captivated by tall, lean, tanned, shaggy-headed Sam.

"So I had cancer," I repeat, and Sam doesn't push for more explanation, because he knows it's on its way, in due time. "Had Edna and I decided to open this shop together?"

"I don't think so."

"Grande Applejack mocha!" I announce, as I spot Terry Lovold, VP of Student Affairs, that plump sexy bitch, marching toward my shop in high heels, swinging her briefcase. I know what's in there.

My customer stares uncertainly at the Applejack mocha.

"Sorry. It's a skinny white chocolate mocha."

"That should be the Edna," Charlotte concurs.

"Last I knew," says Sam, filling a pitcher for me, "you were going to open a shop in the new retail strip by the hospital."

"Isn't that nice, having the milk right there? You're right, I was going to open a shop in the Bluffs. I partnered with Andrea—you remember Andrea, Rick McEwen's ex? I think you knew her—yes?—well?—didn't you?" Sam blushes. "Yes, you did. She and Rick got back together, you heard that? You didn't? You probably didn't know Edna murdered Rick then?"

Sam drops the pitcher. It clanks to the staging shelf, sending a geyser of milk straight up, and straight back down into the pitcher.

"Whoa. Careful there. Extra large iced *decaf* coffee. Next time it's double for decaf," I tell the girl. "I'm serious." I am. "Hey, we got ourselves a Veep in the house. Lady, what can I get you?"

"How about a private office," says Terry Lovold, "where we can talk?"

Three more kids come in. Perfect timing. "I'm pretty busy right now." I kick Sam before he can volunteer to spell me. "Can I give you a call?"

"I'll wait." Terry turns a window chair around to face me and mounts it, somehow crossing her legs inside the cozy confines of her overstuffed skirt without being indecent.

"Okay. Where was I? Let's back up. Andrea was begging to be my partner, business and personal. She was saying all the right things, talking about how we could open all these branches in California or Colorado, with her running the business aspect and me without a real role, spending a lot of time at each shop, guest-hosting behind the bar, keeping the customers happy. At the time it seemed like the only way I was ever going to be able to build my coffee empire, you know?"

"Sure," says Sam.

"Andrea was gung-ho to drop everything and move to Denver or Davis. But even with all the dollar signs dancing in my head, I was pretty sure she was more committed to escaping North Dakota than to running a coffeeshop. So I played it safe and convinced her that we had to get our feet under us here first. Run this shop and the Bluffs, make sure our partnership and our business plan were compatible."

"Conservative stance," Sam compliments me.

"Except I procrastinated so long that Mike gave the Bluffs to Billy-boy. Pissed me off. So at the last second Andrea and I stole it back, right out from under Billy-boy's nose."

"Radical move," Sam praises me. "Who's Billy-boy?"

"Work with me here, Sam. You remember Bill Hernandes? 'Campus' Coffee? Just to bring you up to date, he closed that shop across the river three weeks ago, after we opened here. Not to jump too far ahead, but he did end up with the Bluffs location. And now he's selling it to Starbucks."

"Starbucks? Starbucks is coming?"

"Can you believe it?" says Charlotte.

"It was inevitable," I say.

"You're not worried?" Sam asks.

"Damn right I'm worried. I wouldn't be, so much, if..." I sneak a peek at Terry Lovold, stabbing buttons on her Blackberry, giving some poor bastard hell. I sigh. "Terry," I call out, "you're sure I can't get you anything? Water? Take-out from somewhere? Something to read? No? Okay."

"So," Sam wants clarification, "you and Andrea...?"

"You mean...?" I wiggle my finger suggestively. "I guess we were dating, kind of. I mean, I had cancer pretty bad, and with all the chemo and radiation, I was barely human."

"What about Isabel?"

"I had already dropped Iz. Or maybe it was at about the same time, I forget the timing. She's a freaky lady. You know. Come on," I cajole, "you've heard things."

"There were stories at school," Sam admits, reluctantly. That's the most gossip I've ever heard from him.

"After I dropped Isabel, she started seeing Dennis. I mean immediately, within the hour. Not the Dennis who works for me. Assassin Dennis. By the way, where is the Dennis who works for me?"

"I sent him to Sam's Club for supplies," says Charlotte, a little dismissive.

"And Patti's at the downtown shop? Right?"

"As far as I know," says Charlotte, a little snotty.

"I can't believe you have two stores," says Sam. "How in the world did you get a shop on campus? I thought it was impossible."

"It was all Edna. That's why what's-her-name is here, by the way." I nod at Terry Lovold while turning up the house music—the control console is right at my fingertips, how convenient is that? "Now that Edna's doing thirty-to-life, the College wants to renege on our contract and take possession of this shop. I can't blame them for trying—they paid for most of the construction, and the whole deal was based on Edna generating all this goodwill and publicity. Their high-powered legal team will probably convince the judge to rule in their favor. I need to hire an attorney, but all I can afford is a lawyer."

"An attorney or a lawyer, what's the difference?" Charlotte asks.

"One zero in the price tag." I put up the last two drinks and turn the music back down. "I've been here fourteen hours a day since we opened. I'm making some money, but sure enough, just like I feared, I'm losing business at the downtown shop."

"I'm sure some of it is coming here," says Sam.

"Like Terrence." I nod at my resident writer tucked in the nook beyond the wraparound window. He thinks I had the nook designed specially for him, and I tell him he's right.

"I'm trying to eavesdrop on your story, I hope you don't mind," Terrence calls to me.

"Come on over, pull up a chair."

"How's the writing coming?" Sam asks Terrence as he joins us.

"It's coming. Still plugging away." Terrence is a nondescript guy. So there's no sense describing him. But like I've told you, his writing is pretty darn good. I recently read an article he wrote about the federal farm program's effect on Jamestown-area farmers. It was as good as anything else I read in magazines or newspapers. He submitted it to a few magazines, unsuccessfully.

"He still can't find an agent or a publisher with a clue," I say.

"I'm sorry," says Sam.

"I'm not giving up," says Terrence. "One of these times I'm going to hit the right topic, at the right time."

"So where was I?"

"You were telling us about your relationship with Andrea," says Sam.

"You were talking about why you gave up on the Bluffs," says Terrence.

"No," says Charlotte, "you were *finally* getting to what happened with Edna."

"I think what I was about to say was, I'm a little heavy at the manager position. I'm going to need to fire at least one in the very near future."

Sam nods at Charlotte. "Her?"

"Just try it, and see what happens to these stores," Charlotte threatens.

Edna probably had the right idea paying extra for professional managers like Dennis and Patti, to facilitate rapid expansion. Now that contraction seems to be the direction I'm heading, I'm going to have to go cheap. Charlotte.

"Back to the story," I say.

"I'd call it a disjointed collection of scrambled thoughts," says Charlotte.

"I'm still recovering from the effects of the chemo. It destroys brain cells, you know, so cut me some slack. So, about the time I partnered with Andrea to open the Bluffs shop, I started my second round of chemo. Which I'd still be taking if it was up to that hack Bonilla."

"Dr. Bonilla is my godfather," says Sam.

"You might want to reconsider, if it isn't too late. I'm not sure he's even qualified for godfather duties. So I was feeling awful. And my hair was falling out. I have to admit that got to me a little."

"It looks great now," says Sam.

"Please," says Charlotte. "We've covered that topic enough today."

"Probably true. It is nice though, isn't it?" I point the top of my head at Sam. "Feel it if you want. But then you have to let me feel yours."

"Pass, Sam," says Charlotte. "For the love of God, please pass."

"You'll be kicking yourself later. Terry?" I call over to the Veep. "I'm sorry, but this story is running long. We'll have to meet some other time."

Terry taps her briefcase. "We have to do this." What does she have in there? An attractive buyout agreement? A picture of Edna she'd like autographed? A free pass to Heaven? Make me an offer I can't refuse, Terry.

"Call me," I tell her. "Call Charlotte here, and set up an appointment."

Terry slides off the high chair and tugs at her skirt. That sucker doesn't budge. "I'm sorry we can't do this now, Mr. Lawson. It's only going to get more difficult if we need to involve our attorneys."

"I don't have an attorney. I have a lawyer."

Terry debates whether I'm a stupid jackass or a wily smartass. She hooks a curved fingernail under the lid of an empty cup abandoned on the table in front of her, and like a crane operator pivots to drop it in the trash can. "Take care of our building in the meantime, okay?"

I watch her sashay out the door and down the walk, trying to hate her. "I suppose I'm going to have to give this place up."

"No!" Charlotte yelps. Two girls come through the door and Charlotte dials down her outrage. "You're not giving this up," she growls from the till.

I nod at the kids and whisper, "You don't even like them, do you?"

She checks to make sure the girls aren't listening. "No," she hisses.

"Well?"

"So?"

"I'll make these drinks," says Sam. "You keep telling the story."

"Thanks homey. Alright, so I'm fading fast, from the cancer and especially the chemo. The Bonilla Special, I like to call it. I have absolutely no energy to start a new shop, and it's obvious Andrea isn't going to be any help. And the Bluffs is a terrible location, so I'm desperate for a way out anyway."

Terrence raises his hand. "Starbucks doesn't seem to think so."

"Did you see Terrence raise his hand?" I ask Charlotte. "That's the kind of respect I demand."

"Well you'll never get it, so..."

"Wow do I get angry with you."

"Tough," says Charlotte.

"The fact that Starbucks is going into the Bluffs means that they know they can exploit the hospital's every need, for coffee and pastries and cool frosty drinks and breakfast burritos and lunch sandwiches. And you know I'll never sell sandwiches and breakfast burritos, don't you?"

"Yes," says Sam.

"Plus, they can lose money for years and never bat an eye. That won't be the only Starbucks in town. They probably have plans for a couple more."

"Good Lord," says Terrence.

"You got that right."

Sam shakes his head. "God help us."

"It's not an alien invasion, for crying out loud," says Charlotte.

"Have you ever seen a Starbucks employee?" I ask her. "So anyway," I return to the story, "here was the sweet part about the Bluffs. I didn't put a dime in that store. Mike McEwen financed the construction, and I got Andrea to put up the cash to finish it. By the way, I'm sorry to be the bearer of bad news, Sam, but Andrea took her kid and went back to Colorado. An hour after Rick's funeral, she was gone."

"It wasn't that fast," says Charlotte.

"Close."

"Jamestown's loss," says Sam with a shitty little grin. He puts drinks on the pickup shelf for the two cute coeds. "Here's your iced trio coolers."

"Iced, trio, coolers, on the bar!" The girls jerk their hands back. "No go ahead, take them. I just wasn't sure whether you heard Sam. Can we get some more Squeeze in this mix?! Charlotte! Please!"

Charlotte sighs. "I'll see what I can do."

"So Edna Applejack—you know, the famous basketball player and manslayer, that Edna Applejack—she comes to me with a proposition to open a JRV on campus, and then on campuses across the state. I'm not the savviest businessman, I've proved that a few times in the past. But it sounded like a good idea. So I sold the Bluffs location to Billy-boy and ditched Andrea, in every sense of the word. Then I moved in with Edna. Can you believe that?"

"Impressive."

"I thought so. Turns out she was seeing Rick McEwen the whole time. Daytime friends and nighttime lovers. They were high school sweethearts."

"Is that right?" Terrence marvels. "Wow. Interesting."

"They did a good job keeping it secret. I sure didn't have a clue. Did you know?" I ask Charlotte.

"Nope."

"And Charlotte was Edna's number one groupie, so—yes you were. Probably still are. Charlotte, just admit it. But as it turns out, Rick and Andrea kept *their* love an even bigger secret."

Charlotte shakes her head. "I don't get that. He could have had Edna, and he chose Andrea. I will never get that."

"It's the Small Woman Syndrome," I explain. Everyone looks confused. "It's like toxic shock syndrome. No one believes it, but it's all too real."

Charlotte glares at me. "Brian. No."

"Bad analogy? Okay. It's like Shaken Baby Syndrome." Charlotte doesn't like this one either, but I'm getting a favorable response from Sam. "Small Woman Syndrome. It needs to be eradicated. I'd rank it ahead of prostrate cancer on the national priority list. The government needs an informational campaign to teach men that small women are people too, and they can make it on their own. Men need to learn that it's okay to break it off with a small woman. Before we have more tragedies like this one."

Sam chuckles. "So when did Andrea and Rick break the news?"

"I was on my deathbed. In Edna's bed. Andrea came over to tell me they were tying the knot again and moving back to Colorado. So of course I told Edna."

Charlotte tsks me.

"Hey, I didn't know Edna was giving it up to Rick. Should have—she was having 'business' meetings with him every other night, supposedly to talk about the construction of this shop."

"Yeah, maybe that should have been a tip-off," says Charlotte.

"Cut me some slack here, woman. I was truly dying. Oh, I skipped this part. After the second round of chemo almost killed me, my cancer came back in the shin again. Your godfather wanted to start a third round of chemo. I told him where to go. In the meantime, the cancer spreads. Metastasizes, is the proper medical term. I go in for another checkup, and Dr. Zhivago tells me he'll have to amputate my leg."

"Oh no," says Sam. Then he chortles despite the horror. "Dr. Zhivago."

"Get the connection? Neither of them are real doctors. I was a little bummed to hear about the need to hack off my leg, to say the least." I hike my shorts to an inappropriate height to demonstrate the proposed cut line, at the hip. Sam and Terrence wince, although there's really nothing to see now. My shin is almost the same size as the other one, a little puffy and slightly discolored. It doesn't hurt a bit.

"That's when Brian stopped coming in to work," says Charlotte.

"I was really sick, and really depressed. Charlotte, what's the one thing I hate to do, more than anything else?"

"Die," says world-weary Charlotte.

"Close. Die, with only one leg. Andrea had been working on me to go with her boss's treatment. Dr. Bhani used deadly bacteria to make cancer patients so sick that their immune system attacks anything in sight, including the cancer. It sounded a little medieval to me."

"That's the treatment Brent McEwen tried, isn't it?" says Terrence. He's the storyteller's straight man, supplying the occasional key fact in the form of a question to create a faux conversational feel, never interrupting the flow or forcing the story in an unscripted direction, careful not to ruin the punch line.

"Correct. When I was finally desperate and brave enough to take the treatment—the toxins, that's what Dr. Bhani called them—Andrea anonymously sent me gruesome pictures of Brent's autopsy."

"If it was anonymous," says Sam, "how did you know who sent them?"

"That's where you benefit by hearing this story two months late. All the loose ends have been tied up."

"Check," says Sam.

"The pictures were unbelievably hideous. Brent died of flesh-eating bacteria. Which, as it turns out, is basically the same bacteria Dr. Bhani uses for his cure. Scared the shit out of me. Edna was livid that Andrea tried to spook me, when she knew how successful this treatment could be. I thought Edna was ready to kill her. Keep that in mind, by the way, for later in the story."

"Why did Andrea send you the pictures?" Sam asks.

"Spite." With death no longer imminent, I can cut the crap and call it like I see it. I wasn't fooling Jesus anyway. He and I both know there isn't a charitable bone in Andrea's tiny body. "Spite, for dumping her. She wanted me bad, what can I tell you. And as we continue to learn, hell has no fury like the scorned woman."

"Why Andrea didn't just count her blessings when Brian dumped her, I'll never know," says Charlotte.

"Because Brian's a dreamboat," says Sam.

"Thank you. Actually, I was her ticket out of North Dakota. I don't think Andrea is a fall-in-love type of gal. So anyway, I'm freaked out by the pictures, and then I read all these articles about how other researchers think Dr. Bhani is a mad scientist. How his treatment doesn't work. How dangerous it is. So, of course, I decide to take the treatment."

Sam pauses, about to hit the blender switch for a batch of raspberry mango smoothies. "Why?"

"Partly because I was growing tumors in my back and my groin and my throat and my armpit, and probably a few other places they hadn't caught yet. Mostly because I wanted to live to fulfill my dream of running a chain of campus coffeeshops with Edna. Which has now gone right down the freaking drain, of course."

"That's not why you took Dr. Bhani's treatment," says Charlotte. "Tell the real reason."

I nod to Sam and he hits the switch. There can be no conversation during the running of the blender.

Prematurely, before all the ice has been pulverized, Sam turns off the blender and looks at me. "Are you crying?"

"Maybe." I tried blinking the tears away, and now I have to wipe them from my cheeks. "You got a problem with that?"

Sam snorts a happy "no", finishes the job, and hands the girls their drinks.

"Brian always gets emotional at this point in the story," says Charlotte.

"Charlotte knows I'm going to cry, that's why she has me tell this part."

This, what I would call a secular salvation testimonial, is part of the story, by now scripted almost word for word. It's way too personal for a place of business, but I really want the people I care about to know, and that's the way it works in my shop. "Aaa. Hang on. Okay. After I got the amputation news, and the toxin treatment looked like a sham, I was really down. It was way beyond a depression. I was in a deep hole with a lid on top. I knew I was going to die soon, and I was scared shitless. Most people acquire a strong faith in God right about then. But I went the opposite way. My faith had always been kind of fuzzy. And now it deserted me completely."

I can't describe it without feeling it. I'm back there again, right now, a couple inches, a few days, a missed heartbeat from slipping into Nothingness, that unimaginable world where there is a complete lack of Brian.

"And then," Charlotte prompts.

"And then, all of a sudden, Dad shows up, from California." My voice shakes. "Just Dad. He never travels alone, without Mom. He's committed to his job, hates to leave it. But here he was." I'm wiping tears as I talk. "Dad tells me he's going to hang out with me for a few days. And then he's going to come back...hang on, I'm sorry."

Sam squeezes my arm. "It's okay, Bri."

"Okay. There. Sorry. So...alright, here's the really emotional part. Huh, Charlotte?" I look over and she's crying too. She nods. "I'm telling Dad how sorry I am that I was a failure in the coffee business. I'm confessing that I'm incapable of running more than one little shop...and he looks at me...and he tells me how proud he is of me."

I'm crying way too hard to keep up with the tissue. Customers are coming in, but there's nowhere to hide in this theater-in-the-round setup.

Terrence turns away to hide his tears from the gawking college kids. "Goldammit, Brian, I'll never forgive you for this."

"I know. I'm sorry homey."

"You're going to have to stop telling this here at the shop," says Charlotte. "I think I've cried every day this week." She turns her back on the till to wipe her eyes, and then faces the customers. "What can we get for you?"

"That's a beautiful thing, Brian," says Terrence.

"When Dad told me how proud he is, how impressed he was that I had my own business by the time I was twenty-five, and how I had already taken more risks and succeeded more than most people...maybe he was trying to soothe my soul so I could die in peace, without any regrets. But that's not the way I took it. I believed he expected to see me do something incredible and pull through. Dad made me feel so good about myself...honestly, the thought of dying just disappeared. From that point forward, I knew I was going to live. I just wish I could have taken the treatment with Dad here."

"Isn't his dad amazing?" says Charlotte.

"Is that when you found out Dr. Bhani wouldn't give you the treatment?" Terrence asks.

"No kidding?" says Sam, simultaneously trying to watch me and add the right amount of foam to the extra-dry capp.

"I found out on the way to the rez."

"The rez?"

"The hospital here wouldn't let Dr. Bhani in the building anymore, because of the injunction against him. And the malpractice lawsuit from the McEwens. Mike was sure Bhani killed Brent with his treatment. Everyone was gunning for him. Bhani was afraid to set foot in the state. So his assistant pinch-hit for him."

"Even with the injunction?" asks Terrence the straight man.

"It was a gutsy move."

"I'll say," says Charlotte.

"Dr. Sawyer. Brave, and handsome. Like a young and really small Rob Lowe. Charlotte should move to Minneapolis and contract an incurable disease and let Dr. Sawyer cure her. It would be a beautiful love story."

"Don't tempt me," says Charlotte, out on the floor retrieving dirty coffee cups. "I just might. Assuming he doesn't go to prison."

"Huh?" says Sam.

I hold up my hands requesting his patience. "So an orderly at the hospital converts my van into an ambulance for us."

"Nice," says Sam.

"We're driving to Fort Yates, almost there, when the rez hospital calls and tells us to turn it around. An editorial in JAMA came out that day and ripped on Dr. Bhani and his toxins. Called him a fraud and a quack. Basically called for the police to shoot him on sight. So the rez hospital barred their doors."

"So then what?" Sam prompts me.

"So of course we do it at Edna's house."

"Of course."

"Except Mike McEwen shows up to stop us. The whole McEwen family, except Rick, who's at his folks' house, leveling the pool table."

Sam is incredulous. "The McEwens go to Edna's, to stop your cure?"

"They brought Dennis—not our Dennis; Dennis the Assassin. He came along as the McEwen's enforcer."

"Oh boy," says Sam.

"Luckily I brought one too. Jerry."

"Oooh." Sam is ready to hear about a rumble.

"They were this close to duking it out. I mean they were bumping chests and jockeying for position."

"I'd pay money to see that one."

"The house had to be shakin'," says Terrence.

"From the look on their faces, it was going to be a death match. Meanwhile Doc Sawyer and his nurse are pushing ahead. They rough up the skin on my shin, make it bleed real good, to stimulate the immune system, in preparation for the injection of Bhani's toxins. Jerry's got Dennis contained, and Nurse Ratchet's not taking any shit from Mike. Doc Sawyer is about to stick the needle in me, when the cops burst in. Officer Pilsson and his boys. They separate Dennis and Jerry, and tell the Doc to drop the needle. So he does."

"He dropped it?" Sam verifies.

"He literally dropped it?" Terrence confirms.

"He pretends it's an accident. One of the cops is in a hazmat suit, because the McEwens had them freaked out about these killer bacteria. Everybody runs screaming from Edna's bedroom, certain that the flesh-eating bacteria is coming for them. Doc Sawyer wipes up the spill with a cloth and throws it in a hazmat container. Then he bandages my wound—with a cloth. The cops cart him away, and I start getting really sick. I'm sure this is it, in my cancer death throes, puking my guts out, mostly in the can, some on the floor, a little on the walls. Edna doesn't care, because she's distraught about Rick and Andrea, completely wigged out. Hey, look who's here."

Jerry and Dennis (the Assassin) walk in together. "Look who's back!" Dennis greets Sam. "How was Alaska?"

"Great." Sam nods at me. "We're at the part where Brian is throwing up."

"Which time?" Jerry asks.

"In Edna's house," I tell him.

"Oh, oh," says Dennis, "this is my favorite part. Okay, go on."

"I'm glad to hear you two put down the gloves and made up," Sam tells our latecomers.

"Tensions were high that day, what can I say," says Dennis.

"How about when we all realized Edna is a homicidal maniac?" I ask.

"Thanks to your hunch," says Dennis.

"Too bad my hunch was a little less than perfect. So Edna goes upstairs, and then disappears. During the time I knew her, she got mad at me a couple times, and I would pretend to be afraid she was going to kill me. Suddenly it hits me that it's no joke. I'm sure she's going to kill Andrea. So the cops, the McEwens, everybody—"

"Everybody but you and Isabel," Dennis qualifies.

"So are you and Isabel..." Sam raises his eyebrows.

"She's all yours, Sam," says Dennis.

"I wouldn't recommend it," Charlotte warns.

"You two could have a great time together. Just keep her away from your little sister," I caution. "So I'm too delirious to understand what's really going on in Edna's head, and I send everyone on a wild chase to Andrea's apartment. Isabel's driving me to the hospital, when we notice that the skin around my bandage, my whole leg, is burning red. The worst looking infection you've ever seen."

"Oh boy," says Sam.

"And it dawns on me: Doc Sawyer wrapped my scuffed skin with the toxin clean-up rag. He pulled the old switcheroo."

"No way," says Sam.

"That guy was a quick thinker," says Dennis. Jerry pauses; nods.

"I was undergoing treatment without anyone knowing it. Iz freaked out and tried to tear off the bandage. I didn't let her."

"And she's hard to resist," Dennis testifies.

"I'll bet," says Charlotte, disgusted.

"Iz is driving like a maniac to the hospital, when it hits me: Edna doesn't murder women. She's a mankiller. We fly over to the McEwens. The front door is locked, so we come up through the basement. There's screaming. I didn't know if it was Edna or Rick..."

"I'm leaving for this part," says Charlotte. "I don't ever want to hear this description again. I have nightmares just from hearing about it."

"You're coming back down here if we get customers," I call after her as she heads upstairs. I take a pull from my water bottle. "I don't blame her."

For once Sam isn't smiling. "Pretty bad, huh?"

"I'm glad they had police tape up by the time I got there," says Jerry.

"I've never seen anything like it. Rick was a big guy, but I still don't know how he stayed on his feet. Edna was on top of his shoulders, draped over his head, going to town on his face with her nails. She had torn out his throat, his eyes.... Rick was basically dead on his feet already. But when I tried to convince Edna to let go of him, she stuck the knife in his brain. She stabbed him right through the nose hole."

"Oh my god," says Sam, ill.

"I knew she murdered her husband with her bare hands, but I had no clue. The cops said this was similar to her first go-around. Except for the knife, which as I pointed out to her at the time, was sort-of cheating. But, academic at this point." Sam's eyes are wide. Jerry and Dennis slump in their seats, heads hanging. Terrence studies me. "The cops tackled Edna so hard they fractured her back. She's in a wheelchair in prison."

"I hope they put that cunt in SuperMax," says Dennis, adding extra color to the sentiments I've heard from a lot of people. Jamestown can forgive one cold-blooded murder; two is crossing the line. "Put that bitch in a hole and throw away the key."

"Did you visit her when she was still at the local jail?" Terrence asks.

"I think I would have, if I wasn't in the hospital for so long."

"It's hard to believe Rick is dead," says Jerry.

"Mike and Valerie are a mess. I heard they might move. And seriously about Isabel," I warn Sam, "stay clear. She was a freak before, and she is way gone now. Her folks may check her in for long-term intensive therapy."

After absorbing, Sam says, "So Brian, I suppose you have to be thankful it turned out that Edna was in love with Rick and not you?"

"It's kind of a letdown, actually. It would be like if that couple who raises big cats south of here were to have a tiger get loose. Knowing there's something out there more powerful than man, stalking us...it's exciting."

"I'd like to shoot that bitch between the eyes," says Dennis. "I'd like to hunt her with my Bowie knife. I'd like to jump down out of a tree"—Dennis acts out his fantasy—"and land on *her* shoulders, and start stabbing. That's what the bitch deserves."

We all nod. "So let me see your tumor sites," says Sam. "I heard they just melted away."

"Hey...I thought you hadn't heard anything?"

"I lied," says Sam. "Mom called me every day for awhile there. I even caught a couple of your interviews on TV. I just wanted to hear you tell it."

"Amen, brother." We knuckle-knock. "It was downright miraculous. Your godfather Dr. Seuss couldn't believe what he was seeing. My immune system went ape shit, turned into a cancer blender. I guess they were draining dead tumor soup out of me for a few days. I wish I had been awake for it."

"I heard it got pretty bad," says Sam.

"Practically everybody in town came to see Brian," said Jerry. "You couldn't find any flowers to buy, the stores ran out. People were picking them from Amber's garden."

"Everyone was sure Brian wasn't going to pull through," says Dennis.

"Except his mom and dad," says Jerry.

"A few of us tried to keep all-night vigils in Brian's room," says Dennis. "The nurses were getting cranky. It was amazing. It was like when Donna Bennamin's cat had that calico kitten with Lawrence Welk's face on its belly. People were waiting in line to go see Brian. The hospital gave everyone numbers in the lobby, and then took groups every half-hour up to his room."

I shrug. "What can I say? I'm as big as the Bennamin kitten."

"Poor thing got pneumonia from all the draftiness, having the door open all day," Dennis reports. "It died."

"Pussy. Although I shouldn't talk, because the cure almost killed me. Basically put me in a coma. I actually preferred the coma. Spared me from feeling violently ill for three days. When I came to, I felt great. And the tumors were gone." It had taken me a day to straighten out my thoughts, and separate wild coma dreams from equally wild reality.

"What does Bonilla think about Dr. Bhani's treatment now?" Jerry asks.

I shake my head. "He doesn't. He's treating it like a miracle. From what I can tell, my cure hasn't changed anything. Everyone still thinks Bhani is a fraud. Doc Sawyer is in trouble for violating the injunction. I'm giving a deposition tomorrow. Dr. Bhani called me from a payphone, asking me to play ignorant about what may or may not have been on that cloth bandage. Since he's not going to benefit anyway. Doc Sawyer might avoid jail time if no one can prove that I had the toxins in me."

"Didn't they take blood tests when you were so sick?" Dennis asks.

"They did. But that's the beauty and the curse of Bhani's toxins. They're hard to distinguish from infections people pick up in hospitals all the time. That's the story Bhani and Doc Sawyer are going to stick to. It shouldn't be hard to get them off the hook. Mom and Dad, the McEwens and half the town are convinced I somehow saved myself. With a big helping hand from God."

Sam grins. "But you know differently, don't you?"

"I know I owe Bhani and Doc Sawyer my life. Without a doubt."

At the end of the story, I always get tearful hugs from the women and heartfelt handshakes and the occasional hug from the men. This time is no different.

Charlotte descends the stairs. "Is the gross part over?"

"The coast is clear," says Sam.

"You missed the hugs, though," says Dennis.

"I've hugged Brian enough lately."

"Amen."

Charlotte slugs me in passing.

"So what are you doing with this new lease on life?" Dennis asks.

"Wondering whether there are any golf courses still open. I promised myself on my deathbed that if I somehow made it out alive, I'd beat Jerry's ass repeatedly on the links. I'd like to get started as soon as possible."

"I called Joshua yesterday," says Jerry. "He's helping his dad with harvest. He says their little nine-hole is still open."

"The one with the Astroturf greens and year-round deer season?" Dennis asks. "I want a piece of that action."

"Can you set it up for us, homey?" Jerry nods. "Otherwise…I'm just going to hang onto this shop as long as possible. But it sounds like no one gets in the ring with the College and comes out on top. As far as they're concerned, no Edna, no deal."

"It's true," says Dennis. "They rule the world."

"I don't care," says Charlotte. "I'm just so happy Brian is alive. That's all that matters. It wasn't looking too good there for awhile."

"We'll see if you still feel that way when I fire you."

"Like I said, go ahead and try it."

I've heard comments like Charlotte's a hundred times in the last few weeks, and said it to myself a few more. No matter what life throws at me from this point forward, no matter how little success I have, regardless how little money I make, I should be deliriously and unconditionally happy. Simply delighted to be here.

And I am delighted. I am thankful to Dr. Bhani and Doc Sawyer. They single-handedly saved my life. For Doc Sawyer, at great risk to his career. He's the bravest guy I know. In the Single Moment of Outstanding Bravery category, the award goes to Doc Sawyer.

But I'm a conditional man. I may be delighted, but I'm not going to be *happy* unless I've earned it, unless I succeed to the level I'm capable of. I'll tell you what, I'm going to be hard to live with, if another fifteen years go by and I'm still treading water, still scraping to get by. Dad, thank you for your love and your pride, but I'm afraid you're still selling me short. Getting to where I am now—which is basically where I was ten years ago—wasn't that hard. I haven't done anything exceptional. Here comes Starbucks, to prove it.

Of course it's possible I'll mellow and soften as the years go by, finally settling down with the realization that the world is viciously competitive, regardless whether you live in New York or Jamestown, and this is as high as most of us can get. What are a few equivalents to owning your own coffeeshop? Middle manager at a bank? Regional head of a crop insurance agency? Probably. Salesman of the year for a drug company? That would be ten times the money, with ten times the demons—so as far as success goes, equivalent. Most people top out somewhere in the middle. Most small businessmen are just that. Small, with no franchise-able growth in the cards. So I might not be in such bad shape; just too young yet to realize it.

Dennis, Jerry and Sam leave as the Period Four flock descends upon us. "Thanks for stopping in," I tell them.

"This is the only way we get to see you anymore," says Dennis.

"Not to mention wall-to-wall college girls," says Jerry; and *then* he pauses, out of order, costing him an honest admission. "In any case," he says quickly, "we're glad you're here. The College would be crazy to lose you."

"Amen," says Sam.

I knuckleknock 'em. "I appreciate it, homies."

The first wave of students hits the till. Terrence asks me, "How many Edna interviews have you done, since that day?"

"Five. I have a guy from the Atlantic magazine coming tomorrow. We have six hours blocked off, and then more the next few days if he needs it."

"Don't."

"Okay."

"Seriously." Terrence is agitated. "I want it. I'm sitting on a gold mine. Edna Applejack…her story's got movie rights written all over it."

"She is still alive," I remind him.

"We'll go unauthorized."

"It's true, people are crazy for info on her. And not just North Dakotans."

"Two mocha coolers and a berry smoothie," Charlotte relays an order.

"Two chilly chocolates and a bloody Maggie! Stat!"

Charlotte sighs and apologizes to the customers.

"I would love for you to write this tale," I tell Terrence. "I know you'd do a great job. But when you get right down to it, it's really my story."

"True. True."

"So let's write it together. You and me, fifty-fifty, everything down the middle. We'll even split my acting income when they cast me in the role of Brian Lawson."

"You'd be great in that role."

"I'd nail it."

"Can you write?"

"I can tell a good story. Should we find out if they're the same thing?"

"Brian, you can't write," says Charlotte. "Terrence is our writer, not you."

"I might need a little help with the grammar."

"Editing is my forte," says Terrence. "You just write wild and free, and I'll clean up after you."

"You know," I start dreaming, "we might have something here."

"This could be our springboard to the big time," says Terrence. "Can I drink for free during the collaboration period?"

"No, but maybe you can tax deduct it."

"Would you be willing to go visit Edna with me, once or twice, to see what she's willing to share?"

"They're transferring her over to Mandan. If I'm going to drive all that way, it's going to have to be a conjugal visit."

"You should have married her when you had the chance," says Charlotte. "Instead of living in sin."

"No sin, unfortunately. Maybe we can have a jailhouse wedding."

"She's a killer, Brian," says Charlotte. "For God's sake."

Terrence types into his laptop. He looks up at me. "Okay. Our story has begun. I can see already that there's one question we have to answer. One question everybody wants to know. With everything Edna had going for her, all the basketball success, all the love from the people here and around the state—why did she do it?"

"Of course I've asked myself that question a few times. I even asked her, when she pulled the knife."

Charlotte covers her ears. "You said you were done talking about that."

"Do you mind? We're working here. We're talking character motivation."

"Sor-ry."

"I can recall Edna babbling something about life needing conflict. We could work with that angle. I can craft some pretty impressive theories. Do you have any trouble with me making some things up?"

"Not at all," says Terrence.

"We could take the approach that all big-time athletes are ticking time bombs, ready to blow at any second."

"That's a good angle," says Sam.

"Or that deep down all women are black widows."

"Nice," says Charlotte. "Can I get a grande iced chai and a tall skinny mocha, light whip?"

"You forgot to say 'or else'."

"You know the 'or else'."

"You are not going to come off flatteringly in our book," I warn.

"Flatteringly?" says Charlotte. "Terrence, is that a word?"

"I think so."

"Not a good one. I'd think twice about writing a book with Brian."

"I think we're sitting on a gold mine," says Terrence.

"You think so?" My heart beats faster. "You think we could make some money? You don't think a movie deal is out of the question?"

"This story has it all," says Terrence. "Murder and athletics."

"Sex, drugs and rock'n'roll, baby. Hey mister," I greet Spence as he arrives for his three o'clock shift. "Take over for me, would you? That's the mocha, that's the decaf caramel macchiato." I lean over the counter across from Terrence. "How far back do you think we should go?"

"Let's start with Edna's first murder and work forward, her prison time, her release, her relationship with you, with flashbacks to her playing days."

Charlotte clears her throat. "Brian..." The queue of kids waiting to order and the cluster awaiting drinks have both grown.

"We can interview the JC athletic director," I tell Terrence. "And I'm sure we can track down a few high school and college teammates. In fact, Patti, one of my new managers, used to play against Edna back in college."

"That's good stuff," says Terrence.

"Which means Dennis draws the short straw," I muse.

"Brian," Charlotte's voice is sharper now. "Help, please."

"Damn customers," I mutter. "I gotta go to work."

About the authors:
Allan Harris has written six previous novels, while the other half of his brain works as a finance guy. Jason Gray is a 15-year coffee industry veteran and owner of Crowfoot Valley Coffee in Castle Rock, CO. *A Long Pull* is their second collaboration.